"It matches, or even outdoes, the first story in excitement and drama. . . . Greg Iles has long been one of my favorite writers and he is certainly at his best with this series . . . each page is raging with fever and fervor. These are some of the best characters he has ever created and his plot is southern drama at its most traumatic. Race relations, adultery, murder, parenthood, and friendship are all smashed together to form a searing saga of remorse and revenge. . . . Just savor the sweetness of a good story brilliantly told. *The Bone Tree* is better than *Natchez Burning.*"

"If William Shakespeare lived today in our Deep South, he would probably write similarly to Greg Iles in *The Bone Tree.* . . . Highly dramatic, expertly written, and compulsively readable . . . There are murders, too, but to describe *The Bone Tree* as just a murder mystery is like calling One World Trade Center just a building."

"The second installment of his hard-boiled Natchez trilogy finds Iles' hero Penn Cage on even swampier, and surely deadlier, ground than before."

"Absolutely compelling . . . A beautifully constructed story, some extremely fine writing, and some hard-to-bear tragedy . . . Everything is big about this one: its epic scale [and] its built-in readership based on the success of its predecessor."

NATCHEZ BURNING

"An impressive beginning to what could prove to be an epic exploration of the nation's secrets and hidden sins, and it marks the return of a gifted novelist . . . Like Stephen King . . . Iles has come back from a near-fatal accident to produce his most searching and ambitious work to date. *Natchez Burning* obliterates the artificial distinction between genre and literary fiction with passion, grace, and considerable style. This is Greg Iles at his formidable best. It's good to have him back."

Washington Post

"A well-made thriller. Mr. Iles provides plenty of menace and action and a host of closely observed characters. . . . He delivers a whopping tale, filled with enough cliff-hanging crises for an old summer-long movie-serial. Yet there are still enough unresolved matters at the end of *Natchez Burning* for two already-promised sequels."

Wall Street Journal

"Every single page of *Natchez Burning* is a cliff-hanger that will keep you devouring just one more chapter before you put it down. . . . A mystery rooted in the real-life racial divides of the Deep South, this ambitious, unique novel is the perfect marriage of a history lesson and a thriller."

JODI PICOULT

"An absorbing and electrifying tale that thriller fans will be sure to devour."

Library Journal (★ Starred Review ★)

By Greg Iles

THE
BONE TREE

GREG
ILES

WM

WILLIAM MORROW

An Imprint of HarperCollinsPublishers

"A Change Is Gonna Come" Written by Sam Cooke. Published by ABKCO Music, Inc. Used by permission. All rights reserved.

WILLIAM MORROW
An Imprint of HarperCollins*Publishers*
195 Broadway
New York, New York 10007

Copyright © 2015 by Greg Iles
ISBN 978-0-06-231113-9
www.harpercollins.com

First William Morrow premium printing: March 2016
First William Morrow mass market international printing: June 2015
First William Morrow paperback international printing: April 2015
First William Morrow paperback special printing: April 2015
First William Morrow hardcover printing: April 2015

For
Caroline Hungerford Iles

*I must learn to be content with being
happier than I deserve.*

– JANE AUSTEN, *Persuasion*, paraphr.

The end of man is knowledge,
but there is one thing he can't know.
He can't know whether knowledge
will save him or kill him.

– ROBERT PENN WARREN, *All the King's Men*

PROLOGUE

SPECIAL AGENT JOHN Kaiser stood at the window of the FBI's "tactical room" in the River Bend Hotel and stared at the lights of Natchez twinkling high over the dark tide of the Mississippi. After struggling silently with his convictions for more than an hour, he had decided to use the authority granted him under the Patriot Act to take a step that under any other circumstances would have been a violation of the Constitution—the unauthorized invasion of computers belonging to a public newspaper. He had not done this lightly, and Kaiser knew that his wife—an award-winning journalist and combat photographer—would condemn him if she ever learned what he'd done. But by his lights, the deteriorating situation demanded that he cross the Rubicon. And so he'd quietly risen from bed and, without disturbing his wife, slipped down the hall to where two FBI technicians sat behind computers connected by secure satellite to a high-speed data link in Washington.

This is the Deep South, Kaiser reflected, watching the bow lights of a string of barges round the river bend to the north, from Vicksburg, and push slowly southward toward Baton Rouge. *The real South.* After being stationed in New Orleans for seven years, he'd realized that the Big Easy, while technically a southern city, was in fact an island with a unique identity: a former French possession, deeply Catholic, multiracial, bursting at the seams with joy and pain, corrupt to its decaying marrow. But the farther north you drove out of New Orleans, the deeper you penetrated into the true South, a Protestant land of moral absolutes, Baptist blue laws, tent revivals, fire and brimstone, heaven and hell, good and evil, black and white, and damn little room between.

Natchez on its bluff was a *soeurette,* a little sister, to

New Orleans—not quite as cosmopolitan in this century as it once was, but still an enclave of license and liberality in the hard-shell hinterlands of cotton and soybeans. Yet Natchez had once been the capital of this cotton kingdom, and a hundred years after the Civil War the hatred that simmered in her outlying fields had infected the city, and murder had roamed her streets like a scourge. If you drew a thirty-mile circle around Natchez, it would encompass more than a dozen unsolved murders from the 1960s alone, and twice that number that were officially solved, but begged for deeper investigation.

Kaiser pressed the palm of his hand against the cold windowpane and watched the barge lights through the fog of his breath on the glass. Two days ago, when he'd mobilized a massive FBI corpse-recovery effort here in Concordia Parish, his goals had been to solve some cold case murders and to save the life of a heroic journalist—not to unravel the darkest thread of the Kennedy assassination. But twenty-four hours after his arrival in this embattled parish, that was exactly the position in which he found himself.

Was it possible that a group of long-unsolved race murders in this neglected corner of the South held the key to the biggest cold case in American history? Given what he'd learned in the past twelve hours, it just might be. Texas bordered Louisiana, after all, and in 1963 Dallas had been a fundamentalist redoubt of reactionary political conservatism, seething with rabid Kennedy hatred. More unsettling still, in that era Dallas had been a feudal possession of New Orleans mob boss Carlos Marcello. For decades, finding a link between Marcello and Dealey Plaza had proved maddeningly elusive. But today new evidence had emerged, revealing a credible plan by the Double Eagle group to assassinate Robert Kennedy in April of 1968 as well as actions by the group's founder that suggested complicity in the 1963 assassination. Kaiser had long known of a connection between certain Double Eagles and Carlos Marcello. And while he could not explain his certainty, he sensed that the missing links that would tie Marcello to the dead president would soon be within his reach.

Now that Kaiser had authorized an invasion into the

computer servers of the *Natchez Examiner*, his dilemma was how much information to pass up the chain to Washington. In the three months since Hurricane Katrina struck, he had been operating with near-complete autonomy, and he liked it. The breakdown of basic human services in New Orleans—most notably the evaporation of the NOPD—had created a situation of unprecedented chaos on American soil. A veteran of the final phase of the Vietnam War, Kaiser had pushed into that vacuum and deployed Bureau resources with the independence and assertiveness of a military officer, and Washington had allowed him all the rope he desired. The fact that New Orleans lay in a part of the country that the D.C. nabobs never thought much about had been useful in this regard. But Kaiser knew all too well that once he started passing explosive information up the chain, those same bureaucrats would instantly go into ass-covering mode and force his operation to a grinding halt. And almost nothing was more explosive than evidence tying the New Orleans Mafia and a violent offshoot of the Ku Klux Klan to Dealey Plaza.

What Kaiser most wanted was time and freedom to follow the leads he'd unearthed—to wherever they led, unhampered by oversight and regardless of consequences. J. Edgar Hoover might be long dead, but his paranoid ghost still haunted the halls of FBI headquarters on Pennsylvania Avenue. Already two men had died since Kaiser and his team had driven north from New Orleans to Vidalia, and more had died in the days before that. These deaths had not gone unnoticed in Washington, and by early this evening a few reporters at national newspapers had picked up on the violent doings in the backcountry of Louisiana. None had yet learned that Kaiser had designated the Double Eagle group a terrorist entity under the Patriot Act (which gave him unprecedented power to combat the survivors of the Klan offshoot), but someone soon would, and that would only increase the political pressure to quickly resolve events.

The problem was, Kaiser saw no hope for a quick resolution. The Double Eagle group was tied to at least a dozen unsolved rape, kidnapping, and murder cases in and around Concordia Parish and Natchez, Mississippi.

And while Kaiser had made remarkable progress during the past twenty-four hours, it might take weeks or even months to solve them all. The surviving Double Eagles were tough men who had never been compromised, much less infiltrated. Breaking them would be difficult. The one Eagle who had shown signs of wanting to wash his conscience clean—a terminal cancer patient named Glenn Morehouse—had been ruthlessly murdered by his old comrades two days ago, before the FBI even became aware that he'd opened talks with a crusading journalist named Henry Sexton. Sexton himself had nearly perished in a subsequent attack by unknown assailants, and he now lay in a heavily protected room in the nearby Concordia Parish hospital.

It was Sexton's working files and notes that Kaiser hoped to access by breaching the computers of the *Natchez Examiner*. Early that morning, Kaiser had learned from Sexton's girlfriend that the injured reporter had given a bundle of Moleskine notebooks containing the results of years of Double Eagle investigations to Caitlin Masters, the publisher of the *Examiner*. Kaiser had tried both bribes and threats to persuade Masters to allow him access to those notebooks, but so far she had refused. Just before going to bed, his wife had told him that she'd spoken to Masters (who was a great admirer of her work) about them all being on the same side, and Jordan believed the publisher would allow Kaiser access to the notebooks tomorrow. He'd made up his mind to subpoena Sexton's records under the Patriot Act in any case. But as he'd lain awake in the dark beside his wife, he'd begun to believe that waiting even eight hours for that information would be a mistake.

Though few knew it, Kaiser had twice today visited Henry Sexton in the hospital, and during the second meeting he'd heard a story that had stunned him. According to Sexton, the 1968 kidnapping of two young black men— Jimmy Revels and Luther Davis—had been anything but a simple racist attack by the Ku Klux Klan. Glenn Morehouse, a founding member of the Double Eagles, had told Sexton that Revels and Davis had been kidnapped as part of a plan to lure Robert Kennedy to Mississippi to be assassinated. This plan had come into being after RFK announced his intention to enter the 1968 presidential race, a decision that had enraged Carlos Marcello, who'd been targeted for deportation multiple times by Kennedy, both as a senator and as attorney general. According to Morehouse, Marcello believed that if Robert Kennedy was elected president, he would be permanently deported and lose his criminal empire, which stretched from Dallas, Texas, to Mobile, Alabama. Through case work of his own, Kaiser knew this to be true.

He did not, however, know anything about the rest of Morehouse's Kennedy revelation, which was: first, that Marcello had gone through local millionaire and power broker Brody Royal to recruit his assassin; and second, that the assassin was Frank Knox, the founder of the Double Eagle group. Morehouse claimed that Knox had chosen Jimmy Revels as his victim because Revels had worked tirelessly to register black voters for a Kennedy presidential run, and also because Revels was personally known to Bobby Kennedy. The boy had even spoken to the senator by telephone only days earlier. Frank Knox believed that if Revels were brutally murdered, Kennedy would be unable to resist the temptation to travel to Mississippi to attend his funeral. Only the accidental death of Knox during this operation had prevented the assassination plan from coming to fruition. Despite Knox's death, Revels and his friend Davis had still perished, and horribly. Earlier today, Kaiser's team had brought up Davis's bones from a deep pond after thirty-seven years of submersion, proving that at least one of the young men had been handcuffed to the wheel of his Pontiac convertible and driven into the water after being both shot and tortured. Revels's body remained undiscovered, but Kaiser hoped to find it next—and soon.

The aborted plot to kill Robert Kennedy was not what had triggered Kaiser's present fears. No, it was something Henry Sexton had told him during their first hospital visit, something Sexton himself had learned from Morehouse only eighteen hours earlier. On the day Frank Knox founded the Double Eagles—during the summer of 1964—Knox had drawn three groups of letters in the sand beside the Mississippi River. "The three K's," he'd called them: *JFK, RFK, MLK*. Then Knox had crossed out the

JFK and said, "One down, two to go." To his stunned followers, Knox had then shown a photo of Robert Kennedy and Martin Luther King Jr. standing in a group in the White House Rose Garden, with red circles drawn around their heads.

After Kaiser heard this, every instinct told him that Carlos Marcello's approach to Frank Knox about killing RFK in 1968 was not the first time the mobster had gone to the former marine for that kind of help. In 1961 and '62, Frank Knox had been training Cuban expatriates in a South Louisiana camp funded by Marcello. And in 1963 Marcello had even more reason to believe Robert Kennedy meant to destroy him than he would have in 1968. Given all these factors, Kaiser had come to believe that he was working the most important FBI investigation outside the war on Al Qaeda. In historical terms—given the FBI's abysmal failure on so many civil rights murders, and Hoover's sabotaging of the Warren Commission investigation—it might be the most important case of all.

What complicated Kaiser's effort to redeem the Bureau's record—and honor—was the fact that the Louisiana State Police were working against him. In a uniquely southern twist, the chief of the LSP's Criminal Investigations Bureau was the son of Frank Knox. Forrest Knox had worked hard to distance himself from his family's racist past, and he'd been so successful that many Louisiana politicians supported him as the next superintendent of the state police. For Kaiser, this possibility represented a nightmare. If his suspicions were correct, Forrest Knox was the architect of a statewide criminal organization that used corrupt police officers and ex–Double Eagles to facilitate drug smuggling, gambling, and prostitution—the rackets once ruled by the Marcello organization of old. Whispered rumors that Knox had used a state police SWAT team to wipe out drug competitors during the chaos of Katrina were starting to seem more like fact than fantasy. Worse still, Kaiser had begun to uncover connections between Forrest Knox and the ruthless developers and bankers intent on rebuilding New Orleans as a whiter and more marketable version of itself in the wake of the storm.

"I'm almost through," said one of the technicians

behind Kaiser. "They have better security than I expected. It's run out of the home office in South Carolina."

"John Masters owns twenty-seven newspapers," Kaiser said, the fog of his breath blanking out the glass again. "I'd expect him to spend at least some money on information security."

"Two minutes, tops," said the tech, tapping rapidly at his keyboard.

Kaiser checked his watch, wondering where Caitlin Masters was at this moment. Almost certainly in her office at the *Examiner*, working on the next day's stories, chasing her second Pulitzer. "Will she be able to see that we're inside her system?" he asked.

"No. No worries there."

Kaiser grunted. He liked Caitlin Masters. Earlier tonight, when a state police captain named Ozan had shown up at the Concordia hospital to take over the Sexton case, the slightly built newspaper publisher had gotten right up into his face to challenge his authority and reaffirm federal jurisdiction. You had to admire spunk like that.

The paternal warmth Kaiser felt toward Masters reflected the conflicts he felt about the overall case, and none was more complex than that he felt about the Cage family. Penn and Tom Cage represented a unique problem for him. Penn Cage was not only Caitlin Masters's fiancé, but also the mayor of Natchez, a successful novelist, and a former prosecutor from Houston. Even more impressive to Kaiser, Cage had been the primary mover behind the scandal that resulted in the resignation of FBI director John Portman in 1998. While working a cold civil rights murder, Cage had uncovered criminal actions on the part of the young Portman that could not bear modern scrutiny. By any standard, Kaiser saw Cage as a modern-day hero. And yet, in the present circumstance, the mayor was more a pain in the ass than anything else.

The reason for that was his father.

Tom Cage was almost a relic of a bygone era. A former combat medic in Korea, Cage had gone on to practice medicine for nearly fifty years in Natchez, where he'd worked tirelessly for decades to treat the black community with no thought of recognition or reward. Yet paradoxically, this beloved physician's irrational actions had directly or indirectly triggered every tragedy that had happened over the past three days.

In the wee hours of Monday morning, Viola Turner, Dr. Cage's sixty-five-year-old former nurse, had died in her sister's home in Natchez. After living in Chicago for thirty-seven years, the Natchez native had been diagnosed with terminal cancer and returned home to die in the care of her old employer. Few people had known that Dr. Cage was treating Turner, and even if they had, no one would have expected the explosion that followed her death. That only occurred because Turner's son, a Chicago lawyer, had shown up at the Natchez DA's office and demanded that Dr. Cage be charged not with euthanasia, but with murder. And because the black district attorney, Shadrach Johnson, had a long history of antipathy for Penn Cage, he had obliged the angry son.

Things might have progressed with some semblance of order had not Dr. Cage jumped bail after being indicted by a grand jury with lightning speed. From what Kaiser could ascertain, the doctor had been aided in this task by an old war buddy, a former Texas Ranger named Walt Garrity. Worst of all, within hours of making their escape, either Cage or Garrity had killed a Louisiana state trooper who'd cornered them near the Mississippi River. Kaiser strongly suspected that the dead trooper had been working for Forrest Knox, not the State of Louisiana, when he'd caught up with the two fugitives, but sadly Kaiser could not prove that.

"I'm in!" crowed the tech. "I'm looking at the front page of tomorrow's *Examiner.*"

"Let me see," Kaiser said, turning from the window.

"Give him your screen, Pete," ordered the tech.

The second tech got up and went over to the coffee-maker. As Kaiser took the warm seat, the first tech said, "I routed the front page to you. I'll keep looking for any mention of Henry Sexton's notebooks."

With his aging eyes, Kaiser had to tilt his head at exactly the right angle to read what was on the screen, and he could barely make out what the tech was saying on his left. Kaiser had lost nearly all the hearing in that ear two years ago, when a drug dealer holding him hostage on Royal Street in New Orleans had fired off a 9 mm pistol only inches from his ear.

From what Kaiser could see on the screen, Caitlin Masters had led off her story with the true events at the Concordia hospital. Kaiser had hoped to lull the Double Eagles into making a mistake by putting out the story that the Eagles had succeeded in killing Henry Sexton rather than merely wounding him, but the appearance of Captain Ozan at the hospital had seriously lowered the odds of success. He couldn't blame Masters for printing the truth.

"I've got a folder!" cried the tech. "'Henrys Moleskines' is the name. Jesus, do you think—?"

"She digitized his notebooks!" Kaiser cried, his pulse racing. "Put the folder on my screen."

"Doing it now."

"Can we copy the files?"

"Sure."

"Will they know we did it?"

"If they hire a forensic firm down the road, yes. But not anytime soon. Do you have it?"

A cluster of typical Windows folders appeared on Kaiser's screen. "Just click on it?" he asked, his right hand tingling as it hung over the mouse.

"Sure. Just like your computer."

Kaiser clicked on the folder, but no files opened. "I've got nothing. Is the folder password protected or something?"

"Not that I could see."

Kaiser tried twice more, then clicked on Properties. "The folder appears to be empty on this screen. Are you sure I have access to the file from here?"

"You should have access to everything I do. Hang on."

Kaiser waited, fingers twitching. If he could get immediate access to every note that Henry Sexton had taken over decades of investigation, there was no telling what deductive leaps he might make. Plus, despite Sexton's apparent candor in the hospital, the reporter might have held back critical information, hoping to follow it up himself after he recovered. Kaiser suspected, for example, that Sexton might have some notion of the location of the Bone Tree, a long-rumored dump site for Double Eagle corpses and a killing ground that dated to the pre-Columbian years of the Natchez Indians.

"Oh, no," groaned the tech, his voice taut.

"I don't like the sound of that."

"Somebody erased the files in that folder."

"Just now?"

"Yep. I can see their tracks. Somebody just deleted the file containing what must have been digital scans of Sexton's notebooks. There was thirty gigabytes of data in that folder. Now it's empty. And I think they're still deleting stuff."

"Who the hell would do that?" Kaiser demanded, a bubble of panic in his chest.

"User 23. That's all I can tell you."

"You can't tell who User 23 is?"

"Nope. Sorry."

"Shit!"

"What do you want me to do, boss?"

"Can you copy their whole server drives? Everything they have?"

The tech's eyes went wide. "That's a lot of data."

"That's not an answer, goddamn it."

"It would take a long time. And it would definitely increase the odds of their IT people in Charleston noticing something."

"Do it anyway."

Kaiser was trying to think outside the box when his cell phone rang. He expected it to be his wife, asking where he'd gone, but it was one of the agents guarding Henry Sexton at the Concordia hospital.

"What is it?" he snapped. "Is Sexton still stable?"

"I don't know, sir."

"What do you mean?"

"Sexton's not in his hospital bed. I just walked in and found his seventy-eight-year-old mother lying in his place. She's hooked up to the heart monitors and everything."

"*What?*"

"She used to be a nurse, apparently. When you gave permission for Henry's mother to visit him, he got hold of a cell phone and asked her to bring him a few things to help him sneak out. She did, and Henry pulled it off. He walked out of here wearing his mother's coat and hat. Right past our guards."

Kaiser slammed his hand on the table. "Damn it! What else does she know?"

"We're trying to find out. But I've already learned one thing that's not good."

"What's that?"

"One of the things Sexton asked for was a shotgun. And she brought him one."

Kaiser thought fast. "Could Henry even drive? He was heavily sedated when I saw him earlier today."

"He probably skipped his last doses of meds, except the pain pump."

"Did Mrs. Sexton know where he was going with the shotgun?"

"She claims she doesn't."

"Do you believe her?"

The agent paused. "Yeah."

"Keep her there! You hear me? I'm coming straight over. And put out an APB on her vehicle. The vehicle and Sexton both. Wait—don't do that. If the state police hear that, they'll find Henry and kill him before we get close. He'll just disappear. Tell our guys to hit the streets. Everybody but you. I'll wake up the troops here."

"Got it."

Kaiser clicked END and started to get up, but at that moment his wife touched his shoulder. Jordan Glass was wearing a LEICA T-shirt and sweatpants, but her eyes were glued to the screen in front of Kaiser.

"Has Caitlin already posted tomorrow's edition?" she asked. "I figured she'd be writing right up to the last possible deadline."

For a moment Kaiser considered lying, but experience had taught him that would come back later and bite him on the ass.

"No," he said. "We went into their intranet."

Jordan's gaze slowly moved to him. "You didn't."

"I had to see Henry's notebooks, if I could. Things are happening too fast to wait."

"I told you she was going to show them to you tomorrow."

"You can't be sure of that, Jordan."

His wife gave him a look of infinite reproof. "I *was* sure."

Kaiser endured her gaze as long as he could, out of penance, but then he turned to his techs and said, "Wake everybody up, and I mean everybody. We've got to find Henry Sexton ASAP."

"The Double Eagles murdered the woman he loved earlier this evening," Jordan said. "They were gunning for him, and she died in his place. Whoever Henry thinks did that, he's going to kill them."

Kaiser couldn't believe this. "Henry is the most mild-mannered guy I've met in all this."

"Everybody has a breaking point, John. You know that."

As Jordan turned to leave, half a dozen phones began to ring.

WEDNESDAY

CHAPTER 1

TONIGHT DEATH AND time showed me their true faces.

We spend our lives plodding blindly through the slaughterhouse gate between past and future. Every second is annihilation: the death of this moment, the birth of this moment. There is no "next" moment.

There is only now.

While the pace of life seems stately in the living, we funnel through that gate like driven cattle, fearful, obedient, insensate. Even while we sleep, *now* becomes *then* as relentlessly as a river wearing away a rock. Cells burn oxygen, repair proteins, die, and replace themselves in a seemingly endless train: yet from the womb, those internal clocks are winding down to final disorder.

Only in the shadow of death do we sense the true velocity of time—while adrenaline blasts through our systems, eternity becomes tangible and all else blurs into background. It is then, paradoxically, that seconds seem to stretch, experience becomes hyper-real, and flesh and spirit unite in the battle to remain breathing, conscious, aware—afloat in the rushing stream of time. If we survive the threat, our existential epiphany quickly fades, for we cannot bear it long. Yet somewhere within us, a dividing line remains.

Before and after.

Tonight time slowed down so much I could taste it like copper on my tongue. I felt it against my skin—dense and heavy—resisting every move. Mortality hovered at my shoulder, a watchful beast of prey. Chained to a cinderblock wall, I watched a man older than my father torture the woman I love with fire. I realized then that hell existed; the terrible irony was that *I had created it.* In arrogance, against the counsel of others, I'd wagered all I had and more—the lives of others—to try to save my father. In desperation, I cast away every principle he ever taught me and reached into the darkness in the hope of a bargain.

What did I get in exchange for my soul?

A pillar of fire roaring in the night. The pyre of three men, probably more, visible for miles across the flat Louisiana Delta. Probably even from Mississippi. Not far to the east, my town sleeps along the high ground above the river, but here all sense, all logic is suspended while the fire devours the dead. Two of those men gave their lives for Caitlin and me. *Henry Sexton, reporter. Sleepy Johnston, musician and prodigal son of Louisiana.* One a white man, one black. Allies by chance, or maybe fate. Either way, they're gone forever.

Through the slaughterhouse gate.

I've never witnessed such brutality as that which preceded their deaths, nor such heroism as was displayed in their sacrifices. Yet all I can taste is ashes. Three months ago I felt a lot like this, as a flood of biblical scale swept over New Orleans, the only real city between the Gulf and Memphis. Three hours south of here, hazmat-suited crews are still dragging bodies from mildewed houses. That disaster, like this one, had human causes. Greed, apathy, hubris—even loyalty—all demand payment in the end. Storms will always come, and men will always do evil in the shadow of some other word.

It's how we respond that defines us.

A FEW MINUTES AGO, gripped by a mad delusion of invincibility, I carried Sleepy Johnston out of the basement inferno where this fire was born, and not once while I staggered through the smoke and flames did I doubt I would reach the surface. I hauled a man nearly my own weight as easily as I would have carried my eleven-year-old daughter—but to no avail. Two minutes after I laid him on the ground, Johnston died of his injuries. Now he lies a few yards behind us, staring sightlessly at the smoke-obscured stars.

I did not pray while Caitlin knelt to ease his passing. Anything I said would have been superfluous, for if any God exists, he must surely fold such martyrs into his embrace. I watched in silence while Caitlin reenacted the oldest ritual in the world, cradling the older man's head and murmuring maternal reassurance into his ear. Touching my newly scarred face with my right hand, I drove the nails of my left-hand fingers into my palm. *Pain is proof of life.*

After Johnston expired, I comforted Caitlin as though I had some purchase on reality. But that was only another delusion, though I didn't know it then.

Then . . . ?

With alarm I realize that these events happened only a minute ago, if that. *Does a man in shock know he is in shock? Probably not.*

If I rewind history fifteen minutes, this chaotic mass of fire and smoke was a stunning lake house. Now its owner is being cremated in the ruins of his home, and we two survivors stumble about as reality slowly returns with soul-searing clarity. An imaginary newscaster's voice speaks in my head: *Brody Royal, multimillionaire sociopath, burned to death last night in a fire started by his antique flame-thrower. Sadly, Royal was unable to complete the murders he was contemplating prior to his demise, due to a sudden and suicidal intervention by a man he'd ridiculed as harmless for the past twenty years—*

Brody's house shudders like some giant creature, and then, with the sound of cracking bones, one wing implodes. The heat diminishes for a few seconds, then suddenly intensifies, as though feeding on the evil within. Soon it will drive us farther back, away from Johnston's body.

Caitlin stares at the burning wreckage as though she can't quite grasp what's happening. Five minutes ago we both believed we were dead, yet here we stand. Covered with ash and streaked with sweat, her face has a burn scar to match my own. I want to speak to her, but I don't quite trust myself.

Beyond her, the lake's mirrored surface reflects back an image of the tower of flame, and with a rush of fear I see our future in it. Like the pillar of fire the Israelites followed across the desert, this beacon too will lead men to us.

"Is that a siren?" Caitlin asks, looking away from the raging flames, and toward the narrow lane at the edge of the light.

"I think so." My older ears belatedly pick up the distant whine.

"That way," she says, pointing westward, away from the lake.

I peer through the darkness, but I can't make out any police lights through the orange glare and waves of super-heated air.

"What about Henry's files?" Caitlin asks. "I should hide them."

The charred box that Caitlin salvaged from the burning basement stands a few feet from Sleepy Johnston's body. From the looks of the ashes inside, little of Henry Sexton's journals remains.

"There's nowhere to hide them," I tell her.

"What about the boathouse?" she asks, a note of hysteria in her voice.

"They'll search that. It's too late anyway. A neighbor's coming. Look."

The nearest house is seventy-five yards away, but a pair of headlights has separated from the garage and begun nosing down toward the lane that runs along the lake here. Perhaps emboldened by the siren, the car's driver has finally decided to investigate the fire. *Must have heard the gunshots earlier*, I think, *or they'd have been here long before now.*

The siren is growing louder and rising in pitch. "That's probably the Ferriday fire department," I think aloud. "But the law won't be far behind. I hope it's Sheriff Dennis, but it could be the FBI or the state police. They may question us separately. We need to get our stories straight."

Bewilderment clouds Caitlin's eyes. "We both lived through the same thing, didn't we?"

I take her hand, and the coldness of it startles me. "I don't think it's quite that simple."

"Everything you did in Brody Royal's basement was self-defense. They were torturing us, for God's sake!"

"That's not what I mean. The tough questions won't be

about what happened in the basement. They'll be about *why* it happened. Why did Royal kidnap us? Why did he want to kill us? We've held back a lot over the past couple of days." *And not just from the police*, I add silently.

"What if we just say we don't know?"

"That's fine with me, so long as you don't plan to publish any stories about it in the *Examiner*."

At last, realization dawns in her eyes. "Oh."

A half mile from the lake, the whirling red lights of a fire engine break out from behind the trees that line the levee, then veer onto the narrow lane that runs along the shore of Lake Concordia. A half mile behind it, three vehicles traveling in train quickly follow. The flashing red arcs are much closer to the road on those vehicles, which means they're police cruisers. Our window of opportunity to shape history is closing fast.

"I found Brody Royal's name in Henry Sexton's journals," Caitlin says, spinning her story on the fly. "That led me to interview his daughter. Out of fear of her father, Katy panicked and took an overdose of pills before I arrived to question her, but she still implicated Brody in multiple murders. Katy's husband walked in on us after she passed out—that would have been documented by paramedics, if not police. Up to that point, everything's more or less true. Royal learned from Randall Regan that I'd questioned Katy, and they retaliated to keep me from publishing what I'd learned from her."

This fairy tale might convince the Concordia Parish sheriff, but probably not the FBI. "Too many people saw me go into St. Catherine's Hospital," I say. "They know I spent twenty minutes alone with Brody. Now that he's dead, his family's liable to make all kinds of accusations about me going after him. Kaiser will find out sooner or later."

"Surely you can explain that conversation somehow?"

"I sure can't admit that I tried to cut a deal with him." Under the pressure of the approaching authorities, my mind ratchets down to the task at hand. "What if I pick up where your story leaves off? I went to St. Catherine's Hospital to make sure Royal wasn't going to take some kind of revenge against you for his daughter's suicide attempt. I suspected that he'd ordered several murders during the

1960s, and Katy had verified that to you. I also believed Royal had ordered the hit attempts on Henry at the newspaper and the hospital, and I was worried he'd do the same to you. That makes sense, right?"

Caitlin nods quickly, her eyes on the whirling lights.

I step closer to her. "Are you going to tell the cops about your recording of what Katy said?"

"I might as well, since Brody burned both copies. They're going to read about it in tomorrow's paper anyway."

Closing my eyes, I see Caitlin's Treo smartphone and my borrowed tape recorder being consumed by the fearsome blast of a flamethrower. "You really don't have another copy at the newspaper?"

Her look of desolation is my only answer.

The fire engine has reached the head of Royal's driveway. We only have seconds now.

"What about Brody's confessions?" Caitlin asks. "That he was behind Pooky Wilson's death? That Frank and Snake Knox killed Pooky at the Bone Tree?"

"We tell the cops all of that. Every bit of it helps justify what we did tonight."

Caitlin looks strangely hesitant, which I don't understand. Even if we tell the police about those confessions, she can still publish the story before any other media outlet gets the information.

"For God's sake," I say, "until tonight, no one was even sure the Bone Tree was real. And Royal admitted taking part in the gang rape of Viola Turner. We've *got* to tell them that."

Caitlin gives me a pointed look. "Brody also told us your father killed Viola. Do you want to tell the police that?"

"Of course not."

"All right, then. That's why I'm asking what we hold back. Is there anything else?"

I can't read her eyes. We've kept so much from each other over the past few days that it's hard to know where our stories might diverge if compared to one another.

"The rifles," I say softly. "Those two rifles in the cabinet that he showed us just before you held the razor to his throat. Did you see them?"

"Yes, but I wasn't really paying attention. I was waiting for my chance to attack him."

"There were identifying plaques beneath every other rifle in the gun collection. But on those two plaques there were only dates. Dates, and a small American flag emblem."

Caitlin shrugs. "So?"

"The dates were November twenty-second, 1963, and April fourth, 1968."

She blinks in confusion for a couple of seconds, but then her eyes go wide. "No way. I mean . . . do you really—"

"I don't think so. But if we don't tell Kaiser about them, whatever's left of those guns might disappear tonight. And we'll never know."

Caitlin gingerly touches the burn on her cheek. "Let's hope Sheriff Dennis is in one of those cars, and not the goddamn state police. Not that Captain Ozan."

I reach out and squeeze her shoulder. "Whoever it is, act more disoriented than you are. You really are in shock, but play it up more. When they question you, try to stick to the past hour, nothing more. Act exhausted, and play up your injuries."

Caitlin doesn't appear to like this plan. "I don't want to spend the night in a damned hospital. This is the biggest story I've ever been involved in. I've got zero time to waste."

"I know." Moving forward, I pull her tight against me. An hour ago I made the worst mistake of my life by begging her to suppress part of a story in order to try to bargain with a killer for my father's life. I've got no right to try to control anything she does now. "I'm sorry I didn't listen to you. You tried to tell me something like this would happen. My worry over Dad blinded me."

She shakes her head against my chest. "It wasn't just you. Once I made that recording of Katy, Brody was going to come after us, no matter what."

"But he wouldn't have known about the recording if I hadn't told him."

This is debatable, but Caitlin only draws back and looks hard into my eyes. "Whatever happens now, I need to get back to the newspaper. *Please* do whatever you can to make that happen."

The fire engine screeches to a stop thirty feet from us, and uniformed men leap off and out of it. The hoses come out faster than I would have believed possible, but these guys don't have a prayer of putting out this inferno. One fireman hurries toward the body on the ground and drops to his knees, but I call out to him that the man is dead.

"What happened?" shouts another man from behind me. "Is there anybody still in the house?"

When I turn, I see a fire captain wearing a black hard-hat and a fireproof coat. "Three dead men. That's all I know. Not from the fire, though. There was a gunfight."

His mouth drops open. "Gunfight? In Mr. Royal's place?"

"Brody Royal's one of the dead."

"Oh, no."

"His son-in-law is another. The third is Henry Sexton, the reporter."

The fire captain shakes his head, unable to comprehend what I'm telling him. "Is that it? Nobody else?"

"I really don't know. There's nobody I'd risk my men to save."

The fireman looks at me as if I might be out of my mind.

"They were torturing us," I say. "Before the fire."

"Torturing . . . ?" The captain looks closer at me. "Hey, I know you. You're the mayor of Natchez. Penn Cage."

"That's right."

"Are you okay?"

"I guess so. This is Caitlin Masters, the publisher of the *Natchez Examiner*."

"What the hell started the fire?"

The answer to this question isn't something the fire captain could accept. *Let's see . . . Brody Royal was preparing to burn off Caitlin's arm with a flamethrower. I was chained to the wall, tearing my hands to shreds in my desperation to break free. That's when Henry Sexton, despite his injuries, somehow struggled to his feet and shielded Caitlin with his body. Royal meant to burn him too, but like some medieval martyr, the reporter charged Royal and threw his arms around him before the old man could safely ignite the flamethrower. While the rest of us stared in horror, Henry pulled the trigger and immolated them both, creating a firestorm that no amount of water could smother—*

"Mayor?" says the fire captain, catching hold of my shoulders. "Maybe you ought to sit down, huh?"

"A World War Two flamethrower," I mumble. "Loaded with gasoline and tar."

The man shakes his head in disbelief, then motions for help and starts shouting orders.

The sound of gunning motors makes me turn toward the driveway entrance. Three Concordia Parish Sheriff's Department cruisers roar up behind the fire truck. Two park there, but a Chevy Tahoe pulls around the fire truck and drives up to within ten feet of me before it stops.

"Thank God," Caitlin says in my ear.

Sheriff Walker Dennis gets out of his cruiser and stumps toward us. Three years shy of fifty, he carries himself like a minor-league baseball star gone to seed. He weighs 220 pounds and has forearms that would discourage anyone from betting against him in an arm-wrestling match. The way he wears his brown uniform and Stetson gives the impression that he's been a sheriff all his adult life, but in fact he only took over the job about six weeks ago, after his predecessor was indicted on corruption charges that decimated the entire department.

"Are you okay?" Dennis shouts, striding forward and grabbing my forearm as though to reassure himself that I'm alive.

"Yeah, yeah. Caitlin, too."

The sheriff looks over at the fire. Two crews have trained hoses on the base of the flames, but most of the house is gone already.

"Anybody in there?" Dennis asks.

"Royal and Regan, both dead."

"Shit. They couldn't get out?"

"No."

The sheriff gives me an odd look. "You couldn't get 'em out?"

"I didn't try, Walker. They kidnapped us from the *Examiner* office—or sent two guys to do it. They were torturing Caitlin for information when this guy"—I point at the dead body of Sleepy Johnston—"busted in with Henry and saved us. Royal had a flamethrower in there. It was a miracle we got out alive."

"Henry's dead too," Caitlin says.

Walker Dennis rubs his forehead like a man with an incipient migraine. This has already been one of the worst days of his life, and this event will only compound his difficulties. "I obviously should have pressed you harder about Brody Royal."

"It wouldn't have mattered."

He takes a tin of Skoal from his breast pocket, opens it with some urgency, and jams a pinch beneath his bottom lip. "Who the fuck *is* that?" he asks, pointing at the dead man on the ground.

"Sleepy Johnston. You know him better as 'Gates Brown.'"

The sheriff's eyes widen. Dennis knows "Gates Brown" as the alias of a man who haunted the periphery of our investigations for the past couple of days. Walking closer to the body, he looks down at the face of a sixty-seven-year-old black man who lived in this area as a boy, then fled to Detroit for the rest of his adult life.

"This the guy who called me about seeing Royal and Regan burning the *Concordia Beacon*?"

I nod.

"We need to get the hell out of here. The state police could show up any second, and we need to get some things straight before you talk to them."

I glance at Caitlin, who's watching us closely. I nod, thinking the same thing that she and Dennis must be: *Captain Alphonse Ozan.*

"All right," Dennis says. "Let's get back to the department to get your statements. At least that way I'll be on my home turf if they try to take this case away from me."

"What about the FBI?"

"Agent Kaiser called me just before I got here. He'd just heard about the fire, but he didn't seem to know it was Royal's house yet."

"I'll bet he does by now."

Sheriff Dennis spits on the ground and leans close to me. "We've got a jurisdictional clusterfuck on our hands here. And both our asses are on the line."

"I know."

"You ride with me," he says, pulling me toward his Tahoe. "Ms. Masters can come in the car behind us."

"Hold on." I yank my arm loose. "Caitlin rides with us."

Walker shakes his head. "Sorry. I have to separate you two. A lot of eyes will be watching this. I've got to follow procedure."

"Surely she can ride with us? You can swear we didn't talk on the way."

Sensing danger, Caitlin has come up beside me and taken hold of my arm.

"I'm sorry," Dennis says firmly. "It's got to be this way."

Before I can argue further, Walker leans in close and says, "My brother-in-law will be driving the second car. If you need to call her on the phone, you can. The stupidest thing we can do is stay here and argue. You want Ozan to arrest you two for killing one of the richest men in Louisiana? A friend of every governor for the past fifty years?"

"I'll be fine in the second car," Caitlin says, nudging me toward Dennis's truck. "Let's not waste one more second. Just let me grab Henry's files."

Walker gives her a grateful look, then signals a deputy standing by one of the cruisers behind the fire truck. The man reaches us as Caitlin trots back with her box, and Dennis introduces him as Grady Wells, his brother-in-law. I beg Wells to take care of Caitlin like he would his own flesh and blood, and he promises that he will.

"If the state police try to pull us over," Walker tells Wells, "ignore them. Don't stop until we get back to base. You only take orders from me. Ignore the radio, and if they start yelling at you over their PA speaker, pay no mind. We'll hash out the jurisdictions when we get to the station."

Moments later, six doors slam, and our small convoy begins racing toward Highway 84 and the Mississippi River. Turning to look back through the rear windshield, I see the pillar of fire still towering over the vast alluvial plain, announcing calamity to the world. If my mother and daughter were to look out of their third-floor window high on the Natchez bluff, they would see it in the distance. As I think of my mother, a double-edged knife of guilt and anger slips between my ribs, and I wonder whether my father is within sight of that roaring flame.

CHAPTER 2

TOM CAGE DROVE through the cold Louisiana night in a stolen pickup truck, his .357 Magnum pressing hard against his right thigh. An unconscious hit man lay on the seat behind him, hands bound together and lashed to a gun rack mounted at the rear of the cab. A corpse lay on the floor between them, a bullet from Tom's .357 in his belly.

Tom had taken a Valium and some nitroglycerine, but he was still suffering from tachycardia, and no thought he could summon seemed to calm his overburdened heart. Walt Garrity had almost certainly been killed tonight, trying to extricate Tom and himself from the trouble Tom had gotten them into, and now nearly every cop in two states was combing the highways in search of them, believing they'd murdered a Louisiana state trooper, as well as Tom's former nurse, Viola Turner.

Walt had shot the trooper, all right, but only to stop him from killing Tom in cold blood. Even so, the cold-eyed state policeman had put a bullet through Tom's shoulder before he died, and while that wound had been treated some hours ago, the pain had now built to an excruciating level. Tom didn't dare take enough narcotics to dull the agony. Fifty years of medical experience told him that the gunshot wound had pushed him into a state where he could simply collapse behind the wheel and be dead before the pickup truck came to a stop. Only two months ago he'd suffered a severe coronary and barely survived. In the past seventy-two hours, he had endured more stress than even a healthy seventy-three-year-old man could take without caving under the strain.

Tom could scarcely believe that six weeks ago life had seemed relatively quiet. Having recovered from his heart attack, he'd been looking forward to his son's marriage, which was planned for Christmas Eve. But then Viola Turner had returned to Natchez, trailing the past like a demon in her wake. The cancer that drove Viola back home after four decades in Chicago had reduced the beautiful nurse he'd once loved to a desiccated shadow of herself; despite his nearly fifty years of medical experience, Tom had been profoundly shocked by the sight of her. The grim truth was that Viola had come home to Natchez not to retire, but to die. The first night he saw her, he'd realized he might conceivably be charged with murder in the near future. A merciful act that usually went unreported might well draw the attention of a vindictive sheriff and DA. But not even in his darkest dreams could Tom have imagined that he and Walt would be running for their lives.

The bound man in the backseat moaned. Tom debated whether to stop the truck and sedate the would-be assassin again. The hit man's name was Grimsby, and he was thirty years younger than Tom. If he regained full consciousness, Tom would have difficulty handling him, even with his hands and feet bound. Tom had only managed to tie the bastard by chemically incapacitating him first. Along with his now-dead partner, Grimsby had cornered Tom at the edge of a nearby lake. And though Tom had been armed, he'd resigned himself to death before the two killers ever appeared. But then—by the simple act of checking his text messages—Tom had learned that Caitlin was pregnant. That knowledge had transformed him from an old man tired of running (and killing) into a patriarch committed to seeing his fourth grandchild—and perhaps his first grandson—born. With chilling deliberation, Tom had shot one of the two arrogant hit men as they faced him, then disarmed Grimsby and forced him to carry his dead partner up to Drew Elliott's lake house, in which Tom had been hiding.

After retrieving his weekend bag, Tom had filled a syringe with precious insulin and jabbed Grimsby in the back as he loaded his dead partner into the truck. That put the hit man into insulin shock. While he lay sprawled across the backseat of the truck, barely breathing, Tom had bound his hands with an old ski rope he'd found in Drew's garage, then tied his hands to the gun rack so that

Grimsby couldn't attack him if he revived during the ride. Tom hadn't intended to kill the other man, but his options had been limited, and the pair had surely meant to execute him beside the lake—an emotionless murder for hire. If Grimsby died (or lived out his days in a coma) as a result of the insulin overdose Tom had given him, so be it.

Tom's real dilemma was what to do next. If he pointed the truck toward civilization, he would come to a roadblock sooner rather than later, and there he would be shot while "resisting arrest." To avoid this, he'd driven the truck into the low-lying backcountry between Ferriday, Rayville, and Tallulah, endless cotton fields so thinly populated that they felt deserted, but Tom knew better. He had been born in the southwestern part of Louisiana, and he'd gone to undergraduate school at NLU in Natchitoches, where he'd met his wife. But Peggy Cage, née McCrae, was from an eastern Louisiana farm only ten miles from where he was now. The nearest conglomeration of people to her father's homestead was a tiny crossroads village called Dunston, which lay about forty miles north of Ferriday. This familiarity gave Tom the only sense of security he'd felt in a long time: Peggy had relatives in this area, and Tom had treated them and most of their neighbors for medical emergencies while visiting over the years. He knew he could rely on the loyalty of clannish country folks.

He needed to get rid of the truck as fast as he could. Grimsby and his partner had almost certainly notified their boss that they'd cornered him at Drew's lake house, and that meant Forrest Knox would have an APB out for their truck in no time. Tom felt confident that his wife's brother would help him ditch the truck, but that meant putting another family at risk, and Tom had already gotten people killed by doing that.

Peggy would tell me to do it, he thought.

The real question was what to do if he *did* manage to get safely to ground somewhere. This nightmare had begun when he was charged with Viola's murder, but the death of the state trooper had complicated matters exponentially. Jumping bail on the first charge only made him look more guilty, and further reduced his options. Walt's plan had been to seek help from the superintendent of the

Louisiana State Police (who, like Walt, was a former Texas Ranger) in getting the APB on Tom and Walt withdrawn. But something had obviously gone wrong. Tom had expected Walt back long before the two hit men found him, yet he'd heard nothing.

That left two options. He could try to turn himself in to some arm of law enforcement—preferably the FBI, if he could reach them—and hope to survive the encounter. Or he could do exactly what he'd advised Penn not to do—deal with the devil direct, and try to remove his family from harm's way by any means necessary. Given that he was likely surrounded on all sides by Louisiana's state and local cops, the chance of safely delivering himself into the arms of federal agents was small. Simply using his personal cell phone was likely to bring a state police helicopter down on his head within five minutes, and the last burn phone Walt had left him might well be compromised by now. They had used it too many times already.

The ring of the very phone Tom was thinking about stunned him, and his shoulder began to pound, telling him his blood pressure had spiked at the sound. He stared at the phone for two more rings, then answered.

"Hello?"

"It's me," said a voice that made him sag against the truck's door. "Are you okay?"

"I thought you were dead." Tom craned his neck around to try to see if the hit man had woken up.

"I didn't want to put you at risk by calling you. Even now we shouldn't spend more than a minute on the phone."

"Did you have any luck with Colonel Mackiever?"

"No. And don't say his name again. He got delayed, but he's on his way up here now."

"Up here" meant Baton Rouge.

"FK has already moved against him," Walt said.

Forrest Knox, Tom thought.

"I don't know the details," Walt continued, "but it sounds like they're trying to discredit Mac and take his job."

"So he can't get the APB revoked?"

"Not with a phone call. He needs to hear our side of the story before he can move. That's the next step. But that's not why I called. The colonel just told me something you need to know. Brody Royal was killed tonight, in his house on Lake Concordia. That reporter died with him, Henry Sexton."

"No." Tom's heart began to pound again.

"Yep. And there's more bad news."

The hammering in Tom's chest began to solidify into angina. "Not Penn—"

"No—hell, no. But Penn was apparently there when it happened, and Caitlin, too. They're alive, but that's all I know right now. Mac just caught it over his radio. Royal's son-in-law died there too, and a black fellow I never heard of. Nobody Mac trusts seems to know what really went down."

"Where are Penn and Caitlin now?"

"In custody. Concordia Parish Sheriff's Department. State police heard it from firemen on the scene. Alive and in squad cars, only minor injuries. I'll try to learn more, but you don't hear from me, they're fine. If anything's seriously wrong, I'll call you. Don't call me back except in an extreme emergency."

"Okay."

"How you doing? Melba still there?"

"No. I'm not either."

"What?"

"FK sent two guys to the lake house, and they nearly got me. I'm lucky to be alive, to tell the truth."

"What?"

"He sent them to kill me. I turned the tables. One's KIA, the other tied up in the backseat."

"Jesus. How the hell did you manage that, the shape you're in?"

"A little luck and a lot of drugs. What the hell do we do now?"

Walt only paused for a few seconds. "You need to go to ground somewhere while I talk to the colonel. And don't try to cover any distance—you'll hit a roadblock. Can you think of anywhere close that's safe?"

"Actually, yes. But your part's done. You need to get back to Texas. You've got Carmelita to think about. Just get clear, buddy."

"That's enough of that. Look, we've been on the phone too long already. Let me ask you one more question."

Walt's voice sounded strange.

"What is it?"

"What do you plan to do with the survivor in the back?"

"I'm not sure. I figured I'd ditch him somewhere. Cotton field, probably."

"I don't think that's a good idea."

"Where, then?"

"Nowhere." After a pause, Walt said. "He's KIA. Just like the first one."

It took a moment to absorb Walt's meaning. "I can't do that. Too much has . . ." Tom trailed off. "Too many people are dead already."

"Listen to me," Walt said in a voice that came all the way from their days in Korea. "Mercy is a virtue you can't afford. We already made that mistake once this week."

Tom thought of Sonny Thornfield and wondered if saving the old Klansman had really been a mistake, or whether he might yet play some positive role before events resolved themselves.

In the backseat, Grimsby stirred. Tom looked back but could see little in the darkness.

"Hey," Walt said. "Did I lose you?"

"Now that I think about it," Tom said, in case Grimsby had awakened, "going to Mobile was about the smartest thing you could have done."

"What?" Walt said. "Oh. I get it."

"I wish to God I was there with you," Tom added, meaning it. He waited about ten seconds, then said, "Well, I don't like it, but I guess it's my best chance. Mobile it is."

"That's enough dinner theater," Walt said in a quieter voice. "Listen to me now. Get yourself a new burn phone at a Walmart. Better yet, send someone you trust to get you a half dozen. Then call this number. I want you to use a code to tell me where you are—a basic code. Three steps. Number the letters in the alphabet from one to twenty-six. Then spell out your message, convert it to numbers, and multiply each letter-number by the number of men who died in the ambulance at Chosin. We clear on that number?"

Just the mention of that ambulance made Tom grimace. "Yeah."

"Call and give me a string of numbers, nothing else. Like thirty-six, break, two-seventy-five, break, one-fifty, break. You got it?"

"Yeah."

"Remember, if you don't hear from me, Penn and Caitlin are fine."

Tom nodded wearily in the dashboard light. "It's good to hear your voice, Walt."

"Same here, buddy. Time to go, though. Just remember, you've got one tough thing to do before you do anything else. Finish that son of a bitch. This is war, Corporal."

"Walt—"

"He meant to kill you in cold blood, didn't he?"

"I'll see you soon."

Tom broke the connection and put down the phone.

The revelation that Walt was alive had buoyed him in a way that nothing else could. With Walt still working to get the APB revoked, the most immediate threat to their lives might actually be removed. The news about the killings at Lake Concordia, on the other hand, had deeply unsettled Tom. He knew he bore some of the blame for those deaths, as he did for the earlier ones. Worse, Penn and Caitlin could only have turned up at Royal's house because of their efforts to help him. But it was Henry Sexton's death that most haunted him. To think that Henry Sexton had survived two earlier attacks only to die at Brody Royal's house . . . it seemed almost incomprehensible.

Tom squinted down the twin headlight beams illuminating the narrow road between the empty cotton fields, watching for deer or stray cattle. He couldn't afford an accident that might disable the truck. In his present state, he was incapable of walking to safety.

He tensed as a pair of headlights appeared in the distance, and his heart and shoulder began to pound in synchrony. Unless he stopped dead, turned around, and made a run for it, he had no choice but to continue toward the oncoming vehicle.

As the two vehicles closed the distance, a sharp pain stabbed him high in the back, and his breath went shallow. If whoever was in that car or truck was a cop, Tom knew, he was likely to die in the next minute. His photo—along with Walt's—had been circulated across the state for the past few hours, saturating all media. Any cop who stopped him would recognize him. And what police officer was going to give a fugitive cop killer time to explain a corpse and captive in the backseat? Tom had treated plenty of cops over the years, and in this situation, eight out of ten would shoot first and take the glory.

The skin on his neck and arms crawled as he waited for the bright red flare of Louisiana police lights. His face was pouring sweat, and angina had locked his back muscles by the time the blinding lights flashed past him, and he saw that they belonged to a Louisiana Power and Light bucket truck.

"Christ," he gasped, as his stolen truck rolled out of the sucking vacuum between the two vehicles and plowed back into the darkness.

As his heartbeat slowly decelerated, Tom realized that Grimsby had awakened in the backseat. Some ancient survival instinct had flickered to life and told him that the hit man was now staring at the back of his head, trying to work out a way to kill him. If Tom tried to turn, Grimsby would close his eyes and pretend to be asleep. But Tom knew different. Behind the lids, those eyes would be alive with lethal malice.

What had Walt said? *Mercy is a virtue you can't afford. . . .*

As the truck rolled through the dark fields, Tom reached down and laid his hand on the cold checkered butt of the .357.

CHAPTER 3

THE MOMENT SONNY Thornfield saw Billy Knox standing beneath the lights on the floating dock outside his fishing camp on the Toledo Bend Reservoir, he knew something had gone wrong. Sonny and Snake had just carried out one of the most nerve-wracking missions he'd taken part in since the war, and he was elated simply to be alive. In the dead of night, Snake had secretly flown them via floatplane to a small lake near Ferriday. After being ferried by car to the lawn outside Mercy Hospital, Snake had assassinated Henry Sexton by shooting him through his hospital window. Then, because Forrest had given the order that everyone with direct knowledge of the Sexton attack had to die, they had drugged two boys in their twenties and drowned them in the Atchafalaya Swamp. No one could have seen that crime. Snake had set the plane down in the middle of a pitch-black pool, miles from human habitation.

That can't be it, Sonny told himself, staring at Billy's grim face as Snake taxied the Beechcraft up to the dock. As carefully as he could, Sonny climbed out onto the starboard pontoon and caught the mooring line that Billy tossed him.

Billy didn't look much like his father had as a young man. Snake had always been wiry and hatchet-faced. Billy was stockier and blond, with the shoulder-length hair and beard of a 1970s rock singer. Normally his eyes glinted with an amused light, but tonight he looked as grim as Sonny had ever seen him.

"What's the matter?" Sonny asked. "What's happened?"

"Wait till Daddy gets out," Billy said.

When the pontoon bumped the dock, Sonny stepped onto the floating square of wood. "Trouble?"

Billy nodded once. "Big-time."

A chill raced up Sonny's back.

Snake climbed down onto the pontoon and stepped lightly onto the dock, his inquisitive eyes on those of his son.

"What's the matter, boy? You look like you need a dose of Ex-Lax."

"You won't be laughing when you hear this. You missed Sexton tonight."

"Missed . . . ? Bullshit."

Billy shook his head. "Captain Ozan called. You definitely missed him. You killed his girlfriend, if that makes you feel any better."

"I saw the round hit him in the head!" Snake barked.

"You only grazed him."

"No way. That was a .22 Magnum round, and I drilled him."

Billy shrugged as if tired of arguing the point. "Maybe your eyes aren't what they used to be. Ozan was there, and he knows what happened. The FBI moved Sexton to an interior room—an office—and tried to pretend he was dead, but Ozan got the truth out of a CPSO deputy. Now we've got a world of shit over there."

"Does Forrest know?" Sonny asked worriedly.

"Haven't talked to him. But he sure as hell won't be happy."

"Where is he?"

"New Orleans. He's making his move on Colonel Mackiever."

"Shit, shit, shit." Sonny couldn't hide his fear.

"I hit that son of a bitch!" Snake insisted.

"The window glass must have deflected your shot," Billy said.

"Shut the fuck up!" Snake bellowed. "I know what I saw."

"Why didn't you kill the Masters girl?" Billy asked, ignoring his father's anger. "Ozan says she should have been visible through the window. Killing Sexton's girlfriend didn't do a damn thing for us. At least wiping Caitlin Masters off the board would have bought us a margin of safety, if Sexton told her anything about us."

"The other woman was trying to close the blinds. She filled up half the fucking window! Besides, I figured Forrest would have a stroke if I told him I'd killed that newspaper bitch without his okay. If I'd have known he wanted that, I'd have marched right up to the window and blasted them all."

"Forrest wouldn't have okayed the Masters girl," Sonny said. "That's only hindsight talking." He rubbed his arms and shivered. "How about we get up to the house?"

"Fuck that," Snake said. "We need to head back to Ferriday and finish off Henry. We can't risk him talking." Sonny looked longingly up the slope at the luxurious condo on the shore of the reservoir, where warm yellow light glowed through the windows.

"Forget Sexton," Billy said firmly. "He needs to be finished, all right, but you'd never get close to him now. Forrest will make that decision."

Snake kicked a tackle box that was standing on the dock. "This is bullshit, Billy. What does Brody say? You talked to him?"

"No. We're not supposed to be using the phones, remember? Ozan broke the rules, but he figured we needed to know. You're to stay here in Texas until you get further word."

Sonny waited while Snake cussed and spat.

"Let's just hope," Billy said, "that Forrest is the new superintendent of state police by this afternoon. Then we can start some realistic damage control."

Snake kicked the tackle box into the dark water, then marched up the wooden steps toward the house.

Billy's cell phone rang, and he answered it immediately. After ten seconds, his face went pale. After ten more, his mouth hung slack. He turned away from Sonny and walked a few steps along the pier. Looking up the slope, Sonny saw that Snake had stopped climbing and was hovering near the top step, watching his son. When

Billy hung up, he walked back toward Sonny like a man trying to pass a field sobriety test.

"Who was that?" Snake called, coming back down the steps. "What's happened?"

"That was Ozan," Billy said in a dazed voice. "Henry Sexton's dead."

Snake laughed and pumped his fist. "I told you I got that son of a bitch!"

Billy shook his head slowly. "No, you didn't. Brody's dead, too."

"What?" Sonny whispered.

"Brody, Sexton, Randall Regan, some old nigger from Detroit, a couple of Brody's guards, and a Natchez cop to boot. Brody's house is burning to the ground right now."

"Bullshit!" said Snake.

"Ozan just heard it on fire department radios in Concordia Parish."

"What does Forrest say?"

"Ozan can't get Forrest on the phone. Not since he went into a hotel in New Orleans to meet Colonel Mackiever."

"Oh, God," Sonny breathed, looking for a place to sit down.

CHAPTER 4

SHERIFF WALKER DENNIS'S Tahoe hums swiftly through the Louisiana night, his roof lights dark, his siren silenced. The dry blast of the heater sweeps past my face, the muted crackle of the police radio barely audible beneath it. The heat aggravates the cigarette burn on my left cheek, but after enduring all I have tonight, the pain seems inconsequential.

"I tried to keep a lid on this to delay the state police," Sheriff Dennis says, "but some firemen mentioned names on the radio. It's out now. And when a man as rich as Brody Royal dies, people are gonna want to know everything. We'll be lucky to make the station without state police cruisers flagging us down."

Twelve miles east of us, this highway crosses the Mississippi River into Natchez, but our destination lies several miles short of that. The Concordia Parish Sheriff's Office is housed in the basement floor of the parish courthouse between Vidalia and Ferriday, Louisiana. The highway between those two towns runs through the worst sort of sprawl: small-engine repair shops, oil field service companies, salvage yards, boat dealerships, and an ever-changing line of marginal enterprises. All have parking lots where state police vehicles could lie in wait for us.

"I'm going to videotape your statements when we get there," Sheriff Dennis says, "but I'd just as soon know ahead of time what you're going to say. I don't want to talk you into a corner you can't get out of."

"Thanks, Walker."

"Are you and your fiancée straight on your stories?"

"Yeah."

"Good. Because whatever you say is gonna get picked apart by a lot of agencies."

I nod but add nothing.

"I got the basic gist of what went down, but why don't you tell me who killed who, and in what order."

I take a breath and organize my thoughts before speaking. "Two of Royal's men knocked out the Natchez cop who was guarding the parking lot at the *Examiner* before they snatched us. I think they probably killed him, because I felt no pulse in the van. Once we reached Royal's, those two guys hauled his body away."

"Can you give me a good description?"

"Decent. I'd like to kill the sons of bitches."

"If they killed a cop, you'll have to get in line. Who died next?"

For a moment I can't speak. Walker considers it a given that cop killers will die violently, and he's so caught up in the moment that he doesn't realize he just condemned my father by extension.

"Royal and Regan were torturing Caitlin and me in the basement," I tell him, "in Royal's gun range."

"Jesus, Penn. I'm sorry. I always heard Brody had some kind of million-dollar collection down there. Never saw the place, though."

For an instant the two putative assassination rifles flash behind my eyes. "A million might be low," I murmur. "Royal was trying to find out who had visited Pooky Wilson's mother before she died. He knew there was a witness who could place him at the scene of Albert Norris's death."

"How did he know that?"

"Between you and me . . . I told him, earlier tonight."

Walker gives me an angry glare. "Damn it, Penn."

"I know. I'll pay for that the rest of my life. But it's done now. During the torture, Henry Sexton and Sleepy Johnston busted in to try to save us. We heard gunshots upstairs. They pretended to be SWAT, but Royal didn't fall for it. When Sleepy Johnston came through the door, Brody got the drop on him. After Brody figured out who he was—by calling his lawyer, Claude Devereux—he shot Johnston in cold blood."

"So this Sleepy Johnston was the guy who went to see Pooky Wilson's mother before she died?"

"Right."

"And he was the one who called in tips to me as 'Gates Brown'?"

"That's right. And visited Henry at the hospital."

"How the hell did Johnston know that Royal had kidnapped you?"

"He was watching Brody's house when we were brought there. He'd been following Royal ever since he got down here from Detroit. That's why he was in a position to see Royal and Regan burn the *Beacon* building. He just didn't get up the nerve to call your office until today. Or yesterday, I guess. Technically. Even after living in the North for forty years, Sleepy was still scared shitless of Royal and the Knoxes. He didn't think Brody would ever pay for what he'd done."

"Why did he use a baseball player's name as an alias?"

"After Sleepy moved to Detroit, he was lonely. Gates Brown was a black star of the Tigers, and he'd had some trouble in his youth, just like Sleepy. But he helped the Tigers win the Series in '68, and Sleepy saw him as a role model. But his luck ran out tonight."

Sheriff Dennis, an old baseball player himself, nods with understanding. "Pretty damn sad when you think about it."

"Worse than sad."

"So who died next? Henry?"

"Henry was already wounded from the earlier attacks, but I think he'd got hit again in the gunfight upstairs at Royal's. He could barely hold himself upright. Brody knocked him down and taunted him, then basically forgot him. But when Brody was about to fry Caitlin with that flamethrower—and I was chained to the wall—Henry crawled over there, got to his feet somehow, and protected her with his body."

"Henry did that?"

"You haven't heard the half of it. He went after Brody then. Brody was trying to fire that flamethrower, but once Henry lunged at him, he couldn't fire without risking the flame blowing back on him. Then Henry closed with Brody, and after a brief struggle, Henry pulled the trigger and immolated them both." I pause to get my voice back under control. "It was the most terrible and heroic thing I've ever witnessed."

"God almighty. And Randall Regan?"

After a few seconds of silence, I say, "I killed Regan."

Sheriff Dennis grunts. "Well . . . I guess you can give me the details at the station."

"Thanks."

"But tell me this: if Sleepy Johnston was shot down in the basement, how'd he wind up outside on the ground?"

"I carried him out."

The sheriff looks back at me, his eyes skeptical. "Dead?"

"No. He was hit in the spine. I knew moving him might paralyze him, or even kill him, but he'd have burned alive otherwise." I force back the images of Sleepy Johnston's face as he resigned himself to death in those flames. "I didn't even feel the weight, Walker. It was like lifting a little kid."

Dennis nods slowly. "That's how it is when shit like that goes down."

"All I know is, two good men are dead. Three, if that Natchez cop guarding the *Examiner* was killed."

"I don't envy you the call to Chief Logan. Unless you want me to make it."

I shake my head. "No, I owe Logan that."

"Well, at least Royal and Regan are dead. I won't say I'm sorry to hear that news."

But at what cost? "Caitlin blames me for what happened tonight," I say dully, voicing my deepest conviction. "She'll never say it, but she does. She blames my father, too, of course."

"What about you? Do you blame your old man?"

After a long silence, I hear myself say, "I guess I do. If he'd done anything but what he did, you know? If he'd opened up to me from the beginning, about Viola's death? If he hadn't jumped bail? How many people would still be alive?"

"I don't know, Penn. But wait till you can talk to him before you judge. Your daddy's a good man. I feel sure there are things you don't know. Things that will make all this make sense."

"I tried to write him off tonight, Walker. After Henry died. And Sleepy Johnston. But I can't."

Sheriff Dennis turns and gives me a look of pure empathy. "He's your father, man. He's blood."

There it is. Blood. The empirical, evolutionary imperative. What more can be said? "Walker . . . tonight I asked Brody if he killed Viola Turner, or ordered her killed."

"What did he say?"

"He said no. He admitted that he'd raped Viola, along with some other Double Eagles. Snake Knox and the others. But he said he didn't kill her. He *said . . .*"

"What?"

"I'll deny I ever said this, Walker. But Royal said my father killed Viola."

Sheriff Dennis seems to freeze behind the wheel. Then he bites his lip for a few seconds. "Did he give you any details?"

"He said Dad saved Viola's life forty years ago, but he killed her two days ago. He laughed at the irony of it."

"Do you really believe that sick son of a bitch?"

"He had no reason to lie, Walker. He thought Caitlin and I were about to die, and he'd already admitted ordering the murder of Pooky Wilson."

Dennis watches Highway 84 and takes his time before speaking. "But do *you* believe it? In your gut?"

"I don't know. Could Dad have killed Viola to ease her suffering? Yes. But murder her . . . Not one person I've talked to this week believed that's possible. And in the end, I guess I don't either."

"What did Henry think?"

"Henry believed the Double Eagles killed her. They'd threatened to do it if she ever came back to Natchez, and she did. Henry didn't have any doubt that they fulfilled their threat."

"That's good enough for me, bub."

"I wish it were for me. I've come up with at least three different theories over the past three days. There are so many possibilities. It might even be that Lincoln Turner killed Viola, Dad knows that, and he's covering up for him."

"Lincoln Turner, who accused your old man of murder in the first place? You're saying he killed his own mother?"

"Maybe. Possibly by accident, either in a botched mercy killing, or a layman's effort to revive her with adrenaline."

"But . . . if that's the case, why the hell would your father cover for that asshole?"

"Because Dad thinks Lincoln is his son."

This silences Dennis for half a minute.

"Jesus," he says finally. "This is Tennessee Williams shit, here."

I'm surprised Walker Dennis knows enough about Tennessee Williams even to make that remark. "More like Faulkner, I'd say. *Absalom, Absalom!*"

"Same difference. You know what I think?"

"What?"

"All this crap with Royal and Regan and the Double Eagles is a good thing. For your father, I mean. It's obvious that there's a whole lot more going on than the murder of one old nurse. And Viola was related to that civil rights kid, Revels. If you can just get your dad safely into custody—in Mississippi, not Louisiana—he'll go to trial for killing Viola. Right?"

"Aren't you forgetting the dead Louisiana state trooper?"

Dennis waves his hand dismissively. "Just forget that for a minute. I'm no lawyer, but I've watched my share of murder trials. If your father goes to trial for killing Nurse Viola, all you need is one thing—*reasonable doubt*. Am I right?"

"You're not wrong."

"Are you going to defend him yourself?"

"Hell, no. Quentin Avery's his lawyer."

"Even better. Avery could talk twelve dogs off a meat truck."

"We're light-years from a courtroom, Walker."

"Maybe we are, and maybe we ain't." The sheriff looks back at me, his eyes glinting beneath his Stetson. "All this trouble goes back to the Knox family: Frank and the Double Eagles in the old days, and Forrest and his drug operation now. I say we go back to our first plan. Hit the Knoxes as hard as we can. Bust every meth cooker and mule in this parish. Turn up the heat on the Knox organization, big-time. Before you know it, we'll have a couple of Double Eagles in the frying pan. And once they start singing, I'll have Forrest by the balls. And Quentin Avery will have all he needs to stuff your dad's jury full of reasonable doubt. When Quentin's done preachin', those jurors won't be sure whether they're right-handed or left."

"None of that matters," I say in a flat voice, "if the state police kill Dad as a fugitive."

Dennis shrugs. "They haven't got him yet, have they?"

"We don't know that."

"Sure we do. If they'd caught him and Garrity, my radio would be chattering like my wife's church group. No, my money says that old Texas Ranger has the trail smarts to keep your daddy loose for a while yet."

I don't hold out much hope that any Double Eagles would give up enough information to save my father from police execution. But as the security lights of various businesses flash past in the darkness, a new strategy begins to take shape in my mind.

"How soon could you organize a parishwide sweep of the meth dealers?" I ask.

Dennis looks at his watch. "I can have my people ready to go six hours from now. Just before dawn."

"Are you serious?"

"I did ninety percent of the groundwork today. I told you that yesterday, and now we're here."

The prospect of hitting the Knoxes hard in such a short time frame is tempting. "What about Agent Kaiser? Would you tell him about it?"

The sheriff rolls his shoulders, then sets them as though to take a blow—or deliver one. "After I saw Kaiser tuck his tail between his legs when Captain Ozan showed up at Mercy Hospital? No way in hell. This is you and me, Penn. I'm tired of standing by while the Knoxes shit all over my parish. My cousin's two years gone, and I know in my bones it was Forrest Knox's outfit that killed him. I'm through sitting on my hands."

"Henry didn't believe any Double Eagle would break his oath of silence under police pressure. Kaiser, either."

Walker snorts with contempt. "Forgive me speaking ill of the dead, but Henry Sexton didn't know shit about law enforcement. And Kaiser's a big-picture guy. It's time to keep it simple. I'm a cop, you're a prosecutor. Meth trafficking carries a mandatory fifteen- to thirty-year sentence in this state. Somebody on the Knox payroll will give us a Double Eagle or two to keep their asses out of Angola. And once we have an Eagle in my jail, it's Katy-bar-the-door. Those old bastards are in their seventies now. You think they want to die on Angola Farm with a bunch of black lifers? *Hell*, no. Think about Glenn Morehouse facing cancer. He cracked, didn't he?"

"That's different."

"You think so?" A bitter laugh escapes the sheriff's lips. "Given a choice between dying of cancer in a nice hospital and rotting in Angola with a bunch of pissed-off soul brothers who know I used to be in the Ku Klux Klan? I'll take the cancer every time, bubba. At least you get morphine to cope."

The sheriff just might be right about this. Some accused criminals live in mortal terror of incarceration—dirty cops, for example—but given the racial demographics of American prisons, I imagine former Ku Klux Klansmen rank right up there with child molesters when it comes to those who have real reason to fear going to jail.

"All right," I say softly. "I'm with you."

Walker glances at me, excitement in his face. "Seriously?"

"Let's do it."

"What made you change your mind?"

Since Dennis is going out on a limb for my father, I feel I owe him the truth. "Battle tactics. Forrest Knox is driving the manhunt for Dad and Walt. If we hit the Knox organization as hard as we can tomorrow, and keep hitting them, Forrest will have to devote a lot of energy to defending himself. And every minute he puts into fighting you and me is one less he has to track down my father."

"Damn straight," Walker says. "When in doubt, run it up the middle. Don't even give Forrest time to *think* about your daddy. I just wish we could get Agent Kaiser out of the way somehow, so he can't interfere."

As soon as Walker says this, a memory of Brody Royal describing the murder of Pooky Wilson at the Bone Tree comes to me. "I might just be able to do that. Though not in the next six hours."

"Anything will help. Hey, look." Sheriff Dennis points across the westbound lanes at the jarringly modern silhouette of the 1970s courthouse. "We made it. And no state cops in sight."

As Walker gives me a thumbs-up, I turn in my seat to make sure Walker's brother-in-law is still behind us, and that Caitlin is still his passenger. Thankfully, I can see both their heads silhouetted by the headlights of the vehicle behind them.

"Hey," Walker says sharply. "Earlier today you said you

wanted to ride with me on the busts. Do you still want to do that? Or should you lie low and let me take the heat?"

I don't even have to think about this question. "I've got my mother and daughter well hidden. What's the point in letting you have all the fun?"

The sheriff smacks his steering wheel and smiles. "All right, then. In six hours we hit those sons of bitches. And I'll lay odds that in twenty-four hours we'll have at least one Double Eagle in my jail, begging to tell us everything he knows."

Dennis pulls around to the left side of the courthouse, the site of his motor pool.

"I'd better call Chief Logan now," I say, the weight of dread and guilt in my voice. "He needs to know he probably lost a man tonight."

The smile melts off Walker Dennis's face. "You tell him we're going to get to the bottom of that tomorrow, too. Tell Logan I promised him that."

"I will."

Dennis switches off the engine, then looks at me. The eyes in his fleshy face burn with fearsome conviction. "Before I'm done, Forrest Knox is gonna wish his family never set foot in my parish."

Forrest Knox's ancestors probably arrived here generations before Dennis's did, but the sheriff could not care less about that. Subtlety isn't his strong suit. Special Agent John Kaiser is like a Predator drone, circling high above Forrest Knox and the Double Eagle group with an array of precision-targeted missiles. Sheriff Dennis is more like the iron bombs that dropped from the bellies of B-17s during World War II: dumb and heavy, but deadly enough to bring down a city block. And for my new purpose, Walker Dennis is just what the doctor ordered.

CHAPTER 5

CAITLIN MASTERS HAD wasted no time after getting into the cruiser. The deaths she'd witnessed, the torture she'd endured—all that was working its way through her like slow poison, she knew, but there was no quick antidote. And if what Brody Royal had said about having a mole at her paper was true, then every passing minute might mean more deleted computer files. She prayed that if there was a mole, he had not located the digital scans of Henry Sexton's journals. The fire wasn't even out of sight when she said, "I need to call my editor, Deputy. May. I use your cell phone?"

Deputy Grady Wells pulled a Nokia from his shirt pocket and passed it over. "Walker said you could. I just hope to hell the state police don't find out about this."

"Don't worry, you're on the side of the angels tonight."

Wells grunted skeptically.

Her editor's cell phone rang four times, but then he answered. "Jamie Lewis. Who's this?"

"It's me, Jamie."

"Christ, I was afraid you were dead." Lewis's crisp northern speech sounded alien compared to the drawl of Deputy Wells.

"I almost was. And some people are sure going to wish I was."

"One minute you were here arguing with Penn, and the next you were gone. Now the police scanner's going nuts about an explosion on Lake Concordia."

"I was in the damned explosion. Or next to it, anyway. Don't say anything more, Jamie. Just listen and do what I say."

"Go."

"Shut down our computers, right now. The servers, everything."

"What?"

"Our system's been breached. Somebody's in our intranet, wiping out information. Brody Royal had a mole on our staff. Henry's scanned backup files are probably gone, and God knows what else. You haven't noticed anything weird going on?"

"I did accidentally delete a story about an hour ago."

Caitlin's stomach did a queasy roll. "No, you didn't. They already stole the physical copies of Henry's journals and backup files, right out of our fire cabinet. Have you shut down the system yet?"

"I'm trying to now. We're going to lose unsaved stories people are working on."

"*Pull the fucking plug, Jamie!* We've got to start the whole edition over anyway."

"Okay, okay. When will you be back here?"

"I don't know. I need to read over the hub story I wrote before this happened—I can access the copy I sent to Daddy's other papers via e-mail. Then I'll call you back and try to dictate a new one from here."

"Where is here?"

"I can't tell you that on the phone. But I'll tell you this: I've never worked a story this big in my life. Brody Royal just closed about five murder cases in as many minutes. He shot a black man named Sleepy Johnston right in front of us, a witness to the Albert Norris murder in 1964. I've got Snake Knox for murdering Pooky Wilson and trying to skin him alive. Royal admitted raping Viola Turner, and also killing his own daughter."

"Holy shit. I heard she died in the ICU earlier tonight."

"That's right. Royal knew Katy was starting to talk about his involvement in her mother's murder, and the others, too. Either Royal or his son-in-law did that. Oh, Randall Regan's dead as well, by the way."

Jamie's amazement only silenced him for a moment. "How did Royal know that his daughter had talked to you?"

Because Penn played him the recording of her voice . . . "I don't know," Caitlin lied. "But he did."

"You still have that recording, right?"

"No. Royal burned both copies, mine and Penn's."

"Fuck!"

"I know, I know. But Penn and I both heard him admit the murders. It'll be okay. Tomorrow's edition is going to be like a bomb going off, Jamie. By tomorrow at noon, every media outlet in the country is going to be chasing this story. And the FBI is going to look like the Keystone Kops. I just have to stay clear of certain people until we get the issue done."

"Such as?"

"The Adams County sheriff, for one. How are your dictation skills?"

"Meredith's a lot better. I'll get her ready."

"No. Just you. When Penn and I were kidnapped from the back parking lot, I almost made it back inside, but one of our people locked me out. I don't know who did that, and it could have been a woman as easily as a man. Has anybody left their post tonight?"

"Now that you mention it, Nick has been out of touch for an hour or more."

"Nick Moore, the press operator?"

"Yeah. We figured he went out for some food, since the press obviously wouldn't run for some hours yet."

"Try to track him down. Anybody else?"

"I don't think so. Everybody's working like this is the biggest story of their lives."

"It is. Okay, I'll call you back in two minutes, max, and dictate the new story in case I get arrested. At the very least, I'll be stuck in a police interrogation room for a while. For now, tomorrow's edition is on your shoulders. You're probably going to have to try to reconstruct almost everything that's been written from memory."

"We'll do it, if we have to stay till dawn."

"Count on that. None of us will be sleeping for a long time."

Caitlin hung up and began punching commands into the cell phone's tiny keypad. Only then did she realize that her hands were shaking. Normally, she was an ace with a cell phone, but not now. The trauma she'd endured in Brody Royal's basement was part of it, of course. But the larger part, she knew, was her realization that within an hour or two, Special Agent John Kaiser would learn that Royal had not only verified the existence of the Bone Tree, but also placed the murder of Pooky Wilson there.

Given the massive effort Kaiser had expended to drain the Jericho Hole in search of the bones of the Double Eagles' civil rights victims, what resources might he marshal to locate Pooky Wilson's remains? Two hours ago, Caitlin was certain she'd had the only real chance of finding the near-mythical race-murder site that most authorities considered apocryphal. Now she was likely to be competing with a battalion of National Guardsmen and satellite imagery specialists. As soon as she could get to a safe phone, she would try yet again to call Toby Rambin, the Lusahatcha County poacher who had sworn to Henry Sexton that he knew the location of the Bone Tree. Calling him in the middle of the night wouldn't be ideal, but she had no choice now.

After several curses and mistakes, she finally got into her digital mailbox and called up the file attachment she needed. Blocking out the pain of her injuries, she focused on the tiny screen, processing her own words with ruthless efficiency, deciding which elements of the existing lead story could function as a foundation for the new one she would dictate before they reached the sheriff's department. As she stared at the glowing LCD, it finally sank in how profoundly the world had changed in the two hours since she'd written that piece. The entire story would have to be rewritten.

A wave of exhaustion rolled over her, giving her the sense that she was being smothered. When at last she caught her breath, her stomach rolled with nausea. The only thought she could hold in her mind was of the poacher, Rambin. Only days ago, this stranger had contacted Henry Sexton with an offer to guide him to the Bone Tree for a price. But did Toby Rambin know what he claimed to know? Henry had been misled by greedy "guides" before. And since he'd been attacked the night after Rambin contacted him, he'd been unable to keep his scheduled rendezvous. In a narcotic fog in his hospital room—only minutes before a sniper fired a bullet at his head—Henry had given Caitlin the poacher's telephone number. With a twinge of guilt she recalled altering the entry in Henry's cell phone so that no one else would be able to find the right number if they checked his phone. As ruthless as that was, Caitlin was glad now that she'd done it. She only hoped she could reach Rambin before the poacher heard about Henry's murder and fled the state.

Calm down, she told herself. Caitlin closed her eyes and tried to blank her thoughts, but the image of Henry Sexton immolating himself and Brody Royal only grew more distinct in her mind's eye.

She opened her eyes and punched the keypad of Deputy Wells's cell phone.

"Caitlin?" Jamie said. "Is that you?"

"Have you had any word from the press operator?"

"None. Nick's dropped off the face of the earth."

"With a lot more money than he had last week," she muttered.

"You really think Nick would help somebody hurt you?"

"I doubt he thought they would kill me. But . . ." Caitlin fell silent as another memory from the basement returned to her. "Jamie . . . before he died, Brody Royal was bragging about how little it had cost him to buy one of our people."

"Okay. And?"

"I'm pretty sure he said he'd bought a journalist. A *scribbler*, he said. I remember now. So even if Nick was the one who locked me out, he might not be the only person Royal bribed. I mean, would Nick know where we were keeping Henry's journals? Would he know how to work the computers, navigate our intranet? Would he know the user names or passwords of the reporters?"

"No. But if Nick didn't delete the files, then it could be anybody. How the hell do we go forward from here?"

"Think hard about who you trust. With Royal dead, the mole will assume their payday is over. So from this point forward, they might just go back to doing their job."

"I guess. It still creeps me out, though. And it pisses me off."

A worrisome thought struck her. "There's another possibility. When Royal mentioned the mole, he said he had taken a page out of Forrest's book. He was talking about Forrest Knox, chief of the Criminal Investigations

Bureau of the Louisiana State Police. That means Knox was also paying a reporter somewhere. Probably Baton Rouge, where he lives, I'd guess. Or maybe New Orleans. But if Forrest knows about Royal's mole at the *Examiner*, who's to say he can't extend the arrangement?"

"What if Forrest Knox's mole was at Henry Sexton's paper?" Jamie asked. "Or at half a dozen of them? Why limit a good thing, if you've got the money to spend?"

"You're right. Jeez, that would explain a lot. We'll have to keep our plans confined to a very tight circle. Tomorrow's stories will have to be written on two computers only, yours and mine. No sharing files, no Internet connection for them."

"Okay."

Caitlin looked out at the lights flashing by outside the cruiser. At last she recognized a building. "I'm only five minutes from the sheriff's office. I need to start dictating."

"I'm ready."

"Jamie, this really is the most—"

"You're not seriously going to waste time telling me how big this is, are you? *Go.*"

She took a deep breath, then shut her eyes and began to compose her new story on the fly. "Last night, Henry Sexton of the *Concordia Beacon* laid down his life for a fellow journalist. That journalist was me . . ."

As Caitlin spoke, a soft voice at the center of her mind asked a deeply troubling question: *Could Jamie be the mole?* Almost instantly another voice answered, *No way.* She had known her editor for six years. He was a flaming liberal, a crusader for justice who hated greed and repression in all their forms. But probably more persuasive than this, Jamie—like Caitlin herself—was rich. He'd been born into a family with money, and thus had the luxury of being immune to blandishments that might tempt those less fortunate.

"Caitlin?" Jamie said. "What the hell? Are you there?"

"Yeah, can you not hear me?"

"You stopped talking thirty seconds ago."

"I'm sorry. God, it's been a crazy night. Where was I?"

"The last thing you said was, 'This lone reporter, working from a tiny newspaper in the slowly dying delta of Louisiana, accomplished more than an army of FBI agents did in forty years—' and then you trailed off."

"Okay . . . okay. Ready?"

"Go," Jamie said.

Banishing the mole from her mind, Caitlin picked up the story again.

CHAPTER 6

LIEUTENANT COLONEL FORREST Knox was seventy miles north of New Orleans and nearing Baton Rouge when he considered switching his cell phone back on. He'd spent the past three hours in New Orleans, but he didn't want anyone knowing he'd been there. That's why he was driving an unmarked car, and at the speed limit. Blackmail missions were best carried out under the radar, especially when your target had the kind of connections that Forrest's boss did. Colonel Griffith Mackiever had headed the Louisiana State Police for seven years, and bringing him down was no small task. Forrest would have preferred a couple of more months to get his ducks in a row, but the moneymen in New Orleans who stood to make millions off the post-Katrina reconstruction wouldn't wait. They wanted a full-time state police presence in New Orleans to calm jittery investors (by filling the vacuum created by the dysfunctional NOPD). The most ruthless among them wanted certain human obstacles to their plans neutralized by any means necessary. Forrest knew well the impatience that accompanied ambition, but he would not let recklessness destroy him on the verge of success.

At nearly fifty-four, he had never been closer to achieving his goals. Using unerring instincts and iron self-control, he had worked his way up through the ranks of the most powerful law enforcement organization in his home state. Now he stood within a heartbeat of commanding it. Once he cemented his control of the LSP, he would be as bulletproof as a criminal could be in America. Unlike Griffith Mackiever, who had vainly battled the forces of human nature throughout his tenure, Forrest had leveraged his pragmatic worldview into something unique. By combining his cousin Billy's statewide meth operation with the manpower surviving from his father's Double Eagle days, and then enlisting an army of avaricious politicians and hungry police officers for protection, Forrest had built a criminal network of unrivaled reach and power in the South.

His philosophy was based on principles understood by every cop in the world: no matter what the law did to discourage them, people were going to use drugs, gamble, and fuck whores (both male and female). Any sane government would have legalized all three practices decades ago and co-opted the criminals. But thankfully, the remnants of America's religious ethics prevented that from happening, which left the field wide open for a man of vision. Long ago, Forrest had realized that he was that man.

The only problem was that Hurricane Katrina had shown him just how picayune his vision had been. The ravaged city left behind by the receding floodwaters was a vacuum that attracted the true predators of twenty-first-century America—the real estate developers and bankers. Multimillionaires like Brody Royal had been waiting for a catastrophe like Katrina for decades. For the storm and the flood had accomplished what no human activity could: it had flushed the poor blacks out of the city, like a biblical purge. Royal and his friends intended that those blacks should never return. In place of the dilapidated housing projects and single-story rental houses that had blighted the city, they saw upscale housing and corporate offices with mouthwatering proximity to downtown and the French Quarter. The men who planned this remaking of the Crescent City reckoned their profits in tens of millions, not the paltry numbers to which Forrest was accustomed. And thanks to Brody Royal, they had settled on Forrest as one of the lieutenants who could help bring their vision to fruition.

Moving in this world was surreal to him. This morning he'd been at a brunch with politicians, insurance executives, and hedge-fund managers, and he'd known without asking that not one of them had set foot in Vietnam, unless it was as a tourist with a designer backpack and a Black Card. Yet they were predators, just as he was. Instead of crystal methamphetamine and whores, they dealt in political influence, rigged construction contracts, secret real estate deals, and inside stock trades. And right now—thanks to an accident of weather—they needed him. It was these men who had quietly informed the governor that they would like to see a change in leadership at state police HQ. But tacit support from the capitol was not enough. First, Forrest had to move Colonel Mackiever out of the seat at the top of the pyramid.

It wasn't like the old man hadn't asked for it. Mackiever had been trying to nail Forrest for months now, and if the superintendent made common cause with the FBI, they just might be able to find enough evidence to tie Forrest to the Double Eagles' meth operation and bring him down. Everything that had happened in Concordia Parish over the past three days would make that job a hell of a lot easier. Agent John Kaiser had already used extraordinary measures to bring up 1960s-vintage bones from a sinkhole beside the Mississippi River, and he'd used the Patriot Act to take possession of the corpse of Glenn Morehouse, the Double Eagle whom Sonny and Snake had killed to keep quiet (one day too late, apparently). To effectively fight these tactics, Forrest needed full control of the state police. Only then could he take over the investigation into the sniper attack on Henry Sexton—which he himself had ordered—and sandbag the FBI's efforts to solve the old Double Eagle murders.

Since Griffith Mackiever was virtually incorruptible, Forrest had chosen a tactic calculated to hit the man in the only place he was vulnerable. It was a dirty business, and Forrest would never forget the old man's face after he'd seen the strangling net of false evidence Forrest had meticulously woven together while Mackiever had been working so ineptly to nail him. Only a supreme effort had allowed the old man to choke back tears. An ex–Texas Ranger, Mackiever had worked in law enforcement long enough to know that there were certain kinds of accusations from which no man ever recovered, regardless of what facts emerged in the wake of the initial smear. Forrest had given him forty-eight hours to resign, and he felt sure the old man would cave by midday tomorrow. If he didn't, Forrest had no problem pulling the trigger and destroying the man's career—and his personal life along with it.

Now that he'd moved against Mackiever, Forrest's immediate concern was finishing off Henry Sexton. Forrest could never have imagined that Snake Knox—a trained combat sniper in his youth—would miss Sexton and kill his girlfriend by mistake. The simple truth was, Snake and the other Eagles were getting too old for the work they were doing. That was why Morehouse had cracked: he was dying of cancer and scared shitless. He'd wanted to clean his conscience before he faced his maker. After Snake missed his shot at Mercy Hospital in Ferriday, the FBI had moved Sexton to a windowless hospital room under Bureau guard. Getting to him there would not be easy. But it had to be done. Sexton had spent at least an hour speaking to Glenn Morehouse in person, and then again later on the telephone, and Morehouse had known more than enough to send not only his fellow Double Eagles, but also Forrest himself, to Angola Prison for the rest of their lives, and possibly even to death row.

Forrest also needed to know how much information Sexton had confided to Caitlin Masters, the publisher of the *Natchez Examiner.* The two were competitors and normally would not cooperate on a story. But Forrest worried that with Henry wounded and out of commission, he might have passed what he knew to the girl in order to hit the Eagles as hard and as fast as possible. And no mole, no matter how well placed, could tell Forrest what was inside the girl's head.

WHEN THE POINTED TOWER of the state capitol appeared in the distance, Forrest switched on the encrypted cell phone he'd been using to communicate with Alphonse Ozan. Yesterday he'd ordered Billy's drug organization to begin using "Al Qaeda rules," which meant no electronic contact, only face-to-face meetings. But that wasn't practical for the man sitting at the top of the pyramid. Forrest felt reasonably confident that the FBI didn't know about his satellite phone, but he had occasional nightmares about the NSA and their automated intelligence-collection algorithms. He decided to wait until he reached headquarters to talk to Ozan.

The instant his phone found a satellite, it began to ring. As the LED read out Alphonse Ozan's number, the hair on Forrest's arms stood erect. Ozan should not be calling him. He had no idea what the trouble might be, but the odds were, it involved Concordia Parish. Instinct told Forrest he was behind the curve of events, and that was never a good place to be.

"What's happened?" he asked, holding the phone to his head.

"Colonel, I've been trying to reach you," said Ozan, sounding rattled. "Are you okay?"

"Of course. I've been following the goddamned rules. You ought to try it."

"I couldn't wait. We've got trouble."

"Something to do with Dr. Cage?"

"No. Brody's dead."

Forrest gripped the phone harder. "Brody Royal?"

"Yes, sir."

"Dead how? Natural causes?"

"Nobody's exactly sure what happened, but his lake house burned up. It may have *blown* up. He's not the only one dead, either. It's a mess out there. Son-in-law's dead, too."

Randall Regan? Dead? Forrest felt himself brace for further shocks. "Who else?"

"Three of Royal's security people, plus Henry Sexton and an old black guy named Johnston."

And the hits just keep on coming. Forrest tried to picture what sequence of events could have led to such a nightmare. "This doesn't make any sense, Alphonse. What the hell happened?"

"You ain't heard the worst of it. Somehow, Mayor Penn Cage and his fiancée, the Masters girl, wound up in Brody's basement, and—"

"Don't tell me they're dead."

"No, no," Ozan said quickly. "But they were in there. Looks like Royal may have kidnapped them, or ordered it done."

"Goddamn it!" Forrest gritted his teeth.

"I know. I think maybe Henry Sexton and the old nigger went in there to try to get Cage and the girl out. What happened after that, I don't know. Only Cage and the girl came out alive, and only they know what happened."

"Who was the nigger?"

"His name was Marshall Johnston, Junior, but I don't know what the hell he was doing there. Fire department says there was some kind of explosion, and everything smells like tar."

Forrest instantly thought of Brody Royal's flamethrower, the weapon Forrest's father had used on Albert Norris and his store in 1964. The deadly antique fired a mixture of gasoline and tar, propelled by inert nitrogen gas. *I should have taken care of Brody last night*, he thought. *Or even before that.*

"Where are Cage and the girl now?" he asked.

"Concordia Parish Sheriff's Office."

Forrest was tired of dealing with old men. They were as reckless and sensitive as teenagers. Because of the bruised ego and paranoia of Brody Royal, he now had to contend with a seismic shift in battlefield conditions.

"Alphonse?"

"Yeah, boss?"

"Get your ass over to the sheriff's department and take over the investigation."

"Which one? Brody's house blowing up?"

"No. Everything going back three days. We can't afford to have Walker Dennis poking around in our business any longer."

"You think Dennis will stand for that?"

"You're not going to give him any choice."

"Okay. And the FBI?"

"If Kaiser backs off like he did at the hospital, then we'll know we've got it made."

"And if not?"

"We'll sandbag that blue-flame son of a bitch before he knows what hit him."

"Yes, sir."

"And don't call me again."

"I won't."

Forrest switched off the phone and dropped it on the seat beside him. Despite his best efforts to control the situation, the bodies were piling up fast. With Henry Sexton dead and the Masters girl involved, one thing was sure: a media storm was coming. Any hope of solving his problems quietly would vanish with the publication of tomorrow's *Natchez Examiner*. Forrest pulled the red bubble light from his glove box and set it on the dash, then switched it on and floored the gas pedal. He needed to get to headquarters. Speed was everything now.

CHAPTER 7

I'M SITTING ON a bench outside an interrogation room in the Concordia Parish Sheriff's Office, with Special Agent John Kaiser staring down at me with a mixture of fury and disappointment. The trim and usually well-dressed agent looks like someone shook him awake from a nap in his car: hair sticking up, clothes askew, eyes bloodshot and heavy-bagged. Sleep deprivation is finally taking its toll on him.

There's nothing in the corridor but a battered vinyl couch, a metal chair, and a card table with a plastic Christmas tree and a dying Mr. Coffee standing on it. The coffee in the carafe looks like river mud mixed with tar, but that didn't stop Caitlin from pouring herself a full cup before going into the interrogation room. She's obviously prepping for a marathon of work once she gets out of this place.

Ten minutes ago, I finished my statement to Sheriff Dennis and his video camera, while the sheriff's brother-in-law stood guard over Caitlin in a nearby office. As agreed with Caitlin, I mostly told the truth, while omitting a few dangerous facts, among them Brody Royal's assertion that my father murdered Viola Turner three days ago. By the time Sheriff Dennis called Caitlin into his office, she was nearly crazy to get back across the river to the *Examiner*. She'd been talking to her editor on a departmental landline, and she'd managed to assemble her full staff, which now awaits her arrival. Sheriff Dennis promised to finish with her as soon as possible, but his intentions meant nothing unless we could get clear of this building before the state police or FBI arrived to detain us further. And that was exactly what happened. Five minutes after Caitlin disappeared into Walker's office, Agent Kaiser walked up the hall from the front entrance and called out my name.

In response to the FBI agent's questions, I've given a reasonably detailed summary of the night's events. About seventy percent of what I told Kaiser is true. Twenty percent was lies, and another ten percent I omitted altogether. In the silences between my words and his, I fought to drown out internal echoes of gunfire, Caitlin's screams, and the bone-chilling hiss and roar of Brody Royal's flamethrower.

"I'm glad you're alive," Kaiser tells me, obviously working hard to keep his anger under control. "But we both know that if Henry Sexton and Sleepy Johnston hadn't broken into Royal's house and sacrificed their lives, you and Caitlin would be dead now."

I don't look up from the floor tiles. "That's all I've been thinking about since it happened."

"I warned you to stay out of this, Penn. But you went ahead, and now six people are dead—maybe more."

The guilt I've felt since the fire is so lacerating that Kaiser's words add nothing to the pain. I look up at him without a hint of apology. "As long as we're telling the truth, John, I'd say you've given me mixed messages from the start. This morning at the Jericho Hole I told you I was going to poke a stick in a rattlesnake hole, the same as you. Did you tell me not to? No. You also knew I'd tangled with Regan in the restroom of that café. You warned me to be careful, but that's it. I think you were hoping I'd stir things up *just enough* to get Royal and Regan to incriminate themselves, but not enough to cause a disaster—which, admittedly, is what we have now."

Kaiser returns my gaze with a stony stare. "Okay, I bear some blame for this. But in any case, you're done now. You're the mayor of Natchez, not the district attorney of Adams County. You have no jurisdiction whatever."

"Obviously. If I was the DA of Adams County, the Double Eagles would already be in a cell in Natchez, begging for a plea bargain."

"Then thank God you're not. Because that would be exactly the wrong thing to do."

"How do you figure that?"

Kaiser walks to a folding metal chair opposite me, then sits beside the card table and hangs his hands over his knees. "Penn, we've held a lot back from each other over the past two days, but I'm going to be straight with you now. I knew more about Brody Royal than I let on to you. About Forrest Knox, too. Some I knew before I got here, and the rest I got from Henry Sexton."

"I can't believe Henry told you much."

"Henry had a certain amount of bitterness toward the Bureau, granted. For our civil-rights-era failures, and for the way a lot of agents treated him over the years. But after Glenn Morehouse was murdered, Henry decided that safety demanded he pass me a certain amount of information. It was Henry who told me about the link between Royal and the Double Eagles going back to 1964. He also told me his suspicions about Forrest Knox protecting the Eagles' drug business, and possibly even being a partner. I'd heard a few rumors prior to that, but Henry had more facts than the Bureau did."

I say nothing, still trying to process the fact that Henry confided so much in Kaiser.

"He *didn't* tell me about his backup files," says the FBI agent. "His change of heart didn't extend to that. I think he worried that if he gave his journals to the Bureau, they might disappear forever. He wanted a journalist to have them, so Caitlin got it all. A bad decision, considering what's happened to them."

Earlier tonight Caitlin told me she intended to let Kaiser view Henry's files tomorrow, but given what happened at Brody's house, I don't want to speak for her.

"I visited Henry one last time this afternoon," Kaiser says, "only a few hours before the sniper tried to finish him off. He was pretty depressed, but he told me what Glenn Morehouse said about Jimmy Revels's murder."

I give Kaiser a puzzled look, but he's having none of it.

"The RFK assassination plan?" he says. "Carlos Marcello, all that? Don't play dumb, for God's sake. Not after what's happened tonight."

Before I can reply, Kaiser says, "We need to talk about what you told me about your father when I first called you from New Orleans."

He's referring to me saying that Brody Royal and my father might possess information about the major 1960s assassinations. I only told him that to lure him to Natchez, and now I regret it. I need to sleep and be ready for the drug raid at dawn. But one thing Kaiser does need to know, no matter how crazy it may sound.

"Do you have any agents at the fire scene?" I ask.

"Three. Why?"

"Can they stop the state police from taking evidence away from it?"

"Absolutely. Brody Royal's lake house and property are now a federal crime scene."

To my surprise, relief washes through me. "As soon as the ruins cool, your guys need to grid-search the place and sift the ashes."

"What are we looking for?"

Something makes me put off revealing the most explosive information. To stall him, I lay out some bait that could get him out of my way tomorrow. "Depending on the heat of the fire, you might find the remains of a one-of-a-kind letter opener. Royal told us that Frank Knox carved it from one of Pooky Wilson's arm bones. The blade was bone, and the handle was covered in the tanned skin of Wilson's penis. Or so Royal claimed. He admitted that murder to us, John. He gave the order, Snake and Frank Knox carried it out, and all this happened at the Bone Tree."

"The Bone Tree?" Kaiser says softly. "Most of our agents don't believe that thing even exists."

"It does. Royal was there when Wilson was killed. And his bones are bound to still be there."

Kaiser can't hide the interest in his eyes. "Did he say anything about Jimmy Revels's murder?"

"No. But he admitted taking part in the gang rape of Viola Turner."

"What made Royal so damn talkative?"

"Henry and Sleepy showing up. Brody just had to tell them how pointless their lives had been."

"What a guy." Kaiser slowly shakes his head.

"Could you extract DNA from something like that letter opener?"

"Possibly. But you're deflecting me, Penn. What does a trophy from Pooky Wilson's murder have to do with the 1960s assassinations?"

"Nothing." I prop my elbows on my knees and rub my temples. "This is going to sound crazy, but . . . just before everything went to hell in Brody's basement, he showed us two rifles in one of his gun cabinets. There were brass plaques beneath the guns."

"And?"

I look up, letting Kaiser see that I'm not personally invested in what I'm about to tell him. "Unlike all the other plaques, which gave the make of the weapon, et cetera, these only had dates on them, plus a small American flag."

Kaiser shrugs. "So?"

"The dates were November twenty-second, 1963, and April fourth, 1968."

I expect the agent's face to show incredulity, but what I see is a hunter's excitement glimmering in his eyes. "Did you believe they were real?"

"*Brody* believed they were real. Did I? No. I think Snake Knox sold that old man a pig in a poke. Twice. And I told him so."

Kaiser mulls this over. "Was that truly your gut reaction?"

Thinking back to a story my father recently told me, I reconsider. "I can't say that one hundred percent. Not about the JFK rifle."

"Tell me why."

The realization that Kaiser is more interested in this than in my father's plight makes me want to smack him in the face. "While my father's being hunted down like an animal by corrupt cops?"

The FBI agent studies me for a few seconds, then speaks with maddening calm. "I know how hard you've been trying to save your father. I know what you did tonight, too. You got hold of some leverage against Brody and tried to force him to help your father. After you left me, you went to St. Catherine's Hospital. You offered to bury what you know and keep Brody's name from the cops, and out of the newspapers. Right?"

Kaiser didn't get where he is by being slow on the uptake. "I might have tried that, if Henry Sexton would have gone along with—"

"Oh, bullshit. It was Caitlin holding the sword over Brody's head, not Henry. She made some kind of recording of Katy Royal earlier this evening, didn't she?"

I don't answer, but I can't for the life of me figure how Kaiser found out about that tape.

"Does it still exist?" he presses. "Or did Brody take it from you tonight?"

My expression tells him all he needs to know.

Kaiser's face betrays genuine empathy. "Look, speaking as a man, I don't blame you. Your father's life was on the line, and you had Royal by the short hairs. But look what's happened because of what you did."

I stare at the floor, wishing Caitlin would emerge from the interrogation room.

"If it's any consolation, I think your old man and Walt Garrity have gone to ground somewhere. We'll never find them, and with luck, the Knoxes won't either. Those old coots are safe as houses. That's why your next plan is stupid."

"What plan?" I ask, wondering if he somehow knows that Dennis and I intend to bust the Knoxes' meth operation.

"The deal with Royal didn't work, so now you're thinking about approaching Forrest Knox. Right?"

This assumption actually stuns me. "Hell, no!"

Kaiser rolls his eyes. "Just tell me you haven't already reached out to him."

For once the FBI agent is wrong, so I let my anger fill my eyes. "I'm not that stupid, John."

"Not normally. But you're not thinking straight now. So let me enlighten you. Brody Royal was like a cranky old dog lying under a porch. Forrest Knox is a purebred wolf that will smell you coming from five miles away. Do *not* fuck with him."

I get up from the bench and start pacing the hallway. "Why are you so concerned with those old assassinations? I would think you'd be organizing a search of the Lusahatcha Swamp, trying to find the Bone Tree. You're bound to find the remains of Pooky Wilson, and maybe even Jimmy Revels. That's the way to nail the Knoxes, if you won't go after them from the meth angle. You could arrest Snake on Brody's statement alone."

Kaiser is already shaking his head. "Brody Royal told you Snake Knox killed Pooky Wilson. But there's a 302 report in our files from the 1970s in which a Double Eagle named Jason Abbott swears that Forrest Knox killed Pooky. Also at the Bone Tree, by the way."

"That's got to be bullshit. Forrest was what, twelve years old the year Pooky died? Royal was telling the truth tonight. He had no reason to lie."

"You're probably right. But that doesn't make that 302 disappear. Do you know how Henry Sexton first discovered that Pooky Wilson had probably been crucified?"

"From that 302, obtained through the Freedom of Information Act."

"That's right. Jason Abbott was an older cousin of Forrest Knox, and also a Double Eagle. In 1972, he found out that Forrest had been screwing his wife, both before he left for Vietnam and after he got back. Abbott stood being cuckolded for as long as he could. Then one night he got blind drunk and went to the hotel room of an FBI agent who'd once questioned him. He told that agent that the Double Eagles had intended to skin Pooky alive, but they didn't have the right kind of knife, so after some effort, they gave up and nailed him to the Bone Tree. He said Forrest hammered in the nails."

"That's the way Brody described it, except Frank and Snake were in the lead roles."

Kaiser intertwines his fingers around one knee and speaks like a thoughtful college professor. "My guess is that Forrest was present but only witnessed Pooky's death. Abbott wouldn't admit to being at the Bone Tree himself. He claimed he'd heard the story from another Double Eagle who'd been there. He tried to hang a bunch of other crimes around Forrest's neck, as well—all unverifiable—but he also revealed a lot of valuable information about the Knox family. The FOIA version Henry got was heavily redacted."

"Did the Bureau do anything about Abbott's stories?"

Kaiser suddenly looks uncomfortable. "That was problematic. After he sobered up, Abbott tried to recant. And since Forrest had been screwing his wife, the man had an obvious motive to make false accusations. Even so, two agents set up an interview with Forrest at a military base, to check out the story."

"And?"

Kaiser leans back against the wall and savors his next

words. "While the agents were questioning Forrest, Jason Abbott was run over by a truck two hundred miles away. Hit and run, never solved."

My stomach rolls over. "*During* Knox's interview?"

"That's right. And Forrest was only twenty years old at the time, Penn. I'm telling you, he's as cold as they come."

"Was Dwight Stone one of those two FBI agents?"

"No. Dwight was being railroaded out of the Bureau at that time, so he couldn't help. There is one interesting footnote, though. Once Abbott sobered up, he denied he'd ever been a Double Eagle. But during his wake, someone dropped a JFK half-dollar on his body in the casket."

"I thought the Double Eagles carried twenty-dollar gold pieces."

"Only the older guys, the founding members. The rest wore 1964 JFK half-dollars, most with a hole shot through them." Kaiser raises one eyebrow, Mr. Spock style. "Kind of makes you wonder, huh? Anyway, the Bureau sent an informant to the funeral. The guy watched Forrest Knox walk up to the casket alone."

"You think Forrest put the coin in Abbott's coffin? On the body of the man he'd ordered killed?"

Kaiser's eyes carry some emotion I can't read. "When Forrest was in Vietnam, he carried a little bag of JFK half-dollars with him. Whenever he killed a VC, he'd leave one of those coins in the corpse's mouth, so the Cong leaders would know it was him."

A chill races along my arms. "The Bureau couldn't pin Abbott's murder on him or the Eagles?"

Kaiser shrugs. "J. Edgar Hoover was still director at that time. His last few months on earth, I'm happy to say. The problem was, Forrest was a decorated war hero— something in short supply during that war. I don't think Hoover wanted to cause him trouble."

"Wonderful."

Kaiser makes a sour face. "Here's your takeaway from that story." He holds up his right forefinger. "You cannot bargain with Forrest Knox. He'll eat you alive, Penn."

A little overwhelmed by Kaiser's revelations, I walk over to the door to the interrogation room and lay my ear against its face. Walker Dennis's sonorous voice passes through the wood in a muted drone. Caitlin must be bursting to get out of there.

I turn back to Kaiser. "How the hell could you hold all this back? This morning you acted like you didn't know shit about Forrest Knox."

"I tried to tell you Brody Royal wasn't the real power behind all this. Just three hours ago, outside the hospital, after the sniper tried to get Henry, I told you Forrest was the real enemy. But then I got called away, and you took your chance to bug out. You didn't want to hear it."

He's right, of course, but that's not what bothers me. "But how *long* have you known this?"

Kaiser rubs his stubbled cheek, his eyes distant. "Look, if I told you what I really believe about this situation, you'd think I'm out of my mind."

Given that Walker Dennis and I intend to declare war on the Knox family tomorrow morning, any intelligence I can gather in the meantime could be critical. "We're already in the twilight zone. Cough it up."

Kaiser clucks his tongue softly, then gets up and begins pacing the hall with me. "There's a synchronicity to Forrest turning up in this Double Eagle mess that feels like fate, like it was supposed to happen. I feel like I've been brought to this place—after years of chasing ghosts—specifically to oppose and destroy him."

"I didn't figure you for a Jungian."

The FBI agent smiles strangely. "Hey, I'm a child of the sixties. Seriously, though, this is the third time Forrest and I have grazed past each other, in historical terms. He doesn't even know about the first time."

"When was that?"

"Vietnam. In 1970 I was stuck on a hill on the northern rim of the A Shau Valley, a hellhole called FSB Ripcord."

"FSB?"

"Fire Support Base. Ripcord was one of the last major engagements of the war. A twenty-one-day siege. I was 101st Airborne. We took *beaucoup* casualties during that particular nightmare. You don't hear much about Ripcord, because in the end we sneaked out and let the B-52s carpet-bomb the place into oblivion, but we lost that battle."

"Forrest Knox was there?"

"I didn't know it then, but he was. He was a Lurp."

"A what?"

"A *Lurp*. That's the phonetic version of an acronym—L-R-R-P: Long-Range Reconnaissance Patrol. The Lurps were precursors of the modern-day Delta operators. They weren't at Ripcord the whole time I was, and they had technically been folded into the Seventy-Fifth Rangers by then, but they were still Lurps in every way that counted. And Forrest's army record puts him there during the first phase of the battle. I must have seen him several times—all the time, really—but the Lurps kept to themselves. They were truly elite soldiers, and a few were stone killers. As a unit, the Lurps had a four-hundred-to-one kill ratio."

"Jesus."

"Like I said, you don't fuck with a guy with that résumé. But it's weird, isn't it? I was from Idaho, Knox was from Louisiana, yet fate kept putting us in the same place."

"When was the second time you 'grazed past' him?"

"Hurricane Katrina. While I was out in the field trying to hold the city together for the Bureau, Forrest was theoretically doing the same thing for the state police. But as the situation deteriorated, I started getting reports of crazy shit going on in the wee hours. Vigilante stuff. Scores being settled, prisoners disappearing, sniping . . . Lurp-type stuff, only directed against certain elements of the U.S. population. Black drug dealers, mainly."

"I thought those stories were bullshit."

"Most were, but not all. Between the time the levees broke on Monday and Saturday afternoon when General Honoré got his troops into the city, things literally went to hell. The NOPD virtually ceased to function, and civil unrest was rampant. You saw the daylight stuff on TV. At night it was worse. Bands of predators roamed the streets, preying on desperate people, using the sound of emergency generators to locate victims. Quite a few young black men turned up dead during that time, from head or heart shots, and most got written off as flood deaths or unexplained homicides."

"Forrest was involved with that?"

Kaiser shrugs. "A couple of sources have told me he had a private SWAT crew down there, operating off the reservation. At the time, I assumed that if it was true, it was cowboy law enforcement. After all, Forrest was the son of an infamous Klansman. I figured he and some racist buddies took their chance to declare open season on black drug dealers. But after talking to Henry, I think those killings were *business*."

"Christ, John."

"The thing is, Forrest has gone to great lengths to appear above reproach. He has quite a few fans in state government. There's even talk of making him the next superintendent of state police."

This seems beyond belief. "Will you try to stop that?"

"A week ago, I'd have said I couldn't. Tonight . . . things have changed a bit. Depending on how far he and Ozan stick their dicks out to protect the Knox family, I might just be able to rip Forrest's mask off."

I stop walking and take hold of his arm. "You've held back a hell of a lot more than I have."

"Have I?" The FBI agent looks skeptical. "I could tell you some mind-blowing pathology about the Knox family. History that explains the mutilations and trophy taking—"

"Screw *telling* me stuff! Why haven't you *done* anything about it?"

Kaiser seems surprised by my anger. "I'm doing something now. But it takes time to build a case against cops—especially one as powerful as Forrest."

"Hey, I've been there, you know? But meth trafficking carries mandatory minimum sentences. That's the legal equivalent of a baseball bat. Why the hell would you pursue any other angle? You told me this morning that you're operating under the Patriot Act. So bust every perp you know about in the Knoxes' meth organization and start offering plea bargains. Sooner or later, somebody will cough up a link to Forrest."

Kaiser actually smiles at this suggestion. "You really must be in shock. You worked enough federal task forces to know how cases like this have to be handled. It's like fighting the Mafia. You don't start squeezing peons and hope to work your way up to the top. You've got to find a star witness—a key man with access to the center of operations. Then you build your case, piece by piece. And once *all* your ducks are in a row, you roll up everyone at once, from the bottom to the top. If I went after Forrest your way, he'd either kill my low-level witnesses or skip the country."

Kaiser is right; but that doesn't mean his is the only way. "You're talking about months of work, John. You've got probable cause to start busting Double Eagles tomorrow, and that would instantly put Forrest on the defensive. You might get lucky and flip someone who could help you nail him on RICO charges. Why won't you try that, when hours might mean life or death for my father?"

Kaiser looks back at me for a few seconds, then walks down to the L in the corridor, so that he can see the main entrance. Satisfied, he walks back to mxe and speaks with quiet conviction.

"I guess the plain truth is, I don't want Knox and his relatives going down on a drug charge. I believe the Bureau has a moral duty to the people of this parish— the black people, mainly—to close the cases we failed to solve back in the 1960s. We failed those victims and their families, and we failed the agents who worked those cases as best they could. To get any kind of closure, or redemption, or healing, the Double Eagles will have to be tried and convicted for the race murders they committed—not for peddling crystal meth."

My face feels cold from the blood draining out of my cheeks, and my palms have gone clammy. "Are you serious?"

"Never more so. The same holds true for Forrest. That bastard's not going to Angola for skimming profits off meth sales. He's going down for murder. He will be tried and convicted for disgracing the badge and uniform he wore during Hurricane Katrina. He betrayed every cop who stood by his or her post and acted honorably while others deserted."

Kaiser clearly means every word. But I can't let his argument go unanswered. "John . . . would you really let my father die for your sense of *moral proportion*?"

He takes a deep breath, then lets it out slowly. "Your father put himself where he is now. Dr. Cage has always had the option of turning himself in."

"Bullshit. Knox's troopers would shoot him down before he could even raise a white flag, and you know it."

Kaiser neither answers nor looks away.

It takes several seconds to get my temper under control. "The Treasury Department didn't show these scruples when they went after Al Capone. Income-tax evasion was good enough."

"This is different. When you combine the unsolved civil rights murders with Forrest's modern-day crimes, and then tie that in to the Kennedy and King assassinations through Brody Royal and Carlos Marcello, you're talking about one of the most important conspiracy cases in American history. And if anyone but your father were involved, you'd be making my argument for me."

The realization that Kaiser truly means to move at a snail's pace while the men he claims to be hunting close in on my father engenders a kind of crazed panic in me. Compared to Walker Dennis and me, Kaiser has unlimited power at his control. He can tap the NSA, the DEA, and any number of other resources for support. One of the few things he *cannot* do is control my actions—

"I don't like what I see in your eyes, Penn. Tell me what you're thinking."

I hold up both hands and back away from him. "Hey . . . you hold all the cards. I'm just the mayor of Nowhere, USA, and I want to go home."

His eyes remain on me, but the suspicion in them slowly wanes. "Are your mother and daughter okay? I assume you're hiding them somewhere?"

You're damned straight, I reply silently.

"So long as they're not with your father."

"Fuck you, John." I glance anxiously at my watch. "Walker's got to be nearly done with Caitlin. She's been in there longer than I was."

"Maybe she's more talkative than you. Is Dennis videotaping the questioning?"

"Why? You want a copy?"

As if on cue, we hear the sound of sliding chairs from the interrogation room. Kaiser takes out his cell phone and sends a quick text message.

"Jordan's sitting up front," he informs me. "She thought

she should come along, in case Caitlin was upset. Do you think it would help Caitlin to see her?"

Jordan Glass is Kaiser's wife. A famous conflict photographer from my generation, she was one of Caitlin's idols as a young woman. Now fate or chance have thrown them together in the midst of the kind of story they both live to cover. It was Jordan who earlier tonight convinced Caitlin to turn over a copy of Henry Sexton's backup files to the FBI instead of fighting a federal subpoena—or so Caitlin claimed, anyway.

"It probably would," I say, my mind back on tomorrow's drug raid.

The door of the interrogation room opens abruptly, and Caitlin walks out, her face still smeared with ash. Behind her I see Walker Dennis shutting off the video camcorder he used to record our scripted charades in that little room.

"My God," say Jordan Glass, rounding the corner of the hall and catching sight of Caitlin. "I think we need a trip to the bathroom."

"I'm fine," Caitlin says, giving me a worried look. "What I really need is to get to the newspaper. Like an hour ago."

"I'll drive you over," Jordan offers.

"Hold on," says Kaiser, stepping up to Caitlin. "I wouldn't advise you to cross the river into Mississippi just yet."

"Why not?" she asks, cutting her eyes at me again.

"Because the Royal family has already filed complaints against both of you with the Adams County Sheriff's Department. They're claiming that you caused Katy Royal to take those pills, and that Penn harassed their father at St. Catherine's Hospital." Kaiser looks at me. "They'll undoubtedly claim that you went to Royal's house to persecute him for a crime he never committed."

"And killed a Natchez cop on the way?" I ask.

"Tell them good luck with that," Caitlin says. "Tomorrow's *Examiner* will explode that little illusion."

"I'm sure. But be aware, you're almost certain to be sued over anything you print about Brody Royal in your newspaper. Even if they lose, that family has the money to burn."

Caitlin waves her hand as if swatting a mosquito. "That still doesn't explain why I shouldn't go back to Mississippi."

"Sheriff Billy Byrd," I say in a flat voice, naming one of the three men behind the prosecution of my father for murder. "And Shad Johnson. Right?"

Kaiser nods. "I doubt Sheriff Byrd will miss this chance to harass you. You two ought to take a room at the motel where my field agents are staying. You'll have a lot more peaceful time over here than you will trying to function in Natchez. Caitlin, you can call your staff over there for a briefing."

"No way," Caitlin says. "If Billy Byrd arrests me, I'll slap it on the front page of the paper. Then I'll sue *him*, and my father has the attorneys on retainer to do it. Does Billy really want that action?"

Kaiser doesn't look surprised by her fire.

Caitlin looks at Jordan. "Will you still take me across the river? My staff is waiting."

"Absolutely," Jordan answers, without even looking at her husband.

Kaiser sighs in resignation. "I'm going to have a team follow you over, just in case. I'd suggest sneaking into the *Examiner* building, if you want to have a hand in tomorrow's stories. Otherwise, you're liable to spend all night in an interrogation room like the one you just left—only not as hospitable."

"Should my ears be burning?" Sheriff Dennis asks, stepping into the hall with his Stetson on.

"Not at all," Kaiser replies. "How'd it go, Sheriff? You get everything about tonight documented?"

"In Technicolor."

Caitlin's trying to catch my eye, but I know better than to try to slip anything past Kaiser. The behavioral science veteran is quietly studying us, absorbing nonverbal cues I can't even begin to guess at. Kaiser looks as though he's about to ask a question when his cell phone pings. After checking the message, he looks up with his facial muscles as tense as I've ever seen them.

"What is it?" I ask.

"A state police cruiser just pulled up. Our friend Alphonse Ozan is inside."

"*No*," Caitlin whispers. "I can't spend the night being questioned by that son of a bitch. I'm about to write the biggest story of my career." She looks at Sheriff Dennis. "Can you sneak me out the back or something?"

"No way," Kaiser interjects. "You try that, Ozan will have an APB out on you, same as Dr. Cage."

The sound of boot heels on a tiled floor echoes from the front of the sheriff's office.

"What's your plan, then?" I ask Kaiser. "Are you going to back off like you did at the hospital? If so, tell me now, and we'll take our chances running. Ozan is Forrest Knox's man, and you know it."

Before Kaiser can reply, a muscular man with black eyes and copper-colored skin rounds the corner in highly polished knee boots and a state police uniform. A Louisiana Redbone, Alphonse Ozan radiates a quality of eerie apartness that has nothing to do with his race, but what I perceive as his sociopathic nature. He walks up to the little hall table and taps one of the red Christmas balls on the plastic tree.

"Well, well," he says, looking around the corridor with amusement in his eyes. "Four men burned to death out by the lake, more likely shot dead, and here we've got everybody in the hall having a Christmas party."

Sheriff Dennis pulls his Stetson low over his eyes and drills Ozan with a hard stare. "What can I do for you, Captain?"

Ozan pretends to notice Dennis suddenly. "You? Nothing. Your whole damned parish is falling apart around you, and you seem powerless to stop it. I've come to officially inform you that, as of now, the state police have assumed control of all criminal investigations originating in this parish over the past three days. I want all the relevant files boxed up and ready to go in fifteen minutes."

CHAPTER 8

SHERIFF WALKER DENNIS'S face has gone through about six discernible shades since Captain Ozan declared he was taking over all his investigations—starting at pink and arriving at purple. But when Sheriff Dennis speaks, his voice somehow remains under control.

"We seem to have some jurisdictional confusion, Captain. Those crimes happened in my parish, and I've got the staff and resources to investigate them. That's what I'm doing now. We don't need assistance. Not from the state police *or* the FBI."

A chuckle of ridicule escapes Ozan's thin lips. "Sheriff, you ain't worn that badge but six weeks, and it shows. You can't even manage the pitiful resources you do have. You should have called us the second you heard what happened out at Brody Royal's place."

John Kaiser clears his throat and turns his gaze on Ozan. "Just what do you think *did* happen out there, Captain?"

Ozan smirks, emboldened by his successful intimidation of Kaiser earlier tonight. "Well, I'll tell you, *Agent* Kaiser. We've got one of Mr. Royal's security personnel lying dead out by Mr. Royal's driveway, his throat cut. Then we've got an elderly African-American gentleman gunned down outside the house. The firemen just dragged two more bodies clear of the wreckage, one of whom has a massive shotgun wound. And then there's the basement, which appears to contain the remains of three people—one of whom *might* be Brody Royal. It's still too hot to get down there to get a positive ID. But however you slice it, that's a multiple-homicide scene, and Barney Fife here hasn't got the experience or the budget to properly investigate it."

Kaiser looks sharply at Sheriff Dennis, hoping to stop

him from doing something that could cost him his job. "Captain, under what authority are you taking over Sheriff Dennis's jurisdiction?"

Ozan barks out an incredulous laugh, then hooks his thumbs in his trousers and turns to give Kaiser his full attention. "I thought we'd straightened this out back at the hospital. Murder's a state crime, and that's the end of it. You didn't argue then, and I don't expect any lip now."

To my amazement, Kaiser's face remains calm. In fact, I see what looks like a trace of anticipatory pleasure in his eyes.

"I'm going to have to take exception with your opinion, Captain," he says in a tone of mild regret.

Ozan draws back his head, squinting. "Exception to *what*? You federal boys ain't got a damn thing to do with murder, unless you're invited in by local authorities. Even then you're only there to advise. *We* say who comes and goes from that crime scene. *We* handle all the evidence. And *we make the arrests*. By the way, I'm gonna be detaining both Mayor Cage and his girlfriend for questioning right now. Questioning as *suspects*."

"*What?*" Caitlin cries, her face going red.

Kaiser holds up a restraining hand.

"I'll use one of the sheriff's rooms to start," Ozan continues, "but if necessary, I'll have them transported to Baton Rouge."

Everyone in the hallway is watching Kaiser, wondering if he'll keep playing out the milquetoast role he began at Mercy Hospital. For a moment he purses his lips as though considering Ozan's argument. Then he steps squarely into the state trooper's space and speaks with the calm authority of a military officer addressing a subordinate.

"In conventional situations, Captain, you'd be correct. But as Ms. Masters informed you earlier this evening, the murder of Henry Sexton was a hate crime. That gives the FBI automatic jurisdiction over that case. As for Mayor Cage and Ms. Masters, they were victims of a kidnapping and attempted murder tonight. That kidnapping was instigated by Brody Royal and Randall Regan. While they were hostages, Mayor Cage and Ms. Masters heard Royal confess his involvement with the Double Eagle group dating back to 1964. They also witnessed Mr. Royal murder the black man you mentioned, whose name is Marshall Johnston, Junior, nickname 'Sleepy.'"

While Ozan blinks at the flood of details coming from Kaiser's mouth, the FBI agent says, "You may not know it yet, but the Double Eagle group has been designated a domestic terror organization under Title Eight of the USA PATRIOT Act. Under the provisions of that act, the FBI has assumed full primacy of authority over any and all investigations pertaining to that group. Tonight's events fall directly under that umbrella. The Royal house on Lake Concordia is now a federal crime scene. Should you choose to interfere with our investigation, you will find yourself subject to severe disciplinary measures, beginning with immediate incarceration at the facility of my choosing, *without* due process. Right now, I'm thinking Fort Leavenworth, Kansas."

Ozan's face has gone even darker than the sheriff's did. He's spitting mad, but Kaiser presses on relentlessly.

"Further, under Title Eight of the Patriot Act, kidnapping in connection with terrorism has been reclassified as a terrorist act. The Bureau will be taking the lead on that investigation as well. It might also interest you to know that under last year's Intelligence Reform and Terrorism Prevention Act, special anti-methamphetamine initiatives were passed into law, and those will be vigorously pursued in relation to any and all members of the Double Eagle group, their families, and criminal co-conspirators."

Now Ozan's face is losing color.

"Title *Five* of the Patriot Act," Kaiser continues, "stipulates fifteen-year prison terms for any public official found to have taken a bribe. Any offender's personal assets can be seized under this act. In that connection, under a Title Five National Security Letter, the Bureau's New Orleans SAC has already requested that all state police telephone, wireless, personnel, and computer records on both you and Forrest Knox be delivered to me by four P.M. tomorrow." Kaiser looks purposefully at his wristwatch. "Correction, that's four P.M. *today*. While I'm not legally required to inform you of this, I'd like you to pass the information to your boss at the earliest opportunity." Kaiser let his words hang for a couple of seconds. "Just so we're all clear on where we stand."

After gaping dumbly like a punch-drunk boxer, Ozan shuts his mouth and starts working himself up for a fight, but at the last second his judgment gets the better of his hormones, and he confines himself to a low growl. "You ain't heard the last of this, Jack. This is a states' rights issue."

Kaiser actually smiles at this. "The last time you boys had a serious states' rights problem with Washington, it was 1861. That didn't work out so well for you. But if you want to push it, we'll be happy to oblige."

Ozan looks slowly around at the rest of us, then focuses on the FBI man once more. "You know something, hotshot? The last thing you want to do is make this personal. Especially while you're living down in New Orleans. That's our neck of the swamp."

Kaiser gives me a momentary glance. "Mayor Cage, did you just hear Captain Ozan threaten a special agent of the FBI?"

"I did."

"And will you testify to that fact in a court of law?"

"I will."

"Thank you. Captain, I suggest you avail yourself of the opportunity to leave before I have the sheriff jail you."

Ozan shakes his head as though in disgust at a world turned upside down. Then he turns on his heel and marches away without another word.

"I'll be goddamned," Sheriff Dennis marvels. "He looked like a dog shittin' peach pits. Shakin' all over. In all my years on the job, I've never seen nothing like that."

Jordan Glass laughs out loud, apparently happy to see her husband shed his girdle of self-control.

Kaiser gives Dennis a wry smile. "It was time to send Forrest Knox a message. And I'd had about enough of Ozan's dime-store Nazi act."

I ask, "Did your SAC really request National Security Letters on Knox and Ozan?"

"Not yet. I tacked that on to give Ozan the runs. But after tonight, we'll get them. Too many people are dead. And I want Knox to know that I know what he is. Maybe that'll give him pause before killing anybody else."

Kaiser takes a step toward Walker Dennis and slaps him on the shoulder.

"Sheriff, I look forward to working with you on the Royal case, and I feel sure I can count on the same hospitality you've shown us so far. In exchange, I can promise you full Bureau support, should you have any problem with your comrades from the state police."

Sheriff Dennis gives Kaiser a respectful salute. "I appreciate it, Mr. Kaiser. And I'll be happy to buy you a drink, first chance we get."

"I'll look forward to it."

Kaiser is playing this about as subtly as a used-car salesman. Sensing that Walker Dennis and I are allies beneath the surface of things, he figures that in the glow of his public spanking of Ozan, Dennis might confide our secrets to him. One look into the sheriff's eyes tells me Kaiser's instincts are dead-on. Walker even gives me a questioning look, as though asking for permission. He's probably thinking how much harder we could hit the Knoxes if we had Kaiser on our side.

Before Walker can speak, I say, "I was just telling John he ought to hit the Double Eagles as hard and fast as he can with the meth stuff, while they're off balance. Maybe we'd get one to flip on Forrest, to save himself from dying of old age or worse in Angola."

Kaiser practically whirls on me, frustration in his eyes. "We already went over this, Penn. Give it up, will you? There's no point."

Caitlin and Jordan freeze, their eyes darting from Kaiser to me, then back.

"The Double Eagles are tighter than the Mafia about secrecy," he goes on, looking at Sheriff Dennis. "They're like Islamic fundamentalists."

"They can't *all* be," I say evenly. "Not at the street level."

"Street drones won't know anything about Forrest. It's all compartmentalized."

"Somebody on the street will know about the Double Eagles."

Kaiser turns back to me. "So what? *No* Double Eagle is going to talk, not even to save himself a jail term."

"Glenn Morehouse did."

"To make peace with God, not to send his war buddies to death row. And even if one decided to cut a deal, Knox would kill him before we could get what we need."

"What's going on, guys?" Jordan asks sharply. "What's wrong?"

"Penn's worried about his father," Kaiser says wearily. "Understandably."

I need to cement Walker's mistrust of Kaiser once and for all. "Okay, John. If you believe forcing a plea bargain won't work, then go another way. Direct attack."

"What the hell are you talking about?"

"Use me to sting Forrest. I can do what you think I did with Brody Royal: offer to keep his name out of the papers in exchange for saving my father. And you can record everything he says."

"No!" Caitlin snaps, horrified that I'd even consider repeating this disastrous tactic, or offering compromise in her name. "That's a total nonstarter."

Kaiser's shaking his head. "You haven't heard a word I said. You want to wear a wire on Forrest Knox? He won't say one incriminating word on tape, but as soon as the heat's off—he'll kill you." The anger bleeds out of Kaiser's face, and he speaks with exhausted conviction. "This is a dangerous time to be Forrest Knox's *friend*, much less his enemy."

"I'll bet I can make him talk."

"Even if Forrest agreed to talk to you," Kaiser goes on, "he'd never believe you could muzzle Caitlin and her newspaper."

"And he'd be right," she says, looking stricken. "I can't believe this."

Sheriff Dennis is watching Kaiser with sudden wariness. I only hope Walker has the intestinal fortitude to go ahead with tomorrow's raids as planned.

"Enough of this," Kaiser says. "The bottom line is, thanks to that dead state trooper, Forrest can kill your father with no worries at all. And he means to. All he has to do is find him."

"John!" cries Jordan.

"I'm sorry, Penn," Kaiser says, sounding as though he means it. "But you've got to accept reality. The only good you can accomplish at this point is to find your father and convince him to turn himself in to me. You do anything else—anything related to Forrest Knox—and I'll have to arrest you."

Sheriff Dennis's mouth drops open.

Kaiser nods for emphasis. "I could make an obstruction case right now, and you know it."

"Go ahead. You haven't exactly handled this case by the book yourself."

"You're right. My ass is on the line, too, thanks to what happened tonight. But you'd better pray that Washington doesn't pull me out of here. Because whoever they send to replace me will see you as an absolute liability. They won't give you the time of day, much less help your father."

I wave my hand dismissively and walk toward the hall that leads to the exit. "Can somebody give me a ride to City Hall? Royal's men stole my Audi, but I've got a city car I can use."

"I'll drop you when I take Caitlin," Jordan Glass calls from behind me.

"Thank you."

Kaiser starts to protest, but Jordan shushes him.

After I round the corner, I pause and lean against the cold wall. Jordan Glass's angry voice floats around the corner.

"John, that was too much."

"Somebody's got to save him from himself," Kaiser replies. "Caitlin, are you really okay? I heard it was pretty bad in Royal's basement."

"I'm fine," she answers in a taut voice.

"They got Henry's files, huh?"

She doesn't answer at first. Then she says, "I saved the box with the burned journals in it. But there's not much left."

"Penn told me Royal paid somebody to delete your backup files from the newspaper's computers?"

"That's right."

"If you'd like, I can send you some Bureau techs who might be able to reconstruct those files. If you're still willing to share them, of course."

"Seriously? They can do that?"

"Maybe. Since 9/11, we've spent billions on technology aimed at restoring lost data, or partially destroyed evidence."

"I won't turn down the help."

"Good," Kaiser says, sounding like a kid who's been

told he can open his Christmas presents early. "I've got two techs here in town, and if we need more talent, I'll get some headed this way from D.C."

"Okay. Look, I really need to get back to the paper now."

"All right, but I need to drive Penn myself. He and I aren't finished, as much as he might wish we were."

At these words I nearly bolt from the building, but something keeps me in the hallway. If Kaiser wants to keep talking, he either needs to ask me something more or reveal something he hasn't given up yet. I hope it's the latter.

By the time they round the corner, I'm far down the hall, waiting by the front door. Jordan has taken Caitlin by the arm; she looks like she's escorting an accident victim through a hospital. Jordan smiles as they reach me, but the expression looks forced.

"Hold up, Mayor," Kaiser says from behind them. "I'm going to drive you."

I'm too tired to argue, even for show.

"Hey, Penn!" Sheriff Dennis calls from around the corner. "Come back down here a sec. I forgot to get you to sign a form."

"Go on to the car," I tell Caitlin.

She gives me a fragile smile, and before Kaiser can stop me I trot back to Sheriff Dennis's office. The rusted-spring sound of the front door opening follows me around the corner, and then I see Sheriff Dennis moving quickly up the hall, his big legs churning, a white piece of paper in one hand and a pen in the other. As he reaches me, I hear Kaiser's footsteps behind me.

Walker hands me a pen, then holds the paper up against the wall for me to sign. He's standing so that his big body will be between me and Kaiser, should the FBI agent come all the way around the corner.

"That sucks about your car," he says in a conversational tone. "I'll see if we can find it for you. Those assholes probably dumped it somewhere not too far from Lake Concordia."

"I just hope it's not in the river," I reply loudly. Then I whisper, "Is tomorrow's raid still on?"

"You bet your ass. Be here five hours from now, ready to rock and roll."

"You going to tell Kaiser about it?"

"Not on your life, kemosabe."

My heart swells with gratitude. "Thanks, Walker."

Kaiser's footsteps round the corner.

"Get some sleep, brother," the sheriff says in a man-to-man voice. "You earned it tonight." Then he calls to Kaiser: "You guys keep your eyes open out there."

Stuffing my hands into my pockets, I walk past Kaiser without a word. Seconds later, the FBI agent catches up to me at the front door. When I push it open, a blast of cold wind hits my face, then cuts through my collar like a blade.

"I wonder where Ozan's got to," Kaiser says. "Wherever he is, he's talking to Forrest Knox, you can bank on that."

"I feel like I can still smell the fire," I say to myself, "even though it's ten miles away."

"Closer than that, as the crow flies," says Kaiser. "But you're smelling yourself. That wind stirred it up."

Raising my coat sleeve to my face, I realize he's right. "So what's this about? I thought we'd said all we had to say."

Kaiser turns and gives me a piercing look that has nothing to do with officialdom. "Unfinished business. We're about to go through the looking glass, Mayor. And on the other side, we both tell the truth, regardless of consequences."

He seems to want a response, but I offer nothing.

"What do you say to that?" he asks.

"It's about fucking time."

CHAPTER 9

"COLONEL, WE GOT TROUBLE."

On the roof of state police headquarters, Forrest Knox pressed a satellite phone harder against his good ear—most of the other he'd lost in Vietnam—and spoke in a controlled voice. "Give me specifics, Alphonse."

"I went to the CPSO," Ozan explained, "just like you said, and I tried to take over the case."

"But?"

"That Agent Kaiser was there, the same FBI prick who was at the hospital after Sexton was shot."

"I know who Kaiser is. I know him from New Orleans."

"Well, this time he didn't turn tail. This time he read me the goddamn Patriot Act, chapter and verse. He was talking about seizing our personal phone and computer records, yours and mine. That son of a bitch is trouble, boss. He threatened to jail me on the spot. Quoted some new Patriot Act rules on meth production, which don't sound good."

"What about Mayor Cage and his girl?"

"They were there, but the girl headed back across the river to her newspaper. Kaiser's wife went with her. Cage left with Kaiser. What you want I should do?"

Forrest looked down at his watch. Whatever Caitlin Masters knew about him and the Double Eagles was almost certain to appear in tomorrow's *Examiner*, no matter what he did at this point. Unless . . . "We may need to mobilize the Black Team, Alphonse."

The "Black Team" was a handpicked group of SWAT officers who occasionally functioned as Forrest's private tactical unit. During Hurricane Katrina, the Black Team had done much more than help keep the peace. In the fetid darkness of poststorm New Orleans, they had ruthlessly winnowed the ranks of the Knox organization's drug-dealing competition, using chaos and lawlessness as their cover.

"Sounds good to me," Ozan said. "We can't just sit and wait for the hammer to fall. You want me to make the call?"

Forrest weighed the risks of immediate action against those of watchful caution. "Not yet. Just find out where everybody is."

"Got it."

Forrest thought swiftly. HQ was the wrong place from which to direct tactical action. The best place was Valhalla, the family's hunting camp halfway between Natchez and Baton Rouge. "Get your ass up to the camp, Alphonse. We don't need to take this any further on the phone."

"I can be there in forty minutes. You?"

"About the same."

"Ten-four, Colonel. Any further orders in the meantime?"

"Gather all the intel you can, as quietly as you can. Use only contacts you trust. Talk to our man in Dennis's department. Check Royal's contact at the girl's newspaper. Do you know who it was?"

"Yeah. What about the feds?"

"We'll discuss that when I see you."

Forrest hung up, then walked to the edge of the building and looked west toward LSU's Tiger Stadium and the Mississippi River. From long practice, he'd developed the skill of descending into a state of calm in direct proportion to the scale of chaos. Though Ozan's news had stunned him, his pulse had accelerated only slightly during the call, and it quickly returned to normal. Having honed his instincts in combat, where expediency ruled, Forrest was always first inclined to hit back, hard. In war, if someone attacked you, you counterattacked as quickly and viciously as possible. If someone on your own side screwed up and put your unit at risk, you transferred them out. If you couldn't do that, you sent them home in a body bag. Forrest had once fragged a Yankee second lieutenant in the A Shau Valley who seemed to think he was on the set of a John Wayne movie. Nobody had missed him, either, not even MACV.

Such tactics were more complicated back in the world, of course. For one thing, nearly every death in civilian life brought about some sort of investigation, which meant attention. And attention was anathema to the moneymen in New Orleans. They wanted to remain invisible. Even more troubling, Brody Royal had been a member of their insulated elite. His death would profoundly unsettle men accustomed to feeling untouchable. Worst of all, there were probably traceable links between Royal and his New Orleans partners, and those men would be scrambling to eradicate those links wherever possible. Forrest himself was one. He needed to find a way to assure Royal's partners that he was part of the solution, not the problem.

With a last look out over the city—his city—he headed for the stairs that would take him down to the elevator. It had been a long time since someone had challenged him in any meaningful way. Rival drug dealers were one thing; they could be killed without fear of recrimination. But a veteran FBI agent was something else. A former prosecutor like Penn Cage couldn't be ignored either, much less a newspaper publisher like Masters. Those three together made a formidable alliance, one that violence alone could not counter. Violence would play a part, of course, but what Forrest really needed was a narrative that would shape the perception of recent events. Only in this way could he continue to bend the world to his will, which was all he had ever asked of life.

CHAPTER 10

TOM CAGE PULLED the stolen pickup off the dirt road into an empty cotton field and switched off the engine. He hadn't seen a light for miles. The hit man in the backseat was still playing possum, and Tom decided to play along for another thirty seconds. Barren fields and scrub woods stretched into endless darkness and when Tom opened his door, he smelled the rot of a swamp on the air.

As best he could figure, they were five miles from a telephone, unless there was a farm around here he didn't know about. Even if the hit man reached a phone within an hour, Tom figured he could be across the Mississippi River in less than that—if his brother-in-law was home. And being a farmer, John McCrae was never anywhere else. There was a chance that the state police might have staked out Peggy's Louisiana relatives, but if they had, he'd figured a way around that.

"I know you're awake," Tom said, closing his hand around the butt of his .357 and sliding carefully out of the truck.

Grimsby held to his ruse and said nothing.

Tom felt unsteady on his feet, but after a few seconds, he regained his equilibrium. The pain in his shoulder had not relented, however.

"Get out," he said through the open door. "I'm not going to kill you. I was advised to, and I can't say you don't deserve it, but I've got a better use for you."

At first there was only silence. Then Tom heard a stirring, and the hit man said, "What use is that?"

"Errand boy. You're going to carry a message for me, Mr. Grimsby."

"To who?"

"Your boss. Forrest Knox."

More silence.

"But first you're gonna get that goddamned corpse out of the truck. Move it, son. Double-quick. I don't have all night."

"I'm tied to the goddamn gun rack!"

Tom reached into his pocket and dug out a steak knife he'd taken from the kitchen of Drew Elliott's lake house. He leaned into the truck and tossed it onto the backseat.

"Make it quick. And if you come at me with that knife, I'll put a bullet in your gut, the same as I did your partner."

After half a minute of grunts and struggle, he heard a mechanical *thunk*. Then the rear door on the driver's side swung open. "I gotta tell you, Doc," said the voice behind the door, "you're a walking dead man. You know that, right?"

"Bold words for an unarmed man on the wrong end of a pistol."

The hit man's feet touched the ground, and then he stepped out from behind the door—a tall, thin man with his hands now free, and a knife in one of them.

"You're not gonna kill me?" Grimsby said, obviously trying to decide whether to risk a charge.

"I will if you don't drop that knife."

Grimsby's twitchy eyes moved up and down Tom's frame, assessing his condition. Sensing the man was going to rush him, Tom fired a round at his feet.

"Goddamn it!" yelled the hit man as the deep echo rolled over the fields like a thunderclap.

"Drop the knife," Tom repeated.

The blade hit the pavement.

"Now, get your partner out of that backseat."

"Get him yourself."

Tom waved the gun.

"You won't shoot me."

"I killed your partner."

"That was different. That was self-defense."

Tom laughed. "Remember that, if you're ever asked to testify against me."

"You'll never see a courtroom, Doc. Nobody who crosses Colonel Knox ever does."

Tom figured this was true. "Maybe I'm the exception. I've beat the odds so far." He aimed his pistol at the hit man's shoes. "I can't leave here with that corpse in the backseat. Get him out, or I'll put a bullet in your foot. You probably won't die from it, but this is a Magnum. You might go into shock, and they'll definitely have to amputate."

Grimsby worked his mouth around anxiously, trying to gauge Tom's ruthlessness. After a face-saving moment, he walked back behind the door and bent to his work, which was dragging a dead body off a truck's floor and onto the shoulder of a dirt road. While he worked, Tom stood twenty feet away and gave him his brief, beginning with a lie.

"You're ten miles from the closest human habitation. Even if you run all the way, I'll be long gone by the time you can get to a phone and call Knox. But when you do get him, I have a message for him."

A strained grunt was the only response.

"Did you hear me, shitbird?"

"I heard you, goddamn it. He's heavy."

"There's a reason they call it dead weight, son. Now, listen up. About the stupidest thing Forrest could do at this point is kill me. If he does, my son and Caitlin Masters won't rest until Forrest is rotting in jail or dead himself. That might not scare you, but it will him. Because he's got a brain, like his father. I knew Frank Knox, you see. And Frank was no fool. Now, Forrest has probably already considered trying to silence my boy and his girl. But I've got a better solution for him. Far better. You see, if he'll help me with my problem . . . I'll help him with his."

The dead man's head and shoulders dropped beneath the bottom of the door, hanging in the air like a deer carcass.

"What the hell are you talking about?" asked Grimsby, leaning out of the truck. "How can you help the colonel?"

"I can call off my daughter-in-law and her newspaper. She'll have to cover the deaths that have happened already, and might touch the Double Eagles, but I can keep Forrest's name out of the papers. I can guarantee my son won't pursue him either, and Forrest will know the value of that. It was my son who nailed those bastards running the dogfighting ring out of the *Magnolia Queen*. You remember that?"

"I remember."

"I can't do anything about the FBI chasing Forrest, but that's his lookout. There are also certain things I know that could hurt Forrest, as well as Snake and the others. The old guys will know what I'm talking about. I'll keep those buried, as well."

With a long heave and a steady driving of his feet, Grimsby finally dragged the corpse clear of the truck. The dead man's shoes hit the cold earth with dull thuds.

The hit man straightened up and rubbed his hands together, his breath steaming in the chilled air. "What do you want in exchange for all that?"

"I need Forrest to call off the hunt for me and Garrity. That trooper tried to kill me, and he got what he deserved. Forrest can also clear me of the Viola Turner murder charge."

"How the hell can he do that?"

"By blaming the murder on somebody else."

"Such as?"

"Yesterday I was thinking Glenn Morehouse, but that might be a little close for comfort, considering he was a Double Eagle. Now Brody Royal and his son-in-law look like perfect candidates. Forrest can hang everything on them."

"You don't mind asking for the moon, do you?"

Tom shrugged. "I don't care if he blames the dead trooper on *you*, so long as he calls the dogs off me. Have you got all that?"

Grimsby snorted in derision.

"Tell Forrest I'll be waiting for his signal that he accepts my terms."

"What signal?"

"An announcement on statewide radio and TV. When I hear that the APB has been called off, I'll know he's serious about making a deal. The statement should say that the state police have a new theory and are now pursuing other persons of interest. After I hear that, I'll contact Knox's office at state police headquarters." Tom gestured with the Magnum. "That's it. Back away from the truck."

The hit man folded his arms and shivered in his windbreaker. "Are you really gonna leave me out here? It's fucking cold, man! I could freeze."

Tom thought about the mountains around the Chosin Reservoir. "You think this is cold?"

"Hell, yeah."

"Your friend's a lot colder."

Grimsby looked down at the corpse. "Seriously, Doc. You gonna leave me without a heavy coat?"

"Take your friend's and put it over yours. He doesn't need it anymore."

The hit man looked up in disbelief.

Tom raised his Magnum, and his shoulder screamed with pain.

"You won't make it twenty miles without hitting a roadblock," Grimsby said. "Like I said before, you're a walking dead man."

Tom grinned. "Lab tests have been telling me that for a long time, but I'm still vertical."

Without turning his back on the killer, Tom put one foot on the running board and raised himself slowly into the driver's seat. Grimsby was still staring down at his dead comrade when Tom put the truck into gear, made a painful three-point turn, and drove back the way he had come. The hit man might be right about the roadblock, but Tom didn't have twenty miles to go. John McCrae's farmhouse was less than half that distance away.

With a sudden inspiration, Tom switched off his headlights and slowed down until his eyes adjusted to the moonlight. At this point he'd be a fool to let himself be caught because of being sighted by a chopper or high-flying prop plane. He'd switch the lights back on when he reached the narrow strip of pavement they called the main road around here. The thought made him smile, despite his pain. Whenever anyone asked his wife where she was from, Peggy always said "a little farm in the middle of nowhere." People always assumed she was exaggerating, but she wasn't.

Tom had never been more grateful for that than he was tonight.

CHAPTER 11

NATCHEZ SLEEPS IN silence as we cross the Mississippi River, as silent as Kaiser and I have remained since
we left the sheriff's office. The town looks as it has since I
was a child, a fragile line of lights strung along the rim of
the high bluff, with church steeples standing watch over
the populace. Given the ruckus at the Concordia hospital
early in the evening, a few citizens are probably sitting up,
constantly refreshing the *Examiner*'s Web page, hoping
for a Breaking News update that will tell them once and
for all whether Henry Sexton was killed by a sniper. How
will they react when they learn that Henry survived that
attack only to give his life for Caitlin's hours later? Or that
he was only one of several casualties, among them Brody
Royal?

Looking back at the dark lowlands of Louisiana, I scan
the sky for the column of flame we left behind, but I don't
see it. The levee near that lake stands thirty-five feet tall,
and the flames were probably double that, but now the
fire's burned out of sight.

Kaiser turns onto Canal Street and heads into downtown proper.

"Are you going to keep me in suspense all night?" I ask.
"I'm not going to sit outside City Hall talking till dawn.
I'm wiped out, man."

When Kaiser begins speaking at last, his voice carries a
passion that it didn't back in the corridor of Sheriff Den-

nis's office. "Penn, the FBI had two great failures in the last century, and they irreparably damaged the Bureau in the public mind. The first was the unsolved murders of the civil rights movement. The second involved the major assassinations, particularly that of JFK. Those weren't failures of process, but of *will*. Why did the Bureau fail? Because the director didn't really want those cases solved."

This isn't news to me, but it's a pretty remarkable statement to hear from a serving FBI agent. "When Dwight Stone discovered who was behind the murder of Del Payton in 1968—a big Nixon supporter, as it happened—Hoover made Stone suppress it. "

"I know all about that. Stone's generation of agents saw J. Edgar's sins firsthand. And as a result, there's now a group of retired FBI agents—mostly thirty-year men—who've never forgotten the sting of those failures. They've never let go of the cases they weren't allowed to work as they should have been. The Double Eagle cases were among those."

"And the JFK assassination?"

Kaiser nods. "That, too. These men work quietly, in the background, but they've done significant investigative work over the years. They've even got serious funding behind them now—private money, of course. The current director knows nothing about these guys, but some active agents give them help when possible."

"Like you?"

A brief nod. "Like me."

"Is Dwight Stone part of this group?"

"He is. They don't publicize their activities, so you can't tell Caitlin about it. If it got out that former FBI agents were actively working the Kennedy assassination . . . that's like chum in the water to the media. These men are dedicated pros. Engineer types. They keep their heads down, and they don't get excited. I think of them like retired astronauts. In fact, that's what I call them, when I refer to them at all. They call themselves the 'Working Group.'"

Kaiser turns right on State Street, rolls past Sheriff Billy Byrd's sheriff's department and the courthouse, then turns left again and parks in front of the lit oaks before City Hall.

Dwight Stone's participation in this group legitimizes it in my eyes, but given tonight's events, I can't raise much interest. "Where's this going, John?"

"My astronauts have been pretty quiet for a while. The civil rights murder cases have stalled, and the few remaining witnesses are dying like flies. Even the agents themselves are dying, more's the pity. But when Glenn Morehouse talked to Henry Sexton on Monday, everything changed. *Everything*, Penn. No Double Eagle had ever cracked before."

"Except Jason Abbott."

"That was different. Abbott was just trying to screw the guy who was screwing his wife. But Morehouse was trying to clear his conscience, and in the process he opened a door that the Working Group believed was closed forever. By revealing the connection between Carlos Marcello and Frank Knox—through Brody Royal—he cracked the door on the JFK assassination."

"How? Just what did Henry tell you, exactly?"

"That Jimmy Revels was murdered to lure Robert Kennedy to Mississippi to be assassinated by the Knoxes. Or that was the plan anyway, until Frank Knox was killed in an industrial accident."

"You don't doubt that story?"

"Not at all. Carlos Marcello had hated Robert Kennedy since the McClellan hearings in '59, and he'd wanted him dead since Bobby deported him while attorney general in '61. If JFK's death hadn't neutralized Bobby in '63, Marcello would probably have killed Bobby then. And five years later, when Bobby announced his presidential run, he put himself right back in Marcello's sights. If Frank Knox hadn't died in your father's office in March of '68, Robert Kennedy might have been assassinated in Natchez or Ferriday in April, rather than Los Angeles in June. Carlos could not allow RFK to become president, Penn. If he had, he would have been immediately deported, and lost his empire."

"Empire?" I mutter in frustration.

"You think I'm exaggerating? In 1979, the House Select Committee on Assassinations determined that Marcello's combined operations—both criminal and legitimate—comprised the largest industry in the State of Louisiana.

Bigger than the oil business, bigger than agriculture. Carlos wasn't just a Mafia kingpin. He was a king, every bit as powerful as Huey Long in his day."

Kaiser has raised his voice, and I'm starting to hear the obsessive passion of a conspiracy nut. "I still don't understand what we're doing here, John."

The FBI agent looks at me like I'm playing a game with him. "You're holding back on me, Penn."

"What are you talking about?"

"When you called me Tuesday night, after Henry's stabbing, you told me you thought Brody Royal might be involved in the major assassinations of the 1960s. You also said your father might know something about them. You used the plural both times. It's time to tell me what you were talking about."

I don't want to answer, but my memory of Dwight Stone and all he did for me seven years ago is pushing me to speak. After some deliberation, I decide to break my father's confidence.

"My dad told me a story the other night," I say, not mentioning the incriminating photo that Henry Sexton passed to me earlier that same night—the photo that prompted our conversation. "Back in the midsixties, Dad and Dr. Leland Robb were down on the Gulf Coast at a gun show, and Dr. Robb set up a fishing cruise with Brody Royal. Dad didn't know about it until the last minute, so he couldn't get out of going. Claude Devereux and Ray Presley were also on the boat."

"That's a pretty motley crew."

"I know. Anyway, the one other guy on this boat was some kind of paramilitary CIA type. A contractor, probably. He spoke French. Or cursed in French, anyway."

Kaiser's gaze has turned intense. "What year was this?"

"In '65, I think. No, '66. Dr. Robb was killed in '69, so it was three years before that. Anyway, the CIA guy got trashed during this little voyage, and he and Royal got to talking about Cuba. The Bay of Pigs. They also talked about some coup d'état operations in South America. Then at some point the guy started bitching about 'Dallas' and how the whole thing had been screwed up, like a botched military operation. Dad didn't know what he meant, but it scared the shit out of him, and he made a point never to see Royal again after that. And that's all. That's my story."

"Why would that scare your father unless he thought 'Dallas' referred to the JFK assassination?"

"I know, I know. You're probably right."

"Dr. Cage didn't think this guy was just talking out of his ass?"

"No. Dad was a combat medic in Korea, and he told me he'd seen a certain type of guy over there. The hard type, you know? Professional. He said this guy was like that. No bullshit. A killer."

Kaiser nods slowly and motions for me to go on.

"That's all I know, John. Seriously."

"No, it's not. You saw those rifles in Brody's basement."

"That's meaningless, man. A gullible old man's fantasy. You'll have the rifles themselves soon anyway. The barrels and works, at least. You don't need me for that."

"Earlier you told me you thought the JFK rifle might be real. What made you say that?"

"The fishing story, I guess. I figured there might possibly be some connection between Royal and the kind of guy who'd be involved in an assassination."

"That's all?"

"Maybe after all I've heard about Frank Knox . . . it didn't seem beyond the realm of possibility that he was in Dallas on the day John Kennedy died."

"No shit," says Kaiser. "And he might not have been alone, either. His brother Snake served as a sniper in Korea. I told you that over the past couple of years Snake has bragged to a few people that he shot Martin Luther King."

I groan in protest. "James Earl Ray killed King, John. I don't think there's any serious dispute about that. In any case, I honestly don't care right now. I killed someone myself tonight. I need to sleep."

"Just one more minute. Tell me about the rifles. What kind of guns were they?"

I close my eyes and think back to the awful few seconds between Royal and Regan pushing us toward the indoor firing range and Caitlin going after Royal with the straight razor. "Hunting rifles," I say softly.

"Not military?"

"No. Wooden stocks, hunting scopes."

"What make?"

"I don't know. My father's the gun expert, not me. The rifle on the bottom might have been a Winchester. Yeah . . . and the top one was bolt-action."

"Do you remember which rifle was dated for which assassination?"

"The bolt-action was Dallas. The Winchester-style gun was April fourth. Memphis."

"That's good detail for a quick glimpse. I guess former prosecutors make good witnesses. We'll have to see what comes out of the ashes after the wreckage of Royal's house cools."

"Good luck with that." I reach for the door handle. "I'll talk to you tomorrow."

"Hold up," Kaiser says, betraying some tension. "We're not quite done."

"Damn it, John. Yes, we are. I'm exhausted."

"You didn't think the story about the founding of the Double Eagles was relevant to all this? To the rifles, even?"

"What are you talking about?"

"The sandbar south of Natchez? Nineteen sixty-four? Henry didn't tell you that story?"

I think back to the long conversation in Henry's "war room," but nothing rings a bell. "I don't think so."

Kaiser purses his lips like he's surprised. "Frank Knox founded the Double Eagles on a sandbar south of the International Paper Company in the summer of '64, five days after the FBI found the three civil rights workers in that dam in Neshoba County. That's the first day Frank handed out the Double Eagle gold pieces."

"This is the first I've heard of that."

"Snake Knox was there, and Sonny Thornfield, and Glenn Morehouse. They were having a family campout and practicing with plastic explosives. Just good ol' all-American fun."

"Okay. So?"

"On that day, Frank told the others they were splitting off from the Ku Klux Klan. Then he drew three *K*'s in the sand." Kaiser takes a small notepad from his coat and draws three capital *K*'s as the points of a triangle.

"Morehouse and Thornfield were confused until Frank took out a magazine photo of Bobby Kennedy and Martin Luther King, Junior, standing with President Johnson in the White House Rose Garden."

"Go on."

"Frank had drawn red circles around the heads of Kennedy and King."

"Shit, that doesn't mean anything."

"You don't think so? When Sonny and Morehouse still didn't get it, Frank drew more letters in the sand—two before each *K*."

As I watch, Kaiser adds letters to his notepad. Now the points of his triangle read:

JFK
MLK RFK

To my surprise, the sight of these letters starts a low buzzing in my head. "But it's what Frank said," Kaiser goes on, "that makes me take all this seriously. He scratched an X through the JFK with a barbecue fork and said, 'One down, two to go.'"

A wave of sweat breaks through my skin inside my coat. "Henry didn't tell me anything about that."

"I guess he was too busy telling you other things."

I don't bite on this bait, but Kaiser's probably right. Since the founding of the Double Eagles had nothing to do with my father, Henry didn't waste time telling me about it. I'll bet he didn't tell me half of what he knew that night. He'd been working for twenty years on those cases. Thirty, maybe.

"John, are you seriously working the JFK assassination?"

This time, when Kaiser's eyes meet mine, it's as if I'm truly seeing the man for the first time. The intensity in his gaze is not that of a fanatic, but of a soldier committed to his cause. "Like I said, I'm helping Dwight and his buddies. But you still don't understand. We *know* who ordered John Kennedy's murder. We've been certain for more than two years. We just haven't been able to prove who fired the kill shot."

Now we've come full circle, back to cuckooland.

"That's great, John. But I've got no time for conspiracy theories."

I reach for the door handle again, but Kaiser catches hold of my arm. "Yes, you do. Because your father knows the same thing we do. He's known it for forty-two years."

Kaiser's words don't quite seem real. "If you believe that, you don't know my father at all."

He concedes this with a small nod. "Are you sure *you* do?"

This freezes me in my seat. I want to argue, yet everything that's happened over the past three days has happened because my father has refused to speak about the past—a past that it's becoming increasingly clear is very different from the one I believed in only days ago.

"Penn, your father's being hunted for killing a state trooper. I need very much to talk to him. And ultimately, his only chance to survive is to turn himself in to me."

My heart leaps at this new tack. "Are you saying you'll take him into protective custody?"

"I don't know yet. I was trying to set it up with the director, but after all the deaths tonight, it'll be a hard sell. *However*—if Dr. Cage can link the Double Eagles to the Kennedy or King assassinations, I will make the case and spirit him out of harm's way before the Louisiana State Police even know what happened."

Why does Kennedy's death mean more than all the civil rights martyrs put together? "What about Dad's fishing boat story? The Frenchman talking about Dallas? Is that enough?"

"Too thin. We need more."

"I've got a photograph taken on that trip. Henry gave it to me. It shows Dad, Presley, Royal, and Devereux in the stern of the boat."

Kaiser's eyes widen. "Is the Frenchman in the shot?"

I shake my head.

"Damn. Where is this picture?"

"Caitlin has it. It's probably at the *Examiner*."

"Okay. I'm going to be grilled by the director once more tonight, and I'll do what I can to push protective custody for your father. For now, let's hope I'm right about him and Garrity lying low somewhere safe. But between now and tomorrow morning, I want you to rack your brain, talk to your mother, do anything you can think of to locate your father and Garrity. And if you do, tell Dr. Cage that information about Carlos Marcello and the Kennedy assassination is his salvation."

"Honestly, John, there's no way he's sat on that kind of information for forty years."

"He kept quiet about Brody Royal and the murders of Albert Norris and Dr. Robb, didn't he? Why should the Kennedy stuff be any different?"

I'm not sure I can articulate my feelings about this. "Because that's not . . . personal. Not local. It's history. And history is almost like a religion to my dad."

"All history is personal," Kaiser replies. "I'm betting Dr. Cage knows that." For the first time tonight, the FBI agent's voice sounds almost kind. "Your father was close to Ray Presley for most of his life. Before Presley moved to Natchez, he was a New Orleans cop on the pad for Carlos Marcello."

"I know that."

"Henry told me he told you about the Bureau surveillance reports that mention your father. On at least four occasions, Marcello soldiers drove north to Natchez to get medical treatment from your father in the late sixties and early seventies. Why would they drive a hundred eighty miles for treatment?"

I start to repeat my father's explanation for this, but another answer comes to me—the one Brody Royal supplied. "Whatever Dad did, John, he did it to protect Viola. After her rape, and the murder of her brother, he made some kind of a deal to save her. He must have. The Eagles would have killed her otherwise. Maybe that deal was with Marcello."

"I think you're right," Kaiser concedes. "But we need to know for sure."

After several seconds of silence, he leans across me and reaches into his glove box for a folded sheet of paper. This he patiently unfolds, then hands to me and switches on the Crown Victoria's interior light.

I'm holding a low-resolution grayscale photograph printed on copy paper. It looks like a telephoto image of a man in profile, driving a light-colored sedan that dates to the 1960s. Something about the car is familiar, or maybe the man, but the photo is too blurry for me to figure it out.

"That was taken outside the entrance of Churchill Farms," Kaiser informs me, "a sixty-four-hundred-acre tract of Louisiana swampland owned by Carlos Marcello. Churchill Farms was Marcello's most secluded hideaway."

"Okay. Who's driving the car?"

"You don't recognize him?" Kaiser asks softly. "Or the vehicle?"

"The car looks familiar. The man, too. But it's too blurry."

"That's your father, Penn. He's thirty-six years old in that photo. Nine years younger than you are now."

My heart lurches in my chest.

"And the car," Kaiser goes on, "is—"

"A 1966 Oldsmobile Ninety-Eight," I finish, as a rush of scents and feelings from my childhood pass through me. "Our old family car."

Kaiser nods. "That's right. Your father visited Churchill Farms for sixty-two minutes on April eleventh, 1968. The Bureau's organized-crime unit had routine surveillance set up out there at the time. Also, you can't see him in this photo because of the angle and the graininess, but Ray Presley was sitting in the passenger seat. He went down there with your dad. And Carlos was definitely in residence at the time."

"Jesus Christ."

"I know. I'm sorry."

"What the hell does this mean?"

"I don't know. But we need to find out."

"How long have you had this? Henry never saw this, did he?"

"No. I saw it myself for the first time today. It came in a big transmission of the Bureau file on Carlos Marcello, which is a massive collection."

I'm trying to focus on the micro, not macro. "April of '68 was the month Jimmy Revels and Luther Davis were killed."

"Close enough. They probably died on March thirty-first."

"That's right. And Viola had been raped in March, as well. She was abused again when they were tortured, but

Presley saved her. So my father *must* have made some kind of deal with Marcello shortly afterward, to protect Viola."

"That's why I need to talk to him. He knows a lot more than you think he does about all this."

I close my eyes before I ask the next question. "John, what the hell's going on? Seriously. How did we get from Viola Turner and euthanasia to the assassination of John Kennedy?"

"You know how. Through the Double Eagles. Specifically, the Knox family. Remember what I said about history? It's all personal. In 1963, Carlos Marcello ordered the assassination of John F. Kennedy. It wasn't the CIA, or Castro, or Cuban exiles. It wasn't the Russians or the military-industrial complex. It was Carlos Marcello. The Little Man used the Knox family to carry out the hit, and he did it for the oldest motive in the world."

"Money?"

"No. Survival."

Another question was forming in my mind when the sight of a white pickup truck parked down the block drove it from my head. A few seconds of watching shows me an exhaust plume coming from the tailpipe.

"What's the matter?" asks Kaiser. "Are you looking at that truck?"

I nod. "That's Lincoln Turner's truck. The son of a bitch has been following me again."

"Again?"

"He's been stalking my house."

Kaiser cocks his head, his eyes on the truck. "I tell you what. I've given you a lot to absorb. You go on up to your office and get your keys. I'll take care of Mr. Turner for you. He won't be here when you come back out."

"Really?"

"No problem. You just think about what I said. We'll talk tomorrow."

"Should I just go?"

Kaiser smiles. "Yep. Take off. I'm going to abuse my authority for a minute."

He opens his door and begins marching down the block like a military officer on a mission. Though I'm tempted to watch the confrontation, I exit the car and trot up to the door of City Hall. Lincoln Turner has a big chip on his shoulder and a lot of nerve, but something tells me Kaiser can handle him. For the first time since arriving at the sheriff's office, I think about Annie and my mother hiding out at Edelweiss. They're probably mad with worry by now, and as much as I'd like to check on Caitlin at the newspaper, I know she can take care of herself. I need to hug my daughter, and I need sleep. Tomorrow's battles will be here all too soon.

CHAPTER 12

IN THE END, Caitlin decided to enter the *Examiner* by her usual route, the employees' door at the rear of the building. If Billy Byrd had a deputy lying in wait, Jordan Glass was ready to snap fifty pictures of the arrest with her motor-drive Nikon. As Caitlin walked through the rear parking lot, noting the familiar cars of her reporters, she spied the door that had been locked against her by one of her own staff. Without warning she flashed back to the kidnapping with a clarity that made her pulse pound and her breath go shallow. She saw Penn being held on tiptoe with an arm around his throat and a pistol to his head. Then came a rush of images from all that had followed, from the basement, and the fire.

How close we came to dying, she thought, touching her burned cheek for the first time since the lake. *And if I had died, the child I'm carrying would have died with me, and no one would have known—not unless they discovered it in the autopsy.* Caitlin had only known about the baby herself for twenty hours or so, and she'd only told one soul on the planet about it: Tom Cage, via text message. *Tom hasn't even seen that message,* she thought. *He doesn't have his cell phone on. If he did, they'd have caught him by now. Killed him, probably. In fact, he could be dead already.* As much as Caitlin blamed Tom for the events of the past days, the thought of him lying facedown in a ditch somewhere stopped her breath in her throat.

Sensing her distress, Jordan took Caitlin's hand and squeezed, bringing her back to the present. As her heartbeat slowed, Caitlin started toward the door again. A Natchez Police Department squad car was parked in the handicapped space to the right of it, exhaust rising from its tailpipe. Caitlin waved at the young cop behind his fogged window glass, thinking of the officer who had probably been murdered by Brody Royal's men. She'd known him only as a prone form lying on the floor of the van that had carried them to Royal's house. Stopping at the back door, she raised her hand and turned the knob. Against all logic, it opened.

"I called ahead, remember?" Jordan said, sensing her confusion. "One step at a time, girl."

"Thanks."

THE *EXAMINER* BUILDING SEEMED eerily quiet as Caitlin and Jordan moved up the back hall, but the moment Caitlin walked into the newsroom, the place erupted in applause. She raised her hands to quiet the grinning staff, but new people kept coming in from other rooms, photographers and service people and even one of the advertising girls. They were obviously happy to see her alive, and she was glad to be that way, so she let the clapping go on for a bit.

They were a young group, she realized. Almost no one over thirty. For many years the *Examiner* had served as a sort of farm program for the larger papers in the Masters chain, but during her tenure as publisher Caitlin had changed that. She'd managed to assemble a bright cadre of journalism majors from all over the country, most from top schools. She paid them well and did her best to keep them busy. Whenever she'd lost one to a larger paper, she somehow managed to replace him or her with someone of equal talent. This eclectic group she had supplemented with some of the brightest liberal arts graduates from Natchez, kids who'd wanted to return to their hometown after college.

Now they stood before her, gathered between the computer workstations that lined the walls, fourteen kids with all the talent in the world and a desperate hunger to work on something important. They'd known since Tuesday that something big was afoot. The initial attack on Henry and the burning of the *Beacon* had galvanized them into action, and Henry's backup files had given them something to sink their teeth into. But according to Jamie Lewis, the assassination attempt on Henry in the hospital—followed by the attack on Penn and Caitlin—

had stunned them into a kind of paralysis. They'd read about attacks on reporters in places like Colombia and Myanmar, but murderous attacks on journalists in America seemed incomprehensible. The discovery that the *Examiner*'s press operator had disappeared after probably assisting in Caitlin's kidnapping only added to their collective sense of shock. Yet not one had refused to come in when Jamie called in the middle of the night; indeed, few had left the building during the past forty-eight hours, except to catch four or five hours of sleep.

Caitlin looked at each face in turn: taut lips, worried eyes, the young men with arms folded across their chests, the women biting fingernails, everyone gathered closer together than they normally would. The silence truly was eerie, and then she realized why: the computers had been shut down. She couldn't remember ever having heard the newsroom so quiet. *I must have*, she thought, *during electrical storms*. But of course then there was the drumming of rain and the roll of thunder. Now there was absolute silence—the silence of expectation.

Into that silence, she began to speak.

"Thank you for that," she said. "Every one of you. First, let me say that I'm all right physically, except for this burn on my cheek, and Penn is, too. But it was a near thing, and if Henry Sexton and a heroic man who worked for Albert Norris as a boy hadn't sacrificed their lives for ours, we would both be dead. That's one of the stories we'll be printing tomorrow. We will honor those men as they deserve. But that's only a small part of a much larger duty we have tonight."

She took a moment to gather herself. "It's axiomatic that people in small towns don't get their news from newspapers. They never have. Local papers print stories about Little League baseball and garden clubs and the press releases from the local factory. But the real news— the reasons for layoffs or why someone lost an election or the facts behind a murder—usually travel by a different route: word of mouth. Long before Myspace and blogging, the real news traveled over backyard fences and via telephone, around watercoolers and on golf courses. The newspaper functioned as a Chamber of Commerce billboard advertising the town, while the real story lived behind the glossy sign, off the page, or at best, between the lines.

"My father's newspapers have been as guilty of this irrelevance as any other chain. And even before Dad bought it, the *Examiner* was one of the worst offenders. The old Wise family made sure of that. If you go back and check the week that Delano Payton was murdered in 1968, you'll find a perfunctory story about the bombing, then a follow-up announcing the offer of a reward by his national union—and very little else. If you go back to the week Albert Norris was burned to death, you'll find nothing.

"During my time as publisher, I've tried to change that policy. All of you have helped me. Seven years ago, our Del Payton stories carried the message of justice delayed to the entire world. Now, tonight, we're going to break the biggest story that any of us are likely to touch in our entire lives. As you know, it spans over a dozen civil rights murders committed during the 1960s. The perpetrators of those crimes have been allowed to roam free for forty years, and now they've killed again in their efforts to avoid being exposed and punished for their crimes. The death toll tonight is unprecedented in the history of this area, and a Natchez police officer will probably be added to the list before dawn."

Several people gasped.

"We're going to be dealing with next-of-kin issues, so I'm not sure if we'll be printing names in all cases. But beginning now, we're going to devote every waking minute to doing justice to this epic story. A single edition of the paper can't possibly contain it. So, after physical publication this morning, I hope that those willing to remain will do so and continuously update our online edition. I fully expect that by noon tomorrow—or today, rather—we'll be in the eye of a media storm. This is what we live for, people. For about twelve hours, we're the only news staff in the country in possession of the facts of this story. Television, radio, the blogosphere—they've got nothing. But tomorrow that will change. So . . . right now, I want everyone in this room to take thirty seconds and think about Henry Sexton, who was murdered for his courage and convictions. For those of you who don't know, on the first night he was attacked, Henry had already agreed to write for this paper, so he is your colleague in more ways than one."

Caitlin bowed her head and silently counted to thirty. In the elegiac silence of held breaths and closed eyes, she realized that she blamed herself more than anyone else for Henry's death. For in the end it was her forcing Katy Royal to unburden herself of her secrets that had sent Brody Royal into a homicidal rage. Of course, nothing she could do now would bring Henry back. Sleepy Johnston, either. All she could do now was carry on Henry's cause and try to do justice to their memories. Stealing a glance upward, she saw a few people staring at Jordan to her right.

"Amen," she said in a firmer voice, and every face in the room rose to hers. "By the way, the woman to my right is Jordan Glass, a legend in our business, and I assume she needs no further introduction."

The room burst into applause again, and a couple of the guys whistled.

"Easy, dudes, she's married."

"And I'm too old for you," Jordan added.

After the much-needed laughter subsided, Caitlin said, "Sadly, I also need to bring you up to speed on a very upsetting matter. I know the silent computers have probably freaked you all out. They do me. It's like a 1950s horror movie or something. But there's a good reason for it. We've experienced a major breach of security at the *Examiner*. Earlier tonight, when Penn and I were kidnapped, Nick Moore, our press operator, probably helped the kidnappers commit their crime."

A murmur of consternation and anger rose at this confirmation of the rumor.

"The FBI is hunting Nick now. But I must tell you, I have reason to believe that Nick might not be the only one of our staff who took a bribe from the people we're investigating."

This time there were gasps of disbelief.

"Henry Sexton's files and journals—the files that you spent so many hours painstakingly scanning into our computer system—have been deleted by someone working for Brody Royal."

Many in the audience groaned as though in physical

pain, and Caitlin saw more than a few reporters cursing under their breath.

"Worse yet, the physical files and journals have been stolen and destroyed. However, all may not be lost on that front. The FBI is going to lend us some computer experts who might be able to reconstruct those deleted files."

Caitlin saw incredulity on Jamie Lewis's face. He probably considered this sleeping with the enemy, but he would have to live with it.

"The truly upsetting thing is that the person who deleted those files might still be among us. He or she could be standing next to you right now."

Total silence descended on the newsroom.

"I don't want to create some kind of McCarthy atmosphere of paranoia, but we'd be fools not to take rational precautions until we get this sorted out. So—here's what we're going to do. Our stories are going to be written on three or four notebook computers in the conference room. We will restore limited Internet access out here for research, but that's it. Everyone will take their instructions directly from Jamie or me, and you'll work only on what you're assigned. If you see something suspicious, or feel strange about anything, come to us. Again, I don't want a bunch of tattletales running around. Use your common sense. But make no mistake—we're in a war, folks. They burned the *Concordia Beacon* last night. Now, we'll be looking after your physical safety; we're going to have some serious security around this building going forward. But be smart and be safe. And remember: for those of you who became journalists because of a David-versus-Goliath fantasy, this is your chance."

She saw a few grins at this.

"One thing: you may see Sheriff Byrd show up and arrest me. If you do, just keep on working—after you snap a few shots of the proceedings."

A few more laughs broke the tension.

"As for the news stories, I don't care who you have to roust out of bed for comments or confirmations, or what resources you have to commit—just do it. We will probably be sued over some of this, so try to get it right. But the final responsibility rests with me, so be fearless. Do what Henry Sexton would have done."

Caitlin knew her last assertion was not quite true: final responsibility rested not with her but with her father, who owned the chain. But if he didn't trust her instincts by now—and back her with the full resources of the company—then she needed to find work elsewhere anyway.

"That's it," she said. "Make me proud."

The crowd dispersed slowly, but as a couple of computers were switched on, the newsroom slowly became the fully engaged hive that Caitlin so loved. She pulled Jamie's sleeve until he was following her down the corridor to her private office.

"What now?" he asked. "Gather the conference room team?"

"In a minute," she said, walking faster. "I've used this newspaper as a weapon before. A sort of artillery piece, I suppose. But tomorrow's edition is going to detonate like a dam buster."

"A what?"

Caitlin laughed low in her throat, thinking of her grandfather. "That's a kind of bomb from World War Two. Tomorrow we're going to crack the foundations of a dam that's held back terrible truths for forty years. And once that tide is let loose, a lot of people and careers are going to be washed away."

Her editor's eyes narrowed. "Not ours, I hope?"

Caitlin didn't answer. They'd reached her office door. In the awkward silence that followed, Jamie's eyes filled with an unspoken question.

"What is it?" she asked.

"Did you have to kill anybody?" he asked softly. "You didn't tell me when you dictated the lead story. Who killed who down in that basement?"

Caitlin looked into his hungry eyes for a few seconds, then shook her head. "No. Penn did, though."

Jamie went pale. "Oh, man."

"I'd just as soon forget it, but I know I never will." She took a sharp breath, then exhaled slowly. "Have you thought about who you want in the conference room? Who you really trust?"

Lewis nodded. "Anna, Chris, Tim, and Brit. That work for you?"

"Sure. What about research?"

"Paul and Chesney for the main stuff. The rest can handle background details."

"Fine." She took hold of Jamie's forearm and looked deep into his eyes. "I've got to ask this. Is there anybody you suspect at this point? Someone you really don't trust?"

He shook his head and looked away, but she knew he was wrestling with something.

"Come on, Jamie. Out with it."

He shook his head. "If I know something, I won't hold it back. But I'm not going to start condemning people based on hunches."

"Fair enough. But the stakes are pretty high here. We're all-in on this one."

"I know."

After a few moments' contemplation, Caitlin walked into her office and pulled the door shut behind her.

Coming into the familiar office after being tied to a pole in a basement that looked like some Nazi torture cell was almost like entering a decompression chamber. The moment she sat in her Herman Miller chair, a wave of exhaustion rolled over her. She'd been living on green tea and adrenaline for three days. She tried to add up the hours of sleep she'd gotten since Monday morning, but stopped when she couldn't remember more than a three-hour stretch. At her best she had been functioning like someone with jet lag. Yet now, along with survivor's guilt and anger and a dozen other emotions, she felt the giddy elation of someone who has been "shot at and missed," as her grandfather used to say. The sense of relief was overwhelming. If she sat in this chair another minute without doing something, she would be asleep.

She made a note to talk to Chris Scanlon, an *Examiner* photographer who suffered from ADD, and see if he could spare some Adderall. Then she remembered she was pregnant. Surely speed couldn't be good for a baby? *I'd better Google it*, she thought, turning groggily toward her computer keyboard. Then she remembered that Jamie had killed the paper's Internet access.

My computer isn't even on, she thought, hitting the power switch.

Nothing happened.

Jamie probably unplugged it.

She folded her arms and put her head down on her desk. As though watching a film in her mind, she saw Tom Cage standing in the dark, reading her text message about the baby. That message had been a last-ditch effort to try to persuade him to turn himself in—to come back to his family and put his trust in Penn. As Tom read the message in her vision, an awestruck smile lit his white-bearded face. *I've got to find him*, Caitlin thought. *Surely I can do that. If he's still alive . . .*

"Caitlin?" said a voice, and then someone shook her.

She opened her eyes and found Jordan Glass kneeling beside her chair. "Hey," Jordan said. "You need some real sack time."

"Nooo," Caitlin moaned in protest. "I've got tons of work to do."

"You're no good to anybody like this. You've hit the wall."

"Two hours," Caitlin pleaded. "Two hours' work, and then I can grab a little sleep. Can you help me?"

Jordan sighed heavily, then got to her feet. "What's your poison? More coffee?"

"No. Green tea, strong as you can make it."

The photographer looked down at her with a maternal frown. "It's like looking in a damn mirror. A mirror with a ten-year time lag."

As Jordan walked out, Caitlin remembered that the photographer had been trying to get pregnant for months, without result. Glass had confided this to her on the first day they met, in an unexpected moment of shared confidence. Jordan was Penn's age, so the odds were against her. Caitlin, on the other hand, hadn't even been trying, and she was already knocked up.

If she had the power, she would trade places with Jordan, at least as far as their obstetric situations. She had plenty of time to get pregnant again, but she might never have another career opportunity like this one. The "baby" in her belly was at this point only an agglomeration of cells that would not even begin to show for months. The Double Eagle story, on the other hand, had been fulminating within her like some protean thing, constantly changing shape, growing new faces and revealing hidden ones. Earlier tonight it had almost devoured her. For the next week, at least, she would have to focus on that larger inhabitant. For if she managed to deliver it to the world, in all its depraved ugliness, she would make possible the justice and healing for which Henry Sexton had given his life. And more than that . . . she would have nothing left to prove. Not to her father . . .

Not to anybody.

CHAPTER 13

FORREST KNOX TOOK a remote control unit from his pocket and opened the gate of the Valhalla Exotic Hunting Reserve. Driving north from Baton Rouge always invigorated him, leaving behind the gas flares of the petrochemical plants of Cancer Alley and the haunted fields of the Angola Prison Farm, and climbing into the green hills and hollows of southwest Mississippi, the hunter's paradise. The great river itself lay scarcely a mile away now, beyond a few wooded ridges and the swamp where the river flowed eons ago.

The serpentine access road to the hunting camp wound through acres of second-growth hardwood forest filled with wildlife surveillance cameras and food plots for the game animals. After a descent through broken terrain, the road flattened out on a plateau overlooking the rich bottomland between the westernmost ridge and the Mississippi River. At the edge of this plateau stood the main lodge. Ozan's state police cruiser was already parked in the oyster shell turnaround on its back side. Forrest parked beside him, then hurried up the steps and into the lodge.

He found Ozan in the great room, a vast space lined with the heads of exotic game taken from around the world, though several species had been transplanted here and bred behind the camp's eleven-foot fences. The Redbone sat in a leather club chair, a shot glass of bourbon beside him. Forrest couldn't remember seeing the man so anxious in all the time he'd known him.

"You want a drink?" Ozan asked, moving to get up.

"Later." Forrest sat on the sofa opposite Ozan and put his boots up on an ottoman. "We need to make some fast decisions."

"I've got the Black Team online. Everybody but Pichot.

He's in Florida, but he's heading back as soon as he can get a flight."

"Good. Because Brody put us in a real corner tonight. It's a relief that Henry Sexton's dead, but we have to assume he passed on what he knew to the Masters girl. And we have to assume Morehouse told Henry everything *he* knew."

"Shit."

"And Brody's death is going to rattle the hell out of the money boys in New Orleans."

Ozan's lips parted in silence: this consequence had not yet occurred to him.

"If I'd known all this would happen," Forrest thought aloud, "I might have waited to move on Mackiever, but the iron's in the fire now."

The Redbone took a sip of whiskey, then wiped his mouth. "If that girl is the problem, I can take care of that. I can be in Natchez in forty minutes. By noon tomorrow, she'll have disappeared off the planet. Nobody'll ever find her. It'll be like she never existed."

Forrest admired Ozan's initiative, but the man was no strategist. "No, it won't."

"Sure it will. How many drug dealers have I fed to the alligators? I can do the same to Mayor Cage, and even the FBI man if it comes to that."

"This is different. If high-profile people like that disappear, the story will just get bigger and bigger until it swallows us. If we killed the Natchez mayor, its newspaper publisher, *or* an FBI agent, we'd have a dozen new FBI agents in here the next day. Kill all three, and we'd have fifty. And they'd never stop hunting until they nailed us. No . . . the only people we can kill with impunity at this point are Dr. Cage and Ranger Garrity. The others are practically untouchable."

The Redbone shifted uncomfortably on his chair. "What's the alternative? Sit tight and hope for the best?"

"That's one option, as much as I hate to contemplate it. The other, obviously, is to hit hard and fast, damn the consequences. Scorched earth."

"But you just said they were untouchable."

"I said 'practically.' There's one way you can pull off a hit like that. You need a fall guy. The crime has to be unambiguous, the corpses there for everyone to see, and the killer so obvious that all the carnage looks inevitable in retrospect. Then people move on without ever looking past the surface of things. You understand?"

"Sure. Like Kennedy, right?"

Forrest smiled and nodded, pleased at the irony of Ozan making this leap. The Redbone had learned a lot about Forrest's business in the relatively short time he'd been involved, but he knew nothing about the innermost secrets of the Double Eagles.

"Who the hell could our fall guy be?" Ozan asked. "Brody and Regan would have made good patsies, but they're dead."

Forrest's smile broadened. "They can still be blamed for everything that happened up till tonight. After all, Brody did order that first attack on Henry, at the *Beacon* office. And Brody and Regan burned the *Beacon*. The FBI's bound to prove Brody was behind the kidnapping of Cage and Masters, and also that his guys killed that Natchez cop. How big a leap is it from there to assume Brody sent the sniper to finish off Sexton at the hospital but killed his girlfriend by mistake?"

Ozan grinned. "A damned short one. I like it. But that won't help us with the other targets."

"No. But this is the beautiful part. For those hits, we've got two patsies so perfect they could have been sent over by Central Casting."

Ozan was clearly behind the curve. "Who you talking about, boss?"

"Snake and Sonny. The original Double Eagles. Last of the crazy racist crackers."

The blood drained from the Redbone's face. "Are you shitting me?"

"If we want to go scorched earth, it's the only way. We have to give the FBI somebody they can close the cases on, fast. With no doubters at the table."

Frightened wonder still shone from Ozan's face. "You mean it, don't you?"

"You bet your ass I do. Listen to me. Katrina has given us a chance to get our snouts up to the big trough. One or two deals with the guys I'm rubbing shoulders with now is worth more than everything I ever made out of Snake and Billy's operation."

Ozan still looked unconvinced. "But . . . how can you take those guys down? The second Snake and Sonny figure what you're up to, they can cop a plea and send you to death row. And me along with you."

Forrest shook his head. "Give me some credit, Alphonse. By the time Snake knows what I'm really doing, it'll be too late."

"You'd better lay this out for me, boss. 'Cause I can't see it working."

"You know Snake. A more hotheaded son of a bitch never drew breath. And once he hears what happened tonight, and how much danger we're all in, he'll be screaming for blood. The fact that he fucked up the hit on Henry will make him that much more ready to do it. You agree?"

"That's Snake, all right."

"Okay. Now, he'll be expecting me to hold him back, like I usually do. Only this time I won't, see? I'll tell him the stakes are so high that killing those three is our only hope. And he's the only man to do it."

A tight smile had appeared on Ozan's face. "Snake'll eat that up, all right."

"Here's the twist, though. As soon as Snake has made the hits, we'll leak something that puts the FBI on his trail—but not too close. Naturally, we'll know where Snake's hiding. Sonny's fishing camp would be perfect. It'll be Snake and Sonny, maybe one more Eagle. I'll make a public appeal as Snake's nephew, to get him to turn himself in. I'll have told him to expect that, that I'm just playing the game. But then the FBI will corner them."

Ozan was nodding.

"I'll volunteer to go into the house and talk Snake out. Once inside, I'll stall a little, tell him I'm figuring a way to break him from jail once he goes in. Then, when he's distracted, I'll take him out. Sonny, too."

The Redbone blinked; the rest of him remained as motionless as a cigar store Indian. "You mean kill him?"

"Snake and Sonny both. And whoever else is with them."

The Redbone swallowed hard. "Your own uncle?"

"It's the only way, Alphonse. If I'm willing to kill my own uncle because he committed murder, I'll be permanently safe. Washed in the blood, son. Better yet, that's political gold in this state. You can't buy that kind of press."

"Ain't you forgetting something?" Ozan asked, still looking wary. "What about Billy? You think he's gonna stand by and keep his mouth shut after you kill his daddy?"

Forrest had thought a lot about his cousin during the past hour. "I can't say for sure. But I do know this: Billy knows his father is a hothead. And the last thing he wants on this earth is to go back to prison. Billy did a jolt in Raiford in the eighties, and that was all the hell he could stand. He just might sit still for this, if I put it to him the right way. After all, Snake's had a good run. It's time for our generation to take the helm."

Ozan swallowed the last of his bourbon, then leaned back in his chair. "It's a ballsy plan, I'll say that."

"Can you see any other way to take those people out and stay out of prison?"

As if against his will, Ozan shook his head. "You know I'm up for damn near anything, boss. But when you start killing family . . . I don't know. It's like asking for trouble from the gods."

Forrest barked a laugh. "The *gods*? Alphonse, the only god you need to be worrying about at this point is the god of war. And you know what he says."

"What's that?"

"Kill 'em all and let God sort 'em out."

Ozan gave him a smile, but it looked forced. The Redbone's hesitancy shocked Forrest. He'd watched Ozan commit acts as brutal as anything he'd seen in Vietnam, even among the tribes up in the Highlands. To see him sobered by such a logical proposal gave Forrest pause.

"When will you decide?" Ozan asked quietly.

"I think I already did. The only question is when. It's too late to stop the girl from getting tomorrow's newspaper out. Whatever she knows at this point is going to hit the street. I just have to hope my name is nowhere in it. And that Snake's is."

"It will be," Ozan said with certainty. "I checked with Brody's mole at the paper, like you said. They know Snake killed one of those women in the insurance fraud case. The whistleblowers. Morehouse told Henry the story. They're going with that tomorrow."

A rush of excitement went through Forrest. "God-damn, that's perfect."

"As long as the cops don't arrest Snake before he can take out our targets."

"They won't. What evidence do they have besides a story told by a dead man? No, there's a mile of wiggle room between a newspaper story and an arrest warrant."

Ozan jerked in his chair at the muted ring of a cell phone. He dug into his uniform pants and brought out a black TracFone.

"Who the hell is calling you?" Forrest asked. "Didn't everybody get my order?"

"We got two guys missing, remember?" Ozan said. "The ones we sent to get Dr. Cage at his partner's lake house. I hope to God it's them."

"Is that a burn phone?"

"Yeah." Ozan answered with a press of his thumb. "What's the word?" he asked, then waited for a coded reply. "Okay. What happened?" As Ozan listened, his face darkened. "Where are you now?" he asked after nearly a minute. "Then get here as fast as you can. . . . What? . . . I'll tell him. Out."

The Redbone clicked off and looked at Forrest with something close to fear in his eyes. "This ain't our night."

"What happened?"

"That was Floyd Grimsby, one of the two guys I sent after Dr. Cage. The other was named Deakins. They're off-duty cops from Monroe. They were the closest to where we traced Dr. Cage's nurse's cell phone to."

"And?"

Ozan shook head. "They found the doc there, down by the water. Deakins was about to shoot him when Dr. Cage gut-shot him with a pistol from his pocket. He fired right through the pocket. Floyd went for his piece, but Cage had the drop on him. Then Cage drugged him and dumped him out in a cotton field somewhere."

Forrest felt as though a cold wind had blown through the room. His blood pressure was dropping. "I don't be-lieve that," he said. "Old Dr. Cage?"

Ozan shrugged. "You told me he served in Korea, didn't you? And him and that Garrity did kill Deke Dunn."

"Was Garrity at the lake house?"

"No sign of him, Grimsby said."

"Jesus Christ. We can't catch a break."

"There's one more thing," Ozan said.

"What's that?"

"Dr. Cage gave Floyd a message for you."

"Me? What message?"

"Floyd said it had to be face-to-face. He'll be here in less than an hour."

"My face'll be the last thing that fuckup ever sees."

Ozan got up and started pacing. "What kind of message would Dr. Cage send you?"

"You don't think the FBI has Grimsby, do you? That this is a setup?"

"I don't think he would have given me the right code if it was like that."

Forrest snorted. "A dirty cop from Monroe? Can you put a man down by the gate before he gets here?"

"Sure. I've got four in the bunkhouse."

"Do it. Meanwhile, I'll have a think about Tom Cage, M.D."

"How much do you know about him?"

"A bit. Daddy always liked him. And I know he did some favors for Carlos Marcello back in the day."

"Dr. Cage?"

Forrest shrugged. "It was the sixties, man. Strange times down here. Get that man on the gate, Alphonse. We'll wait down by the river with a radio. If it's the FBI, we'll take the boat."

Ozan pulled on his duty coat and headed for the nearby building where overflow guests stayed when hunters came in large groups.

After the door closed, Forrest walked back to the study where the seven-hundred-pound razorback he'd killed with the atlatl spear glared from behind the desk. His cousin Billy used this desk more than anyone else. In the top left drawer was a box of Cuban cigars. As Forrest sat in the padded chair, he opened the drawer and thought back to the days when his father was alive, an afternoon when Dr. Cage had given Forrest his junior high football physical. He remembered the easy manner in which his father and the doctor had dealt with each other—Frank Knox and Tom Cage, two men from opposite ends of the social spectrum. His father always said they didn't make them like Dr. Cage anymore. If what the cop from Monroe had told Ozan about the gunfight was true, Frank Knox had been posthumously proven right.

Wouldn't be the first time, Forrest thought, lighting one of Billy's cigars and settling in to wait.

CHAPTER 14

WALT GARRITY LAY half-asleep on a double bed in the Sheraton Casino Hotel in Baton Rouge, just inside the downtown levee. He'd planned to spend no more than an hour in the city; now he'd wasted more than eight, and Tom was out on the night roads, wounded and carrying a hostage, with every cop in Louisiana on his trail.

Walt had come here to meet Colonel Griffith Mackiever of the Louisiana State Police, hoping to get the statewide APB for Tom and himself revoked. He had at least some reason for optimism. Long before Colonel Mackiever joined the LSP, he'd served as a Texas Ranger with Walt, and despite the passing years, they still shared the Ranger bond. When Walt arrived at the hotel, however, he hadn't found his old comrade-in-arms waiting, but a faxed note telling him Mackiever had been forced to take an unexpected trip to New Orleans to check out their "mutual problem." Walt assumed this referred to Forrest Knox, and he hoped to God Knox hadn't suckered his old *compadre* into a trap. There was talk that Forrest might be next in line for superintendent of the state police, and Mackiever's death would open up that powerful position sooner rather than later. Untimely deaths were far from uncommon in this godforsaken state.

Garrity had never liked Louisiana: shitkickers in the north and Frenchmen in the south—Baptists versus Catholics, praise Jesus. Driving down Highway 61 from Natchez, he'd thought of Angola Farm out in the darkness between the road and the Mississippi River, glowing like some fortified island of lost souls. Most of the prisoners chained inside the Farm belonged there, but the hypocrisy of harsh punishment for men who'd ripped off a few hundred dollars in Louisiana stuck in Walt's craw. People thought Huey Long had set the high bar for state corruption in the 1930s, but the Kingfish was a latecomer to the public trough. A wise man once said that any territory colonized by the French eventually settled into a state of lassitude and corruption. As regarded Louisiana, he was right. Like some third-world island appended to America, the state had decayed as steadily as an old whore working the darkest den in Marseilles. During the 1950s and '60s, Texas Rangers had viewed certain Louisiana parishes as feudal fiefdoms more akin to the realms of warlords than to American counties, and Walt wasn't sure that the foundations of those fiefdoms had been completely uprooted.

Rolling past the vapor-lit machinery of the refineries and chemical plants along old Highway 61, he'd reflected on what bad odds Mackiever must have faced trying to run the state police in such a place. New Orleans had become so lawless during the 1990s that the Justice Department had considered federalizing the NOPD. The chaotic aftermath of Hurricane Katrina hadn't surprised Walt a bit; the cataclysmic storm had merely laid bare the systemic corruption that had been festering downtown for three centuries, and which had doomed the city itself by allowing a substandard levee system to be built.

With that kind of rot eating away at the state's largest city, no one should have been surprised to learn that rural parishes had also become dens of vice and violence—a perfect environment for predators like Forrest Knox. Clothed in the uniform of the state police, an ambitious sociopath could pretty much do as he pleased in the boondocks. When the officials above him had so many secrets to hide, which of them would risk confronting a man who had a high-tech intelligence division under his command?

Walt had hoped Mackiever could explain how Forrest Knox had risen so high in his organization, but with every hour that passed, his faith that he would see his old buddy faltered. Tossing and turning on the hotel bed, Walt dreamed of his wife, who had begged him not to leave home to try to help his old friend. The night before Tom called, Carmelita had actually dreamed of Walt's funeral. But Walt felt he had no choice about helping Tom, and he'd told her as much. As he drove away from their house, Carmelita had watched with her face forlorn and her arms folded, like a woman sending her husband off to war. Walt had felt an ache like an ulcer in his belly, but he hadn't turned around.

Yesterday, when some Knox-controlled asshole shoved photos of a beheaded family under Carmelita's door to frighten her, it had taken all of Walt's self-restraint not to walk up to Forrest on the street in front of LSP headquarters and blow his brains out. Though Walt now had three old Ranger buddies covering his house in Navasota, every second of fear his wife had suffered stung him like a hornet. Before this mess was through, he would exact retribution for each sting.

Picking up his derringer from the bedside table, Walt rubbed his eyes and headed for the toilet to take a leak. He was zipping up his pants when the landline rang beside the bed. Walt walked out and stared at the phone for three rings, then picked it up and put it to his ear.

"Cap'n McDonald?" said a familiar voice.

Walt said nothing, but his rapid pulse began to subside. "Bill McDonald" was the alias that Colonel Mackiever had instructed him to use when he registered at the hotel. McDonald had been one of the toughest and wisest Texas Rangers ever to wear the star, but he'd died in 1918. It was unlikely anyone else would think to use such a code. Nevertheless, Walt said, "Name a president that Bill McDonald guarded."

"Teddy Roosevelt."

Walt sighed with relief. "Where are you, Mac?"

"Coming up the hall. Sorry to make you wait."

"I'm opening the door."

Walt took his derringer to the door, opened it, then extended the bolt and backed away so that his visitor would have to push open the heavy door to gain entry. Then he stood just inside the open bathroom door and aimed the derringer at head level.

Someone knocked three times, then slowly pushed open the door while a voice behind it said, "At ease, Cap'n. I know you've got a gun back there."

Walt kept his derringer cocked and ready until Mackiever came in and locked the door behind him. One of the colonel's hands was empty; the other carried a bottle of Macallan Fine Oak, which gladdened Walt's heart. Mackiever's hair had gone nearly white since Walt had last seen him, though his trimmed mustache still had a little pepper in it. His old eyes looked dazed, and he shook Walt's hand like a man grasping at a life preserver.

"Damn, I'm glad to see you," he said. "I was up to my ass in alligators before you ever called. But this time I think they've got me. Can I pour you a scotch? I need one bad."

"I won't turn it down."

Mackiever went to the bathroom sink and unwrapped two water glasses. Walt watched him pour—both hands shaking—then took the proffered glass and drank the whisky neat. He savored the burn as it sank toward his stomach, then took a seat on the end of the bed while the colonel poured himself another.

"Dark days," Mackiever said hoarsely.

Walt grimaced. "Let's hear it, Mac."

The colonel sat heavily in a chair by the table before the curtained window. As Walt raised his glass in a silent toast to his old friend, he realized he was looking at a man close to breaking.

"Forrest Knox just issued me an ultimatum," Mackiever informed him. "Step down for health reasons, or he'll ruin me. I've got forty-eight hours."

"Ruin you? How?"

"The son of a bitch has had one of our tech experts— one of my own officers—planting kiddie porn in my computers, both at work and at home. If I don't resign, he'll go public with child pornography charges and drag me through the mud until I choke. You know how it goes with accusations like that. It's almost impossible to prove a negative. You never shake 'em."

"That's bullshit, Mac. A man with your record? He'd never make that stick. You can prove that stuff was planted."

"Not this time. Knox has been setting this up for months. Day by day, in real time. There's an extensive search history, thousands of photographs of young kids, even online conversations. They've already printed out reams of computer logs and placed them secretly into evidence."

"Jesus. I still think—"

Mackiever stopped him with a raised hand. "You haven't heard the worst of it. Forrest's got two underage prostitutes from New Orleans who'll swear under oath that I paid them for sex. *Male* prostitutes."

"*What?*"

The colonel nodded, his haunted eyes glancing at the floor. "He just paraded one of them in front of me in a New Orleans hotel room. The boy was no more than fifteen, if that. I'm screwed, partner. I've got no play."

"I don't know what to say."

Mackiever took another sip of scotch and closed his eyes. "There isn't anything."

"Help me understand this. How the hell did a man like Knox climb so high in your outfit?"

The colonel shook a cigarette from a pack of Salems and lit it. "Forrest joined the force long before I came over from Texas. He worked his way up, making strong connections all along the way. Everybody knew he was Frank Knox's son, but nobody in power gave a damn about that, not back then. Hell, most don't care now. But I wasn't any better. I initially sized Forrest up as a straight shooter. A hardass, sure, but fair—or so it seemed. And he appeared to have no relationship at all with his extended family."

"What changed your mind about him?"

"That's hard to say. After a while, the little man inside just started telling me something was wrong with him. For one thing, he used to keep a samurai sword hanging behind his desk. Like we used to see in Texas sheriffs' offices, remember? Forrest claimed his daddy had taken it off a Japanese officer during World War Two. One day I asked him to tell me the story, and he did. But first he took a couple of photos out of his desk. They were in a frame he kept in his bottom drawer."

"And?"

"The first one showed this Jap officer brandishing a samurai sword. The guy had two human heads tied to his belt. Caucasian heads. I kid you not, Walter."

Mackiever gulped some more scotch. "Why don't you look surprised?"

"I was in Korea, remember? I know about shit like that."

"That's right. Well . . . according to Forrest, these two heads on the Jap's belt belonged to American marines. But the second picture showed a U.S. Marine sergeant holding the same sword with a headless body at his feet. The dead man was the Jap officer from the first picture. The marine was a tough-looking bastard, a real leatherneck. He looked like Forrest, only twice as mean."

"Was it Forrest's old man?"

Mackiever nodded. "Frank Knox. In that photo, he's holding the Jap officer's head up for the camera. By the *hair*. Forrest said when his daddy found the first photo on that Jap officer after an island battle, he cut the guy's head off with his own sword. Forrest kept the photo in his desk. He'd take it out and show it to people when they asked about the sword. And they *loved* the guy for it."

"I've known guys like that," Walt said, thinking of the photos of the beheaded family that had been shown to Carmelita to frighten her.

"Don't be so sure. It's easy to underestimate Forrest Knox. God knows I did. He's a smooth character. I hear he's done some sick stuff to hookers he's arrested—blacks and Asians, mostly—and I've heard talk of even crazier things going on at a hunting camp his cousin Billy runs just over the Mississippi line. The official name is the Valhalla Exotic Hunting Reserve, but they call it 'Fort Knox' amongst themselves. But hell . . . that's not what you're here for."

"I'm here to help you, buddy," Walt said, "and to get your help in return. Tell me what you need, and I'll do the same. My request might overstep the bounds of friendship, but we is where we is."

Mackiever sucked at his cigarette as though it were a narcotic. "Walter, by the end of the day, I'm going to be a private citizen. I won't be able to help you. And there's nothing you can do to help me."

"You're wrong on both counts. When you're in the kind of fix we're in, you do what you've gotta do to get the ox out of the ditch. Tell me more about Forrest. A guy that dirty has to have a weak spot. All of God's creatures have an underbelly."

"If Knox has one, he's wearing armor over it."

"Why's he got such a hard-on to move you out?"

Mackiever lit a second cigarette off the first one and poured himself another scotch. "Walt, you may not believe this, but there are people in this state who saw Hurricane Katrina as a blessing. Divine intervention, even."

"I've heard the talk."

"But do you know what's beneath it? For the past twenty years, New Orleans has been shrinking. Major companies have been pulling out, and white workers have been fleeing across Lake Pontchartrain. The trend seemed unstoppable—until Katrina. The storm destroyed the homes of huge numbers of blacks, and they were bused out of the city in the so-called evacuation. About four days too late, by my count, but that's not my point. That 'evacuation' looked more like the relocation of the Indian tribes in the 1800s to me. That's how it's worked out, too. And the money boys don't mean to let 'em back into the city. They want to raze the Lower Ninth Ward and demolish the housing projects elsewhere, then put up new developments for their kind of people."

"White people?" Walt grunted.

"Or rich colored. They aren't that particular, so long as you've got the green. Point is, the state's elite doesn't see me fitting into this new utopia. They want an enforcer with their own ideology heading up the state police."

"What's the LSP got to do with the city of New Orleans?"

"More than you think. The fat cats have got puppet politicians standing for all the municipal offices, but political authority is still subject to the whim of the voters. The man with my job isn't subject to election. We have a lot of power and discretion, and with the right superintendent—or the wrong one—the state police can function like a paramilitary force. The governor can use us as an intimidation tool, sort of how Nixon used the FBI and the IRS against his enemies."

"I see."

"I first started to suspect what Forrest was up to about

two years ago. I suspected he had my Internal Affairs division compromised, so I handpicked a mean son of a bitch named Alphonse Ozan to infiltrate the Criminal Investigations Bureau. Ozan's a big Redbone, so I figured he'd be immune to Knox's influence, Knox being such a racist, and half Cajun to boot. There's no love lost between those two groups."

"Bad bet?"

"Apparently. Ozan's fed me steady reports ever since, claiming Knox is clean. But about two months ago I started smelling something. I ran a little test, the way the SOE used to do during World War Two, to test the integrity of their people. And I confirmed my worst fear."

"Why didn't you bust Ozan?"

"Better the devil you know, right? Since then I've been quietly trying to scope out just how big Knox's operation is."

"And?"

"He's got his fingers in a lot of pies around the state. He's taking cuts from various crooks to leave their operations alone. Coyotes moving illegals through the Port of New Orleans, drugs coming into the country on speedboats down around the barrier islands, prostitution. You name it, Forrest skims it. And after Katrina hit . . . I think he used a team of SWAT guys to selectively take out some of the competition."

"Man alive. This is the guy the moneymen want to put in your job?"

"Most of Forrest's supporters don't know about the criminal stuff. All they know is, Knox did them some favor or other. Got 'em LSU tickets on the fifty-yard line or sprung their drunk kid from some backwoods parish jail. Hell, I still can't prove anything against him. Nobody will testify against the guy. Everybody either loves Knox or lives in terror of him."

Walt swirled some scotch around in his mouth, then swallowed. "Some of his thugs threatened my wife earlier today. Out in Navasota."

Mackiever shook his head. "I'm sorry, Walt. But it doesn't surprise me. She okay?"

"I've got some retired buddies covering her now."

"Good." The colonel looked around the room like a

man startled from a dream. The daze Walt had seen when he entered the room had never really left his eyes. "Well, I think you see my problem. How exactly can I help you?"

"You know that trooper you lost up in Concordia Parish Tuesday evening?"

"Darrell Deke Dunn."

Walt nodded. "He wasn't yours. He was Knox's."

The colonel quickly gulped from his glass. "Are you positive?"

"I was there. Your APB's right about that, but he was about to murder my best friend in cold blood."

Mackiever looked at the ceiling and cursed.

"I don't know how much pull you still have in this state," Walt said, "but I need you to make that APB go away. If you don't, I can't help you or myself either."

The colonel looked as if Walt had asked him for a million dollars cash. "How the hell can I do that? All the evidence points to you and Cage killing Dunn, and I can't prove Dunn was dirty. I can't pull the APB on suspected cop killers without good reason."

"I did kill Dunn," Walt said bluntly. "So you'll need to make up a reason."

Mackiever's eyes had gone wide. "Christ, Walt. How the hell did you get caught up in this?"

Walt shrugged. "Helping a friend. How else?"

Mackiever leaned back in his chair. "Tell me something. If Dr. Cage is innocent, why did he skip bail on that first charge? Murdering the nurse."

Walt kept his face blank. "All I can tell you is this: if the DA and sheriff up in Natchez had gotten Tom into jail, he'd have died there. The Knoxes aren't the only ones who want him dead. Tom Cage and Sheriff Billy Byrd have bad blood from way back."

Mackiever looked less than satisfied, but Walt had no intention of elaborating. He drained his glass and wiped his mouth on his sleeve. "Here's my proposal. You get rid of that APB, I'll take down Forrest Knox for you. That's the only solution that's gonna work for both of us."

"You can't do it, Walt. Short of killing him, there's nothing you can do." The LSP chief dropped his gaze and let the pregnant silence drag. Then he looked up with a strange glint in his eyes. "Are you willing to go that far?"

Walt looked at his old friend for a few moments, then walked to the window, parted the curtain, and stared down at the street between the hotel and the casino that sat outside the Mississippi River levee. "No. I can't do that, Mac. Knox's men threatened my wife yesterday, and I was about ready to kill him. But I'm not the hothead I once was. I've got a lot to lose now. If Knox comes directly at me or mine, I'll smoke him. But I can't kill him in cold blood. I can't risk leaving Carmelita alone while I rot in Angola. She deserves better than that. So do I."

"Then you might as well go home tonight."

"Home?" Walt turned angrily from the window. "I'm wanted for killing a cop. Look, anybody as dirty as you say Knox is has got records of what he's doing. He has to, just to keep up with his money."

Mackiever waved his hand as if too exhausted to explore this. "Have you searched his home?" Walt pressed.

"Hell, no. The only guys I'd trust to do that and keep quiet about it are my nephew and my son-in-law—both troopers—and I don't want to put either of them that far into harm's way."

"Well, then. I'm your man. And what about that hunting camp you mentioned? If it's way out in the woods, and the Knox family owns it, it sounds like a damned likely place to cache incriminating records."

"You'd need an army to get in and out of there alive."

"Or a warrant."

Mackiever shook his head. "It'd have to be federal. Any local judge is liable to pick up the phone and tip one of Forrest's people. He's that connected."

"There's other ways, then."

The colonel took a deep drag on his cigarette, then held the smoke in his lungs for so long that by the time he started talking again, there was hardly any left. "In theory, I've got five hundred and eleven troopers serving under me. But in practice? Tonight? I trust you and maybe a half-dozen others. And as for going after Forrest, you're an army of one." Mackiever gave Walt an ironic smile. "Sounds familiar, doesn't it?"

Not long ago, Tom Cage had quoted to Walt the unofficial Ranger motto: *One riot, one Ranger.* "There's some truth in that saying," Walt said. "Sometimes one man can accomplish what a whole platoon can't."

Mackiever looked doubtful. "Times have changed, Cap'n."

Walt thought about the situation for half a minute. "You know, two can play the game Knox is running on you. You need to throw away the Marquess of Queensberry rules and look at this thing like our lives depend on it—which they do."

"I'm listening."

"If I'm willing to go into the jackal's den, what about planting some evidence on *him*?"

Mackiever's mouth worked around as though he had something struck in his teeth. "What are you thinking?"

"Come on, Mac. Are you that squeaky clean? Drugs, dirty money, other contraband—I ain't particular."

"Getting hold of something like that would take some time."

"Time's what we don't have. If you can't get something damning in my hands in an hour, it's no use to me."

The colonel thought about it, then shook his head. "If I or any of my loyalists go into the evidence room at this hour, Knox is going to hear about it."

Walt wondered if this was true, or if Mackiever had simply lost the stomach for conflict. "Well, then. The best thing I can do is search Knox's house, then get up to that hunting camp and go through it with a fine-tooth comb. I'll lay odds I find something you can hang him with."

"You're a lot more likely to end up digging a shallow grave at gunpoint. These are some bad boys, Walt."

"Bad boys are my business. Yours, too. Or have you forgotten? You're still a Ranger down deep, aren't you?"

Mackiever sucked long and hard on his cigarette, then looked away. After he exhaled, his eyes found Walt's again. They looked like cloudy marbles lost in dark bags of wrinkled skin.

"If that male prostitute goes on TV and says I paid him for sex, my children and grandchildren will never look at me the same again. I don't want to risk that, Walt. It's not worth it. Not this close to retirement."

"You're not risking anything! Knox gave you forty-eight hours, you said. That's plenty of time for me to get in and out of those places. I just need to know where Forrest is while I'm doing it. Can you help me do that, at least?"

Mackiever nodded. "That I could do. I've got a state-of-the-art GPS tracker on his cruiser. My nephew installed it four days ago. Now and then Knox takes an unmarked car, like this morning, going to New Orleans. But usually he's in his cruiser."

"Okay then. You get me the tracking scope, and I'll know when the coast is clear for me to move on his places."

"You've got a lot more to worry about than Forrest. He's got a wife and a goddamn pit bull at his home. Then there's Ozan, the dirty cops they've got on call, plus God only knows who else up at that hunting camp."

Walt shrugged as if this were of no consequence. "That's my problem, not yours. You just get me that GPS tracker."

"I can have it delivered here in ten minutes."

"That's more like it. Do you know where Knox is now?"

"The hunting camp. He told me he was going to spend the day catching up on work while he waited for my answer, but he's up at Valhalla. He fully expects to be appointed acting head of the state police by five P.M. I think even the governor expects it, though she doesn't know the details."

Walt stroked his mustache, thinking. "And where's his house?"

"Less than five miles from here, near the LSU campus."

"I'll hit his house first, then swing up to the camp after he leaves. Where's Captain Ozan?"

"Probably Concordia Parish. Last night Forrest sent him up there to investigate Trooper Dunn's death, but now he's got that Redbone son of a bitch leading the Henry Sexton investigation."

"Inmates running the asylum," Walt muttered. "What about bugging Knox's cruiser and his phones? Have you tried that?"

"I don't trust my tech division. They work too closely with the CIB. I'm sure Forrest has them checking his phones and sweeping his cruiser regularly. If he found a bug today, he'd release that porn stuff five minutes later. I'd be done, Walt."

"Won't a sweep find the GPS transmitter on his car?"

"They tell me it won't. I borrowed this unit from a federal intel guy I know in Texas. It only transmits coordinates in bursts, at predetermined intervals. Otherwise, it's electronically transparent."

"All right, then. Get the tracker here. I'm ready to move."

Mackiever held the tiny screen of his phone at arm's length so that he could make out the keypad, then punched in a text message. "I wish I could do more to help you."

"You can," Walt said bluntly. "Find a way to kill that goddamn APB. You're still the head of the LSP. I've got false identification, but it's damned hard to move around this state with my face on every TV screen and dashboard computer for three hundred miles."

Mackiever put down his cell phone and nodded. "It won't be easy, but I'll see what I can do."

"Do it fast. Tom and I are lucky to have lived this long."

Mackiever leaned forward and looked at Walt as though trying to penetrate a shell of bravado. "Are you *sure* you want to do all this? Why don't you just go back to Navasota, lock the door, and take care of Carmelita? Let Dr. Cage sort out his own mess?"

The tone of surrender in his old comrade's voice made Walt's throat constrict. "Tom and I served in Korea together, Mac. He saved my life over there. And if I have to die for him over here, well . . ."

Mackiever picked up his glass and raised it in salute, but Walt saw only an empty gesture. He closed his eyes to spare himself seeing how far his old friend had fallen.

"Walt," said the colonel, sensing his friend's disgust, "if you'd seen that pathetic kid in that motel, his face painted up, his eyes dead, you might understand. After a lifetime of good work, I can't stand to see it all tainted by something like that."

Walt gripped Mackiever's shoulders and squeezed to the point of pain, his eyes burning. "You *can't* resign. You hear me? If you cave in to Knox's threat, Tom and I are dead men. But there's more to it than that. You took an oath. The Ranger oath, if the LSP oath don't mean enough. You owe it to every man who ever wore the star to stand tall, no matter what. Don't kid yourself that you have a choice. You don't. You break that oath, you won't be no damn good to anybody. Not your wife, not your grandkids, not even to yourself."

Through the fear in Mackiever's eyes, Walt saw a faint flicker of the old esprit de corps. "I hear you," the colonel said. "I'll do what I can. You just be careful, take care of yourself."

Walt waved off the warning. "Don't waste time worrying about me. I'm taking Knox down, and God help any man who gets in my way."

CHAPTER 15

FORREST KNOX SAT behind the desk in the study at Valhalla, peering into the terrified face of the cop who had lost his partner to Dr. Tom Cage. Floyd Grimsby looked like every other North Louisiana cop who ended up on the take, a bullying Baptist deacon who liked screwing the church secretary on the side. He'd relayed Dr. Cage's message in a voice quavering with equal parts of fear and anger, watching Forrest's face as attentively as a dog waiting for a beating from its master. Forrest was surprised the man hadn't fled the state after a fuckup of that magnitude. He'd probably figured that Forrest would find him eventually, and it was better to face the music and try to make up for his mistake.

Alphonse Ozan stood against the wall beside the door to the great room, maintaining radio contact with the scouts he'd placed at the perimeter of the camp. There was still a chance that the Bureau had sent Grimsby as a stalking horse, so they had to be ready to run for the river on a moment's notice. If the feds brought a helicopter, Ozan had a man outside with a BAR that could take it down. Of course that would mean leaving the country, but Forrest and Billy had always been prepared for that. They had paid-up property in Andorra, in the Pyrenees on the French border, waiting for the day when fate finally caught up with them. But as Forrest had often told his cousin, many times success came from holding your nerve when other men would bail. In this time of maximum danger, Forrest stood to gain more money and power than he could have imagined only a year earlier.

"So Dr. Cage took a phone call while he thought you were unconscious," Forrest said. "How much did you hear?"

"Not enough to know where he was going. I think it

was that Texas Ranger though. Garrity. Later, Dr. Cage told me his friend had told him to kill me."

Forrest smiled. "A wise man. Did anything you heard give you any idea where he might be running?"

"He said something about Mobile. Like Garrity was already there."

"Alabama?" Forrest thought about this. "That doesn't make any sense. Garrity would run to Texas if he was running at all. Do you know where you were when he dumped you off?"

Ozan said, "I've got it pinpointed about as close as we can get it. Catahoula Parish. But given the elapsed time, and the fact that Cage has a vehicle, he could be a hundred miles from that point by now."

"What about our roadblocks?"

Ozan shrugged. "It's the boonies, boss. If Cage knows those roads, he could get a long way without hitting a roadblock."

"And he was born in Louisiana."

"His wife, too," Ozan said. "She grew up right around there. I've sent some guys to check, on the off chance he's hiding with relatives."

Forrest tapped on the desk. "Where the hell *is* Garrity? Why did they split up at all?"

Grimsby shrugged.

"Garrity was a Texas Ranger," Forrest said thoughtfully. "Mackiever was too, back in the day. He only came to Louisiana to take the superintendent's job. I wonder if he and Garrity knew each other? Or even served together?"

Ozan was nodding. "Good thinking. I'll check it out."

"You do that. We've got Mackiever by the balls right now. The last thing we need is a hardass like Garrity giving him hope that he can save himself."

Forrest gave the Monroe cop a last measuring glance. "You let an arthritic old man kill your partner. How does that feel?"

The cop's eyes smoldered with hatred and embarrassment. "Not good."

"You want to kill Dr. Cage?"

"Just give me one shot at him, Colonel."

"You already had your shot. And you didn't take it."

Forrest leaned back in his chair. "Go out to the bunk-house and get a few hours' rest. You'll have new orders when you wake up."

The cop didn't move.

"Go, goddamn it," Forrest said mildly. "Before I have Captain Ozan here give you the punishment you deserve."

The cop stood, and with an awkward salute he left the room.

After the sound of his boot heels faded, Forrest sighed and shook his head. "That's some piss-poor manpower right there, Alphonse. A sad state of affairs."

Ozan let some time pass before he spoke. "What you think about Dr. Cage's message? If he can do what he said, it kind of throws a new light on things, don't it?"

Forrest smiled. "It offers the possibility of a low-body-count solution, which we could sorely use right now. If we start killing public officials, even if we blame it on Snake, we're asking for trouble we may not be able to handle. *But*—Dr. Cage's solution requires trusting not only him, but also his son and the Masters girl to go along with his promise to protect us. And that would take a lot of convincing for me to buy."

Ozan didn't reply to this.

"I've been giving a lot of thought to the good doctor," Forrest mused. "And what I've decided is, I don't know what all the fuss is about. Dr. Cage was never really any threat to me. He might be to Snake and Sonny and the other old men, but he can't hurt me at all."

Ozan looked intrigued by this idea.

"And if he really killed his old nurse, he probably did us all a favor."

"What do you mean *if*?" Ozan asked.

"I'm not so sure he did it. Hell, all we have to go on is Snake's word."

"And Sonny's."

"Sonny Thornfield wouldn't cross Snake—not if Snake told him to lie. And neither of them would want to tell me they'd disobeyed my orders."

"But if Dr. Cage didn't kill the old woman, why did he jump bail?"

Forrest shrugged. "We'll ask him that when we find him. We're talking about a man and a woman, Alphonse.

Ain't no telling what might have gone on between them over the years, or in that house that night. But I *know* Snake wanted her dead. He always did. The Eagles had a death warrant on her if she ever came back to Mississippi. I don't know what she knew, but cancer wasn't quick enough for Snake. He nearly busted a gut when I told him he couldn't waste her. Anyway, my point is, the Double Eagles themselves are more of a threat to me than Tom Cage ever was. The Eagles truly *know* shit about me."

"I think you're forgetting something," Ozan said in a cautious voice. "Dr. Cage and Garrity had Sonny Thornfield in the back of that van before Deke Dunn pulled up and got hisself killed. So Cage and Garrity might know whatever Sonny knows about you."

Forrest couldn't believe he'd forgotten something so obvious. "You're right. So we either have to cut a deal with Cage or kill him, *tout suite*."

"Then we're basically back to our original dilemma," Ozan said. "Sit tight, kill 'em all, or try the doc's approach?"

As Forrest nodded, he realized he'd already decided to hold off on the scorched earth strategy. "I'm going to take a chance on Tom Cage. But step one is to find him. I'm not about to cancel that APB until he looks me in the eye and swears he can do what he claims he can."

"And then?"

"Then we need to verify that his son and the Masters girl will follow suit. God only knows what Brody might've said to them before he died. I guess we might read it in this morning's paper, no matter how fast we move."

"That's one uppity bitch," Ozan said. "At the hospital, she got right up in my face even after Kaiser had backed down. I wanted to pistol-whip her so bad I could taste it."

Forrest shook his head. "That's one pleasure you're unlikely to get. If anybody kills her at this point, it'll be Snake." Forrest got up from behind the desk and stuck the dead cigar in his mouth. "Change the orders to our people. Find Dr. Cage, but don't kill him. Not unless he forces the issue."

"Got it. What about Garrity?"

The specter of Walt Garrity allied with Griffith Mackiever rose to the forefront of Forrest's mind. "If they find Garrity alone, they should waste him. We'll pin Deke Dunn's death on him, and that'll clear the books, freeing us to cut a deal with Dr. Cage. The doc will just have to live with Garrity's death as the price of his freedom."

Ozan seemed to like this solution. "And Snake? When he finally reads what's in the *Examiner* in the morning— and he will, the online version—he'll be ready to kill that Masters bitch, just like you said."

"Leave Snake to me. I'll tell him we're going to take everybody out, but he needs to stay in Texas while we do it. Then if I change my mind, I'll tell him we couldn't bring it off, and we need him to do the wet work."

At last Ozan seemed satisfied.

"Now, find me Tom Cage."

"It can't be that goddamn hard," Ozan declared. "Especially with him and Garrity split up. He's got to still be in Louisiana, probably within twenty miles of where he dumped Floyd. There's no way he crossed the Mississippi River. We've got roadblocks at every bridge, and even a cruiser at the St. Francisville ferry, in case he thinks it's still running."

Forrest wasn't so sure. "He's proved to be a resourceful son of a bitch, Alphonse. If we don't find him in the next two hours, we might need to pull that APB on him and just leave it on Garrity."

"You think that'll bring him out of the woods?"

"Who knows? For now, put every man you can into LaSalle, Catahoula, Franklin, and Tensas parishes. Check out the wife's relatives' houses. And keep the tech division going back over all electronic communications of Dr. Cage, his family, his partners, everybody. If there's a deal to be made, we've got to do it quick. Otherwise, we turn Snake loose and get ready for the Sam Peckinpah ending."

"The what?" Ozan asked.

"Nothing. Get to it, Captain."

As the Redbone left the study, Forrest reflected on the irony that he could probably have a more enjoyable conversation with Tom Cage than with any of the men he worked with every day. That included his cousin Billy, who was a serious reader, at least by Knox family standards. Once more Forrest thought about his father and Dr. Cage joking around while the doc gave him his football physical. Then he banished the thought. For at bottom, he felt strangely sure that before another day had come and gone, he would have to kill Tom Cage, either with his own hands or by sending other men to do his will.

CHAPTER 16

I'M STANDING IN the third-floor bedroom of Edelweiss, the historic house I bought for Caitlin as a wedding present, looking down at my daughter's sleeping face. There's just enough light leaking through the cypress shutters to illuminate Annie's profile against her pillow. I've done this hundreds of times in my life. The nights I remember most were those after Annie's mother was diagnosed with cancer—immediately after getting the news, of course, and then later, after her treatments had failed, and hope failed with them. On those desolate nights, I stared down at my three-year-old daughter and shivered in the strangling grip of mortality, forced to accept that all my hope, faith, strength, intelligence, friends, and money could not even slow the progression of the disease that would take Annie's mother from her and leave me to do a job for which I felt completely unprepared.

Now, eight years later, having brought Annie through that most terrible of traumas, I feel almost as helpless as I was then. Only this time it's not an illness I'm fighting, but my father. The man who guided me through most of my life has vanished, leaving chaos and death in his wake, and I am all but powerless to save him. For now, I must focus on protecting the rest of our family. Thinking back on what Kaiser told me about the lethality of Forrest Knox, I'm thankful for this German chalet perched on the bluff above Silver Street and the Mississippi River. *Whenever possible, hide in plain sight*, a wise friend once advised me. Since I kept this purchase secret from everyone but my mother, it has proved to be a serviceable safe house. How strange it is to remember that if Viola Turner hadn't died early Monday morning, I would be giving Caitlin a key to Edelweiss next Friday—probably with a huge ribbon and bow tied around the massive doors. Now I have no idea when we might be married. In the meantime, my mother and daughter hide here like witnesses in a Mafia trial.

The route I took here from City Hall is testament to the gravity of our situation. First I drove to Walmart and purchased a half-dozen prepaid cell phones. Then I drove through several residential subdivisions, doubling back often to be sure I wasn't being followed. As I did, I pondered all John Kaiser had told me outside City Hall. The FBI agent's goal had been to recruit me to the cause of persuading Dad to give himself up to the Bureau, not for my father's safety, but so that he might reveal to Kaiser whatever he might know about Carlos Marcello. To be fair, he wasn't the only one with selfish motives. I had hoped to persuade Kaiser to organize a search of the Lusahatcha Swamp, with its object the elusive Bone Tree, and whatever dead bodies lay in its shadow. Such a large-scale effort would have kept him out of my and Sheriff Dennis's way while we moved against the Knoxes' meth operations tomorrow. But once I realized that Kaiser's primary focus had become tying the Double Eagles to the Kennedy assassination, I knew the Bone Tree gambit would have been a waste of breath.

A shadow passes the crack of the bedroom door, then pauses to hover there. *My mother.* She's floating outside in the maternal holding pattern all women learn after they have children, one that serves them well after grandchildren come along. When I arrived tonight, I found Mom asleep in the chair next to this bed, her hand on a .38 revolver half covered by a crocheted comforter she brought from home to keep Annie surrounded by familiar things. She did not wake until I knelt before her, laid my hand flat over the pistol, and gently touched her shoulder.

Seeing my burned cheek and smelling the smoke on me, she asked what had happened. I assured her that Caitlin and I were all right, and that we'd learned nothing more about Dad's whereabouts or well-being. Then I gave her an abbreviated summary of what had transpired at Brody Royal's house. I could tell that my description of Henry Sexton's death shook her deeply, but she insisted I go downstairs to the newly remodeled kitchen so that she could make me something to eat. I told her I would be down after a few minutes of sitting with Annie.

Mom's appearance at the door must mean that the food is ready. If so, I've been up here longer than I thought. Not wanting to wake Annie, I leave her without a kiss, then join Mom in the hall. She's holding a drink that looks like a gin and tonic, my tranquilizer of choice when I need one.

"Yours or mine?" I ask.

She holds out the sweating glass. "Yours. It's strong. Knock-you-nekkid strong. You need it."

I take a large swallow of the bittersweet mixture, then follow her down to the kitchen, where a plate of scrambled eggs, grits, and toast awaits me. Picking up the plate, I motion for Mom to join me on the sofa in the sparsely furnished sitting room opposite the kitchen. She folds her legs beneath her to keep her feet from the cold floor and watches with maternal satisfaction as I devour the food.

Without makeup, my mother looks closer to her actual age, seventy-one, but even with silver hair and her slightly fallen face, she looks younger than her contemporaries with all their plastic surgery, makeup, and expensive dye jobs. Long before Caitlin's father bought the *Examiner*, an editor of that paper wrote that when he heard the word *class*, he thought of Peggy Cage. "One part Donna Reed, one part Maureen O'Hara, with a sprinkle of Audrey Hepburn," the journalist described her, and he wasn't far wrong. My mother has aged with rare grace, having settled into a fine handsomeness befitting her age and station. Peggy Cage didn't come from money; she came from a dirt farm in central Louisiana, not far from the land that produced Frank and Snake Knox. But you would never know it to speak to her.

As I finish the meal she prepared, I sense an expectant tension in her. A strange emotion has animated her face. It almost looks like excitement.

"What is it?" I ask.

"I've got something to show you, Penn. While I was waiting for you to come downstairs, I checked my e-mail. I've been doing it every fifteen minutes since Annie and I got here."

"Mom, I told you not to do anything like that."

"Oh, fiddle. I had to, and you'll be glad I did. Five minutes ago, I got a message from your father."

"What?" The last forkful of eggs hangs suspended before my face.

She points to my notebook computer, glowing at the end of the sofa. Grabbing the device, I hit the return button to stop the screen saver. It vanishes to reveal the GUI of Mom's AOL account, which is currently displaying a list of her old mail. In a box in the upper-right corner of her screen is a message from ENGINEERJACK1946.

"Uncle Jack?" I ask, recognizing the AOL user name of my father's youngest brother, who lives in California.

"Yes! Read the message, and you'll understand."

Trying to get my heartbeat under control, I quickly skim the message.

> *Peggy,*
> *A few minutes ago I received a phone call from someone who identified himself as "a friend of your big brother." The caller told me not to mention my brother's name during the conversation. He said that Tom had given him a message for you, which he was going to read to me, and I was to get it to you however I thought best. I called your house and got no answer, so I'm trying e-mail. The caller told me that he'd seen Tom in the flesh, and he was physically all right. I have no idea who the caller was. From traffic sounds, I'd bet he was standing at a pay phone. I don't know what's going on, obviously, but if there's anything I can do, let me know, and I'll fly in. Tell Penn to call me.*
> *   Love, Jack*
>
> *Faithfully transcribed message follows:*
>
> > *Peg,*
> >   *You're going to hear that some people were killed tonight (Wednesday) and that Penn and Caitlin were there when it happened. It's a tragedy, and I surely bear some guilt for it. But as far as I can learn, Penn and Caitlin are safe. I want you to know that I'm safe also. I know you'll be worried to death, but think back to all I told*

*you on Monday, and trust that I'm doing
the right thing for our family.*

*Penn will be very angry. Please
explain to him that while he thinks I have a
choice in what I'm doing, I don't. If we try
to use the system to solve this problem, our
family will suffer terribly. I have a plan to
straighten all this out, and I believe it has
a good chance of success. If I succeed, the
charges over Viola's death will be dropped
and the matter of the state trooper taken
care of. That's the only outcome I'm willing
to accept at this point. You'll understand
why later. Obviously there's a lot I can't
tell you through this medium, but soon I'll
explain in person. You know me, my girl.
I don't always have the answers. But I'm
asking you to trust that I know best in this
case.*

*Tell Penn I'm counting on him to
keep you and Annie safe. That's far more
important than him trying to get to
the bottom of this mess, which would be
pointless. I hope he can protect Caitlin, but
that girl goes her own way, and you can't
tell her anything. That's why she's good at
her work. I'll get home as soon as I can. I
love you, my darling.*
Tom

Long before I finish the message, I'm shaking my head
in disbelief.

"Do you feel any better?" Mom asks hesitantly.

"No. Mom, I told you what happened tonight . . . who
died. A Natchez cop was murdered simply for guarding
the *Natchez Examiner*. He died trying to protect Caitlin
and me."

"Surely you don't blame your father for that?"

"Yes, I blame him. Because the death of Viola Turner
set all this off, and all he's willing to say about it is, 'Trust
me, I know what I'm doing.' People died because he made
the decision to jump bail rather than remain in custody.

And jumping bail led to Dad and Walt killing that state trooper."

"You don't really believe they did that?"

"I'm afraid I do. Out of self-defense, probably, but that won't matter to anybody but us. The lead FBI agent in town would actually like to help Dad, but Dad's making it very tough. It's hard to help a man with a dead cop hanging around his neck."

Mom draws her mouth into a tight frown. "I hate to hear you speaking against your father like this."

"What do you expect? When Dad kept silent about Viola's death, I told myself he was taking some kind of moral stand on euthanasia. When it looked like murder instead, Henry Sexton convinced me the Double Eagles had killed her. When Dad jumped bail, I told myself he had no choice—that we were dealing with a vendetta by the DA and a redneck sheriff, and there was a method to his madness. But *now*? People are dying every day, and Dad and Walt could be shot on sight at any moment. At the very least Dad should be calling Quentin Avery and trying to arrange a safe surrender. But he hasn't. If you want to know the truth, I'm starting to believe that all my faith in Dad—*all my life*—has been misplaced. That I believed in a father who only existed in my head. And yours."

Her eyes plead for understanding. "Penn, please don't talk that way."

"I'm sorry. But anybody looking at what he's done since Monday would see the actions of a guilty man. I'm starting to think Shad Johnson is right: whatever Dad did in Viola's house, he did it to keep something buried in the past. And if it's so bad that he can't tell us about it, then I'm afraid that once we discover what it is—if we ever do—it *will* change our view of him."

I've never seen such sadness in my mother's eyes. Very softly, she says, "It would kill your father to know you've lost faith in him like this."

"He's broken almost every rule he ever taught me. How many chances has he had to do the right thing?"

She closes her eyes and hugs herself. "None of us is the person that others think we are. Not you, and not me. I'm not the woman you think I am."

"Yes, you are. I know nobody's perfect, but this goes so far beyond normal human frailty that I can't even make sense of it."

"That doesn't mean there is no sense to it." Mom's eyes open and fix me with adamantine conviction. "All I know is the man I married. I know what he's capable of, and what he's not."

"No human being can say that with certainty. Not even about a spouse."

My mother takes my hand and speaks across the gulf of a generation. "You and Sarah were married nine years before the cancer took her. I know you loved her. But nine years isn't that long. I've been married to your father since 1952. Fifty-three years. I've earned the right to say that I know him as well as any human being can know another. And I know this—Tom Cage is going to do the right thing no matter what. He can't do the wrong thing. It's not in him."

What would it take to shake such faith? This is like trying to knock down a granite wall by talking to it. My stomach burns with resentment from holding my tongue about so many things pertaining to my father. The right thing? I want to ask. Lincoln Turner believes that he's Dad's son by Viola Turner—and Dad probably believes it, too. This whole crazy nightmare may be happening because Lincoln Turner screwed up a mercy killing and Dad is covering for him. Risking all our lives because he can't bear to watch an illegitimate son punished by the courts . . .

But I say none of that. Instead, I say, "I don't think Dad would ever intentionally do something terrible. But he might deceive himself so badly that he wound up doing something that had terrible consequences. We're all capable of that. And I'm not sure he could bear the idea that our image of him was going to be shattered, or even tarnished."

My mother looks down into her lap, then takes the gin and tonic from my hand and takes two big swallows. "You're right about that much. If Tom thought you'd begun to doubt everything he taught you as a boy . . . it would break his heart. So I want you to promise me something. If you do find him, please don't try to browbeat the truth out of him, whatever it is. That will come in its own good time—if it's meant to. Maybe even in a courtroom, if there's no other way. Will you promise me that?"

I take the glass back from her and swallow some gin. "Yes," I tell her, knowing it's a lie. This is no time for truth. "But you've got to accept that you can't help Dad by going along with his plans. His only chance now is a safe surrender into federal custody. If he contacts you again, please try to convince him of that."

Her gaze falls away from me and settles in a dark corner of the room. "I could never have imagined things would go this far."

"Of course not. How could you?"

She's staring at the foot of the hall staircase, and she looks strangely preoccupied.

"Mom? I'm getting the distinct impression that you know more than I do about all of this. Do you?"

She doesn't answer. I'm not even sure she heard me.

"Dad's message said remember all he told you on Monday. What did he tell you?"

She slowly shakes her head. "Nothing that would help you. Just that Viola's life had been tragic, and her death was, too. He didn't want to burden me with anything I might have to lie about."

Great. Realizing I'm going to learn nothing further about Viola, my mind skips back to my disturbing conversation with John Kaiser. "Mom?" I say gently. "Did Dad ever talk to you about knowing a man named Carlos Marcello?"

For a moment her face remains transfixed, but then the tiny webs of wrinkles move, and her eyes focus on me. They're filled with surprise.

"Uncle Carlos?" she says.

"*Uncle Carlos?*" I echo. "Mom . . . are we talking about the same man?"

"The boss of New Orleans?"

Stunned speechless, I can only nod.

"Oh, I don't know anything. Just a story your father told me. You know Tom did an externship at the parish prison in New Orleans during his final year of medical school. He was the jail doctor, and there was a lot of excitement. He once saw a crazed prisoner shot right in front of him."

"Mom . . . what about Marcello?"

"Oh, yes. Well, Tom once told me a story about Carlos Marcello serving time in the prison. He said New Orleans policemen delivered his meals every night, from the best restaurants in New Orleans. Marcello even had women visit him in his cell. The godfather lived better in jail than most people did at home, and everybody called him 'Uncle Carlos.' The whole thing was like a big joke."

"Yeah," I murmur, but this is anything but funny. "What year would this have been?"

"Nineteen fifty-nine, of course. The year Tom graduated from LSU med school."

The year before I was born. I'd forgotten that my mother and father lived in New Orleans for four years. This means that Dad could have met Carlos Marcello as early as . . . 1955. In any case, he surely met the don in 1959, and not as a random student, but as the parish prison physician. *My father treated Carlos Marcello.* What the hell would Kaiser make of that information?

"Did Dad mention Marcello any other times?"

An almost wistful look comes over my mother's face. "No, but . . . I actually met him a couple of times. Both times in restaurants. Tom and I couldn't afford to eat out back then, you know. I was teaching across the river, just to pay the rent on our little apartment in the French Quarter. But one night Tom took me to Felix's Oyster Bar, and this short, grinning man came over to our table and asked if everything was all right. He spoke like an illiterate tradesman, but after he left the table, Tom told me he was the Mafia boss of Louisiana."

I can scarcely take this in as my mother continues.

"The second time was near Waggaman. A nice, homey Italian restaurant called Mosca's. The same thing happened. And I think Tom may have told me that Mr. Marcello owned that place. I'm not sure."

"Do you remember whose idea it was to go there?"

"Oh, Tom's, of course. It was our anniversary. Seventh, I think."

"I see," I tell her, which is a lie.

"Why are you asking about Carlos Marcello?" Mom asks, suddenly worried. "He's been dead for ages, hasn't he? What could he have to do with anything?"

For a moment my mind fills with the blurry image of

my father visiting Carlos's swamp hideaway in 1968, but it would be pointless to ask my mother about that. Whatever really took my father to Churchill Farms in 1968, he'd have told Mom nothing about it. And it would serve no purpose for me to tell her now. While I ponder this, my mother squeezes my right hand in both of hers.

"I wish I could help you, Penn. I wish I knew more. And I especially wish you could trust your father." She wipes tears from the corners of her eyes. "And don't you wear a hair shirt over that man you shot tonight. I've heard plenty over the years about Randall Regan, and how he abused his wife. You only did what any husband would have done, considering what they did to Caitlin. What any man worth the name would have done."

This is exactly what I'd expect to hear from my mother, who carries genes and mores forged in the Scottish Highlands. I wonder how many mothers said similar things to their handcuffed sons in the Houston jail while I was preparing to prosecute them?

I lay my hand on her shoulder. "Tomorrow's going to be a big day, and you and Annie need to be ready for it. Sheriff Dennis is going to hit the Knox family hard, and I'm going to help him. They're involved in a major crystal meth operation in Louisiana, and Walker's going to arrest as many low-level people as he can. By threatening them with mandatory prison sentences, he hopes to force a Double Eagle to turn state's evidence. If one of them knows who killed Viola Turner, we might be able to force Shad to drop the murder charge. Then hopefully Dad's jumping bail will seem more defensible."

Mom is looking at me like she doubts either my sanity or my intelligence. "But isn't that exactly what your father said *not* to do? He said it was pointless for you to try to get to the bottom of this mess."

All I see in her eyes is adamant refusal to question her husband. "Doesn't that make you even the slightest bit suspicious? Don't you get it, Mom? What Walker and I are doing tomorrow may be Dad's only hope."

Fear flashes across her face. "I don't see that at all! None of those old klukkers is going to confess anything. They don't really believe they'll be sent to jail. They never have been before."

"You're right, but that's not my real goal. If we can hit them hard enough—really hurt them—then we'll knock them off balance and force them to defend themselves. Forrest Knox is the power behind the Knox drug business, and the one who stands to lose the most if things go south. He's also the one leading the hunt for Dad and Walt. A wave of arrests will be a major distraction for him, and that should ease the pressure on Dad and Walt. Maybe enough for them to get somewhere really safe. Now, if—"

Before I can get out another word, my mother throws her arms around me and hugs me so tightly I can scarcely breathe. "When is Sheriff Dennis carrying out these drug busts?"

"In about four hours."

She draws back, her eyes wide. "We've got to get you in the bed. You need to be rested for that."

"I am exhausted," I admit. "But my thoughts are spinning so fast, I'll probably just lie there until dawn, waiting for the alarm."

Without a word Mom goes into the kitchen, fishes loudly through her purse, then returns with a bright yellow pill in the palm of her right hand.

"What's that?" I ask.

"Temazepam. It's like Valium. I take one every night. Take this now, and I'll wake you up at five fifteen."

"I don't think I should risk oversleeping."

"Take the damn pill, son. Sometimes I take two, if your father has the TV up loud enough, and you outweigh me by nearly a hundred pounds."

"You're not trying to keep me from going with Sheriff Dennis?"

"No. I think you're right about knocking the Knox family off balance. That can only help Tom."

I take the pill and swallow it with a big gulp of gin.

My mother pulls me to my feet and ushers me downstairs to one of the guest bedrooms in what I call the basement, though technically it's the first floor of the chalet. At the threshold, she gives me a hug and says, "I'll wake you at five fifteen."

Then she whisks herself back up the stairs to see to Annie.

Whether it's the sleeping pill, the alcohol, or the exhaustion produced by the battle at Brody Royal's lake house, I can barely stand erect through the ritual of brushing my teeth. By the time I reach the guest room bed, I can't even pull back the quilt. I simply fall facedown onto it, my mind cycling between total blankness and nightmare images from the smoke-filled hell of Royal's basement. Behind these pictures drones the voice of John Kaiser, but I can't make out his words. Through the black boiling smoke I don't see the burned corpses of Henry and Royal, but rather my father and mother, young and improbably beautiful, sitting in a homey restaurant while a grinning man with stony black eyes hugs them and raves about his red sauce. A fat accordion player steps forward and begins to play, drowning out Kaiser's voice, and then with a final slap on my father's back, Carlos Marcello struts back into his kitchen, the big door with the round glass window swinging behind him.

CHAPTER 17

BY THE TIME Tom Cage reached Jefferson County, Mississippi, exhaustion, his various illnesses, and his bullet wound had pushed him into a sort of trance. The road in front of the unfamiliar car he was driving wavered in the darkness, his headlight beams an illuminated tube into which startled deer charged with alarming regularity, nearly sending him off the shoulder more than once.

Tom's short-term memory had gone haywire; the events of the past hour flickered through his head like a piece of film with random sections spliced out by a drunken editor. After dumping the Knox assassin in a barren field, he'd driven away with his headlights extinguished, making for the home of his wife's brother. Tom had meant to approach the farmhouse carefully, but in the end he'd just turned into the driveway and honked his horn. He hadn't the strength for more than that.

John McCrae had emerged from his farmhouse with a shotgun in his hand. The McCraes were clannish folk, driven out of Scotland during the Clearances, and congenitally mistrustful of authority. But Tom would never forget the look of compassion on McCrae's face when he realized that the bloodied man sagging against the wheel of the strange pickup was his sister's husband. McCrae's wife had been terrified by Tom's sudden appearance, and what it might mean for her family, but John had only asked Tom what he needed and how he could help. Tom told his brother-in-law that he couldn't stay; the risk for them was too great. Neither could he seek medical care or turn himself in to the police. What he needed was to get back across the river into Mississippi.

Once Tom had established that objective, John McCrae bent his will toward it, and within one hour he'd made it happen. McCrae was the kind of southerner who had only left the parish of his birth to serve his country in wartime or to carry bulls across the state for mating purposes. Enlisting his son's help, he'd ditched Tom's stolen pickup in a ravine already littered with junk cars and trucks. Then he'd concealed Tom himself beneath a carpet of hay in a horse trailer (along with one gentle horse standing over it), spirited him through a state police roadblock, and driven him across the Mississippi River at Vicksburg. McCrae's son had followed a mile back in a different vehicle—the old Chevy Nova Tom was driving now. Once they were safely across the river, they'd given Tom the Nova and promised to pass a message to Peggy through Tom's brother in California. Tom remembered his brother-in-law's face as he shut the Nova's door and bade him farewell. John McCrae had clearly believed he was looking at a doomed man.

The trip from Vicksburg to Jefferson County was a blur. A fever had begun rising in Tom, and perhaps that was the culprit where his memory was concerned. All he could focus on was his goal: eighty acres of wooded land in a corner of the county that had elected Charles Evers the first black mayor in Mississippi. As Tom drove, lines from Frost's "The Death of the Hired Man" ran through his overheated brain: *Home is the place where, when you have to go there, they have to take you in. . . .*

The land and house he made for now were not his home in any legal sense, but he felt sure that the owner would take him in. There were other places he could go: the homes of patients whose lives he had saved, whose babies he'd delivered, whose families he had treated for three generations. But wherever he went, he would carry danger with him, and maybe even death. In his mind's eye Tom saw helicopters circling suburban houses like birds of prey, shining spotlights into the windows. That was why he'd refused shelter from his brother-in-law. He'd never have been able to forgive himself if he got John McCrae hurt or killed.

The place he was running to now was different. The man who owned this sanctuary was a soldier of sorts, though he'd never worn a uniform. But during his own years at war, he'd called upon Tom when he needed help, and Tom had answered. Now the tables had turned, and Tom believed that his old friend would return the favor.

Yanking the steering wheel right to avoid a scuttling armadillo, he centered the Nova as best he could on the narrow road. A fresh sheen of sweat had broken out on his face, and he clumsily wiped his forehead to keep it out of his eyes. His need for sleep was like a dark tide swelling around him. He felt as though he were treading water, barely keeping his eyes above the surface.

Home, he thought again, trying to remember what the word meant. The house he considered his real home— the one that contained his treasured library—had been destroyed seven years ago, burned to the ground by the man who'd once helped him save the life of Viola Turner. The houses Tom had known before that one flared in his mind like cars on a passing train: the clapboard army box at Fort Leonard Wood, the married officers' quarters in Germany, the French Quarter apartment he and Peggy had shared while he was in medical school, the dorm of the little college he'd attended in northwestern Louisiana. Somewhere back behind all those lay the tiny house where he'd been raised with his brothers, just up the road from the stinking creosote plant where he'd worked as a boy, sweating alongside the local Negroes until he'd managed to get hired on as an usher at the local movie theater—a job not open to his fellow creosote workers. He'd made good friends among those men, and he credited them with teaching him that human beings were pretty much the same, no matter what color they were.

The gate Tom was searching for rose out of the darkness like a mirage, then vanished behind him. Braking carefully, he stopped, reversed direction for a few yards, then drove slowly back to the metal obstruction and parked. He didn't know what he'd do if the gate was locked. He would never be able to walk the half-mile-long driveway that led to the house. And calling the owner was not an option, since under the circumstances his phone might well be tapped.

Climbing carefully out of the Nova, Tom trudged up to the gate and grabbed the upper crossbar to keep himself erect. He nearly cried from joy when he saw a simple chain loop holding the gate to the timber post. After lifting the chain with great difficulty, he pushed open the gate, then returned to the Nova and drove through. He considered simply driving on to the house, but he forced himself to get back out and close the gate, knowing that even the smallest lapse could kill him at this point.

Tom drove slowly up the gently curving driveway, through the bare woods, toward the winter home of Quentin Avery, his lawyer and, more important, one of his oldest living friends. Though Quentin was an attorney of national reputation, and a hero to many who remembered his role in the civil rights movement, Tom knew him best as a patient. Quentin suffered from severe diabetes, and Tom had shepherded him through progressive peripheral neuropathy, two leg amputations, retinal problems, dangerous hypertension, and a half-dozen other maladies that came along with age and African-American genes. Through most of these battles, Quentin had fought valiantly, maintaining his good humor and acute intellect. But losing his second leg had nearly done him in. The loss of mobility, combined with sexual issues and a much younger wife, had pushed him into clinical depression. There were times Tom had feared the old lion would end his life rather than struggle on with diminished capacity. But so far, Quentin's survival instinct had prevailed.

At last Tom's headlights washed over the front of Avery's Tudor-style manor. Like so many of the newer homes in Jefferson County, it had been financed by settlement money from the famous fen-phen diet pill lawsuits. Quentin had represented more than a few of the plaintiffs, and he'd profited handsomely from its stunning resolution. After one of his clients squandered every cent of his settlement, the man had been forced to sell this house at a near-panic discount. With the most sympathetic face he could muster, Quentin had consented to take the showpiece off its desperate owner's hands.

Tom drove up to the garage and shut off the Nova's engine, then sat for a couple of minutes, marshaling his strength for the walk to the door. Once he felt capable, he got out, struggled through the chilly wind to the arched timber door at the side of the house, and rang the bell twice.

Nearly a minute passed before a light came on inside the house. By the time someone peered through the little window set in the door, Tom had sagged against its face.

When the curtain rustled, he stood up straight so that he could be seen clearly. Muted voices spoke behind the wood, but then at last the handle turned and someone pulled open the door.

Quentin's wife, Doris, stood there in her housecoat, a black pistol in her hand. An attorney herself, Doris Avery was almost thirty years her husband's junior. Tom figured Doris was about forty, but she had the same coloring as Viola Turner, the darker side of café au lait. In his confused mental state, Tom perceived her as an avatar of Viola, whom he hadn't seen between the ages of twenty-eight and sixty-five.

"I'm so sorry," he said.

"Dear God," Doris Avery whispered. "Quentin, it's Tom Cage."

Tom heard the whir of a motorized wheelchair. Then his old friend appeared behind his wife, smiling up from his chair as though finding Tom on his doorstep was only what he'd expected.

"Man, you look dead on your feet," Quentin said. "Get yo' ass in this house before I freeze to death."

Doris didn't look so sure about this invitation, but after a sharp whisper from Quentin, she helped Tom inside and led him to a sofa in a beautifully appointed den. When Tom collapsed into the padding, he felt something in him give way. He could scarcely follow the words being exchanged only ten feet from him. After a minute or so, the voices began to rise with emotion, and he realized that Quentin and Doris were arguing. He tried to speak, but a moan was all that emerged from his mouth. Then a warm hand touched his face, and he felt glass against his lips. He opened his mouth and swallowed instinctively. Cool water poured down his throat like ambrosia.

"He's feverish," Doris said. "Tom, you've got a fever. Do you have any drugs in that truck?"

Tom nodded. "Bag," he whispered. "Cipro . . ."

He sensed Doris moving away from him. Then he felt a cooler hand take hold of his, and Quentin Avery's warm, rich baritone, which had swayed so many juries in its day, spoke near his ear.

"I'm here, buddy. You just take it easy. You're gonna be all right."

"I'm sorry for coming here, Quentin."

"Hush that nonsense. Is anybody following you?"

Tom laughed inside his head. "Everybody. But nobody followed me here. I just need sleep, Quentin . . . sleep."

"You need a lot more than that. But sleep would be a good start."

The next thing Tom remembered was Doris forcing a pill into his mouth and making him drink again.

"That was Cipro," she said. "That's a broad-spectrum antibiotic, isn't it?"

Tom nodded and opened his eyes long enough to see Doris's worried eyes. "Thank you. I'm sorry . . . nowhere else to go."

"Lie back, Tom. Just rest there on the sofa. We'll figure this thing out."

Tom tried to follow the subsequent conversation, but his mind slipped underwater again. Then a sharp cry brought him to the surface. Doris Avery was clearly afraid—as John McCrae's wife had been—and she was arguing that they could call someone she knew and arrange to surrender Tom to someone trustworthy in Jackson, the state capital. Tom tried to sit up, but he couldn't manage it. He did, however, bring himself awake enough to hear Quentin's reply. The old lawyer spoke quietly but with absolute conviction.

"Doris," he said, "you're my wife, and I love you. But you weren't born until 1965. While you were in your mama's belly, I was down in Liberty, Mississippi, challenging the county government on voter registration. Lionel Hill was down there with me, working secretly with CORE and the SNCC. Lionel was a wanted man in Mississippi. The Klan had been after him for a year. But at night he'd go into homes and churches and talk to the people, trying to buck up their courage and get them to risk registering to vote."

"Q, that's ancient history," Doris broke in. "It's got nothing to do with here and now."

"You're wrong, baby. It means everything. About a week into this work, the local cops heard Lionel was in town, and they started hunting him. The Klan, too. One night they got onto our tails, and we had to run for it in an old, broken-down Rambler. Lionel's daddy had run whiskey up in South Carolina, and he was a hell of a driver. We got away from those white boys on a dirt road that ran across a flooded creek. But just after we got clear, Lionel skidded off some gravel and hit a tree. Ripped half the scalp off his head, broke some ribs . . . he was out cold for ten full minutes. We carried him to an old logger's shack and got him awake, but he needed real help. The problem was, where to go? Any hospital in the state would have called the cops the second we walked in. They'd have jailed Lionel without putting a stitch in his head, if the Klan didn't get there first and take him."

"Quentin—"

"Let me finish. Then make your decision."

Doris huffed in exasperation, and Quentin went on: "Lionel wanted to try for New Orleans, but there was no way we were going to make it out of Mississippi that night. Natchez was only twenty-five miles away. That old logger sneaked us out of Amite County on roads hardly wider than a deer track. Then he drove us to the edge of Natchez. I'll never forget that night. I used a pay phone at the Minute Man just past the Johns Manville plant to call Dr. Tom Cage. And what did Tom do? He got out of bed, met us at his office, and worked on Lionel for two hours straight. That's right. He risked everything he had to help us out of that jam. He risked his *family*, Doris. In *1965*. Do you understand what that means?"

"Yes, I do. But I also understand the penalties for aiding and abetting a fugitive—especially one wanted for killing a state trooper. You'll lose your law license, Quentin. So would I. Maybe forever."

"Maybe," Quentin conceded. "So maybe it's best if you go on and leave this to me."

"To you?" Doris snorted at the suggestion. "Between the two of you, you haven't got the strength to get Tom into a bed, much less do anything substantive to help him."

"I just might surprise you," Quentin growled. "You go if you need to go. Just don't tell me what I'm risking to help this man. If the police come for him, I'll sit in our front door with the Constitution in one hand and a rifle in the other. At least until somebody convinces me he'll make it to a courtroom alive. After that, I won't need a damned rifle."

"You're a hardheaded old fool," Doris said, but Tom heard love beneath her frustration. "I don't know why I put up with you."

"Yes, you do," Quentin said. "Let's get him to a bed."

"No," Doris said.

"What?" Quentin asked, sounding truly worried for the first time.

"I don't think he can make it to a bed. I'll get some quilts and a pillow. He's going to sleep right here. And if he's still alive in the morning, we'll decide what to do then."

As the swish of Doris Avery's slippers receded, Tom felt Quentin's hand close around his again. "That's a good woman right there," Quentin intoned. "Between you and Doris, I've been a lucky man. You gonna be all right now, Tom. Just let go. Let go of everything and trust old Q."

Tom squeezed his friend's hand. Then he let go and slipped beneath the surface for the last time.

THURSDAY

CHAPTER 18

SHERIFF WALKER DENNIS and I are roaring down a Louisiana back road at ninety miles per hour in a supercharged Ford sedan, a SWAT van struggling to keep pace with us. I feel a little like I've stepped onto the set of a 1970s Burt Reynolds movie, but none of the other cast members seems to be in on the joke.

Walker Dennis certainly isn't playing games. At 5 A.M. he assembled twenty-four deputies in a staging area beside the Concordia Parish courthouse. Half wore SWAT gear, and all were armed to the teeth. From the warmth of my car in the main courthouse lot, I watched Walker brief his troops. After a short speech, he got into his cruiser and drove toward my car, while his deputies broke into teams and climbed into several different vehicles. As they drove out to Highway 15 and turned left or right depending on their destinations, Walker pulled up beside me and motioned for me to get into his cruiser. When I did, I found a plastic bucket of cell phones on the passenger seat. There were at least twenty handsets in the bucket, of every imaginable make.

"Sorry," he said, lifting the bucket into the backseat.

I got inside the car, my left thigh brushing against a cut-down shotgun mounted in a rack between us. "What's with the phones?"

"I collected them before I told anybody where they were going."

I'll be damned, I thought. "How'd they take that?"

"Not well."

"Do you think you got every phone?"

"Yep." Sheriff Dennis winked, then backed out of the

parking space. "My brother-in-law walked behind the ranks with a scanner while I was giving my speech. I'm pretty sure the two who had extra phones are having extramarital affairs, but I'll double-check it later. For today I've paired them with reliable partners." He stopped and put the powerful cruiser in Drive. "Fasten your seat belt, Mayor. This is gonna be a hell of a morning."

During the next hour, I listened to Walker direct a parishwide assault on the Knox family's meth operation. His tactical teams rousted users and dealers out of their beds, busted cookers in the midst of their work, and searched a half-dozen probable storage sites for illegal chemicals. By 5:55, twenty-seven people had been arrested without a shot fired. Walker handled the whole operation with absolute professionalism, save for one detail: he'd failed to get wiretap warrants on any member of the Knox family prior to the raids. Had he done that, he probably would have gathered enough evidence in the first hours to put Snake, Billy, and Forrest Knox in Angola Penitentiary for twenty years apiece. But the sheriff explained his oversight pragmatically. The judge who'd granted the search warrants (and kept his mouth shut about them) hated the Knoxes enough to help Walker take a shot at their meth operation, but not enough to sign wiretap warrants on the Knoxes on the basis of rumor alone. Apart from arousing the ire of the state supreme court, that might make him a target of violent retaliation.

After a team of female deputies ferried the prisoners back to the station in vans to begin processing them, Walker told me we were about to lead a tactical team out to the western edge of the parish, where he had a man keeping watch on a suspected Knox drug warehouse. And that's how I found myself riding shotgun in this rattling car as it threatens to lift off the pavement on every sweeping turn.

"There it is," Walker says, pointing through the windshield.

All I see is a white metal storage building about the size of a small gymnasium standing at the edge of a fallow field. Walker keys his radio and says, "This is Whiskey Delta. Give me a sitrep."

His radio crackles, and then a male voice says, "I see you. I'm in the ditch to your left. Nobody's gone in or out since I've been here."

"Did you see any lights before dawn?"

"Negative. I think it's empty."

The SWAT van pulls up beside us, and Walker signals for its driver to get out. Seconds later, a tactical team wearing full body armor and black face screens stands lined up beside the car. As Walker gets out and walks around to address them, I crank down my window a couple of inches.

"No sense wasting time," the sheriff says. "There's an overhead door on the far side, plus one regular door. Three of you cover that side while the breaching team blows the front. Eyes front, Deputy!"

One of the men wearing the black masks was staring at me. He snaps his head back toward Sheriff Dennis.

"We think this building's empty," Walker says, "but we never assume anything. You go in there like you expect a Russian Spetsnaz unit waiting."

"Yes, sir," says one of the deputies.

"Go."

As the deputies fan out around the building, Walker gets back behind the wheel and says, "Did you just send a text message?"

"I'm just keeping Caitlin up to date. We want all the coverage we can get on these busts. I only wish we had Henry with us."

Dennis nods, still watching his men. "He's looking down on us right now, brother."

I wish I believed that, but rather than express my doubt, I give Walker a smile. At this point I don't want him thinking of me as anything but a solid partner. We sit in silence for about a minute, and then a voice crackles over the radio, "We're in position."

Walker looks at me, and I nod, my pulse quickening.

"Door team go," says Walker.

Two men carrying 10-gauge shotguns step up to the front door of the warehouse and lay the muzzles of their weapons against its hinges at a downward angle.

"Those Remingtons are loaded with Hatton rounds,"

Walker says to me. "Turn to dust as soon as they penetrate the door."

"Glad to hear it."

"Breach," Walker says into his radio.

Even with the doors of the cruiser closed, the shotgun blasts buffet the air in my lungs. The four men behind the shotgun team crash through the door yelling loud enough for us to hear it in the car.

"What you got, Alpha?" Walker asks in a wire-taut voice.

His radio crackles twice, but I can't make out the response.

"This is Whiskey Delta," Walker repeats, "what have you found?"

"Sir, we've got a pile of fifty-five-gallon drums here. Could be precursor chemicals, or just plain old herbicide. We're gonna need some lab rats for this."

"I'm coming in."

As Walker grabs his door handle, a shock wave that dwarfs the one generated by the shotguns rocks the car. A gaping hole has opened in the near end of the metal building, orange flame and black smoke jetting from it like the breath of a dragon.

"Booby-trapped," I mutter. "Just like a pot field. There could be a secondary device—"

"Get out of there!" Walker shouts into his radio. *"Move, move, move!"*

"We've got two men down, Sheriff!"

"Get out NOW!"

The second explosion isn't as powerful as the first, but it produces twice the smoke and flame. *Incendiary bomb.*

"Goddamn it!" Walker shouts, pounding the steering wheel.

He scrambles from the cruiser and starts running toward the warehouse. As I leap from the car and sprint after him, I pray that the men inside somehow escaped the brunt of both blasts. But the calculating part of me knows this tragedy will bring about one change that can only help my father. After this, the Double Eagle group and the Knox family will no longer be able to operate in the shadows, not even with their political protection. As my father learned yesterday, when you kill a cop, you cross into a zone where neither aid nor mercy can be expected. Though they probably never intended it, the Double Eagles have joined the war.

CHAPTER 19

FORREST KNOX OPENED his eyes in the dark. The susurrant sound of his wife's breathing reassured him that nothing was wrong, at least not in the bedroom. The faint blue LCD screen on his encrypted mobile phone had awakened him. He shook his head to clear his thoughts. For the last thirty-six hours he'd been popping "Whoa" and "Go" pills, as he had in Vietnam. Speed to stay alert, benzos to knock himself out. Lifting the phone from his bedside table, he got out of bed and walked to the door. His wife, long accustomed to the routine of a trooper's life, did not even stir.

"Knox," he said quietly.

"It's me," said Alphonse Ozan. "We got more problems. Big problems."

"Did Sheriff Dennis turn up something unexpected in the ashes of Royal's house?"

"No. They didn't even go there."

"What?" Forrest moved down the hallway toward the kitchen.

"Dennis played us, boss. This morning he lined up every deputy he's got and took away their cell phones. Then he handed out tactical plans for a parishwide bust of every known or suspected meth cooker, dealer, mule, and storehouse."

"Son of a bitch."

"Yep."

"Did he bust any Eagles?" Forrest asked, thankful that Snake and Sonny, at least, were out of the state.

"Doesn't look like it. None of the front shops got searched, either. But they busted all the lower-level people."

Forrest's usually steady nerves had begun to fray. He was fighting an urge to punch the refrigerator door. "Find out every location and person that Dennis hit, then do a liability assessment of who and what they knew. You'll probably have to talk to Snake and Sonny to do it, so be careful in your communications."

"Will do. But look, some busts are still going on. Dennis still has a tactical squad out in the field. SWAT."

Forrest switched on the coffeemaker. "For what?"

"Don't know. I got all this news late, thanks to Dennis confiscating the cell phones. But most deputies are back at the station now, processing prisoners, so our guy got clear and went to his home phone."

Forrest wondered what the hell had gotten into Walker Dennis. "Any FBI or DEA involvement?"

"Not so far. It seems to be Walker Dennis on his own hook. But I did hear one strange thing."

"What's that?"

"Mayor Penn Cage rode in the car with Dennis during the busts."

Forrest froze with his hand on the refrigerator door. "*What?*"

"That's what my source said. Cage was riding shotgun. Joined up with Dennis at the station before the first busts."

"Well, well. I'll have to think about that." Forrest set the milk on the counter, then took a croissant from a white cardboard box and bit a hunk off the buttery roll. "I wonder why they didn't hit any Double Eagles . . ."

"I'll get on Mayor Cage's—" Ozan's voice stopped, then started again, but seemingly farther away. Forrest realized he was speaking on another line. After twenty seconds, Ozan said, "I'll call you back, boss. I think the shit just hit the fan, but comm is spotty. I'll call you right back."

"No, I'll wait."

Ozan's voice rose in pitch as he barked out a series of rapid-fire questions. From what Forrest could hear, someone had been killed in the field, but he couldn't tell who. Thirty seconds later, the Redbone was back on the line.

"It's bad, boss. Shit."

"Tell me."

"Sheriff Dennis sent his SWAT team into a warehouse on the road to Jonesville. Somebody had precursor chemicals stored in there, and the damned place blew up. Looks like it was booby-trapped. CPSO's got one deputy dead on scene and three more in critical condition. Two are being airlifted to Alexandria, one to Baton Rouge."

"The Jonesville Road? Well, at least that's none of our concern."

"I'm not so sure, boss. One of the Double Eagles owns a warehouse on that road. Initials L.S."

L.S.? Forrest thought about the initials. *Leo Spivey?* In his mind he saw a heavyset man with a ready grin, a Double Eagle since his father's days. "Fuck, Alphonse. Did he go into business for himself?"

"I'm betting yeah. I just checked the address online, and it matches. L.S. must have got greedy. And paranoid enough to booby-trap the place."

"Unbelievable."

"What you want I should do?"

Forrest had been glad that Snake and Sonny were at Toledo Bend, on the Texas side of the reservoir, but now he wished Snake were close to hand. He would know where to find Leo, and how best to dispatch him. There was always the Black Team, but that seemed like over-kill.

"Spivey's a problem. Once they track him down and threaten him with a mandatory meth-trafficking sentence . . ."

"I know."

"That can't happen, Al."

Ozan said nothing for several seconds. Then he said, "Don't worry 'bout it, boss. I feel like that old man's al-ready dead."

As always, the Redbone had gotten the message.

"How do you think he died?" Forrest asked with irony in his voice.

"I figure he killed himself as soon as he heard the news. But you never know. Maybe rival drug dealers killed him to send a message. What you think?"

"I think he killed himself, Alphonse. That's a message all its own."

"I hear you. Anything else?"

"Yes. If Dennis picked up that many foot soldiers, it's time for a little negative reinforcement. Have somebody round up a couple of their kids and hold them somewhere. Don't hurt them or anything. Just let the word spread through the jail. That'll stop any talk."

"Consider it done."

"How long would it take you to assemble the Black Team for action in Concordia?"

"Two hours. I alerted everybody last night. They're pretty much on standby. You want me to make the call?"

"I'll call you back when I decide. What about Mackiever? Is he home yet?"

"Not yet. I'm running cruisers by there regular. Just his wife's car at the house."

"Where the hell did he go? I expected his resignation call before now."

"He'll turn up. You scared him half to death with that kiddie porn stuff."

Forrest recalled the ashen face of his superior when he saw some of the pictures that could now be found on his home and office computers. "We need him to resign by noon," Forrest said. "I never should have given him forty-eight hours."

"Reckon you ought to go ahead and leak the story? That would flush him out of the bushes."

Forrest thought about it, more instinctively than rationally. He'd always relied on instinct during battle, and that's what this was shaping up to be.

"No," he said. "But I'm going to call a press conference and announce that I've been carrying on a long investigation of a high-ranking state police officer, after members of the Technical Division brought certain workplace computer traffic to my attention. Also the disappearance of confiscated evidence checked out of the evidence room in violation of departmental procedure. When Mackiever hears that, he'll feel the branch creak."

Ozan laughed heartily. "What about them French Quarter boy toys?"

"We'll keep them in reserve. That's the nuclear option."

"He'll crack before noon. All a guy like the colonel has is his reputation. His wife's a big churchgoer, too, and he goes with her."

"That still leaves one loose cannon rolling around the deck. Tom Cage."

"I got no idea where the doc is, boss. It's like he fell off the planet."

A couple of hours ago, Ozan had sent patrolmen to the houses of Peggy Cage's Louisiana relatives, but no one they talked to seemed to know anything, and they'd seen no sign of Grimsby's pickup truck.

"He's still on planet Earth," Forrest thought aloud. "And we've got to find him."

"Are you still thinking about the deal he offered? I figured after Dennis and Penn Cage declared war on us, you'd be ready for the scorched earth plan."

"Not if Dr. Cage can do what he says he can. Anything that ups the body count at this point is asking for more trouble. We've got to stabilize the situation."

"Why don't you just revoke the APB, like Dr. Cage asked for? Then Cage will come to us."

"I can't afford to go that far. Once we revoke that APB, we undermine the image of Dr. Cage as a cop killer. I won't do that until I know he can neutralize the threat from his son and the Masters girl."

"I see."

"Send Grimsby back out to Drew Elliott's lake house in case the doc heads back there. I don't think he would, but you never know."

"Will do. That it?"

Forrest listened to Ozan's expectant breathing over the line. While the Redbone waited, another thought occurred . . . "I wonder if Dr. Cage could have made it back to Mississippi somehow. Did you ever get hold of the data from the Mississippi River bridge cameras?"

"Not yet. Homeland Security told Tech Division they're having trouble with their data links. At first I thought it was legit, but they sure seem to be dragging their feet."

Forrest thought about this. Technical glitches weren't uncommon with high-tech surveillance, but this didn't feel right. Did anyone have the power to interfere in the relationship between the state police and the Department of Homeland Security? If so, their power had to be federal. And last night Ozan had said Kaiser had somehow invoked the Patriot Act. . . .

"Alphonse, I want you to get me everything there is

to know about Special Agent John Kaiser. And I mean everything."

CAITLIN MASTERS HAD RARELY experienced a media frenzy like the one that began Thursday morning, and never in a small market. Henry Sexton's work had penetrated much deeper into the national media consciousness than she'd suspected, and his violent death had caught the attention of journalists from coast to coast. The fact that it was associated with a violent Ku Klux Klan offshoot and unsolved civil rights murders pushed the story toward critical mass. But it was the deaths of Brody Royal, Royal's daughter and son-in-law, Sleepy Johnston, and a Natchez police officer that magnified the story to epic proportions. Reporters were converging on Natchez from every corner of the country, and even from overseas. All the major national papers were sending people, and the TV networks had been calling without letup. Friends Caitlin hadn't spoken to in years were calling to get an inside track on the story, and she simply hadn't time to spare for them.

Special Agent Kaiser had taken over the *Examiner*'s conference room and turned it into an FBI command center. There were now nine special agents spread across Natchez and Concordia Parish, plus a half-dozen technicians of different types, and more manpower was on the way. FBI computer experts had begun the laborious task of trying to reconstruct the deleted scans of Henry Sexton's files and journals from the *Examiner*'s servers. And while they did that, Kaiser had been working with Jamie Lewis in an effort to identify a possible second mole among Caitlin's editorial staff. She felt conflicted about giving the Bureau access to personnel records, but she couldn't risk another security breach while they were working such critical stories.

The proximity of Kaiser and his team had made it tough for Caitlin to contact Toby Rambin, the poacher who'd offered to guide Henry Sexton to the Bone Tree. Three times during the night she'd risked calling the number Henry had given her, but each time she'd gotten no answer. By researching the numerical prefix, she learned that the number was a landline, so she figured Rambin might be out in the swamp plying his trade. Caitlin also wanted Kaiser out of the building so that she could review Henry's most recent journal—the one she'd saved from the burned ruins of the *Concordia Beacon*—but she wasn't about to risk Kaiser discovering that. Along with Henry's journal containing his leads and meditations on the Bone Tree (which, thankfully, she'd kept separate from the group that had been stolen and burned), this was all that remained of the brave reporter's original records. Right now the two Moleskine journals lay atop Caitlin's tall office credenza like holy relics hidden from an invading pagan army. Those journals—along with Toby Rambin—represented her only investigative advantage over the FBI, and the crux of her head start against the army of journalists descending on Natchez.

Just before dawn, Kaiser had told her that he was trying to organize a massive search of the Lusahatcha Swamp, in hopes of locating the Bone Tree and the bodies that might still lie there. This prospect gave Caitlin hives, and she'd felt immense relief when Kaiser slammed down her desk phone and complained that Washington had denied his request. A few minutes later, Jordan Glass confided to her that the director's position wasn't exactly unreasonable. Within twenty-four hours of sending "his best New Orleans agent" to Concordia Parish, half a dozen bodies had piled up, and the director was afraid that more would follow. He wasn't about to organize a military-scale search in Mississippi without more cause than Kaiser had given him so far. He wanted to proceed with "cautious deliberation."

Caitlin wasn't sure Kaiser had given up his plan for the swamp search until word came in that Penn and Sheriff Dennis were sweeping up Concordia Parish's meth cookers and dealers. It was then that she saw what John Kaiser looked like when he truly lost his temper. She didn't envy Penn being on the receiving end of that anger. While Kaiser fumed, she pled ignorance and went about her business, thanking her stars that the Bone Tree would remain undiscovered by the FBI for some time yet.

At 7:45 A.M. Caitlin received one request she could not ignore: a summons to appear before the Adams County sheriff, Billy Byrd, for questioning. After telling Kaiser to send the cavalry if she hadn't returned in an hour, she went out to her car, trusting that Henry's journals would be fine where they were until she returned.

Turning east onto Main Street, Caitlin checked the Motorola cell phone she was currently using—she'd sent one of her advertising people out to replace the Treo 650 that Brody Royal had burned—and saw that she'd received twenty-six text messages in the past fifteen minutes. For the next few days, she was going to have her hands full merely evading friends, much less the remainder of the media locusts. If she couldn't find a way to set her team's course for the day and then get out of the office—preferably to meet Toby Rambin—she would be overrun.

As she turned onto Wall Street, Caitlin saw two TV trucks parked in front of City Hall: one from WAPT in Jackson, the other from WLOX on the coast. After passing the trucks, she glanced right and saw two more parked in front of the courthouse: KNOE out of Monroe and WBRZ from Baton Rouge. There were more to come. When she turned west onto State Street, she saw a big CNN truck parked between the sheriff's department and the district attorney's office, and beyond that was a mini-van that read MPB—the Jackson PBS station.

Slowing to scan the block for parking spaces, Caitlin saw Shadrach Johnson giving an on-camera interview on the steps of his building. As usual, he was dressed to the nines and standing as straight as a man announcing his candidacy for governor. When she looked left, she saw Sheriff Byrd doing the same on the steps of the ACSO building across the street from Shad. At least five reporters had microphones jammed into Byrd's face, and he looked as happy as a pig in slop.

Caitlin parked around the corner near Judge Noyes's chambers, then walked back to the ACSO building. Byrd was winding up the interviews as she approached, and he motioned for her to follow him inside. She soon found herself sitting before his desk like a schoolgirl called to see the principal. Her chair had been chosen to drop male visitors half a head lower than the potbellied sheriff, so she was forced to sit ramrod straight to achieve any sense of being on equal terms.

Squinting down at her like a caricature sheriff from some 1960s western, Byrd announced that he'd brought her there because of complaints filed by the Royal family, who claimed she'd broken into Katy Royal Regan's house and harassed the woman until she committed suicide. However, it quickly became apparent that the sheriff's real objective was discovering why Penn had been riding shotgun in Sheriff Dennis's cruiser during the drug raids. Caitlin only smiled and asked whether Sheriff Byrd planned to make a similar sweep of Adams County. Bristling, Byrd declared that Adams County had no significant meth problem, which was ridiculous, since only the river separated Natchez from Concordia Parish, and traffic flowed over the twin bridges twenty-four hours a day. Caitlin only smiled and kept pressing him.

After Byrd realized she wasn't going to give him anything on Penn, he began questioning her about the stories in the morning edition of the *Examiner*. Byrd was obviously accustomed to women deferring to him, so Caitlin played the game, hoping to discover how much or how little he knew by way of his inept questioning. The risk was negligible. Fooling Billy Byrd was child's play compared to dealing with Kaiser.

Ninety seconds of back-and-forth told her that Byrd knew nothing of the real situation, and she was trying to think of a way to gracefully extricate herself from his office when his cell phone rang. He held the phone away from him and squinted at its LCD, then took the call. After listening for a few seconds, he turned pale and sat up straight.

"How many?" he asked, his face darkening.

Caitlin took the opportunity to check her cell phone, which she'd silenced before entering Byrd's office. The last text message was from Penn. It read: *Disaster at the warehouse. One deputy dead, others critical. I'm ok, headed to C hospital w Dennis.*

Caitlin felt the blood drain from her face.

"Call me as soon as you know more," Sheriff Byrd said, and slammed the phone down on his desk.

"What happened?" Caitlin asked, fighting the urge to bolt from the office.

Byrd cursed and rubbed his forehead. "Sheriff Dennis

just lost a man in an explosion. Looks like a booby-trapped drug warehouse. He's got three more men in critical condition, some being airlifted out."

"I'm sorry to hear that. I know you'll have a lot to do." Caitlin got to her feet and headed for the door.

"Where the hell do you think you're going, missy?"

"Back to work," she said, wondering how long it had been since she heard that archaic term.

"Hold it right there. You've haven't answered one damn question I asked, and now people are dying across the river. What the hell is your boyfriend up to over there?"

Caitlin turned back to the red-faced sheriff. "Helping Sheriff Dennis do his duty. At least on that side of the river, they have a sheriff who *knows* his duty. Not one who wastes his time playing games with the law."

"I'm not playing any damn game."

She walked back to his desk and spoke with cold conviction. "Bullshit. You and Shad Johnson are using the law to settle your personal scores. Penn thrashed Shad in court and an election, and Tom helped your first wife get away from your beatings. You and Shad want to punish them for that." Caitlin nodded for emphasis. "Tell me I'm wrong."

Byrd blinked like a man confronting some animal he'd never seen before. Then his expression hardened and he got to his feet. "You have no idea how much trouble you're biting off."

"I know you're a big man in this county. You've got an army of deputies, your own private crime lab, your jail. And I'm just a newspaper publisher. Nothing to be afraid of, right? But you forgot one thing. Yours is an elected position. The voters put you behind that desk, and they can snatch you right back out of here. My father owns twenty-seven newspapers across the southeast. And I—"

Caitlin jerked back as Byrd came around the desk, his bloodshot eyes blazing. "You sassy bitch. I don't care how much money your old man's got. I run this county, and you're about to find that out."

"You're right about one thing," she said evenly. "I *can* be a bitch. And up till now, I haven't taken much interest in you. But that's about to change. There's a reporter who works for one of our papers in Alabama—a twenty-five-year-old black girl named Keisha Harvin. Last night, Keisha told her boss she was taking her vacation, then drove all night to get here so that she could work on the Double Eagle case. I trained that girl, Sheriff, and she is *hungry*."

Byrd snorted in apparent derision, so Caitlin gave him the rest of it. "I'm going to feed you to Keisha Harvin, Sheriff. She's going to crawl so far up your butt you'll feel like you had a weeklong colonoscopy. Then I'm going to post the results of her investigation for everyone to see. The next time you go to a meeting of the Mississippi Sheriffs' Association, your oldest buddy won't walk within twenty feet of you. Any plans you have for reelection will be as dead as that deputy across the river. Am I making myself clear? Or do you want to harass me some more?"

Sheriff Byrd aimed his finger at her like a pistol and spoke softly, but with implacable malice. "Listen to me, hon. Sometime in the next few hours, I'm going to hear one of two things: either Tom Cage was shot, or he's on his way to my jail. You'd better hope it's the first one. Because if he winds up in my jail, you're going to come back here and *beg* me to go easy on him. Then you'll find out how things really work in this county."

Byrd's mention of Tom's plight had shaken her, but Caitlin pressed down her fears. "Oh, I think everybody knows that already. And they're sick of it."

Byrd's face went purple, but he made no move to arrest her when she turned and reached for the doorknob.

"You'll be back," he said with certainty. "And you'll be begging."

Caitlin opened the door and went out, her heart in her throat.

TOM AWAKENED WITH A desperate need to urinate, but when he opened his eyes, he had no idea where he was, or how to find a bathroom. Only when he saw a large framed portrait of Doris Avery did he remember that he was inside Quentin's house, sleeping on the sofa. The heavy curtains had been drawn, but daylight leaked through at the edges. Tom tried to raise his arm to look at his watch, but pain knifed from his shoulder to his fingertips. He groaned and dropped his arm. He didn't think he could get to his feet, much less make it to the bathroom.

After the pain receded, he looked toward his legs. Someone had laid a quilt over him during the night—Doris, he was sure—and a glass of water stood on the coffee table within reach of his right hand. Three pill bottles stood beside the water glass. As carefully as he could, Tom extended his right hand and pulled the water glass across the open space and leaned it against his hip. Then he pulled the pill bottles near. One held Cipro, and he swallowed one of the big white pills. Another held Vicodin, which he'd prescribed for Quentin one month earlier, according to the label. The third bottle held nitro tablets, but only three, which would not last him long under his present stress load. Tom chewed up a Vicodin despite the bitter taste, then swallowed the fragments. Then he picked up the water glass and drank steadily until it was empty.

Looking once around the large living room, he slid the glass under the quilt and unzipped his fly. After several surgeries, Tom was an old hand at using a urinal, and a tall glass was close enough. After he'd finished, he set the glass on the floor and fell back on the sofa, his back and shoulder seething with pain.

As he stared at the vaulted ceiling, he remembered he was supposed to text Walt a message that he'd reached safety, and also pass on his location. A coded message, he recalled. The problem was, he was supposed to get a new burn phone before he sent it. Given the two alternatives—taking a chance that someone had discovered the numbers of their burn phones, or Walt wondering if the hit man in Tom's backseat had killed him—Tom decided to split the difference.

Without pencil or paper ready to hand, he closed his eyes and thought of the simplest message he could send that would allay Walt's fears. He finally settled on "*Safe. Loc to follow aft new fon.*" Once he had that, he popped the flimsy back off his cell phone and removed the SIM card, then switched on the phone. While it tried in vain to make contact with a nearby tower, he began to key in the message. One letter at a time, he converted each to its alphabetical number, then, as Walt had instructed, multiplied those numbers by the number of soldiers who had died in the ambulance outside Chosin, which was seven. Shutting his mind against the memories of that night, Tom did the math in his head, then entered the digits on the tiny keypad, putting a hyphen between each one. After the message was entered, he reinserted the SIM card and waited for the phone to acquire a tower. As soon as it did, he pressed SEND. When the LCD read "Message Sent," he killed the phone again, then removed the battery and dropped the pieces on the floor beside the couch.

These actions had utterly expended his energy. He felt light-headed enough that he worried about his blood sugar, but he hadn't the equipment to check it. He thought about calling out for Quentin, who was diabetic, but Quentin and Doris were probably still asleep. For a few seconds Tom saw an image of the would-be killer he'd abandoned in the dark cotton field last night: the anger in the man's features, the childlike desolation in his eyes. Had that man reached Forrest Knox yet? Had he even tried? Or had he feared the punishment for failure so much that he'd simply run for his life?

"Time will tell," Tom muttered. Then he slid back on the couch and slipped into unconsciousness.

CHAPTER 20

THE CONCORDIA HOSPITAL emergency room is a Babel of frightened wives, wailing children, and deputies so furious they're ready to kill someone—anyone who might have played a part in the warehouse explosion. In the wake of that lethal blast, the most the hospital staff could do was try to stabilize the injured deputies and evacuate them to the nearest urban hospitals via helicopter. Walker Dennis has been circulating among the families of his men, doing what he can to instill calm, but it's a tough job with one deputy dead and at least one other barely clinging to life. I can't help but think of last night, when an unknown sniper killed Henry Sexton's girlfriend just down the hall from this ER and came close to killing Henry himself. Walker is standing in the door of one of the treatment rooms, comforting the sons of one of his less seriously injured men. I'm trying to decide how long I should hang around when Special Agent John Kaiser marches through the main ER doors, scans the area, then homes in on me.

"What in God's name possessed you to do something this stupid?" he asks, taking little care to keep his voice low.

"We obviously didn't believe it was stupid," I counter, motioning for him to quiet down.

"I told you last night how risky this kind of attack would be. And pointless."

"We didn't attack anybody. Sheriff Dennis simply enforced the law, which has been a neglected practice in this parish of late."

Kaiser glances at Dennis, whose back is to him, then looks back at me. "Oh, bullshit. You hit the Knoxes, and they hit you back. Nothing surprising about that."

"I'd bet money Forrest Knox was surprised this morning."

Kaiser shakes his head in exasperation. "Do you realize I had the director sold on a massive search of the Lusahatcha Swamp? He was talking to the Mississippi National Guard commander and the sheriff of Lusahatcha County. He'd even contacted Dwight Stone to consult about the 1964 search. If you hadn't started this fiasco, we might have found the Bone Tree by sundown today. We might have had Jimmy Revels's and Pooky Wilson's remains. But now? There's no way I can leave to run that effort. I'm stuck doing damage control. Only this time the damage is so great, I don't know if it's fixable."

"We're not your problem, John. You're working a massive case that could take months or years. We're going after some drug dealers and crooked cops. It's that simple."

"More bullshit. You're going after the same targets I am, only you're doing it in the stupidest possible way."

My temper is starting to rise, which tells me Kaiser might be taking his life into his hands if any of the nearby deputies are listening. "We're taking the shortest distance between two points, which in my experience is a good strategy. Besides, after last night's conversation, I thought you were after Carlos Marcello, not the Knoxes."

At last Kaiser lowers his voice to an angry whisper. "I told you I was after Forrest Knox. It's all the same case anyway." Before the FBI agent can vent more fury, Sheriff Dennis walks over from the treatment room. "Can I help you, Agent Kaiser?"

Kaiser manages to rein in his anger slightly. "I'm sorry for what happened to your men, Sheriff. But I have to ask: what did you really hope to accomplish with these raids?"

Dennis squares his shoulders like a man preparing for a fight. "Aside from upholding the law and protecting the people of this parish?"

"You've confiscated some precursor chemicals, and you've got a truckload of low-level perps locked up. Do you really think they're going to give up the Double Eagles? Do you think they even know anything *worth* giving up?"

Walker gives a surprisingly calm shrug. "Since they're facing mandatory minimums, I'd say there's a good chance that one or more will talk."

Kaiser shakes his head. "You have no idea what you're

up against, Sheriff. The punks you arrested this morning don't know enough to jail one Double Eagle, and they
don't know jack shit about Forrest Knox."

"I reckon we'll see," Dennis drawls. "But I'm betting at
least one of them knows more than you think."

"Bad bet, Sheriff."

"John," I cut in, hoping to prevent further escalation,
"I don't think we're going to find much common ground
this morning. You ought to think about vacating the
premises. Some of these deputies are . . . in a highly ir-
ritable state of mind."

"I'll go you one better," Dennis says aggressively. "I'm
gonna call in the Double Eagles for questioning today."

The FBI agent clearly can't believe his ears. "You mean
get warrants for their arrest?"

"No, no," Walker says. "Just ask 'em nicely to come in
for a chat."

Kaiser actually laughs. "How are you going to contact
them?"

Dennis shrugs again. "It's a small parish. I'll figure a
way. If they've got nothing to hide, they shouldn't mind
coming in."

"I'll save you the trouble, Sheriff. Snake Knox and
Sonny Thornfield are in Texas, at Billy Knox's fishing
camp. It's on the Toledo Bend Reservoir. And they won't
come back here to talk to you, no matter how nicely you
ask them. Especially after this morning. Because they *do*
have plenty to hide."

Sheriff Dennis works his lower lip around his dip of
snuff. "Well . . . I reckon I'll ask anyway. Can't hurt none."

"You're wrong," Kaiser says in a grave voice. "If all you
guys were doing was jumping the gun on a drug case, I'd
shut up and go back to New Orleans. But you're throwing
a wrench into one of the biggest conspiracy cases the Bureau's ever been involved with, and I can't stand by while
you do it."

Dennis cuts his eyes at me, but I offer nothing. "You
wanna explain that statement?"

When Kaiser doesn't answer, I say, "Our junior G-man
thinks he's working the JFK assassination."

Dennis's eyes narrow. After squinting at Kaiser for fifteen seconds, he says, "Why not the Lindbergh baby?"

Kaiser angrily shakes his head. "What you guys don't know . . . Jesus."

"Do you *see* what's going on in this parish?" Walker asks, waving his hand to take in his casualties and their families. "I've got good men down, and one dead. Bastards who murdered people forty years ago still killing people today. And they've got their kids helping them. When I saw you draining the Jericho Hole yesterday, I figured we were on the same side. But it's starting to look to me like you're just in the way."

"That's because you've got blinders on," Kaiser says, not the slightest bit intimidated. "Penn, could I speak to you alone?"

"I don't think so. We're in Sheriff Dennis's jurisdiction. I'm just the mayor of Natchez, as you reminded me last night. And I'm not really interested in the Kennedy assassination right now."

"No?" Kaiser lowers his voice again. "What if I told you that one of the rifles we took out of the ruins of Brody Royal's house was a 6.58-millimeter Mannlicher-Carcano, just like the rifle Oswald fired from the Texas Book Depository? It's the exact variant, 40.5 inches long."

I think about this for a few seconds. "I'd say you found yourself a replica that Brody bought to add to his little collection. Like a model of the starship *Enterprise*."

"That Carcano's no replica. It's a genuine Italian surplus war rifle that was probably made within a few months of the one Oswald bought through the mail in 1962."

"Does it have a serial number?"

"It does. It also has fingerprints on it."

"How is that possible? The fire would have—"

"This rifle wasn't in Royal's basement." Kaiser's eyes shine with triumph. "We found it in a gun safe in the old man's study, on the main floor of the house. Everything in that safe was in pristine condition. Agents from our Legat in Rome have contacted the Italian government to trace the records. The odds are that Royal's rifle was shipped to the U.S. for retail sale, like most of the other Carcano surplus in the fifties."

"Great. But I'm not interested."

"Penn, how sure are you about the type of rifles you saw in that special display case?"

To my surprise, Sheriff Dennis seems to be listening closely.

"I know neither was a Mannlicher-Carcano," I tell Kaiser. "Any Texas prosecutor has talked to enough JFK conspiracy nuts to know what Oswald's rifle looked like. The Carcano has an extended trigger housing and a fore-stock that nearly reaches the end of the barrel. It's basically a crappy weapon. The rifles I saw in that display case were expensive hunting rifles with quality scopes. Surely you've identified them by now?"

"We think so. But let's double-check." Kaiser pulls a folded piece of paper from his back pocket and shoves it at me. "Have a look and see if you can ID the two rifles you saw in that case."

While Dennis stares with knitted brows, I take the inkjet-printed sheet. It shows a column of eight rifles in full color and good resolution. At first they look very similar, but the closer I study them, the more differences I see.

"I'm pretty sure this is the one that had the MLK date under it," I say, pointing to a lever-action hunting rifle. "What is it?"

"Winchester Model 70," says Kaiser. "Classic sniper rifle. What about the one dated November twenty-second?"

After narrowing the remaining weapons down to two, I point at the one that looks most like the image from my memory. "This one."

Kaiser gives a half smile. "Right both times. That's a Remington Model 700. A hot load in that rifle drives a bullet close to four thousand feet per second, depending on the caliber. Perfect for the Kennedy head shot. And that's one of the rifles we found. Minus the incinerated wooden parts, of course."

"Then why the hell are you making such a fuss about the Mannlicher-Carcano from Royal's study?"

"Because it raises so many questions. And if I'm right, it's going to connect the Royal-Knox-Marcello group directly to Oswald and Dallas. I'll bet you any amount of money that the final shipping destination of that rifle was Louisiana, Mississippi, or Texas."

"I told you, John. Not interested."

"Hold up a second," says Sheriff Dennis, his eyes on Kaiser. "Are you saying Brody Royal had something to do with the assassination of President Kennedy?"

"I am. But that's confidential case information, Sheriff. And not just Brody Royal."

"Who else? The Knoxes?"

Kaiser shakes his head. "I shouldn't say more at this time."

"He thinks the Knoxes and Carlos Marcello had a hand in it," I say. "Crime of the century."

Kaiser glares at me, but Sheriff Dennis is studying the FBI agent intently. "You're serious, aren't you?"

"Do I look like a joker to you, Sheriff?"

"No, sir, you don't. And I know a little bit about the Marcello clan. If you really believe you can solve the Kennedy case, I can respect that. But you've got to grant me the same courtesy. You probably don't know it, but I lost a cousin to these bastards in a drug buy gone bad a couple of years back. A dirty cop killed him. And Forrest Knox covered for that bastard. I mean to make those Knoxes pay, you hear? We've put up with their crap for too long in this parish. I drew the line this morning, and there's no going back. So, I wish you well with your work. If there's any way I can help you with your case, I will. But I won't stop my own work on the Double Eagles. And you'd do well not to try to interfere. Okay?"

Sheriff Dennis doesn't wait for an answer. He turns and walks back through the door to the treatment room, where one of the deputy's sons is crying.

"Small-town sheriffs," Kaiser mutters.

"Didn't I hear you started out as one?"

He gives another exasperated sigh.

"We're moving forward, John. You can either get in the game with us or sit on the sidelines and watch. Either way, Forrest Knox is going to feel the heat."

Kaiser steps close to me. "If you keep pushing Forrest—and Snake and the others—this morning's casualties won't be anything but a warm-up for the main event. Take a word of advice, Penn. Hide your family in a deep hole. Because there's nothing Forrest won't do to stop you."

In my mind I see Annie and my mother looking worriedly after me as I left Edelweiss and headed out to my car. "I'll do that."

Kaiser turns without another word and walks toward the exit. Before he passes through, he turns back and says, "Let me know if Dennis gets an answer from the Double Eagles on that voluntary questioning."

"I thought you said there was no chance."

"Yeah, well . . . this is Louisiana. Crazier things have happened." He shakes his head miserably, then walks out.

I follow Walker into the treatment room and find him sitting with the two young boys. Their wounded father is wearing an oxygen mask over his mouth. Walker is holding the hand of one of the boys. His face is wet, and his big neck is bright red. With embarrassment I realize that the wife is saying a prayer beside the bed. I bow my head.

After she finishes, Walker rises and leads me back to the main ER area.

"How *are* you going to contact the Eagles?" I ask him.

"I'm gonna call Claude Devereux, their lawyer. That Cajun bastard has always been too slick for his own good. If he doesn't cooperate, I'm gonna find a way to lock him in the trap with the rest of them."

This is actually a good idea. "Kaiser's probably right about Snake and Sonny being in Texas. Surely Devereux will tell them to stay put?"

"If they stay in Texas, that tells us something, doesn't it? Meanwhile, I'll be grinding away at the punks we brought in this morning. Sooner or later, one of them's gonna want to trade something."

"Do you want me to help you with the questioning?"

"Not after what happened at the warehouse. Too many people will be watching me. You steer clear for today. If somebody decides to flip on a Double Eagle, I'll call you. Fair enough?"

"Yeah. I need to tighten up my family's security anyway, and I've got a huge backlog of work at City Hall. I'm sorry again about your men."

I start to leave, but Walker takes hold of my arm, then steps even closer, his eyes hard on mine. "How come you didn't tell me about that JFK angle?"

"Because it's just a pig trail. Even if Kaiser is onto something with that rifle, it's ancient history."

Dennis clucks his tongue twice. "Murder's never ancient history, Penn. You know that. And that one caused more harm than most. A lot more. If there's a chance of finding out who really killed the president that day in Dallas—or why—I'm all for it. I'll do anything I can to help."

"I hear you, Walker."

The sheriff lowers his big head another inch. "Don't keep anything else from me. Okay?"

"I won't."

After a long moment, he nods, then walks back to his injured deputy's cubicle.

Small-town sheriffs, I say silently. *Jesus.*

CHAPTER 21

WALT GARRITY HAD been staking out Forrest Knox's house since before dawn, and he was tired of waiting. Knox's wife was asleep inside, which prevented an immediate search, and there was also a large pit bull penned in the backyard. Forrest himself had driven from Valhalla to Baton Rouge at about 5 A.M., and Walt had followed the whole journey on the GPS tracking scope Mackiever had given him. The new toy was nice, but Walt was worried that his target intended to sleep the morning away. That might seem improbable to some people, given the present situation, but in Walt's experience career criminals often possessed the ability to sleep through anything.

As Walt cruised past Knox's well-tended ranch house, his burn phone pinged. Picking up the TracFone, he saw a text message from Tom. The message contained only a sequence of numbers, as Walt had instructed him to use, but the mere sight of those numbers relieved some of the strain Walt been suffering since he'd heard Tom had a hit man tied up in his backseat.

Pulling out of the affluent neighborhood, which stood less than a mile from the university, Walt turned into a service station and parked near the car wash. He felt reasonably secure in the truck, since he'd stolen a new plate from a similar model in a Lowe's parking lot. Satisfied that no one was watching, he took a notepad from his bag and began decoding Tom's message. A minute later, he read the words: *Safe. Loc to follow aft new fon.* He wished Tom had gone ahead and given him his location, but his old friend was wisely waiting until he had a 100 percent secure telephone. Taking one of Tom's cigars from his shirt pocket, Walt lit the expensive beast, then settled back in his seat and watched the entrance to the quaint little haven that sheltered the most dangerous cop in the state.

FORREST KNOX SAT AT the Dell computer in his home office, working on notes for the press conference he would call at noon. Inkjet printouts of child pornography pulled from Colonel Mackiever's work computer lay spread on the right side of his desk. Forrest should have been at headquarters by now, but something was nagging at him down deep. The obvious problems were bad enough. Henry Sexton's death had triggered a media storm, and Caitlin Masters's newspaper coverage had only magnified it. (Today's online edition of the *Examiner* hovered just behind the Word document containing Forrest's notes for the press conference.) Thankfully, Masters had focused primarily on Royal and the Double Eagles, and stopped short of accusing Forrest of anything. But that wouldn't last.

What had kept him at home were the two phone calls he'd received a half hour earlier. The first was from a contact he had in the New Orleans federal court. The woman hadn't identified herself, but she hadn't needed to. She simply told Forrest that the FBI had filed National Security Letters requesting the phone and e-mail records on Forrest Knox, Alphonse Ozan, and two other officers in the Criminal Investigations Bureau. Forrest had hung up without a word, but he couldn't pretend the call hadn't rattled him. Had he not had that contact, he would never even have known the Bureau was digging into his past. Before he could fully process this news, the second call had come, this one from one of the wealthiest developers planning the post-Katrina transformation of New Orleans. Brody Royal's death—and the scandal brewing in its wake—had hit those multimillionaires where they lived, and their answering message to Forrest was clear: get Mackiever out of his job ASAP and tamp down the trouble in Concordia Parish by any means necessary. If he couldn't, their support for him would evaporate like smoke.

A loud barking from behind the house startled Forrest. Traveller, his pit bull, was letting him know he was running late. Forrest forced himself to ignore the dog and focus on the Word document. He was glad when his encrypted phone distracted him from the computer screen.

"What is it?" he said, reading a sentence that needed to be a lot better than it was.

"Mackiever's back home," Ozan informed him. "About ten minutes now."

"Any idea where he's been?"

"Nope."

"I should have had him followed from New Orleans."

"Spilled milk, boss. You think he'll go in to HQ today?"

"I wouldn't." Forrest glanced down at the naked little boy on his desk.

"He's a proud old bastard," Ozan said. "He's liable to go over to the governor's office to personally hand in his resignation."

"She's ready to accept it."

"What about your press conference?"

Forrest suddenly knew what he was going to do. "I've changed my mind about that."

"What do you mean? You gonna wait? Give him the full forty-eight hours?"

"No. I'm going to leak the full story."

"Who you gonna give it to?"

"Don't worry about that. Just call me when you hear it's circulating."

"Got it."

"No word on Dr. Cage?"

"Negative. Bermuda fucking Triangle."

Forrest grunted. "Keep looking. Out."

He pressed END, then deleted the document he'd been writing. Taking his regular cell phone from his pocket, he called a former vice detective he'd partnered with long ago. The man answered after three rings.

"Yo, Colonel. You the boss yet?"

"Not quite. Are you still tight with that woman at the *Advocate*?"

"Sure."

"And the TV station? WAFB?"

"You know me. Finger on the pulse."

"I know the pulse that finger likes to take."

The detective barked a laugh. "I ain't changed, partner. Who does? You want me to pass something on?"

"Yeah. But not on the phone. I'll give you an envelope."

"Sounds dangerous."

"You won't believe it when you see it."

"Who's the target?"

"The cowboy colonel."

The detective was silent for a moment. "Sounds like I'm doing you a real service."

"You know I'm big on gratitude."

"That I do, old buddy. How about one of those weekend hunting trips with *diablitos* and whores included?"

"Do this and you're comped."

"Oh, hell yeah. Where's the handoff?"

Forrest thought about it. "How about the Home Depot parking lot, College Drive? I'll be in my cruiser. Twenty minutes."

"That's quick, but I can make it. Can't wait to see it."

Forrest heard the floor creak behind him, then a sharp scream. He knew without turning that his wife had made the sound, but it took him a moment to realize why. When he did, he swept the photos on his desk into the top drawer. His wife was accustomed to seeing grisly crime scene photos, but the kiddie porn that Ozan and some of the guys in vice had pulled off a server in the Netherlands was truly sickening.

"What *was* that?" his wife gasped.

"A case," he said gruffly.

"I don't want that in our house."

He looked up at the woman who knew his own proclivities about as well as any woman who still walked the earth. But even for someone of her experience and disillusionment, those photos were beyond the pale.

"I don't either," he said.

"Why do you have them?"

Forrest decided to test his strategy. "Tech Division pulled these off Colonel Mackiever's computer. He's been downloading them at work for months."

His wife's hand flew to her mouth. "I don't believe it. Griffith Mackiever?"

He nodded once, watching her closely.

"Dear Lord." She shook her head as though she could

never accept the idea, but then she said, "I guess you never know anybody, do you?"

Forrest shook his head, but he was smiling inside.

KEEP WALKING, WALT TOLD himself, moving steadily up the street with his picklocks nestled in his inside jacket pocket. *Straight and steady, like an old man out for a constitutional.*

Knox had left the neighborhood first, his wife about five minutes later. But the most welcome sight had been the silhouette of the pit bull in the backseat of the state police cruiser. Given this gift from the gods, Walt had decided that the best tactic would be to simply walk along the street with a normal gait, then turn up Knox's driveway as though he were a meter reader or repairman. Mackiever had assured him that no call from Knox's home security system would alert anyone. It was wired directly to state police headquarters, and Mac had assigned his nephew to disable the connection through the departmental computer system.

Knox's driveway was fifteen feet ahead.

Walt emptied his mind of doubt, then turned and walked up into the carport, through the picket gate in the breezeway, and into the domain of the now-absent pit bull. He was an old hand at B&Es, and French doors were particularly easy. With the alarm system neutralized, the dog was the only thing that could have complicated his entry. Hearing no alarm, he unlocked the door and moved quickly inside.

Walt's initial plan had been to search the house itself, then try to break into Knox's home computer. But as he passed the door of what appeared to be a home office, he saw something he never expected: the computer screen glowing softly, a Microsoft Word document showing.

Charging across the room, he stabbed the keyboard to keep the screen saver from popping up. If it did, a password would almost certainly be required to re-access the computer. As he stood there panting, he wondered at his good fortune. Surely Knox had not left his computer unprotected?

The wife, he thought. *His wife must have used the com-*

puter right after he left. Tensing, Walt minimized Word and checked to make sure he wasn't logged on to the wife's account, but no—the account name was *NBFKnox.*

"Nathan Bedford Forrest," Walt said softly. "Who's your daddy, asshole?"

He sat down and began working through Knox's file directory. His folders contained the usual stuff: work letters, tax records, to-do lists. Walt wanted to go through the e-mails, but Knox's Gmail account required a password. Conscious that the wife might come back at any time, Walt moved on and searched for all images stored on the hard drive. Knox only had a couple of hundred photos on the computer, and Walt didn't see anything that looked suspicious. There was some pornography, but it was typical heterosexual fare. Moving on, Walt searched for video files.

This yielded more interesting results. Knox had quite a few videos that appeared to be training films for state troopers, familiar stuff to Walt. Many dealt with shooting techniques, while others depicted SWAT instructors clearing buildings during hostage situations. Walt was nearing the end of the list when a video that looked very different expanded to fill the screen.

The grainy image showed an open dirt field with a line of trees in the distance. After about five seconds, two horses with men on their backs galloped into the frame. The men carried long spears, and they spurred their horses toward a black blob in the middle of the field. Suddenly the blob disintegrated into several animals racing in different directions.

Hogs, Walt thought.

Two more horsemen galloped on-screen, with smaller blurs running at their flanks. *Dogs.* From the motion of the dogs, he guessed they were pit bulls or blackmouth curs. Real hog hunters put vests on their dogs so the boars wouldn't rip their guts out. One good rip with those tusks could easily eviscerate a dog. Walt had seen it.

The four horsemen quickly singled out the largest hog and, with the help of the dogs, began trying to hem it in. After several feints and charges that dropped one smaller dog, the big razorback cut between two horses and broke for the tree line. Just as Walt thought the hog might make it, another horseman charged from the trees and with expert skill forced the hog to check its momentum and turn 180 degrees.

By then the other horses were closing in. When the hog turned and began slashing at the dogs with its tusks, the fifth horseman drove his spear down into its ridged back, between the shoulder blades, like a matador finishing off a bull. The razorback staggered, took a few steps, then collapsed and lay still as a boulder. The dogs went mad, circling the kill, but the men only climbed leisurely off their horses and shook hands with one another.

Drawing back a couple of inches, Walt squinted at the man who had killed the hog. Despite the graininess of the image, he was pretty sure that man was Forrest Knox.

Walt nodded slowly, recognizing that they were up against a certain kind of man. There was nothing illegal about hunting hogs with spears. Some crazy sons of bitches hunted them with *knives*, leaping out of trees to make the kill. From somewhere deep in his memory, the word *atlatl* rose in Walt's mind. That was what the old-time hunters called the tool that normally hurled the spear Knox had used during the hunt.

He clicked on the last video in the folder. Compared to the hunting footage, the final video was about as exciting as a television test pattern. It showed a small house in the dark, and it appeared to have been shot through a telephoto lens. Unlike the hunting film, this video had sound. Walt heard human breathing, as if the man shooting the film was breathing right into the microphone. As Walt stared at the screen, he noticed it was raining. Unlike Hollywood rain, these drops were difficult to see.

Nothing else happened. The rain continued to fall, and the cameraman kept breathing. Just as Walt was about to switch off the video, he realized that there were numerical markings superimposed over the scene. They were *range markings*. While he tried to figure this out, the front door of the little house opened and three young black men walked out. Two were carrying a box, while the third carried a semiautomatic rifle, a CAR-15. As the men walked, Walt realized there was water lapping around their feet.

What the hell . . . ?

"Target visible," said a voice with a Cajun accent,

and Walt nearly jumped out of his skin. "Two hundred twenty-one meters."

"Acquiring," said a second voice, as cool as a fighter pilot's. "Target acquired."

On-screen, the three black men—oblivious to the camera—moved toward an SUV parked next to the house. The one with the carbine unlocked the rear hatch of the SUV. Walt recognized a high-tech scale sitting on the box in the other men's hands. The kind of scale used by high-volume drug dealers.

"Cleared to engage," said a third voice. "Engage when ready."

The breathing stopped.

The flat crack of a supersonic bullet told Walt that a rifle had been fired. A silencer had muted the muzzle blast, but the exploding head on-screen relegated that thought to something he would only recall later.

"Reacquiring," said the shooter.

"Fire at will," said the second voice.

The two young men carrying the box had whipped their heads around at the sound of the crack, but they had no idea what had happened. By the time they looked down and saw their companion lying facedown in the water, the shooter had fired again. A second man shuddered, then staggered back and fell into the black water.

The third man dropped his end of the box and ran for the driver's door of the SUV. Walt expected a flurry of shots, but none came. The SUV backed up with frantic speed. As the driver stopped to shift from Reverse into Drive, a third bullet shattered his window and blasted half his head across the passenger seat.

"Targets neutralized," said the emotionless voice.

"Thirty points," said the third voice. "Outstanding."

The picture froze, and the sound stopped.

Walt sat staring at the screen, his heart pumping like a fist squeezing his trachea. What had he just seen? His gut told him military or police snipers operating during Hurricane Katrina, but he had no way to be sure. As his mind whirled in confusion, he heard a noise from the interior of the house.

Reaching down through the neck of his shirt, he pulled out the leather thong that held his derringer around his neck. Then he moved quickly into the hall. He heard the noise again, a loud clunk that he now recognized as the sound of an icemaker.

"*Fuck,*" he breathed, going back into Knox's office.

Taking his seat again, he rifled through Knox's drawers in search of a flash drive. In the third drawer, he hit pay dirt. A half-dozen thumb drives lay in a pile of old pens, yellow highlighters, and other office junk. Walt suppressed the urge to pocket them all, and instead inserted an orange one into the USB slot on the Dell. A minute later, he had a copy of the sniping video. He copied the hog-hunting video for good measure, then pocketed the flash drive and carefully replaced everything on the desk as he'd found it.

He was walking to the hall door when he heard a car engine on the street outside. The car seemed to slow near the Knox driveway, leaving Walt frozen like a statue in a cemetery, not daring to breathe. *I'm too old for this shit,* he thought. By the time the car drove on, Walt had abandoned his plan to search the house. He needed to get that video to a safe place before fate intervened and made it something the police found in a pocket on his corpse.

As he made his way back to the French doors that led to the patio, his derringer in his hand, a breathtaking inspiration struck him. A smile stretched his mouth. *I'm holding the gun I used to kill Trooper Darrell Dunn. The murder weapon. Ballistics can prove it. How perfect would it be for that weapon to be found hidden in the home of Lieutenant Colonel Forrest Knox?*

Walt stopped walking and looked around for a place to hide the gun.

CHAPTER 22

CAITLIN HAD HOPED to find Kaiser gone when she returned from Sheriff Byrd's office, but as she pulled into the employees' lot, she saw his black Crown Victoria parked against the wall. Pulling around the building, she parked in the visitors' lot and headed for the front door.

As she passed through it, she came upon some sort of altercation between a haggard-looking woman of about seventy-five and Jackie Cullen, the paper's receptionist. Jackie gave Caitlin a quick shake of her head, as though she should hurry past, but before Caitlin could manage it, she heard the overwrought woman say that no one but Caitlin Masters could possibly help her, and she wasn't leaving what she'd brought with anyone else.

Something plaintive in the woman's tone made Caitlin pause. Without taking time to think, she said, "Maybe I can help you, ma'am. What is it you need to see Ms. Masters about?"

"Oh, for God's sake," the old woman said, whirling on her.

As soon as the frustrated eyes lit on Caitlin's face, they changed. "You're her," she said, her face softening. "Aren't you?"

The old woman hadn't a dab of makeup on her wrinkled face, and she was clutching a manila envelope to her chest like it held the deed to her ancestral home. She looked like nothing so much as a woman from one of Dorothea Lange's photographs from the 1930s. A Dust Bowl wife. Caitlin forced a smile and said, "I am. And you are . . . ?"

The woman closed her eyes and wavered on her feet as though about to collapse. Then Caitlin saw tears trickle from the corners of her eyes.

"Virginia Sexton," said the woman. "I'm Henry's mother."

Caitlin froze for a second, then rushed forward and put her arms around Mrs. Sexton to support her. The receptionist's mouth dropped open, but Caitlin didn't bother to explain. She was scanning the newsroom behind Jackie, searching for FBI agents. Seeing none, she took Mrs. Sexton by the wrist and led her into the nearby advertising office, which was about the only room John Kaiser was unlikely to enter.

"I need the room," Caitlin said to the two salespeople sitting in the office. "Don't tell anybody I'm in the building, and tell Jackie to say she hasn't seen me. Got it?"

The younger of the two women nodded as she left the office.

"I'm so sorry you had to wait," Caitlin apologized, leading Mrs. Sexton to a rather uncomfortable chair. "We get a lot of cranks demanding to see me or the editor, so the receptionist is overly cautious."

"I understand," said Mrs. Sexton, breathing too fast. "You can imagine what kind of nuts showed up at the *Beacon* to give Henry an earful."

Caitlin smiled and nodded, but she felt tears on her own cheeks. For the thousandth time she saw Henry disappear into a roaring fireball, giving his life to save hers. "I can," she said, wiping her eyes. "Mrs. Sexton, I have more respect for your son than any reporter I ever met."

As the aged eyes took her measure, Caitlin felt the ruthless appraisal of someone who has nothing to gain or lose. Virginia Sexton had already lost everything, and nothing could compensate her for it.

"I'm sure you do," said Mrs. Sexton. "I tried to warn him, you know. Two, three times a week I'd try to talk him into letting go of all that history and just getting on with life. But he couldn't turn it loose. He was like a loggerhead snapping turtle. Stubborn, like me. I wouldn't admit it while he was alive, but it's true."

Caitlin didn't know what to say, so she simply vocalized what was in her heart. "Mrs. Sexton, Henry gave his life to save mine last night. I wouldn't be here if it weren't for him. Literally. I feel so guilty about that."

The old woman nodded, obviously bereft. "You feel guilty? I took him my car and that shotgun last night. I went to his room and helped him out of that hospital bed . . . helped him fool the monitors." She dabbed at her eyes, looking away from Caitlin. "I used to be a nurse, you see. So don't blame yourself. If I hadn't done those things, my boy would still be alive."

As Caitlin reassured Henry's mother, her eyes settled on the manila envelope still clutched in the wrinkled hands.

"What was it you wanted to see me about?"

Mrs. Sexton slowly took the manila envelope away from her chest and set it on her lap. "I haven't been able to sleep since last night. I've been going from room to room, cleaning up. I've always kept Henry's old room pretty much like it was when he was a boy, even though he's a grown man. After his father passed, I never really needed the space, so . . . well, I don't know. I have some happy memories of the things in that room."

"Is that where you found the envelope?"

The woman looked down as if she'd already forgotten what she held. "No. Henry had this in his weekend bag at the hospital. It was stuffed under the plastic bottom. I found it when I was unpacking the bag, and . . . I made the mistake of looking inside. It's a letter to you. My first instinct was to go out back and burn it in the trash can."

Inwardly, Caitlin shuddered.

"But Henry wouldn't have wanted that. I know he chose you to carry on his work after they beat him up, so I decided to bring it to you. There's pure evil in this envelope, and no mistake. I don't think you should fool with it. But I imagine you're like my Henry was. You've got to get at the truth of things, even if it kills you."

"I'm afraid you're right."

Caitlin stepped forward and gently lifted the envelope from Mrs. Sexton's hands. The old woman seemed to shrink within her skin when she let go of the paper. However much she hated Henry's work, she understood that giving it up meant giving up the surviving essence of her son.

"I'm so sorry for what happened," Caitlin said uselessly. "And I'll never let the world forget what Henry did."

Mrs. Sexton shook her head. "Henry didn't care about that. My boy didn't do what he did to see his name in the paper, like some."

Caitlin's cheeks burned, though she didn't get the feeling the comment had been directed at her.

"He just believed everybody deserves the same break. I don't know where he got that idea. Not from his daddy, that's for sure. And I learned a long time ago, if you're going to wait for this world to be fair, you're going to be waiting in the grave."

"Yes, ma'am."

The old woman started to leave, but Caitlin touched her arm and checked the foyer first, to make sure no FBI agents were close. Before she let Mrs. Sexton go, she said, "Did Henry's, ah, *partner* know about this envelope?"

"You mean that Sherry Harden?"

Caitlin nodded.

"I don't know. She might have brought some of those papers up there to him. I don't know how else he would have got them. But she couldn't have seen the letter. He wrote it after Sherry was shot, and he woke up in the special hospital room. It doesn't matter now, does it? She's beyond doing anything about it."

Unless she told Kaiser about the papers before she was killed. But if she had, surely Kaiser would have found them after Henry escaped from the hospital.

"I suppose I'd better go to her funeral," Mrs. Sexton said, "if only for her boy."

"Do you have any idea when Henry's service will be?"

"I reckon Saturday. We have some people up in Kansas who'll probably want to come. I haven't even been to the funeral home yet."

For a moment Caitlin thought the poor woman would finally collapse, but she didn't.

"Mr. Early told me there's really nothing left of Henry," Mrs. Sexton said softly. "Bones and ashes. It's like he was cremated already."

Caitlin didn't need to be told this; she'd seen it happen. "If there's anything you need done, or taken care of—anything at all—please call me. I mean that, Mrs. Sexton. If there's any question of funds—"

"Henry had a little insurance," the old woman said, lifting her chin with pride. "I know you mean well, but we're not destitute. We bury our own."

Caitlin blushed again, but as soon as Mrs. Sexton left

the office, she closed the door and hurried back behind the advertising desk. With Kaiser in the building, the journey to her office was too risky. This office door had no lock, but with FBI agents and techs roaming the newsroom and halls, this was as safe a place as any in the building.

Caitlin heard the blood rushing in her ears as she opened the manila envelope and spread its contents across the desk. There were only a few sheets of paper inside. An inkjet-printed photograph grabbed her attention and held it. A craggy-faced man with hollow eyes and cracked, tanned skin stared out at her with unsettling intensity. He reminded her of John Brown, the wild-eyed abolitionist. Or maybe Abraham Lincoln without a beard. She turned over the page and saw block letters written in pencil: *ELAM KNOX*. After looking once more into the wild eyes, she checked the rest of the pages.

One long, folded piece of paper turned out to be a hand-drawn Knox family tree, beginning in the late 1800s. An FBI document that looked to be the heavily redacted version of the 302 detailing Jason Abbott's 1972 interview about the Double Eagles and Forrest Knox came next. Then finally she found four sheets of notepaper covered with Henry's now-familiar script, though in this case it looked as though he'd been drunk while he wrote. The first page began "Dear Caitlin." She centered the letter before her and began to read at lightning speed.

> *Dear Caitlin,*
> *Forgive me if I ramble. I'm weaning myself off the pain drugs, but my mind's still foggy. Sherry's dead, and the FBI's put me in an office they converted to a hospital room. But I'm not going to stay here. I've thought a lot about the last three days, and either Royal or Forrest Knox had to be behind this attack. I believe it was Royal, and I'm going to confront him tonight. I've sat on the sidelines too long. I don't know if I'll survive the encounter or not, so I'm leaving this for you.*
>
> *John Kaiser came to see me earlier today, before you. I trust his motives, for the most part, even though he's FBI. He told me some things about the Knox family, which you'll find in a separate note,*

*and I told him most of what Glenn Morehouse told
me on Monday. About Jimmy and Luther being
murdered as part of a plan by Carlos Marcello to kill
RFK, about Brody's part, Frank Knox's death, all of
it. Kaiser looked shocked, but when he answered, he
shocked me even more. He asked whether I thought
Carlos could have hired Frank Knox to kill John F.
Kennedy in 1963.*

*As dumb as it may seem to you, I'd never really
considered this possibility. You've read my files,
so you know that on the day Frank founded the
Double Eagles, he talked about killing JFK, RFK,
and MLK. It seems obvious now, but at the time
Morehouse told me about the RFK plan, I was totally
focused on Brody Royal. For so many years I'd been
working to find out who killed Albert Norris that I
missed the bigger picture.*

*Once Kaiser raised the JFK idea, I couldn't stop
thinking about it. The relationship between Frank
Knox and Carlos Marcello dated to well before the
Bay of Pigs. If Marcello wanted the president dead,
Frank would have been a natural choice, so long as
Carlos trusted him. Carlos obviously did, because he
went to Frank when he wanted to murder Robert
Kennedy in '68.*

*Now we come to the point. Though I suspected
Kaiser was right, I didn't tell him any more than I
originally had. But I knew more. When Morehouse
called me back Monday night, he told me something
I didn't even put in my journal. After he told me
about the RFK plan, he told me Frank Knox had
something on Marcello, something he'd kept as
insurance, to protect himself in case things ever went
bad between them. Remember, Brody used to lend the
Double Eagles to Marcello as muscle on Florida real
estate deals, so there was a long history there. And it
was when I went to New Orleans to check out those
deals that somebody sent me the photo with the rifle
scope printed over my face. At the time, I figured
that was Royal protecting his crooked deals, but now
I think he or Forrest was keeping me away from the
old conspiracy.*

When I asked Morehouse what Frank had kept for "insurance," he said it was a letter or document of some kind. Morehouse had seen it once, but he couldn't read it because it was written in a foreign language. Snake once told him it was Russian, but he didn't know for sure. Whatever the paper was, he said, it dealt with something so big that everything else paled in comparison—even the RFK plot. I thought that was bullshit, and I told him so. If there was anything bigger than the RFK plan, nobody would have left any paperwork. Morehouse told me that whatever the paper was, Frank kept it at the Bone Tree, so nobody could find it.

The night I talked to Morehouse, I made my first and only contact with Toby Rambin, who promised he could take me to the Bone Tree. But at that time I wasn't thinking about Frank's "insurance." I was thinking about all the bodies that might have been dumped at the Bone Tree. Jimmy and Luther, Joe Louis Lewis, Pooky. It was only after Kaiser talked to me today that I realized how important Frank's "insurance" might be, and that it must have to do with John Kennedy.

You've got Toby Rambin's number now. I was stoned on Dilaudid when I told you about it, but I know you got it, because when I checked my cell phone, I saw you'd changed his last name and number in my contacts list. You've been a naughty girl, but I'm in no position to criticize. I held back a lot from Kaiser myself. If I'm honest, I guess down deep I'm as ambitious as you are.

If these pages reach you, then I'm probably not around anymore. If so, take them with my blessing and do what you can to get to the bottom of all this. If Kaiser finds them I guess that's the second-best outcome. I'm tired now, and I've got a journey ahead of me. Maybe a fight, too. However it goes, you take care of yourself.

    Henry

P.S. Don't try to find the Bone Tree alone. You've got too much to live for.

Caitlin looked up from the papers, her eyes wet and her heart beating fast. The letter in her hands was a voice from the grave. Henry had felt alive to her as she read his words, but he was not. He was dead, now and forever. He had foreseen the possibility, and he had passed his torch to her. No one else alive knew about Toby Rambin and his offer, and no one else would—

Her heart lurched as the door opened and Jackie Cullen stuck her head inside.

"Agent Kaiser is looking for you," she said. "I told him I hadn't seen you, but I wouldn't count on privacy for long."

"Thanks, Jackie. Go."

Caitlin gathered up the pages and photos and slid them back into the envelope. Then she flattened the brass closure tabs, went out into the lobby, and opened the door to the hall that led to her office. She was ten steps away when John Kaiser came around the corner beyond her door and waved.

"You look like you just translated the Rosetta stone," he said. "Want to let me in on it?"

He stopped and waited beside her office door. Flustered speechless, Caitlin went into her office and dropped the folder on her credenza as if it meant nothing, then sat behind her desk.

"Everything okay?" Kaiser asked. "Seriously. What's going on?"

"Nothing," she said, too sharply. "I'm just functioning on zero sleep."

"What's in the envelope?"

"Business crap. Advertising reports. The paper shuffling doesn't stop just because I'm working on the story of a lifetime."

"That's for sure," Kaiser said, taking a seat in the chair opposite her. "I've got one of my agents doing nothing but filing reports for the rest of us. A total waste."

"What can I do for you?" Caitlin asked. "Have you found my mole?"

"No. But we will. I should tell you that the original deleting of files was done by 'User 23,' and that ID belongs to your editor, Jamie Lewis—"

"Jamie!"

"Relax, he didn't do it. He's a rich, liberal Yankee, and

I questioned him myself. Somebody hacked into Lewis's intranet account, which I'm pretty sure is well beyond the abilities of your missing press operator, Nick Moore."

"Do you have any idea who it could have been?"

"Not yet. It could be an employee, but it could also have been someone who hacked in from outside. You just leave the mole hunt to us. Why don't you go home and grab a nap?"

"Are you kidding? This town's filling up with reporters so fast that we'll run out of hotel rooms. I'll sleep when this story's finished."

The FBI agent crossed his legs and toyed with a shoelace as if he had all day to sit there.

Caitlin shifted uncomfortably in her chair. "What's on your mind, John?"

"Henry Sexton's journals."

She kept her features immobile.

"I've been watching our tech try to reconstruct your server's drives, which is a bit like watching children try to reconstruct shredded pages one strip at a time. We're making progress, and getting a pretty good idea of how the journals lay out. There's just one problem."

"What's that?"

"None of the pages seem to describe any of Henry's work over the past two months. I can only conclude that we must be missing a journal."

Caitlin pursed her lips and pretended to think about this.

"Did Henry say anything to you about his most recent one?" Kaiser asked bluntly.

"No," she answered truthfully. After all, she'd discovered that journal on her own. The Moleskine had been in Henry's pocket when he was attacked outside the *Beacon*, and she'd found it in the ashes of the *Beacon* fire later that night.

"It just seemed to me from reading your stories this morning that you had a lot of detail on the Jimmy Revels case. The RFK plot, all of that."

"I've got a good memory."

Kaiser smiled. "Also the murder of Pooky Wilson. The crucifixion. Royal told you that happened at the Bone Tree?"

"That's right."

"But he didn't say where the tree was? Other than the Lusahatcha Swamp?"

"It wasn't that kind of conversation."

A thin smile. "No. I imagine not." The FBI agent looked at her for a long time without speaking. "I spent seven years in the ISU, Caitlin—what they used to call the Behavioral Science Unit. And this just doesn't add up. Henry Sexton was a creature of habit, like all of us. There has to be a last journal, and it's got to be somewhere. It's too bad that sniper's bullet killed his girlfriend."

Caitlin made a sympathetic noise and blanked her mind. As impossible as it was, she felt strangely sure that if she thought of the slightly scorched Moleskine lying atop the tall credenza behind her, Kaiser would see it too—in his mind. As he studied her, she thought, *I should be put in jail. I'm like a raging id with a body—no governing conscience at all.*

"Was there anything else?" she asked.

Kaiser's eyes stayed on hers. She could almost feel the pressure of his gaze. "Have you talked to Penn recently?" he asked.

"Only for a second. It sounded pretty bad across the river."

"Penn's not too happy with me right now. Nor I him. We both think each other's priorities are screwed up."

Caitlin shrugged. "We've all got different agendas. The way of the world, right?"

"Jordan said the same thing."

"Smart woman. Wait, that was redundant."

Kaiser rolled his eyes.

"I figured I'd see a lot of Jordan today," Caitlin said, fishing.

"You probably would have, if I weren't here. She's a little upset with me right now." He glanced at his watch. "She's still a pro, though. She's photographing everyone who shows up at Glenn Morehouse's funeral as we speak. Did you know she's scheduled to go to Cuba tomorrow, to photograph the Castro brothers?"

"She mentioned it."

"She said something about maybe pushing back the trip for a day, which I couldn't believe. Any idea why she'd do that?"

Caitlin remembered giving Kaiser's wife a backhanded

offer of employment, but she never thought the photographer would really consider it. Jordan Glass had multiple Pulitzers in her bag, and a Robert Capa award to boot. *Is this story getting* that *big?* she wondered.

"None. You'd better ask her that."

"You'll probably see her before I will," Kaiser said. "I'm heading out to take care of some other business. I've rented an empty warehouse in Vidalia to use as an evidence storage site. So much stuff came out of the Jericho Hole that we're going to sort, identify, and tag everything we can here, then ship selected pieces to the crime lab in Washington."

"Can I send a photographer over for some shots?"

Kaiser gave her a wry smile. "No, but I'll have Jordan shoot a few snaps for you."

"Thanks. And keep your eyes open. I don't think your credentials would stop the Knoxes from taking a shot at you."

Kaiser got to his feet. "You're right about that. But I'd be a lot more worried if I were Penn or Sheriff Dennis. Or you," he added, giving her a meaningful look.

He went to the door, but after he passed through, he turned back and said, "Don't try to solve this thing on your own, Caitlin. What you wrote this morning was read by a lot of people, some of whose lives are now at risk because of you. And every one of those bastards knows where you live and work."

She nodded as though this were old news to her. "I'll be careful."

Kaiser gave her a casual salute, then walked down the hall.

Caitlin desperately wanted to read the rest of the papers inside Mrs. Sexton's envelope, but she opened her top right drawer to put them away until she could be sure Kaiser would not return. A shining new silver Treo 650 lay inside the drawer. Stuck to the smartphone was a yellow Post-it with a note from Allison Oswalt, the advertising sales girl she'd sent to replace her favorite device.

Here's your new phone. You can find your new number inside. Your security code is the year I came to work here. Enjoy!

Caitlin picked up the gleaming phone and gave it a grateful kiss. At last she had a secure line she could count on, at least for a while. Now she could call Toby Rambin from inside the building—and talk to him if she reached him!

While the Treo powered up and searched for a tower, she thought about Henry's letter. Was it really possible that the Bone Tree—which the FBI didn't believe existed—concealed evidence of Double Eagle involvement in the assassination of John Kennedy? Henry Sexton had never been a muckraker or sensationalist; on the contrary, his reputation as a serious journalist had been above reproach. And Henry seemed to believe that Morehouse had told him the truth. Of course, Henry had been under the influence of Dilaudid while he wrote that letter—

The Treo had acquired a tower. Caitlin glanced at her office door, then dialed Toby Rambin's number—which she had memorized—and waited. Yet again it rang in vain, as it had the previous three times. She wondered whether Rambin might have fled the state after hearing about Henry's death. She couldn't blame him if he had.

"Come *on*," she muttered. "Do poachers really work that hard?"

How long until Kaiser leaves the building? she wondered. She was dying to take Henry's Bone Tree journal down from atop the credenza. Instead, she removed a page at random from the manila envelope, a piece of hospital stationery. At the top Henry had written *ELAM KNOX* in bold pencil lines. She started to read the tightly packed paragraphs, but a knock at her door made her jump. She shoved Henry's stuff into her drawer, then went to the door. Though she'd expected Kaiser again, she found Jamie Lewis waiting in the hall.

"I've got some news," her editor said. "Can I come in?"

She backed up and motioned him in. Lewis shut the door behind him.

"On the mole?" she whispered.

"No, sorry. But something pretty radical just came over the wire. The *Baton Rouge Advocate* is reporting that a highly credible source inside the state police Criminal Investigations Bureau is claiming that Colonel Griffith Mackiever, the superintendent of state police, has been downloading explicit child pornography onto his work computer for months. There's been no official confirmation, but several politicians are calling for a public investigation, and one state congressman has already demanded Mackiever's resignation. Do you think that's related to Dr. Cage's story in any way?"

Caitlin thought about it. "It's bound to be. Forrest Knox wants that job, and he's already the chief of the CIB. He's got a certain amount of support across the state, especially in New Orleans. He's also behind the hunt for Dr. Cage, and he's the son of the founder of the Double Eagles. You dig into that, Jamie. Don't give it to somebody else."

Before he could reply, another knock sounded at the door. Caitlin rolled her eyes, and Jamie opened the door a crack as though to send the supplicant away. But then to her surprise he pulled it wide.

Keisha Harvin stood there, her face glowing with vitality, her eyes with quick intelligence. "Have you got a sec?" Keisha asked. "I want to pitch you something."

"Take a seat," Caitlin said, beckoning her inside. "Pitch away."

As Keisha perched on the edge of the chair across the desk, Caitlin reflected that there was a world of difference between twenty-five and thirty-five. Harvin wore her hair in a tight, no-nonsense bob, but she still managed to look glamorous. The Alabama native wore practical shoes, yet her jeans were Sevens, and her top expensive silk. Caitlin knew from the months she'd spent training Harvin that the reporter pinched her pennies to be able to afford such style. Keisha had always possessed the same fire Caitlin did—the desire to make her mark in her chosen field—but now she seemed driven by an even more powerful passion, the hunger to right a wrong against her people.

"Right now Jamie has me working background on Sheriff Billy Byrd, and that's cool. I get it."

Caitlin almost blushed with guilt. She'd texted Jamie to assign Keisha that job on her way back from Byrd's office. "But you really want to work on something else."

Keisha inclined her head.

"Which is . . . ?"

"I've reviewed everything that's been reported so far,

and I've talked to the staff about the angles they're working. And given that . . . it's become clear to me that one part of the story is being completely ignored."

"What's that?"

"The crime that started it all. The murder of Viola Turner."

Caitlin felt her cheeks heat up. She felt shock, anger, embarrassment . . . and each emotion had hit her on at least two levels. Various replies to Harvin's request rose in her throat, but Caitlin clamped her mouth shut before any could escape. Because Keisha was right: Viola's story *was* being ignored. And there could only be one reason for that. Caitlin's staff had sensed that she'd marked it off-limits. Silently perhaps, but absolutely. Otherwise people would have been all over that story. The chief murder suspect in the Viola Turner case was *the mayor's father*, for God's sake. The problem for her staff was, because Caitlin and Penn were engaged, the mayor was the boss's future husband.

It struck Caitlin then that Jamie had known what Keisha was going to say before she walked through the door. He might even have advised her to do it, thinking Caitlin would be reluctant to blast a young black reporter for raising the sensitive subject. Not that it mattered, of course. Now that they'd brought the unpleasant reality to her attention, she could not ignore it.

"Okay," she said to Keisha. "How do you want to handle it?"

"I'd like to interview Dr. Cage. Obviously that's not possible at this time, so my first fallback would be to interview Mayor Cage."

Caitlin took a deep breath and kept her voice under control. "I honestly don't know if Penn will talk to you. Even though you work for me, he'll probably take the same position he would with any reporter. While his father's life is on the line, he won't discuss it."

"Will you at least ask him?" Keisha pressed.

God, this girl has balls, Caitlin thought. She wondered if she'd had that kind of courage at twenty-five. *Yes*, she decided, *I did*.

"I'll ask him," she said. "But I'd get busy finding a second fallback, because I don't think Penn will talk to you."

"I'm trying to reach Viola Turner's family right now."

"Who? The sister?"

"And the son. Lincoln Turner."

Caitlin's stomach fluttered. She forced a smile, then tapped her hands on the desktop. "That sounds like a plan. Anything else, guys?"

Keisha gave her an emotionless smile. "Nope. Thanks."

After the reporter went out, Caitlin tried to pretend like nothing unusual had happened, but after a few seconds, she gave up. She stood and looked Jamie in the eyes. "You set that up, didn't you?"

"No."

Caitlin held the eye contact for a few uncomfortable seconds, then went to her refrigerator for a Mountain Dew. After taking a long drink, she said, "She's right, of course. We have been ignoring the story, and it's no accident. I don't like being a pawn in the political games of Shad Johnson and Billy Byrd. But . . . we have to cover it."

"I agree. If we don't, we look biased."

She gave a reluctant nod. After another sip of Mountain Dew, she said, "Tom didn't murder Viola, you know."

"Of course not," Jamie said, much too quickly.

"You'll see. It may take some time, but you'll see."

Jamie sighed as if letting out a long-held breath. "I hope you're right, boss."

CHAPTER 23

AFTER LEAVING THE Concordia hospital, I checked in at City Hall and took stock of the work I'd ignored for the past three days. In the face of that, I decided to go over to the district attorney's office and see how the events of the past twenty-four hours had affected our DA's view of the pending murder prosecution against my father. The TV trucks parked outside the courthouse and DA's office should have told me what to expect. After I brusquely marched through the knot of journalists, Shadrach Johnson made me wait half an hour to see him, and now I wish I hadn't wasted my time. According to Shad, Dad has the same chance of reaching his custody alive as any other cop killer—about one in a hundred—but if he somehow survives, Shad intends to try him for Viola's murder as though the events of the past three days have no bearing on that case. The man knows how to hold a grudge, I'll give him that.

As I leave the DA's office building, the cold wind brings me wide awake. I trot down the steps through the shouting reporters without a word, turning left toward City Hall, which abuts the southeast face of the courthouse. Just as I think I've cleared the feeding frenzy, someone catches hold of my arm. I whirl in anger, then find myself facing an elderly black woman huddling in a jacket.

"Yes, ma'am?" I say. "How can I help you?"

"Isobel Handley," she says with a smile. "I want to know when you're going to do something about the schools, Mayor. You got elected saying you were gonna fix 'em, but right now it's a crying shame how few children who go into the first grade make it through the twelfth for graduation. And you've been in office two whole years!"

The reasons for this state of affairs are both simple and unimaginably complex, and I certainly don't have the resources to go through them on a cold sidewalk. Not today, anyway. But conversations like this one are the daily fare of a mayor.

"I'm talking about the *public* schools," the woman goes on. "Not the private white schools where the only black kids are football players."

"Yes, ma'am," I say hopelessly. "I'm working as hard as I can on the issue, I promise you."

"If your little girl wasn't in a private school, you'd work harder."

"Mrs. Handley, I—"

"You don't have to explain, baby, I understand. But you take a stick to them selectmen and supervisors, if you have to. That's what they need. Sometimes I think the schools were better before integration. At least we learned the fundamentals, and we graduated knowing how to read."

There's no point trying to explain that I have no authority over the county supervisors or the state board of education. "Sometimes I wish I could do exactly what you suggested, Mrs. Handley. Now, you'd better get out of this cold. And Merry Christmas to you."

At last she smiles. "You too, Mayor. God bless. And don't pay these reporters no mind."

I look toward the door of City Hall as I move on, hoping to avoid more conversations, but that's too much to ask. This time it's not a journalist or member of my constituency who buttonholes me, but John Kaiser. The FBI agent is sitting on the steps beneath the lamppost, obviously waiting for me.

"Don't you have anything better to do?" I ask. "A meeting with Oliver Stone, maybe?"

He makes a sour face. "I've got some news for you."

My blood quickens, more out of dread than hope. "My father?"

"No, the Double Eagles. Leo Spivey is dead."

"Who the hell is Leo Spivey?"

"The Eagle who owned that booby-trapped warehouse. A hotel maid found his body in a room across the river. He appeared to have put a bullet through his own head. The hits just keep on coming."

"Was it really suicide?"

"Fuck, no. Knox's goons got him. Sheriff Dennis's men

are over there now, working the scene as a homicide. To the best of their abilities, anyway."

"Maybe Spivey killed himself rather than be punished by Knox or his buddies."

Kaiser shrugs. "Either way, the cause is the same. You and Dennis hit the Knoxes' drug operations. Soon we'll have bodies piling up everywhere."

"I know you wanted everything to keep running nice and smooth while you worked on recruiting a star witness against Forrest, but my dad doesn't have six months to wait on you."

I start to move past him, but Kaiser stands and blocks my way.

"One more bit of news. Our Legat agents in Rome tracked down the serial number of the Mannlicher-Carcano from Royal's house."

"And?"

"It was shipped into the Port of Los Angeles in 1962, one shipment after the lot that contained Lee Harvey Oswald's rifle. Our next stop will be finding the U.S. retailer. That might take a little time, but the director's with us now, and we're pushing hard."

"The director doesn't think you're nuts?"

"It's pretty hard to deny physical evidence."

"I told you earlier . . . I'm not interested."

"And if we track that rifle to Louisiana?"

I turn up my hands in exasperation. "What do you want me to say? My only concern right now is my family. If you want to spend your time trying to crack the Kennedy case, have at it."

"Do you feel the same way about the murders of Albert Norris, Pooky Wilson, and the others?"

"We know who killed those guys now, or who ordered the hits, anyway. Brody Royal, and he's dead. If you want to nail Snake Knox and the other Eagles, you need to get on *our* side. Because Walker and I are going to be squeezing those guys' balls before you even get your plan into first gear."

Again I try to move past him, but Kaiser raises the flat of his right hand to my chest. "I know you don't want to listen to me. But will you listen to Dwight Stone?"

God, is this guy pulling out the stops. "You think a phone call from Stone is going to make me reverse course on busting the Double Eagles?"

"Not a phone call. Stone's flying in today on a Bureau jet."

This actually stuns me. "*In*? Here? For what?"

"To talk to you. He's been trying to find a way down here since Tuesday night, when I told him about the bones coming out of the Jericho Hole. He was looking into chartering a plane. But you seeing those rifles in Royal's basement and hearing Royal say the Knoxes killed Pooky Wilson at the Bone Tree convinced the director to authorize a Bureau flight to bring Dwight down here to consult. He's only going to be here for a few hours."

"Why such a short stay?"

Kaiser takes a long breath. "Because he's dying, Penn."

A sick feeling hits me high in the stomach. "What?"

"Liver cancer."

"I had no idea."

"You know Dwight. Old school. A lot like your father, I imagine. He's scheduled for an operation tomorrow. This visit is the Bureau's way of giving back a little of the respect Hoover took when he fired Stone in '72. Before Dwight goes under the knife."

"Goddamn it, John. When's he coming in?"

"He ought to be here by six P.M. Can you spare him an hour of your time?"

Kaiser's revelations are almost too much to process quickly.

"The way I heard it," he says, "it was Stone who made it possible for you to solve the Delano Payton case seven years ago."

I nod. "He did more than that. Stone saved my life up in Colorado."

"So will you come by?"

I have no choice, and Kaiser knows it. "Yeah. But only because it's him. I think you guys are crazy to believe those rifles are real."

"The evidence will tell, one way or the other."

"What does he want to ask me, John? He's not going to change my mind about anything."

"I don't know. I doubt any man alive knows more about the JFK case than Dwight and his colleagues. He was posted in Mississippi and Louisiana multiple times during the sixties, so there's no telling what he might know about the Double Eagles, Carlos Marcello, or even your father. I suspect Dwight wants to give you the Working Group's theory of how what happened in Dealey Plaza grew out of Louisiana. Once you hear that, you might be as reluctant as we are to jeopardize any chance of achieving justice in that case."

"Does Dwight understand the jeopardy my father's in now?"

"Of course. And he's trying to convince the director that Dr. Cage should be brought under Bureau protection as a witness in the Kennedy investigation."

I should have known Dwight would be doing what he could for me. "What are the chances of that happening?"

"Better with Dwight involved. But I won't lie to you. No sane FBI director wants a public battle with a state police agency over a reputed cop killer, especially with the legal grounds for protective custody being the JFK assassination. That's a publicity nightmare. The point is, Stone's doing all he can to help your father. So am I."

I restrain my temper with some difficulty. "If you really were, you wouldn't ask me to waste an hour humoring an old man with an obsession."

Kaiser gives me a sad look. "You're not seeing this thing straight, Penn. Your fear about your father has distorted your perception. You're like a guy looking through the wrong end of a pair of binoculars. Seventy percent of all Americans believe John Kennedy died as the result of a conspiracy. Justified or not, people believe this country swerved into darkness on that day, and we've never recovered from it."

"Sixty percent of Americans believe in UFOs. Fifty percent believe AIDS was invented by the government."

The FBI man grabs my left arm. "You're pretty glib, aren't you? After Dallas . . . almost anything became possible. I lived through one of the results in Vietnam. So did Forrest Knox. So before you discount this as a waste of time, consider what the fuck you're talking about."

In the face of his burning intensity, I raise my hands in symbolic surrender, but Kaiser's having none of it.

"Over the past forty years, the JFK assassination has

become the vessel of America's darkest anxieties. If we can cut through all that crap and give the people the truth—in all its banality, once and for all—then we'll have done a lot more than atone for the sins of the FBI. We'll have cut a tumor from the soul of this nation."

Kaiser obviously feels great passion about his subject, but passion means nothing on the topic he's discussing. "You're wrong about the unknown, John. People need a mystery on which to project all their free-floating paranoia. If you pull back the curtain on the Kennedy assassination, people will just project all their angst onto something else."

"Maybe I've got more faith in people than you do."

"Maybe so. Politics has changed me, I'll admit that."

I pull my coat tighter and scan the streets and windows surrounding the courthouse and City Hall. Not much Christmas cheer in the air today. "JFK's been pretty battered as a symbol, John. He's no longer King Arthur cut down in his prime. He's more like a spoiled prince we never really knew. I feel like people are almost angry at him now, for not living up to their dream of him."

Kaiser shakes his head. "They still want the truth."

"Heady conversation for the steps of City Hall, huh?" I say, trying to lighten the tension. "I need to get upstairs to work."

"But you'll come see Dwight?"

"I will. I owe him that. I'll call you about five thirty?"

"Thanks. And please give me a heads-up if you and Sheriff Dennis decide to make any more arrests today."

I nod acknowledgment but make no promises.

As the FBI agent walks back to his car, I walk up the six steps to the door of City Hall, then pass through the lobby and jog up the staircase to my office on the second floor.

"You alone?" asks Rose, my secretary, peering around me at the hallway door.

"Sure, yeah."

"That FBI agent is gone?"

"Yes. Why?"

"You've got visitors," Rose says in a cryptic tone.

I raise my eyebrows.

"Go back to the lounge. I didn't want to put them in your office, in case Agent Kaiser came back."

Irritated by her caginess, I walk back to the little kitchen we call our lounge. There, I find Dr. Drew Elliott and Nurse Melba Price waiting for me. Drew looks very uncomfortable, but Melba appears relieved to see me.

"What's going on?" I ask. "Have you heard from Dad or something?"

They look at each other. Then Drew says, "We've got something to tell you, Penn. Your father spent yesterday at my house on Lake St. John."

At first I think he's telling me he's just discovered this, but almost immediately I realize that this is a confession. "When did you find this out?"

"We knew Tuesday night." Drew's guilty countenance does nothing to ease my anger or sense of betrayal. "I'm sorry, man," he goes on. "Tom asked me for help, and he was wounded. I didn't feel I had a choice."

My face is hot, and my heart has begun pounding. "Wounded how?"

"Through-and-through gunshot. Left shoulder. I treated him, and Melba nursed him until last night."

My eyes switch to Melba Price. "And you couldn't call me?"

Melba closes her eyes in what appears to be shame.

"Tom specifically asked me not to," says Drew.

"So? You think he's in his right mind right now?"

"He appeared to be."

"Jesus . . . we've been friends since we were kids."

Drew turns up his palms. "Tom's my partner, Penn. I'm sorry. I see now that it was probably a mistake. Especially since . . ."

"Since what? What's happened?"

"I don't think he's there anymore. Melba was with him until last night, like I said, but he sent her away."

Dad's nurse looks at the floor and nods.

"Melba?" I prompt.

She looks up at me with eyes no one could argue with. "He needed my help. You know your father. I wasn't about to say no."

"Did he give you any idea of his plans?"

"Captain Garrity drove to Baton Rouge to meet with the head of the Louisiana State Police. I know that much."

"Why'd he do that?"

"I think he was going to try to get that APB revoked. For the killing of that trooper. Captain Garrity knows the head of the state police down there."

"I see. And what about Dad?"

"He was waiting for Captain Garrity to get back. But the captain was late, way late. Dr. Cage made me leave a little after midnight. He was worried we might be found by those old Klansmen."

That Drew and Melba would keep Dad's whereabouts from me when his life was at stake is almost incomprehensible. And yet . . . why would I expect anything else? Their willing deception tells me just how many options my father must have when it comes to finding aid and comfort in his home territory.

"Why don't you think he's still there now?" I ask.

"I've been calling the house phone all morning," Drew explains. "No answer. Tom could be there, of course, but my gut tells me no."

"Mine, too," Melba agrees.

"Maybe Walt got back and they moved on?"

Melba slowly shakes her head. "I think Dr. Cage believed Captain Garrity was already caught. Maybe even dead."

"Jesus. I need to get over there."

"Do you want me to come with you?" Drew asks. He reaches into his pocket and brings out a key. "I brought this."

"No." I pluck the key from his hand. "You've done enough already."

"Penn—"

"At least you told me now. Christ, you guys. Swear to me that you'll call me if he contacts you again."

They both nod with the sincerity of the guilty.

With a heavy sigh, I hurry to my office for the keys to the city car.

CHAPTER 24

WHEN WALT SAW Griffith Mackiever sit down opposite him in the Waffle House on Lee Drive, he knew he was looking at a broken man. The restaurant was nearly empty, and Walt had taken a corner booth, but Mackiever spoke in a cracked whisper so soft that Walt could hardly make out his words.

The gist was that Forrest Knox had leaked the story about Mackiever downloading child pornography, and he'd supplied images to the press. Reporters started calling the colonel's house immediately, and within half an hour TV trucks had laid siege to his front yard. Mac had only reached this rendezvous by sneaking through his neighbor's backyard and having his nephew pick him up, and he was anxious to get home to his wife as quickly as he could. He'd only come because he'd put Walt in harm's way and felt he owed it to him to personally release him from any obligation.

"What do you mean?" Walt asked, trying to keep the anger out of his voice. "You sound like you're giving up. You're not going to resign, are you?"

"What else can I do?"

"Fight, goddamn it."

"How do you fight a fire hose of filth? Knox has been laying this computer trail for months, using my actual computers. How can I prove I didn't do those searches?"

"Did you do them?"

"Of course not!"

"Then you can prove it. You've just got to calm down enough to approach it systematically."

"Walt, I don't have that kind of time. If I don't resign, Knox will have those male prostitutes talk to the press. They'll swear I hired them. I'm sure Forrest has access to all my movements for the past year, and all the dates will jibe."

"Fuck him. You need to stab that prick in the gizzard."

Mackiever cradled his face in his hands. "With what?"

Walt took the flash drive out of his pocket and laid it on the Formica between Mac's elbows.

"What's that?"

"A video of snipers murdering three black teenagers during Hurricane Katrina."

The colonel dropped his hands and blinked in disbelief. "Are you kidding?"

"No. They're trained snipers, either military or police. I'm betting state police. The shooter used a silencer."

A light came into Mackiever's eyes. "Can you see their faces?"

"No. The footage was shot through a scope. Probably a spotting scope. But you can hear voices on the tape."

"Clearly enough to recognize them?"

Walt thought about it. "I think so. With all the high-tech tools available now. If you're lucky, one of the voices on the tape is Knox's."

Mackiever was clearly tempted. "If that's true, it would not only destroy Knox, but the reputation of the state police."

"Beggars can't be choosers, Mac."

Mackiever looked miserable.

"Don't give Forrest any clue that you have this, or he'll have time to make up some bullshit story to explain it."

The colonel looked at Walt a couple of more seconds, then hung his head.

"What the hell did you expect when you brought me into this?" Walt demanded, looking around the restaurant. The fry cook behind the counter was staring at them.

"I thought I had forty-eight hours," Mackiever said. "That's what Knox told me in New Orleans. But he didn't even give me twelve."

"He's being squeezed. His drug operations got hit in Concordia Parish this morning."

"Really?"

Walt nodded. "I'm betting Penn Cage is behind it. Knox isn't invincible, Mac. But you can't fight a guy like that halfway. It's kill or be killed, just like the old days."

"I just wish we had something lethal, something that would damn Forrest alone."

Walt thought about the derringer he'd planted in Knox's house. Then he thought about the man he saw before him. Looking at the bloodshot eyes and resigned face, he saw nothing of the stalwart Ranger he'd once known.

Walt patted his own chest. "You remember what I always keep around my neck here, don't you?"

Mackiever nodded dully. "A five-shot derringer."

"That's right. Let me run something by you. I was thinking . . . if you were to order a search of Knox's home, and the search team found the gun that killed Trooper Dunn hidden there . . . that would change the game quite a bit. Wouldn't it?"

Mackiever's eyes had gone wide. "That derringer was the gun you used on Dunn?"

"You're asking the wrong question, buddy."

"You'd go back in and plant it?"

The fucking thing is already planted, you amateur, Walt thought dejectedly. "I told you, this is kill or be killed. Survival."

"How could I explain telling the team what to search for? How would I know or even suspect the gun was there?"

"Get the judge to write the warrant as generally as you can. You know how to play that game."

Mackiever's face told Walt that his old friend was simply overwhelmed. "Walt . . . I appreciate all you've done. And I'm going to take the video, get it analyzed. But trying to pin Trooper Dunn on Forrest would be just about impossible. He was nowhere near that crime. And why in God's name would he keep the gun if it was a murder weapon?"

"Possession's nine-tenths of being screwed," Walt said bluntly. "You're overthinking this."

"You're oversimplifying. Knox has been planning his play for months. We're not going to beat him by improvising at the last second. For one thing, you could get caught going back in there to plant the gun."

Walt considered telling Mackiever that the derringer was already planted, but he decided against it. "Knox is at headquarters right now. I checked the GPS before I came in."

"His wife could walk in on you."

"A meteor could hit the Waffle House. What's happened to you, Mac?"

The colonel gripped his coffee mug and swirled it on the table. "The world isn't what I thought it was. I knew things were bad, but . . . shit, forget it. What about your derringer? Is there any way they could trace it back to you?"

"No. I got it from a friend in Texas who used it as a throwdown gun for years. It's as cold as they come."

Mackiever considered this for close to a minute. Then he shook his head and said, "I'm not going that way. I've still got a couple of allies in my corner, if this porn thing doesn't drive them away. A senator and I teach Sunday school together."

Walt reached across the table and squeezed his old friend's wrist. "You're hoping for a miracle, Mac. In my experience, those are damned far between in this life."

Mackiever stared at him in silence for a while. Then he threw a ten on the table, pocketed the flash drive, patted Walt on the shoulder, and walked out of the diner.

THE SECOND TIME TOM awakened, he saw Doris Avery's lovely face hovering just above his own. She might be an attorney, but he saw the compassionate concern of a natural nurse in her brown eyes.

"How do you feel?" she asked.

Tom tried to say, "All right," but his throat was parched, and all that came out was a croak.

"I brought you more water." Doris held a straw to his lips. "How's that shoulder?"

Tom drank several sips from the straw. After he'd finished, he said, "Not too bad, actually. I woke up earlier and took a pain pill."

"I saw you did," said Quentin Avery with a laugh.

Tom turned his head to the right and saw his old friend sitting in his motorized wheelchair on the other side of the coffee table.

"Couldn't make it to the bathroom, huh?" Quentin asked, pointing at the glass on the floor.

"Sorry about that."

The lawyer grinned. "Oh, I can relate, baby."

"Is anything wrong?" Tom asked. "Has anything happened?"

"No. Everything's quiet."

Tom breathed a little easier.

"You don't feel like you have a fever anymore," Doris said. "Are you hungry?"

"I could eat. But I don't want to be any trouble."

Quentin laughed heartily. "We're way past that, old friend."

Doris said, "How about a grilled cheese sandwich?"

Tom's stomach growled.

"I'll fix one," she said, giving Quentin a meaningful look. "I'll leave you two to talk."

"Fix two," Quentin said.

After she left, the wheelchair hummed, and Quentin piloted it around the table until he sat near Tom's feet. Now Tom could talk to him without having to crane his neck.

"How are you, really?" Quentin asked. "Medically speaking."

Very carefully, Tom tried to move each of his limbs. The pain was bad, but if he didn't have a fever, he was a lot better off than he could have been.

"My heart's still beating. That's about the best I could hope for."

"And the shoulder?"

"Better than I have any right to expect."

Quentin's eyes filled with concern. "No shit, man. How bad is it?"

Tom forced himself to smile. "I'll be all right. After the army, gunshots are something I know a lot about."

"You're not a twenty-year-old GI anymore."

"A lot of grizzled old vets got hit in Korea. They made it."

"Grizzled old vets of thirty-five."

This time Tom's smile was natural. "I treated indigenous Koreans, too. Plenty of old men survived having their legs blown off by land mines."

"I'd still feel a lot better with you in a hospital."

As Tom looked back at his old friend, he realized what was about to happen. "You're leaving, aren't you?"

Quentin nodded slowly. "I've got a doctor's appointment in Jackson, but that's not the real reason. I read your future daughter-in-law's stories in the paper when I woke up. A man named Sonny Thornfield has made a statement that he saw you and Walt Garrity kill that Louisiana state trooper."

"That's a lie. He didn't see anything."

"That's good to know. But if the police come here and find you, I'll lose my law license, even if I don't go to jail. And Doris could lose hers as well. I can't do you any good if I can't represent you in court, Tom. And if guns are what you need to protect you, I'm betting you know men a lot better with them than I am."

"I understand, Quentin."

"Let me finish. You're welcome to use my house as long as you need to. If Doris and I aren't here, no one can argue that we aided and abetted. My deepest wish is that you'd let me arrange a surrender to a district attorney, or even a U.S. attorney. But you're not ready to do that, are you?"

"Not yet, I'm afraid."

"All right, then. When you get ready to fight this case, or plead the charges down to something manageable, you call me."

"I will."

Doris's shoes clicked on the floor, and she brought in a plate with a hot cheese sandwich on it. She set the plate on the coffee table, then some iced tea beside it.

"Thank you," Tom said.

"Where's mine?" asked Quentin.

"You get a salad."

Quentin groaned, but then he said, "Doris put your car in our garage, so nobody can see it from the air. And there's a laptop computer on the floor by your pee glass. We've got Wi-Fi in the house. You ought to be safe here for as long as you need to stay. Just promise me you'll call somebody if that shoulder starts getting bad."

Tom sat up a little and gave them a brave smile. "I've got some people I can call. I'll have help here soon. You two already went beyond the call of duty. You saved my life."

Doris laid a warm hand on Tom's bearded cheek. "You think hard about your options, Tom. Don't sacrifice yourself for the wrong reason."

He didn't know what to say to that.

Quentin reached out and squeezed Tom's foot beneath the quilt. "I'll be thinking about you. And you think about me. I've still got one good murder trial in me. Two, if there's no other way."

"I'm counting on that. You two take care."

With that, Quentin squeezed his foot once more, then whirred out of sight.

Doris sighed, then stood up straight. "Does your wife know where you are?"

"No. But she knows I'm safe."

"I doubt she's resting easy."

"No. But it's her I'm doing this for, as much as anyone."

Doris looked at Tom for a long time. Then she said, "I hope I see you again soon, and in far better circumstances."

Before he could reply, she turned and walked back into the kitchen.

Tom listened until the back door closed. A minute later, the soft sound of an engine reached him. It grew louder for a few seconds, then faded fast.

He was alone.

His first thought was of Walt. His old friend had not acknowledged receiving the "safe" message, nor had he asked for information on Tom's exact location. That meant one of three things: either he was busy, he did not trust his or Tom's current mobile phones, or he was dead. Tom prayed it was not the latter. If so, he would carry the burden of Walt's death for whatever remained of his days.

Tom's next thought was for himself. If he didn't get help soon, he would die in Quentin's house. Above all, he needed a safe telephone, preferably several burn phones, and he had no hope of getting these himself. Second, he needed more nitroglycerine and antibiotics than Quentin had left on the table.

His options were few.

He could call Penn, but Penn would insist that he turn himself in to the authorities, which was out of the question. Tom couldn't even consider that until he'd learned the result of Walt's meeting with Colonel Mackiever. Peggy would do anything he asked, of course, but he wasn't about to put her in further jeopardy. If he died, or was killed while on the run, at least she would remain to represent their generation in the family. A primitive thought, he reflected, but that was what he felt.

Drew Elliott had helped him once, but Tom had a feeling he'd stretched Drew's loyalty about as far as he dared. No, what he needed was unswerving loyalty. A hundred patients came to mind, but Tom couldn't bring himself to put them in lethal danger. Once he faced that reality, only one person remained.

Melba Price.

Melba hadn't wanted to leave him last night, at the lake. Thankfully, she had finally relented, or the confrontation with Knox's killers might have gone differently. Tom hated to ask more of her, but the grim truth was, Melba was single, her children were grown, and her loyalty was beyond question. Tom had only to close his eyes to remember what a wreck Melba had become when her husband left her for a younger woman. She'd drunk so steadily and suicidally—with various pills added to the mix—that she put even Tom's worst excesses to shame. But with Tom's intervention and help, she had survived. He didn't think of the present situation in terms of her repaying any debt; he simply knew that if asked, Melba would come.

She was like Viola that way.

CHAPTER 25

WAITING UNTIL KAISER left the building had required almost heroic self-denial on Caitlin's part. Even after Jamie assured her that the FBI agent had gone, she ran to the back window and checked the back lot to make sure the black Crown Victoria was gone. Satisfied that it was, she'd hurried back to her office, locked her door, then climbed onto her chair to verify that Henry's two surviving journals were where she'd left them. Finding the Moleskines safe, she took them down and laid them on her desk, then opened her top drawer and removed the manila envelope Henry's mother had brought her. No one else in the world knew these artifacts still existed, and that knowledge was intoxicating.

While her heartbeat returned to normal, she put a pot of water on her cooking ring, knowing that tea would steady her nerves. As the water heated, she picked up Henry's most recent journal. The feel of its charred leather cover gave her a thrill of anticipation. She opened the Moleskine and flipped through the dense handwritten notes and finely detailed sketches.

After decades of patient investigation, Henry had spent the last month of his life rushing from revelation to revelation. The death of Pooky Wilson's mother, the appearance of a mysterious witness to the Norris bombing, and finally the confessions of Glenn Morehouse had given Henry potential keys to some of the most heinous unsolved murders in American history. Last night's events had brought partial closure to some of those cases, but many mysteries remained.

As footsteps passed back and forth beyond her door, she dropped a bag of green tea into her mug and settled in behind her desk. Then she took out the sheet labeled *ELAM KNOX* and began to read Henry's notes. The writing on this sheet was much clearer, which told her Henry must have written this shortly after seeing Kaiser, before the sniper's bullet grazed his head.

I always knew that Abbott's redacted 302 contained something important, but I never could have imagined what it was. According to John Kaiser, Jason Abbott told a lot of lies about Forrest Knox in his effort to incriminate him, but Kaiser believes that some of what he said was true. Abbott told his FBI interviewers that in 1966, Frank and Snake Knox murdered their father, Elam, at the Bone Tree. Abbott said Elam had died a particularly brutal death, even by the standards of the Double Eagles. As for the motive, all he knew was that Elam had been killed for betraying his family. But Elam Knox's death was held up as an example of how far the Knoxes would go to avenge treason. According to Abbott, the old man's bones were left among all the others at the Bone Tree, as a perpetual warning to would-be traitors.

Kaiser believes that Elam Knox was murdered by his sons, but he's not convinced that he died at the Bone Tree. Like Dwight Stone, Kaiser doubts that the Bone Tree exists. He thinks it more likely that the term refers to a man-made cross or torture post in the Lusahatcha Swamp, or even a "torture house" that many FBI agents were told about in the 1960s. Kaiser told me that anecdotal evidence suggests Elam Knox was not only a violently abusive man, but also a sexual predator. He was the kind of itinerant preacher who seduced women in every town where he ever set up his revival tent. Many of his paramours were underage, and if rumor could be believed, not all were female. Both his sons were often in trouble for violent offenses, some sexual in nature. Kaiser theorized that Elam might have crossed some sexual or moral line that Frank would not tolerate and was punished for it. But I'm not so quick to believe this. I always heard that Elam was a bad-tempered drunk, and it might be that he simply passed on information that ended up hurting the family or the Double Eagles.

> *Kaiser also believes that a cache of "trophies"*
> *of Double Eagle violence exists somewhere, such*
> *as the military tattoos cut from Jimmy Revels*
> *and Luther Davis. After hearing my summary of*
> *Morehouse's revelations, he thinks that cache might*
> *be at Valhalla, in Lusahatcha County. Of course, I*
> *told Kaiser nothing about Morehouse verifying the*
> *existence of the Bone Tree, or his assertion that some*
> *sensational historical artifact might be hidden there.*
> *On balance, I believe the Bone Tree exists. At the*
> *very least, the bones of Jimmy and Pooky and Joe*
> *Louis Lewis probably lie there. As for Frank Knox's*
> *"insurance" against Carlos Marcello, I won't know*
> *that until I find the tree myself. I asked Morehouse*
> *about Elam on the phone Monday afternoon, but he*
> *refused to say anything. I could tell he was holding*
> *something back, and I suppose now I know why. The*
> *truth would have opened Snake Knox to a murder*
> *charge, and not for just any murder, but patricide.*

Caitlin licked her lips and set the stationery to one side. Then she picked up Henry's Bone Tree journal and opened it with almost reverent care. Reading these Moleskines was like being given the key to a hidden library, one in which the secret histories of Natchez and Concordia Parish had been recorded by a monk working in fanatical solitude. And out of all the tales Henry had meticulously documented, none had lodged in her mind like that of the huge, hollow, centuries-old cypress hidden in a swamp near Athens Point, Mississippi.

According to Henry's research, the mysterious "Tree of Bones" dated to pre-Columbian times, when the mound-building Natchez Indians were said to have traveled south to conduct rituals beneath a great cypress in a swamp that lay to the east of the Father of Waters, between two natural clearings that would later become the towns of Woodville and Athens Point. In that swamp, said the Indians, dying deer and panthers had chosen certain hollow trees in which to spend their final hours, over time creating and sanctifying "bone trees." One particularly large specimen had been woven into several area legends, from that of pirate Jean Lafitte in the early 1800s to Al

Capone's bootlegging operation in the 1920s, which had flourished up and down the Mississippi River.

While Henry was skeptical about these likely apocryphal stories, he'd clearly believed reports that Confederate raiders operating in the area in 1862–1863 had used the Lusahatcha Swamp as a haven to escape pursuing Union troops. Those raiders had reportedly hanged at least three local Yankee collaborators from what one officer had called "the Bone Tree" in his diary. Lieutenant Richard Wadsworth, CSA, had noted that slave hunters punished runaways beneath the same tree (which slaves called "the Chain Tree") by whipping, maiming, or worse. Henry had also established a Ku Klux Klan connection to the Bone Tree. According to Special Agent Dwight Stone, one Klan informant had spoken of African-Americans being hunted for sport in the Lusahatcha Swamp, those hunts ending in castration or murder beneath the tree itself. In 1964, Stone and a team of FBI agents had searched the swamp for three days with boats and dogs but had found nothing. At that time Agent Stone had concluded that the term "Bone Tree" referred to a man-made cross that the Klan had constructed for torture purposes, and not to an actual tree.

Caitlin realized that the archetypal image of a sacrificial tree would be irresistible to rumormongers, but she couldn't escape the feeling that some of the stories must be based in fact. Henry noted that the bald cypress belonged to the redwood family, and one specimen in Florida had been documented as thirty-five hundred years old. Caitlin shivered when she read that line, for if it was accurate, then all the bloody legends of the Bone Tree could be true. She wondered whether her fascination with the tree might be rooted in her morbid curiosity about the most atavistic human impulses. Tales of castration and crucifixion conjured the horrors of the Belgian Congo and Rwanda. As unpleasant as those thoughts were, some rogue region of her brain had always hungered to peer into the psychic abyss that yawned beneath these depraved acts.

According to Henry's notes, some residents of Lusahatcha County had claimed to know the location of the Bone Tree, but in fact they had "known" only that the tree lay somewhere in the Lusahatcha Swamp. That was like saying you knew where a particular New York brownstone was by pointing to the island of Manhattan. Henry Sexton had made one personal effort to find the Bone Tree, using as his guide an Athens Point native who claimed to have been shown the notorious cypress by his grandfather. But after an exhausting day of trolling through acres of swamp that straddled federal timberland and a private hunting preserve—all of it choked with thick stands of ancient, moss-bearded cypress, and infested with venomous snakes and alligators—Henry had returned home no wiser than he'd left.

Clearly, if Dwight Stone and a platoon of FBI agents in boats had failed to find the Bone Tree in three days, Caitlin's only hope of success lay in Toby Rambin. If the Lusahatcha County poacher turned out to be another con man hoping to cash in on the hopes of a gullible outsider, she would be screwed. Within a day or two, the army of outside reporters would make up her head start on the Double Eagles case, and she would own the story no longer. Finishing her lukewarm tea, she picked up her Treo and dialed Toby Rambin's number once more. She tried to stay calm, but even the prospect of making contact with a man who had seen the Bone Tree made her pulse speed. The phone rang twelve times without an answer, and at last she hung up.

Opening Henry's journal again, she flipped to a sketch he had made of a giant cypress with an opening like an inverted V in its trunk. He'd filled in the opening with black ink, and that blackness bled into the water he'd drawn around the tree, where cypress knees jutted upward like the limbs of half-buried bodies. Caitlin touched the drawing with her fingertip, feeling the rough page that Henry had pored over while he was alive.

The legend of the Bone Tree reminded her of the mythical "Raintree" from the movie *Raintree County*, starring Elizabeth Taylor and Montgomery Clift. Part of that overripe Civil War film, which itself had been haunted by tragedy, had been shot about thirty miles from Natchez, at the burned ruins of Windsor. Only a few weeks after Caitlin and Penn had fallen in love, they'd spent a magical day walking among the ghostly Corinthian columns that, along with the famous Staircase to Nowhere, were all that remained of the once-majestic mansion. To Caitlin, the Windsor ruins conveyed the tragic grandeur of the Old South far more viscerally than the perfectly preserved mansions of Natchez, which gave the illusion of beauty to a society built on the bloodied backs of slaves.

The producers of *Raintree County* had obviously felt the same. On Windsor's steps, Taylor and Clift had struggled through some of the worst lines in movie history, trying in vain to repeat the success of *Gone with the Wind*. You could almost sense the enveloping darkness that had swirled around the failed production. Ross Lockridge, the author of *Raintree County*, had committed suicide at age thirty-four—one day before his book reached number one on the *New York Times* bestseller list. Like Montgomery Clift, who'd recently had his face scarred in a car crash, the author never got to enjoy the success he'd struggled to attain. And Elizabeth Taylor was already being troubled by the demons that would haunt her for the rest of her life. But despite these chaotic elements, Caitlin had always recalled the story that had given the film its title.

In Lockridge's novel, the mystical Raintree was given several origin stories. Folklore claimed it was an exotic plant brought from the Orient by an idealistic community of pioneers, and that only a single tree had survived, hidden deep in an Indiana swamp. All who found the tree supposedly discovered love under a rain of yellow flowers. A second legend told of a ragged preacher who had planted apple seeds throughout his travels. In his bag, that preacher—later called Johnny Appleseed—had also carried one rare and precious seed: that of the Golden Raintree. "Luck, happiness, the realization of dreams," said the legend, "the secret of life itself—all belong to him who finds the Raintree." Was it merely chance, Caitlin wondered, that the Yankee legend of a mystical tree was empirically optimistic, while the southern version was a dark tapestry of blood, betrayal, and murder?

Flattening her left hand over Henry's sketch, she picked up her Treo and dialed the poacher's number yet again.

The phone rang five times . . . seven. She was moving her thumb to the END button when a surprisingly deep voice barked from the Treo's little speaker.

"Hello!" she said, jerking the phone to her ear.

The cigarette-parched voice of an older black man said, "Hey, now. Who dis be?"

"I'm a friend of Henry Sexton," Caitlin said. "I've been trying to reach you since last night."

Silence.

"Are you there, Mr. Rambin?"

"I been workin'. What you want, lady?"

"I want to find the tree that Henry Sexton was looking for. Do you know what I'm talking about?"

More silence. Then the voice said, "Might do. Might not. I read in the Natchez paper a little while ago that Mister Henry be dead. Burned up, it said. I don't wanna get burned up."

"I don't either. And I wrote that newspaper story, by the way."

"Huh. How you know about Henry and me?"

"I was working with him. And I can certainly make the trip worth your while."

This time the silence stretched too long.

"You can name your price," she said quickly, afraid she would lose him like a fish nibbling on a line.

"Henry was gon' pay me two thousand dollah."

Caitlin doubted this, but she said, "I can match that."

After a couple of seconds, Rambin said, "Price gone up now, though. Hazard pay."

She closed her eyes but did not sigh. "I see. What's the new price?"

"Double. Fo' thousand. Take it or leave it."

After what seemed a suitable interval—which she hoped would mask the fact that she would pay forty thousand dollars to find the Bone Tree—she said, "Four thousand it is. But I want to go this afternoon."

"No way, lady. I got work this afternoon. Can't get loose. Plus, I got to make sure the coast is clear. We'll go tomorrow morning. After that, I'm clearing out. Too dangerous round here. Gettin' like the old days again."

The idea of waiting a full day galled her, but Caitlin sensed that upping her offer wouldn't persuade Rambin to change his mind. "You know what tree I'm talking about, right? Are you positive you know where it is?"

A harsh squawk of a laugh came through the phone. "Lady, they ain't nothin' I don't know 'bout this old swamp. I was birthed on the edge of it, and lived jes' about every day in it. You jes' bring your money, hear?"

"Where?" she asked quickly.

"Ain't but one decent road leads down to the swamp from the state road. There's others, but you'd never find 'em."

"I'll be there. Is eight A.M. all right?"

"Six thirty," Rambin said. "And bring cash. I don't take no damn bank check."

"I will."

"What's your name?" Rambin asked.

"Caitlin Masters."

The old poacher took his time with this. "I see it right here in the paper," he said finally. "All right, then. You wear a red bandanna around your neck. You see a rusted old school bus, you'll know you goin' the right way. Park where the road ends. If I feel like you're on the level, I'll let you see me. And no *po*-lice. You hear?"

"I'll be there," Caitlin promised. "Without police."

Rambin clicked off without another word.

Caitlin sat up, her eyes on Henry's journal. She was excited, but the reality of tomorrow's rendezvous presented certain problems. For one, she would have to craft a cover story that would guarantee both secrecy and freedom of movement, one that would satisfy both Penn and Kaiser. At least she had a decent amount of time to come up with something credible.

She suddenly remembered Henry's warning that she not try to find the Bone Tree alone. Yesterday the reporter had actually made her promise not to do so. Would it be wise to keep that promise? Who could she trust to keep their mouth shut about her mission? Jamie? She needed her editor running the paper in her absence. Keisha Harvin, perhaps? The hungry young reporter would kill to go on an assignment like this one, but Keisha was simply the wrong color. A black girl prowling the back roads of Lusahatcha County in the company of a white woman would attract unwanted attention.

While Caitlin considered other alternatives, an image of Jordan Glass rose into her mind. Jordan would be the perfect companion: the photographer was a veteran of countless war zones and wouldn't be intimidated by anything they might encounter. The problem was, Glass was married to Kaiser. And even though Jordan had told Caitlin that she kept some things from her husband, Caitlin was unwilling to trust her best lead to a woman she'd only just met—even if Glass was a personal hero to her.

Caitlin jumped when the landline on her desk rang. The second she picked it up, Jamie Lewis said, "Kaiser's headed back to your office, and he doesn't look happy."

"Thanks."

She opened her drawer and swept the journals and envelope into it, then switched off her light and unlocked her door. As she curled up on the little sofa against the wall, a knocking sounded on her door.

Caitlin didn't move.

The FBI agent waited a few seconds, then turned the knob and leaned into the room. She could almost sense Kaiser's eyes adjusting to the darkness.

"Caitlin?" he said softly.

She didn't stir.

"Caitlin."

She gave him nothing. Kaiser stood there in silence, making judgments she could only guess at. While she waited, the mind-boggling reality of what she'd arranged with Toby Rambin sent a chill up her spine. If she did everything right—and if Rambin turned out to know what he claimed he did—then by tomorrow at noon she might be cracking open the biggest story of her career. In a single day she could vindicate Henry Sexton, bring closure—and possibly justice—to the families of several civil rights martyrs, and rack up another Pulitzer Prize. You couldn't do a better day's work than that.

After some fraction of time she could not guess at, John Kaiser went out and pulled the door shut behind him. Caitlin remained on the sofa, breathing deeply, trying to slow her pounding heart. Now that she'd finally connected with the poacher, whatever had kept her going all these hours without sleep finally let go, and exhaustion washed over her. In the darkness of her mind, she saw the wild-eyed face of Elam Knox staring in fury from the black V in the trunk of the Bone Tree.

"I'm coming for you, you bastard," she whispered fiercely. "And there's not a goddamned thing you can do about it."

CHAPTER 26

DREW'S LAKE HOUSE was locked when I arrived, so I opened it with the key he'd given me. Inside, I found nothing but evidence of a hasty departure. There were dirty dishes in the sink, and the chairs and sofa looked as though someone had gotten up and left the room only minutes ago. One bed had been slept in, and in the bathroom lay a pair of pants on the floor that matched my father's size. Back in the den, I found something far more disturbing: a plastic bottle of nitroglycerine tablets. Dad usually keeps a couple of tablets in a pocket, but it was hard for me to imagine him voluntarily leaving that bottle behind. The only scenario that made sense—other than his being killed or kidnapped—was him running for his life, leaving so fast that he left critical medication behind.

After searching every room, I went out to the closed garage. Drew had told me I might find his old pickup truck there, but it was gone. Instead, I found Walt Garrity's Roadtrek van. The sight of it stirred something in me. It was so easy to imagine Dad and Walt rolling down the highway, laughing and smiling. But necessity had separated them, and since the police had a description of the unique vehicle, they'd been forced to leave the Roadtrek behind.

Since I had no key to the big van, I picked up a brick in the corner of the garage and smashed the passenger window. My throat locked up when I opened the door, so afraid was I that I'd find my father's body inside. But I found only clothes, a couple of cash cell phones, and quite a bit of high-tech gear that Walt must have brought from Texas. Nothing that would tell me where my father had gone.

I was walking down to Drew's boathouse when I noticed some dark smudges on the dead grass to my left.

Kneeling, I found that they were bloodstains, and the realization nauseated me. *Did my father die here?* I wondered. As best I could determine from the depressions in the soft ground, at least three men had faced one another at the edge of the lake. But exactly what had happened I had no way to tell.

Unable to find any other clues, I screwed up my courage and opened Drew's boathouse, again expecting to find Dad inside. But again I found no sign of him. No less afraid, I walked the forty yards out to the end of Drew's pier and gazed desolately over the lake.

Here I have stood for twenty minutes, watching the wind ruffle the black water and trying to get my mind around all that has happened since Shad Johnson called me Monday morning. One of the hardest things to accept is that a friend as close as Drew Elliott would lie to me in such a situation. Could he not see that Dad stopped making sound decisions long ago? The most bizarre development, though, is John Kaiser's sudden obsession with the JFK assassination, and his belief that Dad might somehow be involved. I can accept that my father probably knew Carlos Marcello, as Kaiser claimed the surveillance photo he showed me proves. After all, my mother verified it last night, or at least that Dad had treated Marcello in the Orleans Parish Prison and Marcello was grateful for whatever Dad had done for him. But that's a long way from my father knowing anything about a presidential assassination. Still, Kaiser's stubborn persistence tells me he's not going to let the subject drop. And if Dwight Stone is really flying in from Colorado to talk to me about it, then they must know a lot that I don't. That, or else both men have crossed the line into conspiracy psychosis.

I remember the day John Kennedy died. It's one of my earliest memories. I was sitting on a white vinyl sofa beside my mother, watching our black-and-white TV. My sister was at school, but because I was only three and a half, I still spent my days with Mom while Dad worked at his new job in Natchez. I didn't really understand that, of course. In my mind, we were still living on the Missouri army base where he'd been stationed after returning from Germany. I don't remember the assassination announcement on TV, but I do remember my mother suddenly getting more upset than I'd ever seen her, hugging me and sobbing, then frantically trying to reach my father by telephone. We'd recently returned from West Germany, and my parents were acutely aware of the dangers of the Cold War. My sister was crying when she got home, and that evening she and I sat on the floor while Mom and Dad watched the news and spoke in hushed tones. It was only much later that I truly understood what had happened in Dallas, but the emotional crux of it sank into me right then. From that day forward I knew the taste of loss, and I'll carry the memory with me—in the somber black-and-white of our old television, not the saturated, horrifying color of the Zapruder film—until the day I die.

Three days after the assassination, I watched John Kennedy Jr. salute his father's coffin. "John-John" was seven months younger than I, but he knew enough to salute when the horse-drawn caisson passed by and his mother prompted him. I didn't understand much more about the world than he did, but I did realize one very frightening thing: if a boy as special as he was could lose his father, then I could lose mine, too. His dad might have been president, but mine (in my mind, at least) was in the army. I couldn't know then that my father had already survived the greatest dangers he was ever likely to face, in Korea. But time and fate change all things. Now, forty-two years after JFK died, Dad is running for his life. And in a twist almost beyond understanding, a senior agent of the FBI believes that he may know the truth behind John Kennedy's death.

Is it possible? I wonder. *Could the brutal, unsolved murders that Henry Sexton was working in this quiet corner of the South for decades actually conceal a deeper secret? The truth behind the biggest cold case murder in American history?*

"No," I say to the wind. "Oswald killed Kennedy, and he acted alone. That's the sad truth."

As I walk back up the pier toward the shore, I reflect that Hannah Arendt had it right: evil is incomprehensibly banal. The existentialists went her one better: it's also absurd, and terrifyingly so.

Before I reach the bank, the sound of voices pulls me from my reverie. Looking up, I see two men walking down the hill toward the pier. Both are tall and appear to be about forty. One is wearing orange-tinted Oakley sunglasses, and they give him the look of a bird of prey. Both walk with a surly self-assurance that makes me think of cops, though if they are, they're wearing plainclothes.

My heart has kicked into overdrive, and only the reassuring hardness of the .357 jammed into the small of my back keeps me from jumping into the water to try to escape. Our paths intersect where the wooden walkway meets the grass, near the blood on the ground.

"Who are you?" asks the man in the Oakleys, who's standing on my left.

"Penn Cage. I'm the mayor of Natchez. Who are you?"

"Police."

"Not Ferriday police."

"That's not your concern," says the man on my right, who looks like he hasn't slept for days.

"It certainly is my concern," I counter, trying to get a read on their intentions. "I used to be an assistant DA in Houston, and I know my rights. I also believe a crime was committed here last night."

"What crime is that?" asks Oakley.

I point to my right, at the blood on the ground. "Murder, it looks like."

The other man laughs. "You're right about that."

The certainty in his voice chills me. "Was somebody killed here? Where are you guys from?"

Oakley smiles and shakes his head, then takes a .38 from a holster beneath his coat. "Now, just what the hell are you doing here?"

"I'm looking for my father. Dr. Tom Cage."

The two men look at each other. Then Oakley says, "He ain't here, Mayor. But he's wanted for killing a cop. So you'd best get the hell out of here, before you get hurt."

I respond in a steady voice that I hope hides my fear. "Look, I just want to find my father. I want him to turn himself in. Is there anything you know that would help me?"

"Slow, ain't he?" says the man on my right. "You sure you were a lawyer? 'Cause you don't seem to understand the situation."

Oakley doesn't bother playing this game. He jerks his .38 at me and says, "You're going to have to come with us."

I hold up my hands, wishing I'd drawn my gun before I reached the head of the pier. Before I can say anything, the man on my right says, "I think he's carrying."

Oakley points his gun at my face. "Are you?"

"No." I'm hoping to lull their vigilance for a couple of seconds, but it doesn't work. Oakley waves his gun, indicating that I should turn around. If I do that, one of them will lift my jacket and see the butt of my .357 sticking out of my pants. But I have no choice. I'm about to turn when the rumble of a heavy engine rolls down the hill from the house. When I look up, I see a white pickup driving about thirty miles per hour down the slope toward the pier.

Clearly confused, Oakley's first instinct is to conceal his weapon, which tells me he's probably not a cop. The two men back onto the pier as the truck barrels toward us, and while they do I draw my pistol and hold it along my leg.

"Who the fuck is that?" yells Oakley.

Before his partner can answer, the brakes screech, the truck slides to a stop, and Lincoln Turner leaps out of the driver's seat, a sawed-off shotgun in his big hands. He loses no time pointing the gaping barrel at the man nearest him, which is Oakley.

"Throw down your guns, motherfuckers!"

The two men look at each other, then one pistol hits the boards of the pier.

"Kick it in the water," Lincoln tells me.

I do.

"Yours too, shithead!" Lincoln barks, jabbing his shotgun at Oakley.

Oakley's pistol hits the pier, and I kick it into the water as well.

"Check their ankles."

Oakley is wearing an ankle holster with a .25 automatic in it. I draw that and pocket it, then take out the men's wallets. In short order I learn that they *are* police officers, both from Monroe, Louisiana. Oakley's last name is Kennard, and his buddy's is Grimsby.

"They're city cops from Monroe," I say, walking over to Lincoln's side and facing the men. "Who sent you here?"

Neither answers.

"Forrest Knox. Right?"

The flicker of surprise in Kennard's eyes tells me I'm right. Turning to his partner, I say, "You know what happened last night. You were here, weren't you?"

Grimsby's eyes keep flicking to Lincoln's shotgun. "Who the fuck is this?" he asks.

"No friend of yours," Lincoln bellows. "Although you probably figured that when you saw my color."

"Dad was here last night," I tell Lincoln. "I think this asshole was, too. We need to know what he knows."

Lincoln steps forward and cracks Grimsby across the jaw with the barrel of his shotgun.

The man staggers but manages to hold his feet, blood dribbling from his mouth. Rage brews in his eyes, but Lincoln just laughs and says, "You cops ain't used to that kind of treatment, are you? That's how the other half lives."

"You're a dead man," says the cop in the sunglasses.

Lincoln's half smile vanishes, and he steps up to Kennard. The man flinches when Lincoln raises his hand, but instead of hitting him, Lincoln yanks off the Oakley sunglasses and crushes them in his hand. "I'll tell you boys right now, there ain't no percentage in staying quiet. Next man who refuses to answer a question get his jaw broke."

Kennard shakes his head, but I can tell Grimsby is afraid.

"What happened here last night?" I repeat.

"Your old man shot my partner," Grimsby says. "Late last night. Right there." He points at the bloodstains on the grass.

Lincoln and I share a glance, but I can't read his eyes. I know this, though: if Dad really killed another cop, he's thrown away whatever chance he had of survival.

"How did that happen?" I ask. "How did he get the drop on two cops?"

"He had a pistol in his pants pocket," Grimsby says. "We didn't know it was there."

"Why did he shoot?"

The cop's eyes go wide. "I don't know!"

"He wouldn't have shot except to save his own life. You were about to kill him, weren't you?"

"No!"

"Bullshit," says Lincoln, stepping closer to Grimsby. "Who told you to kill him?"

"Nobody, I swear!"

"I'll fuck you up," Lincoln says, raising the shotgun over Grimsby.

"Go ahead," says Kennard. "Kill him. You'll be doing him a favor, compared to what would happen if he tells you what you want to know."

Lincoln gives me a questioning look.

Taking out my cell phone, I start looking for John Kaiser's number.

"Who you calling?" Lincoln asks.

"FBI."

"No," says Kennard. "Don't do that."

"Tell us who sent you here."

Neither answers.

"You work for Forrest Knox. Nobody else would scare the piss out of cops, except maybe Brody Royal, and he's dead. And you two are way too young to be Double Eagles."

Kennard is looking hard at his wallet in my hand. *Is he stupid enough or desperate enough to try to escape?* I point my .357 at his belly. "Where were ya'll when I pulled up?"

"Neighbor's house," says Grimsby. "Nobody home over there. Our car's on the far side of that house."

"What you want to do with them?" Lincoln asks. "Give them to the FBI?"

Grimsby shakes his head and says, "I'll tell you anything you want to know if you'll let us go."

"Tell me what happened last night. Everything."

The man takes a deep breath, then looks over at the blood on the grass. "My partner was going to shoot your old man. We had orders, that's all I'll say about that. But at the last second, the doc shot my partner in the stomach using a pistol in his pants. Then he put the gun on me. He made me carry my partner up the hill, then drugged me with something. Later on he dumped me out in the middle of nowhere, and the body with me."

"If you guys had been working as legitimate cops at the time, that would have been all over the news. In fact, I still don't know why Forrest wouldn't put out a release saying Dad killed another cop. What kind of game is Forrest playing?"

Grimsby shrugs, and Kennard doesn't look like he knows the answer either.

"Why the hell would you come back here?" Lincoln asks.

"Forrest ordered him to," I guess. "Right?"

Before Grimsby can answer or evade the question, Kennard breaks to his right and sprints past me, running in a zigzag pattern. Lincoln fires his shotgun, but only into the air. Seeing this, Grimsby bolts as well.

Lincoln aims after his retreating figure. "Want me to shoot him?"

"No. I've got their IDs."

"I can hit him in the legs."

"We don't need the hassle." I shove the cops' wallets into my pocket.

As the men disappear around the neighbor's house, Lincoln lowers the shotgun. "Whose house is this?"

"Drew Elliott's. One of Dad's medical partners."

"Have you searched it?"

"I didn't find anything that would tell me where he's gone. And it looks like he was taken against his will. He left medicine behind. But if that guy was telling the truth, maybe he was just under stress."

Lincoln peers deeply into my eyes.

"That's all I know, seriously. I'd rather him be on trial for killing Viola than running from a thousand cops. Besides, you probably just saved my life."

The silence that follows this statement is strangely awkward. While Lincoln stares at the blood on the grass, I search his face for similarities to my father's, or even my own. I remember our conversation in CC's Rhythm Club, the juke joint by Anna's Bottom, and his promise to take a DNA test. If I had a Q-tip or a plastic bottle to store a twig in, I'd ask him to scratch a sample from his inner cheek right now.

"You followed me here, didn't you?" I say at last. "You were hoping I'd lead you to Dad."

Lincoln looks up the slope, toward the lake road, as though he's considering leaving. "Yeah. But you don't know shit, do you?"

I remind myself to be more careful the next time I visit Annie and my mother.

Lincoln cradles the shotgun and looks back at me. "All anybody's talking about now is that dead reporter, Sexton. And Brody Royal. A couple of white men die, and my mother's forgotten. No surprise, I guess. This is still Mississippi."

"Do you really still believe my father killed your mother?"

"Nothing's happened that would change my mind."

"What about all the killings in the last three days?"

"What about them? I read the paper this morning. Don't mean shit."

"Did you read about Glenn Morehouse?"

"That old Klansman who talked to Henry Sexton?"

"He wasn't a Klansman. He was a Double Eagle."

"Same difference to a black man."

"I think your mother was killed for the same reason Henry was. She knew too much about the Double Eagles, and they were afraid she was going to act on what she knew."

Lincoln looks past me, back over the lake.

"Unless you killed her yourself, that is," I add.

His face whips back to me. "What are you talking about?"

"I know my father a lot better than you. It was totally out of character for him to run rather than face the charges against him. He'd never do that to protect himself, only someone else."

"He's ashamed," Lincoln says, "and his shame's made him cowardly."

"No. He has his faults, but cowardice isn't one of them. He's protecting someone. And maybe that someone is you."

Lincoln looks as though I slapped him. "Why would he protect me?"

"He believes you're his son."

The black man's eyes narrow, and for the first time he looks at me with serious interest. "You've finally accepted it, haven't you?"

"No. But Dad has. I think your mother told him he was your father, and that was enough to make him believe it. I think she was trying to help provide for you after she was gone. I don't blame her. And I don't blame you if you tried to ease her passing with morphine."

Lincoln's dark cheek twitches.

"But if you made some kind of mistake and gave her that painful death by adrenaline—and then tried to blame Dad for it—then for that I blame you. Is that what you did? Did you have second thoughts and try to revive her?"

Immeasurable contempt radiates from Lincoln's eyes. "If I'd done that, and Dr. Cage meant to protect me, why would he run? Why wouldn't he just plead guilty and take his sentence?"

"I'm not sure. He probably figured her death would be recorded as natural, and there'd be no autopsy. He certainly didn't expect any videotape. And he probably expected you to show some gratitude and keep your mouth shut. But instead you pushed for a murder charge. And Dad knows that both the Double Eagles and the Adams County sheriff would like to see him dead. I don't think he was ready to die in a jail cell."

"Why would I press charges if he was protecting me?"

"Bitterness. You clearly still hate him. You saw a chance to get some payback for the pain you believe you suffered at his hands, and you took it. It's a human response. But things have gone too far now, Lincoln."

He shakes his head as though he's tired of dealing with a crazy man, then starts walking back to his truck.

"Aren't you even going to deny it?" I ask.

"What's the point? Even after everything that's happened, you can't admit to yourself that he might have killed my mother."

"You haven't given me any facts!"

Lincoln shrugs and gets into his truck. "The truth will out, my brother. Sooner or later. I'll see you 'round."

The big engine roars, Lincoln backs up, and then the white pickup climbs the slope and turns onto the lake road. The rumbling drone lasts half a minute and then fades to silence. Standing alone by the stained grass and the water, I wonder if it's remotely possible that Lincoln Turner and I have the same blood flowing through our veins. It doesn't seem so, and yet . . . it's become clear over the past few days that the history I've believed was mine wasn't nearly the whole story.

With shaking hands I slide my .357 back into my pants at the small of my back, then start up the hill. If Lincoln is still following me, and Forrest Knox is dispatching dirty cops to commit murder, I need to find a more private place to hide Annie and my mother than Edelweiss. Hiding in plain sight is a good principle, but it can't work forever. The Natchez bluff has too much tourist traffic for someone not to notice that somebody has taken up residence in the famous house. How long before someone gets curious and climbs the steps to the gallery to look through the windows?

Hiding Mom and Annie somewhere safer will require serious thought, and probably some very quiet negotiation with someone I can trust with my family's lives. But for now I need rest. If I go back to Edelweiss, I won't get it. Annie is bound to be bored out of her skull, and she'll talk to me nonstop. City Hall is no refuge either, especially after three days of ignoring my mayoral duties. In this moment, the only place that seems to offer sanctuary is my town house on Washington Street. There I could get some peace.

As I reach my city car, I decide to call Caitlin and ask her to meet me at home. We haven't seen each other since last night's nightmare, and while I know she's probably working at a fever pitch, no one who went through what she did in Brody Royal's basement can be all right. More to the point, I feel a strong urge to reconnect with her before events spin any farther out of control. In situations like this one, we're almost always pushed apart by the things we're forced to keep from each other.

The vibration of the starting engine comforts me a little, but the car has sat too long for the heater to provide any warmth. As I pull onto the road, it strikes me that Grimsby was telling the truth. Dad shot and killed his partner last night. If Forrest Knox isn't exploiting this fact, it can only be because he's working a more subtle plan. In my present state of ignorance, I have little chance of guessing what that might be. I only pray that Walt and Dad possess enough information to unravel Forrest's intent. If they don't, they're certain to wind up right where he wants them, which I assume is dead.

CHAPTER 27

CLAUDE DEVEREUX HAD lived a long life, but the old lawyer had never been as afraid as he had since last night, after hearing Brody Royal had died. Yet that fear increased as he walked into the Baton Rouge headquarters of the Louisiana State Police. Unlike most people who dealt with Forrest Knox, Claude Devereux had known his father. And he knew that the will and anger that drove Frank Knox burned in Forrest also. Claude did not fancy bearing bad news to Frank's son.

Worse yet, the FBI was investigating the recent deaths in Concordia Parish, as well as those dating back over forty years. Though Claude had worked hard to insulate himself from the more violent activities of his clients over the decades, remaining immaculate was impossible. If the Bureau looked hard enough at Brody Royal's dealings, they would find enough to send Claude to prison.

Claude was shown into the office by Forrest's Redbone acolyte, a fairly recent recruit who made Claude's skin crawl. Claude took a seat before Forrest's desk, ignoring the plaques, awards, and shooting trophies that adorned the walls and focusing on the single samurai sword that hung behind Forrest's head—one of the *katanas* that Frank had brought back from the Pacific in 1945.

To Claude's surprise, a pit bull sat like a statue beside Forrest's desk. *Surely there must be a rule against that*, he thought. Then he guessed that Forrest must be testing the boundaries of the authority he hoped to make official in a short time.

"You look nervous, Claude," Forrest said.

"Oh, I am."

"Because Brody was killed? Surely you expected that, as reckless as he's been lately?"

Claude glanced over his shoulder. The Redbone had

taken up a station beside the office door, like a second attack dog. "In all honesty, it's a relief that he's gone, though I'll miss the fees. I didn't think he'd go as far as he did last night. Kidnapping Penn Cage was suicidal. But that's not why I'm nervous."

"What is it, then?"

"I'd rather discuss that in private. I have some news."

Forrest motioned for him to continue. Clearly, Alphonse Ozan was going nowhere.

Claude cleared his throat. "Sheriff Walker Dennis asked that I relay a message to Snake and the other Double Eagles."

Forrest laid his elbows on the desk. "What message?"

"He'd like the surviving Double Eagles to come to his office tomorrow morning to answer some questions."

"Voluntarily?"

Claude nodded.

"Is he serious?"

"Deadly serious. He's lost a deputy. Another one's in critical condition."

"He should have left well enough alone," Ozan said from behind Claude. "He let that Penn Cage get him into trouble."

"Is that what I should tell him?" Claude asked.

Forrest shook his head. "Does he want Billy to come in, too?"

"He didn't mention Billy."

Forrest pursed his lips as he mulled this over. Claude tried not to stare at the mutilated left ear. He'd often wondered why Forrest hadn't gotten plastic surgery to mask the injury. His best guess was that it served as a primitive badge of combat experience.

"What's the latest from the moneymen?" Forrest asked, changing the subject. "Any word on the housing-project decision?"

"I spoke with a couple of attorneys during the drive down. Getting a public housing project rezoned for mixed use is no small matter. A lot of money is changing hands. A lot of favors are being called in."

Forrest gave him an expectant look. "But I'm still in the deal."

"As of now, yes. But I would venture to say that if things worsen in Concordia Parish, that might change."

Forrest Knox's flat stare chilled Claude as much as Frank's ever had. "I have no say in the matter," Claude said. "Most of my time's been taken up trying to sort out probate issues with Brody's estate. The children are already fighting over it."

"Not one of them's worth a cup of spit. Who gets that Italian turboprop?"

"The plane will be sold, I'm afraid." Claude forced a smile. "May I ask how things are progressing with Colonel Mackiever?"

Forrest reached down and scratched his pit bull between the ears. A low sound of satisfaction came from the animal's barrel chest.

"Mackiever was holed up in his house until about twenty minutes ago," Forrest said. "The press had surrounded him like Indians around a wagon train. But he managed to slip out."

"How did he do that?"

Ozan said, "His son-in-law, his nephew, and three or four older guys from the Highway Division blocked in the media with their vehicles. The colonel and his wife got out during the melee. Where they are now, nobody knows."

Claude didn't like the sound of this. "He hasn't contacted you about resigning?"

"Not so far."

"Have you tried to reach him?"

Forrest shook his head.

"Does he have any political support I don't know about?"

"I don't think so."

"You don't . . . you don't think he'd go to the FBI?"

Knox studied his fingernails. "It's possible, but there's no way he can refute that evidence. We spent months creating that trail. If he forces my hand, his life is over."

Claude didn't share Forrest's confidence. "Then why hasn't he resigned?"

"Let me worry about that. After you leave here, I want you to contact Billy. Tell him I want Snake and Sonny and at least two other Eagles at Valhalla by five P.M. They can use the plane, obviously."

"Why do you want them back?"

"Because tomorrow morning they're going to do just what Sheriff Dennis wants them to do."

Claude heard the Redbone gasp behind him. He took a moment to compose himself. "As an attorney, I'm not sure I'd advise that course of action."

"It's a good thing you're not my attorney, then. You were Brody's attorney, and he's dead. I'm alive, and I intend to stay that way."

Claude considered what Forrest was asking him to do. "Do you really think Snake will return to Louisiana and walk into the sheriff's office of his own accord?"

"He won't know anything about it until he talks to me. You're going to tell Snake you're not sure why I want him at Valhalla. If he pushes you, tell him you're worried I'm ready to kill every mother's son—and daughter—who poses a threat to us. You know Snake. He'll come back for that."

Claude nodded. "Without doubt."

"You tell him anything else, Claude, and I'll pickle your liver. Are we clear?"

"Absolutely, Frank." Claude felt his face go red. "I mean Forrest. I'm sorry . . . I had a senior moment. You look so much like your father."

Forrest grinned. "Take it easy, Claude. I take that as a compliment."

A cell phone rang behind Claude, and he heard Ozan walk out of the office to answer it.

"Just tell me one thing," he said to Forrest, taking advantage of the sudden privacy. "What do you hope to gain by sending Snake and the others into the lion's den?"

"Time, of course. Meanwhile, I'm going to cut a deal to keep the people who could hurt me quiet."

"With whom?" Claude asked. "Who has the power to keep those people quiet?"

An almost serene expression came over Forrest's face. "Thomas Cage, M.D."

Claude sat silently for several seconds. Then he said, "I see. Yes . . . I believe I do see. That makes me feel a little better. I suppose you'll blame as much as you can on Brody and Regan?"

Forrest inclined his head. "You have any problem with that?"

Claude sighed. "Not as long as you keep me out of it. I may have to leave the country in any case. Brody kept too many mementos around."

"Just like Snake and the rest. I've kept a couple myself, to tell the truth. But Brody seemed especially careless about it."

"That's actually what's making me nervous," Claude said quickly, glancing back at the closed door. "I think the FBI has the rifles from Brody's basement. The special rifles. You know the ones I mean?"

"Dallas and Memphis?"

Claude nodded.

"How many people did Brody show those rifles to over the years, Claude?"

"Almost none. There was a panel over that display case whenever guests were there."

"Exactly. Brody was like the guy who pays an art thief to steal a Rembrandt for him, knowing he can never sell it. He was content to stand in front of that case and say to himself, 'I helped change the history of this country.'"

"That may be, but the Bureau has whatever remains of them now."

"So what?" Forrest said, flicking his hand. "Those rifles won't tell them anything that can hurt us. Do you think Carlos Marcello ran this state for thirty years by being stupid?"

"No. But . . ." Claude trailed off as Forrest got up and walked around behind him. He felt the younger man's powerful hands on his shoulders, then his neck.

"I don't like nervous men, Claude. Nervous men make bad decisions."

"I only wanted to make sure you were aware of the rifle problem."

Forrest clicked his tongue twice, and the pit bull growled ominously. "I'm not worried about that, Claude. But tell me this: was there anything in Brody's house I *should* be worried about?"

Claude tried to look up, but with his neck in Forrest's grip he couldn't manage it. "Not that I know of. But in all honesty, I think we both should be ready to leave the country on short notice, just in case."

Forrest laughed. "I'm always ready. But I'm not going anywhere. I'm about to break Griffith Mackiever into pieces even his kids won't want to touch. Then I'm going to shut down the mess in Concordia Parish. You tell the moneymen in New Orleans to batten down the hatches for two or three days. With luck, I'll cut a deal with Dr. Cage and there'll be no more casualties. But if there does have to be more bloodshed, I've got that covered, too. No mud or blood will touch the Mardi Gras kings. Okay?"

Claude nodded as vigorously as he could.

At that moment Alphonse Ozan came back into the office.

"I just got a call from Grimsby. Penn Cage showed up at the Elliott lake house, poking around. Grimsby and his partner were trying to find out if he knew where his daddy was when a big nigger in a white truck pulled up with a sawed-off shotgun and ran them off."

Forrest dropped his hands from Claude's neck and walked back to his desk. He was nearly to his chair when he kicked it across the room. The pit bull sprang away, startled into confusion.

"A big jig in a white truck," Forrest muttered. "That sounds like Lincoln Turner to me."

"Yep," Ozan agreed.

"What the hell is he doing protecting the son of the man he wants to send to death row?"

"I got no idea, boss."

Forrest sat down on the desk and began tapping out a rhythm on his knee. "Claude, you do just what I told you. Except you tell Billy I want him to fly over with his daddy. Got it?"

Claude nodded, impressed by the decisiveness in that voice. Forrest Knox truly was his father reincarnated.

"Alphonse, I'm going to leak the rest of the story on Mackiever."

Claude cocked his head, curious as to what this might mean.

Forrest smiled. "We've got a couple of male prostitutes who'll swear under oath that Colonel Mackiever paid them for sex on multiple occasions. They're both underage, and all the dates match up. Nobody can give old Griff an alibi."

While Claude stared openmouthed, Forrest clapped his hands and stood. "Okay, everybody knows what to do. I expect Snake and the boys at Valhalla by five. If Snake gets ornery, tell him he can bring his sniper rifle. That'll give the old bastard a hard-on. By the time they touch down, he'll think he's in a Charles Bronson movie."

Claude couldn't help but chuckle. Forrest knew his uncle well. "May I go?"

Forrest gave him a sidelong glance, then an easy smile. "Sure, Claude. Just don't go too far."

Claude cleared his throat. "Meaning?"

"Don't leave the country. If I call, you come. Are we clear?"

Devereux nodded, then shook the younger man's hand and hurried out of the office as though urgent business awaited elsewhere. Truth be told, he had tickets for a Virgin Atlantic flight leaving New York tonight. But he wasn't about to use them now. If he disobeyed Forrest Knox's edict, no country could provide him sanctuary.

MELBA PRICE PULLED INTO the parking lot of a Walgreens drugstore, got out, and walked inside to the rack of *Natchez Examiner*s near the cash registers. Half an hour earlier, the office receptionist had told her that a caller identifying himself as the husband of "Doris Avery," an old patient of Dr. Cage's, was asking for her. Melba had never heard of any such patient, but the surname was enough to make her expect to hear Quentin Avery's voice when she picked up the phone. Once she got on the line, though, she quickly recognized the voice of Jack Cage, Tom's younger brother from California. Pretending to be "Fred Avery," Jack gave her a list of drugs and other items that "his wife" needed, and asked if there was any way Melba could drop them by Doris's house that afternoon. He knew that was asking a lot, he said, since their house was near Fayette, but Doris really needed the medicine.

With a shiver Melba realized that Tom must be hiding at Quentin Avery's house in nearby Jefferson County. She told Jack that she was sorry Doris was hurting, and promised to get the medicine to her as soon as possible.

During the next twenty minutes, Melba had bagged several bottles of drugs from the sample room, then told Dr. Elliott that exhaustion and stress had overcome her. She needed to go home and lie down. Once Drew released her, she'd headed for the Walgreens to get the newspaper. Tom had not put this on his list; she'd made this stop to check whether she could spot anyone following her.

As she paid for the newspaper, Melba recalled her promise to call Penn if Tom contacted her again. But she had no intention of doing that. Personal loyalty meant more to Melba than any abstract concept of right and wrong, and Tom would have to do more than he'd been accused of thus far to make her abandon him.

Standing a few feet back from the glass doors, Melba scanned the parking lot for familiar cars. Then she looked across the bypass, toward St. Catherine's Hospital. She realized then that she'd chosen her location poorly. This section of town had some of the heaviest traffic in the city.

After taking a deep breath, she walked back out to her car, started the engine, and set off for the Walmart two miles away. The cash cell phones were the most important item on the list, Jack Cage had told her, as important as the drugs. Melba hoped she would find Quentin Avery with Tom when she finally reached his home. She was of two minds about the wily old lawyer, but she knew one thing for sure: no attorney in the country stood a better chance of keeping Tom out of jail. As she drove north, Melba kept her eyes on her rearview mirror.

CHAPTER 28

CAITLIN'S CAR IS parked outside Washington Street when I arrive. When I unlock the front door, I find her standing on the other side, wearing a smile like a hastily painted door on a storm-damaged house. The circles beneath her eyes are so dark that her makeup can't mask them, and the Band-Aid on her left cheek reminds me of the painful burn beneath it.

Without a word I pull her to me. She's stiff at first, but after a few seconds, her muscles give way and she sags against me. She feels so light that I know she must have been skipping meals for days, as she does whenever she's immersed in a story. When she begins to sob, I pick her up and carry her to the guest room on the ground floor, then lay her on the bed and enfold her in my arms.

We hold each other in silence for several minutes, and I lose myself in the smell of her dark hair in my face. After she quiets down, she asks if I've had any word of my father. I tell her about Drew and Melba lying for Dad last night, and Caitlin doesn't seem at all surprised. She guesses at least a few hundred more people would be willing to lie for him, and that the odds of us—or the Double Eagles—finding him and Walt are almost zero. I'm not nearly so sure, but I don't argue the point with her. I tell her about my trip to the lake, the face-off with the Monroe cops, their story of Dad's gunfight, my rescue by Lincoln. She listens closely but says little, her mind recording every word with the mechanical dispassion she often shows when she's working. She does ask if my mother and Annie are adequately protected. I tell her they are, and that I plan to move them somewhere safer still as soon as I can arrange it. Caitlin doesn't ask where they are or where I mean to take them, and I know why. If she were to be taken during the next few days, she wouldn't be able to tell anyone where they are.

To lighten the atmosphere, she describes a morning confrontation with Billy Byrd, then updates me on the FBI's progress in reconstructing Henry's files. She seems most excited by my news that Kaiser will be staying in town for the next twenty-four hours, tending to Dwight Stone. I assume this is because she hopes to see and possibly interview Dwight, whom she got to know during the Del Payton case. I soft-pedal the JFK stuff, making it sound as though Stone has a pet conspiracy theory about the assassination and because he's ill, Kaiser is humoring him. Caitlin does ask whether Dwight might be willing to answer some questions from her, but I tell her it's doubtful. I use his cancer and impending surgery to avoid giving my real reason, which is keeping Caitlin out of Kaiser's JFK quest altogether. If she gets her teeth into a story that sensational, she'll lose whatever remains of her perspective, and everything else could go by the wayside. But she will not be deterred.

"How seriously is Kaiser taking the Kennedy stuff?" she asks, lightly touching my mouth. "Does he think those rifles we saw last night were real?"

"He's doing his due diligence, treating them as though they might be. Honestly, I think he may share some of Dwight's conspiracy theories."

Caitlin's finger stops moving. "What makes you say that?"

I can't find it in myself to lie to her completely. "Well, the director has refused to offer Dad protective custody for information on any of the civil rights cases, but Kaiser told me that if Dad has knowledge pertaining to the JFK assassination, he probably could get him protection."

"What?" Her eyes have filled with disbelief. "What the hell could Tom know about the JFK assassination?"

"Nothing. I think Stone and Kaiser have convinced each other that the Double Eagles had something to do with killing Kennedy, and since Dad was their doctor, he might know something."

"Oh." Caitlin lies back on the covers. "That sounds like nothing but a shot in the dark."

"Exactly."

"Unless . . ." She rolls over and looks at me. "How could the Double Eagles be tied to the JFK assassination?"

Now there's no avoiding it. "Stone believes Carlos Marcello, the New Orleans godfather, ordered Kennedy's death. And the Double Eagles apparently did occasional muscle work for Marcello over the years. Through Brody Royal, I guess."

"I see." Caitlin's bright green eyes are impossible to read. "And is there any indication that Tom knew Carlos Marcello?"

This is where I draw the line. I'm not going to have Caitlin digging into my father's past in New Orleans, upsetting my mother and making me crazy. I'll be doing enough of that myself. "Dad and Mom lived in New Orleans while he was at LSU med school. Dad did an externship at the parish prison, and Marcello was the don of the city at that time. But that's all they've got. The flimsiest imaginable connection."

Caitlin watches me in silence for several seconds, then says, "If that's all they have, then Tom's got nothing to worry about. On that score anyway."

"Exactly."

"Him treating the Double Eagles who worked at Triton Battery and Armstrong Tire is something else, though. I can imagine him hearing things about the civil rights murders that might be important."

"Well, if we ever find him, we'll ask him about that."

Lying on our backs, staring at the ceiling, we fall into an exhausted but companionable silence. After only a couple of minutes, I feel myself jerk at the edge of sleep.

Caitlin laughs softly. "I'm tired, too. What if we set an alarm and sleep for two hours? Do you think we'd feel better or worse?"

"Worse. I need sleep, but I've got to get Mom and Annie moved before I can rest."

"Okay. You're right."

"I wish Stone weren't coming down here. Not in the middle of all this. I've been trying to think of a way to persuade Kaiser to head down to the Lusahatcha Swamp and hunt for the Bone Tree. That would keep him out of my hair for at least a couple of days. Walker and I would have a lot more freedom to pressure the Knoxes that way."

After a couple of seconds, Caitlin makes a sound of acknowledgment but offers no comment.

I feel my breathing deepen. As consciousness begins to dim, I fight against sleep. "The Bone Tree is out there somewhere," I murmur. "Brody wasn't lying when he told us about Pooky dying there. And Kaiser has the resources to find it. Surely Dwight would love to find it, too. Have you found any clue in Henry's notes as to where that tree might be?"

Caitlin doesn't answer. At first I think she's asleep, but then I hear the sound of a zipper. As I blink my eyes against the light, she arches beside me, then works her jeans down over her feet.

"I thought we didn't have time to sleep," I say.

"We don't. This is the next best thing."

She rolls on top of me and peers down into my eyes. "It's been a long time," she says, looking surprisingly awake. "Are you really that tired?"

In truth, I am. But she's right. It has been a long time. As she straddles me and begins unbuttoning my shirt, it strikes me that the only respite I might find from my chaotic thoughts would be inside her. Caitlin clearly feels the same, and within a minute she's put me there. As she labors purposefully above me, the world contracts to the boundaries of her eyes, and sensation blots out thought as surely as intravenous morphine.

HALF AN HOUR HAS passed since Caitlin climaxed and lay across my chest, her face buried in my neck. She's sleeping as soundly as a child who's stayed up past her bedtime. I haven't had the heart to wake her, nor have I fallen asleep myself. My thoughts have been occupied with finding a truly safe haven for Annie and my mother.

In the past, I've moved them as far as Texas to get them out of danger, but this time I want them close enough that I can stay with them at night. No hotel would be safe, or any local B&B, though I know of several secluded ones. With Sheriff Billy Byrd and Forrest Knox on the hunt, any public or even semi-public accommodation will ultimately be traced. I've just about decided to leave them where they are when I remember that Sam Abrams, one of my best childhood friends, recently moved his parents to a retirement community in south Florida—Sea Haven Towers, or something like that. Sam was raised in Natchez's once-thriving Jewish community, and he and I found we had a lot in common in high school. Like me, he's one of the few successful members of our class who returned to Natchez as an adult. Sam has helped me during difficult times before, and most important, he makes the cut for what I call my "foxhole friends," guys I'd trust with my life no matter what the circumstance. If I died tomorrow with no money to my name, Sam Abrams would make sure Annie made it through college with everything she needed. Since I'm now at war with Forrest Knox, that's the kind of friend I need.

I'm about to prod Caitlin awake when I notice a Treo sticking out from behind the base of the lamp on her bedside table. Since Brody Royal destroyed her Treo last night, along with my BlackBerry, she must have gotten another. Moving smoothly, I reach over and slide the phone off the table, then enter her old passcode.

The phone rejects the code.

For a moment I lie staring at the screen, wondering why she would change her passcode. But since her previous phone was in the possession of more than one person before Royal destroyed it, perhaps she simply took the precaution of changing it when she got a new one.

Replacing the Treo on the bedside table, I get up and walk into the kitchen, where we keep a small laptop for recipes and shopping lists. The sweat on my skin evaporates quickly, chilling me enough to make me shiver. Booting up the computer, I check my e-mail, something I haven't done nearly enough since losing my BlackBerry. My box contains more than thirty messages, but my quick scan stops instantly at the third most recent. The sender is *KaiserJohn@fbi.gov*. Opening the mail, I wait several seconds for it to download, then read the following:

Penn,
We traced several fingerprints on Brody Royal's M-C
to a Cuban émigré from New Orleans. You'll recall
that this M-C was part of the lot shipped from Italy
after the rifle LHO bought via mail from Klein's

*in Chicago. It was wholesaled to a Dallas retail gun
store, and the earliest it could have been sold was
August 1963. Cuban émigré was one Eladio Cruz,
a student reported missing on November 21, 1963.
(Yes, you read that right.) Cruz was never seen
in the U.S. again. We're now trying to determine
whether Cruz was pro- or anti-Castro. Don't miss
the meeting with Stone. I told him you were coming,
and we may have a decision on getting protective
custody for your father by then.*

*P.S. Keep your eyes open and stay indoors when possible.
Caitlin, too. Snake Knox could shoot you both from
600 yards, maybe more, and we can't be positive he's in
Texas. His flying skill gives him a lot of mobility.*

Kaiser's mention of Caitlin makes me wonder if he
knows I'm with her now. Is there an FBI agent outside my
house, giving Kaiser regular reports? Or possibly a static
surveillance camera? Right now I don't really care, but I
don't want to be followed all afternoon. Kaiser's warning
about the danger from the Double Eagles only strength-
ens my resolve to hide Annie and my mother somewhere
safer. As soon as Caitlin and I separate, I'm going to call
Sam Abrams and try to arrange a move.

Rereading Kaiser's e-mail, I wonder why he bothered
to code anything when the overall meaning of the message is so clear. Maybe he was in a hurry. "M-C" obviously
refers to the Mannlicher-Carcano, and "LHO" is Lee
Harvey Oswald. The six-month separation between the
sale of the two rifles must have miffed Kaiser, but the fact
that Cruz went missing one day before the Kennedy assassination would have more than made up for that. That
the Carcano was purchased by a Cuban student living in
New Orleans is doubly provocative. First, because New
Orleans was the private preserve of Carlos Marcello,
and second, it throws Cuba into sharp focus in relation
to the assassination. The answer to whether Eladio Cruz
was pro- or anti-Castro will push Kaiser's theory either
toward or away from Fidel Castro and Russia. Away from
Castro would mean toward the Cuban exiles who landed
in the Bay of Pigs, and their CIA and Mafia backers. John

Kaiser—and Dwight Stone's Working Group—must be salivating over this possibility.

I'm suddenly more sure than ever that I don't want to open this can of worms with Caitlin. After double-checking that I've signed out of my e-mail account, I switch off the laptop, then return to the guest room, take hold of her upper arm, and gently shake her.

She makes no sound.

I shake her again. This time she groans like a teenager who doesn't want to get out of bed on a school day.

"Caitlin?" I say sharply. "Wake up."

"*Nooooo*," she moans. "I feel like hell."

"I know. But we've got to get moving."

She raises her head and brushes black hair out of her eyes. "Did you even finish? I don't remember."

"Yes."

"Good." She smiles lazily. "For half a second there I felt guilty."

With a deep sigh she rolls over and sits up on the edge of the bed. The ladder of her spine shows through her skin. "This *sucks*," she says.

"Yep."

"I'm *freezing*." She flips back her hair and searches the covers for her panties. I try not to laugh while I watch this familiar ritual. At last she finds them, tangled in the sheet near the foot of the bed. As she pulls then on, she says, "Do you realize if all this hadn't happened, we would be getting married in nine days?"

"I do."

"I guess we'll get there eventually."

"We will." While I pull on my own pants, it strikes me that once I've moved Annie and my mother out of Edelweiss, I could take Caitlin over there and show her what would have been her wedding present.

"You know what?" I stand beside the bed. "If we can find half an hour later on, I could show you a real surprise."

She pauses with her bra halfway on and stares at me with narrowed eyes. "What kind of surprise?"

I realize I'm grinning stupidly at her. "A one-of-a-kind surprise."

She looks suspicious for several seconds, but then she

seems to intuit that I won't reveal my secret no matter how hard she presses me. "I'll see what I can do. Call me after eight or so?"

"Before sundown would be better."

She draws back her head, once again mistrustful. "What did you do?"

"You'll see."

"Before sunset is tough. There's too much going on, and too much competition in town. Plus, we already stayed here too long—my fault, I know. Are you sure it can't be later than that?"

"I guess later's okay. But it won't be as good."

She sighs and snaps her bra, then begins hunting her shoes. "Later will have to do. Story of our lives, right?"

Right.

CHAPTER 29

WALT GARRITY PAUSED behind a large oak tree and stared up a hill at the Valhalla hunting lodge. He'd been working his way through the forest of Lusahatcha County for nearly ninety minutes, and he was winded. He'd cut through the game fence a mile south of the main gate, then taken a circuitous path through the hunting camp to avoid the wildlife cameras he saw mounted on pine trees at regular intervals. He could still see the gate in his mind, an enormous wrought-iron thing set between stone pillars. A brass sign on one of the pillars read:

VALHALLA EXOTIC HUNTING RESERVE
Absolutely No Trespassing

Nailed to a tree to the right of the gate was a smaller wooden sign with letters burned into it. Those letters read: FORT KNOX. Beyond the gate, an asphalt road led deep into the forest. Walt had given the road a wide berth, but during his hike into the hunting camp, he'd crossed several logging roads that led nowhere, food plots for game, and always the cameras, affixed to trees with plastic flex-cuffs.

When the lodge appeared through the trees, he approached it with extreme caution. Though the GPS tracker in Drew's truck had told him Forrest was back at state police headquarters in Baton Rouge, there might be anything from a gang of Double Eagles to a full complement of visiting hunters staying at the camp. As Walt neared the big building, the hum of a central heating unit reached his ears. He paused behind a large thornbush and watched for another five minutes, then made a careful circuit of the house.

Its rustic appearance was merely an illusion. The

rough-hewn timber building was served by both power lines and a massive backup generator, while the telephone wires, satellite dishes, and various antennas made it look more like an army outpost than a hunting camp. Walt saw no vehicles, which encouraged him. Then, to his amazement, he saw that a sliding glass door on a deck at the side of the lodge was standing partly open. Taking a Browning 9 mm from the holster at the small of his back, he moved quickly up to the door and scanned the interior.

The great room of Valhalla looked as he'd expected: dozens of stuffed animal heads adorned the walls, many of them of African origin. Some appeared to be threatened or endangered species; a fully grown mountain gorilla stood in one corner as though pondering a charge toward the center of the room. A staircase led up to a broad landing on the second floor. Following his instincts, Walt slipped inside, bypassed the stairs, and moved along one wall to a cypress door at the far end of the room.

Near the door, he noticed a display of weapons on the wall. Most prominent in the rack were four *katanas*—samurai swords—that appeared to be antiques. To the right of the rack hung the framed photographs Mackiever had told him about early that morning: a Japanese officer with two Caucasian heads hanging from his belt, brandishing a samurai sword; and beside it Sergeant Frank Knox beheading the same officer, who knelt like a slave at his feet. Walt suspected that one of the swords on the wall was the one from the photos, but he didn't waste time finding out.

Beyond the door, Walt found an office containing an antique desk that might have belonged to Teddy Roosevelt. The room's appointments also seemed to fit that era, but what dominated the room was a massive feral hog stuffed and mounted on a polished stand against the wall opposite the desk. Walt had hoped to find filing cabinets, or even a safe, but he saw nothing like that. Taking a seat in the black leather chair behind the desk, he quickly went through the drawers. He found little: some ledgers pertaining to Billy Knox's legitimate business interests, particularly a television program about hunting; a messy drawer filled with pens and office supplies; a bottle of Wild Turkey bourbon; a few tins of Skoal; and a box of Cuban cigars. There was also a letter from Jimmy Buffett's management company, expressing doubt that their artist could perform for a private birthday party in Mississippi, regardless of the fee.

Walt was about to get up and start working his way through the rest of the lodge when he noticed that a rectangular section of the floor beneath him was lighter than the rest. Standing, he looked down, trying to work out why this was so. It appeared that the hardwood around the rectangle had been darkened by sunlight, while the rectangle had escaped this aging, as though a rug had covered it for a long period. As he stared, Walt realized that the rectangle was exactly the size of the base upon which the big razorback had been mounted—which now stood on the opposite side of the office.

Kneeling, Walt found a small hole in one plank that went right through the floor. The hole was smaller than his little finger. He searched the desk again until he found what he hoped for, a metal rod with a hook on one end. Inserting this hook in the hole, he lifted a concealed trapdoor about two by three feet wide. His heart began to pound when he saw what lay beneath: two heavy floor safes with combination locks set in their faces.

He was gauging his chances of breaking into those safes when the rumble of a low-flying airplane sounded over the lodge. After twenty seconds it faded, then returned, though at diminished volume. Walt's heartbeat had just about returned to normal when he heard the *whup-whup-whup* of a helicopter approaching. This was a different engine. The rotor-driven craft flew directly over the lodge, then hovered and began to land in the clearing outside. With no time to flee the building, Walt dropped the trapdoor, replaced the hook in the desk, and ran for the staircase in the great room.

THE LAST THING BILLY Knox wanted to do while Concordia Parish was turning into a redneck version of Fallujah was return to Louisiana, especially in the company of his father. But since his cousin had sent the invitation, remaining in Texas wasn't an option. At Forrest's

command, Snake had flown Billy and Sonny over in the
Baron, while three more Double Eagles had set out from
Toledo Bend by car and would arrive in five hours or so.

Snake had spent most of the flight offering theories for
why his bullet hadn't killed Henry Sexton at Mercy Hospital, all of which amounted to detailed but pathetic ex-
cuses. Only Claude Devereux's hint that Forrest planned
to retaliate for the morning's drug busts by killing Penn
Cage and his girlfriend had brightened Snake's mood.
He was furious that "that newspaper whore" had written a story claiming he'd murdered and mutilated Pooky
Wilson in 1964. That Snake was in fact guilty of the crime
seemed not to matter to him, but Billy had learned long
ago not to demand reason from his father. While Snake
went on and on, Billy had simply put on his headphones
and listened to Steve Earle for the remainder of the flight.

Forrest's Redbone enforcer had met them down at
the landing strip in an SUV, then ferried them up to the
lodge. Now they trooped into the great room like GIs
summoned to a pre-mission briefing. Billy had never
served in the military, but everybody else had, and there
was no mistaking the martial air of this meeting. Snake
made quite a thing of laying his rifle case on the coffee
table, as though it held some ceremonial weapon about to
be consecrated.

Forrest straddled a heavy wooden chair at the center of
the room, facing the sofas and club chairs. Ozan played
waiter and got everybody their preference in alcohol,
but even before it arrived, Snake launched into a monologue on the ways he might remove the human threats
to their organization. Forrest let Snake run, but Billy
hardly looked at his father. He sensed that Forrest had
something very different in mind. Finally, after a couple
of shots of bourbon, even Snake began to sense something
amiss. When he finally stopped talking, everyone sat in
awkward silence, which was unusual at Valhalla, where
family members and Double Eagles had always felt completely at home.

Forrest looked at each man in turn: Billy, Sonny, and
finally Snake. Then he began to speak, softly but with
absolute authority, as if it were understood that no one
would interrupt him. This was no mean feat when Snake

and Sonny were a generation older than he. Billy could never have pulled this off without his father butting in, but Forrest was different. He always had been.

"We're under attack from at least four different directions," he began, "and probably more. The FBI is after us, both for what the Double Eagles did back in the day and for our current operations. The Masters girl is trying to crucify us with her newspaper. Penn Cage wants us because of the threat to his father. And Walker Dennis wants revenge for the cousin he lost a couple of years back. To that you can add a whole department that wants blood because of the deputies that died from the bomb in the warehouse this morning."

Forrest looked directly at Snake. "While my instinct when attacked is to counterattack, violently, I've decided that we're not going to dump gasoline on this fire. We can't afford to."

Billy saw his father gearing up to argue, but Forrest raised his right hand a few inches to forestall him. "Brody apparently lost his mind last night. I should have seen it coming, but I didn't. He did us the favor of taking Henry Sexton off the board, but we don't know what information he might have passed to others, or what our current exposure is. We don't know what Morehouse told Henry before you guys took him out, but we have to assume the worst. We also don't know what Viola Turner may have told Dr. Cage or Henry Sexton before she died. So . . . we're pretty much in the dark when it comes to the exact nature of the threat. The body count is already unacceptably high. Even if we suspend operations and nobody else gets killed, it'll be weeks before the FBI pulls out of the parish. And that is what we are going to do. I've already given the orders to my people, and you guys will do the same."

Snake's face had gone red, but to Billy's amazement, he didn't rush to fill the vacuum of Forrest's first pause.

"The fact that what's been in the paper has focused on the 1960s is encouraging," Forrest went on, "because proving any of those crimes in court would be virtually impossible, especially with all the witnesses dead. One of you guys would have to turn state's evidence for them to get a conviction, and I assume that will not happen."

"You're goddamned right it won't," Snake vowed.

Forrest acknowledged his fury with a nod. "But that doesn't mean we're in the clear. This morning's busts will allow Dennis to put a lot of pressure on your mules, cookers, et cetera." Forrest looked at Billy. "What do you think our exposure is from those people?"

"Zero to minimal," Billy said. He'd been thinking about this all morning. "Hardly any of them can hurt us, and we're holding wives or kids of the few who could. They won't talk."

"Good. Make sure our men in the CPSO reinforce that. If one man tries to cut a deal, mamas and babies start dying. Just the fact that we have people on the inside will scare the hell out of them."

For the first time, Snake nodded in satisfaction. Probably at the coldness in Forrest's voice, Billy thought.

"As for the bigger picture," Forrest continued, "we're going to play it very cool. There'll be a lot of moving parts to my response. First, I've called up the Black Team. They'll start arriving here today. If anybody needs to be threatened or hit in the short term, they'll handle it. The Bureau has no idea who they are, as opposed to you guys. Second, I need time. First, to get Mackiever out of his job. But there are other reasons, too." Forrest flexed his fists and looked around the room. "To that end, you guys are going to have to do something you won't want to do. But we have no choice."

Snake's eyes had narrowed in suspicion.

"Sheriff Walker Dennis has asked that you guys and four other Eagles come in to the CPSO tomorrow for voluntary questioning."

Billy's stomach flipped over. Snake looked like he was about to bust a gut, but still he waited to hear what was coming. Sonny Thornfield was obviously terrified.

"Why me?" Billy asked hoarsely.

"Not you," Forrest said. "I misspoke there."

Billy nearly fell out of his chair with relief.

"At seven tomorrow," Forrest said, "Snake, Sonny, and the other named Eagles are going to do exactly that. To my knowledge, Dennis has no plans to arrest you. This amounts to harassment, plain and simple. But you're going to put up with it, because I need the time."

When Snake finally blew his top, it was like a storm being unleashed from above. He could cuss more in sixty seconds than any man Billy had ever seen. Forrest simply sat there and took it, like a man waiting for a tornado to pass. Sonny looked like he might collapse from the strain at any moment. But at last, like even the most violent of hurricanes, Snake blew himself out.

Forrest waited a bit, then said calmly, "There's no risk of arrest, Uncle Snake. Zero."

"For you," Snake snapped. "That goddamn Masters girl already accused me of murder in the newspaper!"

Forrest actually chuckled at this. "Yeah, well, you've been bragging in bars that you killed Martin Luther King. Did you think that shit was never going to come back on you?"

"This is different!"

"You're goddamn right it is." Forrest's eyes looked like lasers burning into Snake's face.

Snake looked at the broad plank floor. "What are you gonna be doing while all this is going down?"

"I'm glad you asked, Uncle. I'm going to be cutting a deal to make all this trouble go away."

"Who with?"

"That you don't need to know. Not right now. Nobody does."

"Bullshit we don't," Snake said, looking around for support. "If you think I'm gonna walk into the sheriff's office without knowing—"

"I do think that," Forrest said with icy calm. "Because it's your only option. Do anything else and you look guilty. Kill the mayor or the Masters girl or, God forbid, John Kaiser, and we'll have an army of federal agents in here for a year. They'll be like that posse in the Butch Cassidy movie. They'll hound us until we're dead. So you and your old buddies are going to walk into the CPSO like you have nothing to hide."

"No goddamn way," Snake muttered. "That's suicide."

When Forrest laughed again, Snake looked apoplectic. "I tell you what," Forrest said. "I was going to keep this a surprise, but to ease your mind, Uncle, I'll give you a little heads-up. Ten minutes after you walk into the sheriff's office tomorrow, Walker Dennis won't be the sheriff anymore."

Snake's mouth fell open. "What do you mean? Is the Black Team gonna kill him?"

"That's none of your concern. All you need to know is that by the time you walk in there tomorrow, Walker Dennis will have ceased to be a factor in our situation."

"Who'll be the sheriff, then?"

Forrest grinned. "A friendly face."

Billy drank off his whiskey, leaned forward, and waited for his cousin to lay out the plan. He expected a classic Forrest Knox gambit: ballsy as hell, yet as intricately choreographed as a ballet. But Forrest said nothing. He had no intention of telling them anything. Billy expected his father to raise hell, but after staring at Forrest's face for nearly a minute, Snake settled back in his chair with a malevolent smile. It was as though Forrest had cast a spell over him.

"So," Forrest concluded. "We're all clear? Tomorrow you walk in there for questioning?"

Snake laughed. "I reckon so, nephew. I reckon so."

"Good. Now, I want to discuss a couple of things with Billy. We're going to take a walk down to check the food plots."

Billy started to get up, but Snake said, "Hold up one minute. I heard you've changed your orders on Tom Cage. No more shoot to kill, they say."

In an instant the beast that lived behind Forrest's imperturbable mask revealed itself. "Who told you that?" he asked in a barely audible voice.

But Snake was not intimidated. "Never you mind, nephew. Is it true?"

"It's true."

Snake looked at Sonny as if to say, *You see?* Then he said, "And why would that be?"

"Tom Cage is one of the moving parts in the deal I'm making to save your ass."

Snake slowly went red again. "You mean to save your real-estate deals down in New Orleans, don't you? This ain't about saving us up here at all."

Forrest looked at the floor as though by so doing he could bleed his fury into the wood. After half a minute he composed himself and looked up again, focusing on each man in turn once more.

"The crystal meth business is for suckers," he said. "You found out why this morning. Every man they brought in is facing a mandatory minimum sentence. You may be right that none of them will turn on you— this time. But sooner or later, somebody will give you up. If we stay in that business, we're going to end up in Angola one day. You guys may be willing to take that chance, but I'm not. The deals Brody has got me into will make the money we've earned in the past look like a joke. I'd be better off paying you to stay *out* of business than to risk you staying in. You understand? And I'm willing to do that, for a reasonable amount of time. What I won't do is stand by while you go rogue and try some crazy shit like Brody did, and bring more heat down on our heads. Because the day you become a liability to me . . ."

Forrest didn't finish this sentence. He didn't need to.

Snake was shaking his head, but when he finally spoke, he only seemed to have one thing on his mind. "I want Tom Cage dead," he growled. "The rest of it I can live with, but not that. I think the doc knows enough to put us all in Angola, and he'll do it, too."

"Why?" Forrest asked, sounding genuinely interested. "Why would he do that?"

"Because of what we done to that nurse of his back in '68." Snake looked hard at Forrest. "You know what I'm talking about. You were there."

Forrest acknowledged this with a nod.

Billy was pretty sure they were talking about a gang rape, but he had no desire to know more.

"Dr. Cage might feel some bitterness about that," Forrest conceded. "But he cares about his family a lot more than he does revenge. You leave him to me."

"To him that nurse *was* family," Snake said. "He loved that nigger, and he had a natural child by her. Why else would he have gone so high up to keep us from killing her?"

Billy had no idea what Snake was talking about.

"He probably did love her," Forrest said. "I don't give a shit about that. I care about security. Dr. Cage wants to watch that granddaughter of his grow up for as long as he can. He'll do a lot for that privilege."

Snake held out a shaking hand and pointed at Forrest. "Mark my words, boy. You try to cut a deal with Tom Cage, and he'll fuck you in the end."

Forrest looked more intrigued than angry. "Why is that, Uncle?"

Snake sat so still he looked carved from stone. "I've never trusted that motherfucker. Not since your daddy died in his office."

For the first time Forrest looked rattled. "What the hell's that supposed to mean?"

"It's just a feeling I always had. I don't like that that nigger woman was in there when Frank died, especially so soon after what we done to her."

Forrest sneered and shook his head. "You're nuts, Unc. Daddy was doomed the second those batteries fell on him. The pathologist told Mama that."

"Yeah, well . . . fuck him, too."

Forrest's voice hardened. "You're the one who took Daddy to Dr. Cage's office. You should have taken him to the hospital. That's something else the pathologist told Mama, if you want to know."

"Fuck the pathologist!" Snake roared. "I know what I know. And I want Dr. Cage *dead*. The rest you can have your way on, but I want that SOB in the swamp!"

Forrest stood, then walked over to Snake and spoke in a voice so soft and sibilant that Billy was reminded of the warning hiss of the moccasins for which his father had been nicknamed.

"Listen to me, Uncle. I say who lives and dies in this outfit. Not you, and not anybody you might call in the dark of the night. *Me*. Anybody crosses me on that, he'll be chewing over old times with Leo Spivey. Am I understood?"

Billy wasn't breathing. Forrest had just threatened his father with death. To Billy's surprise, Snake didn't jump up screaming, but instead merely mumbled a reply. Billy couldn't make it out, but apparently this response satisfied Forrest, because he turned and walked over to his chair to get his coat.

Billy got up to go for the "walk" Forrest had proposed, but Snake suddenly stood, grabbed his rifle case off the coffee table, and said, "Don't get up, Billy. I wouldn't want you youngsters to get a chill. Sonny and I will check the food plots. I might see a buck on the way down. At least that way I won't have brought my gun for nothing."

As the obviously shaken Sonny followed Snake to the door, Forrest called after them, "I will give you this, Uncle. If I can't get this deal done, and quick, there *will* be some killing to do. Mayor Cage, the Masters girl . . . even Kaiser. So keep your gun warmed up, because you never know."

Snake stopped and looked back at his nephew. "Agent Kaiser? You serious?"

Forrest nodded. "I'm digging into Kaiser right now. I've got a funny feeling about him. It may be that even if I do a deal to spare the Cages, Kaiser will need to have an accident. But until I know, you play it my way. Agreed?"

The wild light Billy knew so well flickered in his father's eyes.

"Deal," Snake said. Then he went out. Sonny pulled the door shut behind then, and then Billy was alone with Forrest.

Billy had no idea what was coming, but he knew it was serious when Forrest motioned for Ozan to leave the room and refilled Billy's whiskey glass himself. Forrest poured himself a straight vodka, then turned the big wooden chair around and sat with his legs crossed, his eyes on Billy's.

"How you doing, William?" he asked.

"Ah, I'm good," Billy almost stammered.

"Do you think I was too rough on your old man?"

Fuck yeah, Billy thought. But in his calmest voice he said, "Nah, I get it. It ain't easy keeping him calm, and we damn sure got enough heat on us already."

"That's right. And for that reason, I need to make sure you and I are on the same page."

Billy's eyes strayed to the windows that faced the deck. He worried about his father and Sonny trying to eavesdrop.

"Alphonse will make sure nobody hears us," Forrest said. "Here's the deal, Billy. I told them the truth. I'm moving up to the next level, where the kind of money and power your father never dreamed about is everywhere. There's room at that table for you, brother, right next to me. You've done a good job of straddling the line between the legitimate and criminal worlds. And you're good with money, especially cleaning it."

Billy swelled with pride. His cousin never gave compliments.

"At the same time, thanks to the actions of . . . the past generation, we're in more danger than we've ever faced. I told the truth about the drug business, too. It only ends one of two places, prison or the cemetery."

Billy took a gulp of bourbon. He'd served time in Raiford Penitentiary in Florida, and the term "prison rape" was not academic to him. He hadn't watched a prison movie since.

"In some ways," Forrest went on, "we're our father's sons, you and me. We got some good qualities from them. But they had some bad ones, too. Your father's is his temper. Agreed?"

Billy nodded soberly.

"We can't let that temper put us at risk, William."

Billy shook his head. What else could he do?

Forrest leaned toward him, and Billy felt as though the temperature in the room had risen five degrees. "I'm going to do all I can to keep us all out of prison," Forrest said. "But it's not a perfect world. The day may come when we have to make a choice, you and me. Between our father's generation and ours. You understand?"

Billy felt the blood drain from his face. This was the point of the whole conversation. "I do, yeah."

Forrest let the silence stretch until Billy felt he could hear himself sweating. Then he said, "I need to know that if that day comes, you'll be ready to cut loose anybody who's a liability. And that includes your father."

Billy could no longer speak. It was all he could do not to start shivering on the spot.

"I know that's a tough thing to contemplate," Forrest said. "But we may face that choice a lot sooner than we'd like."

Billy tried to think of something appropriate to say, but his mind had gone blank with fear. Forrest seemed to understand this, and he said, "One more thing. If things should go tits up, we might have to pull the ripcord on our escape chute. We need to make sure our Andorra option is ready to go. Do you feel everything's good on that front?"

"Absolutely," Billy said, thankful for the reprieve.

"Good. Well, what about that choice I was talking about?"

Billy got up and walked a few steps away from Forrest. He hated the eyes of all the dead animals staring down at him; he always had. He wasn't a born killer like his father or Forrest. In fact, if it wasn't for the TV show, he'd probably have quit hunting game a long time ago.

"When you say cut them loose," Billy said, "do you mean let them go to jail? Or . . ." His voice died in his throat.

"You know the answer to that. In spite of all their talk about blood oaths, those old men aren't going to sit in Angola while nigger gangs torment them. One of them will talk. Glenn Morehouse proved that."

In Forrest's dark eyes Billy saw not a shred of doubt or mercy. He might as well have been looking into the eyes of his uncle Frank, who despite being long dead, still dominated the family like an unquiet ghost.

"Do we understand each other?" Forrest asked.

"Yeah," Billy said, knowing further hesitation could be fatal. "I'm not going back to prison. I can't."

"I'm glad to hear that, brother."

Billy felt some of the nauseating tension drain away. "Since I'm not turning myself in, can I go back to Texas now?"

Forrest got to his feet. "Sorry, no. I need you to ride herd on the old men until tomorrow. You speak for me, William. I'll make that clear. Everything depends on them going to Walker Dennis's office in the morning."

"I got it. Where will you be?"

"Concordia Parish. Out of sight, but close enough to take over if things spin out of control tomorrow. I'm going to leave Traveller out here tonight. I may not be able to take him everywhere I'll need to go. You look out for him?"

"Sure," Billy said, adding the dog to his endless list of responsibilities. He took another slug of bourbon. "Do you really think you can cut a deal? I mean . . . is there a real chance?"

"A good chance. Tomorrow Walker Dennis is going to get the surprise of his life. And with luck, by then my deal will be in place." Forrest walked over and patted Billy on the shoulder. "Okay?"

Billy felt the drink shaking in his hand. "Okay, Forrest. I'm with you."

WALT LAY BENEATH A bed in one of the second-floor rooms, his heart thundering in his chest. He'd scarcely reached the second-story landing when the front door of the lodge opened and booted feet marched into the great room. As he'd turned to slip down the hallway, he'd peered back around the corner and caught sight of the last man into the room: a uniformed state trooper with dark hair, a hard jawline, and a mutilated ear. *Forrest Knox.* And trailing at Knox's heel was the large pit bull Walt had seen back in Baton Rouge.

Once Walt reached his present hiding place, he'd heard muted voices below, yet as hard as he strained to hear, he couldn't make out the words. Any hope that the conversation would be short faded as the minutes dragged on. Eventually, the helicopter outside spooled up again and noisily departed, but after the beating of its rotors faded, at least two voices droned on below. More disturbing still, when Walt checked his cell phone, he found he had no service. This puzzled him, since he'd checked his phone several times during the walk in and seen three bars of reception.

As carefully as he could, he slid out from under the bed, tiptoed to the window, and peered through a crack in the curtains. A dog that appeared to be Knox's pit bull was sitting in the yard, alert as a hungry wolf. The sight chilled Walt's blood. He'd worked with K-9 units enough to know that the canine sense of smell was a truly fearsome thing. He had no chance at escape while that dog patrolled the yard.

Walt took out his burn phone and checked it again, but being near the window hadn't improved his reception. *At least I know Tom's okay*, he thought. *Even if I don't know where he is.*

As he tiptoed back across the floor, he realized that, depending on what the men below did next, he might have to spend quite a while in this place. Lowering himself to his knees, he rolled onto his back and slid slowly under the bed.

CHAPTER 30

"THIS HOUSE LOOKS just like it did twenty-seven years ago," Mom says, looking around the living room of Sam Abrams's parents' Duncan Avenue home. "I remember coming to one of your senior parties here. My god, you and Sam were just boys."

"How come I've never been here before?" Annie asks, looking wide-eyed around the unfamiliar house. "If you're such good friends with Mr. Sam?"

"His parents are older than Gram and Papa, punkin. That's why they moved to Florida."

"But they kept this house? And the furniture?"

"That's right. So they can come visit their kids during holidays."

"Jewish holidays?"

"I imagine so. Why don't you run upstairs and check out the bedrooms? That's where they all are."

Annie looks toward the ceiling, then sniffs suspiciously. "It *smells* like old people."

"Well, they lived here fifty years, at least."

As Annie wraps her mind around this, I know my mother must be thinking of the house she and my father lost to arson seven years ago.

"Come on, Gram," Annie says. "Let's see where we're going to be living this time."

Mom waves her toward the front foyer and stairs. "You go on, honey. I'll be up in a minute."

Annie rolls her eyes, then takes my mother's suitcase from her. "I'll carry your bag up."

"Thank you, muffin."

At age eleven, Annie must be pretty tired of being addressed as *punkin* and *muffin*, but she rarely protests so long as none of her friends are around. She disappears in search of the stairs, and then I hear the *clunk-clunk-clunk* of a heavy case being dragged up carpeted steps.

My mother gives me a look that communicates many things: guilt and regret most of all. "I hate losing the Abramses. But we've lost most of Natchez's Jewish families over the last twenty years. All their children settled elsewhere."

"Like most of my classmates."

"Won't the neighbors think George and Bernice have come back to town?"

I can't help but chuckle at this. "Sam called the nosiest one and told her he's rented the house to a visiting professor from Alcorn State University."

"That was smart."

"The only question the neighbor asked was whether the professor was white or black."

Mom smiles and shakes her head. "The closed garage is nice. I was a little worried people would recognize your car downtown, even tucked back behind the fence and bushes."

"This is a better safe house by every measure. It's totally untraceable, so long as you and Annie stay inside and keep the curtains closed."

I walk into the kitchen and pull the curtains almost shut. The Abramses' house stands on Duncan Avenue, facing a park donated to the city in the nineteenth century by one of the "nabobs of Natchez." It's one of the most peaceful streets in the city, since it faces the back nine of the golf course and thus has houses only on one side. Beyond the links, I can make out the Little League ball fields where Drew Elliott and I played Dixie Youth baseball.

Mom walks up behind me and squeezes my upper arm. "It's going to be all right, Penn. I really believe that."

Before I can answer, my new BlackBerry rings. After seeing Caitlin's Treo earlier, I realized I couldn't live without at least occasional access to my e-mail accounts. As soon as I set up the phone, I gave the number to Caitlin and Walker Dennis, telling them to use it only if they couldn't reach me on one of my new TracFones.

"Who's calling?" Mom asks anxiously.

"Sheriff Dennis, from Vidalia."

She looks grave, and I realize she must fear the worst every time the phone rings.

"What you got, Walker?" I ask. "How are your deputies doing?"

"The second one just died. Terry Stamper was about to go into the OR over in Alexandria. Turns out his aorta was torn, and he bled out while he was on the gurney."

"Jesus, Walker. I'm sorry."

"Three kids, Penn. Oldest is six."

"Is it about Tom?" my mother whispers, probably terrified by my expression.

I shake my head and cover the microphone hole. "Nothing to do with Dad. I may be a while. Why don't you check on Annie?"

Mom nods and heads for the staircase.

"I'm so sorry, man," I repeat, sitting at the banquette in the corner of the kitchen. "I wish we hadn't gone to that warehouse."

"That's the job," Dennis says stoically. "My men knew that. And we're gonna finish this particular job."

"I'm with you."

"Good. I finally got ahold of Claude Devereux. I told him I wanted the Double Eagles in my office at seven A.M. tomorrow. All of them I could get, but for sure Snake Knox and Sonny Thornfield."

"What did he say?"

"That he'd pass on my request—if he could find them."

"He'll pass it on, all right. He probably called Forrest Knox two seconds after you hung up. But Kaiser's right. I wouldn't expect to see the Eagles tomorrow."

"Well, I'm going to question them one way or another, even if I have to extradite them from Texas. You could probably help me with that, huh?"

"Yes, but that's a slow process. Have you found anything useful in what you confiscated during the busts?"

"Nothing against the Double Eagles. Going through the computers is slow work. But if we find something, it's gonna be there."

"What about your interrogations of the people you busted this morning?"

"Not one of them's talked yet. They're scared to death, Penn."

"That tells me they know their employers well."

"Yeah. But I've never seen anything like this. I feel like I could walk in there with a blowtorch and they wouldn't say a word."

This takes me back to my days as an ADA in Houston. "Have you checked out their families?"

"What do you mean?"

"I was thinking about hostages. Sometimes you see that in the drug trade. The Double Eagles might be holding some wives or kids, to ensure silence."

"Oh. I get it. But tracing these families could be tough. Quite a few of these folks are illegals."

"Do what you can. What about Leo Spivey's death? Anything come from that?"

"It was probably murder, but there's nothing pointing to anybody in particular. I'll tell you something peculiar, though. I noticed it when I talked to Claude Devereux."

"What's that?"

"Claude sounded scared, too. Especially for a cocky old lawyer."

I remember Pithy Nolan telling me that calling Claude Devereux a snake would be a slander to the serpent. "Lawyers who walk the line between both sides of the law tend to build up liabilities over the years. Maybe Devereux's afraid that his note's about to come due."

"It is, if I have anything to do with it."

"Are you going to tell John Kaiser you called Devereux?"

"I will if I hear the Eagles are coming in. Short of that, I got no use for Kaiser."

"The FBI could help you with those computers you confiscated."

Walker pauses for a moment. "I'll think about it. What's your plan?"

"I need to sleep, like you said. I'm about to pass out. But I can come over to the station if I can help you with anything."

"Nah. Get some rest. If the Eagles do come in tomorrow, it's gonna be a long day, and I want you there."

"Thanks. And again . . . I'm sorry about your deputy."

"Tough times, bud."

Sheriff Dennis hangs up.

The sound of Annie's footsteps comes through the

ceiling. As I walk back into the den, television voices float down from the upstairs. Then my TracFone rings as I'm walking to the garage door to be sure it's locked.

This time it's Jewel Washington, the coroner. For a second I wonder if the final toxicology report has come in on Viola Turner, but that process usually takes weeks.

"Hey, Jewel," I answer. "What's up?"

"Are you close to a radio?"

"Uh . . . I don't know. Hang on. What's happening?"

"Just tune in to WMPR in Jackson. 90.1 on the FM dial."

Walking back into the kitchen, I find no radio. But in the den stands an ancient console sound system, the kind where you lift the heavy wooden lid and find a turntable and radio. I switch on the system and wait for the tubes to warm up.

"I'll have it in a few seconds, Jewel. Won't you tell me what's going on?"

"I don't want to ruin the surprise."

A crazy thought hits me. "It's not Dad, is it?"

"God, no. The opposite."

Turning the big dial to 90.1, I hear a disc jockey's voice, rich with the rhythms of black Mississippi.

". . . folks will tell you times have changed down here, but no sooner do the movers and shakers get that out of their mouths than something happens to give the lie to their words. To illustrate my point, we've got Mr. Lincoln Turner with us. Mr. Turner is the son of the victim in that doctor murder down in Natchez. He was born in Chicago, but his family goes way back in this town. And it's a good thing he came back home to Mississippi when he did, because otherwise the powers that be would have swept his mother's death right under the rug. Yes, sir, that big white rug they spread out to cover anything they don't want the world to see. Well, it's out again, my brothers and sisters. So let's hear firsthand what's going on down there in the old slave capital of the Magnolia State. . . ."

"Has Lincoln been on the air yet?" I ask Jewel.

"Oh, yeah, baby. They're running it in a continuous loop. I just caught the end of it, but they said they were going to run it again."

"How bad is it?"

"It's not good. He's saying there's a huge cover-up to protect your father, and he aims a lot of his anger at your better half."

"Great. Does Caitlin know?"

"I texted her a minute ago."

Lincoln Turner's voice rises from the old speakers.

"The problem down here," he says, "is that the accused, Dr. Tom Cage, is the father of the mayor. And the mayor is set to marry the publisher of the newspaper. So even though the Natchez DA is supporting this prosecution, the citizens know almost nothing about it."

"I've read their online edition," says the disc jockey. "There's a lot of stuff in there about old civil rights cases, which is admirable. The publisher seems to support getting justice for the cold cases worked by that reporter that got killed across the river, Henry Sexton."

"Yes," says Lincoln, "but those crimes are forty years old. And to Caitlin Masters, the hero of all those cases is the dead white reporter. There's hardly anything in there about Sleepy Johnston, who came all the way from Detroit to nail Brody Royal for killing his friend. And there's no story focusing on my murdered mother, or the case against Dr. Cage, or any more than a passing mention that he's jumped bail and remains on the run from the law."

"Amen," says the disc jockey. "She treats that like a minor detail."

As I listen, a female arm slips around me and switches off the console.

"That's enough of that," says my mother.

"Who was that talking?" asks Annie from behind us.

"A disc jockey in Jackson," I tell her. Then I say to Jewel, "I'll talk to you later. Thanks for the heads-up," and disconnect my call.

"Was he talking about Papa?"

"Yes," Mom says. "But it's all lies. And we don't listen to lies."

Mom's response does little to reassure Annie. "This is the kind of thing that goes on during big legal cases," I explain. "People try to use the media to sway people who might become jury members down the road."

Annie nods but says nothing.

"Did you find a good bedroom up there?"

She nods. "The bedrooms smell like old people, too, but they're nice. Gram gave me the one with the TV. Do you want to come watch a show with me?"

"Sure. What about your schoolwork, though? Are you keeping up?"

Annie smiles. "Piece of cake. I've never had this much free time before."

I wonder how long the story of a vacation with my mother is going to hold the St. Stephen's administration at bay.

"Come on, Dad," Annie says, taking my hand. "Let me give you a tour."

Mom says, "I'll get the groceries from the car and make some sandwiches."

"I'll get the groceries," I tell her, but she shakes her head and pushes me after Annie.

"I'm not so old I can't carry two grocery bags."

By the time Annie and I reach the top of the stairs, Lincoln's voice has faded from my mind. In its place I hear Walker Dennis telling me that another of his deputies has died. By the time Annie gets the TV tuned to a documentary on the Discovery Channel, my eyelids are at half-mast. Instead of penguins marching across the Arctic tundra, I see John Kaiser and Dwight Stone on their knees, scrabbling through the ashes of Brody Royal's house, searching for scorched artifacts from the fall of Camelot.

"Are you that sleepy, Dad?" Annie asks, poking my shoulder.

"Um . . . I haven't been sleeping at night."

"You're going to miss your sandwich."

"Sandwich? Oh, yeah. I'll eat it when I get up."

In less than a minute I'm sinking into oblivion again, but something startles me back to alertness. It's my internal body clock. Kaiser told me that Dwight Stone, my old savior, would be in town by six, and I promised I'd meet them at Stone's hotel.

"Boo," I mumble, "I need to wake up at six."

"Tonight?"

"Mm."

"That's only like an hour and a half from now."

"I don't have a choice."

She groans in frustration and disappointment, but after a moment she says, "Okay. I'll get you up."

I feel myself sinking again. "Don't forget."

"Don't worry. You sleep. I'll watch over you."

CHAPTER 31

TOM'S HEART THUDDED when he heard the car engine outside Quentin's house, but two short blasts on a horn told him his visitor was probably Melba. A minute later, the same pattern was repeated from behind the house. It took Tom longer than that to reach the back door, but the more he moved, the more his stiff muscles relaxed. By the time he looked through the peephole and saw his nurse, he felt half human again, and when he opened the door, he hugged her as if he were a prisoner being visited on death row. The upwelling of emotion surprised him, but Melba was squeezing him as tightly as he was her. After they separated, he wiped his eyes and led her back to the living room sofa that had become his home.

"Is Quentin here?" Melba asked.

Tom could tell she'd hoped to find the lawyer at home. He shook his head. "If the police found him here, he'd lose his law license. I can't let that happen, especially now." Tom eyed the Walmart bag in her hand. "Did you get the phones?"

"I bought four."

"Thank god. Let's get one activated. I need to let Walt know where I am. He gave me a kind of code, and I can text him where we are using that."

"How did Captain Garrity's meeting go?" Melba asked. "With that state police man?"

"I don't know yet. Apparently, that fellow's got his own problems, and with the same people who are trying to kill Walt and me."

Melba shook her head almost hopelessly.

"Can you open up one of those phones for me, Mel?" Tom asked. "My arthritis is kicking up bad."

"Sure." She got out one of the plastic packages and

began to explore its seams. "I need to tell you something, Doc."

"What?" he asked, sensing trouble.

Melba looked up, her eyes filled with guilt. "Dr. Elliott and I went and talked to Penn."

Tom's chest ached suddenly, and his breath went shallow. "Why did you do that?"

"We were afraid something had happened to you. Dr. Drew had been calling his lake house all morning, and nobody picked up. We figured the best thing would be to send Penn over there."

"Did you tell Penn where I am now?"

"No, no. I didn't tell Dr. Elliott, either." Melba was clearly in distress. "I promised Penn I would call him if you got back in touch with me, but . . . I couldn't bring myself to do it."

Tom placed a nitro tablet under his tongue. "Okay," he said, trying to breathe deeply. "Okay."

"I'm sorry," Melba said. "This is hard, Doc. I'm scared for you. I knew I shouldn't have left you before, and I was right. It's a miracle you're even standing here now."

Tom gave her a reassuring smile. "You know I'm hard to kill, Mel. I've outlived at least two serious diseases already."

"I'm not talking about disease."

"I know. But . . . this is one of those times when we just have to hold our nerve. I know you don't understand, but you're better off not knowing more than you do. I'm asking a lot of you, I know. And you can go back home, now that you've brought me these supplies. I've already asked too much."

Melba sat on the arm of the sofa, folded her arms, and looked at him like an angry sister. "You think I drove out here just to leave you with no help? In the shape you're in? I know you know better than that." The nurse sighed and looked around the opulent living room. "Lord, Quentin Avery's got more money than anybody has a right to. You can't make this kind of money doing the right thing."

"Maybe not," Tom conceded. "But he's done more good for more people than most of us ever will. I figure he's earned the right to sell out just a little at the end of his life."

Melba gave Tom a chiding look. "That's not how it works with right and wrong, Dr. Cage. And you know it."

Tom looked back at her for a few seconds, wanting to explain himself. But in the end he turned away without speaking.

CAITLIN WOKE FROM A dead sleep on her office sofa with no idea what time it was. She'd switched off the ringers on her phones, but still her dreams had been troubled: she'd been frantically treading cold, black water as dark figures with yellow eyes floated around her in an obscene ballet. Cypress knees like gnarled wet knuckles jutted from the water, giving her the feeling that a great hand waited to snatch her below the surface, and when she looked up to escape this sight, she saw twisted limbs and feathery leaves hanging over her like the hair of some terrible witch.

"Caitlin?" said a voice.

Someone poked her shoulder, then shook her, and bright light burned away the dark world that had enveloped her.

Jamie Lewis stood beside the sofa, staring down at her. "Are you okay?" he asked, starting to kneel.

"Don't get too close. I have bad breath."

Lewis straightened up. "Gary Valentine's on the landline for you. He said he had a private message for you."

"Okay," she said, rolling groggily off the sofa. Gary Valentine was the computer technician she'd dispatched to watch Drew and Melba after Penn told her that both had seen Tom and then lied about it.

"I told him we didn't have time for games, but Gary still wouldn't tell me what he wants."

"Blame me, not him." Caitlin got to her feet and gave Jamie a smile that triggered a shock of pain from the cheek burn. "Some things you don't need to know. Hand me the cordless phone, would you?"

Jamie flipped her the bird, then picked up the phone and gave it to her. "Don't do anything crazy, okay? You nearly died last night. Let's not go for an encore."

Caitlin motioned for him to get out.

From the door, Jamie said, "Oh, did you see my text about the state police thing?"

"No."

"Man, you really were out. The *Advocate* is reporting that a fourteen-year-old male prostitute from New Orleans claims he was paid for sex by Colonel Mackiever on multiple occasions. Mackiever's home has been under siege by the media. Some officials are already calling for his resignation."

"Forrest Knox has got to be behind that. Stay on it, Jamie. Keep digging into Knox's background. You'll find something we can use against him."

As Jamie went out, she thought about Forrest Knox. The man was obviously making an all-out effort to destroy his superior and consolidate his own power. And that would put him in the best possible position to help the Double Eagles survive the attack by Penn and Sheriff Dennis—not to mention protect himself from Mackiever or the FBI. Pushing these thoughts from her mind, she put down the cordless phone, took her Treo from her pocket, and called Gary Valentine.

"Hello?" she said, after the door had closed. "Gary?"

"Thank God," said the tech's excited voice. "I think I hit pay dirt."

"What do you mean?"

"I followed one of the people you asked me to watch. She just went into a place that my gut tells me is what you're looking for."

Melba must have gone to Tom again. . . . "Where is she?"

"I probably shouldn't say on the phone, right?"

Damn, Caitlin thought, realizing she must not be fully awake. "I think this line is safe, but can you give me a clue nobody else could decipher?"

"I've been thinking about that. She's at a private residence. It's a house that belongs to somebody I'm pretty sure you know. Here's the clue: the owner's initials are the same as those of the first two words of the TV show that Gabriel Vance used to rave about."

Gabriel Vance was a gay reporter who'd worked at the *Examiner* until he moved to the New Orleans *Times-Picayune*. He'd done heroic coverage of Hurricane Katrina, but what popped into Caitlin's mind almost without thought was Gabe's favorite cable show: *Queer as Folk*.

"Have you got it?" Gary asked.

Caitlin almost said "Q-A" aloud, but checked herself. Despite her exhaustion, it had taken her less than five seconds to arrive at *Quentin Avery*. "I think I have it," she said. "I've never been there, though. Are you looking at it now?"

"You can't see it from the road. I figured out the owner using Google. You ought to check Google Earth."

Caitlin glanced at her watch, calculating how long it would take her to reach Quentin's wooded compound in Jefferson County. Twenty minutes, minimum, and at least twice that to be sure she had no tail.

"I'll be there in an hour. Forty minutes if I'm clean when I leave here."

"I'll be cruising up and down the nearest main road."

"Thanks, Gary. And don't tell a soul. Not Jamie, not anybody."

"I know, boss."

"Thanks."

Caitlin hung up and opened the purse on her desk. The .38 Tom had given her years ago was inside it. For a few seconds she considered calling Penn, but in truth her decision was a foregone conclusion. Like Drew and Melba, she would not betray Tom's location without his permission—not even to his son. Not until she'd heard what he had to say, anyway. Pulling on her jacket, she slung her purse over her shoulder and opened her door.

She nearly jumped out of her skin when she found Jordan Glass standing less than a foot away from her.

"Hey, hey!" Jordan said, catching hold of her arm. "I didn't mean to scare you."

"No, no," Caitlin said, flustered. "I just wasn't expecting anybody."

"Obviously. Looks like you're headed out, huh?"

Caitlin forced a smile and tried to think of a credible lie. Glass was wearing a black down jacket over a white *Synchronicity* tour T-shirt splashed with red, blue, and yellow—a relic of the mid-1980s. "I'm just headed home to get a shower," Caitlin said lamely. "This is the first time things have slowed down at all."

Jordan's understanding smile both noted and forgave the lie. "I came by to talk to you," she said. "Have you got a minute?"

Caitlin didn't, but she backed up and motioned for Glass to enter her office.

Jordan shook her head, then pulled her close. "Not in there," she whispered. "Let's go to the ladies' room."

It took Caitlin only seconds to realize what was worrying Jordan. Nodding once, she followed the photographer down the hall and into the female employees' restroom. It held two stalls, two sinks, a tampon machine, and nothing else.

"Is my office bugged?" Caitlin asked.

"I don't know. It could be."

"FBI?"

"I really don't know."

"But you're obviously worried."

Jordan anxiously ran her hands through her hair. She was clearly conflicted about something, and Caitlin guessed it had to do with her husband.

"Last night I asked if you ever hold things back from John. You said you did."

Glass nodded. "Of course. And he does the same. More than I suspected, I'm afraid."

Caitlin saw pain in the older woman's face. "Can you be more specific?"

"Not without damaging things I still care about." Jordan turned on the cold water tap and let it run. "But I'll say this . . . one of the downers in life is finding out that people you thought you knew well can always surprise you, and not in a positive way."

A worm of anxiety was turning in Caitlin's stomach. Jordan Glass wasn't the type to worry about trivialities. "You're positive you can't talk about it?"

"There are things I can't say. I don't want you to think John isn't on your side, because he is. But he takes this case—or cases, plural—very seriously, and he's not about to give up any advantage he might be able to get over the Knoxes."

"I wouldn't either. Is that what you came to tell me?"

Jordan swallowed and looked at the floor. "No. Do you know where Penn is now?"

Caitlin looked at her watch. "Probably meeting your husband and Dwight Stone."

Jordan looked up sharply. "So he told you about that?"

"Why wouldn't he?"

"What did he say they were meeting about?"

"He said Dwight has some conspiracy theory about the Kennedy assassination. Penn didn't know if John is humoring Dwight because he's ill, or if John believes the same theory."

Jordan nodded slowly. "That's not exactly the truth."

Caitlin thought about Henry Sexton's letter to her, and Kaiser's theory about Carlos Marcello and JFK. "What is?"

"Dwight Stone is part of a group of retired agents who work cold cases. *Major* cases. Jimmy Hoffa, JFK, like that. Something they learned in the last two days has convinced them that the Double Eagles here were involved in the Kennedy assassination. I don't know many specifics, but they seem to think the whole plot was run out of New Orleans."

"By Carlos Marcello."

Jordan's eyes widened. "Did Penn tell you that?"

"Not exactly. He made it sound like a fringe theory."

Jordan smiled with what looked like bitter resentment. "Look, you were obviously headed somewhere. Were you taking advantage of Penn and John being busy to follow whatever lead you hinted at last night at the hospital?"

Caitlin was tempted to tell the truth, but she didn't dare—not with Tom's life at risk. "Why have you told me this, Jordan? Are you and John having problems or something?"

The photographer shrugged. "Not exactly. Maybe I want you to have a level playing field. We're both journalists, and I've been exactly where you are, only without help. I wanted you to know you need to be careful about more than your enemies. You might be an intelligence target."

"I appreciate it. So . . . is John going to simply abandon the civil rights cases that remain unsolved?"

"No way. He's trying to get approval for a massive search for the Bone Tree, and he's doing overflights of the Valhalla hunting camp in the hopes of finding it empty."

Caitlin almost gulped at the mention of the Bone Tree, but she quickly moved away from the subject. "Why would Valhalla need to be empty for him to search it?"

"It wouldn't, for a normal search. But he wants to do what they call a sneak-and-peek search under the Patriot Act. That way Forrest Knox won't know how much scrutiny he's under."

"Man. The gloves are off, aren't they?"

"Oh, yeah."

"Well, what's your plan?" Caitlin asked, glancing at her watch again and thinking of Melba and Tom.

"I haven't got one. I spent way too long today photographing geriatrics at Glenn Morehouse's funeral. No Double Eagles showed up, by the way. Not known ones, at least. Now I'm pretty much at loose ends. Tomorrow evening I fly to Havana to shoot Fidel Castro and his brother, but till then . . . nothing."

Glass obviously wanted to be asked along on Caitlin's trip, but Caitlin wasn't ready to trust her completely. "Listen," she said awkwardly, "what I'm about to do, I have to do on my own. But if you can get away later tonight . . . come back and see me. I do have a plan for tomorrow, and you might be able to help."

The smile that lit Jordan's face warmed Caitlin inside. Yesterday the photographer had talked like a burnout case, but there was no denying the excitement in her eyes.

"I'll be here," Jordan said, turning off the tap. "You make sure you get back safe. These are serious people you're trying to dismember in your newspaper. Have you still got your gun?"

Caitlin nodded. "And I won't hesitate to use it."

"Good girl. And good luck."

Caitlin hugged her old idol, then left the restroom and ran for the back door.

CHAPTER 32

ANNIE DUTIFULLY AWAKENS me at six o'clock, and Mom sends me on my way with a mug of coffee made in the Abramses' 1970s-vintage percolator. Annie begs me to take her along, but I explain that I'll be working in a place that, while not physically dangerous, is no place for an eleven-year-old girl. She isn't happy about this, but she doesn't try to guilt-trip me over leaving.

Night has fallen as I approach the Mississippi River. An hour ago, the sun's last rays bled red and orange into the clouds over the westward-flowing bend south of town. It's too late now to show Caitlin Edelweiss at sunset, as I'd planned, but before I feel too guilty, she sends me a text saying she's tied up and won't be able to meet me for several hours.

Dwight Stone has checked into one of the new hotels situated in the flood zone between the levee and the river on the Vidalia side. I park near the front entrance, my mind filling with memories of the two weeks in 1998 that Dwight Stone and I teamed up to break the most important case of my career. Without his selfless help, I not only wouldn't have solved the case—I wouldn't have lived to hear the verdict. As I walk to the door, I notice two black SUVs with FBI stenciled on the doors. One has two high-tech satellite dishes deployed on its roof. One points skyward, but the smaller one is pointed at the hotel. This reminds me of the microcassette recorder in my coat pocket. Since I have no idea how long our conversation will last, I decide to switch it on just before entering Stone's room.

Kaiser gave me the floor and room number, so I'm surprised to find him in the lobby. He's talking on his cell phone, but he waves and motions me over to him. "Thanks for coming," he says, slipping his phone into the inside pocket of his sport coat. "I know you didn't want to, but it means a lot to Dwight."

"I owe it to him."

"That was an assistant director of the FBI on the phone. I want you to know that I'm pushing hard to get a protective custody deal for your father. That's what that call was about."

"And?"

Kaiser winces. "It's a tough sell, Penn. You know that. But the director hasn't ruled it out. Stone is pushing as well."

"Does the director know about Stone's Working Group?"

"He does now. After the discovery of those rifles in Royal's basement, I decided to pull the trigger and bring him into the circle. But last night's deaths created a lot of anxiety in Washington. The director's pretty pissed off, but he's not going to ignore what we've found. I think he'll get there on your father as well."

"It's not like Dad's got a lot of time, John."

"I know." He pats my arm. "Why don't we go upstairs?"

We move toward the elevators. "Any idea how long this will take?"

"If you let Dwight speak his piece without interruption, an hour ought to do it."

"He's going to tell me about Carlos Marcello and the Kennedy assassination?"

"And your father."

"What about my father? What haven't you told me already?"

Kaiser looks uncomfortable as we step into the elevator. "Look," he says, pushing 4, "when it comes to the Kennedy case, it's Stone's show. Let him tell you his way."

I don't even try to hide my exasperation.

"By the way," says Kaiser, as the car starts to rise, "Stone got the skinny on Eladio Cruz, the Cuban student who ordered the Mannlicher-Carcano Royal ended up with, and then disappeared in New Orleans. Somebody in the Working Group knew an old FBI informant who worked undercover against Castro in Havana. He said Eladio Cruz was a DRE agent for Castro. Cruz's job was recruiting high school and college-age kids who'd come to

America with their parents. He disappeared on November nineteenth, 1963, but he wasn't reported missing until the twenty-first. At the time, his friends assumed that either exiles had killed him or he'd gone back to Cuba. But Cruz never returned to Cuba, not in 1963 or later. So he didn't just disappear from New Orleans. He disappeared off the face of the earth."

The elevator stops, and the doors open to the fourth floor.

"Where do you think he went?" I ask, motioning for John to walk ahead of me into the orange-carpeted corridor.

"Into the sixty-four hundred acres of swamps behind Marcello's Churchill Farms," he says, "just like a lot of other guys did."

As Kaiser takes the lead, I slip my hand into my inside pocket and hit the RECORD button on my Sony. That's one advantage of the old analog units; the buttons are big enough to operate by touch. "Did his disappearance have to do with the Carcano?"

Kaiser points to his right. "Room 406."

"Come on, John," I say, following him.

"Are you serious? A known pro-Castro agent buying a rifle exactly like the one that would be used to kill John Kennedy, then disappearing only days before the assassination?" Kaiser holds up his hand and stops me a few paces from Stone's door. "Listen, you may not realize how bad Dwight—"

My TracFone is ringing. Kaiser pauses, waiting for me to answer.

"Go on in," I tell him. "I'll be right there."

He sighs with frustration.

Retreating down the hall toward the elevators, I click SEND. "This is Penn."

"It's Walker Dennis. I'm headed out to another warehouse fire on Frogmore Road. But that's not why I'm calling."

My gut hitches in dread. "What's happened?"

"I just got a call from Claude Devereux."

"Brody Royal's attorney? What did he want?"

"You won't believe it. That old Cajun bastard told me that Snake Knox, Sonny Thornfield, and the other

Double Eagles on my list will be at my office at seven A.M. tomorrow to surrender themselves for questioning."

For several seconds I'm speechless. "That's hard to believe."

"Well, they're coming. Devereux didn't call them Double Eagles, of course. He claims they have nothing to hide, and that they want to clear their names as soon as possible."

"Did he say Billy Knox would be with them?"

"Billy wasn't on my list. We don't have anything on him yet."

"What do you have on the others?"

"Not much, to be honest. Leo Spivey's home computer has turned up some suspicious accounting—coded stuff—and we've found a few suspect connections to the old guys. We still have a lot of evidence to go through, and I'm pressuring the hell out of the cookers and dealers we rounded up this morning."

"Walker . . . those punks know that ratting out the Knoxes means a bullet in the head—if they're lucky. Stay with the computers."

"We will. I just wanted to make sure you're gonna be at my office in the morning. If those fuckers have their high-dollar lawyer present, I want to make sure I've got mine."

A rush of conflicting emotions floods through me. I still believe in my strategy of pressuring Forrest Knox so that he'll have to turn his attention away from the hunt for my father. But something tells me Dwight Stone wouldn't have traveled all the way here without having something important to say. And now Kaiser has hinted that it may be about my father. Until I hear Stone out, I'm reluctant to commit to what he may think is a serious mistake. In the silence of my thoughts, I hear Walker breathing impatiently.

"You're not getting cold feet, are you?" he asks.

"No, no. I'm just thinking this may be more complicated than I first thought."

"Tough shit. You're the one who got me started on this drug war, and now I've got two dead deputies and the state police crawling up my ass. We're fully committed. So make sure you're standing outside my interrogation room at seven A.M. Otherwise, you get no more information or assistance from me *henceforth*."

"Don't worry, I'll be there."

He clicks off.

Looking back toward Stone's room, I see Kaiser still standing in the hall, watching me. I'm pretty sure he couldn't have heard anything I said.

"Everything okay?" he asks as I approach.

If I related Walker's news about the Double Eagles to Kaiser, he would blow his top, and probably upset Stone in the process. "Yeah, no problems."

"About Dwight," Kaiser says, blocking the door with his hand. "He looks pretty rough. He's on the transplant list, but they haven't found him a liver yet. His tumors are growing, and this operation tomorrow is sort of a last-ditch holding action. I gather his odds are about fifty-fifty going in. It was crazy for him to come here, but nothing was going to stop him. I lobbied the director to give him this last gift."

I hadn't realized things were quite that bad. "How's his mental state?"

"Oh, he's still sharp as a razor. That's the tragedy of it. He may run on a little about the JFK stuff, but be patient with him. You'll know a lot more about your father when you walk out of here than you did when you came in."

With that cryptic comment, Kaiser drops his arm and ushers me into room 406.

After moving through the short passage between the closet and the bathroom, I see a man who bears little resemblance to the one who saved my life in 1998. Back then Stone was a tough, tanned, wiry old bird who looked like he could whip men twenty years his junior. Now he's so jaundiced that his face and hands look as though someone swabbed them with Betadine. He's propped against the headboard with the covers pulled up to his waist. His eyes have sunk deep into his skull, and his silver hair looks thin and wispy. I haven't seen many men who look this far gone emerge from a hospital again.

"Hello, Penn," he says in a reedy voice that's but an echo of his once powerful baritone. "Come over here and shake my hand."

I walk around the bed and carefully take his right hand in both of mine. Gently squeezing the papery skin, I notice bruises at both inner elbows, probably from multiple needle sticks. His face, too, is bruised in places, but his hollow eyes still burn with the light of a gas flame. In my peripheral vision I note a plastic urinal behind the lamp on the bedside table and a folded wheelchair leaning against the wall. It's hard to believe this is the man who took a bullet while trying to save my life in the icy river that ran beside his Colorado cabin.

"I appreciate you coming," he says, obviously meaning it.

"Wouldn't have missed it, buddy."

Kaiser sits on a small sofa beneath the picture window on the wall to my left. Behind him the lights of Natchez glow high on the bluff across the dark river.

Stone gives me a weak smile. "I'd ask about your father, but John has brought me up to speed. You know, back in 1998, after your trial was over, Tom and I had lunch together. We found we had a lot in common. We're exactly the same age, and we both spent 1950 freezing our asses off in Korea."

"I'd forgotten that."

"I know you're probably baffled by his recent actions. I hope I can give you some insight into why he's behaved as he has."

"I sure need it. Is the answer good or bad?"

Stone drops his hand and takes a measured breath. "Once we get to the final truth, I believe that whatever Tom did will ultimately prove justified."

"Are you referring to the Viola Turner case? Or the Kennedy stuff?"

"Both, I hope. Why don't you sit down, Penn? I don't have the wind I used to, so we'd better get to it."

"Do you want me to sit on the bed? Or can you talk loud enough for me to use the chair by that desk?"

"The chair's fine."

As I move back to the desk chair, it strikes me that I'm sitting with the veterans of two wars: Korea and Vietnam. By being born roughly a decade after Kaiser, I won the lottery that spared my generation combat. Neither man comments when I take my .357 Magnum from the small of my back and lay it on the veneer desk.

As I settle back in the chair, Stone folds his hands in his lap, looks down at them, and begins to speak in the voice of a man who has paid a great price for his wisdom. "This meeting may be the last significant thing I do in my life outside a hospital. If it is, I'll have no complaints. I've been certain who gave the order to kill John Kennedy for nearly two years. But I couldn't prove it, because I didn't know how he arranged it or who fired the kill shot."

I glance at the sofa, where Kaiser is silently pleading with me to be patient. "Lee Harvey Oswald killed Kennedy, Dwight. From the sixth floor of the Texas School Book Depository. Anything else is fantasy."

"No," he says. "Oswald was in Dealey Plaza that day, and he did shoot President Kennedy. But he didn't *kill* Kennedy."

"Then who did?"

"Before I tell you that, let me tell you how I know Oswald didn't. I'm not here because some old FBI gomers got together in the rest home and came up with a conspiracy theory." He gives me a small smile. "Although I suppose you could make that argument. We're old enough to have read most of the five million pages of public records pertaining to the assassination. But my group has also gained at least limited access to most of the ten thousand records that will remain sealed until 2017."

This is the first thing I've heard that's surprised me. "Is that where you got your new assassination theory? From the sealed records?"

Stone snorts with disdain. "God, no. Most of those records remain sequestered for one of two reasons. They deal with CIA and FBI operations that either were illegal or showed gross incompetence by still-living officers. Some of it makes waterboarding and drone strikes look like a tea party, but it's ass-covering, Penn. Nothing more. Every conspiracy nut waiting to find the Dealey Grail in those sealed records is due for some serious disappointment."

"Then why are we here? How do you know Oswald didn't fire the kill shot?"

"*I'm* here because of one forensic fact. It's been right in front of us—in front of the whole world—ever since we saw the Zapruder film."

"It's simple ballistics," Kaiser interjects. "And undeniable proof of a conspiracy in the Kennedy assassination."

"Well?" I prompt.

"Oswald fired three shots in Dealey Plaza," Kaiser says. "He only hit President Kennedy with one of them—in the back. That was the so-called magic bullet that produced seven wounds between Kennedy and Governor Connally, and remained 'fairly pristine.' You remember that?"

"I saw the movie. How could I forget?"

"Exactly. Oliver Stone's film did an even greater disservice to the head shot—the kill shot. District Attorney Jim Garrison created the theory of the improbable 'magic bullet,' then tried to prove that the shot to Kennedy's head was fired from the grassy knoll. You remember?"

"Back, and to the left," I say, quoting Kevin Costner from the movie. "*Seinfeld* even had an episode mocking that."

Dwight nods in the bed. "Oliver Stone almost single-handedly elevated two glaring forensic errors into myth, which always trumps truth in the public mind."

"What were his errors?"

"First, the magic bullet wasn't magic at all. Oswald was firing fully jacketed rounds designed for winter war in the Alps, meant for penetrating multiple layers of heavy clothing. His bullets were slow—eighteen hundred feet per second—but very powerful. In Dallas, they performed exactly as they were designed to."

"The *real* magic bullet," Kaiser says, "was the head shot. It blasted open Kennedy's skull, blew out a third of his brain, and left only tiny fragments in the skull case."

"And practically vaporized in the process," Stone finishes. "Which no Mannlicher-Carcano 6.58 round ever did after hitting a human skull at eighteen hundred feet per second. We've verified that under the most rigorous field conditions, and also through exhaustive research."

"There had to be another shooter there," Kaiser asserts. "One firing a rifle with a muzzle velocity greater than three thousand, two hundred feet per second, the speed required for a bullet to reliably and effectively explode. A rifle like the Remington 700 you identified from Brody Royal's basement. A hot load for that rifle can reach four thousand feet per second."

"Why didn't ballistics experts see this long ago?" I ask.

Stone smiles sadly. "The forest and the trees, Penn."

"Contrary to popular belief," Kaiser says, "Oswald had the skill to make that shot. What he didn't have on that day was the rifle or the bullet."

"But Dwight said Oswald hit Kennedy in the back," I point out.

"Even a blind pig finds a truffle now and again," says Stone.

"That was luck," says Kaiser. "The scope on Oswald's Carcano was a cheap Japanese add-on, and it wasn't even zeroed. In fact, it *couldn't* be zeroed. It only had two screws holding it on. But even if it could have been, that Carcano couldn't fire a bullet fast enough to explode, and Oswald wasn't using frangible rounds."

"Okay, let's say I buy all that. If Oswald didn't kill JFK, who did?"

Stone and Kaiser share a long look. Then Stone says, "Frank Knox."

I shouldn't be surprised to hear this, but the conviction with which Stone said the name has rattled me—not least because I know my father knew Frank Knox.

"On November twenty-second, 1963," Stone goes on, "Frank Knox—the ex-marine from Ferriday, Louisiana, and founder of the Double Eagle group—fired the bullet that blew John Kennedy's brains out. Knox was sent there by Carlos Marcello. He fired from a lower floor of the Dal-Tex Building, probably the second floor. He fired one reasonably silenced shot from deep within the room, and he accomplished his mission, just as he'd done so often during the war."

Stone sounds as sure of this as any man has ever been sure of anything.

"Can you prove that?" I ask.

"Some of it. With your father's help, I think we can prove the rest."

My skepticism quickly morphs into an almost frantic exasperation. "Dwight . . . I love you, man. But this is pretty hard to take. Last night John told me that you think Dad knows who killed Kennedy."

Stone shakes his head. "No, it's worse than that, I'm afraid. Your father actually made Frank's shot possible."

These stunning words trigger the disorientation of an unexpected blow, when your brain tries haltingly to fathom the cause and extent of the damage. Stone closes his eyes as though he feels the same pain I do, but when he opens them, I realize that he doesn't even see me. He grimaces in agony, and then his hands go to his emaciated belly.

"Dwight! Are you okay?"

"I need to get to the bathroom," he croaks.

Kaiser has already sprung to his feet. He unfolds the wheelchair, and together we transfer the old agent from the bed to the chair. Dwight's quivering muscles tell me he barely has the strength to hold himself erect. With Kaiser's help, moving him into the bathroom isn't that difficult, but once he's there we stand anxiously outside the door, listening closely in case he should pass out.

"I can't believe he flew down here in such bad shape," I whisper.

Kaiser shakes his head, then whispers back, "This really may be his last ride. That's how much this case means to him."

Sobered by the nearness of mortality, I blow out a rush of air. "John . . . what the hell was he talking about? My dad made Frank's shot possible? Even if Knox *did* shoot Kennedy, that's just nuts."

Kaiser gives me a long look, then shakes his head. "Let's just wait for Dwight, okay?"

This doesn't reassure me. "I haven't got all night, man."

"It won't take that long. But you've got time for this. Stone wants to solve this case, but he also wants to help your father if he can. So how about you make time for him?"

A groan and a thud come through the door.

"Oh, fuck," says Kaiser, grabbing the knob.

CHAPTER 33

BILLY KNOX SAT on the front deck at Valhalla, staring out through the cold dusk toward the Mississippi River. Billy had his chair tilted back, his feet on the rail, and a big glass of bourbon in his hand. His father sat in a teak glider to his right, Forrest's pit bull curled up beside him, and Sonny Thornfield stood at the rail beyond Snake. The cheep of crickets and the calls of night birds filled the air, but Billy was listening for the deep rumble of barges passing on the river, a mile to the west. Most of the land directly across the river was unpopulated wildlife refuge, but the clouds had begun to glow to the southwest as the lights of Marksville, Louisiana, came on.

The past two hours had been the most uncomfortable of Billy's life, outside of prison. After Forrest and Ozan flew away in the big state-police helicopter, Snake had begun saying all the things he hadn't had the guts to say to his nephew's face. Worse, he kept looking to Billy for agreement, and even prodding him for information. Billy had claimed that Forrest had spent their time alone giving him instructions on how to protect their financial assets during this crisis, but his father wasn't buying it. And the more Snake drank, the nearer he came to what Forrest would consider treason.

"You know what I think?" Snake mumbled into his glass. "I think he's got Dr. Cage already. That's why nobody can find him. I think Forrest has the doc holed up in some safe house, and he thinks he's working some kind of deal. But what's really happening is the doc is working *him*."

When no one responded, Snake jabbed Billy's shoulder with his fist. "What do you think, son? Only stands to reason, don't it?"

"No," Billy said wearily. "If Forrest had Dr. Cage, he'd be a lot less worried than he is."

"So you say. And another thing. I don't like Forrest bringing his SWAT guys into our business. What the hell do we need them for?"

"Keep your voice down," Sonny said. "We don't know who the hell might be out here right now. Or whether there might be microphones around here."

Snake waved his hand as if to brush these worries away. "And why's he jamming the cell phones? Huh? Who's he afraid we'll talk to?"

Billy had puzzled over this himself (and he'd actually switched off the jammer momentarily to make a couple of calls). "Forrest told me it was to help block FBI surveillance. But I think that's probably for the Black Team as much as anything. He doesn't want anybody being able to prove they were here, later on."

Snake grunted, obviously dissatisfied with his explanation. "I tell you, those Black Team bastards wouldn't hesitate to kill us if Forrest ordered them to. In fact . . . that might be why he's calling them in. You ever think about that?"

"You've had one too many drinks, Pop. Seriously."

"Black Team, my *ass*," Snake went on. "I can outshoot every one of those pissants. They never shot nothing but nigger dope dealers through a night-vision scope. They don't know nothing about *war*."

Billy looked over at Sonny, who looked older than ever with a white frizz of stubble on his normally clean-shaven face. Sonny was staring back with naked fear in his eyes.

"You boys listen to me," Snake said. "Walking into the CPSO tomorrow to get arrested don't make no damn sense, with meth charges waiting for us. I don't care what Forrest has planned for Walker Dennis. That's just plain suicidal. I think Forrest *wants* us in jail."

"That's crazy, Pop," Billy said finally. "What's Forrest got to gain from you going to jail?"

"It'd take the heat off him, for one thing. You seen his name in the newspaper yet? No."

"Forrest can't let you go to jail. You could rat him out any time you wanted."

"If we lived long enough." Snake clutched Billy's arm. "Forrest could have us killed *in jail*."

"Come on. . . . You need to get some sleep."

"He's done it before." Snake's eyes flashed with certainty. "I know that for a fact. So do you."

Billy was thinking about Forrest's final words to him, but he forced himself to chuckle. "He couldn't kill all of you, could he?"

"He wouldn't have to," Snake said, his eyes still shining with animal cleverness. "If he killed me, the rest would fall right into line." Snake looked back over his shoulder. "Ain't that right, Sonny?"

Sonny Thornfield swallowed audibly. "I say we're already *in* line. I don't see what the problem is. Forrest will take care of us. Let's just get this thing done tomorrow, then start the move to the businesses Forrest's talking about."

"Sonny's right," Billy said. "All Snake told me after you guys went out was to keep you calm and get you there in the morning. Forrest isn't looking to kill you. He's trying to save you. We're family, for Christ's sake."

Snake let his hand fall from Billy's sleeve and slumped in his chair, his gaze once again lost in the vast darkness over the river. Half a minute later, he sat up suddenly, his head cocked like that of a hunting dog. Traveller came to his feet, puzzled but curious.

"What is it?" Billy asked.

"I heard something," Snake said. "*Listen.*"

WALT HAD BEEN LYING beneath the bed for so long that his back and legs were numb. Just once he had crawled out to check if the pit bull was still outside—it was—and then to listen at the door for the drone of voices.

The men below were still talking.

Walt's only consolation was that a half hour ago he'd received a coded text message from Tom telling him his location. He didn't know how the message had come through, since he'd begun to suspect the presence of a cell frequency jammer. But apparently Tom had found a way to cross the river and had made his way to Quentin Avery's house in Jefferson County. This gave Walt a destination to aim for, if he could ever get out of this place. But the transmission of that message had also put Tom at risk. Walt had deleted it immediately, for if the men downstairs dragged him out from under the bed, they would find his phone before they killed him.

Though he was almost frantic with the desire to escape Valhalla, he knew he'd be insane to do anything but lie as still as he could and sweat as little as possible. If the pit bull outside caught his scent, he was doomed. Walt was wishing he'd hid his truck better when the sound of a helicopter coming over the trees reached him. Seconds later, the window began rattling as the chopper settled over the lodge as though preparing to land.

Walt dragged himself from beneath the bed, then struggled to his feet beside the window. Through the crack in the curtains, he saw the chopper disgorge six men and one German shepherd. Clad in black, the men moved easily beneath the rotor blast, and each carried a heavy gear bag as he trotted toward a building about thirty yards to the south. Walt felt a wild compulsion to use the cover of the rotors to run downstairs and make a break for the woods, but he knew better. Those rotors meant nothing to a dog's nose, and now there was more than one dog down there.

He had no choice but to sit tight.

SONNY THORNFIELD WATCHED THE state police JetRanger bore in low over the trees and hover above the lodge, blasting leaves and pine straw and other debris into the air in a mini-tornado. Its rotors buffeted the air so hard that Sonny felt the waves like a bass drum in his chest.

"Why don't he land down at the goddamn strip?" Snake shouted, flipping the bird to the pilot. "Lazy motherfucker!"

Sonny watched the big helo settle earthward on the other side of the lodge. Five seconds later it disappeared from view, and the noise dropped by 50 percent.

"That's the beauty of having a chopper," Billy said, a note of envy in his voice. "You can land where you want."

Snake grumbled something unintelligible.

"I better go check on them," Billy said, getting to his feet. "Forrest told me to make sure they had everything they needed."

"Yeah, jump to it, Hop Sing," Snake said. "Make sure they've all got butt wipes and a hair dryer."

As Billy opened the sliding doors and walked back through the house, Snake shook his head and muttered, "SWAT, my ass. A SWAT team oughta be able to live on bugs in the middle of hell for ten days. These assholes need a goddamn babysitter?"

Sonny didn't bother answering.

Suddenly Snake got up and walked down the steps of the deck, then made his way to the corner of the lodge and disappeared around it. Forrest's pit bull followed at his heels. Sonny reluctantly got up and went after them.

The big JetRanger had landed in the clearing before the lodge. Three men clad in black were trotting between the chopper and bunkhouse, heads ducked beneath the spinning rotors.

"We got a problem, Sonny," Snake said, loud enough to be heard over the rotors. "You know that?"

Sonny shifted uncomfortably. "I'm not so sure. Don't you think maybe we ought to let Forrest try it his way first? Let him de-escalate the situation?"

Snake looked back at him like he was a fool. "Boy, you wanna close your eyes and follow the cattle right into the kill chute, don't you? Anything's better than facing the truth, I guess."

"What truth are you talking about?"

"The fork in the river, Son. The parting of the ways."

"I don't know what you're talking about!"

"Blood, boy. It don't mean the same thing to everybody."

"Huh?"

Snake spat and turned back toward the chopper, which looked like a gigantic metal insect that had risen out of the swamp. "You'll find out soon enough. Mark my words, Son. I just hope I'm still around to say I told you so."

Snake stepped from behind the wall and started toward the chopper and the bunkhouse.

"Where you going?" Sonny called. "Snake!"

Snake looked back and grinned. "Just bein' friendly. I'm gonna make these boys feel at home, like Forrest said to."

Then he began to trot toward the chopper, one hand raised in greeting.

CHAPTER 34

THE NOISE KAISER and I heard from the hotel bathroom was Dwight falling off the toilet. When we reached him, he was bruised and angry but basically no worse than before. After Kaiser and I lifted him back onto the toilet, I cleaned him up and wheeled him to the bed while Kaiser wiped up the vomit he'd left on the floor. Without the headboard to support him, I don't think Stone could hold himself up, yet the unquenchable light still shines from his sunken eyes and yellow face.

Despite my internal distress, I sit in the desk chair and wait for Kaiser to take his seat on the sofa beneath the picture window. After he does, Stone begins speaking with slightly diminished volume. "Penn, I know why you're still sitting here. You want to know what I know about your father. I'm going to tell you that. But you have to trust me about something. Without context, the information would be almost useless to you. To understand Tom's involvement, you've got to understand and accept what happened in Dallas, and why."

"You mean that Carlos Marcello killed Kennedy? What if I tell you I do accept that?"

A faint smile touches Stone's lips. "You don't really believe it. Think like the prosecutor you once were for a moment. Glenn Morehouse and Henry Sexton have given us a unique opportunity here. John Kennedy was shot forty-two years ago. Some members of my group have been working that case almost all that time. We've made real progress, but two years ago we hit a wall. Some of us have died in the interval since. I've been afraid *I* would die without knowing the truth, or worse, that it would never be known. But now we have a chance. Not only to discover the truth, but to *prove* it."

"I understand, Dwight."

"Do you? Because this opportunity is very fragile. If Tom is killed running from the police, the truth could die with him. If you push the Double Eagles too soon, or too hard, Forrest Knox could move to bury whatever evidence remains. That might mean killing some of his own family, and I don't think he'd hesitate. We have to move quickly, but with the utmost care."

Again the pressure to back off from the Double Eagles. "Just tell me what you need to, Dwight. I came here because of you, and I'm ready to listen."

"It's not easy to condense twenty years of investigation into an hour, but I'll try, for both our sakes. First, I want to dispense with the existing conspiracy theories. To do that, you must stop thinking of the word 'conspiracy' as meaning a large number of people. Large conspiracies usually fail, and when they do succeed, they never stay secret for long."

"Agreed."

"Second, I want to explain a principle that a colleague of mine calls 'Stone's Razor.' It's a way we deal with coincidence."

"All right."

"Nearly every JFK conspiracy theory depends upon one critical and unacceptable coincidence: President Kennedy's motorcade passing beneath the building where Lee Harvey Oswald worked. Oswald got that job randomly, through the friend of a friend of his wife, and only thirty-seven days before the assassination. Kennedy's motorcade route was chosen by the Secret Service only *seven* days before the assassination."

"And it wasn't made public until three days prior," Kaiser clarifies, "after being printed in the *Dallas Times Herald* on Tuesday, November nineteenth."

"The point," Stone continues, "is that Oswald getting the Book Depository job and the choice of motorcade route were *causally unrelated.* That's been proved as conclusively as any fact in history. No one could have placed Oswald in that job in that building with the intent to kill JFK, because no one knew at the time he got the job what the motorcade route would be. Consequently, any conspiracy involving Lee Harvey Oswald that depends upon inspiration or planning prior to November fifteenth is *de facto* impossible."

"Which is all of them, right?"

"Except Oliver Stone's. Since he claimed that everyone from the CIA to the military-industrial complex was in it together—right up to LBJ—Oliver was claiming that they could have controlled the motorcade route and put Kennedy in Oswald's sights."

"Yeah, well . . . let's come back to planet Earth."

"How about halfway back?" Dwight says with a smile. "If I asked you to list the main conspiracy suspects in the assassination, you'd probably give the same ones most Americans would."

The usual suspects, I think, recalling Kaiser's list from last night outside City Hall. "The CIA, Cuban exiles, Castro, the Russians, the Mafia, and the military-industrial complex?"

"Right. And while the House Select Committee cleared the CIA, the Cubans—both pro- and anti-Castro—and the Mafia as *organized groups* in 1979, it did not rule out the possibility that individual members of those entities had carried out the hit in Dallas."

"And your Working Group?"

"We picked up where the Select Committee left off. Let's dispense with the CIA first. Most top-level agency people were relieved or even happy to hear JFK was dead, but they had no reason to kill him. Kennedy had never made good on his threat to splinter the agency in a million pieces, beyond firing Richard Bissell and Allen Dulles. Nor did the agency need to cover its attempts to assassinate Fidel Castro, as is often proposed. Both Kennedy brothers had been partners with the CIA in that effort since taking office. Robert Kennedy had personally signed off on Operation Mongoose, so the Kennedys stood to lose even more than the agency did by exposure. That whole theory is nonsensical."

"Who else can you eliminate?"

"I won't waste thirty seconds of breath on the 'military-industrial complex.' Contrary to popular belief, John Kennedy was no liberal saint, but a dedicated cold warrior. Therefore, defense corporations had no reason to kill him. That theory also violates the large-conspiracy rule. They never could have kept it secret."

"And as for the Russians," Kaiser offers, "by assassinating a sitting president, they would have risked global thermonuclear war. There's zero chance they did that."

"What about the Russians sending Oswald to do it?"

"*Less* than zero," Stone declares, becoming more animated by the give-and-take of discussion. "Oswald had a neon paper trail behind him that led straight to Moscow. Besides, because of his defection to Russia, the KGB knew better than anyone how unstable Lee was."

Stone uses Oswald's first name as easily as a man who knew him all his short life. "And Castro?"

This time Stone's answer is slow in coming. "That's another kettle of fish. Castro knew that the CIA and the Mafia had been trying to kill him, and he had intel reports that those attempts had been sanctioned by the Kennedy brothers. In early '63, Castro actually said publicly that elected officials who engaged in those types of activities could become targets of such activities themselves. In the very year of Kennedy's assassination, he'd threatened to retaliate in kind."

"Well, did he?"

"There's no evidence that he did. Oswald probably hoped that killing JFK would make him a hero in Havana, and thus facilitate his entry to the country. But that's all."

Stone's eyes and voice betray emotion when he speaks of Oswald and Castro, and I sense that we're nearing the crux of his theory. "What's the rest of it, Dwight?"

"Let's cross off the Cuban exiles first, the men betrayed at the Bay of Pigs. They were shot to pieces on the beach or imprisoned because Kennedy wouldn't send air support. A lot of them wanted to punish him for that, and they had the training and weapons needed to pull off Dealey Plaza. However, our considered opinion is that none did. Do I need to go into detail as to why?"

"No. So, where does that leave us?"

"La Cosa Nostra," says Kaiser.

Stone nods. "From the Mafia, the Select Committee singled out Carlos Marcello, Santo Trafficante, Sam Giancana, Johnny Roselli, and Jimmy Hoffa as serious suspects. It recommended that all be investigated further, but I'm sorry to say that no law enforcement agency ever officially fulfilled that charge, including the Bureau."

"Except your guys."

"With a vengeance, I'm proud to say. In summary, each of those mobsters had a motive to want JFK dead, and each rejoiced at the news that he *was* dead. *But*"—Stone leans forward like a professor making a salient point—"just because you want someone dead doesn't make you a murderer."

"If it did, I'd be in jail myself."

"Exactly." Stone drums his fingers on his legal pad. "Of the mobsters, Sam Giancana had particular reason to hate Kennedy. 'Momo' had helped get JFK elected president in 1960, by pushing key wards in Chicago and West Virginia Kennedy's way. Being persecuted by brother Bobby after that election must have pushed him close to violent retaliation. This was aggravated by the fact that Sam and JFK shared a mistress—Judith Exner—but Momo never acted on his hatred."

"You sound pretty sure."

"We had the Chicago Outfit under electronic surveillance for years before the mob even knew about planted microphones—both before and after the assassination. Sam G. and his crew bitched and ranted endlessly about both Kennedys, but there was never even a hint that they'd moved against them."

"Jimmy Hoffa wanted Kennedy dead more than anyone else," Kaiser says.

Stone concedes this with a nod. "Hoffa was heard many times to threaten both Kennedys, and he asked Sam G. and Marcello to whack JFK. But in my group's opinion, that never came to anything either. Hoffa was a hothead, a loose cannon. If Momo or Marcello had moved against Kennedy, they would have done it for their own reasons, not as a favor to Hoffa. All testimony to the contrary by mob lawyer Frank Ragano was fabricated. Ragano made up those stories years later, trying to get a book deal."

I have to fight the urge to ask him to skip ahead to my father. "So, that leaves Marcello and Roselli?"

"And Santo Trafficante. Johnny Roselli was the main link between the CIA and the Mafia during their attempts to kill Castro. He was close to both Giancana and Trafficante, but nothing ties him or them to Dallas and Dealey Plaza. Frank Ragano told a story about Trafficante ordering him to tell Marcello they'd screwed up by killing

JFK—that they should have killed Bobby instead—but that was more bullshit. As a coda to that line of inquiry, Giancana was murdered in 1975, shortly before he was to testify before a Senate Select Committee investigating mob-CIA collusion in the JFK assassination. It sounds suspicious, I know, but Giancana was actually killed over a dispute about Iranian casino revenues. One year later, Roselli *did* testify before that committee, about the CIA-mob efforts to murder Castro. Days later he was found floating in an oil drum off Miami. Roselli knew a lot about his bosses, but nothing about the JFK assassination."

"I guess we're down to Marcello, then?"

"'Uncle Carlos,'" Stone intones. "The king of New Orleans, and the most powerful don in the United States."

His timbre sounds weirdly like affection, and reminds me of my mother's use of that nickname. I think of my father and his time in New Orleans. If Marcello really was that powerful, and Dad was in a position to do him favors at the parish prison, how could a lowly medical extern have resisted?

"If the story I'm about to tell you sounds like it was written by Mario Puzo," says Stone, "that's because there's a lot of Carlos Marcello in *The Godfather*."

The old FBI man begins to speak in a soft but spell-binding baritone that reminds me of the agent I knew in another life. "In 1910, Carlos Marcello was born Calogero Minacori in Tunis. His parents were Sicilian, but Carlos himself never went to Sicily. He once famously said to another mobster who tried Sicilian on him: 'I don't talk dat shit, only English.'"

Kaiser chuckles from the sofa. "That sounds just like Carlos. I've heard the BRILAB tapes."

Stone presses on like a man who knows he has only so much stamina remaining. "When Calogero was an infant, his parents emigrated to a plantation near Metairie, Louisiana. The boy changed his name while very young to better assimilate with the children in his new country. As a boy he hauled vegetables in the swamp parishes south of New Orleans, but he soon figured out that crime paid better. As a teenager, he ran an armed robbery gang that preyed on the surrounding towns. Carlos carried a sawed-off shotgun on a sling, and he killed anyone who got in his way or questioned his leadership. The bodies usually went into the nearby swamps, into the bellies of alligators."

Kaiser gives me a pointed look. "Sound familiar?"

"At eighteen," Stone continues, "Carlos was sentenced to nine years in Angola Prison for robbery and assault. The state let him out after five, and he went right back to his old ways. This is the period during which Brody Royal and his father came to know Carlos. At twenty-seven, Marcello was arrested with twenty-three pounds of marijuana in his possession. He got another stiff prison sentence and a seventy-five-thousand-dollar fine, but this time he was released after only ten months. Why? Because somehow, he had attracted the notice of Frank Costello, head of the Genovese crime family in New York.

"That connection was the making of him. After cutting a gambling deal with Huey Long, Costello chose Carlos to move illegal slot machines into New Orleans. Using his six brothers, local muscle, and the influence of the Long political machine, Carlos eventually forced one-armed bandits into every redneck honky-tonk, black juke joint, Cajun dive bar, and whorehouse from Grand Isle to Raceland—five thousand in all. Within ten years, he'd seized control of all gambling rackets in Louisiana."

"He also developed an association with Meyer Lansky," says Kaiser. "Through the Lansky connection—as reward for services we're still not sure of—Marcello was awarded a percentage of the skim from the Outfit's Vegas casino operations. And they don't hand that out for nothing."

Stone nods. "Carlos was also awarded an interest in the mob's Havana casinos under Batista. He got that cut by providing muscle to Santo Trafficante on Florida real estate deals, a job that the Double Eagles would take on years later. Anyway . . . by 1947, Carlos had become not just a made man, but a bona fide member of the national *Commissione*, and one of the richest of all the bosses."

I suddenly recall several images I once saw of Marcello, way back when I was investigating Ray Presley. The mobster known as "the Little Man" was short, but as thick and tough as a cypress stump. His face looked quick to anger, and several photographers had captured his chilling glare during the 1960s and '70s.

"When Fidel Castro liberated Cuba in 1959," Stone

continues, "Carlos lost untold millions, just like Traffi-cante, Giancana, Lansky, and the other bosses. Hoping to take those casinos back, they helped fund training camps for the Cuban exiles prepping to retake the country in the Bay of Pigs invasion. That's probably where Carlos first came into contact with Frank and Snake Knox, who worked as combat instructors at Carlos's training camp near Morgan City."

"*Ping*," Kaiser says softly, imitating a submarine's sonar.

"Despite the failed invasion," Stone goes on, "Carlos was nearing the height of his power. By the midsixties his cash inflow would reach two billion dollars per annum. That's more than *twelve* billion in today's money."

"Jesus."

"Carlos owned trucking lines, shrimp fleets, untold amounts of real estate—much of it held by third parties who served as blind trustees for him. Interestingly, a lot of those were poor black families who felt complete loyalty to the old tomato salesman from Jefferson Parish."

"He was a folk hero to those people," says Kaiser. "Like Pablo Escobar to the Colombian poor. A benevolent dic-tator."

I nod. "They do like their dictators in Louisiana."

Stone raises a forefinger and points at me. "That's something a lot of people miss. After Louis the Fourteenth and Napoleon, Louisiana never really assimilated into America, not fully. The law here is *still* based on the Na-poleonic Code. They seceded from the Union in 1861, and in the 1930s they got Huey Long. After Huey was assas-sinated, they got Carlos Marcello. Carlos had learned the patronage system under the Kingfish, and he perpetuated it with cash in one hand and a gun in the other. He spread the wealth to every official in the state, from the governor and senators down to the lowest justice of the peace, and nobody—but nobody—bucked him."

"And yet," Kaiser interjects, "despite all that power, in 1963 Carlos found himself under mortal threat from the attorney general of the United States."

Stone nods grimly. "As attorney general, Robert Ken-nedy initiated the most aggressive battle against organized crime in U.S. history. He attacked several mob bosses, but none with more personal animus than Marcello."

Kaiser takes the baton from his mentor. "In 1959, Carlos was called before the McClellan Committee. Senator John Kennedy was a committee member, but Bobby was its chief counsel. You should see the film. Bobby barks and growls like a pit bull, and Carlos treats him with utter contempt. Carlos pled the Fifth a hundred and fifty-two times and smirked throughout the hearing. He claimed he was nothing but a tomato salesman, and on paper he was—through his Pelican Fruit Company." Kaiser laughs dryly. "Salary, fifteen hundred bucks per month."

"Carlos lived to regret that performance," says Stone. "As soon as JFK made Bobby attorney general, Bobby set out to destroy Marcello. He attacked the don on two legal fronts. The first was an IRS case for back taxes. If fraud could be proved, that would land Carlos in federal prison. But the more dangerous prosecution involved Carlos's immigration status. Unlike his brothers, Carlos had never bothered to become a citizen, which kept him out of the army and making millions during World War Two. But in the end that cost him dearly. To gain some legal status, he'd bribed the government of Guatemala—the source of his fruit and marijuana imports—to issue an official birth certificate. But that lie also made Carlos vulnerable."

"I know about Bobby Kennedy illegally deporting Carlos to Central America in '61," I tell them. "As a prosecutor, I read quite a bit about his anti-Mafia tactics."

Stone looks grateful that he can skip the details. "As soon as Carlos got back from that little excursion, Bobby indicted him for falsifying his birth certificate, and *United States versus Carlos Marcello* was set in motion. Between 1961 and 1963, Carlos did all he could to put off the day of reckoning, while Bobby and the INS steadily ratcheted up the pressure. Marcello's Washington lawyer was Jack Wasserman, former chief counsel of the INS. He was the best immigration lawyer in the country, but there was only so much he could do. Carlos *had* bribed the Guatemalans, and Bobby's team could prove it."

"If Marcello played that immigration case by the rules," Kaiser says, "he was guaranteed to lose. And the result wouldn't be simple deportation. If he was forced out of the country, he would lose his empire. That's why he had another lawyer on his payroll—a New Orleans lawyer. One who played by New Orleans rules, by which I mean no rules at all."

"We're getting ahead of ourselves," says Stone, holding up a hand. "What matters is that Bobby had Carlos dead to rights. Carlos knew that if he was deported, the remaining Marcello brothers could never hold his empire together. So long as Bobby Kennedy headed the Justice Department, it was only a matter of time before Carlos's stranglehold on the South was broken and his multibillion-dollar kingdom was carved up by his fellow dons. For Carlos Marcello, deportation was the equivalent of death."

"I get it. So that's the basis of your theory? Marcello had the president killed to sabotage RFK's prosecution?"

"Yes," Stone says simply.

"Tell him the dog story," says Kaiser. "It always makes me think of Brando playing Vito Corleone."

Stone waves his hand almost angrily. "It can't be verified. I don't want Penn thinking about Hollywood bullshit. This is history."

Kaiser looks suitably chastised, and this brings me some satisfaction.

"Try to imagine the rage Carlos must have felt at this state of affairs," Stone says. "Unlike mainstream America, he'd never bought into the myth of Camelot. He knew this country was corrupt to the marrow. He'd bought and sold politicians in Washington, put senators at the head of major committees. He knew that Joe Kennedy had made his fortune as a bootlegger. To Carlos, JFK was a bootlegger's son, no more, and Bobby was a self-righteous hypocrite."

Stone gives me a piercing stare. "Many scholars dismiss the idea of mob assassination because in some crime families it was forbidden to murder any state official, even a prosecutor. They figure that since mobsters balked at killing judges or even cops, killing a president was totally beyond the pale."

"The exception to that rule," says Kaiser, "was betrayal in a criminal enterprise. And *that's* what this conversation is really about. The actual relationship between Carlos Marcello and John Kennedy."

"Did they *have* a relationship?"

"Of course they did," Stone replies. "It was carried on at a distance, but it was as valid as any other, and it had very clear rules—though John Kennedy doesn't seem to have understood that. The crux of it was Cuba. As I said, the Kennedys had used the CIA and the Mafia to try to murder Fidel Castro, and Carlos was part of that."

"And Castro was a head of state," says Kaiser.

Stone nods. "That Kennedy-CIA effort legitimized the assassination of a head of state as a tactic in Carlos's eyes. It lowered his threshold of action to almost zero."

"But John Kennedy was a president," I remind them. "Not a gangster."

"Carlos saw himself as a head of state," Stone says. "That's what I'm trying to tell you. In his own mind, he was the equal of John Kennedy."

"I think that's a stretch, Dwight."

"Do you remember Joe Valachi?"

"Sure. The first 'made man' to testify about the workings of the Mafia."

"One month before the Kennedy assassination, Valachi was asked on the stand about Carlos Marcello. He said only that he'd once planned to visit New Orleans during Mardi Gras, and as a formality he'd mentioned his plans to Vito Genovese. Genovese told Valachi not to go. The Mafia boss of New York told a made man that nobody was allowed to travel in Marcello's territory without Carlos's express permission—not even Genovese himself. 'It was an absolute rule,' Valachi said." Stone holds up a shaking finger. "Carlos Marcello was the only don in America who could make men without approval from the national Commission. He was *sui generis*, Penn. And nobody crossed him."

"Except Bobby Kennedy," I say softly.

Stone nods. "JFK's ingratitude after Giancana's election help was serious, but that's politics. His failure of nerve at the Bay of Pigs lost the mob a lot of money, but that was business. But *Robert* Kennedy's single-minded quest to permanently deport Carlos was a matter of survival. By pushing that trial to its limit, Bobby Kennedy signed his brother's death warrant."

For the first time since entering this room, I feel a chill racing over my shoulders.

"Christ, what I'd give for a shot of scotch," Stone says. "Of course it would kill me, but that might not be a bad way to go." The old FBI agent looks like he's about to laugh, but instead he clenches his jaw in pain.

A strange silence has fallen on us. Though I fight the urge, I glance at my watch again. Three-quarters of an hour has already slipped by. "Guys, we're still a long way from Dealey Plaza, and I haven't heard one thing about my father."

Stone holds up his right hand. "You're about to. But do you accept the premise that Marcello had sufficient motive to kill John Kennedy?"

I shift on my chair, a little reluctant to say anything that might upset my old friend. "I can see why he would hate the Kennedys. I'm not sure that takes us to the assassination of a president as a means of stopping his little brother."

"Tell him the dog story," Kaiser says again.

"I know the fucking dog story!" I snap. "Carlos was supposedly ranting about Bobby Kennedy once, and some goombah said he ought to kill him. Carlos said, 'If a dog is biting you, you don't cut off its tail. You cut off the head. Then he don't bite you no more.'"

"Who told you that story?" Kaiser asks.

"Half the prosecutors in Texas know it! Jesus. Just like the one where Marcello supposedly said in Sicilian, 'Will someone take this stone from my shoe?' The problem is, I heard he didn't know any Sicilian."

"He knew it," Stone says with authority. "He was raised by Sicilian parents. He just didn't speak it."

"Whatever. Look, I didn't come here to listen to a radio version of the History Channel. If you guys have any evidence of contact between my father and Marcello, it's time to tell me about it."

Stone takes a deep, labored breath, then turns and looks at Kaiser. "He's right."

"We haven't even started on Oswald and Ferrie," Kaiser objects.

"*Oswald?*" I cry, getting to my feet. "Are you kidding? I don't care about that little rat."

When Stone looks to Kaiser again, as though for permission, I finally lose my patience. "Goddamn it, guys.

That call I took earlier? Before I came in here? That was Sheriff Dennis. Claude Devereux had just told him the Double Eagles will be in his office at seven A.M. tomorrow for voluntary questioning."

Both men stare at me as though I've just announced the Second Coming.

"Bullshit," says Kaiser. "I don't believe that."

"They're coming. Devereux claims they've got nothing to hide."

Kaiser is angrily shaking his head. "Nothing to fear, more like. They wouldn't be coming if they had anything to worry about. Something's wrong, Penn. Forrest has put in the fix somehow. You and Dennis are walking into a trap."

"What kind of trap?"

"I don't know. But I know Forrest Knox."

"John's right," says Stone. "This is trouble. The Knoxes have more to hide than you can possibly imagine."

After staring at both men in stony silence for a few seconds, I sit back on the edge of my chair. "Tell me what you know about my father and Marcello. Then I'll decide how to handle tomorrow's meeting. Otherwise I walk out now. I'm sorry, Dwight, more than you know. But that's the way it is."

Kaiser starts to argue, but Stone raises his hand to silence him. Then he lifts the top page of his legal pad, picks up a white sheet of paper, and passes it to me. It appears to be a photocopy of a small rectangular business form. The image quality is poor, but at the top of the rectangle a logo reads "TBC." That means nothing to me, but at the bottom I see a cursive signature I instantly recognize.

Thomas J. Cage, M.D.

"What's this?" I ask, my face tingling with heat.

"An excuse form," Stone informs me, almost sadly. "From the Triton Battery Corporation in Natchez, Mississippi."

"Notice the dates?" asks Kaiser.

Despite my father's scrawled handwriting, I can just make them out: *Nov. 18–22, 1963.* Below this line are the words *Chronic Hepatitis.*

"What does this mean?" I ask.

"It's pretty obvious, isn't it?" says Kaiser.

"John," Stone says sharply. "We don't know what it means, Penn. What we do know is that your father signed a medical excuse for Frank Knox to be absent from work at the Triton Battery plant from the Monday prior to John Kennedy's assassination through the Friday he was killed in Dealey Plaza."

"A full week," says Kaiser. "Plenty of time to reconnoiter Dealey Plaza and settle on the Dal-Tex Building as his sniper's nest. You see? Frank Knox wasn't the primary shooter. Oswald was already set up to use the School Book Depository, and Frank was his backup."

"No, I don't see. Not at all."

"Slow down, John," says Stone. "Penn, we obviously need to know whether your father had any idea what Knox was actually doing on those dates."

My ears roar as I shake my head in denial. "Can you prove Frank Knox was in Dealey Plaza on that day?"

"No."

My head snaps up. "Can you prove he was even in Dallas?"

Stone slowly shakes his head. "We can't even prove Frank Knox was in Texas. Not yet, anyway. Of course we just got on this track. All we know for sure is that he wasn't at work, and he almost certainly wasn't at home."

"That's not all we know," says Kaiser.

I look back at the paper in my hand. "How did you even get hold of this? There's no way Triton Battery saved this kind of crap from 1963."

"You're right, of course," Stone concedes. "Your father's written excuse form was in Knox's personnel record. It turns out I requisitioned a copy of that back in 1965, while working some other cases. Knox was still pretending to be part of the mainstream KKK at that time, and for some reason I decided to keep his file along with a few others. If I hadn't done that, we might have solved the Kennedy assassination years ago."

"What do you mean?"

"I mean that the concerted efforts of our team—some of the best investigators in the world—were stymied by the kind of clerical accident that often sways history, without anyone being the wiser. When I was fired from the Bureau in 1972, that record I'd requested in 1965 was

still in the Jackson, Mississippi, field office. The murders
I had investigated were still open cases. When the Working Group came together in the mideighties and began
investigating cold cases, its members couldn't request
Bureau files. They had to rely on what files they'd kept—
illegally—or whatever active agents would photocopy or
smuggle out for them. We did send an agent into the Mississippi field office to locate all the old civil rights records
he could—which included Double Eagle files—and he got
quite a few. But he was told that some had been shipped
back to Central Records in Maryland. He took a quiet
look around the building for them, but he found nothing.
That excuse remained lost."

"Then how did you locate it?"

Kaiser leans forward and says, "This morning, after I
convinced the director that Stone's group is onto something, I sent two agents up to the Jackson field office in
a pickup truck. By this afternoon, I had six crates of files
dating back to the 1960s. They found them in the basement. One of those crates contained Frank's Triton Battery file. It had been sitting there since 1965, with that
medical excuse inside it."

The irony is obvious, but something else is tickling my
brain. "Is this excuse form all you have on Frank Knox
that relates to Dallas?"

Stone shakes his head. "We put Frank and Snake
Knox through the wringer years ago. They became
suspects in the Kennedy investigation the moment we
learned that Frank was listed on the CIA payroll of
JMWAVE/Operation Mongoose."

I faintly remember Henry Sexton telling me this.
"Frank Knox worked for the CIA?"

"It wasn't as cloak-and-dagger as it sounds. The agency
ran its own anti-Castro training camps prior to the Bay
of Pigs. As for the private camps, the agency didn't want
to have to rely on what the bosses like Marcello and Trafficante told them. So they paid some vets to hire on as instructors. To Frank Knox, that just meant two paychecks
instead of one. All he had to do was give his CIA contact
a call now and then and update him on progress in the
camp."

"Would Marcello have known Knox was doing that?"

"No. Frank wasn't stupid. The point is, we discounted Frank and Snake Knox as suspects in the JFK assassination years ago. We figured them for racist rednecks who'd killed a lot of black people, but not much more. Even after we came to suspect Marcello, we didn't see Frank as a soldier or employee of his, because in theory he'd been informing on Marcello to the CIA."

"They didn't know about the Brody Royal connection," Kaiser explains. "Royal was the cutout between Marcello and the Knoxes in later years. But once Glenn Morehouse exposed that connection, everything clicked into place. Marcello's plan to lure RFK here in '68 and use the Eagles to kill him was like a billboard pointing back at 1963."

"When I saw that medical excuse," Stone intones, "I knew Frank had done it."

"This is bullshit," I insist. "There's no *way* my father knowingly took part in a criminal conspiracy, much less a presidential assassination. No way in hell."

"I'm sure you're right," Stone says softly.

Everyone in this room knows my father probably withheld critical knowledge about the murders of Albert Norris and Dr. Leland Robb for nearly forty years. But that doesn't change my conviction.

"Is this all you've got?"

Kaiser starts to say something, but Stone stops him. "The thing is, Penn, even if Tom didn't knowingly assist Frank Knox in wrongdoing, he may know things of critical importance. He just might not know he knows them."

This is slightly more palatable, but I can't tell whether Stone really believes it.

"In any case," says the old agent, "I'm certain that one or more surviving Double Eagles know what Frank Knox did in 1963—most likely his brother, Snake. Snake might even have helped Frank bring off the assassination. Even if he didn't, he may well know the truth about your father and that medical excuse."

"Where was Snake on November twenty-second?"

"We don't know. Some people have told us he was at work, but we can't verify that. Nevertheless," Stone says, his voice wearing away my resistance like a steady flow of water, "now you can see why all the Double Eagles must be handled with the utmost care."

In my mind's eye I see Walker Dennis, the ex–baseball player and newly appointed sheriff, clumsily trying to break Snake Knox in a CPSO interrogation room. The prospect makes me light-headed.

"*Now* you're getting it?" says Kaiser.

Shit.

CHAPTER 35

AS CAITLIN COASTED along the great concrete crescent before Quentin's Tudor mansion, she saw faint light glowing at the edges of one of the window blinds on the side of the house. She wished she had some way to warn Tom that she was no threat to him, but honking the horn might alert neighbors she couldn't see. As she got out of her car, she realized that it had been four days since she'd seen Penn's father. Last Sunday, she and Penn had taken Annie over to eat a late dinner. Peggy had pulled out all the stops and cooked one of her classic southern feasts, including "Ruby's Fried Chicken." Now, only four days later, the world in which such a simple domestic scene could occur had been blown apart by the actions of the family patriarch, whom she would confront in less than a minute. Trying to stay calm, she walked around the house to a side door and knocked three times, as normally as she could.

Nothing happened.

She knocked again, this time giving the child's version of a "secret knock."

Putting her ear to the door, she was surprised to hear a shuffling sound behind it. Then a woman's voice said, "Who is it?"

"Melba, it's Caitlin Masters," she said loudly. "I'm alone."

Several seconds of silence followed. Then she heard a dead bolt slide back, and the door opened to reveal Tom Cage standing in the crack with a pistol pointed through it. Caitlin could see Melba's tall form in the foyer behind him.

"Jesus Christ!" Tom gasped. "How did you find me?"

He looked back at Melba to see whether she had betrayed him.

"I had an employee following Melba. Shouldn't we get inside before some FBI helicopter sees the light?"

Tom grunted and backed out of the gap so she could pass through. When she had, he closed the door and led her into a contemporary kitchen area she recognized from a party photograph she had seen at Tom and Peggy's house. Melba stood by the counter, looking wary.

"Is Penn with you?" Tom asked anxiously.

"No."

"Where is he?"

Caitlin saw nothing to be gained by mentioning Dwight Stone and the FBI at this point. "He's with Peggy and Annie, somewhere safe. He's sleeping."

"Where?"

"I don't know myself. For safety's sake."

Tom processed this, then nodded. "Good thinking." He set the pistol on the counter. "Why didn't you tell him you'd found me?"

"At first I wasn't positive that I had."

"And now?"

"I want to hear what you have to say. I guess Melba and I have a lot in common."

The nurse gave Caitlin a sidelong look.

"Tom, if I can find you, the bad guys can, too."

"You're right," he said, looking preoccupied. "I need to move as soon as Walt gets back."

"Have you heard anything from him? Has he made any progress?"

Tom glanced at Melba again. "He's made some, but he can't move right now."

"Well, I don't think Colonel Griffith Mackiever can do much to help you. He'll be lucky to save himself. He's about to be forced to resign over a scandal that was probably manufactured by Forrest Knox."

In the silence that followed this statement, she realized that the towel over Tom's left shoulder concealed a broad wrapping of gauze bandages. "How bad is your wound?"

"He ought to be in the hospital," Melba said. "Or at the very least home in bed."

"I'm fine," Tom insisted, taking a seat on one of the heavy leather bar stools. "It's a through-and-through, and

Melba and Drew gave me better treatment than I'd have gotten at the hospital."

"Did this happen anywhere in the vicinity of that dead state trooper?"

Tom met her gaze but did not answer.

Caitlin wanted to get Melba out of the room before asking certain questions, but she didn't want to be rude. She decided to edge toward the difficult questions. "Will you answer one question?" she asked. "Off the record?"

"That depends."

"Why in God's name did you jump bail? It seems completely counterproductive for your case."

Tom sighed and braced his elbows on the dark granite counter. "It was my best option at the time."

"Were you afraid you would have died in Sheriff Byrd's jail?"

"That's certainly possible."

"But that wasn't your reason?"

"Let's just say that . . . at that time I had options I no longer have."

"Because of the dead state trooper?"

"Mostly. Once he was killed, there was no clean way out for Walt and me."

Caitlin laid her hand on his back. "Forrest Knox's police obviously hope to kill you before you can get into custody. Why are you making it easier for them?"

"I don't have a choice. Walt wouldn't be in this fix if he hadn't tried to help me. There's no way I'm letting him go to trial for that."

"But there's no other way out of this. Griffith Mackiever can't wave a magic wand and make that murder charge go away."

Tom looked back at Melba and said, "Mel, is there any chance you could make some tea?"

The nurse looked glad to have something to do.

"I don't have a lot of time," Caitlin said, as Melba held a kettle under the tap. "There are FBI agents at the *Examiner*, and the longer I'm gone, the more suspicious they'll get. Plus, Penn could decide to come looking for me."

"Then get back to work. There's nothing to be learned here."

Caitlin felt a stab of anger. "Tom . . . it was Viola's

death that started all this. If you didn't kill her, nobody can prove you did."

"Centuries of history would beg to differ."

"Oh, Christ. Yes, people get wrongly convicted. But not with the kind of lawyers you'd have in your corner. Penn? And Quentin Avery?"

With obvious effort Tom turned the stool toward her. "Even if I were to fight the murder charge on Viola—or plead guilty to a reduced charge—that dead trooper would still be dead, and Walt's life would be at risk."

The idea that Tom might plead guilty to a lesser charge made her curious. "Will you tell me what really happened at Viola's that night?"

"No offense, Cait, but if I wouldn't discuss it with Penn, I'm not going to tell you."

Caitlin glanced at Melba, who was gazing at Tom like a worried wife. She wondered then if there was more between the doctor and nurse than friendship. It seemed odd that in this time of crisis Tom would repeatedly call upon his black nurse; yet somehow Caitlin had known to have Melba watched. Was Melba Price the new Viola Turner?

"I need to ask you some personal questions," Caitlin said. "Very personal. I have to. And you might prefer to be alone. Sorry, Melba. It's up to Tom."

Tom shifted on the stool as though his shoulder had sent a bolt of pain through his body. Then he looked over at his nurse, who was watching the kettle on the gas stove.

"Mel, do you mind watching TV in the bedroom for a few minutes?"

"I've got a glass of wine over on the coffee table," the nurse replied. "I'll finish it on the back patio."

"It's pretty chilly," Caitlin said.

"I could use some air," Melba said, a little curtly. "Can you finish making the tea?"

"Sure."

"I'd rather you stay inside, Mel," Tom said. "This house is huge, and we don't know who might be outside. Caitlin found us, after all."

"Doc, if anybody's out there, we're done for already. I guess I'll be the back-door lookout."

Melba collected her wineglass and walked toward some

double doors behind a broad curtain. Then she slipped through the crack and went outside.

Fighting the temptation to look away from Tom, Caitlin said, "Exactly how close are you and Melba?"

He looked so genuinely shocked by the implication of her question that Caitlin instantly realized her error. "You asked Melba to leave the room for that?"

"No. Tom, last night Penn and I were nearly murdered. Brody Royal almost killed us. Henry Sexton saved us."

"I know." He motioned toward the sofa. "Melba brought me a copy of this morning's paper."

"Before he died, Brody told us two things about you. He said that you saved Viola's life back in 1968. And he said you killed her four days ago."

Tom's lips parted slightly.

"Brody had no reason to lie, Tom. He thought we were going to die. And he thought the irony was hilarious."

Tom turned away and shook his head. "Brody Royal . . . that psychotic bastard."

"I agree. But why would he say that to us, Tom?"

Tom looked down at his hands for some time, then raised his head and looked into Caitlin's eyes. "He told you the truth, Cait. But don't ask me any more about it."

Caitlin suddenly felt cold. "You . . . you killed her, Tom?"

"As I said before, I'm not going to speak about what happened in her sister's house that night. If I couldn't tell Penn, I certainly can't tell you. No offense."

"Then what the hell are you going to do? Just sit here until they come for you?"

"That's my concern, not yours."

Caitlin felt a hot rush of anger. She walked away from the counter, then turned and spoke with more hostility than she'd intended. "Penn met Lincoln Turner yesterday. And then again today. Did you know that?"

Tom turned and squinted as though a bright light had been shined in his face. "Penn and Lincoln, together?"

She nodded. "For close to an hour in a nightclub out in Anna's Bottom. Lincoln told Penn that he's your son. By Viola, obviously."

Tom answered in a low voice. "I wish I could refute that, but I can't."

"You believe Lincoln Turner is your son?"

"You don't?"

"No. How long have you known about his existence?"

"Since the night Viola died."

Caitlin nodded with satisfaction. "Did Viola show you any proof of paternity?"

"What kind of proof could she offer, other than the timing?"

"Tom . . . in some ways, I respect you more than any man I've ever known, but you have always been a soft touch. Sharp customers have always taken advantage of you, and you've always let them. Peggy told me that years ago, and I've seen it with my own eyes many times."

"Viola wasn't a con artist, Caitlin."

"No. But she was a woman. And if she truly had a son by you, do you really believe she'd have kept it secret from you for forty years?"

"Yes, I do."

"I disagree. She knew what kind of father you are. Sooner or later, she would have told you about the boy. And if not you, she would have told the boy himself. And he would have sought you out. I don't buy this, Tom. Not any of it."

The kettle began to whistle. Caitlin had to tear her gaze away from Tom's face, and she sensed that he was grateful for the break. She poured the water into the mugs Melba had set out, then dunked two bags of Earl Grey. Tom took a pink packet of sweetener from a rack on the counter, poured the contents into his tea, and gently shook the mug.

"So Viola suddenly made it up. That's what you're saying," said Tom. "Why would she lie to me about that?"

"Oh, dear Lord. She was dying, and she had a son she was worried about! She knew that one word in your ear would ensure that Lincoln would never want for anything for the rest of his life. By telling you what she did, Viola provided for her son in perpetuity."

"That's pretty cynical."

"I'm a woman, Tom. Just like Viola."

"You think all women are the same?"

"No. But about the fundamental things, we're pretty similar. I'm sure Viola was noble and selfless, but all women are selfish when it comes to providing for their children."

"Lincoln is my son, Cait. Have you spoken to him yourself?"

"No. But I want to. One of my reporters is trying to find him right now. I hope she doesn't, to be frank."

Tom sipped from his mug but said nothing more.

Caitlin decided to try a different tack. "Does Peggy know about Lincoln?"

Tom's eyes went flat, opaque. "No. Not yet."

"I advise you to keep it that way, at least until you have a DNA test performed."

"I've already initiated one."

This shocked her. "How did you do that? Have you had personal contact with Lincoln?"

"No. And I didn't doubt Viola, but I knew Peggy would demand proof. And Penn too—as they should, of course."

"Then how . . . ?"

"Viola had some keepsakes from Lincoln's childhood. One of them was a little pewter box that held a few baby teeth. I took that the night she died."

Caitlin had a feeling Tom had said more than he intended. "Did Viola know you were going to do the test?"

"No."

"When will it be completed?"

"Soon, I hope. I use a Baton Rouge lab for my clinical tests. I have a friend who's a part owner. He said he'd rush it for me. Three or four days from now is possible."

She was glad to know Tom hadn't completely abandoned reason. "I know you said you won't talk about Sunday night. But do you know what Penn thinks about Viola's death?"

Tom's silver eyebrows went up.

"He thinks Lincoln tried to euthanize his mother, but somehow screwed it up and killed her painfully. Maybe he had second thoughts and tried to revive her. Penn thinks you figured that out, and you're protecting Lincoln out of guilt over forty years of neglect."

The flatness in Tom's eyes gave way to an unreadable depth, as though a crust of ice had melted away to reveal bottomless ocean. Caitlin's first thought was that Penn's theory had struck home, but then something in Tom's face changed her mind.

"That's not what happened, is it?"

"Why do you say that?"

"Because when I said it, you looked like that idea had never entered your head before."

"You read minds now?"

"What would you think if I told you Lincoln saved Penn's life today?"

"*What?*"

"One of the men who tried to kill you last night pulled a gun on Penn at Drew's lake house. Penn went out there after Drew told him you'd been there. Two guys were staking it out, in case you came back."

Tom looked stricken. "Oh, no."

"They got the drop on Penn, but Lincoln pulled up out of nowhere with a shotgun and ran the guys off. They were off-duty cops. Apparently, Lincoln has been following Penn in the belief that Penn knows where you are."

"With a shotgun . . ."

"Mm-hm. They told Penn that they'd tried to take you last night, and you killed one of them. A Monroe, Louisiana, cop. Is that true? Have you killed two cops now?"

Tom waved his hand angrily. "I did what I had to do."

Caitlin took two steps toward him and spoke as gently as she could. "Remember last Sunday's dinner at your house?"

Tom nodded like an amnesiac suddenly recalling a bit of reality.

"Now look at where we are. You're the author of all this insanity, Tom. And you've got to stop it before somebody else gets killed. Like Penn."

Tom's breathing had grown labored. "I intended to."

"How?" she demanded. "I see no method whatever in the madness of your actions."

Tom slid carefully off the bar stool, then picked up his mug and carried it into the den. Caitlin followed and watched him set the mug on a coffee table that had been pulled close to a comfortable sofa covered with quilts and pillows. With a groan he sat heavily on the upholstered sofa.

"Was that your idea of a strategic retreat?" she asked, sitting in the club chair nearest the sofa.

"The geography's pretty limited."

She sipped her tea, giving Tom time to process all she'd told him. Her eyes played over the prescription bottles that stood like little soldiers around a laptop computer. At length she said, "Since Griffith Mackiever is unlikely to be able to help you, what option do you have other than arranging a safe surrender?"

Tom rubbed the back of his neck for a while before answering. Then he turned to her with his startlingly clear eyes and said, "You want the truth, Cait? If Colonel Mackiever can't help us, then there's only one person who can."

Caitlin tried to guess who he was talking about. When it came to her, an electric chill raced over her skin. "Not Forrest Knox."

Tom nodded gravely.

"Why in God's name would Forrest help you? He's trying to kill you."

"The same reason anybody makes a deal. I'd have to offer him something in exchange for his help."

"Good Lord. You don't understand. I just went through this with Penn. He tried the same thing with Brody Royal, and that's what nearly got us killed. It *did* kill Henry and the others. You're talking about the very same idea—offering to bury information in exchange for protection."

This time Tom said nothing, but she saw the truth of it in his face.

"A promise like that is worthless unless you can guarantee that *I* won't do anything to hurt Forrest. That I'll stop the newspaper's investigation."

Still Tom remained silent, and the longer he did, the more horrified she became. "I won't do it!" she cried.

Tom's gaze was like a hot lamp, making her ever more uncomfortable.

She shifted in her chair. "Like father, like son, huh? Unbelievable."

"How much evidence do you really have against Forrest?" Tom asked. "Not the Double Eagles. Just Forrest Knox?"

"Some. Not as much as I'm going to have. Because I'm going to get it all. And if I can prove that Forrest—and by extension Trooper Dunn—are crooked, *then* Quentin can get you and Walt acquitted for shooting Dunn."

Tom seemed to be exercising great forbearance. "Do you really believe Forrest Knox will let you do that? And even if you survived to see your story printed, do you think you'd bring Forrest down before his men killed Walt and me?"

A wave of heat flashed over her neck and face. "If you'd let us arrange a safe surrender, yes!"

"I see. And where would this safe surrender take place?"

"If you'd call Penn, I think he can get the FBI to set it up for you."

"Not after the death of that state trooper."

"You don't understand. There's an agent named John Kaiser who could set it up for you. Penn is with him right now. And not only Kaiser, but Dwight Stone. Do you remember him?"

Tom's mouth had fallen open. "Dwight Stone? But you—you said Penn was with Peggy and Annie."

"I lied. He's meeting with Kaiser and Stone right now, trying to arrange a safe surrender for you. And to be honest, I don't think they give a damn about Viola Turner or that state trooper. They're obsessed with the Kennedy assassination."

Tom had gone pale. "The Kennedy assassination!"

She nodded. "Yes, and Carlos Marcello and the Knox family. Kaiser and Stone seem to think all that is tied together."

Tom was shaking his head. "Jesus Christ . . . after all these years?"

Caitlin heard something strange in Tom's voice. "What do you mean? Do you know something about all that? Because Penn said they might well offer you protective custody in exchange for information about the assassination."

"Caitlin . . . you have no idea what you're dealing with. Neither do Kaiser and Stone. If they get too close to the Knoxes, Forrest or Snake will kill them, too."

"You think Forrest Knox would murder FBI agents?"

"Without hesitation."

She was starting to think Tom had entered the realm

of paranoid delusion. "I'm sorry, I just don't believe that. You kill an FBI agent, you're asking for a life on the run."

"Not if you can blame someone else for the crime. And the Knoxes are very good at that sort of thing."

"Are you saying that's what happened to you?"

Tom lifted one of the quilts and pulled it over his lap, as if he'd gotten cold. Then he murmured, "The Knoxes have been killers for generations."

At last they had come to the heart of things. In his desire to persuade her to break faith with herself, Tom had unwittingly taken their conversation into the territory he'd been avoiding for years.

"How long have you known that?" she asked softly.

"Longer than I'd care to admit. Even to myself."

"Tom . . . Henry Sexton told me that he tried to interview you several times, and you always refused to see him."

"I couldn't," he said simply. "I had enormous admiration for what Henry was doing. He was the bravest reporter ever to come out of this area. But look what happened in the end. He met the same fate you're courting now. I blame myself, of course. Partly, anyway. But that doesn't alter the equation as it pertains to you. If you go after Forrest Knox, you'll die."

Tom leaned forward, opened two prescription bottles, and swallowed two pills with his tea—one green and yellow, the other large, oblong, and white.

"Are you having chest pain?"

He smiled sadly. "Fact of life, my dear. But that was a pain pill and an antibiotic."

"Tom, you can't go on like this."

"You're right. And I don't plan to."

"Oh, that's right. You want to make a bargain with the murderer you tell me is too dangerous for me to go after with my newspaper. Tom, even if you physically survived that encounter, you'd die a different kind of death. You'd die on the inside. That son of a bitch is evil."

"You have no idea, Cait. Snake Knox is clinically insane, and he comes by it honestly. Forrest can't have fallen far from the tree, either. But that doesn't change the fact that Forrest Knox is the only man short of the Louisiana governor who can make that APB go away, or blame someone else for Viola's murder. And I won't accept any solution that doesn't extricate Walt from the trouble I've got him into."

At last one of the main reasons for Tom's intransigence was sinking in. "I understand how you must feel about that. But Tom . . . Forrest is corrupting the whole law enforcement system of Louisiana."

"Louisiana has been corrupt for three hundred years, Cait. Forrest Knox is nothing new."

His voice sounded very like her paternal grandfather's, filled with both disillusionment and wisdom. But she would not let that sidetrack her. "You knew Forrest's father, didn't you?" she asked, watching him closely. "Frank Knox?"

"Yes, Frank was a patient of mine." Tom's voice had altered slightly, but she couldn't read the tone.

"I read in one of Henry's notebooks that Frank died in your office."

Tom went still, then regarded her curiously.

She pushed on in spite of feeling anxious. "Did you know that Frank Knox murdered Jimmy Revels in the hope of luring Robert Kennedy down here to be assassinated?"

Tom blinked once, slowly. "I never heard anything like that. Is that true?"

"What if I told you that Frank Knox planned that operation at the request of Carlos Marcello, the Mafia boss?"

"Who told you that?"

"Henry Sexton figured it out. But I think the FBI believes the same thing." Caitlin decided to go for broke. Maybe that would shake Tom from his delusion of coming to some détente with Forrest Knox. "You were no stranger to Marcello yourself, were you?"

Tom's eyes had gone flat again. "Leave it alone, Caitlin. Please."

"I wish I could. But people are dying. And your son is out there risking his life trying to save you. This morning he and Walker Dennis busted every meth cooker and mule in Concordia Parish. And tomorrow morning they're planning to interrogate the Double Eagles at the Concordia Parish Sheriff's Office."

Tom's face grew so pale that she feared he might collapse. "Why the hell is he doing that?"

"He thinks that by putting Forrest on the defensive,

he'll buy you enough time to do whatever the hell you're trying to do. He loves you so much that he's willing to go to war against the Knoxes to save you."

Tom dug his fingers back through his hair like a man trying to hold his brain inside his skull.

Caitlin decided to press on. "Did you already know Brody Royal was guilty of the murders I wrote about in today's paper?"

Tom lowered his hands into his lap and spoke without looking at her. "No. Not for sure."

"Did Dr. Leland Robb tell you that Albert Norris implicated Brody Royal in his murder before he died? Henry believed he did."

The stunned look in Tom's eyes told her she was close to the truth. Caitlin kept her eyes on his, not wanting to give him enough respite to disengage. "You knew Dr. Robb well, didn't you? Before he died in that plane crash, you traveled to gun shows together in his plane."

"Henry obviously did his homework."

"He wanted justice for those victims, and their families. He believed you knew that Royal had killed Albert and Dr. Robb, but you never told the police or the FBI. Henry couldn't square that with what he knew about your character, and neither can I. But now . . . my gut tells me that it's true."

Tom seemed to have aged visibly during the past minute. "Maybe I'm not the man you think I am."

"Maybe not. I've tried to imagine what might keep you silent about something like that, but I've come up empty. The only thing that seems relevant makes no sense to me. According to Henry, there are FBI records that you treated some of Carlos Marcello's gangsters during the late sixties and seventies. The report says they would drive up from New Orleans, and you'd treat them for free. There are actually FBI surveillance reports of that."

"Dear God." Tom cradled his head in his arthritic hands. "I guess nothing we do ever stays buried, does it?" After half a minute, he looked up, his face heavy with what seemed to be grief—or perhaps guilt. "Caitlin . . . if I go further now, what I say is off-limits. You don't print it. You don't speak to Penn about it . . . nothing. Ever."

She wanted to say, *I don't care about that*, but she knew she would be lying. Tom would know it, too. "Never?"

"Not until Peggy and I are dead, anyway."

"All right, then."

"Give me your word. On the child you're carrying."

His demand sent a chill through her. "I won't say that. It scares me." She held up the little finger on her right hand. "Pinkie swear?"

To her surprise, Tom looked as though he might break down. "My daughter used to say that, when she was little."

"Come on, Tom. I'm the most sympathetic audience you'll ever have, other than your wife."

He stared at her for several seconds longer, like a man pondering jumping from a bridge. Then he said, "Viola killed Frank Knox. And I helped her."

Caitlin felt as though she'd levitated off the chair. "You . . . what?"

"Viola murdered Frank Knox. Out of revenge. And I helped her. I covered it up for thirty-seven years. Henry never figured that out?"

She shook her head. "I don't think so. He spoke about Frank's death last night, just before he died. Maybe the possibility had crossed his mind. But I don't think he really got that far. We were talking about Viola's rumored gang rape by the Double Eagles, and whether or not it had really happened."

Tom's reply was hoarse with emotion. "It happened. They raped her two different times, gang rapes both times. Frank Knox ordered it the first time, and Snake the second. The second time was beyond any horror you and I can imagine."

Caitlin drew in a sharp rush of air.

Tom rubbed his white beard, his eyes brighter than they'd been all night. "But Frank paid in full," he said. "On the floor of my office. Yes, sir . . . he paid. But so did we all, I suppose."

"Tell me."

Tom did.

CHAPTER 36

DWIGHT STONE AND John Kaiser have spent ten minutes trying to persuade me to tell Walker Dennis to call off tomorrow's questioning of the Double Eagles, but so far I've refused. Truth be told, I can't get my mind off the Triton Battery medical absence form signed by my father. When set alongside the photos I've been shown in the past few days, my mother's admission that Dad knew Carlos Marcello in 1959, and the fact that Dad probably remained silent about the Double Eagle murders of Albert Norris and Dr. Robb for forty years—it surely suggests something unsavory. Of course, the medical excuse *could* be only what it appears to be, and the only meaningful part of Dad's contact with Marcello might be whatever deal he made to save Viola Turner. At the moment I'm only thankful that Kaiser and Stone know nothing about my father's early contact with Marcello in New Orleans.

My dilemma is what to do next. Part of me wants to simply walk out and leave all this behind. But Kaiser and Stone clearly know more about Dad than they've revealed so far. How can I leave without knowing just how dark the picture gets? And if I'm going to confront Snake Knox in an interrogation room twelve hours from now, I need to know everything that might help me manipulate him. Otherwise, he'll be manipulating me.

"I know this looks bad," I say to Stone. "But there's nothing I've seen in the past three days that can't be explained by scenarios well short of Dad being involved with the Knoxes or Marcello in any criminal way."

Stone gives me an understanding smile, but Kaiser looks far from convinced.

"He was a goddamned war hero!" I practically shout.

"Frank Knox was a war hero," Kaiser says relentlessly. "Snake, too."

"Dwight," I press, searching for sympathy from my old friend, "Dad is the least racist white man in this town. He voted for Kennedy in 1960! All this stuff you've been telling me is pure supposition. You said yourself, you can't even prove Frank Knox was in Dallas. For all you know, he really was home with hepatitis."

"No, he wasn't," says Kaiser. "I spent part of this afternoon tracking down Knox's old neighbors from that era. Most are dead or long gone from here, but I found two women still living in this area. One has Alzheimer's. But the other I found in the Twin Oaks nursing home. Mrs. Johnzell Williams."

"Twin Oaks? Dad used to be the doctor for that facility."

"Mrs. Williams remembers Dr. Cage well. She thinks he walks on water, just like everybody else around here."

"That's nothing to scoff at," Stone says. "Many a man could wish for the same."

"What the hell could she remember from forty years ago?" I ask.

"Forty-two," Kaiser corrects me. "We're talking about the day Kennedy was assassinated, Penn. *Everybody* remembers where they were on that day. Right?"

I don't answer.

"Mrs. Williams had another reason to remember that weekend," Kaiser goes on. "She told me that Frank's oldest son, Frank Junior, was interested in their daughter, Nancy. He was seventeen, but she was only fourteen. On the night of the day the president was shot, Nancy Williams didn't come home until three A.M. *Mr.* Williams was ready to kill Frank Junior, but his wife persuaded him to talk to the father. Well . . ." Kaiser gives me a cagey look. "It seems Frank Knox, Senior, couldn't be found. Nor could his father, Elam. Mrs. Williams didn't think too highly of Elam, by the way. But what matters to us is that Frank Senior didn't appear until late Saturday afternoon. And no one had seen him for days."

Kaiser takes a small digital recorder from his pocket and starts fiddling with its tiny buttons. "I taped our conversation. Thought you might like to hear this part about Frank Junior. I've got it cued up . . . right here."

The scratchy voice of an octogenarian white female comes from the tiny speaker. *"That boy wasn't right. He was all the time goin' to the church house, but he didn't have the Lord nowhere in him. There was something bad in that house. The Knox house, I mean. I was glad when that boy joined the army. I hated he got killed over there, but . . . well, it was a good thing for my Nancy that he never come back. She married a welder from Jonesville, a good Christian man."*

Kaiser's deeper voice floats from the recorder: *"What do you think the bad thing was in the Knox house?"*

"I don't know. And I don't care to know. We minded our own business on Green Street. Folks ought to do more of that nowadays."

"Was it the boy only, or his parents?"

"It's always the parents," croaks the old woman. *"The Good Book says, 'Train up a child in the way that he should go, and he will not depart from it.' Well, I reckon the opposite is just as true. Always seemed so to me, anyway. But what do I know? I'm old."*

"Not a day over seventy, I'd swear. But as for Mr. Frank Knox? You're positive that he wasn't at home on the weekend the president was killed? Maybe sick in his bed?"

"Didn't I say that? Why, my husband raised such a fuss on their porch that Frank would've come a runnin' if he was within half a mile. But nobody had set eyes on him in nearly a week. Some people thought he'd run out on his family. But he was prob'ly just off cattin' around."

"Thank you, Mrs. Williams."

Kaiser clicks off the recorder. "I found that woman in one day. In a week, I'll have Frank Knox pinned to Dallas like a butterfly to a display board."

Stone seems embarrassed by Kaiser's pushiness. "Penn, forget what we don't know. Let's look at what we do. On the day Frank Knox founded the Double Eagles, he wrote RFK, MLK, and JFK in the sand. Then he crossed out JFK's name and said, 'One down, two to go.' We know Brody Royal financially backed the Double Eagles. We also know that Royal—who employed Frank Knox to commit other murders during the 1960s—had two rifles in his house that were possibly related to the JFK assassination. We also know Brody Royal was a longtime associate of Carlos Marcello. Granted?"

I nod but say nothing.

"We know the Kennedys meant to destroy Marcello.

We know Frank Knox worked as a military instructor at a Cuban exile training camp funded by Marcello. We know your father knew Frank Knox from his work for Triton Battery, and that he kept quiet about at least one Knox family murder for forty years. We also know that Tom personally visited Marcello in 1968, and that he treated some Marcello soldiers in Natchez. Finally, we know he signed the medical excuse form that got Frank Knox out of work for the week prior to the assassination in Dallas."

This ruthless recitation leaves me speechless, but Kaiser piles on with more facts. "Henry Sexton had a photo of your father with Frank Knox and Ray Presley at a Natchez KKK rally in 1965. There's the fishing boat photo of your father with Royal, Ray Presley, and Claude Devereux from 1966. Penn, if that many pictures survived to support these relationships, then what are the odds that those were the only times Tom ever saw those men?"

"I don't care," I insist, my voice filled with irrational defensiveness. "You'll never convince me that my dad was part of any plot to kill Kennedy. Would he screw his black nurse, or even fall in love with her? Sure. But knowingly participate in an assassination? *Hell* no."

"As I said before," Stone says quietly, "Tom might have done something without understanding what the consequences would be—until it was too late. You know how the Mafia works. They do you a small favor, and the next thing you know, you're in up to your neck. They lend you money, but when you go to pay them back, you find out they don't want money in return. They want a name, or a key to a building—"

"Or a medical excuse," says Kaiser.

"Fuck you, John." I keep my gaze on Stone. "I thought you said you believed it would turn out that Dad hadn't done anything."

"I said his decisions would turn out to be *justified*." An embarrassed sadness seeps from the old agent's eyes. "Penn, I'm as human as the next man. You know my record. I did a lot of things I'm not proud of, and often for no good reason other than whiskey. But if I feared for my family's safety, I doubt there's much I wouldn't do to protect them."

The universal motivation gives me pause. It might even be the reason Dad is still doing crazy things today.

"Brody Royal told you that Tom saved Viola Turner in 1968," Stone says. "The only person with the power to save that woman from the Double Eagles was Carlos Marcello. Nobody else could have muzzled Snake Knox."

I can't argue this point.

"That simple truth," says Stone, "begs one question."

I know what he's suggesting. "What did Dad do in exchange for Marcello saving Viola?"

"No," says Stone, surprising me. Then he speaks like an oncologist delivering a devastating diagnosis. "The question is, why did Tom think Marcello would help him in the first place?"

With these words, a black abyss yawns open at my feet.

"I know all this has been a blow," Stone goes on softly. "I wish I could have padded it, but I don't have the time."

Without realizing it, I've begun pacing out a path of futility in the little room. Part of me wants to bust out of this hotel and run for miles along the river. But where would I go?

"What do you want from me, Dwight? I know something's coming."

Kaiser nods at the older man.

"You're right," says Stone. "Penn, I don't mean any offense, but . . . I can't accept that Tom is completely out in the cold. He wouldn't leave your mother without some kind of reassurance. If you don't know where your father is, then your mother does."

For the first time in a long while, laughter bubbles up my throat. "Man, you do not know my parents. Mom's faith in my dad is unshakable, almost absurdly so. As for Dad, he thinks Mom is safer not knowing where he is, and he knows she's tough enough to stand the waiting."

Stone ponders this for a bit. "And you?"

I shrug. "I don't think he's thinking about me at all. He's got other things on his mind."

"You're wrong about that. And I think you're wrong about your mother. Ask her, Penn. Push her. You might be surprised."

I step closer to the bed, my sympathy for Stone's plight forgotten. "You've got some nerve, man. You accuse me of lying, then ask me to push my mother into telling you where my father is . . . but you can't even protect him if he did decide to come forward. I've been searching for him from morning till night, even though I'd like to kill him myself. But here's the bottom line: if you can't guarantee to keep him alive while we try to get to the truth, then I won't do a damned thing to help you. Not either of you."

"You're upset," Stone says.

"You're goddamn right I am." I look from Stone to Kaiser, then back at my old friend. There's something I'm missing, still. "You guys are still holding back on me, aren't you? That medical excuse doesn't prove any kind of complicity, or even guilty knowledge. But last night John told me that Dad *knows* who killed Kennedy."

They share another glance.

"Come on, damn it! Out with it. What have you got to lose at this point?"

"We do know one more thing about your father," Stone says quietly. "It's not damning, but it does prove guilty knowledge."

"For God's sake, Dwight. Tell me."

The old man finally gives me an unguarded look, and in his eyes I see a fear that's almost pathetic. "I'm afraid that if I do, you'll walk out that door and never come back."

"So what? Do you expect me to stay here all night?"

"No. I only want you to listen to John for ten more minutes."

I turn to Kaiser. "What for?"

This time Kaiser doesn't speak. He's waiting for guidance from Stone. The old agent looks like he's come to the end of his rope. I feel strangely guilty for fighting him, but he's left me no real choice.

"Penn," he says finally, "you and I are both standing at the doors of mysteries. You want to know why everyone wants your father dead, and why he won't come in from the cold. I want to know what happened in Dallas and why. But I believe that once we get those doors completely open, we're going to find that our mysteries are the same. All my instinct tells me that."

"I don't see how," I say wearily.

"Stay for ten more minutes and find out. I'm asking you as a friend."

"You're holding me hostage to information about my father. Is that what a friend does?"

A flash of guilt crosses his face, but then his gaze hardens. "This is bigger than we are, son. Bigger than your family, even. Help me put this case to rest."

I'm about to tell them I'm leaving when Kaiser stands and walks up to me.

"I know you don't want to listen to me anymore," he says. "But I want you to know that I'm not against your father. In fact, I think he's innocent of killing Viola Turner."

My mouth falls open. This is the first time Kaiser has even hinted at this possibility. "Why are you only telling me this now?"

"Because I knew it would drive you crazy that I couldn't do anything about it. Once your father and Garrity killed that trooper, my hands were tied."

"You're just trying to manipulate me. You want me to talk Walker into backing off from the Double Eagles tomorrow."

"Yes, I do. But that's got nothing to do with my opinion about your father."

"Who do you think killed Viola?"

"I think Forrest Knox gave the order."

"Can you prove that?"

Kaiser turns up his hands. "If I could, I'd have done it already. But Forrest was sixteen when Viola was raped, when her brother and Luther Davis were killed. I think he took part in those crimes. And if he did, then he had every reason to want Viola dead."

I don't know how to respond to this new tack.

"Whatever deal your father made with Carlos Marcello kept Viola safe until Marcello died," Kaiser says. "After that, force of habit was probably enough. Viola was way up in Chicago, and she hadn't said anything about the Knoxes in twenty-five years. But once she moved back to Natchez, and Henry Sexton started visiting her . . . that was too much. The Knoxes had to kill her, exactly as they'd threatened to do."

"John . . . goddamn it. If you really believe that, surely you can do something to protect Dad?"

The FBI agent shrugs helplessly. "My faith buys him nothing with the director. Your only currency is information we can use."

"Information about the assassination?"

"That's the gold standard today."

As I look from him to Stone, I realize the time has come to gamble on the integrity of these two men. I don't like risking my mother's privacy or feelings, and I don't want to implicate my father any further, but his survival is more important than his guilt or innocence.

Taking a seat on the edge of Stone's bed, I say, "In 1959, my dad worked as a medical extern in the Orleans Parish Prison. At one point Carlos Marcello was a prisoner there, and my dad treated him. Later that year, in some Italian restaurant, Carlos came over to their table to make sure they were happy. He seemed to know Dad. I only just learned about this. My mother told me last night, when I asked her about Marcello. She thought it was funny, just a colorful story. The point is, Dad knew Carlos at least four years before the assassination. So he may very well know things you want to know."

"Christ," Kaiser exclaims. "I knew it. I mean, I believed there'd be something like this. I'll bet the restaurant was Mosca's."

I think he's right, but I don't confirm it. I feel like a traitor for revealing any of this. Strangely, Dwight Stone's face shows none of the excitement of the younger agent's.

"What's the matter?" Kaiser asks him. "Are you okay?"

Stone raises his hands and plows them through his wispy hair as though trying to force his brain to work better. "No. Because Carlos Marcello wasn't incarcerated in the parish prison in 1959, or any year that Tom Cage was in medical school. By that time he was untouchable. The NOPD practically worked for him."

Stone's statement stuns me. The old agent obviously knows what he's talking about, but then what does that say about my mother's memory? Or her intent? Surely she could gain nothing by telling me a lie that tied Dad to a mobster?

Kaiser's face has fallen. "Something must have got lost in translation in the story. Maybe Mrs. Cage was mistaken. Maybe one of Marcello's guys was the prisoner, and Carlos was visiting him."

"Maybe."

"He still came to their table and treated Dr. Cage like he knew him. We need to talk to her."

Stone nods silently.

"No way," I say forcefully. "My mother's off-limits. You want to know what Dad knows about Marcello, you get him protective custody."

"What's the harm in a conversation?" Kaiser asks.

"Forget it! She doesn't know anything."

"You don't know that, Penn," Stone says sadly. "We haven't even talked about the deeper New Orleans dimension of the plot. And by that I mean Lee Oswald."

"Is that what the ten minutes you wanted is about? Oswald?"

"And your father. And New Orleans. That's the one thing Oliver Stone got right. The whole key to the JFK assassination was hidden in New Orleans."

"In plain sight, I suppose?"

"No. This part was as secret as anything ever gets."

They've got me, and they know it. Though I couldn't care less about the Kennedy assassination right now, I can't leave this room without knowing the full extent of my father's exposure. Besides, I really have nowhere to go. Caitlin is busy for the next few hours, and while Annie would love to have me home, if I were there, all I would be thinking about is what Stone and Kaiser didn't tell me. Before I agree to hear any more, however, I need to do one thing.

"Give me five minutes in the hall."

"Take your time," says Stone. "I'm afraid I need another trip to the bathroom. These drugs are killing me."

Kaiser looks worried, but I don't know whether it's because he's afraid I'll take off, or because he's dreading cleaning up more vomit from the bathroom floor.

Once in the hall, I move far enough down so that the peephole lens in the door won't allow Kaiser to monitor my actions. Then I take out my tape recorder and check it. The tape ran out before I left the room. I only hope it recorded Kaiser saying that he believes that Forrest Knox, and not my father, killed Viola Turner.

Opening the machine's cover, I flip the microcassette, hit RECORD, and then slip the Sony back into my inside coat pocket. It may not make a great recording, but I've used it in that pocket before and gotten usable tape. If Stone and Kaiser are about to reveal classified information about the Kennedy case—or make exculpatory statements about my father—I want a record of it. If they do the opposite, I can always toss the tape into the river as I cross the bridge back to Natchez.

As I walk back toward Stone's door, Kaiser leans out and says, "Dwight's back in the bed."

"You thought I'd bolted," I tell him, walking slowly back toward 406.

"The thought crossed my mind."

"Mine, too."

CHAPTER 37

CAITLIN PERCHED ON the edge of the coffee table, Tom's hands in her own. He had told her a tale of love and hate and rape and murder that she could not begin to imagine living through.

"That's why I could never speak to Henry," Tom concluded. "Or the FBI, or anyone. I knew Brody Royal belonged in the gas chamber. The Knoxes, too. But I couldn't risk trying to put him there—for the same reason Viola couldn't. She had a child, and I had two. But there was something else. Because Frank Knox had carried out the worst of the killings, and because Viola and I had killed Frank, at times I felt like we'd done our part to balance the scales. Something, anyway. Sacrificing ourselves to try to do more wasn't going to bring anybody back from the grave."

Caitlin was almost overwhelmed by emotion. "I understand now," she said, squeezing his crooked fingers softly.

Tom pulled back his hands and once again ran them through his white hair with frantic energy. "Earlier today, I think I passed out, from the pain meds or exhaustion. While I was out, I dreamed or hallucinated some things. I think I remembered something Ray Presley told me, years after all this happened. About Viola's rapes."

"What did Ray Presley know about that?"

"It was Ray who rescued Viola from the Knoxes. The second time, after Frank died. I didn't know who else to go to."

"I remember now. Brody told us that you and Ray Presley had saved Viola."

Tom nodded. "Snake went mad with rage after Frank died. He ordered Viola kidnapped and taken to the machine shop where he was holding her brother and Luther

Davis. They ran all kinds of rednecks through that machine shop, giving them a peek at the festivities. God only knows what horrors Viola suffered. She saw her brother shot, I know—wounded, not killed. And that tattoo cut off his arm."

"Brody Royal was there, too," Caitlin said. "He told us that. Bragged about it."

Tom grimaced like a man suppressing bone-deep pain. "She never told me that. I'd have killed that son of a bitch, if she had. Maybe she knew that. . . . Anyway, Ray found the bastards somehow. He faced them down with a gun. He managed to get Viola out, but not her brother or Luther." Tom shook his head. "Viola never forgave me for that."

"You said you remembered something Ray said, when you passed out today?"

"Yes. Ray told me there was a kid in there when he went in to get Viola out. A teenager, maybe sixteen, with dark skin, like some Cajuns. Creole blood, you know?"

Caitlin felt a premonitory tingle on her neck. She reached out and took Tom's hands again, trying to comfort him as he relived this terrible memory.

"And earlier, Walt told me he'd learned from a buddy of his that Forrest Knox is a dark-skinned man. As soon as I thought about the ages, it clicked in my head that the teenager Ray saw in that machine shop was Frank's son. His second son. His first died in Vietnam in the midsixties."

"You're saying Forrest Knox was present when Revels and Davis were tortured and killed?"

"And for Viola's rape, yes. I think he was there when they raped Viola in her house, too. The night Viola died, she told me one of her rapists that first time had been only a boy."

"My God." Caitlin squeezed Tom's hands so hard he jerked them back in pain. "And this is the man you want to make a deal with?"

"I've made deals with worse." He looked down.

A rush of butterflies in Caitlin's stomach told her she was nearing the heart of the whole complex mystery. "Tom . . . who are you talking about?"

He shook his head, said nothing.

"Are you talking about Carlos Marcello?"

"Cait, please leave it alone."

"I wish I could. But you know I can't." Her mind was racing now, filling in missing connections in the likely sequence of events. Vague memories of what Brody had said about Viola's survival were coming back to her. "What happened after Ray rescued Viola? Just freeing her physically wouldn't have saved her."

"No."

"Even after you got her to Chicago, the Eagles would have found her. Why didn't she contact the FBI then? Or even years later? They'd killed her brother. She could have put them in the gas chamber."

Tom looked at her with something like pity. "You still don't get it. The woman Ray brought out of that machine shop wasn't the same woman who'd been dragged in. She'd seen firsthand what those men would do. She knew there was no protection from them. But the maternal instinct is as powerful as any in this world. She did what she had to do to raise her son. Our son."

Caitlin sensed that they'd come to the final knot. "The Eagles found her in Chicago," she thought aloud. "They warned her they'd kill her if she ever came back to Natchez. But they didn't kill her there. Why not, Tom?"

Tom braced himself on the coffee table, then stood, his creaking knees protesting. After steadying himself, he walked over toward the counter, then looked back at her.

"Don't you know?" he asked in a voice thick with self-disgust.

She did. "You cut a deal with Carlos Marcello. The only man with the power to restrain Brody Royal and the Double Eagles."

Tom nodded. "Ray had once worked for Carlos, when he was a cop in the NOPD. Ray and I had done each other a few favors back then. I hated being indebted to him, but once Viola's life was on the line, I had no choice."

"Tom . . . what did you do for Marcello in return for protecting Viola?"

He blew out a long rush of air. "I sold my soul. A little of it, anyway. Mob men need doctors like anybody else, and Natchez is only three hours from New Orleans. I didn't supply them with narcotics or anything. But I treated some gunshot wounds, stab wounds, that kind of thing. And I didn't keep any records of it. By the late seventies, when Penn was graduating from high school, Marcello's power was starting to wane, and the relationship faded away."

Caitlin took some time to process this. She wasn't sure Tom had told her everything, but one thing seemed clear: Tom Cage was a good man who'd gotten himself into a bad situation, and he'd done what was necessary to protect both his family and the mistress he'd loved—a mistress who had desperately needed protection. "Tom . . . I don't know what to say. I'm so sorry, for you and for Viola."

Tom seemed lost in his own world. As Caitlin studied him, she suddenly realized why he was willing to bet everything on a deal with a devil like Forrest Knox. Tom had made a similar bargain in the past, and it had achieved the desired result. But this time, she somehow knew, such a deal would not work. The world had changed since the 1960s, and not all for the better. An old-time godfather might have honored such a bargain in his day, but Forrest Knox wouldn't hesitate to betray or kill anyone who was a threat to him. Tom had said it himself.

An idea suddenly struck her. She got to her feet and walked to within an arm's length of him. "Tom, if you had that kind of contact with Marcello—and you knew the Knoxes so well, as their doctor—maybe that's enough to buy you protective custody from the FBI. They seem to think Marcello was behind the assassination."

Tom blinked like a man snapping out of a trance. "I don't know anything about the Kennedy assassination."

"Maybe not, but *they* don't know that! Just play what you do know for all it's worth, get to safety, and then straighten out everything else."

"That won't help Walt. Until I can protect him, I'm not going to do anything. I can't make a separate peace."

Christ, Caitlin thought, cursing his integrity for the thousandth time in her life. "Tom, you can't make a bargain with Forrest Knox. You told me yourself he's insane."

"If Forrest is his father's son, he has a practical side."

"But you have nothing to bargain with!"

"That's not strictly true." He stared at her for several seconds, then walked back to the couch and sat down. The intensity of his gaze triggered deep misgivings within her. "Will you sit down for a second?"

Caitlin walked reluctantly back to the coffee table and sat down.

"You're in a unique position to help me resolve this nightmare," Tom said. "There's a solution to this dilemma that can achieve both safety for our family and justice for the dead. A way that I can make a deal with Forrest—and honor it—but still have him go to prison, preferably to death row. Also without you stopping your investigation, by the way."

Despite his last statement, she still felt profoundly uneasy. "I'm listening."

"It's simple. Instead of printing the results of your investigative work on a daily basis, you could feed it to the FBI. Let this Agent Kaiser take Forrest down. It's his job to take that risk, after all. If you're willing to do it that way, I can promise Knox that you won't be tearing him apart in the *Examiner*. Along with Penn and Dennis laying off the Double Eagles, that should be enough to get Forrest to cancel the APB, and possibly even blame one of the dead Eagles for Viola's death. The FBI can use whatever you've uncovered to destroy the Knoxes, but our family won't be blamed. Walt and I can safely return home, and you and Penn will live to get married and raise children."

Caitlin was stunned speechless. She got up and took five steps away from the sofa, her cheeks filling with blood. "You're asking me to compromise every principle I hold dear."

Tom's eyebrows went up again. "Am I? I don't think so. I'm just asking you to forgo the glory of breaking the case—and only for a little while, really. You could still write a book about the case, after Forrest was in prison. Or dead."

The blood drained from her cheeks. She felt as though he'd slapped her face.

"I'm sorry to put it so bluntly," Tom said gently. "I know your work is your passion. It means more to you than almost anything else. Maybe more than everything." He smiled sadly again. "Only you know the answer to that."

Caitlin wanted to argue, but she couldn't find her voice. Her throat felt like something had lodged in it, blocking the air. But the worst thing was that Tom had read her innermost desires as accurately as a gifted physician diagnosing a disease. She brushed back her bangs and looked around the room like someone seeing the world for the first time.

"I can see the idea doesn't appeal to you," Tom said. "But before you decide, let me make the existential argument. Because despite what happened at Brody Royal's house last night, you don't seem to grasp the reality of the danger. Think about your baby, Caitlin. Think about Penn and Annie. Think about Peggy and me. Is anything more important than that?"

"The truth," she said in a taut voice, but the word sounded hollow even to her.

Tom took another deep, labored breath. "Most times I'd agree with you. But please believe me: if you go after the Knoxes as you intend to, they will kill you. Penn will lose his second wife, Annie her second mother."

"Don't do that!" Caitlin snapped. "Don't put that on me."

"That's where we are," Tom said sadly.

"Because of you!"

"Absolutely. The guilt is mine, inescapably and forever."

He said this with such desolation that guilt knifed through her own heart. "Tom—"

"Melba must be frozen solid by now," he said, getting to his feet and walking toward the kitchen.

"Wait." Caitlin darted after him and grabbed his arm. "What will you do if I won't help you?"

Tom shrugged, refusing to meet her gaze.

A paralyzing fear had bloomed in her belly. "Tell me you won't just wait here for them to find and kill you. Promise me that right now, or I'm calling Penn."

Tom took hold of her hands. "No. That's not it."

Caitlin realized she had tears in her eyes. "Don't lie to me. Please. Do you think that if you're shot while on

the run, the investigation into Viola's death will end and
everybody else will be safe?"

Tom sighed heavily. "Last night that thought actually crossed my mind. When those gunmen showed up
at Drew's place . . . I thought about simply letting them
finish me." He squeezed her hands tight again. "Then
I got your text message about being pregnant. And it
was like a switch being thrown in my chest. I knew I
had to survive, Cait, for as long as I could, anyway. For
that child, for you and Penn . . . for Peggy. Less than a
minute later, I killed a man because I wanted to live so
badly. So, don't worry that I'm going to throw my life
away."

As Caitlin wiped tears from her eyes, Tom smiled
through his white beard and gripped her shoulders with
surprising strength. "I'm glad you're pregnant."

"Without benefit of clergy?"

He laughed deep in his chest. "I won't have it said I'm a
man of hidebound morals."

Caitlin wanted to laugh, but she felt tears running
down her face. "Goddamn it, Tom. Can't we just call
Penn? If something happens to you out here, he'll never
forgive me for it. Never."

"I'm sorry to put you in that position," he said. "But
I've got to remain free until Walt gets back. And there's
no way Penn would allow me to do that. All he sees is his
father in danger. Walt's who I need now."

"What do you really think Walt can do? I've told you
Mackiever can't even save himself."

"It's not just Walt," Tom said soothingly. "Think about
where you are. It's Quentin, too. That's a lot of legal firepower, Cait."

"Quentin thinks you're doing the right thing?"

Tom nodded, his eyes as steady as she'd ever seen them.

"Jesus, you make life hard. How long do you expect me
to keep this from Penn?"

"Twenty-four hours. If I can't do what I need to by
then, I'll go to the FBI and tell them *I* killed John Kennedy, if that's what it takes to get protection."

A hysterical laugh escaped Caitlin's throat. She knew
she shouldn't agree to be complicit in his deception, but
after refusing his request to hold off on covering the

Knoxes in the *Examiner* while covertly helping the FBI, she couldn't bring herself to deny him this. "You swear?"

Tom grinned. "Cross my heart."

"God." She shook her head and broke eye contact with him. Tom Cage had to be the most persuasive man she had ever met. "Let's get Melba back in here."

"Wait," he said sharply. "What are *you* going to be doing for the next twenty-four hours? I know you won't be content just sitting on the sidelines, writing stories based on Henry's work."

"No. I have a line on the place where Pooky Wilson's body may have been dumped. And maybe Frank and Snake Knox's father's as well."

All the levity went out of Tom's face. "Elam Knox? Where's that?"

She thought about holding her silence, but Tom couldn't betray her secret to anyone. "Have you ever heard of something called the Bone Tree? Before reading my newspaper story, I mean?"

Tom focused somewhere in the space between them, like an old man looking deep into the past. "Ray Presley once told me he'd heard that story about the Wilson boy being crucified out there."

Caitlin wasn't surprised. "Did he know *where* the tree was?"

"No. But he spoke of it like a real place."

"Is that all you know?"

Tom sat on a bar stool and drank some of the tea she and Melba had made. "It's gone cold."

"Tom . . . come on."

He set down the cup and looked steadily at her. "I once treated a young woman from Athens Point, Mississippi. That's Lusahatcha County. She looked white, but she was African-American. Her mother-in-law brought her in. The woman had some female trouble, but her real problem was psychiatric. She refused to see a psychiatrist, but I managed to get a few things out of her."

"Such as?"

"Her husband had been murdered by the Ku Klux Klan down that way. And she'd been assaulted the same night. Just as Viola had—a gang rape. Her recollections weren't very coherent. She and her husband were taken scene by boat." Tom closed his eyes as if to ⌐⌐⌐ more clearly. "But she did describe a tree. A ⌐⌐⌐ with chains hanging from it. And either she or her mother-in-law used the term 'Bone Tree.'"

"Was that crime ever reported to the police?"

"I'm pretty sure they told the FBI about it. But they never found the husband's body. The tree, either. The local police down there took the position that it was all a lie made up to cover the fact that the husband had run off with another woman."

"Christ."

"That's the way it was back then, Cait. I wish I had more details, but I don't."

She nodded thoughtfully. "Well, I'm going down there tomorrow. Maybe I'll see if I can find that woman."

Tom's expression made plain what he thought of this idea.

"Do you remember her name?"

"No. And I don't have records of it, either. This was thirty-five years ago." Tom looked over his shoulder at the patio door. "Let's get Melba. She's gone far beyond the call of duty tonight."

Caitlin nodded, but she didn't go to the door. She looked up at Tom and said, "You are loved by more people than you'll ever know. By me, by your family, by thousands of patients you've taken care of. Can't you trust us to take care of you this time?"

Tom's knees creaked like horsehair ropes as he slid off the bar stool and stood erect. When he took Caitlin in his arms, the familiar smell of cigars seemed to come from his pores. "They can't help me now," he said. "I told you how you could, but you can't go against your nature, any more than I can go against mine."

She tried to pull away, but he held her tight.

"The past is always with us, darling," Tom went on. "Sometimes we carry it lightly, but other times it's like dragging a wounded brother behind you. I've got a debt to pay, and nobody can pay it but me."

Caitlin's throat ached like it had when she was a little girl and her father told her he was moving out of their house.

"Forget what I asked you to do," Tom said. "Print anything you want, except that you found me. Just give me time to do what I must for our family."

She thought about Penn's desperate worry for his father. Keeping Tom's location from him seemed unthinkable, and yet both Drew and Melba had done it. Their actions—and her own quandary—were testament to how much belief Tom inspired in people. She thought of Jamie and Keisha and all the reporters working practically around the clock to find the truth at the bottom of the Double Eagle murders. If she granted Tom's request, she would be betraying both their faith and their work. But after weighing all in the balance, she realized she had no choice.

"Twenty-four hours?" she asked into his chest.

"Yes."

"One minute longer and I'm calling in the Marines."

Tom squeezed her once more, then kissed her forehead, walked to the patio door, and rapped on its glass.

Three seconds later, Melba slid open the door and walked in shivering.

"I'm sorry, Mel," Tom said, lifting an afghan off the back of the couch and draping it around her shoulders.

"I'm fine," the nurse said. "You two get this mess straightened out?"

At the same moment Tom said, "I think we did," Caitlin said, "I'm afraid not." Melba heard both answers and realized the situation had not improved.

Caitlin looked at the nurse. "Are you going to stay the night with him?"

"I'm going to stay until Mr. Garrity gets back."

Caitlin nodded gratefully. "I hope that's sooner rather than later."

A shadow had fallen over Tom's face. "I do, too."

"I'm heading back to the paper. If you change your mind about anything we said, you call me, and I'll send the cavalry."

Tom managed a smile. He'd always loved western metaphors.

Caitlin kissed him on the cheek, then turned and walked to the side door. Only when she reached it did she realize that Melba had followed her. The black nurse's large brown eyes had fear in them, she realized.

"How badly is he hurt?" Caitlin whispered.

ked her lips between her teeth and shook her
lliott did a good job on the wound. But Dr.
many co-morbid conditions, it's a miracle
he's alive on a normal day, much less under these circumstances. He needs a week in the hospital."

"I tried, but he won't listen to me."

"He don't listen to nobody," Melba said bitterly. "Sometimes that's good, but not now."

"I promised him that I wouldn't tell Penn where he was. Do you think I should break that promise?"

"I can't answer that. I swore to Penn that I'd tell him if Doc called back, and I haven't. I guess that's partly because Doc asked me not to. But I'm not sure Penn could really do much to fix things now."

Caitlin squeezed the nurse's forearm. "Do you have any idea what Tom is really up to?"

"I don't. All I know is, he's hurting in a way I've never seen before. Deep down in his soul, he's sick like. It hurts me to see it."

Caitlin nodded in commiseration.

"How much danger do you figure we're in?" Melba asked.

Caitlin spared her nothing. "If the police find Tom, they'll kill him unless he surrenders. And if those old Klansmen find him, they'll kill him no matter what he does. And you with him."

Melba nodded soberly. "That's no news to me, baby. But Doc's pulled me through some tough times, and I aim to stick by him. I just hope Mr. Garrity gets back soon." The nurse sighed with a resignation that sounded as if it had been inherited over dozens of generations. "But I've made my peace with Jesus, and if it's my time . . . I'm ready."

Tom's voice boomed across the room. "What kind of plot are you two hatching over there?"

"Mind your own business!" Melba snapped back.

Caitlin hugged the nurse, who felt as solid and strong as any man. "Thank you, Melba."

"You be careful. And don't waste no more time. You and Penn go down to the courthouse tomorrow and tie the knot. Life don't wait around for people. Get on with it while you can. Don't worry about us old folks."

"You're not old," Caitlin said, forcing a laugh.

But as she slipped through the door and hurried out to her car, she heard the bolt snap shut, and she felt a chilling certainty that a door had slammed between her fate and those of the two people hiding in the house behind her.

CHAPTER 38

WHEN I WALKED out of the hotel by the river, I stepped into a different world than the one I'd left upon entering. It wasn't merely that I'd been converted from a lone-gunman disciple to a believer in the possibility that John Kennedy had been murdered as a result of a conspiracy—and an eminently rational one. No, what shattered me was something personal. After ninety minutes of cagey give-and-take, Stone and Kaiser finally revealed their hole card: something that convinced me that for most of my life, my father hasn't merely been hiding an extramarital affair (and its unintended offspring), or even information about a murder he happened to learn about by accident. If Stone and Kaiser are right, then Dad not only played a role in the Kennedy assassination, but he knew it and kept silent about it.

Now I'm sitting alone in Caitlin's office at the *Examiner*, wondering where the hell she could be. No one on her staff will admit to knowing where she is, not even Jamie Lewis, her managing editor. And something tells me she's somewhere she shouldn't be.

With nothing to do but wait, I dig in Caitlin's desk until I find a pair of earbuds, then plug them into my tape recorder. I'm not sure what I'm looking for, but as convincing as Stone's and Kaiser's spin on the Lee Harvey Oswald story was, something about it rang false. I don't feel like they lied to me, but rather like they might be missing something themselves.

Leaning back in Caitlin's chair, I kick my feet up on her desk, I press PLAY and close my eyes. The voices instantly take me back to the hotel room beside the river, with my juvenile-sounding voice trying—and failing—to poke holes in the assertions of the two older men. As their words drift around me like smoke, I recall the smoldering eyes and sallow skin of Dwight Stone, a man intent on uncovering the truth before tomorrow afternoon, when death will hover watchfully above his OR table in Denver.

STONE: Carlos's deportation trial was set for November of '63 in New Orleans Federal Court. It began on November first, and believe it or not, closing arguments would begin and end on November twenty-second.

ME: Is that true?

STONE: Yes. And let's stipulate that by, or during, the summer of 1963, Carlos had spoken to Frank Knox about killing Kennedy in the event that nothing else could be done to prevent his deportation in the fall.

ME: Fine. How does Oswald come into it?

STONE: A man named David Ferrie was the link between Marcello and Oswald, and we owe John for figuring out how. A few people suspected the nature of the link, but it was practically impossible to pursue as a lead.

KAISER: Remember I told you that Carlos had a New Orleans immigration lawyer on his payroll? His name was G. Wray Gill. Gill is only important because of two men he had listed on his payroll as investigators for the Marcello trial. One was a private detective named Guy Banister. The other was a former Eastern Air Lines pilot named—

ME: David Ferrie.

STONE: Do you know anything about Ferrie?

ME: Joe Pesci played him in the movie.

STONE: People who knew Ferrie say Pesci actually did an uncanny job, though Ferrie was tall and gangly in real life. Next to David Ferrie, Joe Pesci was a male model. Ferrie suffered from alopecia, and he wore the most horrible pasted-on eyebrows along with his hairpiece. Anybody who saw Ferrie never forgot him.

KAISER: That's for sure. The Bureau has a surveillance photo of Ferrie leaning against a Ford Fairlane. I'm telling you, leaning against those big tail fins, he looks like the forward scout for an alien invasion of hairless Martians.

I bolt forward and hit STOP on the recorder, my heart clenching like a fist in my chest. *That's* what I missed the first time I heard it. My parents owned a Ford Fairlane back in the early 1960s, a red-on-white behemoth with long tail fins like something out of Flash Gordon. I only know this because I've seen the car in very old family pictures, my parents looking young and carefree on a vacation, my older sister cradling me in front of it. They sold the flashy Fairlane around 1964 or '65, I believe, so I don't remember riding in it. But something about that car itches at my brain, like a thought trying to find its voice. There's no way David Ferrie would have been in or near my parents' Fairlane, of course. I don't think they even got it until after they got back from Germany in 1961, and they never lived in New Orleans after that. But there's something . . .

Unable to make the connection, I press PLAY again and lean back in Caitlin's chair.

STONE: Ferrie was a crackpot in a lot of ways, but one thing he wasn't was dumb. He'd worked as a contract pilot for the CIA, running guns into various countries and narcotics out. He ran guns to Castro before Fidel declared himself an ally of the Soviet Union. But at that point Ferrie became Castro's mortal enemy.

KAISER: Without that angle, Ferrie wouldn't have been allowed within a mile of Carlos Marcello. He was an aggressive and unstable homosexual who'd been fired from Eastern Air Lines for giving young men free rides on Eastern planes in exchange for sexual favors. Also for molesting young men within the company. It's difficult to imagine any less useful assistant on an immigration case than David Ferrie. He had no legal training whatever, yet Marcello admitted under oath he'd made at least one payment of over seven thousand dollars to him in November of 1963, for what he called "paralegal services."

STONE: It was Guy Banister who brought Ferrie into Marcello's orbit. Banister was a shady bastard. I'm embarrassed to say that he was the former special agent-in-charge of the Chicago FBI field office, the second largest in the country. I met him when I first joined the Bureau. He liked to tell you how he'd been present at the shooting of John Dillinger. He was a rabid anti-Communist. John Birch Society, the Minutemen, you name it. A real hater.

ME: How did a former FBI SAC wind up working for Marcello?

STONE: After Banister retired from the Bureau, he moved to New Orleans and became assistant superintendent of the NOPD. In 1955, you didn't get that job without kissing Carlos's ring. Banister was dismissed from the force for violent instability, and that's when he opened his private detective shop at 544 Camp. It didn't take him long to get into the anti-Castro business.

ME: What were Banister and Ferrie really doing for Marcello's lawyer?

STONE: Managing Carlos's illegal effort to beat the deportation case. Specifically, working to bribe judges and prosecutors, intimidate jury members, negotiate with crooked politicians in South America, et cetera. Carlos had Jack Wasserman for the actual legal work, but not even Wasserman could turn water into wine.

KAISER: That's why Frank Knox was on tap. Frank was the court of last resort—the final solution, should all other efforts fail.

STONE: I doubt Ferrie or Banister knew that in the summer of '63, although both men would have known Knox from the Bay of Pigs training camps. And neither Ferrie nor Banister was stupid. Sooner or later, they would have realized that their boss wanted Kennedy dead.

ME: So they approached Lee Harvey Oswald? That's absurd.

KAISER: It's not as crazy as you think.

At this point Kaiser gave Stone the floor. The old man paused as though to gather all he'd learned over decades and distill it to the most comprehensible narrative he could. His entire affect changed, as well. Talking about "Lee" seemed to bring him fully to life, and nowhere was this more evident than in his voice, which grew in both volume and power.

STONE: Lee Harvey Oswald was a creature of New Orleans. He was born there and raised there for the most part. He had the archetypal troubled childhood. Lee's father was his mother's second husband, and he died while Lee was still in his mother's womb. Lee was largely raised by his aunt Lillian and uncle Dutz Murret. Now, Dutz Murret was a runner for a Marcello bookmaking operation. He worked for Sam Saia, out of Felix's Oyster Bar in the French Quarter.

The mention of Felix's hurled me back to last night, when my mother told me about my father and her meeting Carlos Marcello there (a meeting I did not mention to Stone and Kaiser).

KAISER: What is it, Penn?

ME: Nothing. I've been to Felix's before, that's all.

KAISER: Some people argue that Oswald didn't see his uncle much, or that he, Ferrie, and Banister wouldn't have known one another. But if you know anything about New Orleans back then, you know that's ridiculous. The French Quarter was a village within a small town. Everybody knew everybody. Metairie was the same way. Oswald's own mother, Marguerite, dated two different men who worked for Marcello. One was a lawyer who arranged for Lee to join the Marines while still underage. Bottom line, Marcello himself would have known all about Dutz Murret's skinny, mixed-up nephew who spouted Marxism and then joined the Marines.

ME: But did Oswald know David Ferrie? Isn't that the question?

KAISER: Yes. And that's what brought me into this case. Back in the early nineties, I was consulting with Dwight about an old murder in Louisiana. We got to talking about criminal psychology, and he figured out pretty quick that I had special knowledge, based on the years I'd spent in the Behavioral Science Unit. During our third conversation, he told me about the Working Group, and he asked whether I'd be willing to make use of my presence in New Orleans to do some work for them, off the books.

STONE: And thank God we did. Because John's behavioral science experience is what broke the case for us.

KAISER: They wanted me to try to prove a connection between David Ferrie and Lee Oswald in the summer of '63. There'd been dozens of reports of the two men being seen together. For example, Guy Banister's secretary claimed Lee had worked out of Banister's office with Ferrie and Banister. But after exhaustive work, I found that nearly all those reports either had been discredited, were unprovable, or came from unreliable witnesses.

STONE: We desperately needed that link. I'd studied Ferrie and Oswald like a goddamned biographer—especially Lee, all the way from childhood—but I couldn't find it. Lee always had difficulty in school. When he was twelve years old, his mother moved him from New Orleans up to the Bronx to live with his half brother. He caused havoc there and had to be psychologically evaluated. A reformatory psychiatrist described Lee as immersed in a "vivid fantasy life, turning around the topics of omnipotence and power, through which he tries to compensate for his present shortcomings and frustrations." She diagnosed a "personality pattern disturbance with schizoid features and passive-aggressive tendencies" and recommended continued treatment. Needless to say, he never got it. Mama took him straight back home to New Orleans.

KAISER: Which eventually delivered him into the grasp of David Ferrie. I started looking into Ferrie's life as a favor, but the more I did, the more the case began to consume me. The only provable link between Ferrie and Oswald dated to 1955 and '56, when Oswald was sixteen and a member of the Civil Air Patrol at Moisant International Airport. Ferrie had been the commander of that unit for some time. In *Case Closed*, Gerald Posner wrote that Ferrie and Oswald couldn't have known each other, because they were never in the CAP unit at the same time— that Ferrie had been removed from his position prior to Oswald's entry. But the very year Posner's book was published, a photo surfaced that showed Ferrie and Oswald in a small, relaxed gathering around a CAP cookout fire.

STONE: Ferrie lost his job as CAP chief, for molesting young cadets. We've verified that. He was a documented pedophile. Ferrie had initially hoped to be a priest, but he was kicked out of seminary for the same kind of nocturnal recreation—teenage boys. He almost certainly took that CAP job because hundreds of teenage boys came through the program.

ME: You believe Ferrie molested Oswald as a teenager.

STONE: Yes.

KAISER: In 1963, David Ferrie told Jim Garrison that he'd never met Oswald. After being confronted with the Civil Air Patrol link, he backed off and said he simply didn't remember him. Penn, I'm sure you had plenty of experience with pedophiles in the Houston DA's office. Do you think a predator like David Ferrie didn't remember every boy who came through his unit? Especially a vulnerable kid like Oswald? No father, insecure, confused sexuality, so desperate to be different that he's spouting Marxist theory at sixteen?

ME: Ferrie would have zeroed right in on him, no question. But you don't have any objective evidence? No witness statements? Nothing?

KAISER: Only deduction. I had to ask myself what kind of relationship could have—or would have, by necessity—remained secret for years. Like you, I've worked more murder cases than I can count, and that experience taught me that illicit sex is the one thing people will stay silent about, if they possibly can. Especially molestation of a minor. And remember, this was the 1950s. There were no cell phones, no text messages, no e-mail, none of the crap that traps people nowadays.

STONE: Oswald sure wasn't going to tell anybody about it. He took a lot of teasing from guys saying he was queer, all the way through the Marine Corps.

KAISER: Neither was Ferrie. The stigma from a homosexual relationship could be lethal back then, even in New Orleans. More telling still, if you look at Oswald's life after the summer that CAP photo with Ferrie was taken, the kid's downward spiral really accelerated. He couldn't do his schoolwork the following fall, and he dropped out of the tenth grade.

ME: Hmm.

KAISER: Trying to emulate his big brother, Lee tried to join the Marines at sixteen, but they turned him down. He then went to work at a dental lab. He remained in New Orleans until the following July, when his mother moved him back to Fort Worth, Texas. Obviously, Ferrie could have been having sexual liaisons with Lee throughout the period prior to this move, or only sporadically, or not at all. We just don't know. But that next fall, at Arlington Heights High School in Texas, Lee only made it to the end of September before dropping out. Does that not sound like a kid who might have experienced something too big to process? Like an affair with an older man?

ME: It does. But that's still supposition.

KAISER: I don't deny it. But tell me it doesn't feel right.

ME: Look, you're preaching to the choir here. After my years as a prosecutor, this is the easiest part for me to believe. But you still haven't sold me that Carlos Marcello would employ this mixed-up kid when it came to a serious crime, much less an assassination.

STONE: It wasn't Marcello's idea. It was Ferrie's. Marcello's JFK plans had nothing to do with Oswald. But Ferrie was working at the heart of Carlos's effort to avoid deportation, and that's what led to Oswald being brought in.

ME: How?

STONE: Let's fill in the years between Lee's Civil Air Patrol summer and the summer of '63. This is the trajectory everybody knows. Marine sharpshooter qualification at seventeen. Working at the U2 base in Japan, two courts-martial for self-destructive accidents. First marine to defect to Russia . . . marrying Marina while in the USSR. Disillusioned by the reality of Russia, Lee returned to America without being arrested or even debriefed—which we still can't explain, I'm afraid— and settled in Dallas. Marina fell in with the Russian émigré community, but those people couldn't stand Lee. During this time, he mail-ordered the pistol and rifle he would later use on November twenty-second. With those weapons he promptly stalked and nearly succeeded in killing General Edwin Walker, the right-wing extremist. It was in the wake of that failure that Lee came up with the idea of defecting to Cuba. His first step in this process was to move back to New Orleans, which he did on April twenty-fourth, 1963, seventeen days before his pregnant wife and his child came to join him.

ME: That all sounds familiar. So what about the summer of '63? You couldn't find any proof of contact between Oswald and Ferrie? Or Oswald and Marcello?

KAISER: I did find one reliable source. An old Marcello soldier told me that Oswald worked part of that summer as a runner for Sam Saia, out of Felix's Oyster Bar, just like his uncle Dutz had. But he wouldn't testify to it, and he died two months ago. Oswald worked as a maintenance man at Reily Coffee for a while, but they fired him, so the runner job makes sense. He had no other source of money. And there's no doubt that the old crowd knew Lee was back in New Orleans. He was making a real ass of himself, handing out Fair Play for Cuba leaflets on the street, getting into fights with anti-Castro Cubans, and going on TV for a debate. If you accept the exploitative sexual relationship back in 1955 and

'56, you've got to figure it was only a matter of time before David Ferrie came around to renew contact with his long-ago victim.

ME: I buy that, all right.

KAISER: Even if Ferrie didn't initiate contact, I think Oswald would have sought him out. Lee had no real friends in New Orleans, and based on all my experience as a profiler, he would have been dying to tell Ferrie about all the big things he'd done since he'd last seen him.

ME: Oswald wouldn't have felt any attraction for the guy who'd taken advantage of him when he was a kid, would he?

KAISER: Probably not, though it's possible. But let's assume Lee hated Ferrie. The summer of '63 was still his chance to tell his abuser that he'd grown up and married a hot Russian girl, which proved he'd gotten past his sexual confusion. He had the baby to prove it.

STONE: What does your gut tell you, Penn? As a prosecutor, listening to a story?

ME: If you accept the secret sexual relationship, then further Ferrie-Oswald contact that summer makes sense. But even so, we're back to square one. If Carlos had Frank Knox ready to kill Kennedy as a last resort, why bring Oswald into it at all?

STONE: Desperation.

KAISER: Genius, on Ferrie's part. Think about *his* position. Marcello's deportation trial was set for November first. Ferrie and Banister were trying to figure a way to fix the verdict, but they weren't having any luck. Carlos was expecting them to pull a rabbit out of their asses, and they didn't have one. Neither did Jack Wasserman in D.C. With every passing week, it looked more like it was going to be *arrivederla* to Carlos Marcello come November. But if Ferrie met Lee that summer, and Lee caught him up on his recent past, then Ferrie would have seen instantly that Oswald was a gift from the gods.

STONE: Only three pieces of information had to pass between Oswald and Ferrie for this theory to be valid. One, that Lee had taken a shot at General Walker in April. Two, that he owned the scoped Mannlicher-Carcano he'd taken that shot with. Three, that he was trying to defect to Cuba.

ME: You're saying Oswald wasn't brought in as a patsy, but as the main shooter? And a signpost pointing to Castro?

KAISER: I don't think Lee was brought in at all at that point. I think Ferrie just filed the information in the back of his mind and let it simmer. It represented a potential manipulation, that's all. For one thing, Lee wasn't exactly stable. And he was trying to get into Cuba. Even if Ferrie had the idea that early, he would have to wait and see how the Cuba thing worked out before he tried to sell Marcello on using the kid.

ME: Go on.

KAISER: On September twenty-sixth, after a truly shitty summer, Lee left New Orleans for Mexico City, hoping to get a visa to Cuba. Marina had left New Orleans three days earlier with an older friend, Ruth Paine. She was pregnant and tired of Lee's bullshit. She moved back to Texas to have her baby.

STONE: For three days in Mexico Lee tried without success to get a visa for Cuba, so that he could defect. He visited both the Cuban and Russian embassies. He had no luck at either place.

KAISER: This would have been a major stressor, coming on top of several others. Lee left Mexico by bus, in despair. He didn't go back to New Orleans, but to Texas, where Marina was living with Ruth Paine and her husband. Marina didn't want Lee back, of course. But two weeks later, a friend of Ruth's got Lee an interview for the job at the Texas School Book Depository.

STONE: At that point, John Kennedy had thirty-seven days to live. But Lee Harvey Oswald had no idea he would be a part of his death.

KAISER: Marcello was scared shitless by this time. His trial started on November first, and every night was consumed by strategizing for the proceedings. Banister had been working a deal to bribe one of the jurors, but Carlos couldn't rely on that. He had to be thinking about pulling the trigger with Frank Knox.

STONE: We know for a fact that Carlos spent the two weekends prior to Kennedy's assassination at Churchill Farms. We also know that Ferrie was there with Carlos for one of those weekends. That was the bill I mentioned, for "legal services." And Marcello actually paid it.

ME: Isn't this pretty late in the game to be planning something?

KAISER: It *had* to be late in the game. Remember Stone's Razor? This is the only timeline that eliminates coincidence from the plan.

ME: So when and how did Oswald get recruited for Frank Knox's job?

STONE: The final weekend. November fifteenth through seventeenth. There's no other possibility. The motorcade route was finalized on Friday the fifteenth. It wasn't made public, but Dallas police officers were made privy to the route on that day.

KAISER: The Joseph Civello mob in Dallas had hundreds of cops on their payroll. They could easily

have passed that information to Marcello. He was
their overboss, after all. By Commission law, Carlos
owned Dallas.

STONE: Imagine that final weekend. A heatwave had
just broken in New Orleans that November. They've
turned on the heat out at Marcello's swamp house.
Ferrie's there with him, sweating like a pig. Marcello
is crazed with rage. He can give orders to judges,
governors, even senators, yet Bobby Kennedy is about
to kick his butt out of the country. It was intolerable,
and I think that sometime on that last weekend—
probably Friday night—Carlos snapped. Maybe the
scheme to bribe the juror fell through, or maybe Carlos
just didn't trust it. But he made the decision to have
Frank Knox kill JFK. Of course, he needed a cutout
to send the message to Frank, and also to pass on the
motorcade information. And who was ready to hand?

ME: David Ferrie.

KAISER: Ferrie was a good courier because he was
an ace pilot. And Carlos had easy access to planes.
He was a big-time marijuana smuggler. So it would
be easy for Ferrie to fly up to Natchez or Vidalia
with Frank's go order.

STONE: Only Ferrie didn't take that flight.
Because after Carlos gave him the motorcade info—
which had to be either a map or a list of streets and
turns—Ferrie had the epiphany of his life.

ME: Oh, my God.

STONE: You see now? Ferrie saw that the
presidential motorcade was going to run right past
the warehouse where Lee Harvey Oswald was
working. He was one of the few people in the world
who knew that.

ME: How did Ferrie know? Oswald told him at
some point?

STONE: He must have. We're not sure how. My guess is by letter. Lee was a big letter writer, and I think Ferrie would have told him to send word about whether he'd made it to Cuba or not. If Lee wrote to Ferrie any time between October fifteenth and November twelfth, Ferrie could have received the letter and learned where he was working.

KAISER: Ferrie could have visited Lee sometime during those four weeks. I wouldn't rule that out, but there's no need to go that far. All we need is for Lee to have let Ferrie know he'd gotten the job at the Book Depository.

STONE: When Ferrie saw that motorcade route, he must have felt like he was witnessing divine intervention. Like God was reaching down to save him and Marcello at the last possible moment.

KAISER: I think Ferrie turned it over in his mind for one night. Using Oswald would be a risk, but the advantages were too great to ignore. Lee had a rifle and the ability to use it. The attack on General Walker proved that he had the *will* to use it. And best of all, Lee had spent the summer publicly agitating for the Castro regime. Hell, he'd defected to Russia! And he'd tried to defect to Cuba. If Lee killed JFK, nobody was even going to *think* about Carlos Marcello.

STONE: And with any luck, the whole country might start screaming for LBJ to invade Cuba, which would get Marcello and the mob their casinos back.

ME: That's how he sold Carlos.

STONE: Bingo. The whole Oswald-as-patsy, blame-it-on-a-nut angle has always been too much of a stretch. There was a Sicilian tradition of using mental defectives to take the fall for gang murders, but Carlos wouldn't have taken the risk had he not had a lot more to gain from Oswald than that.

KAISER: Remember how desperate Carlos was. He was within days of being booted out of America. I think Ferrie pitched his plan as God's deliverance, the miracle they'd been praying for. Carlos would have remembered Dutz Murret's nephew, of course. You don't get where Carlos was by forgetting people.

STONE: Marcello might have been skeptical at first, but it was hard to find a downside in Ferrie's plan. If Lee lost his nerve or missed, Frank Knox could still take out the president, and Lee could still be blamed.

ME: But what if Oswald was captured? What if he talked?

STONE: I don't think Lee was meant to live more than fifteen minutes after the assassination. The safest plan would have been for Frank to kill him shortly afterward. But that's where the operation went wrong. When Oswald saw Kennedy's head explode through his crappy little scope, he knew he hadn't fired that shot. At that point, he probably panicked. Lee skipped whatever post-hit rendezvous he was supposed to make—probably with Ferrie, in his mind—and there Marcello's plan went off the rails.

KAISER: It still worked. And Oswald died anyway.

ME: Let me guess. The mob had to hire Jack Ruby at the last minute to shut Oswald up before he could give away anything?

STONE: It's possible. Ruby has been tied to the Civello mob, and through them to Marcello's people. But it might be that Ruby was just what he seemed—a pissed-off loser who thought the world would call him a hero for killing the man who'd shot the president. Oswald actually died the way he did because he panicked, went home for his pistol, then killed Officer Tippit during his senseless flight.

ME: Wait—back up. When did Ferrie sell *Oswald* on killing Kennedy?

STONE: I think he flew to Dallas on Saturday, November sixteenth. Instead of flying north to give Frank Knox his go order, he flew west to Dallas.

ME: Is there any record of Oswald's movements that weekend?

STONE: No. Those two days have always been a black hole in his timeline. No one has ever been able to pin down where Lee was either Saturday or Sunday. He disappeared Friday after work and reappeared Sunday night at the Paine house. Ferrie had plenty of time to sell him on the idea.

KAISER: And to buy the second Carcano.

ME: There's no documented record of Ferrie being in Dallas between November fifteenth and the twenty-second?

I remember Stone and Kaiser looking at each other when I asked this. Then Kaiser nodded, and Stone seemed to make some silent decision.

STONE: No known record. In fact, there are two relevant reports that have never been seen by the public. One is among the sealed assassination records in Maryland. The other is in a special FBI archive in Washington. It was never turned over to the Warren Commission or the House Select Committee.

ME: What do those records say?

STONE: The sealed record contains a statement by FBI agent James Hosty, who was surveilling Oswald because of his earlier defection to Russia. Lee was just one of Hosty's responsibilities. Anyway, that weekend, Hosty claimed to have sensed other surveillance on Oswald, or even on the both of them. Hosty—and Hoover—assumed this was probably CIA surveillance. But given what we know, my theory is that Hosty sensed either David Ferrie looking for a safe opening with Oswald, or Frank Knox.

ME: And the second record?

STONE: During Jim Garrison's investigation of Clay Shaw in 1965, an FBI agent based in Dallas saw a close-up picture of David Ferrie. At that time he told his SAC that he believed he'd seen Ferrie in Dallas on the weekend prior to the assassination— at a diner, alone. With Ferrie's fake eyebrows and hairpiece, it's hard to believe that agent could have been mistaken.

ME: What happened to that report?

KAISER: Hoover ordered it buried.

ME: But why would Oswald have agreed to kill Kennedy for Ferrie? It may seem an obvious question, but I'm not sure I understand his motive.

STONE: This is where the psychologists are right. Lee strongly prefigured the later killers such as John Hinckley, Mark David Chapman, and the school shooters. His life had been one long string of failures. Emigrating to Cuba was his final fantasy. The Russians didn't want him, employers didn't want him, his wife had left him. When the Cubans said no to his defection, he basically had nothing left. Three weeks before the black hole weekend, Lee actually attended a rally where General Walker spoke, almost as if he was planning to try once more to assassinate him. Lee was truly ready for anything at that point, so long as it was sensational.

KAISER: In behavioral science parlance, Oswald was decompensating. He'd endured stressor after stressor. Killing Kennedy—who had been actively trying to overthrow and even kill Castro—would have made Lee a hero to Castro and the Cuban people. I'm sure Oswald could see himself driving along the Malecón with Fidel in a big convertible, waving to the adoring crowds.

ME: What about the Cuban student, Cruz? The one who bought the Carcano that was in Brody's house?

STONE: I think Ferrie came up with that angle the night he thought of the Oswald plan. If the goal was to sell the world on a Cuban plot—and Marcello on his plan—then they needed a Cuban conspiracy. The way to create that was to pin a rifle like Oswald's to another loyal Communist—ideally, a native Cuban.

KAISER: One with a criminal record, so his prints would be on file.

ME: You make Ferrie sound like a criminal genius.

KAISER: Some Cuban exiles actually called him "the master of intrigue." His brilliance is exaggerated, but he was a devious guy. In any case, all Ferrie had to do to get that second Carcano was walk into a Texas gun shop and buy one.

STONE: And two boxes of ammunition. Western Cartridge Company 6.58-millimeter, manufactured in the U.S. for Italy during the war.

KAISER: Right. The ammunition's key.

ME: So how did they frame Eladio Cruz? They killed him and put his prints on the rifle?

KAISER: And dumped him in the swamp. You nailed it. Probably on the night of Tuesday, November nineteenth.

STONE: But first Ferrie had to carry the revised mission order to Frank Knox. He probably flew out of Dallas on the Sunday after seeing Oswald. We're trying to check his movements during that period, but access to a Marcello plane means he could have traveled as his schedule allowed, with no one the wiser.

ME: You think Frank Knox just went along with the Oswald scheme?

STONE: Frank was a soldier. He would have seen the advantages. He simply went from being the primary shooter to the backup.

ME: But that second Carcano was never found. It was never associated with the assassination in any way. What was the point in getting it? Was Knox supposed to use it against Kennedy?

STONE: I think he was. But Frank would have known better than to trust a critical shot to a junk rifle. My guess is that he told Ferrie he'd leave the Carcano at the scene, but he wasn't going to shoot with it. Otherwise, Marcello might have gotten angry when things didn't go the way he expected.

ME: Then why wasn't the rifle found?

KAISER: Maybe Frank didn't want to risk carrying two rifles into the Dal-Tex Building. That's a serious tactical challenge.

STONE: Or maybe he worried that the FBI or CIA had forensic abilities he knew nothing about. Frank would have known that a presidential assassin's rifle would be subjected to more scrutiny than any weapon in history.

KAISER: Or he might have kept it as insurance. Frank knew he was dealing with the mob, and he knew how those guys handled loose ends. Maybe he figured he could use the Carcano as leverage later.

ME: So why didn't Marcello blow up when Frank didn't leave the rifle at Dealey Plaza?

STONE: [chuckles] When we think about mobsters like Carlos Marcello, we inflate their powers in our minds. We see them as fearless. But Carlos had watched Frank Knox train Cuban exiles at his camp. He'd heard the stories of what Frank had done in the Pacific. The medal-winning assaults, the mutilation of prisoners, the black market skulls. Compared to Frank Knox, a Mafia hit man with a snubnose .38 was a clown.

KAISER: There are some guys it doesn't pay to go to war with. Especially when they only live three hours away from you.

ME: But the ballistics . . . How could the bullet fired from Frank's Remington match the bullets fired from Oswald's Carcano?

STONE: Ferrie would have provided ammunition to both Oswald and Knox. That would further tie the two shooters in an apparent conspiracy. Lee was poor as dirt, so he wouldn't have bought new ammo if he didn't have to.

ME: You're missing my point. If Frank didn't use that second Carcano, then he couldn't have used the bullets that matched Oswald's lot. You said he needed a rifle that fired a super-fast round, didn't you? How did the metallurgy of Frank's bullets—fired from a Remington 700—match the bullets Oswald fired from his 6.58 Mannlicher-Carcano?

STONE: That's where Frank Knox proved his genius. Frank's bullet was designed to explode on impact with Kennedy's skull, remember? It left very little trace. But the metallurgy of the fragments *did* match Oswald's bullet. New tests were done only a few months ago. There are a couple of ways that this match could have been accomplished. You get into complex gunsmithing work and reloading issues, but Frank was an old hand at all that stuff. All the Knoxes were. The only requirement would have been that Frank had a sample of the ammo Oswald used, and he did. With that, he could have used any rifle he wanted. Trust me, Penn—it can be done.

ME: I'd rather hear the explanation.

Leaning forward, I fast-forward past the complex ballistics and stop on the revelation that floored me. I dread hearing it again, but I want to evaluate it once more before Caitlin arrives and distracts me.

STONE: Tell him, John. He's gone beyond the call for us.

KAISER: I told you I sent two agents up to the Mississippi field office today. That's how I found the Triton medical excuse. But once the director was on board, I also put out a Bureau-wide request for any and all files of any type on all the principals in this case. Late this afternoon, a clerk at the Jackson field office sent me a digitized copy of one more file.

ME: Which was?

KAISER: In 1993, a file clerk at the Triton Battery Corporation requested the return of Frank Knox's personnel record.

ME: So?

KAISER: They didn't do that out of the blue. They'd been contacted by a former company physician who wanted to see the record. You know who that was.

ME: Bullshit.

STONE: It was your father, Penn. About a month after Carlos Marcello died in New Orleans, Tom

requested Frank Knox's Triton personnel record
from the company. You see, he had no idea that the
Bureau would have the file.

ME: And what do you conclude from that?

STONE: Well. Either Tom had just figured out
what he'd been a part of, and wanted to check it,
or . . .

KAISER: That's not it, guys. I know you don't want
to hear it, but he wouldn't risk asking for that file out
of simple curiosity. Dr. Cage knew what he'd done
back in '63. And once Marcello was dead, he did
what he could to wipe out the traces. He just didn't
count on the Bureau having that record.

STONE: John—

KAISER: He nearly got away with it, too. Because
nobody at the Bureau could find the file when Triton
Battery made their request. They simply reported
back to Triton that the file couldn't be found. If a
conscientious Bureau clerk hadn't decided to open a
file to note the unfulfilled request, the whole event
would have been lost in the sands of time.

As I listen to Stone try to ameliorate the effects of Kaiser's accusation, my cell phone vibrates on Caitlin's desk.
The incoming text reads: *I just pulled into the lot. I see your
car. Be inside in a sec. Love you!*
I switch off the recorder, glad to be spared the last two
minutes of conversation. My argument with Kaiser was as
intense as it was pointless. I won't know what prompted
Dad to request that medical record until I can question
him directly, and until he'll tell me the truth. But what
lingers in my mind is the lump in my throat as I took leave
of Stone. Though the old agent put on a brave face, and I
tried to match it, I couldn't suppress the conviction that
I would never see him again. And though he'd brought
me unwelcome news, I knew that Stone's heart had always
been in the right place. The tragedy was that his news

had made me confront even more starkly the question of whether the same was true of my father.

I've barely gotten my recorder back into my pocket when Caitlin's office door flies open and she steps inside, obviously looking for me.

"Are you okay?" she asks.

"Yeah. Where have you been? I've been worried."

It's instantly obvious my tone has angered her. "I went to see a couple of my contacts in the black community," she says, setting her purse down on the desk.

I try to make eye contact, but she turns away and begins heating water for tea. She speaks with her back to me.

"The Jackson radio station has been running that Lincoln Turner interview all day, and I heard he's been swaying some people—persuading them I've been protecting Tom in the *Examiner*. As I told you this afternoon, some of my own reporters seem to believe the same thing."

"And what did you find out?"

"Reverend Ransom says most of his flock still love your father, but that doesn't mean they don't think he's human. What they call 'outside children' are a fact of life, especially from white fathers, so they have no problem buying that Lincoln could be Tom's son. That obviously might have led to some real problems between Tom and Viola."

"Great."

Caitlin finally turns back to me, her arms folded across her chest almost defensively. "How's Dwight Stone doing?"

"Worse than I expected. I don't think he has long. Days, at the most."

"God. I should go see him."

Not wanting to encourage this, I say nothing.

"If he's that sick, what's he doing here?" she asks, fixing me with her gaze.

And here we come to it: do I lie or tell the truth? After all I heard in room 406, I've got no desire to tease through every new fact with Caitlin, especially those dealing with Dad's possible complicity in crimes. Nor do I want her hounding a dying man for a scoop on the JFK assassination. "After Henry's death and all John's discovered, he couldn't stay away. I think this trip was Dwight's last hurrah on the unsolved cases from his past. That's probably all that's keeping him going now."

"The JFK thing? Or the civil rights cases?"

"The Double Eagle stuff, mostly."

Caitlin looks almost disappointed by my answer. She turns and drops a tea bag into her mug, then looks over her shoulder and says, "So . . . what's this big surprise you wanted to show me?"

"You'll see, sooner or later. It's really too dark now."

She shrugs. "Your car has headlights, doesn't it? What is it we're trying to see?"

Since Edelweiss stands atop the bluff facing the Mississippi, the combination of streetlamps, the house lights, my headlights, and the moon might be enough to create quite a dramatic reveal. And since the last thing I want to do is sit in this office while she probes me about my meeting with Kaiser and Stone . . .

"Come on!" I say, bouncing up from the chair and taking her hand. "Let's get our minds off all this bullshit for half an hour."

The sound of her sudden laugher is almost a shock after the last couple of days. "*Where are we going?*" she screeches as I try to drag her into the hall. "Wait!"

She darts back into the office long enough to turn off her teapot, then follows me down the hall. Hand in hand, we run through the newsroom together, laughing with near hysterical relief, not knowing why, only sensing that the terrible weight of the past few days has been lifted for a few precious moments. Caitlin's reporters and staff people look up openmouthed, but a few of them smile. For them, the Double Eagle murders are just a story—a big one, to be sure, but only a way station on the long careers they see ahead. Whereas for Caitlin and me . . .

The stakes are life and death.

CHAPTER 39

SHADRACH JOHNSON AND Sheriff Billy Byrd had been talking in the DA's office since Byrd walked over at 5:45 P.M. Neither man could quite believe the turns that the Tom Cage matter had taken, or the casualties that had swiftly mounted in and near their jurisdictions. Together, they had worried every thread of the Viola Turner case until Sheriff Byrd pulled a flask of bourbon from his pocket and started drinking.

For Shad, meeting with Billy Byrd was always a little uncomfortable. For while they shared common cause against the Cage family, Billy was no good old boy with his heart in the right place. He was an unreconstructed redneck who—if it were thirty years earlier—would have liked nothing better than to horsewhip Shad for daring to walk on the same sidewalk with him. Beyond that, Byrd wouldn't have been able to get hired as a janitor at Harvard Law, while Shad had the school's diploma hanging on his wall. Yet in the present circumstances, Shad was forced to treat the corpulent, Skoal-dipping sheriff like an equal.

Shad was about to suggest that Byrd continue his drinking elsewhere when he heard pounding feet on his staircase. Five seconds later, someone threw open the door with such force that Billy Byrd grabbed for his gun.

"Goddamn it, don't do that!" the sheriff cried, pointing his flask at Lincoln Turner, who stood in the door like an angry juke-joint bouncer.

Lincoln ignored Byrd and looked straight at Shad. "I think I've found Tom Cage."

"Where?"

"That big green house at the top of Silver Street, looking over the river? Looks like a Swiss chalet or something."

"That doesn't make any sense," Shad said. "Nobody lives there."

"Maybe not. But I just followed Penn Cage and that Masters girl to it, and they walked right up on the porch like they were playing a scene in a movie."

Shad couldn't believe the speed with which Sheriff Byrd heaved his bulk from the chair and bolted through the door.

"Wait!" Shad cried, yanking open his top drawer in search of his car keys. "Wait for me, damn it! A lot of people go up there to look at the river! *Don't do anything crazy, Billy!*"

CAITLIN FELT AS THOUGH she were trapped in a surreal romantic comedy, or even a farcical one. Penn had driven her down Canal Street, then turned onto Broadway and parked just past the head of Silver Street, where tourists often stopped to gaze over the Mississippi River before driving down to the Natchez Under-the-Hill district. Penn's city car smelled stale, and it nauseated her. She looked to her left, at Edelweiss, which had been her favorite house since she'd first visited Natchez seven years earlier. In a city filled with Greek Revival mansions, the three-story chalet with its wraparound gallery on the second floor seemed to float above the bluff like a clean-lined ship. The mere sight of it usually lifted her mood, and tonight was no exception. Owned by an elderly woman in a nursing home, the 1883 gem had been falling into disrepair for years. Only recently had some mystery buyer begun restoring it to its former splendor.

"What are we doing here?" Caitlin asked, perplexed to be parked in the dark.

"I want to show you something down on the river," Penn said.

"At night? That's my surprise?"

"Mm-hm."

She could tell he was suppressing a smile. "Well, why don't you drive down Silver Street?"

"You have to be up here to see it. Let's get out."

He opened the driver's door of the smelly car. With a

tired groan, Caitlin got out and started toward the fence at the edge of the bluff.

"No, over here," Penn said, walking halfway across the street and beckoning to her. "Let's go up on the porch of Edelweiss. It's a lot higher up."

"Are you sure the house is empty? Somebody bought it, didn't they?"

"I don't think the restoration's finished. Come on."

She crossed the street and followed him up one of the twin staircases to the broad gallery of the chalet. The cold wind racing up the face of the bluff cut mercilessly through her clothes. Penn went to the rail and looked westward, toward Louisiana. She stood shivering beside him, gazing out over the distant lights, trying to guess where in that dark landscape Brody Royal's house had stood. From here you could see more than ten miles of the Mississippi River during the day, but all she could think about now was the Jericho Hole, the burned-out ruins of the *Concordia Beacon*, and the hospital where Henry had died.

"Some view, isn't it?" Penn said. "Even at night."

She lowered her gaze a little. Two strings of barges were making their way along the river in a delicate ballet of drifts and pauses. The twin bridges blazed with light, and Highway 84 twinkled like a line of Christmas lights fading into the distance.

"Yes, but it's the one I'm used to. What am I supposed to be looking for?"

Penn shrugged. "What *are* you looking for?"

She pulled her coat tighter and tried to keep her face calm. Had he brought her up here to interrogate her? Did he have some idea that she'd seen Tom? "What are you asking me?"

"Take it easy. Nothing weird. We've just been in full-on panic mode since Monday morning. After the insanity of last night, I felt like we needed to remember what our lives are really about. Because tomorrow the craziness is going to start all over again."

He took her hand and squeezed, and after a couple of seconds, she squeezed back. But one phrase replayed in her mind: *what our lives are really about*. Though she would never voice the thought, it was during tumultuous times like these that Caitlin felt most alive. What they had endured last night might be terrible from an objective point of view, but she had spent much of her life dreaming about working on stories like the Double Eagle murders, and she wasn't sure she would undo that suffering even if she could. Penn was different. While trying capital cases in Texas, he'd experienced triumphs and losses she couldn't begin to match, yet he'd walked away from that life and never looked back, except to analyze some of his experiences in the novels he'd written later.

With a start Caitlin realized Penn was no longer gazing at the river, but at her. She reined in her thoughts and looked back at him.

"Have you ever found out who's restoring this place?" she asked.

He smiled. "I have."

"Is it some actor, like the rumors say? I've heard everybody from Morgan Freeman to John Grisham."

Penn laughed. "No. Morgan Freeman's staying up in the delta, and Grisham's still in Charlottesville, Virginia."

"Just so long as it's not some out-of-towner who'll stay for a year and then bail. Although, come to think of it, that might not be bad. We could get it for a steal."

"We'll never get this place for a steal. But then again, we don't have to."

"What do you mean?"

"We already own it."

A strange numbness came over her as she tried to figure out whether he was joking. "Penn . . . ?"

"I'm serious," he said, his eyes shining. "This house is your wedding present. I guess now we'll call it your Christmas present."

As Caitlin looked back into his face, a hundred little clues and inconsistencies from the past months suddenly fell into place. Disbelief turned to an effervescent bubble of excitement in her chest. She'd thought herself beyond clichéd romantic reactions, but the bubble pressing upward in her chest broke into a thousand tiny ones, and she felt wetness in her eyes.

"You *do* remember we were supposed to be getting married next week, right?" Penn asked.

"Oh, I remember." She smiled broadly. "You're a better liar than I thought."

"Well, give me a damn hug or something!"

She wrapped her arms tight around him, but even as she did, the reality of all that had been lost during the past few days crashed down on her. She'd held back so much from him that she couldn't even begin to explain her feelings. For one thing, he didn't even know she was pregnant. *Talk about being a good liar.* Worse, she'd just spent an hour with his father and said nothing about it. The trickle of tears on her face became a stream, and she buried her face in his chest.

"Hey," he said, squeezing her gently. "Are you okay?"

Caitlin nodded but said nothing. She was standing on the gallery of her dream house, yet she felt miserable.

"Caitlin?" he murmured into her ear. "What's going on?"

She shook her head against his chest, wondering, *How did I get here?*

"Talk to me," Penn said, separating them enough for him to see her eyes, which had probably become the usual raccoon mask of running mascara.

"Are we really going to live here?" she asked.

"Of course we are."

"I can't believe it."

"It's just everything that's happened. That's why I wanted to show it to you. To show you we're going to get past all this. That normal life is waiting for us."

Normal life. "Does Annie know?"

"Afraid so." He grinned. "Mom and Dad, too. Everybody knows but you. I actually hid Mom and Annie here until I moved them this afternoon."

Caitlin thought back to Tom asking her about her pregnancy at Quentin's house. Even knowing that, he hadn't breathed a word to her about Edelweiss.

"Don't you want to see the inside?" Penn asked, obviously itching to show her all he'd done to the place. "It'll take your breath away."

"No!" she said quickly.

His smile faded. "Why not?"

"That's like the groom seeing the bride before the wedding. It's stupid, I know, but I don't want to jinx anything."

"Okay, okay. I guess I can wait. Annie would want to be here anyway. I just wanted you to know that it's ours."

Caitlin shook her head, still unable to believe that he'd done this, or that the family had managed to keep it from her. "I really can't process it," she said, still crying.

"But you're okay with it, right? You're happy?"

She nodded.

"Well, let's get out of here before you go into terminal depression."

He led her to the head of the right-hand staircase, where she paused. Miles of empty space opened to the west of them, seemingly endless darkness broken only by twinkling lights. She looked upriver and thought of Tom, hiding in the deep forests of Jefferson County with Melba Price.

"Are you really all right?" Penn asked. "Is there anything you need to tell me?"

For a few seconds she considered telling him everything. Penn would be furious, of course, but in the end he would be glad she'd told him the truth. Yet something kept her silent. She supposed it was her promise to Tom: the twenty-four hours of peace she'd sworn to give him. But truth be told, she wasn't sure.

"What are you thinking about?" Penn asked.

The truth pressed against the back of her throat like a lump of food that refused to go down. "I'm just worried about Tom. I'm sorry."

"I'm worried, too. Let's just hope Walt is back with him."

She stood on tiptoe and kissed Penn lightly. "I love you."

"I love you more."

"Oh, *God*," she groaned, as she always did when he showed sentimentality.

He laughed so hard that he didn't notice the cars racing up Broadway, but Caitlin could see them over his shoulder. Seconds later the sound of roaring engines made Penn whirl.

A sheriff's cruiser screeched to a stop in front of Edelweiss. The second vehicle, a white pickup that Caitlin felt strangely certain belonged to Lincoln Turner, stopped some fifty yards back, beyond the head of Silver Street.

Sheriff Billy Byrd got out of the cruiser, looked up at the gallery, then crossed the sidewalk and marched up the right-hand staircase. He was red-faced and out of breath by the time he reached the main floor.

"What do you want?" Penn asked him.

"Your father," Sheriff Byrd said. "Go inside and tell him to come out."

Penn looked at Byrd like he was crazy. "What are you talking about? Who told you he was here?"

"That makes no difference. Open the door."

Penn considered the order for a few seconds, then said, "Go back to your office, Sheriff. You've got no business here."

Byrd took a step closer to the big cypress door. "I said open that house."

Penn moved between the sheriff and the door. "Do you have a search warrant?"

Something in Penn's posture made Caitlin's stomach flutter.

"I don't need a warrant," Sheriff Byrd said. "I've got probable cause."

"Not from where I'm standing."

Caitlin's heart began to pound. If she hadn't known Tom was hiding in the next county with Melba Price, she would have assumed, like the sheriff, that Penn's behavior meant Tom was inside the chalet.

"I'm the sheriff of this county, Cage," Byrd said, hitching up his gun belt. "Being mayor don't mean shit compared to that. Open the door, or I'll open it myself."

Caitlin heard a door slam at street level. Looking down, she saw Lincoln Turner climbing out of his truck, his eyes on the gallery.

She whipped her head to the left. Penn had backed against the door as though he intended to die defending it. *Why is he doing this?* she thought frantically. But almost as quickly, she knew the answer. Penn had felt impotent for so long in this battle over his father that a corrupt sheriff had become the focus of his frustration. He would make a reckless stand over something meaningless in order to gain some control over the situation.

"I'm going around the back!" Lincoln called from the ground. "Dr. Cage might be trying to get out that way."

"Who's down there?" Penn asked Caitlin.

She dreaded answering, but she knew she had to. "Lincoln Turner."

Penn shook his head and glared at Byrd. "Is that who's calling the shots over at your office now?"

"Get out of my way," the sheriff said, his right hand settling on his pistol. "I have reason to believe you're aiding and abetting a fugitive wanted for killing a Louisiana State Police officer. I'm going to search these premises no matter what you say."

"Let him search, Penn!" Caitlin cried. "Your dad's not in there. What does it matter?"

Byrd looked back at Caitlin as though suspicious she was playing him. Then he turned to Penn again. "Listen to her, Mayor."

"This is my property," Penn said evenly. "I'm refusing you entry without a search warrant. Now, get off my porch."

"Boy, you've lost your mind," said Byrd, disbelief in his voice.

"I told you to get off my property, Sheriff."

"Are you threatening me?"

"Take it as you will."

For a few seconds Sheriff Byrd seemed nonplussed by Penn's defiance. Then he backed up two steps and lowered his gaze to Penn's feet. "Are you armed, Mayor?"

"I'm licensed to carry a firearm."

"Goddamn it!" Byrd cursed, jerking his pistol out of his belt. "Get on the floor! Get down, I said!"

Penn didn't move. Caitlin had no idea what to do. Her own pistol was in her purse, back in the car. She was about to ask Penn to do as Byrd had ordered when tires screeched in front of the house. She looked down and saw Shad Johnson leap from his black BMW and run to the foot of the nearest staircase.

"Hurry!" Caitlin shouted, amazed to find herself relieved to see a man she despised.

The DA froze when he reached the top of the steps. "Why is your gun out, Billy?" he asked.

"Cage is packing!" Byrd snapped. "I told him to get on the floor."

Shadrach Johnson held up his hands as though to calm

both men, but it was Penn's unnatural calmness that was actually driving the crisis.

"Put your gun away, Billy," Shad said. "Right now. Put it away and go back down to your car."

"The hell I will! You don't give me orders."

"I'm the district attorney of Adams County, Sheriff. And I'm telling you to go back to your car."

"I take orders from the governor, not you."

"Tonight you take them from me," Shad said, with surprising steel in his voice. "Move your ass, goddamn it."

Shaking his head as though the world had turned upside down, Billy Byrd stumped over to the stairs and, after one last look at Penn, marched back down to ground level.

Still keeping his hands up, Shad took two steps toward Penn and said, "What's going on, Penn? Are you okay?"

Penn shrugged. "I'm fine."

"Is your father in this house?"

"No."

Shad turned to Caitlin. "Is he?"

"I don't think so."

"Then what the hell is this about? Why wouldn't Penn let him in?"

"Penn bought me this house as a wedding present. It was a secret. He was showing it to me for the first time, as a surprise. Suddenly Billy Byrd showed up and started acting like Dirty Harry. That's all I know."

Shad studied Penn with apparent concern. Unlike Billy Byrd, he was perceptive enough to see that all was not right with the mayor.

"I tell you what," Shad said. "I'm going to send Billy back to his office, and I'm going to go back to mine. You two take a few minutes together, and then one of you call me and let me know everything's all right. Okay?"

Caitlin nodded quickly, thankful for the DA's restraint.

A deep voice shouted, "What the hell's going on up there? Make him let you in!"

Shad turned and yelled over the gallery rail at Lincoln Turner: "If you don't get out of here right now, I'm ordering *your* arrest."

Caitlin expected Turner to stand his ground, but he

apparently heard the same resolve in Shad's voice that she had. After a few seconds, Lincoln turned and walked back to his truck, then started the engine and drove away.

"Okay," Shad said. "I'm going now. Call me and let me know everything's okay."

"I will," Caitlin promised.

"Dr. Cage isn't in there, right?"

"No," said Penn. "I don't know where he is."

"That's cool. Okay."

With that the DA turned and retreated down the stairs.

Caitlin rushed to Penn and hugged him, then reached behind him to open the door. His body felt unnaturally stiff, and the door was locked. She rattled the knob hard, her whole body shaking.

"Take it easy," Penn said, taking his keys from his pocket.

"Take it *easy*? What was that? Huh? What the *fuck* was that?"

Penn shrugged again. "I'd just had all of that son of a bitch I'm willing to take."

"Oh, really? Well, that stupid redneck could have shot you. He *would* have! Are you really carrying your gun?"

Penn lifted his right leg and placed her hand on his ankle, where the bulge of a heavy revolver suddenly became obvious. This hard proof of what had nearly happened made her dizzy.

"*Why?*" she asked. "Why would you do that?"

"I told you."

"Oh, come on. Has something happened that you haven't told me about?"

"No." Penn's eyes didn't waver.

"Did Dwight tell you something upsetting about Tom?"

Penn shook his head.

Caitlin hugged him again, but as she laid her face against his chest, she wondered if she could continue to keep Tom's location from him. If Tom being missing had made Penn this irrational, then shouldn't she do what she could to defuse that tension? Yet almost as soon as she had this thought, another more insidious connection closed in her brain. If she did tell Penn where Tom was, then father and son would be joined within an hour. And if that happened—against Tom's will—there would be two men trying to persuade her to give up her coverage of the Double Eagle murders while Tom tried to cut a deal with Forrest Knox. Last night Penn had proved that he was willing to try to bargain with the devil to save his family, and his effort had nearly killed them. Now Tom wanted to go down the same road, one that almost certainly led to death. She could not let Penn join him on that journey.

"Why don't you show me the house?" she said, not knowing what else to say. "I do want to see what you've done to it."

"I thought you didn't want to jinx it."

"Oh, I was just being stupid. You're right, we need to be reminded of normal."

Penn laughed as though nothing out of the ordinary had happened. Then he put a big square-headed key in the lock and opened the door to what had once been her dream house. When he turned, lifted her effortlessly, and carried her over the threshold, she felt wings beating wildly in her chest. Passing through the door, she realized that the first time someone had done that in this house, Queen Victoria had been sitting on the throne.

Caitlin smelled new paint and plaster, lemon oil and varnish. Yet as Penn carried her deeper into the house, she had a sense that dreams and reality had begun to diverge at some inaccessible level where nothing could be influenced by human action. Whatever was going to happen had been determined at some point in the past—perhaps decades ago, or maybe only a few hours—but either way it was irrevocable. From this point forward, she sensed, choice was illusory. All they could do now was ride out the waves of consequence.

"What do you think?" Penn asked, his eyes filled with pride.

She blinked and tried to focus on her surroundings, but all she could think about was tomorrow's rendezvous with Toby Rambin, the poacher who had sworn to guide her through the trackless swamp to the Bone Tree.

"I don't want to think," she whispered, recalling this afternoon at Penn's house, when she'd used sex to stop him asking questions about the Bone Tree. Now she needed it to take her mind off the same thing, and to connect with the man she felt slipping away from her. "Is there a bed upstairs?"

"Of course. This is a *wedding* present."

She looked up the long, narrow flight of steps that led to the third floor. "Can you carry me up those?"

Without a word he swung her in a circle and started up the stairs, his legs pumping as though they would never tire.

Caitlin shut her eyes like a little girl on a carnival ride, but inside she felt like a traitor.

CHAPTER 40

FORREST KNOX HAD not yet gone to Concordia Parish, as he'd told Snake he meant to do. After pulling back onto Highway 61, he'd decided to return to Baton Rouge and check on how things were progressing at headquarters without Colonel Mackiever, then go home to pack a bag and make sure his wife hadn't been too rattled by the kiddie porn she'd seen on his desk. He also packed a briefcase with sensitive material he had removed from Valhalla, and to this he added certain files and digital media from his home. He would deposit the briefcase in a nearby storage unit that he rented under another name. Given that he was locked in battle with Colonel Mackiever, he could not risk a surprise search turning up material that could destroy him.

When his bags stood packed by his office chair, he began skimming the online edition of the *Natchez Examiner* for updates. He'd scarcely gotten through page one when his departmental cell phone rang.

The caller was the duty officer of the tech division at LSP headquarters, a man from Shreveport named Keith Caton.

"Sir, I've been going back over all the digital records on Dr. Tom Cage. His family, known associates, some patients—everybody we know about."

"And?"

"On Monday, Dr. Cage made two calls to an attorney named Quentin Avery. Those were cell to cell. I've recently gotten the phone records of City Hall in Natchez, and I show a flurry of calls to Quentin Avery from there also, to three different numbers. One was to his cell, another was to his residence in McLean, Virginia."

"And the third?"

"To a house in Jefferson County, Mississippi. Avery's got a residence there also."

Forrest felt something shift in his gut—a familiar sensation that always accompanied the discovery of a fresh track. "Who made those calls?"

"Some came from what looks to be the office of the mayor. This past Monday."

"Quentin Avery must be Tom Cage's lawyer," Forrest thought aloud. "The Viola Turner case was just unfolding then. It's natural that they would try to get hold of Avery."

"Yes, sir. But I've also been analyzing the call patterns on the Jefferson County house, and also the Internet traffic."

"And?"

"I can't see the searches, but this morning about three A.M. somebody logged on to the Internet and stayed on for two and a half hours. That's totally anomalous, relative to the normal pattern."

"You can't see the actual searches that were done?"

"Not yet, sir."

Forrest thought about this. "What do you know about this house?"

"I checked it on Google Earth. It's very isolated. Practically a mansion, for that area. It's sitting on eighty acres of forestland."

Certainty clicked in Forrest's mind like a trap snapping shut. He thought about Tom Cage's last known position—dumping that stupid cop Grimsby in a northeast Louisiana cotton field. To reach Quentin Avery's Mississippi estate, Cage would have had to pass through one of the roadblocks guarding the bridges over the river. Motorists had complained so much about the bottleneck those barriers had created that he'd finally had to take them down, but there were still the bridge cameras.

"Have you guys been working the relatives of Dr. Cage's wife, like I told you to?"

"Yes, sir. Augustin handled that. He spoke to all the known relatives, then went home around fifteen minutes ago. He didn't think anybody acted suspicious."

Lazy prick, Forrest thought, marking his underling for later punishment. As he thought about the geography of Jefferson County, a new thought struck him. "Sergeant, I want you to find every vehicle registered to any of Mrs.

Cage's relatives, then see whether any have crossed the bridge at Vicksburg in the past twenty-four hours."

"Not at Natchez?"

"Natchez and Vicksburg, but give Vicksburg priority. How long will that take?"

"I'm not sure. We've been having trouble getting the records of the camera data from Homeland Security. They say it's a technical glitch."

"Do you have the data now?"

"Let me check Augustin's box. Yes, sir, it came in twenty minutes ago."

"Run the plates."

"Yes, sir. You want me to call you back?"

"I'll wait."

Forrest put the phone on speaker and got up from his desk. He didn't know much about Quentin Avery, but he knew enough not to rule out the possibility that Cage had run to his lawyer's house for sanctuary. The two men were close in age, and while Avery was a rich lawyer now, he'd been a civil rights activist in his youth. At one point the regular Klan had been hunting him across the state. Forrest remembered his father talking about it.

"Colonel, I've got it!" said the excited voice. "I got a hit."

"Let's hear it."

"A plate belonging to a John McCrae crossed west to east last night at one twenty-two A.M. That's the wife's brother."

Forrest's blood quickened. "What kind of vehicle is that?"

"It's not a vehicle, sir. It's a horse trailer."

Forrest smiled. "That's it. Has it crossed back over into Louisiana?"

"Yes, sir. It crossed back in fifty-eight minutes after it left."

"We've got him," Forrest said softly.

"What was that, sir?"

"Forget everything you just told me, Sergeant. Sequester that data. We may need it, or we may need it to disappear. I want you to prepare for both eventualities. Understand?"

"Understood, sir."

Forrest pressed END, then picked up his encrypted phone and called Alphonse Ozan.

"Hey, boss," said the Redbone. "What you got?"

"I think I found Dr. Cage."

"Where is he?"

"His lawyer owns a house in Jefferson County, Mississippi, near Fayette. It's way out in the woods. I think he's there. Deploy the Black Team."

"What's the mission? Snatch or terminate?"

"I'll call you back. Just get 'em in the air and headed north."

TOM HAD SPENT MOST of the afternoon and evening sleeping. He rested a lot better with Melba Price watching him. The knowledge that his nurse was awake and alert meant that he didn't have to start at every unfamiliar noise, of which there were many in Quentin's mansion. After enough sleep, a good meal of bacon, eggs, and toast, and a generous regimen of various drugs, he'd begun feeling human again. Melba had even gotten him off the couch to make several circuits of the house. Thankfully, he managed this without getting angina, and his shoulder pain had been dulled to an endurable throb.

After they settled themselves on the living room couch again, Tom had told Melba she needed to think about heading back to Natchez. She'd done more than he had any right to ask of her, and he assured her that he was feeling better. But Melba wouldn't hear any talk of leaving. She'd abandoned him the night before, she said, and he'd nearly died because of it. Tom pointed out that she might have been killed at Drew's lake house as easily as he when the gunmen arrived. But Melba argued that the killers never would have sneaked up on Tom while she was there to keep watch.

After a few minutes, he took a rest from trying to persuade her and clicked on his current burn phone to see whether Walt had sent him any further messages.

There were none.

Melba got up and made a trip around the darkened interior of the house, peering out of each window until her eyes adjusted and she felt confident that no one was outside. Tom appreciated her effort, but Caitlin's earlier visit by car proved just how quickly someone could appear at one of the doors. If Knox's people showed up to storm the place, there'd be nothing he or Melba could do to stop them.

"*Why* won't you leave, Mel?" he asked, after she'd returned to the sofa. "At a certain point, loyalty becomes foolish. Your first loyalty has to be to yourself."

His nurse smiled wistfully. "A minute ago," she said, "I probably couldn't have told you why. But when you asked me just now, I realized the answer."

"Will you tell me?"

"Back when Roderick left me—for that *girl*—and I sunk so low that I was just a shadow of myself . . . when I was drinking so much and thinking crazy thoughts . . . Do you remember that?"

"I remember."

"That night you came to my house to keep me from doing something stupid? And I threw myself at you?"

"Oh, Mel, no you didn't."

She looked up sharply. "Hush. You know I did. We never talked about it after, but I never forgot it."

"Mel—"

"Would you let me say my piece?" She folded her hands together and stared off into space, as though looking deep into the past. "Lord, that was back when I still looked good, and you were young enough to do something about it."

Tom's shoulder throbbed when he laughed, but he couldn't help himself. "Those days are long gone, I'm afraid."

"For you and me both, baby."

"You've got some good living left, Mel."

"Just be quiet, old man. That night, when I let you know you could have whatever you wanted . . . you were nothing but a gentleman. I don't think many men would have walked away from me in that state, to tell you the truth. But you did."

Tom recalled the night with perfect clarity. Melba *had* been a very attractive woman then. But her most alluring quality—to him—was that she'd reminded him of Viola. When she unbuttoned her robe and walked to him, trying to kiss him, for the briefest moment he'd relived the feeling of falling into Viola's embrace. But then he'd smelled the reek of gin, and the memory evaporated.

"That wasn't what you needed," he said.

"I know. But I thought it was." Melba reached out and laid a warm hand on his arm. "I knew about Viola even then. From what the older nurses had said. I think I wanted you to love me the way you loved her."

Tom wanted to comfort her, but Melba raised her hand to keep him silent. "I don't think you ever loved anybody like you did Viola. And I say that with all the respect in the world for Mrs. Cage."

Tom sagged back against the sofa pillows, his mind drifting. "There are different kinds of love. That's one thing I've learned in this life. I don't know if concepts like *more* come into it."

"Yes, they do," Melba said earnestly. "Sooner or later, it always comes to a choice. My Roderick made his, and I learned what a fool I was."

"Well, I made my choice, too."

Melba's luminous brown eyes peered deeply into his. "Did you?"

Tom nodded. "I did. I don't want to say more than that."

"All right, then."

Tom rubbed his eyes to break the spell of remembrance. "Are you planning to spend the night here or what?"

"I think we're both legal," Melba said, smiling again. "And it's not like Quentin's short of space. Are you sleepy yet?"

"Actually, I feel pretty good. Thanks to the drugs, the sleep, and your nursing."

"How about we watch some TV then?"

"Fine by me."

"What you want to watch?"

"Anything but a medical show. What about you?"

"Anything but the news or reality TV. I'd love to see one of them old shows that takes my mind off things, like *The Rockford Files*."

Tom couldn't hide his amazement. "*The Rockford Files*? You're a fan of that show?"

Melba tucked her chin into her chest and fanned her face with her hand. "I love me some James Garner, now. That's one handsome white man."

Tom laughed so hard that he thought he might have to take another Vicodin.

"Go back and watch him in *The Great Escape*," Melba said, "when he was young and pretty. Even my mama thought so."

"Well, let's see what we can find." Tom picked up the remote control and clicked on the widescreen television.

Before he could press the GUIDE button, a news crawl at the bottom of the screen scrolled: *Three-state manhunt continues for accused cop killers Walter Garrity and Thomas Cage, M.D. Both men are considered armed and extremely dangerous. Do not approach these fugitives or seek to apprehend them. They may appear elderly, but are suspected of murdering an armed Louisiana state trooper. If you have any information, contact the Louisiana State Police or dial 911 Emergency.* . . . The crawl went on to announce a severe thunderstorm alert in northeast Mississippi.

"Dear Lord," Melba said. "What you gonna do, Doc?"

Tom swallowed hard and made himself press the buttons on the remote. "Wait for Walt. That's all I can do, at this point."

"Do you really believe he's still alive?"

"His message said he's okay."

"Are you sure that was real?"

Tom sighed and gave her a pleading look. "Please go home, Melba. You don't have any business being here for whatever the next act is."

"And you don't have any business being here alone. Find us a TV show. I told you I didn't want no reality."

WALT GARRITY HAD NOW lain beneath the bed for so long he was worried about getting a blood clot. At some point he was going to have to try to get out, because it didn't look like the Valhalla lodge was going to be empty for a long time.

He was about to switch on his burn phone to test for reception again when he heard a metallic *thunk* outside, and then the big turbo sitting atop the helicopter began to spool up. With painful effort Walt dragged himself out from beneath the bed and pulled himself up to the curtained window. This time he saw the scene he'd watched

earlier played in reverse. Black-clad SWAT troopers ran
from the far building to the chopper's door, their German
shepherd alongside them. Every man carried at least one
assault weapon.

Gut-churning fear awakened in Walt. He saw no
reason for this kind of action unless someone had located
Tom. Every fiber of his being told him the time had come
to bolt and find someplace with cellular reception, but it
would be stupid to try before the chopper left. Worse, he
could see the goddamn pit bull leaping and barking at the
cops as they boarded the helicopter.

Walt rubbed his forehead and cursed quietly, thinking
of his wife back in Texas. If he were ten years younger, and
single, he would make his break as soon as the chopper
departed. He'd kill the dog if it made a sound, and then
rely on his wilderness skills to get him to his vehicle ahead
of any pursuers. But there was no point kidding himself.
He wasn't that man anymore. He would have to make the
best of the situation and the skills he still had.

And Tom would have to do the same.

CHAPTER 41

THE EMOTIONAL TRANSITIONS I've made today have left me shaky and hypersensitive to almost all stimuli, but the past few minutes have gone a long way toward healing that. Annie and I are eating sandwiches and watching TV in the bedroom she commandeered in our makeshift safe house, the Abramses' old place on Duncan Avenue. My mother made the sandwiches: tuna fish with apple slices, like those she used to make for my friends and me when we were kids. Since Annie was unable to find an episode of *Grey's Anatomy* or *House, M.D.*, she settled on *Logan's Run*, the sci-fi movie starring Michael York and a boyhood crush of mine, Jenny Agutter.

"How come they chose thirty to be the oldest you could get?" Annie asks, munching on a triangular half of her sandwich. "I mean, you turn thirty, and then you walk into this thing where they kill you?"

"The people in the bubble city don't know they're going to die. They think they're going to be recycled, sort of."

"But the people who run don't believe that."

"Right. The writer probably chose thirty because at that age you still feel pretty much like you did as a teenager. Also, there used to be a saying: 'Never trust anyone over thirty.'"

Annie knits her brows. "Huh. Weird."

Despite all I've been through today, I can't help but laugh.

While a young Farrah Fawcett welcomes Michael York to a plastic surgeon's office, Annie says, "This no-school deal is pretty sweet."

"Don't get too used to it."

"I know. But I miss talking to my friends. Are you sure I can't call anybody? Just for a couple of minutes?"

"I'm sorry, babe. You can't risk it."

She stares at me for several seconds without speaking, then turns her attention back to the movie. Soon she's lost in the drama of Sandmen chasing Runners, and my mind wanders back to the brief conversation I had with my mother when I arrived.

Despite the drama of the confrontation at Edelweiss, what dominated my mind after reaching the safety of this house was my memory of the Ford Fairlane my parents owned when I was a toddler. The more I thought about that gleaming car, the more I realized how incongruous it was, given my mother's tales of penny-pinching frugality and part-time jobs during the early years of their relationship. While Annie went upstairs to find us something to watch, I sat Mom down in the banquette in the corner of the Abramses' kitchen and asked where she and Dad had got "the old Ford that's in all the family pictures."

"The Fairlane?" she asked.

"The car with the tail fins."

"Oh, Lord. We got that when we were in New Orleans."

A wave of heat flashed across my neck and shoulders. "Really? I thought you only got it after you got back from Germany."

"Oh, no. We needed a car long before that. And back then the army would carry your car over on a ship. I'm so glad we had it overseas. I'd have never made it to the hospital to have you without that car."

"So where did you buy it? That was a pretty flashy car for that time. You didn't get it new, did you?"

Mom's eyes widened. "*New?* Lord, no. But it was only a year or two old, and in really good shape. I think it was a 1957. Maybe a '58. That's one of the few great deals Tom ever made. He actually saved his money without telling me, and then one day he brought it home as a present. It was our anniversary, I'm sure of it. 1959."

"The anniversary you told me about last night? When you guys went to that Italian restaurant?"

"Yes!" A smile of authentic pleasure revealed her still-white teeth. "Oh, that was such a grand time. You don't know what something like a car really means until you've been poor and had to walk everywhere, rain or shine."

I could scarcely keep my mind on what she was saying. All I could see was squat, saturnine Carlos Marcello with his arms wrapped around them both at Mosca's, asking how they liked the spaghetti with clam sauce.

"You know what I remember most?" she asked, her voice laced with nostalgia. "In Germany they told us never to let our gas tank get below half full, in case the balloon went up and the Russians invaded."

"Wow," I said dully. "That must have been scary."

"Oh, your father wasn't scared. He said his army unit had nuclear artillery shells, and they could stop the Russians. But I didn't believe that. Neither did the Germans. If you even said the word 'Russian,' those women would shiver."

"So you don't know where Dad got the car?"

"I guess I don't." Her smile faded into concern, then worry. "Why are you so concerned with that car?"

"I don't know."

Mom watched me in silence for a few seconds. "Is it something to do with Carlos Marcello?"

"Why do you ask that?"

"Because you were asking about him last night. But he didn't have anything to do with that car. Tom saved up and bought it."

"Oh, I'm sure you're right. Forget about it."

But I knew she wouldn't. No more than I would.

Before I went upstairs—while Annie helped Mom make the tuna fish—I walked into the backyard and made two phone calls on my burn phone. The first was to Dr. Homer Dawes, a Natchez dentist who'd been in dental school in New Orleans while my father attended med school. They became good friends, and later, by chance, ended up settling in the same town. After Dr. Dawes's wife brought him to the phone, I told him I was working on a novel and needed to know what Dad's salary might have been for working in the Orleans Parish Prison in 1959. Dr. Dawes laughed and said he knew exactly how much that job paid, because he'd been the dental extern for the prison in 1958. "Most of our compensation was room and board," he said. "Beyond that, they gave us a stipend of fifty dollars a month."

Fifty dollars a month. A *month*.

I thanked Dawes and got off as quickly as I could, assuring him that Dad was doing fine and his "trouble" would soon be straightened out. Then I called Rose, my secretary, and asked her to find out how much a 1957 or '58 Ford Fairlane would have cost in the year it was made.

"*Daaad*," Annie almost whines. "You're not paying attention, are you?"

She's right, but a quick scan of the TV screen and my memory tells me where we are in the movie. "The central computer just changed Logan Five's life clock to flashing red early. Now he has no choice but to become a Runner himself."

"You're right. But doesn't he kind of like that Jessica Six girl enough to run anyway?"

"I think he probably does, yeah."

Annie's eyes settle on me. "Are you sure I can't call my friends?"

"Sorry, babe. It's only for a few days, hopefully. Is there somebody you really miss talking to?"

"All my friends, really. But something happened just before you pulled me out of school, and I want to know what the teachers did about it."

"What happened?"

"Somebody stole Jody Campbell's cell phone. I think it was Haley Winters, the meanest girl in my class. But when the teachers finally went through the lockers, they found it in Maria's locker."

"Maria Estrada?"

Annie nods. "She's the only Mexican girl in our whole school. I think Haley put it in her locker to get Maria in trouble. I think that's the whole reason she took the phone."

"Do you have any proof?"

Annie frowns and sighs angrily. "No."

"Did somebody tell you Haley did it? Or did she brag about doing it?"

"No. I just know Maria wouldn't have done that. She doesn't have a cell phone, but she's not stupid. She'd know she couldn't use it without getting caught, even if she would steal it—which she wouldn't."

"Does Haley Winters have a cell phone?"

"*Please.* She's got every gadget a kid can have. She's spoiled rotten. That's just it. She knew nobody would suspect her because of that. See?"

"Oh, I see."

"I just hope Maria's not in trouble."

"Tomorrow I'll call somebody on the school board and check on it."

Annie smiles. "Good. Thanks."

Having rid herself of this psychological irritant, Annie returns her attention to the movie. I try to do the same, but I cannot. Something about her story has disturbed me, like a fish displacing sediment at the bottom of a pond. While Michael York leads Jenny Agutter down a long tubular corridor that reminds me of a gerbil cage, a blast of pure instinct hits me.

"Will you excuse me for a couple of minutes, Boo? I need to make a phone call."

"Noooo. You'll miss the movie. There's no PAUSE button on this old TV."

"I've seen this one enough times to know what happens."

Annie folds her arms and pouts. "Well, how come you get to make calls if I don't?"

For this question I have no answer she will accept. "I know it's not fair, but it has to be this way for now. I'll be as quick as I can, I promise."

Out on the landing of the staircase, I speed-dial Walker Dennis, and he answers on the second ring.

"Make it fast," he says. "I'm busy as hell, still out at Frogmore. Looks like it was precursor chemicals that blew. Definitely arson, though."

"Nobody hurt this time?"

"Thank God."

"Who owns that warehouse?"

"A front corporation, but Leo Spivey had a part interest."

"Can you connect it to the other Eagles at all? The Knoxes maybe?"

"Tough to do with the courthouse closed. Why'd you call, Penn?"

"To save your ass, maybe."

"What?"

"I've been thinking about the Eagles agreeing to come in for questioning tomorrow. Kaiser's right. It makes no sense that they'd do that. Not while they're safe in Texas. They know you lost two deputies today and you'll be loaded for bear."

"I don't have time to second-guess those assholes."

"You'd better make time, buddy. The Knoxes know I spent time with Brody Royal last night. And they know from Caitlin's articles that Royal confessed some things before he died. They also know Caitlin and I spoke to Henry before he died, and Henry spoke to Morehouse before they killed him. Plus they're scared of what Dad might know, because he was treating Viola at the end, and I could be in contact with him. Finally, they know I'm working with you. Bottom line, there's no *way* they're walking into your office tomorrow like steers to the slaughter."

Walker barks an order to someone, then returns to our call. "I figure they'll be lawyered up and ready to post bond on any charges I might make. They gotta be thinking I'll be forced to show 'em my hand, maybe jump the gun on charges, like Kaiser's worried about."

"I don't think that's it."

"Well, shit. What do you think?"

"I think they're buying time while they hunt Dad down and push Mackiever out of his job. And I think Forrest has figured a way to take you out of the equation. If he can do that, the state police can take over the investigation. And Forrest might well be running the state police by tomorrow."

"Take me out how? You mean kill me?"

"They could, but I'd bet it's more subtle than that. Forrest may have some way of making you look incompetent, or even guilty of a crime. If he could do that, maybe someone in your department that's loyal to him could be appointed in your place."

"Yeah. I didn't like the way Ozan was talking last night."

"Exactly. I think they're planning to sandbag you, buddy."

"But how?"

"Well . . . I was watching a movie with my daughter, and she told me a story about something that happened at school. One girl framed another, purely out of meanness. If I were Forrest Knox, and I wanted you out of the way, that's what I'd do."

"Spill it, man."

"Have you got a K-9 unit?"

"Sure, yeah. My cousin's old dog."

"Okay. If I were you, I'd get that dog and run him through my house, my yard, and any other property I owned, like a storage room or fish camp."

The silence that follows this is absolute. "You think they're gonna try to plant something on me?"

"They're in the meth business, bud. And it sure would be an easy sell, wouldn't it? A parish known to have meth problems turns out to have a sheriff that's neck deep in the trade? Especially with the recent history in your department." I pitch my voice like that of one of the old bench-sitters at the farming co-op. "*'Well, I reckon old Walker was always as dirty as the rest of 'em. It just took longer to smoke him out.'*"

I can almost see Dennis snap to attention in the flame-streaked darkness over Frogmore. "Christ, Penn, I'm twenty miles from home, with nobody there but my wife and boy!"

"Take it easy, man. Just send a deputy you trust to watch your house, then head this way and pick up that drug dog."

"I will," he says, his voice tremulous. "Goddamn, this is a hell of a note."

"You're going to be okay, Walker. We've been a step behind these guys up till now, but maybe this time we're one step ahead."

"Are you home or what?"

"No comment. I've got my burn phone with me. Call if you find anything."

"Count on it. Hey, should I take a deputy with me on the search? As a witness or something?"

"No." My answer came out of instinct, not legal analysis.

"Well . . . you're the lawyer. I'll call you back."

"I hope I'm wrong, Walker."

"If you're not, I'm going to break some heads tomorrow."

"Just keep cool, man. This is a chess game now, not a street fight."

"That's where you're wrong."

Dennis hangs up.

I start to walk back into Annie's bedroom, but as I slip my burn phone back into my pocket, it bumps my Black-Berry, and I decide to check my e-mail. There's some risk in doing it, but I want to know if Rose has answered my query about the Fairlane.

As soon as I open my inbox, I find her reply.

> *In 1957, Ford made several models of Fairlane, and the price would depend on various options. But if the car wasn't a convertible, figure $2,000 being the minimum price. If it was a '58, up to $2,500 is possible for a nonconvertible sedan. Hope that helps. If you give me more specific details, I can get closer to the actual price.*

Two thousand dollars, I think, switching off my Black-Berry. *On a salary of fifteen dollars per week?* My mother was teaching then, but by her own admission she knew nothing about the car, so she wasn't helping save for it. Some very quick math tells me that, even allowing for some depreciation, it would be like buying a forty-thousand-dollar car on a salary of a thousand dollars per month. That's a serious stretch, especially given the proposition that Dad somehow saved up that money without Mom feeling the pinch and realizing he was up to something. And I know from my father's stories that none of my grandparents ever helped them buy a car or home.

With a queasy feeling in my belly, I walk up to the second-floor bathroom and sit on the commode. *Where could Dad have gotten the money to buy a two-thousand-dollar car in 1959?* I know how John Kaiser would answer that question.

Taking my tape recorder from my pocket, I look at the tiny reels behind its plastic window. After Caitlin interrupted me at her office, I never listened to the final minutes of the hotel conversation. I don't want to hear my farewell to Stone, but the denouement of the assassination plot still haunts me. It's got nothing to do with my parents' Ford Fairlane—nothing overt, anyway—but the implications of that final act weigh upon me like a funeral shroud. When I press PLAY, Dwight Stone's weary voice echoes through the tiled room like a voice from the grave. I turn the volume wheel to 1, then hold the little speaker to my right ear.

STONE: Carlos's deportation trial was winding down fast. The lawyers were set to make closing arguments on the morning of November twenty-second. On that day in Washington, Bobby Kennedy was chairing a meeting of district attorneys from around the country. They were strategizing in their war against organized crime. Bobby hoped to come back from lunch and announce the conviction and imminent deportation of Carlos Marcello. Instead, a bailiff walked into the federal court in New Orleans and gave the judge a note. Judge Christenberry then announced that President Kennedy had been shot. Less than an hour later, the jury acquitted Carlos Marcello on all charges and allowed him to stay in America.

ME: Jesus.

STONE: Do you know who was sitting at the defendant's table with Carlos and his lawyer? Guy Banister. I've got the pictures to prove it.

ME: Where was David Ferrie?

KAISER: About to leave for Houston, which was five hours from New Orleans, in the middle of a heavy thunderstorm. Supposedly to go ice skating.

ME: I remember that from the movie.

STONE: He went to a skating rink but didn't skate at all. He spent the whole time on a pay phone. Calls untraceable. He died in New Orleans four years later, within days of Jim Garrison's JFK investigation being made public. He may have died of a berry aneurysm, but we can't rule out murder. In any case, although he told Garrison there was a conspiracy, there's no question why he would have remained silent about the details while pushing the DA toward the CIA. No one alive knew better than David Ferrie that the price of betraying Marcello was death.

Here I said nothing. What could I say?

STONE: The last tragic act on November twenty-second was that Robert Kennedy canceled the afternoon session of his anti-crime unit, and it never met again. Once JFK's funeral was over, J. Edgar Hoover never spoke to Bobby again in his capacity as attorney general. Not once. Robert Kennedy might as well have been a janitor at the Justice Department. His anti-mob crusade went nowhere. He'd lost all his fire, and he had no backing from the Bureau.

KAISER: Carlos's strategy had proved sound. He'd cut the head off the dog, and the tail was dead forever after. At least until Bobby announced for president in 1968.

STONE: Without that second Carcano being found—which meant no link between Dealey Plaza, Eladio Cruz, and Castro—the picture that emerged of Oswald became the lone-nut theory. If that rifle had been found—a direct link to a Cuban agent—I think LBJ would have invaded Cuba within sixty days.

ME: You're saying we might owe Frank Knox for saving us from nuclear war?

STONE: We just might.

I click off the recorder to avoid the final exchange. Dwight asked me once more to press my mother to reveal any line of communication she might have with Dad. If she denied it, he said, would I consider allowing either him or Kaiser to question her? I gave him a flat no, and he did his best to hide his disappointment. As I walk back to Annie's room, Kaiser's final words play in my mind. I had dropped Stone's feverish hand and started for the door, and Kaiser said, "What about tomorrow? The Double Eagles coming in for questioning. What are you going to do?"

I stopped at the mouth of the little passage that led to the door, turned back, and said in a low voice: "I'm going to pin those bastards to the wall and squeeze their balls until they beg for mercy. Metaphorically speaking, of course."

Kaiser's face darkened, but before he could say a word, I walked to the door and made my exit. I no longer cared what he had to say, and as for Stone . . . there's no good way to say farewell to a dying friend.

As I leave the bathroom to return to Annie's room, my mother calls my name from the landing halfway down the stairs. She stares up at me, her eyes freighted with deep concern. *Could she have heard any of that tape?* I wonder.

"What is it, Mom? Are you okay?"

"Why did you ask me about our old Fairlane? Is it something to do with Carlos Marcello?"

"I honestly don't know. The thing that confuses me about Marcello is that you told me Dad treated him in the Orleans Parish Prison back in 1959, but as far as I can find out, Marcello didn't serve a day in jail while you and Dad lived in New Orleans."

Her eyes narrow, and she rubs her hand over her mouth, but even before she speaks I know my mother is not trying to deceive me. I've seen that look ten thousand times. She's simply thinking back, trying to be sure of her memory.

"I guess I could have been mistaken," she says finally. "But I don't think so. Tom told me *some* story about treating Marcello at the jail, because when we saw him later on at those restaurants, Tom said that was the only reason 'Uncle Carlos' knew who he was."

"It's okay, Mom. Don't keep worrying about it."

The concern carved into her features tells me how little chance there is that she'll follow my advice.

"Is Annie all right?" she asks.

"She's doing good. We're watching a movie."

"You spend all the time with her you can. I think she's more upset than she's letting on."

Aren't we all?

"I will. You try to get some sleep. I'll wake you up if I have to go out again."

"Is there any chance of that?"

"I hope not. But if I have to, I'll wake you. I promise."

Mom nods, but her eyes are still troubled. "We needed that car, Penn," she says softly. "But there was nothing improper about it. I'd tell you if there was."

"I know you would." *If you knew about it.* "Don't sit up thinking about it. I know how you are."

She sighs heavily, then turns and walks back toward the kitchen.

"Dad?" Annie calls from the top of the stairs.

CHAPTER 42

DESPITE TOM'S EDICT that they not watch any medical show, he and Melba were on their second episode of *House, M.D.*, a program that his granddaughter had always begged him to watch. While some of the social situations were outrageous, Tom had to admit that the medical dilemmas were real enough, and Hugh Laurie's sarcastic disdain for bureaucratic meddling was something every doctor in the world could relate to.

About twenty minutes ago, during a commercial break, Melba had thought she'd heard a helicopter in the distance. Tom had been unable to hear it, but that was no surprise, given his progressive hearing loss, and she'd heard nothing since. He told her it was probably nothing to worry about. Statistically, Mississippi had some of the worst drivers in the nation, so LifeFlight helicopters were common at all hours, even over rural counties.

Tom had thought Melba felt reassured, but five minutes ago she'd left him on the sofa and begun her long circuit of the ground-floor windows again. Waiting alone was starting to bother Tom. He wanted to switch on his old burn phone and check to see if Walt had sent any additional messages. The cell phone was in his hand when he heard a strange, muted *phtt* sound from the garage side of the huge house.

"Mel?" he called.

She didn't answer.

"Melba!"

Nothing.

With his heartbeat picking up, Tom switched on the new burn phone and waited for the device to find a tower. As soon as it did, a single text message came through, and popped up on the tiny screen.

*Almost sure trouble's headed your way. SWAT team
deploying. Get out ASAP. Sorry I'm late. Phone
jamming here. Listen for chopper on your way out. Good
luck. Text me when safe. Walt.*

"Listen for chopper," Tom whispered, and then his
heart hammered in his chest. The hard-pumping blood
made his shoulder scream with pain, but two seconds later
he was on his feet with his .357 in his hand. He wanted to
call out to Melba, but she hadn't answered the first time,
and if there were men in the house, his shout would only
bring them to him.

As quickly as he could, Tom moved toward the darkest
part of the living room, a short pass-through that led to
the hall that ran half the length of the great house. His
only hope was to find Melba and get outside into the dark,
then into the nearby forest. A SWAT team would have
night-vision devices, but the dense trees might be enough
of a shield to conceal two fleeing figures.

As Tom reached the spot where the pass-through made
a T with the main hall, a man wearing a black mask and
body armor appeared in profile less than a foot away from
him. Knowing the head would turn toward him at any
moment, Tom jammed the .357 under the man's chin and
said quietly: "I'll pull the trigger if you do anything but
drop your gun."

He meant it, for surrender would mean not only his
death, but Melba's also. Tom jabbed the barrel of his pistol
hard under the mandible of the SWAT officer and kept
pressing until he heard the thud of metal hitting carpet.

"Now what?" the man croaked, his eyes obscured by
his insectile face mask. "You've got no play, Doc."

"Where's my nurse?"

"Who?"

Tom didn't like being exposed in the hall. He was
about to drag the guy back into the pass-through when a
voice with an accent he recognized from medical school
in New Orleans shouted from the kitchen at the right end
of the corridor.

"Let him go, Doc! Nuttin' to be gained by killin'
nobody."

Tom looked up the hall at the man who'd yelled at him.

He, too, wore a mask and body armor and carried a short submachine gun in his hands. His accent was pure New Orleans—Brooklyn sautéed in crawfish.

"Then why'd you bring all the guns?" Tom asked.

"We didn't know what we'd find here."

Tom felt panic kicking like a crazed animal in his chest. Having lived through last night, he didn't fancy dying here, and he couldn't live with Melba's death on his account.

"Where's my nurse?" he shouted. "Bring her out here where I can see her!"

As he stared down the hall, waiting, the man raised his right hand as though trying to calm him down. While Tom's eyes adjusted to the dimness, he realized there was another man standing behind the first, and he held a large bulbous rifle in his hands. *A sniper rifle.*

"Who's your senior officer?" Tom called.

"I am," said the man with his arm up.

The animal in Tom's chest was kicking harder. With every passing second he became more certain that he had no way out of this situation—not alive, anyway. He heard a sliding sound from down the hall behind him. He turned, careful to keep his gun at the masked man's head, and saw Melba Price lying motionless on her side while a SWAT trooper dragged her across the carpet. *They were trying to hide her body from him!*

"You sons of bitches!" he yelled, nearly pulling the trigger on the man under his power. "You killed her!"

"No!" shouted the commander. "She's not dead. We just darted her."

"Bullshit!" Tom screamed.

"I swear to God, Doc! We're just here to pick you up, to deliver you to Colonel Knox—alive. He wants to talk to you."

"That's a lie! That wasn't the deal. The deal was that if he wanted to talk to me, he'd call off the APB first. I saw the news twenty minutes ago, and they're still running an alert!"

"I don't know anything about that," the commander shouted, his hand still in the air. "But you've got to see there's no point shooting anybody. Just put down your gun and go take the woman's pulse."

"Sure," Tom said, almost unable to think. "And this bastard breaks my neck on the way down the hall."

"Take him with you. Keep your gun on him."

"Why are you holding your arm in the air?" Tom asked, sensing something wrong. "Is that some kind of signal?"

When the man didn't answer, Tom turned to try to gauge his chances of dragging his hostage down the hall to check Melba's pulse.

He'd never make it.

The sight of her prone body brought tears to his eyes. "Bring her to me!" he yelled. "Tell your man to drag her down here, or I pull the trigger. I've got nothing to lose. I'm going to die anyway."

His hostage shouted, "He won't kill me, Major. Take him!"

Tom moved the gun two inches to the right and fired a round into the ceiling. His hostage screamed and recoiled, but before he could break away Tom stabbed the gun barrel into his neck again.

"Next one goes into your brain," Tom said, his whole arm alive with energy.

"Don't move, Sergeant," called the commander. "I know that tone well. Doc, you take it easy. I'm going to take off my helmet so you can see my eyes."

Tom heard the sliding sound behind him again. When he turned, he saw the trooper at the other end of the hall dragging Melba out of sight. A wild emotion he'd never experienced surged through him.

"Stand down!" shouted the commander. "Let that woman lie!"

Grief and fury had taken possession of Tom. Whirling back toward the commander, he felt his gun hand tense to pull the trigger. But even as he did, the commander dropped his right hand, and a flash blanked out Tom's dilated eyes. Pain exploded in his right shoulder, and his gun arm went limp as boots pounded toward him. His hostage twisted the .357 from his hand, then propped him up before he could fall.

"*Target taken!*" shouted the commander. "*Air one, exfil at the front crescent.*"

Tom blinked again and again, his thoughts scrambled into chaos.

"Get everything he had!" someone yelled. "Clothes, drugs, phones—everything."

"What about the nurse's car?"

"Leave it."

In the confusion of Tom's mind, one clear image rose: Melba lying motionless while men leaped over her as though she were no longer worthy of notice. Pain radiated through him like arcs of fire, and when he looked down, he saw a single bright bloom of blood on what had been his good shoulder. Someone jammed two fingers under his jaw to feel his carotid, but by then his last reserve of strength had given out, and everything went black.

CHAPTER 43

CAITLIN WAS WORKING alone in her office when Jordan Glass knocked, then slipped inside with two go-cups from Hammer's Drive-Thru in Vidalia.

"Vodka and cranberry," she said. "You up for it?"

Caitlin hesitated, suddenly remembering her pregnancy, but a perverse instinct, combined with her deep anxiety, made her reach for the sweating plastic cup with the colored umbrella sticking out of it.

"How'd your errand work out?" Jordan asked.

"Awful and wonderful at the same time, I'd say. Does that make sense?"

"In my experience, it's always that way. Nearly every great photo I ever shot cost me dearly, one way or another."

"This is costing me, all right. I've never been as torn about something as I am tonight."

"Should we go back to the ladies' room?"

"No need. I just had this room swept by someone who knows what he's doing."

"Good. So . . ." Jordan slid into the seat opposite Caitlin's desk. "You're holding things back, right?"

Caitlin hesitated, then nodded.

"From John and the Bureau? Or from Penn?"

"From everybody."

Jordan turned up her palms. "Well, that's the job, isn't it? At least until it's time to publish. The question is, who and what gets hurt by you holding back? Is it just a matter of bruised male pride? Or will trust be damaged long term? Are you risking someone's life by withholding information?"

"I honestly don't know. I'm definitely risking Penn's trust. As for the rest . . . haven't we all been at risk from the moment we took on the Double Eagles? After what I saw last night, how do you even gauge the risk? You know the stakes in this story. How much risk is justified?"

"I'm afraid only you can answer that. Or your loved ones, if you wind up getting killed."

Caitlin looked deeply into the photographer's eyes. "John did something that really shook your faith in him, didn't he?"

Jordan took a deep breath and sighed. "Yes. It was an end-justifies-the-means kind of problem."

"I can relate." Caitlin drank her first swallow of vodka, puckering from the cold sting. "Right now I've got a problem with conflicting promises. To keep one, I have to break another. The question is, do I keep the one to my future husband, because he is my future husband? Or do I keep the one that I feel is right?"

"You know the answer to that."

"Do I?" She thought of Tom and Melba hiding in the forest in Jefferson County. "The thing is, the path I think is right could lead to disaster. Unforgivable disaster."

Glass rattled the ice in her cup. "You're in a war. There are going to be casualties. The real question is motive. What is it you're working in service of? Justice? The truth? Revenge for Henry Sexton? Or is it just the story?"

"All the above. But the story means a lot to me, I won't lie about that."

Jordan smiled knowingly. "No need, girl, not with me. But I warn you, not everyone else will be sympathetic to that choice."

Caitlin sagged in her chair. "I know."

"You told me you had a plan for tomorrow. A lead of your own. Are you still going to follow through with that?"

"Will my answer leave this room?"

Jordan gave her a conspiratorial shake of the head. "Not via me. Scout's honor."

"Were you a Girl Scout?"

"For about five minutes. Oxford, Mississippi."

Caitlin laughed, and the laughter felt good. "I can't believe it."

"I can build a fire in the rain like *that*," Jordan said, snapping her fingers. "That's what I got out of that experience."

"Good thing to know."

"It saved my ass more than once." Jordan hung her hands over her knees and leaned forward. "So are you up for company on this quest of yours?"

Caitlin sipped her vodka to hide her expression. The plain truth was, she needed somebody with her on tomorrow's trip. She'd promised Henry Sexton she wouldn't go into the Lusahatcha Swamp alone, and she'd be a fool if she did. Yet some juvenile compulsion urged her not to tell a soul about her trip. The lure of whatever Henry had called Frank Knox's "insurance" against Carlos Marcello made her heart beat faster, and she swallowed some more vodka. Then, before she could second-guess herself, she said, "Be here at five thirty tomorrow morning if you really want to know. If we find what I'm hoping to find, you'll be hanging another Pulitzer on your wall."

Jordan waved her hand dismissively. "I'm over that crap, honey. But I'd like to see you get a second one. That's when you know you've proved yourself."

Caitlin couldn't help but grin.

"The only problem," Jordan said, "is my Havana trip. I need to get to the New Orleans airport by four thirty P.M. Can I go with you and still make that?"

Caitlin nodded. "The place we're going is south of here, so it's on the way. I can ride with you, then call one of my reporters to pick me up while you drive on to New Orleans."

Jordan tilted her head and pursed her lips in thought. "I know of two interesting things south of here. The Lusahatcha Swamp and the Valhalla hunting camp."

Caitlin ignored this bait. "What are you going to tell John?"

Jordan looked into her drink and thought about it. "That I got an earlier flight to Havana. The Castro brothers can't wait to see me again."

"Again?"

"I met Fidel about twenty years ago, and he flirted shamelessly with me."

Caitlin laughed, wondering what it would be like to move in Jordan's journalistic circles.

"John will want to send an escort with me, so I may have to get creative."

Caitlin drank off the last of her drink. Then, emboldened by the alcohol buzz, she asked, "Did John say anything about his meeting with Dwight and Penn?"

The photographer shook her head. "John's still at Dwight's hotel. I think he's afraid Dwight won't survive tomorrow's surgery. And even if he does, he's facing a liver transplant."

Caitlin shut her eyes, trying to push away premature grief. "God, I hate that. Dwight's one of the good guys. Maybe that's why Penn was so upset tonight."

"What do you mean?"

"He kind of flipped out earlier. He tried to pick a fight with Sheriff Byrd, and there was no real reason to do it. Something had pushed him to a place where he was ready to lash out, regardless of the consequences."

"You couldn't find out what it was?"

Caitlin shook her head. "He wasn't in the mood to answer questions. We made love, and he worked his anger out that way. I honestly don't know if I've ever seen him this tense."

Jordan looked thoughtful. "John, too, in his own way. I'll tell you something you might find interesting. John gave me a couple of questions to ask Fidel if he shows up at the shoot."

A fillip of excitement went through Caitlin. "Seriously? About what?"

"The Kennedy assassination. What else?"

Caitlin's pulse picked up and stayed there. "Jordan, what the hell's going on? Are they really close to breaking new information about the assassination?"

"I don't know. John's pretty good at his job, and Dwight's no slouch."

"What were the questions he gave you?"

Jordan winked at her. "Sorry. I can't go that far. Even if we are partners."

Caitlin groaned in frustration.

"I may only see Raúl, depending on Fidel's health. Rumor is, the maximum leader is drifting toward the minimum state. But I hope I get both of them."

"You'll really ask Castro about the JFK assassination?"

All the levity went out of Jordan's face. "What year were you born, Caitlin?"

"1970."

"I was born in 1960."

Caitlin had a feeling she knew where the photographer was headed. "Surely you don't remember anything about President Kennedy?"

Jordan shook her head. "No. But do you know who my father was?"

"Sure. Jonathan Glass. He disappeared while on assignment in Vietnam. In . . ."

"1972," Jordan finished. "He was actually in Cambodia, just over the Mekong River. But he started as a photojournalist at the age of twenty. He was actually in Dealey Plaza the day Kennedy was shot."

Caitlin sat up. "Really?"

"Mm-hm. He took a famous photograph of two Secret Service agents guarding Jackie Kennedy at Parkland Hospital."

A brief black-and-white image flashed through Caitlin's head: the Praetorian Guard and their widowed queen. Caitlin no longer knew where Jordan was going.

"Daddy wasn't home much when I was growing up," Glass said. "He was always on assignment somewhere, from Asia to the Congo. But after that day in Dallas, he came home to Oxford and stayed almost a month. All he did was drink. I remember him lying on the couch, stinking of gin, unshaven, his eyes glued to the TV while the phone rang and rang. I asked my mother about it when I was older, and she said everything I described was accurate. She also told me that he'd been within two hundred feet of the limo when Kennedy was shot. I don't know exactly what he saw . . . but whatever it was wounded him in some way. We're talking about one of the best war photographers in the world, remember—a man who'd seen everything. But something went out of him that day. He was collateral damage of those gunshots. Daddy was no gullible romantic; he was as cynical as they come. But he'd believed in Kennedy and the possibilities he represented."

Jordan stared into her cup as if at a screen playing footage from her past. "When I was older, I found a cache of pictures from that trip. JFK and Jackie getting off the plane, the president speaking at the Hotel Texas in Fort Worth the previous day. Daddy didn't save many prints, but he kept those. And every shot communicated either resolve or optimism, which definitely wasn't what he usually memorialized on film."

Caitlin expected the story to go on, or to end with some insight or revelation, but Jordan simply stopped speaking. As she stared into the cup, Caitlin said, "Did you ever get to ask him about it?"

Jordan shook her head. "He'd already been missing for four years when I discovered the pictures. I found out a few years ago that he survived his wound and lived on until 1979. Over there. But I never saw him again."

"I'm sorry."

"It's okay. He wasn't the same man. I doubt he even remembered me." At last Jordan looked up, her jaw set tight. "As for your question . . . yes, I will ask Fidel Castro John's questions. This new line of inquiry could be bullshit, but somehow I don't think so. And if I can help get to the truth, then I intend to." Jordan reached out and set her empty cup on Caitlin's desk. "Do you keep any vodka at the office?"

Caitlin shook her head. "Sorry."

"That's a tragedy."

Caitlin smiled, but her brain was racing. As soon as Jordan left, she was going to get out Henry's letter and journals and highlight every fragment of information about John and Robert Kennedy, Carlos Marcello, Marcello's contacts with Brody Royal, and the "insurance" Frank Knox had kept to protect himself against Marcello. Perhaps most tantalizing of all was Snake Knox's statement to Morehouse that the "insurance" document had been written in Russian. Something told Caitlin that while she'd been focused on the civil rights murders that had preoccupied Henry Sexton for so many years, the real story had been unfolding at a much deeper level.

"We'd better get some sleep," she said. "We're pulling out before dawn."

Jordan closed her eyes for a moment, then stood and zipped her jacket. "Maybe I can get to sleep before John gets back to the hotel. I don't fancy a long night of lying."

"But you'll do it if necessary?"

Glass gave her a crooked smile. "Same as you, right?"

CHAPTER 44

TOM AWAKENED IN a fog of pain and terror. A swarm of black, insectile faces hovered above him, peering down as if they meant to devour him any second. He fought to get off his back, but a flurry of strong hands pressed him back down. When his eyes adjusted to the backlighting, he saw one human face in the alien crowd. A boy, earnest and sweating, leaning over his left shoulder. The boy was working on his gunshot wound.

A syringe floated into his field of view, then stung his shoulder. Blessed relief washed through him. He hadn't realized how painful his wound had been until the local anesthetic took effect. With relief from pain, his surroundings took on more detail. An IV line ran fluids into his right wrist. For a few seconds he wondered if he was in some kind of ambulance, but then he remembered that the black masks belonged to a SWAT team—the same killers who had broken into Quentin's house and shot Melba.

"Melba," he croaked.

"Don't try to talk," the boy advised. "You're severely dehydrated, and your heart's in bad shape. Let me take care of this wound."

"Is she dead?"

"What's he saying?" asked one of the masked faces.

"I think he's asking about the nurse," answered another.

"Don't worry about her," said the first man. "She's fine."

They're lying, Tom thought. *Melba's dead.*

He jerked as the boy medic probed flesh that was not quite numb. Then his stomach rolled as the chopper began to descend rapidly. He wanted to ask the boy a question, but it kept drifting out of his head, like a flashlight fading into darkness. Then all was night once more.

"IS MELBA ALIVE OR DEAD?"

"Does it matter what I say? You won't believe me either way."

"Tell me the truth."

"She's fine, Doc. They just darted her, same as they did you."

Hope flamed in Tom's chest, but he tamped it down, wary of being manipulated.

VOICES IN THE DARK.

One more powerful than the others . . . *An officer being deferred to by noncoms and enlisted men.*

This time Tom kept his eyes closed.

"What's his status?" asked the officer's voice.

"He needs to be in a hospital, Colonel. No shit. We're lucky that dart didn't stop his heart."

"What about his bullet wound?"

"I pumped him full of antibiotics. If his heart doesn't give out, he should be okay for a couple of days. But he's also diabetic. Somebody needs to be checking his sugar regularly."

"For the next twelve hours, that's your job. Clear?"

"Yes, sir."

"All right. Give me a minute with him. Then we'll move him out of the chopper."

There was a shuffle of boots on metal, and then someone squatted on his haunches beside Tom. Tom heard the knees creak.

"Hey, Doc," said the officer. "You can quit playing possum. I got your message. If you want to make a deal, open your eyes."

Tom did.

He saw a dark, intense face and a deformed ear that barely qualified as one at all, in the cosmetic sense. Beneath the face he saw a lieutenant colonel's oak leaves on the epaulettes of a state trooper's uniform. The uniform threw Tom back to the borrow pits, and Walt killing the trooper beside the van.

"Do you know who I am?" asked the man.

"I don't recognize you. But I'm guessing you're Frank Knox's son."

The trooper smiled. "That's right. Forrest Knox."

"What happened to the ear? War wound?"

Knox looked almost pleased by Tom's frankness. "Lost it in the Vietnamese Highlands."

"You didn't want to fix it?"

Knox shrugged. "I like keeping the civilians off balance. You know?"

Tom didn't answer. He knew the type all too well.

"So, you want to make a deal," Forrest said.

"That's right."

"You offering to guarantee I stay squeaky clean if I can get you out of hot water on this cop killing? Is that about it?"

"Not just that. I want you to close the Viola Turner murder, too."

Forrest nodded as though intrigued. "I suppose you didn't kill her?"

"That no longer matters. The only question now is who gets blamed for it."

Forrest smiled. "You have a suggestion?"

"I say blame the dead. Easiest for everybody."

Now Knox grinned. "A man after my own heart. I like that plan, Doc."

"So what do you think?"

Knox shifted his weight onto his haunches. "I think I need to get in touch with your son. The problem is, I can't find him."

"I don't know where he is," Tom said. "And vice versa. Safer that way."

"Maybe up till now. But the thing is, Doc, while I trust your motives—and your follow-through, up to a point—your word doesn't mean a damn thing if you can't call off your son and his fiancée at the newspaper. Right?"

"I can do that. I talked to Caitlin tonight."

"And she said she'll drop the story?"

Tom tried to hold his facial expression neutral. "She's open to it. I think Penn and I together can persuade her."

"I hope so, Doc. For your sake." Forrest leaned down over him, his gaze disturbingly intimate. "My daddy always liked you, Doc. He respected what you did in Korea. Do you remember him?"

Tom let himself think back to the early sixties. "I remember Frank, all right."

"Nothing good to say, though? Even now?"

"We were more different than alike."

Forrest grinned again. "No doubt about that." He raised his hand and tapped his forefinger hard on Tom's forehead. "I'd hate to have to hurt you, Doc. I really would. I remember you giving me my football physicals back in the day. But if you and your boy can't straighten out that Masters cunt before she goes too far . . . she's gonna pull the same train Viola Turner did back in '68. Only she won't come out of it alive."

While Tom tried to suppress his memory of Viola's wrecked state after those events, Knox signaled through the chopper's wide hatch. "Let's get him out!"

Three masked SWAT team members clambered through the hatch. Forrest moved aside so they could slide Tom onto a stretcher. They lifted him easily, then manhandled him through the door and out under the starry sky.

Tom smelled the stink of old crude oil and the sticky mud some men called gumbo. Turning his head to the right, he saw the long black arm of a pumping unit rising and falling like a black bird drinking from a puddle, the cyclic hum of its engine strangely comforting in the dark.

"Oil field," he murmured, as the men carried him through the night.

"Yep," Forrest said from above him. "Brody Royal owned this land, but he won't have much use for it now. There's an old well-checker's shack through the trees. I was going to leave you there, but considering your present condition, I think we'll give you the better alternative."

Tom followed Knox's pointing hand.

Parked in the dark about forty yards from the well was Walt Garrity's silver Roadtrek van. They must have sent someone to collect it from Drew's lake house garage.

"Where's Walt?" Tom asked.

"I was hoping you could tell me that."

Tom shook his head. "I lost touch with him a long time ago."

"Come on, Doc. You're going to make me doubt you'll stand by any deal."

Tom felt angina tighten the muscles of his back as they neared the big van. Forrest opened the Roadtrek's rear doors. The sound made Tom think of Walt threatening Sonny Thornfield in this van only two nights ago. How swiftly the tables had turned. The stretcher banged against the van, and he tensed against the pain.

"Hold it," Forrest said, and then he leaned over Tom once more. "You were with my daddy when he died, right?"

Tom nodded, wondering where this was going.

"Did he say anything at the end? I was only sixteen, and nobody ever mentioned any last words. But Snake said Daddy was in and out of consciousness when they took him to your office, and I've always wondered."

Tom shut his eyes and saw Frank Knox gasping on the floor of the little surgery room as his blood poured onto the tile and the air embolism hit his heart like a sledgehammer. For the first time in his life, Tom took pleasure in the memory.

"No," Tom said, opening his eyes. "He passed out when I started working on him, and never regained consciousness. Frank was tough, but his injuries were catastrophic."

Forrest stared into Tom's eyes for a few seconds, then nodded slowly. "That's what I figured."

Tom heard the men holding the stretcher breathing harder.

"I've gone out on a limb for you, Doc. The easiest thing would have been to take you down and hang Viola around your neck. I hope your son wants you back as bad as I'd like to see my daddy. If he doesn't, this RV's gonna wind up at the bottom of the river. And you're gonna be in it."

Forrest gave the stretcher-bearers a hand signal, then walked away. Tom felt a hitch as the SWAT troopers lifted the stretcher high, then slid him into the tomblike darkness of the van.

CHAPTER 45

IT WAS NEARLY midnight when Sheriff Dennis called me back and told me to meet him in the parking lot of the Ferriday Walmart Supercenter. He didn't tell me the reason, but the near-panicked urgency in his voice told me I'd been right about the planted drugs. It took all my strength to haul myself out of bed and walk down to my car, and it took most of the drive over to Louisiana to bring myself fully awake.

Driving west on the dark, flat artery of Highway 84, I suddenly spy the Walmart glowing like a fluorescent island in the vast black fields between Vidalia and Ferriday. Fewer than twenty vehicles dot the parking lot when I pull alongside Sheriff Dennis's cruiser. As I get out and cross between our two cars, I see a black cat with three kittens crouching in the shadow of a parked tractor-trailer, eating from a wet McDonald's bag.

A hot wind escapes from Walker's cruiser when I open his passenger door, and when I close myself inside, I see that the sheriff has mounted a sawed-off shotgun in the floor rack between us. His police radio chatters on low volume, and a dashboard computer glows softly with a screen saver that reads: *GO TIGERS!*

Dennis appears barely in control of his emotions, so I speak in the calmest voice I can muster.

"Hey, bud. Looks like you're sweating bullets. Why don't you turn the heater down?"

Dennis wipes his face like a man waking from a trance. "You're right. Shit, I didn't realize."

After he turns the heater to low, I turn and brace my back against the passenger door. "What did you find, and where did you find it?"

The sheriff shakes his head in disbelief. "A shitload of

crystal meth, cooked and bagged and ready for sale. Right under my goddamn house!"

"How much is a shitload?"

"Three-quarters of a pound. Enough to put me in Angola for thirty years, not counting corruption charges."

A strange serenity flows over me at this news.

"You were *right*," he says, an edge of hysteria in his voice. "Those goddamn Knoxes."

"Well, at least we have our answer. This is why the Double Eagles agreed to come back for questioning. They think you'll be busted by your own men before you ask them your first question."

Sheriff Dennis goes pale. "My own men?"

"Unless Forrest brings in the DEA—which I doubt— I'd bet on it. I imagine one of your deputies will receive an 'anonymous' tip sometime prior to tomorrow's interrogations. A team will drive over to your house to search it, with the expectation of 'discovering' the hoard you found tonight. And if the dope was there, you'd have helped teach your colleagues a valuable lesson: crossing the Knoxes is career suicide for a cop."

"And you figured this out from a story your kid told you?"

"That triggered it, yeah. Kaiser's certainty about the Eagles not coming had been bothering me all evening. To submit to questioning, they had to have some kind of insurance. Subconsciously, I must have been wondering what the easiest way to move you off the board would be. I saw drugs planted on cops in Houston before. With this parish's history of corruption, that would have been a slam dunk."

Sheriff Dennis wipes the sheen of sweat from his forehead with his uniform sleeve. "So what now?"

I don't answer for a while. Then, after some thought, I say, "Are you asking me as the mayor of Natchez? As a former prosecutor? Or as a friend?"

"A friend, goddamn it."

"These are the same guys who killed your cousin, right?"

"Yep."

"They booby-trapped the warehouse that killed two of your deputies."

Dennis nods soberly.

I turn and look over at the harsh light spilling out of the Walmart doors. "An elegant solution came to me while I was driving over the bridge."

"What's that?"

"Send that meth right back where it came from."

Walker's voice goes quiet, as though someone might hear us. "Plant it back on the Knoxes?"

Turning back to him, I answer with words I can't quite believe are my own. "Put on a pair of latex gloves, then divide the meth into separate packages. You know how to make it look authentic. Stash those packets in or around the homes of the Double Eagles we're going to question tomorrow. At least Snake and Sonny, anyway. Make sure the amount meets the standard for trafficking charges."

"That wouldn't be any problem with this load. What about Billy Knox?"

"Something tells me Billy's likely to have serious security around his place. I'd leave him out of it. But Snake and Sonny won't, and I doubt they're back from Toledo Bend yet."

Walker looks away from me, his jaw muscles working hard as he grinds his teeth. Then he nods suddenly. "Fuck 'em. I'm gonna do it."

"Good."

Now his eyes seek me out. "Have you ever done anything like this?"

"No. In all my years as an assistant DA, I never broke the rules. I never looked the other way when a cop did, either. Not on a single case. I was a goddamn choirboy. And I don't know why I'm advising you to do this now, except . . ." I trail off, unsure whether even I know the answer. "Tonight Billy Byrd tried to search my house, and I almost pushed him into a gunfight. It was stupid, but I couldn't stop myself."

"Sometimes the only way to fight fire is with fire," Dennis says softly. "If the bad guys are wearing white hats while they break the rules . . . you throw the rules out the window."

"I guess that's it."

"Part of it. The truth is, you're worried about your father. If we can keep up the pressure on the Knoxes, it'll definitely increase his chances of survival."

I nod slowly, watching the mother cat and her kittens scamper from the shadow of the parked truck to a deeper shadow beside a Dumpster. "Once this is done, you'll need somebody to make an anonymous tip call to you about the meth at Snake's and Sonny's houses, preferably from a pay phone to your home. In case a defense lawyer checks later. Do you have someone you can trust?"

"I think so, yeah."

"Be sure you trust them, Walker. If you're caught doing this, you'll go to the penitentiary, if the Knoxes don't kill you first. If it's the only way to be sure, I'll wake up and make the call myself."

"I don't want you to take that risk. I can get it handled."

"All right. I guess we're done, then."

"What about tomorrow morning? You're gonna be there for the interrogation, right?"

"Kaiser says I have no authority to question the Eagles. And technically, he's correct."

"Screw that. I want you in that room. Consider yourself a special deputy of Concordia Parish. I'll swear you in tomorrow. I'll even pin a tin star on your chest."

A childish thrill of satisfaction runs through me. Walker Dennis is smarter than people give him credit for being. "I didn't think about that. You know, with trafficking charges against Sonny and Snake, we'll have some real leverage. Because of the mandatory sentencing minimums, you won't even need the cooperation of the DA to charge them."

"You're goddamn right. What about Kaiser, though? Do you think he'll show up and try to stop us?"

I think back to the discussions in Kaiser's hotel. "I don't know. He's got a lot of other things on his mind. But he's worried we'll screw things up for him, so I wouldn't be surprised to see him."

Dennis shakes his head, obviously troubled by something. "You know, that Kaiser's a pretty tough dude. He fought in 'Nam."

"Yeah."

"He also worked in the Bureau's profiling unit, but he transferred out after attacking a convict they were interviewing. A child killer. He's probably got a lot of experience with interrogation."

"So do I, Walker. Don't worry. With trafficking charges against the Eagles, you won't require much finesse. And Kaiser won't be able to interfere. Just make sure you don't screw up while you're planting the stuff."

"I won't."

"Where's the meth now?"

"In the trunk."

A bolus of pure terror blasts through my veins to my heart. "*This* trunk?"

"Shit, where else was I gonna put it?"

An almost overwhelming urge to leap from the car grips me. "Okay, okay," I say, closing my hand around the door handle. "Just get the job done as fast as you can. And be careful. This isn't some prank, man. They'll kill you if they catch you. They won't hesitate."

Sheriff Dennis leans forward, his eyes burning with long-suppressed rage. "That cuts two ways, brother. I owe these motherfuckers from way back. They come at me tonight . . . I'll kill 'em. You can sort out the mess with a judge in the morning."

This prospect doesn't excite me, but I raise my hand and pat him on the shoulder. "Just watch your back, okay?"

"Just be at my office at seven A.M. You don't want to miss their faces when I slap that meth on the table."

I can't help but smile. "You're right about that. I'll see you tomorrow."

"Hey, wait," he says as I pop the door handle.

When I turn back, Walker is holding out his hand to me. In it gleams a gold star with *Concordia Parish Sheriff* engraved in the metal. He's taken the star from his own chest and offered it to me.

"I can't take that, Walker."

"Hell yes you can. In case you beat me to my office tomorrow. Consider yourself a sworn deputy."

After a moment's hesitation, I take the badge and slip it carefully into my pocket. "Thanks. Remember what I said, now. Watch your six."

Dennis grins and gives me a quick salute. "Adios, hombre."

CHAPTER 46

BILLY KNOX HAD been drinking bourbon at his desk for so long that he'd started talking to the big stuffed razorback standing against the opposite wall. Forrest had planted the spear in that animal's back as deeply as he'd planted the metaphorical one in Billy's. Surely there was a rule against asking a man to betray his own father in order to succeed, or even to survive? But rules meant nothing to Forrest. They never had.

Billy had expected his dad to give him hell when he heard the chopper taking off without being told why, but all Snake had done was walk into the study and ask where the bird was headed. When Billy denied knowing its destination, his father had accepted his answer and disappeared. But Billy had known that couldn't be the end of it.

Sure enough, as he sat staring at the glazed eyes of the hog, the study door opened and Snake stepped into the room wearing a black sweatshirt and weathered Levis. He raised his right hand in greeting, then took a seat across the desk from his son.

"You've made a hell of a dent in that whiskey," Snake said. "Something bothering you?"

"Nah," Billy lied.

A fleeting smile crossed his father's features. "Listen to me, boy. I'm not gonna fill you with a bunch of bullshit. I'm here because we've come to the fork in the river."

Billy stirred from his anesthetized stupor. "What do you mean?"

"No games, son. You know what I'm talking about. We're at the place where some go one way, and the rest go the other. Forrest means to leave all this behind him. And by 'this' I mean 'us.' He wants to go with the moneymen and the power whores in New Orleans and Baton Rouge. He thinks he can step right up into that life and it will be great. And he's gonna tell you that you can do it, too, if he hasn't already."

Billy wished he would simply pass out, so he wouldn't have to lie anymore. He could hardly believe that three days ago he'd been trying to hire Jimmy Buffett for his forty-fourth birthday party. Now he couldn't imagine celebrating anything, except staying out of prison.

"The truth is," Snake went on, "you'd do better in that world than Forrest ever would. Because Forrest has got something in him that you don't."

"What's that?"

"Self-destruction."

Billy blinked and leaned forward. "What are you talking about? Forrest is the most careful guy I know."

"You think that because you don't really know him."

"What? I've known him all my life."

Snake reached out and took a slug straight from the bourbon bottle. "How much do you remember about Granddaddy Elam?"

"Not much. I remember that weird hat he'd wear, like something from pilgrim times. *The Scarlet Letter* or something."

Snake chuckled darkly. "Yeah. He was a lay preacher, and he wore that thing to impress the suckers. God only knows how many offering plates he robbed and children he fucked in that old hat."

Billy blinked in surprise, unsure that he'd heard correctly. "What are you talking about?"

"Nothing but life. The truth of it. And one truth is, when your own daddy fucks you in the ass, you ain't ever the same."

When your own daddy fucks you in the ass . . . ? "Are you saying Uncle Frank was molested by Granddad?"

"Not just Frank. Frank, some of the cousins, God knows how many kids in Elam's various flocks . . . and me, of course."

It was all Billy could do to stop himself from disgorging the liquor he'd drunk. "*You?*"

"Sure. I was there, wasn't I? And I was too little to stop him. That's all old Elam needed, boy." Snake shook his head and sucked his teeth the way Robert Duvall sometimes did in the movies.

As far as Billy was concerned, this was no longer a two-way conversation. His father had the floor. Snake seemed to sense this, because he began to speak without prompting.

"When that kind of shit happens to most people, they either bury it and move on, or it buries them. I've seen it bury people. We had a cousin who killed herself when she was fourteen. But Frank . . . he buried it. Most people never suspected a thing."

"And you?"

Snake waved his hand. "I'm different. I didn't have to bury it. It's like prison, you know?"

Billy's stomach rolled again. He did know, and he didn't want to be reminded.

"That kind of shit's generally gonna happen when you're inside," Snake said, "and if it does, it does. Ain't no different than getting stabbed or having your head stove in, if you look at it right. Except it tends to happen regular until you find yourself some protection. Anyway . . . Frank buried what your granddaddy done and moved on. But it was always part of him. You follow?"

"I guess."

"See, what people sensed in Frank was this burning thing, but cold at the same time, like a cold flame. Some things he did during the war—crazy, heroic things—I knew it was that pain driving him. Even if *he* didn't know . . . *I* did.

"But it's a funny thing, Bill. You can hate the person who does that to you, and yet still become like them. It's like you absorb part of them with their damn spunk—part of their black soul. Especially if you're young."

"Daddy, I don't think I—"

"Oh, you're gonna listen," Snake said. "You've got to hear this. See, when your old man does that to you, the way Elam did us, it can turn you inside out. At some level, you realize that you came into the damned world through that man's dick. Then you find yourself lying under him with a pillow or a sock stuffed in your mouth, screaming while he's shoving it into you. . . . That's about as painful as it gets, in every meaning of the word. That's what taught me the first law of the damned universe."

"Which is?"

"Pain begets pain, boy. If that ain't in the Bible, it ought to be."

Billy looked at the liquor bottle, but when he nearly lost his supper, he focused back on his father. "Daddy, why are you telling me this?"

"I'm trying to save you. And myself. People think I'm crazy, I know that. Hell, I *like* 'em to think that. It makes life easier in a lot of ways. And I may *be* a little crazy. Who ain't? But I'm crazy like a fox, Billy boy. Because I always rein it in before things spin quite out of control. A crop duster don't get to be my age without knowing how to rein it in.

"But Frank . . . he was the opposite. Ninety-nine percent of the time, he was cool as ice. But one time in a hundred, he was gonna jump off the rails and do something so extreme you couldn't believe it."

"Like?"

"Hell, it don't matter now. Things somebody like you couldn't even imagine. My point is, Forrest has that in him, too."

Billy shook his head, not quite believing this.

"You ever notice how he is with women?"

Billy had heard stories, but he motioned for his father to continue.

"Sure, I'll slap a woman around if she gives me attitude," Snake said, "and I like rough pussy. But Forrest is different. He'll really hurt a woman, and worse, he'll enjoy it. Not just physically either. He likes breaking women down."

"He's been with his wife a long time."

"His *second* wife. The first one died. And it's a good thing nobody looked too close at that. But there's two reasons that second wife has lasted. First, he learned some things the last time around. He don't let the demon all the way out with wife number two. But more important, that woman *likes* being broke down. She don't show it, but she does. There's women who love pain, son, and she's one. She's also got the same ambition Forrest does. She likes shopping in Dallas and New York with those trust-fund bitches from New Orleans."

"I don't see where you're going with this, Dad."

"Yeah, you do. Because you think the same way. All

that bullshit sounds exciting to you. You want to fly around with rock stars and gamble in the private rooms in Vegas. But I'm here to tell you, Forrest can't live that life long without blowing it up. It's just his nature."

"Why are you so sure?"

"Because Elam got Forrest, too."

Billy's face felt hot. "What?"

Snake leaned forward, his eyes burning with conviction. "You only missed it because you were born so late. Elam died in '66—right about the time he would have started on you. But not before he got Forrest, and also his big brother, Frank Junior."

Billy still couldn't quite accept this. "Has Forrest ever talked to you about it?"

Snake shook his head with regret. "No. I tried to talk to him a couple of times, but he wouldn't have it. But I know. I've seen it in him, man . . . that same cold fire that was in Frank."

"Then you don't know for sure."

"Yes, I do. Listen close now. I'm only gonna tell this once. Forrest's big brother—Frank Junior—enlisted in the Corps in '64, and he went to Vietnam in '65. I can't tell you how proud Frank was of that boy. Junior was the reincarnation of his daddy, a born soldier. All the news we got from over there was good. The race war had heated up pretty good over here by '64, so we were pretty busy with the Double Eagles. Old Elam came and went like he always did. He was in his sixties, but he was still a rounder and still getting in trouble—sometimes with the law. Brody got him out of the pokey a few times, as a favor to Frank. Kept him out of prison." Snake paused, reflecting silently, then went on.

"In 1966, everything changed. Frank got a visit from a casualty team. Frank Junior had been killed. At a place called the Rockpile."

"I've heard about that."

"Not the real story, you ain't. The government said young Frank had charged straight into machine-gun fire to save four members of his squad. He got hit getting the second guy, but he kept going back out. The fourth time he ran out there, the gun chewed him to pieces. There was talk of a Medal of Honor. In the end they gave him a posthumous Silver Star."

Billy actually had heard all this before.

"You'd think Frank would be able to handle something like that," Snake said, "as much war as he'd seen. But he started drinking, and he didn't stop. He could always hold his liquor, but he was drinking enough to kill most men. Enough to put himself out every night. Then the letter came."

"What letter? About the medal?"

"No. A letter from Frank Junior. He'd mailed it before he died. It had got delayed somehow, but it finally came."

"What did it say?"

Snake sighed and took another pull from Billy's bottle. "Basically, Frank Junior told his daddy that he had no intention of coming back home. Junior was messed up in his head, he said; he always had been, but he'd never had the nerve to talk about it. But once he got to Vietnam, and saw war up close, he just didn't care anymore."

"Because of Granddaddy Elam?"

Snake nodded. "He told Frank that Elam had been messing with him since he was a little boy. The old bastard done everything imaginable to him, and he'd threatened to kill us all if Junior told his mama or daddy about it. And Elam was so damn crazy, that poor boy believed it."

"Jesus, Pop."

"Junior had made up his mind he was gonna push it in battle until he found some peace. He said he was gonna give the gooks all the hurt he could until his own hurt stopped." Snake nodded once. "And that's what he did."

Billy sat blinking in horror, not knowing what to say.

"Something busted in Frank when he read that letter," Snake said. "He blamed himself, see? And I blamed *my*self. Because I was scared as hell the same thing had happened to you."

"It didn't. At least I don't think it did."

"I know. I made it my business to find out."

"How'd you do that?"

Snake dug in his pants pocket and brought out a bent cigarette, which he lit with an old silver lighter. He blew out a long stream of blue smoke, then began speaking softly.

"Elam was preaching in East Texas when that letter

came, but he was due home in a couple of days. I started checking on Frank every few hours, worried he might kill himself or something. But the day Elam was due back, I went over and found my brother a changed man. Frank was sober as a judge. He told me we were gonna talk to Elam. He told me to get a few of the boys together. Glenn, Sonny, a couple more, and have 'em at his house about dark.

"Elam got home about eight. Me and Frank went by his house and went in without knocking. Frank told Daddy we had an operation set up. We was gonna lynch a nigger that night. Well, old Elam was always up for that kind of party, so he came right along.

"We came out here to Valhalla and got in two boats. Then we headed to the Bone Tree. Elam was drinking moonshine from a clear jug. I still remember that, the jug in the moonlight. When we got to the tree, I climbed out with a rope, and Frank got out with a toolbox. Just as we got to the opening in the big tree, Elam stopped drinking long enough to holler, 'Where's the nigger, boys?'" Snake shook his head, a strange smile on his face. "I'll never forget what happened next. Frank finally looked old Elam in the eye, and he said, 'You're the nigger tonight, Daddy.'"

An electric chill raced up Billy's spine. "Jesus Christ . . ."

"Frank knocked the old man down to the ground, then squatted over him and told him about Junior's letter. Elam tried to deny it, but what the hell could he say? Me and Frank had been through the very same thing with him, till we got big enough to push him off."

"What did you do?"

"I didn't have to do much. Frank had gone off the rails, boy. It was like we was back in the Pacific. He told Elam he'd betrayed his family and his vows to God both. And for that, he was gonna get a special punishment. Then he tied Daddy's hands, dragged him inside that hollow tree, and hung him upside down by his feet. After Elam'd been hanging awhile, with his face all red and about to bust, Frank nailed him to the wood in there. He had some ten-penny nails in his toolbox, and he did old Elam just like the Romans done Jesus. Crucified him upside down, you see? He'd seen something like that in a book once. He said that was the only fitting punishment for a preacher who done what Daddy had."

"I saw those bones," Billy said. "The only time I ever went there. You remember? You told me they were some nigger's bones."

"Well, they ain't. After Elam rotted, Frank wired 'em together and put 'em back up so nobody would ever forget what happens to somebody who betrays the group. But I didn't want you knowin' who it was, if I could help it."

"Does Forrest know about this?"

"He knows," Snake said. "Hell, he's been to that Bone Tree more than any of us. But I didn't finish the story. That night, while Daddy was hanging in the tree, we made a fire outside it and sat talking, mostly about Frank Junior, but also about some of the things Elam had done to us as boys. To Mama, of course. Elam hollered till he lost his voice: first threatening us with fire and damnation, then begging for forgiveness. He begged for water, too, but Frank would just throw swamp water on him now and then to keep him awake I stopped going in with him after the first couple of times. Elam died just after dawn."

Billy looked longingly at the bourbon bottle in his father's hand, but he knew he'd had enough.

"The thing is," Snake said, "killing Elam didn't really help Frank get over his boy. He still blamed himself. From 1966 till the day he died in '68, he was drunk. I think they only kept him on at Triton out of pity, because of Junior being a war hero. Dr. Cage even tried to get Frank to take a year off, but he wouldn't listen. Frank was drunk the day that forklift dropped the pallet on him."

"You're sure Elam molested Forrest the way he had Frank Junior?"

Snake nodded. "He confessed it to Frank before he died."

"God*damn*."

"Forrest puts on a good front, Billy, but deep down, he's got that demon in him. And you don't want to hitch yourself to that."

Billy didn't know what to say. He couldn't tell his father what Forrest had said to him earlier. Snake might do something truly crazy. So he just said, "Thanks for protecting me from that, Daddy."

Snake grunted as if in protest. "I wish I could take credit for it. But I can't. It was just dumb luck, like I said. You were lucky being born last."

Billy rubbed his jaw and tried to swallow. His tongue felt like a forty-year-old shag carpet. "You're right about that. And I get what you're saying about not hitching myself to Forrest. Is that what you came in to tell me?"

"Most of it." Snake leaned back in his chair. "But I also need something from you."

Billy nodded warily. "What do you need?"

"Forrest's got us walking blind into the Concordia sheriff's department tomorrow. And for all we know, Walker Dennis has enough evidence to jail us the minute we cross the threshold."

"I hear you."

"We can't go in blind like that. I need an ace up my sleeve. Insurance."

"What do you have in mind?"

Snake sat up again, then flexed his hands like a man about to take control of some machine. "I need to know where Dr. Cage is. I know the Black Team went to get him. That's the only reason that chopper would have lit out of here like that. Don't waste time telling me you don't know where they went, 'cause I know you do."

A lump had risen into Billy's throat. "Did you ask Forrest?"

Snake snorted. "I called him. He said I was better off not knowing."

Billy closed his eyes, wishing he could somehow escape this room. Looking past his father at the speared hog, he empathized with the animal yet again.

"I'm gonna ask you once more," Snake said. "Where's Forrest taking the doc?"

CHAPTER 47

TOM LAY ON the six-foot square bed in the back of Walt's Roadtrek. Forrest Knox had left long ago, and the SWAT helicopter had departed shortly after that, leaving three team members behind to guard him. One was the young medic, and Tom was grateful for that. The kid had done a good job on his shoulder, stabilized his blood sugar level, and relieved his angina with close monitoring of his heart and careful administration of nitroglycerine.

The other two cops had spent their time in the captain's chairs at the front of the vehicle, playing cards over a small dining table. The passenger window had been smashed somehow, and patched with a square of tarp and some duct tape. If Forrest gave the order to kill him, Tom knew, one of those two men would carry it out. That was why they were keeping their distance. Tom had done what he could to bond with the young medic, who had asked him a dozen questions about his trade. But he was under no illusions that this boy would—or could—protect him against the guns or knives of his comrades.

Tom wasn't sure what time it was. Despite his best efforts, he had drifted off several times. Relief from pain tends to do that to you. While awake, he'd thought back to his visit with Caitlin and wondered whether she would keep her promise not to tell Penn about their meeting. At this point he hoped she'd break it. Because if she told Penn about Quentin's house, Penn would go there and find Melba, or her dead body. If she was alive, Penn would get her medical attention, and if not, at least he would come into the open so that Forrest Knox could make contact with him. Tom didn't know whether Penn would agree to any deal with Knox, but he would surely have the sense to *pretend* to make one—until Tom could get himself and Walt out of harm's way.

Tom was trying to think of a way to probe the medic for information when someone knocked on the Roadtrek's side door. All three SWAT cops had their guns out before Tom had fully registered that a newcomer had arrived. The two men up front communicated with hand signals alone. When they were satisfied, one stood just out of the line of fire of the door and called: "Who's there?"

"Snake Knox!" came the reply. "Forrest sent some beer and food for you guys. He says you may be here longer than he first figured."

"Shit," muttered one of the cops, lowering his gun.

He reached out and flipped the door handle, and someone pulled it open from outside. Then a wiry old man wearing jeans, a black sweatshirt, and a John Deere cap climbed the steps into the van. He had white whiskers, but his black eyes darted throughout the van, taking in everything at a glance.

Snake Knox, Tom thought, remembering a much younger man.

"Bring that box, Sonny!" Snake called. "These boys are probably hungry."

Sonny Thornfield followed Snake up the steps, a grease-stained cardboard box in his hands. He was clean-shaven and looked scared. Tom could hardly believe only two days had passed since he and Walt had tortured Thornfield in this vehicle. His pulse began to accelerate.

"What you got there, Snake?" asked the SWAT cop.

"Burgers and chicken. Better than nothing, right?"

"You're damn right." The SWAT cop holstered his pistol and pulled a chicken leg from the box.

The central aisle of the van had filled with men.

"Hey," called the medic from beside Tom, "pass me a hamburger."

Somebody tossed a wrapped sandwich back to the bed.

"You want something, Dr. Cage?" asked the boy.

"No, thanks."

"A burger won't hurt your sugar. You gotta keep your strength up."

"Do I?" Tom asked with frank skepticism. "I hope so."

The medic averted his eyes.

Tom turned his head and sought out Snake Knox among the bobbing heads in the front of the van. He couldn't make out anything but a green cap sandwiched between black ballistic nylon, LSP logos, and Velcro utility straps. The sound of men eating voraciously turned Tom's stomach. He found himself worrying that Snake and his partner would relieve the SWAT cops, leaving him at their mercy. Thanks to Walt, Thornfield knew exactly where the miniature blowtorch was stored in the van. God only knew what kind of revenge he would take on Tom if given the opportunity.

Tom was asking himself whether he'd done the right thing in saving Thornfield from Walt when he heard a man gasp in surprise. Jerking his head to the right, Tom saw the SWAT cops trying to back away from something in the narrow aisle. They had nowhere to go.

"Not one move," somebody said. "Or I blow his goddamn brains out."

"You've lost your fucking mind, old man," said a younger voice.

"I guess we'll see about that. Take their guns, Sonny."

As Thornfield plucked big semiautomatic handguns from black holsters, the medic beside Tom reached slowly for the pistol on his belt.

Tom whispered, "Don't try it. You can't shoot in here without hitting your buddies, and Snake Knox is crazy."

The medic's hand touched the butt of the pistol.

"He'll empty his gun back here," Tom hissed. "He wants me dead anyway, but there's no sense in you dying."

The young cop dropped his hand just as someone jerked the rear doors open from outside the van, and a cold wind rushed through the RV. Tom looked back and saw two men in their seventies training guns into the van. One held a long-barreled revolver, the other a shotgun. Tom was pretty sure he had treated both men in an earlier decade.

"Sorry, boys," Snake said to the SWAT cops. "But if you was earning your money, I'd already be dead. I need you to go outside and lie down on the ground."

"Colonel Knox is going to spread you across Louisiana in pieces," said the biggest of the cops.

Snake laughed. "I wouldn't expect any less. I taught my nephew everything he knows in that line. Now get the fuck out, shitbird."

After the cops filed out of the van's narrow side door, Snake walked down the little aisle and stood looking down at Tom. Looking up into his eyes, Tom saw the wild light he would have expected in the eyes of Quantrill's Raiders, men who'd rebelled against all authority and who in anger and defeat had burned towns and slaughtered women and children.

"Well, Doc," Snake said in a sandpaper voice. "I hear you and your Texas Ranger buddy gave Sonny a rough time in this van the other night." Snake raised a boot and planted it squarely on Tom's chest, then pressed down until Tom gasped for air. "I'm glad to be able to return the favor."

Tom grabbed the heavy boot and tried to pull it off his chest, but he hadn't the strength to even shift it.

Snake grinned beneath the brim of the John Deere cap. "This is how death comes for you, Doc. I never trusted you. No matter what the others said. You liked that nigger nurse way too much. And now it's me that God sends to cut your string. Ain't that something? I can't say I won't enjoy it."

Tom knew Snake Knox would give no quarter. "If there is a God," he gasped from beneath the crushing force of the boot, "I hope there's a hell, too. Because that's where you're bound."

Snake only laughed.

Tom's breath was failing and his mind growing dim. "At least I left something good behind me," he whispered. "My son . . . my daughter. At least I helped some people. All you brought into the world was death and pain . . . and that's all you'll leave behind. It won't be long, either."

The glow in Snake's eyes rose like a stoked furnace. Snake drew a pistol from his pants and aimed the barrel down at Tom's face.

"Snake, don't!" cried a frightened voice from somewhere in the van. "You can't do it! Not yet. Think about Forrest. Think about tomorrow!"

"Fuck him," Snake said. "You know the score. It was always gonna come to this."

I COME OUT OF blackness grabbing for the cell phones on the bedside table, but all are dark. Propped on my elbow, I try to orient myself in time. Only after I switch on my new BlackBerry and read its face do I see that it's two thirty in the morning.

What woke me up, if not a cell phone?

Swinging onto the edge of the bed, I pull on my pants and shoes, then take my .357 from the table and walk onto the landing outside my bedroom.

A quick glance into Annie's room tells me she and my mother are fine, their fragile forms outlined beneath a chenille bedspread. Moving carefully, I descend the narrow staircase with my gun at the ready and alight on the ground floor of the Abrams house. Ambient light from the outside streetlamps leaks through the cracks in the curtains, giving enough illumination to navigate the furniture.

After checking the ground floor, I open the back door and slip into the backyard. The cold night air raises the hair on my skin, but I move steadily around the perimeter of the house, my eyes focused in the darkest parts of the yard. My eyes will pick up movement in the lighter areas; it's the pools of blackness where death may wait. My forefinger twitches against the thin metal curve of the trigger. I'd hate to have to explain firing a .357 Magnum in the middle of town, but better that than the alternative.

After making a full circuit of the house and finding nothing, I return to the front yard and gaze out over the old ninth hole of the Duncan Park golf course, a long, misty slope that falls away from Duncan Avenue, then terminates at the fences where I played Little League baseball as a boy. The sight triggers one of those temporal dislocations I've sometimes experienced since moving back to my hometown. At my back stands a house where I studied for advanced chemistry exams with my high school friends, yet now it's a makeshift safe house that protects my family from men who were killing people while I was learning how to make a double play on the baseball field down the slope. How is it that, decades later, it falls to me to bring those men to justice? Perhaps it's only fitting. This is my town, after all. And its legacy is the one my father and his contemporaries left me and mine: a community crippled by unresolved conflict, anger, and grief.

I wish that I felt equal to the task, but in truth I feel as lost as I've ever been. I began this week by investigating a relatively simple murder. Now I find myself caught in a skein of connections I never knew existed. Through my father's secret actions, and possibly by blood, I am bound to Viola Turner's family, to the Knox family, and through them to the Royal and Marcello families, and their crimes. At the farthest reach of this tangled web may lie the assassination of a president.

Surely I must stand at that hinge point where in novels and films the hero suddenly reexamines his situation and discovers that the answer has been staring him in the face all along. Alas, I feel no looming epiphany. All I possess is a plan for disruption: sow discord among the enemy and pray for a miracle.

Centuries ago, Heraclitus made a famously sweeping assertion: *Character is fate.* Almost without fail, men make choices based on instinct, eternally proving his maxim. As a lawyer I exploited this knowledge to dissect defendants, opponents, and even judges. As a novelist, I use it as a charting compass. But to profit from the principle in my present circumstance—to see where I must go and what I must do—I need to know *my own* character.

And what is character but the sum of our genes and the pressures of human interaction? Our parents are the door through which we enter the world. In coming together they fix our essential natures, but it's after we become self-aware that they begin weaving the narrative that will ultimately shape the people they send into society. If our parents lie to us—not merely by omission, as all do, but by commission—then how can we ever know ourselves?

For most of my life, my father's character seemed a static and transparent thing, a multifaceted diamond whose essential trait was clarity. Then four days ago, that stone cracked along some pre-existing fault and became milky, opaque. It happens. Even fine diamonds contain flaws, inclusions invisible to the naked eye that weaken the whole. But the revelations about Viola Turner were only the beginning. Soon the milky stone had broken in two. As I tried to piece the halves back together, Henry Sexton began tapping at them, fracturing each into still smaller fragments. Then tonight Kaiser and Stone shattered those fragments into jagged shards, each reflecting light in all directions, creating interference patterns I may never be able to penetrate. Even if I do, how can I possibly piece the original stone back together, when I know my memory of it to be flawed?

Only my father can put himself back together. And if he dies before he does that, I will never truly know him. I will never *have* known him. Which means I may never know myself. I'll be a man without a past, and a man without a past is like a nation without a history, or worse, with a myth of one. If the narrative of my life has been woven from lies, then how can I choose my next move? What crimes were my father's lies told to conceal? If Shad Johnson is right, then simple, selfish murder. If Kaiser and Stone are correct, then murder on a historic scale. The latter proposition seems incredible, but the ties binding my father to the Knoxes, to Royal, and even to Marcello and beyond have been established beyond doubt. At least I'm not alone in my ignorance. If murder has haunted my family, it has also haunted my country. From the humblest victims—forgotten black boys vanishing into the night—to the most privileged and high—President Kennedy cut down on national television—these killings and the darkness that enshrouds them deny us the truth about ourselves.

Standing here in the darkness, my best hope may be to heed Carl Jung's admonition: *If you bring forth what is within you, it will save you. If you do not bring forth what is within you, it will destroy you.* Though I am poorly informed and inadequately armed, this now must be my quest, whatever the cost. Men still live who shared the secret paths of my father's hidden history, and the history of this nation. Soon I will face some of them across an interrogation table. And this I know: to learn what *they* know, I will stop at nothing.

The howl of a dog from the shadows makes me whirl toward the house, but I see no sign of the animal. Looking back at the street, I half expect to see Lincoln Turner's white pickup rolling along the pavement, but the scene is almost ghostly in its stillness.

I still don't know what awakened me. Yet as I walk back to the door, I'm gripped by a certainty that something terrible has happened on this night. And since my mother and child are with me—and Caitlin is safe at the *Examiner*—I can only surmise that the object of this jarring premonition is my father.

Locking the door behind me, I realize that sleep will not return soon. I switch on my laptop in the kitchen, check my e-mail and find that the most recent is from John Kaiser. It reads: *If tonight didn't persuade you to hold off on questioning the Double Eagles, then at least you should go into battle prepared. Do your due diligence and read the attached file.*

With bleary eyes, I open the attachment and find a typed letter headed KNOX FAMILY PATHOLOGY. The first subject line reads: *Nathan Bedford Forrest Knox. 1876–1927.* With a long-suffering sigh, I turn on the coffee percolator, then carry my computer to the little banquette, turn down its screen brightness, and begin to read.

FRIDAY

CHAPTER 48
_____

IT WAS NEARING dawn when Walt Garrity finally managed to slip out of the Valhalla hunting lodge, and he only made it then because the humans inside had either left the camp or gone elsewhere on the property. After drumming on his legs to wake them up after hours under the twin bed, he sneaked down the stairs and out the front door, then worked his way through the trees toward the main road, where Drew Elliott's truck waited. In the forest, he'd avoided the same half-dozen game cameras mounted on trees that he'd detected on the way in. The problem was, he'd almost certainly missed at least one. While they probably weren't part of the security system, whoever reviewed the SD cards in those cameras would eventually realize that he had been on the property, and the time stamps would tell them when.

Don't sweat the small stuff, he told himself. _You'll be lucky if you're alive by then._

From Lusahatcha County he drove north up Highway 61 to Natchez, then through it and on into Jefferson County. Quentin Avery's estate lay in the northwestern corner of the county, not too far from Fayette, which had once been the realm of Mayor Charles Evers. Walt tried Tom's burn phone twice on the way, but he got no answer. That in itself wasn't a bad sign; Walt had warned Tom not to leave the device on. But still . . . knowing Tom, he would have expected some additional reassurance after such a long period apart. He prayed that his old friend was laid up in his lawyer's softest bed, swallowing Vicodin with Maker's Mark for a chaser.

Walt had been watching the woods to his right for a

mile when he saw a turn that looked likely. He took it and soon found himself entering a circular drive before an imposing Tudor mansion, which looked almost absurd in the Mississippi backwoods. With a Glock pistol in his hand, he walked to the door and tried the knob.

It turned.

Bad sign. With practiced stealth he moved quickly through the ground-floor rooms, and in half a minute he found himself standing over the body of a black woman at the end of a short hallway.

"Goddamn it," he muttered, recognizing the nurse who had cooked him fish at Drew Elliott's lake house. "Melba Price . . ."

He knelt over the supine form, certain that Nurse Price was dead, but when he touched her arm he felt warmth in her skin, not the marblelike otherness of death. Encouraged, he patted her cheek, then pinched it.

Melba flinched, then began to cough.

"Melba?" he said. "It's Walt Garrity. You're safe now. Can you hear me?"

Her eyes opened, bloodshot and filled with fear.

"It's me, ma'am, Tom's friend."

"Captain Garrity?" the nurse rasped.

"That's right. Do you know where Tom is?"

She shook her head, then gripped at her right breast. "Oh, Lord, it hurts. They shot me, I think."

"Move your hand," Walt told her, noticing something odd on her blouse. As carefully as he could, he tugged at a small bloom of orange and red. As soon as he touched the filaments, he knew he was holding a tranquilizer dart.

"They shot you," he told her, "but not with a bullet. They darted you, like they would a dangerous animal."

She blinked in confusion for several seconds. "I guess I didn't turn out to be very dangerous."

Walt tugged out the dart, and the nurse barely noticed. "Did you see anybody before they got you?" he asked, tossing the dart against the wall.

"A man in black. He had a black mask on, and he was holding a gun. That's all I know. I didn't even have time to shout a warning."

"Sounds like a police SWAT team. And I know there's

one working for the other side. I was pinned down less than fifty yards away from them last night."

Melba carefully raised herself on one elbow. "Tom's not here?" she asked, clearly afraid to hear the answer.

"No. They took him. But since they darted you, I'm hoping they only did the same to him."

"God, I hope I didn't lead them to him."

Walt didn't care what had led Knox's storm troopers here. It had always been a matter of time, and he told Melba as much, not that it made her feel better.

Getting to his feet, Walt helped the nurse up and into the living room. He laid her on a large sofa, then quickly searched the rest of the house, but he found nothing useful.

"I hope they took his medicine," Melba said when he returned to the living room.

"I didn't see any, so I assume they did." *What should I do now?* Walt wondered, fighting the exhaustion that last night's tense hours had caused.

"Have you talked to Caitlin Masters?" Melba asked.

Walt's eyes popped wide open. "Caitlin? What would she know about Tom?"

"She was here last night."

He couldn't believe it. "How did she find this place?"

"She had somebody following me. Tom asked her not to tell anyone where he was, not even Penn."

"I'll bet she didn't. Otherwise Penn would have been here long ago." Walt took out his safest burn phone and called the *Natchez Examiner*. The receptionist told him Caitlin wasn't available. It took some time, but he finally persuaded Caitlin's editor to call her wherever she was and tell her to call the number Walt gave him.

While Walt waited, he got Melba a tall glass of water.

She took a long sip. "What do they mean to do to Dr. Cage, Captain? He seemed to think they wanted him dead."

Walt wanted to reassure her, but he found that his breath wouldn't come. His diaphragm felt paralyzed. After years of thinking of his friend as invincible, he suddenly realized that this time Tom's luck might have run out. "I hate to say it, Melba, but . . . depending on Forrest Knox's plans, Tom could be dead."

Melba covered her eyes with her free hand and shook her head.

"But don't count him out yet," Walt added. "Not till you see him laid flat in a coffin. Tom could talk a fox out of eating a chicken if he put his mind to it. If he can get in front of Knox, face-to-face, then maybe he can talk his way into a deal. I've been in some pretty tight spots with him, and we always found a way out."

"He's old and tired now, though, Captain. Bone tired. I saw it in his eyes."

Walt gave her a fierce grin. "He's no older than I am, girl. We still got some kick left in us." He squeezed Melba's hand. "You watch and see."

Walt jumped when his burn phone rang, but it was only Caitlin calling him back.

"Tell me it's not bad news," she said.

"It's not the worst," Walt said. "Not yet, anyway. But I'm where you were last night, and our mutual friend is missing."

"Oh, God. What about Melba?"

"She's here. Hurt, but not permanently. It sounds to me like a SWAT team took Tom, but I've heard nothing about any arrest. What about you?"

"No. Oh, Walt . . . this was my worst nightmare."

"I'll bet it was."

"Real cops would have arrested Melba, too, wouldn't they?"

"That's affirmative."

"Jesus. Have you spoken to Penn yet?"

"Not yet."

"Walt, please . . . don't tell Penn I was there last night. I haven't told him, and if he finds out I kept that from him, he'll never forgive me. Never. It was a hard decision, but Tom made me promise not to tell Penn anything."

"I won't tell him you were here, if I can avoid it."

"God, thank you. What are you going to do now?"

"I'm not sure. I've got a line on Forrest's location, so I'll probably go to where he is. If Tom is still alive, he may be with or near that bastard. Where are you now?"

"Almost down to the Lusahatcha Swamp. John Kaiser's wife is with me, but Kaiser doesn't know that. I don't want

Penn to know, either, unless you're forced to tell him I'm down here."

"Got it. But what are you looking for? I was just down there myself. You don't need to go anywhere near that Valhalla camp."

"I'm not. But I am following a story. Are the Knoxes at their hunting camp?"

"They were last night. Some have left, but others could still be there. Don't go near that place. And wherever you go, keep your eyes wide open and one hand on your gun."

"Walt, I feel so guilty about Tom. Do you think I should turn around? Is there anything I can do to help the situation?"

"Not really. But if you want to be safe, you'll turn around. I know you better than that, though."

"Guilty as charged, I'm afraid."

Walt's mind moved to an obvious but unpleasant reality. "As soon as I get Melba squared away, I'm going after Forrest. If you or Penn don't hear from me in"—Walt glanced at his watch—"four hours, assume Knox got me. In that case, tell Penn I said to cut his losses and take care of his family."

"Walt, wait—"

"I mean it, darling. We're up against it, now. Don't take stupid risks. And don't trust anybody."

"I won't. Call me if you hear anything important. They tell me cellular reception is crap down here, but try anyway."

Walt said he would, then hung up.

Melba was watching him like someone afraid to hope for even small mercies. He felt a desperate compulsion to race out to his truck, but somehow he suppressed it.

"Caitlin doesn't know anything about Tom," he said. "Now, tell me the truth, have you got the strength to drive back to Natchez? Or do I need to drive you myself?"

"Aren't the police still looking for you, too?"

"They are. But I've got no choice."

"I can get myself back. Where is that Forrest Knox?"

"A GPS tracker I've got tells me he's on the shore of Lake Concordia in Louisiana, fifteen miles from Natchez.

Probably at a lake house like the one we were hiding in on Lake St. John."

"You think he's holding Tom prisoner there?"

"I hope he is. Because the alternatives are too depressing to think about."

Melba nodded. "Whatever you find out, I want you to call me. Good or bad, I have to know. All right?"

Walt squeezed her shoulder. "I know. Now, get your things together. Every minute counts now."

Melba stood, but instead of moving, she looked hard into Walt's eyes. "What will you do if you find they have Dr. Cage prisoner over there? Can you call the police? Or the FBI?"

Walt debated whether to answer honestly. In the end he decided the nurse wanted the truth. "It's the police who have Tom, Melba. If I find them, and they're holding him . . . I'm gonna kill 'em."

The nurse stared at him in silence for several seconds. Then she said, "I'll be praying for you, Captain. God help me, but I think that's the only way now."

Then she turned and went to gather her things.

CHAPTER 49

THE TRIP FROM Natchez to the Lusahatcha Swamp took only an hour, yet it had already proved an adventure, not only for Caitlin, but also for Jordan Glass. John Kaiser had insisted on having an FBI agent drive his wife to the New Orleans airport. Jordan had resisted so strongly that they'd fought over it, and ultimately Kaiser had agreed to let her go on her own. But soon after leaving her hotel that morning, Jordan had noticed an FBI tail behind her, with two agents in the car. At that point she'd called Caitlin and asked for an address that had a back driveway out. After a couple of minutes' thought, Caitlin told her about an antebellum home that butted up against a 1950s-era neighborhood. Armed with this information, Jordan had driven into the place as though for a visit, pulled around the mansion as if to park, then zipped down a narrow lane that cut through to the residential neighborhood. The agents tailing her didn't figure out her scheme until after Jordan texted her husband that if she was capable of flying to Cuba and meeting the Castro brothers on her own, she could damn well drive herself to the airport. After picking up Caitlin from a street corner two blocks away from the *Examiner*, Jordan had started south on Highway 61 at the speed limit, confident that her tail was frantically driving south ahead of her, trying to "catch up" to its quarry.

Caitlin spent the first twenty-five miles giving Jordan a detailed history of the Bone Tree, describing the part it had played in the history of the Double Eagle group and recounting Henry's abortive attempts to find it. Jordan had smiled upon learning that Caitlin had kept the secret of poacher Toby Rambin to herself. When Caitlin paused her narrative, Jordan almost tentatively asked exactly what she hoped to find at the Bone Tree. By this time they were far enough from Natchez that Caitlin decided to trust her new friend with the crown jewels.

"It's not just the bones anymore," she said. "Not just the civil rights cold cases. I mean, that's a huge part of it, absolutely. But after Henry died, his mother brought me some other material she found. And some of that had to do with what John and Dwight are working on."

"You mean the Kennedy assassination?"

Caitlin nodded.

"Can you tell me about it?"

For the next five miles, they traded the information they'd gleaned from their respective sources, which merged to form a compelling scenario in which Carlos Marcello had hired Frank Knox to serve as a primary or backup shooter in Dealey Plaza on the day Kennedy died.

"But what does that have to do with the Bone Tree?" Jordan asked.

"Glenn Morehouse told Henry that Frank Knox didn't trust Marcello. Knox supposedly kept some souvenir from Dallas, a document or trophy of some kind, and that totally fits with the Knoxes' psychology. This artifact was something Frank must have felt he could use against Marcello if he ever needed to, so it protected him."

"Do you have any idea what it was?"

"Snake Knox told Morehouse that it was a letter or document of some kind. But the crazy part is . . . it was in Russian."

Jordan's eyes went wide. "Russian!"

Caitlin nodded, her pulse picking up. "Last night I read everything I could find about the assassination, and Russia can only come into it two ways. First, if Russia or the KGB played some part in the killing. But I totally discount that as fantasy. The second way is through Oswald."

Jordan simply waited for her to continue.

"Lee Harvey Oswald lived in Russia for two and a half years after he defected. He'd taught himself the language, and at least some letters that he wrote—like those to his Russian wife—he wrote in Russian. You can see them on the Internet."

Jordan remained silent, processing what she'd heard. "But how could a letter or document stay hidden in a tree for forty years?"

Caitlin shrugged. "No idea. The best I can come up with is something like a mason jar."

"No. Water always finds a way in. I once hid some pot in a mason jar and buried it. One month later, the jar was half full of water."

"Well . . . within a few hours, we may know the answer. I wanted you to know that we're not just out here looking for Jimmy Revels's bones, as awesome as it would be to find them. We may actually find the key that Dwight spent half his life searching for. We might even find proof that Frank Knox killed John Kennedy."

Jordan drove in silence for several seconds. Then she said, "I know that cost you. You don't really know me well." Glass looked to her right. "I won't tell John about it. I promise you that."

Caitlin felt a rush of gratitude and relief. "Thank you."

Soon after this, they left Highway 61. Following a map Caitlin had printed from Google Earth, they turned west toward the Mississippi River on MS 24, a narrow asphalt lane barely wide enough for two cars. Then they turned south on something called Lusawatta Road, which turned out to be a neglected gravel lane worn down to red clay. After leaving that, they found themselves on a dirt track hemmed in by trees and undergrowth. They still had not seen water, but Caitlin sensed the swamp was near. Ever since leaving Highway 61, they'd been going downhill, and the oak, elm, and pecan trees had gradually given way to cottonwood and cypress. Caitlin had rarely experienced a more startling transformation of landscape than she had during the last few miles.

Despite the winter month, many of the trees in this area were still choked with kudzu and other undergrowth, and now and then a rusted truck or tractor would peek out of the foliage like some sentient observer. The most surreal moment of their journey had come when ten- or eleven-foot wire fences had risen out of the grass on both sides of the road, giving them the feeling they were traveling through a prison compound. Soon after, they'd begun to spy strange animals through the wire. Caitlin had seen moose, antelope, buffalo, and other creatures that looked only vaguely familiar. With her African work experience, Jordan had recognized several as oryx, springbok, gemsbok, and impala, but other species left even her stumped. Caitlin was reminded of a story she'd read as a child—Jules Verne, perhaps—in which the farther the heroes traveled upstream on a certain river, the deeper back in time they progressed. This trip felt exactly like that.

At least it had until Walt called her. When Caitlin heard that Tom had probably been kidnapped, a black dread had begun to ooze from someplace within her. What she felt was guilt—guilt that she'd known where Tom was but had kept it to herself, and away from Penn. Last night, after they'd made love at Edelweiss, Penn had sensed that she was holding something back, and she'd denied it. If Tom died now, and Penn discovered that she might have prevented it . . . he would never forgive her.

She might never forgive herself.

"Look!" Jordan cried, pointing out the windshield. She hit the brakes and moved slowly into a dirt turnaround. Forty feet from the car, greenish-black water lay across the ground, and farther on, it led back into a forest of cypress knees and overhanging branches.

They had found the swamp.

Caitlin had Jordan drive almost to the water's edge and park. This was the place Toby Rambin had described to her. A rusted old school bus that had once been yellow protruded from the trees to her right. Dying kudzu vines lay across the bus like strangling ropes. Caitlin reached into her bag and pulled out the red bandanna that Rambin had requested she wear.

"Where's our poacher?" Jordan asked, climbing out of the car.

Caitlin shrugged and tied the bandanna around her neck. Then she got out, her mind still on Walt's terrible revelation. The sulfurous stink of the swamp struck her with surprising force, filling her nose and lungs. She hadn't expected that noxious fume in the chilly weather, but then, she had no experience of swamps. Jordan, on the other hand, was scanning the clearing like a professional surveyor.

"He was supposed to be here fifteen minutes ago," Caitlin said.

"I've been in this situation a hundred times," Jordan

said. "I set up a guide to take me into a war zone, and he shows up four hours late, if at all."

"Let's hope this isn't a war zone," Caitlin said, half under her breath.

Jordan peered into the shadows under the distant trees. "After all you told me about the Bone Tree, this feels like some kind of elephant graveyard thing."

"After what we saw on the way in, an elephant wouldn't surprise me."

"Wait." Jordan cocked her head and held up her hand. "Do you hear that?"

Caitlin listened hard, but she heard only birds and frogs. "What is it?"

"Motorcycle. Was Rambin coming on a motorcycle?"

"I don't see how. He's supposed to bring a boat."

Jordan reached into the car and brought out a 9 mm pistol.

Caitlin could hear the motorcycle now. It was definitely coming toward them, probably on the same road they'd traveled. The whining engine rose and fell like a chain saw cutting up a fallen tree, but soon the whine became constant and steadily ascended the scale. Then suddenly the cycle flashed out of the trees and skidded to a stop beside their vehicle.

The rider wore a silver helmet, but he took it off immediately, revealing the face of a black boy who looked no older than fifteen. He jumped when he saw Jordan's pistol, but then he settled down, as though accustomed to being around handguns.

"Which one of you's *Masters*?" he asked, his eyes curious.

"I am," Caitlin said, stepping up to him. "How do you know my name?"

"Toby sent me."

Caitlin cut her eyes at Jordan. "Toby who?"

"Toby *Rambin*. Old Toby."

"Where's Toby himself?" Caitlin asked.

"He had to leave town." The boy smiled. "In a hurry."

Jordan looked at Caitlin as if to say, *Didn't I tell you?*

"What are you doing here, then?" Caitlin asked.

The boy surveyed her from head to toe without shame. He seemed to like what he saw. "Toby told me I should bring you something."

Jordan walked up to the boy. "Hand it over, then."

The boy shook his head, his eyes on her pistol. "Hold up, now. Toby said you gotta pay first."

"How much?" Caitlin asked.

"Toby say a thousand."

"*Shit*," Jordan scoffed. "In your dreams. What are you selling?"

"Map," said the boy. "Toby drawed you a map. He say what you lookin' for be marked with an X. All you need is a boat to find it."

Caitlin and Jordan shared a look.

"I was going to pay him four times that to guide me to the tree," Caitlin admitted. "But this is way short of that."

"A thousand bucks for a hand-drawn map?" Jordan asked.

The boy shrugged. "That's what Toby said. He said if you don't pay, I should ride back to town and forget about all of it."

Caitlin took the fat bank envelope from her back pocket and stared at it. Inside were forty hundred-dollar bills. The money meant nothing to her.

"Wait," Jordan said. "You have no way of knowing whether the map is real, even if he gives you one."

"What choice do I have?"

"That's right," the boy said. "You gots to pay to play, right?"

"*Not always*," said a much deeper voice from somewhere out of sight.

Jordan brought up her pistol with lightning speed, but neither she nor Caitlin saw a potential target. The boy's eyes had gone saucer wide, and he started to bolt, but the voice stopped him where he stood.

"*Dontae Edwards, this is Deputy Carl Sims. If you try to run on that bike, I'll call your mama and have you in jail by noon. Now get off that thing and get the map out of your jacket, if there is one. And you put down that weapon, ma'am.*"

Caitlin nodded with excitement. "Carl's a friend! A good friend. I called him last night to check out Toby. I forgot to tell you."

Jordan reluctantly laid the pistol on the car's front seat.

"*Get off the bike, Dontae!*" shouted the voice.

The boy shook his head, then got off the motorcycle and set its kickstand.

Caitlin turned toward the sound of rustling undergrowth and saw a handsome young black man in a brown uniform step from behind the overgrown school bus. He looked about twenty-five, and he grinned and waved at them to reassure them he was no threat.

"Carl!" she cried, running forward. "What are you doing here?"

Sims smiled and hugged her. "Did you really think I'd let you meet some damned poacher down here without checking to be sure you were okay?"

A frightening thought hit Caitlin. "You didn't call Penn, did you?"

"No, though I probably should have. I did just like you asked and quietly checked out Toby Rambin. But Toby's not exactly a sterling character. I figured I'd better make sure this little deal went through as planned. And it obviously didn't."

Jordan offered her hand to Carl, who shook it with a smile.

"This is Jordan Glass," Caitlin said. "She's a big-time photographer."

Carl's smile spread into a grin. "Oh, I know the name. Proud to meet you," he said, shaking her hand again. "You were in Fallujah for a week when I was there."

"Army?" Jordan asked.

"Marine sniper."

Jordan smiled and stood easy. "How about we take a look at this alleged map? I'm starting to feel like I'm stuck in *Treasure Island*."

Carl held out his hand, and Dontae Edwards finally pulled a folded piece of paper from his inside jacket pocket. He handed it to Carl, who unfolded it. The map looked as if it had been drawn on a paper towel taken from a dispenser in a public restroom.

"Looks real to me," Carl said, studying curving lines that made Caitlin think of a child drawing with a crayon. "This area here looks like the Valhalla hunting camp, and over here is the federal wildlife refuge. Toby's got one of the game fences marked here, about in the middle. And where this X is, is a deep stand of cypress. It's one of the thickest parts of the swamp and covered with water most all year round."

Caitlin nodded excitely. "That sounds like what we're looking for."

Carl gave her a penetrating look. "I did what we talked about last night, but I didn't learn much. Nothing that would confirm a location."

On the phone last night, Carl had offered to have his father, a local pastor, discreetly question some members of his Athens Point congregation about the Bone Tree. Since the church was 100 percent African-American, Caitlin had felt it was worth the risk to gain good information. But apparently Reverend Sims had learned little.

Jordan poked her thumb at Dontae Edwards, who was paying close attention to their conversation.

"Scoot!" Carl ordered. "And forget you ever saw this map, or you'll be hauling ass out of town like Toby did. Only you haven't got the money to do it."

The boy jumped back on the motorcycle and kick-started it, but Caitlin yelled "Wait!" before he pulled on his helmet. As he watched impatiently, she took five one-hundred-dollar bills from the envelope and handed them over. A grin spread across the boy's face. He waited a half second, then snatched the bills, stuffed them into his jacket, and tore out of the clearing with a scream of his engine.

"So what now?" Jordan asked. "We don't have a boat."

Carl smiled, his white teeth gleaming in his coffee-colored face. "I think I can probably do something about that."

"Such as?"

"My man Danny McDavitt is doing a check-ride in the LCSO chopper this morning. He could pick us up and have a look for Toby's X for you."

Caitlin blinked in disbelief. Danny McDavitt was a retired air force pilot who flew the helicopter for the Lusahatcha County Sheriff's Department. She'd met him two months ago, when the pilot had assisted Penn in fighting against the criminals operating the *Magnolia Queen* casino. McDavitt had gone far beyond the call of duty to try to locate Caitlin after she'd been kidnapped by those men. "Carl, are you serious?" she asked. "Would he help us today?"

"Sure. Just let me call him."

"You wouldn't have to tell Major McDavitt anything about what we're looking for, would you? I trust him, but this is a special case of secrecy. Not even Penn knows I'm here."

Carl nodded thoughtfully. "I can play it off like I don't know myself."

"Can you trust the major to keep quiet about the search? At least for a few hours?"

The deputy smiled. "Danny's good people. You know that. He can keep a secret."

Caitlin was sorely tempted, but the prospect of complications worried her. "But what if we *find* the Bone Tree?"

"Well . . . at that point it's going to become a law enforcement matter one way or another, isn't it?"

"Yes. But I'd like at least an hour there before we call anyone else in. And we'll have to call the FBI, even if we call your sheriff as well. Would that put your job at risk?"

"That I don't know. For now, we'll chalk this flight up to hunting for marijuana fields. If we find that tree . . . maybe Danny and I will scoot and leave you two to report it."

Caitlin's pulse raced in anticipation of the hunt, but she also felt conflicted. If Tom's life was at risk, what was the point of searching the swamp for a tree? On the other hand . . . what could she really do to help find Tom? Walt had already told her she could do nothing. While Carl spoke to Danny, Caitlin tried to call Walt back, but her phone wouldn't work. When she checked the screen, it said NO SERVICE.

"Danny's coming," Carl said, drawing Caitlin's attention away from her Treo.

"I can't get a tower," Caitlin said. "Do you have AT&T or Cellular South?"

Carl grinned and tapped the radio on his collar. "Neither. I've got the Lusahatcha County Sheriff's Department radio net. I used a channel nobody monitors."

Caitlin's face fell.

"Sorry," Carl said. "Reception in this swamp is practically nonexistent. You need to make a call?"

She shrugged. "I don't feel good about taking off on

this little jaunt if I can't monitor the situation back home. Penn's father . . ."

The deputy's smile vanished. "I know. When we get to altitude, your phone will find a tower. Danny can make sure of it."

Jordan walked over and took Caitlin's hand. "It's your call. We can keep going, or you can head back to town and I'll go on to New Orleans."

Caitlin looked into the cypress trees and pressed down all guilt and doubt. "Screw it," she said. "Let's go."

FORREST KNOX SAT ON the elevated deck of a five-thousand-square-foot lake house overlooking Lake Concordia, a steaming cup of chicory coffee and a cordless phone on the table before him. Five miles away lay the Concordia Parish courthouse complex, which held the sheriff's office and the jail, where Penn Cage and Sheriff Walker Dennis planned to interrogate Snake, Sonny, and four other Double Eagles. As soon as the Eagles left Valhalla this morning, Billy had gratefully abandoned his babysitting job and flown himself back to his retreat at Toledo Bend, Texas. Forrest didn't want to take any chances on someone arresting his cousin. Only after Sheriff Walker Dennis had been removed from his position and the state police had taken over his duties would Forrest tell Billy to return to Mississippi.

Forrest had sent no attorney to the CPSO. He wanted it to look as though the former Double Eagles meant to cooperate fully, right up until the moment Sheriff Dennis was arrested by one of his own deputies. As soon as that was accomplished, Forrest would make contact with Penn Cage and find out whether or not there was a deal to be made. Now that he had the ultimate bargaining tool in his back pocket—in the form of Tom Cage—the son would have no option but to negotiate. Whether such negotiating would result in a deal remained an open question, since Forrest's real worry wasn't the mayor, but Cage's goddamned fiancée.

He owed his knowledge of Mayor Cage's whereabouts to Sheriff Billy Byrd, who had assigned one of his deputies to follow Kirk Boisseau, the former marine who'd accompanied Penn when he confronted Brody Royal at the hospital on Wednesday night. At 6 A.M. that deputy had followed Boisseau to a house that turned out to be owned by the parents of an old schoolmate of Cage's. Boisseau and Cage had walked one circuit of the house, then had gone inside for five minutes, after which Boisseau returned home. A half hour later, binocular surveillance had revealed the mayor's mother as she'd briefly parted the curtains to look outside. Thankfully, rather than storming the house in search of Tom Cage, who he believed was hiding there, Sheriff Byrd had called Forrest about his discovery. He claimed to have done this out of a sense of obligation to a fellow officer who'd had one of his men murdered in the line of duty by Dr. Cage. Nevertheless, it had taken some creative manipulation for Forrest to persuade Byrd that no immediate action should be taken against that house. Forrest, of course, knew that Tom was currently on ice at the Royal Oil field near Monterey, Louisiana. But he couldn't tell Billy Byrd that. Instead, he'd told the hyped-up sheriff that two plainclothes police officers had checked the Abrams house with infrared technology and determined that it contained only an adult woman and a juvenile female. This, and a promise to keep Byrd updated hourly, had proved sufficient to forestall a SWAT assault.

Forrest looked down at the wrought-iron patio table, where a copy of the *Natchez Examiner* lay open. While yesterday's sensational stories had made no mention of him, today's main article had reported that Colonel Griffith Mackiever was under fire for child pornography allegations and quoted an unnamed "FBI source" who claimed that Mackiever's second-in-command might be behind those charges. A side article by Caitlin Masters suggested that dirty politics lay at the root of this scandal, and Masters had taken great pains to point out the connections between Forrest and his extended family, nearly all of whom had been members of the Ku Klux Klan, and some even suspected Double Eagles. Forrest had a feeling that Masters's FBI source was John Kaiser, the same agent who had drained the Jericho Hole. He was starting to think he'd been behind the curve where that particular FBI agent was concerned. He needed a line into Kaiser's plans, and he had a good idea how to get one.

As his coffee went cold, Forrest began to feel a little anxious. He'd expected the call informing him of Sheriff Dennis's arrest by seven A.M., and it was ten past now. The deputy in charge of the bust hadn't checked in since before six. Forrest took out his cell phone and speed-dialed the moron.

"Hunt here," said a country-ass voice.

"You know who this is?"

"Yes, sir!"

"What's the holdup?"

"The sheriff's still in his house, Colonel. He's usually in his office by now, and already drunk his morning coffee. I don't know *what* the holdup is. You want me to just knock on his door with the K-9?" Deputy Hunt asked. "I could tell him we got an anonymous tip?"

Forrest looked at his watch. "No, hell no. Maybe his wife decided to give it up this morning. Give him ten more minutes."

"Yes, sir."

"Where are you parked? Can he see you?"

"I'm down the street in a friend's SUV. No markings. Sheriff won't recognize it."

"And you have backup?"

"Yes, sir. Parker and McGown. They're out of sight, too."

"Okay. The questioning's going to start pretty soon over at the department, so ten minutes is the limit. If he's not outside by then, bust him right in front of his family."

Hunt made a noise that sounded like a gulp.

"Are you up for this job, Deputy?"

"Yes, sir. No problem."

"All right, then. If you see anything suspicious, call me. Otherwise, follow orders. Out."

Forrest hung up and looked out over the narrow lake. A glittering gold bass boat arrowed along the opposite shore, trailing a silver wake that rolled gently into the cypresses. He sipped his coffee, then held his hand high in greeting.

Across the lake, the fisherman waved back.

CHAPTER 50

"PENN? PENN, WAKE UP."

My mother's face materializes above mine, only inches away. It takes a few moments for reality to assert itself, and longer for my sense of time to reengage. Then I glance at my watch, and a rush of adrenaline blasts through me.

"It's nearly seven! Did you oversleep?" I sit up in the bed, unintentionally giving my mother an accusatory look.

"No," she says purposefully.

Of course she didn't. She's fully dressed, and I can smell coffee and bacon all the way from the first-floor kitchen. Undoubtedly Annie is down there eating breakfast. "Then why didn't you wake me earlier?"

Mom sits beside me on the bed, her brow knit with worry. "Are you sure you need to go question the Knoxes? You said there would be other law enforcement people there. The FBI even. Do they really need you?"

"Sheriff Dennis wants me there. I told you last night I needed to do this."

"I know you did. But I have a bad feeling about it. I don't usually pay attention to that kind of thing—women's intuition and all that. But today is different. That Knox family is bad news. We lived fifty miles away from Ferriday and never left the farm, but our men knew about Elam Knox. They kept their daughters home when he came around with his ratty old revival tent. And the apples apparently didn't fall far from the tree."

While she was speaking, my mind slipped back to the hotel room with Dwight Stone and Kaiser, and their surreal narrative played behind my eyes like a black-and-white sequel to *JFK*. At this point, there's nothing Mom could say that would stop me from keeping my appointment at the Concordia Parish Sheriff's Office.

"Mom, I have to go. It's that simple, and it's my best shot at helping Dad. Now, what do you think about sending Annie back to school?"

"It's a terrible idea. We're fine right here."

"Are you sure it's not too much? I can have patrol cars watch the school. Chief Logan will do that for me."

Mom actually snorts at this idea. "She's not half the trouble you were. She's staying right here."

"All right. But I'm going to have Kirk Boisseau come over and sit with you."

"Kirk Boisseau? Why not one of those policemen your father treated?"

"We need a different skill set than that. Kirk was a recon marine. He can handle real trouble."

Mom sighs as though this is unnecessary, but she doesn't argue further.

As I power up my burn phone, a text pings through. It's from Sheriff Dennis, and it reads: *I left a present at your house. OOOO. I dropped the keys through the mail slot. See you at seven.*

"The keys?" I murmur. Then it hits me: the four *O*'s in his text are meant to be the Audi rings. "Walker found my S4!"

"What?" asks Mom, looking worried. "Who found what?"

"I think Sheriff Dennis found my car."

"Oh. I thought that was something about your father."

I shake my head. "Wherever Dad's hiding, he's doing a good job."

Her eyes betray both anxiety and satisfaction.

"Tell Annie I'll be down in one minute."

Whipping the sheet off the bed, I wrap it around me and hurry into the bathroom. There's no time for a shower. Unless Walker Dennis ran into a problem I don't know about, sometime during the last hour he busted the senior surviving members of the Double Eagle group on meth trafficking charges. And if he did, then everybody who thought the shit hit the fan yesterday is going to have their mind blown today.

CHAPTER 51

"HELICOPTER," SAID JORDAN Glass, cocking her ear. "Sounds like a JetRanger."

Caitlin spun around, scanning the tops of the cypress trees. She saw nothing but looming clouds in the gray morning sky, but Carl Sims was clearly impressed by this deduction, staring at Jordan with a mixture of curiosity and admiration.

Caitlin heard nothing at first. Then she caught the whup-whup-whup of rotor blades slicing the air. The sound grew steadily louder, and suddenly the engine was roaring and the chopper came in over the tree line, pointed straight at them.

"Is that Danny McDavitt?" she asked.

"Who else?" Carl pulled the women toward his truck as the JetRanger flared and settled into the dirt clearing in a roaring cloud of dust.

Caitlin instinctively looked at Jordan for guidance, but the photographer was already running in a crouch toward the helicopter. She obviously knew that the most comfortable place in relation to a chopper was inside the machine, not out of it.

Once Carl shut Caitlin inside and she put on the headset Danny McDavitt handed her, the noise dropped considerably. Danny was a handsome man with a craggy face, close-cropped steel-gray hair, and kind eyes that missed nothing. He was basically a more rugged version of John Kaiser. Pulling off her headset, Caitlin motioned for Jordan to do the same, then gave her a sanitized version of their pilot's personal history, taking care to leave out a few details that had become the feast of local gossips some time ago. She described Danny as a retired air force major—and decorated veteran of Afghanistan—who'd married the widow of a local physician. Jordan looked as

if she wanted to ask for more details, but Carl was signaling that they should put their headsets back on.

"I appreciate you helping us out, Major," Caitlin said
into her headset.

"All we're doing is a little marijuana-crop seces-
sary." Danny said with a wink in his voice. "No thanks."

"Can we set down and pick someplace find any?"
Jordan asked.

Carl Sims laughed, then leaned between them. Satis-
double-checked that both women were still
fied, he nodded to McDavitt, who eased forward on the
collective and lifted the bird into the air.

Long shafts of sunlight streamed down through breaks
high in the clouds, but there was a gray wall to the east.

"Do you think it's going to rain?" Caitlin asked.

"In an hour or two," Danny said. "If you go into the
swamp today, you're going to get wet."

Carl handed Danny the map and pointed at it, probably at the X, Caitlin figured. Danny nodded and banked
to the west. Caitlin saw patches of grassy land between
the cypresses below, and spooked game ran everywhere.
At least thirty deer burst from cover as they roared over
a dense thicket, followed by enormous black animals that
looked like giant hogs.

"They hunt those damn pigs from horses at Valhalla,"
said Carl. "With *spears*. Some of 'em weigh eight hundred
pounds."

Caitlin was going ask Carl about Valhalla, which she'd
read about in Henry Sexton's notebooks, but Danny said,
"Carl's just jealous. The farmers around here pay him to
shoot those hogs at night with his sniper rifle, to keep
them from eating their crops. Every one a hunter gets is
less money in his pocket."

"True enough," Carl admitted.

"Hey, look!" Jordan cried, pointing down at a wide
circle of water.

Caitlin saw an old man in a green johnboat staring up
at them with what appeared to be shock and even fear on
his face.

"What's he doing?" Jordan asked.

Carl laughed. "That's Mose Tyler. He's a local fisherman. A little like your man Toby Rambin. I think we surprised Mose setting out a treble-hook trotline, which is illegal in these waters. He probably thinks we're game and fish wardens. He doesn't see so good anymore."

Danny ascended a hundred feet and left the fisherman in peace. Caitlin was about to ask Carl about Valhalla—and the Knox family—when Carl said, "I asked my daddy about that story you told me last night. About a black woman from Athens Point who got raped out in the swamp. He'd heard a little about it, but he knew another preacher who knew the details."

"What's this about?" Jordan asked. "You didn't tell me this, did you?"

Caitlin shook her head.

"A brother from down here married a colored girl from Chicago back in the early sixties," Carl said. "She was real light-skinned—so light that some folks around here thought she *was* white. Well, for a while it wasn't nothing but dirty looks and such. But in 1963, the Klan took notice. One night they kidnapped the couple from their house. They blindfolded them and put them in boats and took them out to this cypress that the old-timers call the Bone Tree."

Caitlin felt as though her body temperature had dropped twenty degrees. Why had Carl mentioned the Bone Tree? Was he simply passing on a shocking story that his father had learned last night, confident that McDavitt wouldn't suspect any connection to their present search? Or had Carl already told the pilot what they were really after?

"They tied the husband to the tree and started beating him with bean poles," Carl went on. "They beat him bad, and while it was going on they started hollering things. Well, the wife finally figured out they were beating her man for marrying a white woman! She started yelling that they were making a mistake, but the Klan boys wouldn't listen. Finally she's trying to tear them off her husband, screaming, 'He ain't done nothing wrong! I'm a nigger, too! I'm a nigger, too!'"

"Jesus," Jordan breathed. "That really happened?"

"Not five miles from where we are, if this map is right. And after they tired of beating the husband, they raped the wife. All of 'em. The husband ended up dying. And believe it or not, they dumped the woman on the road. They'd beat her too, and she had no idea where she'd been. And of course the sheriff at that time had no interest in pursuing that crime. Since it turned out that the woman was black, the law didn't even see it as a crime. Not the unwritten law, anyway, which was the only one that mattered back then."

Caitlin suddenly felt dislocated from her surroundings. "Does your father know where we can find this woman?"

Carl's helmet shook back and forth. "I don't think he'll tell you."

"Why not?"

"The woman's pastor says she has no idea who attacked her, and more important, no idea where that tree was."

"Caitlin?" Jordan asked over the headset. "Are you okay?"

"I'm sorry if I was too coarse," Carl said. "I forgot about . . . well . . ."

Caitlin held up her hand to reassure the deputy, but she knew the gesture wouldn't help Carl. Deputy Sims had been guarding her when she was kidnapped only months ago. And though Caitlin hadn't been raped herself, she had been forced to listen while a woman separated from her by only a thin partition had been repeatedly violated.

Caitlin took out her Treo. It showed one bar. She'd received eight text messages since leaving Natchez, but all were from employees of the *Examiner*. None from Walt Garrity, and none from Penn, either. A wave of guilt made her face flush. Should she try to call him? If she did, what could she say? That last night she'd had the power to send Penn to his father's side, but now it was too late and Tom might well be dead. *No* . . .

Looking across the chopper's deck, she saw Jordan studying her with deep concern. The photographer's eyebrows went up in a silent question: *Are you okay?*

Caitlin shoved the Treo back into her pocket and looked out the chopper's window again. There was a lot more water than earth beneath them now, and McDavitt seemed to have slowed their forward speed quite a bit. After a few seconds, Caitlin realized he was following a game fence that zigzagged between the trees. Somewhere not far away, she realized, stood the tree where Jimmy Revels and numberless others had died, where a woman she did not know had watched her husband beaten to death, and where Frank Knox might have hidden the key to the assassination of a president.

The Bone Tree.

EXCHANGING THE MUSTY OLD city sedan for my Audi S4 was like climbing into a speedboat after poling a raft for two days. As I drove west toward the Mississippi River bridge, my mind downshifted into the automatic mode I learned first as a law student and then a prosecutor. While I don't have a photographic memory, I do have an uncanny ability to retain blocks of text, particularly when presented in the form of cases or reports.

The assessment of the Knoxes John Kaiser e-mailed me last night is a perfect example. Because it was filled with detail that might be useful in today's interrogations, my brain recorded it as accurately as a tape recorder, despite my fatigue. Kaiser didn't write in the sterile, jargon-heavy prose of an FBI report, but the language of a personal journal. I suspect he developed this habit during his stint in the Investigative Support Unit, which focuses heavily on human psychology and cares little about the formality of the rules-based bureaucracy of which it's nominally a part.

> So far as I can discover, the root of the Knox pathology begins with Frank Knox's grandfather, Nathan Bedford Forrest Knox. Nathan was an abusive sociopath who fought in the Spanish-American War. He took scalps during the fighting in Cuba and probably murdered several people in the decades afterward. Nathan had two sons: Nathan Jr. (killed at Belleau Wood in 1918) and Elam (who fathered Frank and Snake). Nathan Jr. took some German scalps before he was killed, for which he received only minor discipline.
>
> Elam Knox became a lay preacher, a sometime farmer and trapper, a wifebeater, and a child abuser. He was decorated for bravery during WWI, and

his army record notes that he was a savage trench fighter. There are no records of trophy taking by Elam Knox, but he probably carried on the tradition, because the practice showed up in both his sons, and with a vengeance.

Elam's son Frank was probably sexually abused by his father. He was beaten often and had a generally violent childhood. Frank led a life of petty crime, had constant run-ins with the police, yet he never spent more than a night in jail. There were burglaries, probable rapes, and countless assaults. Frank was ejected from several high school football games for fighting. He was about to be charged with rape when World War II came along. The local authorities were so glad to be rid of him, they let him enlist in the Marines. Not even the victim's family complained.

Frank was sent to the Pacific along with schoolmates Glenn Morehouse and Sonny Thornfield, and there he flowered. Frank was a born killer, and there was plenty to be done on the islands. The more brutal the soldier, the better his officers liked him, and Frank Knox had no equal. He racked up medals faster than most men did blisters on their feet. But Frank didn't merely take human trophies—as his father and grandfather had—he started a business selling them to the Merchant Marine. He and his buddies would bleach the skulls of Japanese soldiers they'd killed and sell them to sailors for a hefty profit. They also carved trinkets out of other bones, made bracelets out of teeth, took ears, cut off foreskins, anything that would sell.

Snake Knox was eight years younger than his brother and consequently served in Korea. Part of the time he spent as a sniper, but Snake also fought hand to hand. His army record contains several notes about one-man incursions he made behind the Chinese lines. One night a foxhole buddy told Snake he was getting frostbite because his boots couldn't keep out the cold. That night, Snake sneaked through the

Chinese lines and brought back a pair of boots with the feet still in them. He said he'd left the feet in to keep the leather warm.

Given this history, it's no surprise that when the Knoxes turned their hands to racial violence, they would use the same tactics they'd employed in Asia. The mutilation of Jimmy Revels and Luther Davis by removal of their service tattoos is a particularly egregious example, but the Knoxes employed torture against multiple victims, and even against whites who they felt had betrayed them.

Frank Knox's second son, Forrest, became the first Knox to conceal his savage nature under a mask of refinement. But evidence of the Knox pathology abounds during Forrest's younger years, particularly while he served as a LRRP in Vietnam. While most Lurps living behind enemy lines avoided contact and reported on enemy movements, Forrest did the opposite. If he thought the odds were remotely in his favor (which might mean two dozen VC regulars against a six-man LRRP team), he would either set up an ambush and take them out or follow the VC patrol and pick them off one by one. A few of his men complained, but any soldier who showed initiative and upped the body count was protected in Vietnam. Forrest gave MACV intel they couldn't get any other way, and several superiors misused his unit as a hunter-killer team (a not uncommon occurrence with LRRP units, which had a 400:1 kill ratio).

The classic Knox pathology was revealed in a killing ritual Forrest observed in combat. He carried a bag of Kennedy half-dollars in his ruck, and always left a coin in his dead enemy's mouth. Pretty soon, the VC in his area believed some kind of ghost or demon was operating there. Command didn't think the coins were particularly crazy. It beat cutting off ears. Of course the army brass couldn't know that the JFK coin was the talisman of the younger Double Eagle group members back in the States. Not that they would have cared. . . .

A loud *thunk* startles me as my Audi ramps up onto the westbound bridge and the river opens a hundred feet beneath me, spreading right and left like a broad valley filled with liquid bronze. Suddenly the horizon is miles away rather than a few hundred yards, and the effect is like gulping cold water. I'm tempted to call Walker Dennis and find out whether he's actually busted the Double Eagles for the planted methamphetamine, but I can't take the chance. If anyone is monitoring his calls, I could find myself tied to a serious felony. With an impatient sigh, I force myself to focus on the remainder of Kaiser's psychological assessment. I can wait five minutes to find out whether Snake Knox and Sonny Thornfield are about to be facing mandatory thirty-year sentences. If they are, I won't need to try to take them apart by applying pressure to well-hidden emotional cracks. . . . I'll have a legal bludgeon that would pucker the sphincter of a hardened con.

God, let that be the case. . . .

WALT DROVE SLOWLY PAST the Bouchard lake house for the second time. The GPS tracker had shown this as Forrest Knox's current location, a fact supported by the state police cruiser parked beside a Mercedes convertible at the end of the home's long driveway.

Walt paid more attention to the house on this second pass. Though two stories tall, the structure appeared long and low. The modern design stood out strongly from the ranch houses and A-frames that dotted the shore on this side of Lake Concordia, especially its metal-clad walls, which gleamed in the winter sun. The name *Bouchard* had been painted in a festive script on a sign below the mailbox, which was the custom along this lake. Walt cursed Mackiever for the hundredth time for not bugging the interior of Knox's cruiser. He wished he'd done it himself. If he had, then he would already know where Tom was being held—or at least his final fate. If he was damned lucky, it might turn out that Knox was holding him inside this luxury retreat.

Since trees obscured his view of the Bouchard house, he shifted his gaze to the house next door. It was a typical ranch-style suburban built on a lot so narrow it didn't even have a carport. Walt felt a rush of hope as he saw there were no vehicles parked at that house.

An ideal observation post if ever I saw one, he thought, slowing to turn.

CHAPTER 52

BY THE TIME Forrest's phone rang again, he sensed that something was wrong. He wasn't sure what it might be, but he never doubted his intuition. As soon as he answered, he heard the high pitch of panic in Deputy Hunt's voice.

"Calm down, son," Forrest said. "What happened?"

"There's no stash under the sheriff's house!"

"Bullshit," Forrest said, his mind speeding through possibilities. Who the hell would have the nerve to rip off crystal meth from cops? "You must have missed it. Talk to whoever planted it."

"*I* planted it. That's how I know. It's gone! All four bags."

Forrest thought about this. "How is that possible? Could anybody have seen you plant it?"

"No, sir. No *way*. It was pitch-black."

"Somebody had to. What about Dennis himself?"

"He was twenty miles away!"

"Where is he now?"

"He left for work ten minutes ago. His wife and kid left at the same time."

"Was anybody with you when you planted it?"

"Kyle Allard drove me."

"Then Allard's got it."

"I don't think so, Colonel. Kyle ain't crazy. And he knows he'd be crazy to cross you."

"Either Allard's got it, or he warned Dennis about it."

"Due respect, sir . . . no way. Kyle hates the sheriff."

"Well, you talk to him, then. Tell him if he doesn't come clean, I'll have Captain Ozan cut it out of him. You hear me?"

"Yes, sir. Loud and clear. But this don't make no damn sense."

Forrest hung up and speed-dialed Claude Devereux at his home in Vidalia. The phone rang six times, and then an answering machine picked up. Forrest listened to the old lawyer's oily voice and waited for the beep.

"Claude, this is Forrest. If you don't call me back within five minutes, I'll make sure you spend the few years you have left handling death row appeals pro bono from your cell in Angola. Have a nice day."

Forrest hung up.

Twenty seconds later, Devereux returned the call.

"Jesus," said the Cajun, "you don't have to get my blood pressure up like that."

"Take a goddamn pill, Claude. I need you to get down to the CPSO and advise some clients who are about to be questioned."

"You mean Snake and Sonny and the others?"

"That's right."

"But—I thought you had that taken care of."

"I do. You're my secret weapon."

Devereux muttered under his breath. "Are they in custody?"

"I don't know. Doesn't matter."

"Shit, Forrest . . . the damned FBI's in town. And this isn't 1964. What are you getting me into?"

"You scared, Claude? You used to laugh at the FBI."

"Thirty years ago. I was young and stupid. Those sons of bitches have more power now than they ever did under Hoover. If the FBI is in on this questioning, I might need a lawyer myself. And the tide has turned against loudmouths like Snake Knox, in case you hadn't noticed."

"Stop flappin' your gums and get over there, Claude. You don't have a choice."

After some grumbling, Devereux said, "All right, all right. I suppose I can."

"That tone doesn't inspire confidence."

"Forrest, Christ . . . I'm too old for this."

"The alternative is worse, I promise you."

Forrest was pretty sure Devereux had stopped breathing.

"You getting your tie on, Claude?"

"As we speak."

"Call me with a report, soon as you can."

"I will. Let me get going."

Forrest hung up, then blew out a rush of air. He didn't like it when things didn't go according to plan. It had been years now since anyone had dared to challenge him directly, but Penn Cage, John Kaiser, and Walker Dennis seemed to be intent on doing just that. He wondered whether Claude Devereux still had the stones to handle adversaries of that caliber. Claude had been a slick operator in the old days, as connected as anybody in Louisiana. He'd kept many a sticky-fingered politician out of prison, from sitting governors to U.S. senators. But Penn Cage was an accomplished attorney with a stellar record as a prosecutor, and Forrest didn't like the fear he'd heard in the old man's voice.

A disturbing thought struck him. What if Devereux didn't even go to the sheriff's office? What if he tried to rabbit? Then it would be up to Snake to handle whatever surprise those three Boy Scouts had cooked up for the Double Eagles. The more Forrest thought about this, the surer he became that he wasn't the only one who'd arranged a surprise for today. He got up from the table, tossed the dregs of his coffee over the deck rail, and speed-dialed Alphonse Ozan.

DEPUTY HIRAM HUNT HAD phoned Colonel Knox from underneath Sheriff Dennis's house, and he was still there, checking for the ninth or tenth time to be sure he wasn't mistaken about the crystal meth. But he knew he wasn't. He'd duct-taped the trash bag containing the packets between two floor joists, right where the return air duct descended from the living room floor.

Now nothing remained but the residue of the duct tape. Hunt could feel the tacky glue on his fingertips. Could some scavenging animal like a raccoon have taken the bag? Possibly, but an animal would have ripped it open on the spot to discover whether it contained any food.

"Shit *fire*," Hunt muttered, knowing his life was on the line.

Pocketing his flashlight, he scrabbled backward out from under the house, emerging near the air-conditioning unit. He hoped to God that Kyle Allard knew something about the missing meth, because if he didn't, that Redbone bastard Ozan would probably kill him trying to squeeze out the truth.

As Hunt straightened up, he figured he could wait two minutes to call Allard. He wanted to get away from the sheriff's house before any neighbors saw him. If something *had* gone wrong, the last thing he needed was Sheriff Dennis asking what he'd been doing under his house that morning. Hunt strode around the corner, then stopped cold.

Walker Dennis stood there with another deputy, a recent hire named Wilkins, a kid fresh out of the Marines.

"What's up, Hiram?" asked the sheriff, a strange glint in his eyes. "You lost?"

"Uh, no, sir."

"Well?"

"I was just looking for you, sir. We, ah, got an anonymous tip that there was some drugs under your house. We knew it was bullshit, of course, but we figured somebody ought to crawl under there so we could say we'd checked it out."

"I see. Who's 'we,' Hiram?"

"Uh, you know . . . Randy, I think." Randy Frey wasn't on the Knox payroll, but he was stupid, and the sheriff might believe the deputy was lying if he denied it.

Sheriff Dennis gave Wilkins some kind of head signal, and the new guy drew his pistol and covered Hunt with it.

"Hey now," Hunt said nervously. "What . . . what's going on?"

Sheriff Dennis smiled, but the look in his eyes made Hunt's bowels shift.

"You're going to get plenty of time to answer that question, Hiram. Yes, sir. Now, hand me your weapon."

"Listen, Sheriff—"

"*Hand it over!*"

With shaking hands, Hunt drew his weapon with his thumb and forefinger and passed it butt first to the sheriff. Dennis looked down at it, then grimaced and handed the weapon to the new guy. Hunt was trying to think of something intelligent to say, but nothing came to him.

"Give me your phones," Dennis ordered. "*All* of 'em."

Hunt unclipped the departmental cell phone from his belt. Then, after some hesitation, he removed the StarTac burn phone from his trouser pocket. It had been his only safe link to Forrest Knox, and now it might just hang him.

Dennis snatched the StarTac from his hand. "Cuff him, Wilkins. Hands behind your back, Hiram."

Hunt felt tears in his eyes. "Sheriff, please—"

Walker Dennis drove his fist into Hiram's gut, driving every bit of air out of his lungs. He doubled over, tried to keep his feet, then collapsed on the sheriff's lawn. He felt the new guy cuffing his wrists behind him, then Dennis's hot breath in his ear.

"This is my *home*, you cocksucker. The bastards you work for killed my *cousin* and two fine deputies—*unlike you*. You think about that while you're riding to where you're going."

"You taking me to jail?" Hunt asked, gasping for breath.

"Ohh, no," said the sheriff in a strange voice. "We're way past that now, Hiram. Yes, sir."

WALT GARRITY WAS SCANNING the Bouchard lake house through a 10x Leupold scope when his burn phone rang. After more than a dozen attempts to reach Griffith Mackiever, the man had finally called him back. Walt set down the scope and answered the phone.

"Tell me you've done something with that video," Walt said, skipping the small talk.

"I'm trying," Mackiever said. "I'm having a hell of a time getting anybody to meet with me. Those damned kiddie porn accusations have made me toxic. No government official wants to have anything to do with me. Most won't even take my calls."

"You can always take it to the media yourself," Walt suggested. "Or scare the hell out of Knox with it."

"Hell, I haven't even ID'd the men in it yet."

"Have you tried?"

"I'm working on it, Walt."

"Work faster, damn it. There's a lot more than your reputation on the line, or the image of the state police."

"I hear you."

Walt was about to give his old comrade a stern dose of reality when an F-150 pickup swerved into the driveway of the Bouchard lake house and rolled toward the built-in garage.

"I'll call you later," Walt said, dropping the phone and picking up the scope again.

He sighted in on the driver as the Ford passed and recognized Alphonse Ozan behind the wheel. So . . . the servant had come to the master. Walt saw no passengers in the truck, but when the garage door rose and swallowed the F-150, he began to worry that Tom might be lying on the backseat, on the floor, or even wrapped in a rug in the truck bed.

He had to get closer to that house.

FORREST STOOD STIFFLY ON the lake house deck and stared down at the cell phone he used to talk to the moles he maintained in various parishes around the state. Hiram Hunt should have called back by now. Forrest needed to know what was going on. Something told him not to try to reach Hunt, but that didn't mean he shouldn't try one of his other sources in Walker Dennis's department. Yet Forrest continued to stare at the phone without touching it. He almost felt as though the device had been turned against him somehow, that the tool he used so often to spy on others now made him vulnerable to attack.

As Forrest stared, the cell phone began to ring.

His heartbeat skittered, then stabilized. Odds were, this was Hunt calling to report that he'd discovered the fate of the planted methamphetamine. The phone rang again. Out on the lake, another bass boat skated by with a midrange growl, but Forrest's eyes remained locked on the cell phone.

He made no move to answer it.

CHAPTER 53

I PULL INTO the motor-pool bay of the sheriff's department, which is located beneath the western end of the Concordia Parish courthouse. As I show my ID to a mustached deputy at the basement entrance, I notice a large number of inmates being held in fenced pens beyond the parked cruisers. The pens have a makeshift look, and most of the men inside are wearing street clothes.

"Who are those guys?" I ask. "Trustees about to go work on the highway?"

"Naw," says the deputy. "Most of 'em are the meth cookers and mules we hit yesterday, the ones who ain't made bail. Some we just busted this morning. They're waiting for their initial appearance upstairs. This circus could take all damn day."

"Why are they out here in those pens?"

"The fed upstairs wanted the jail empty 'cept for the boys they're gonna question up there."

The fed upstairs? "Do you mean Agent John Kaiser?"

"Kaiser . . . yeah, that's him."

"Is he with Sheriff Dennis?"

"No, the sheriff ain't made it in yet."

I check my watch, trying to mask my worry. If Dennis's plan was to plant meth on the Eagles before this interrogation, then there could be a lot of bad reasons he's not here yet. "Have the men he's going to question shown up?"

"Not that I know of."

Shit. "Sheriff Dennis told me he was going to be here fifteen minutes ago, if not earlier."

"He usually is. And we need him this morning."

The deputy hands me back my ID, and I walk up the staircase beyond the door. The staircase terminates in an open-plan office. About half the desks are empty, but at the one nearest the front sits a young deputy with the burly build of a baseball player. Unlike the potbellied deputy down in the motor pool, this guy looks like the twenty-first-century version of the southern lawman. He has strapping forearms and wears a mustache and goatee trimmed nearly to the skin, with a baseball-style sheriff's department SWAT cap pulled low over his blue eyes. Far behind him I see a steel security door that leads to the cellblock, and to the right of that, the mahogany door that Henry and I walked through to visit Sheriff Dennis on Tuesday morning.

"Morning, Mayor," says the young deputy, half rising to his feet and offering his hand. "Spanky Ford. I used to watch you play ball with Drew Elliott when I was a kid. St. Stephen's had a hell of a team in those days."

I walk up and shake his hand, which is thickly padded with muscle.

"That was a long time ago, Deputy."

"Call me Spanky."

"Why hasn't the sheriff gotten in yet?"

Ford's smile disappears. "Not sure. He called about an hour ago and told me he might be late. Told me to put Snake Knox and his geriatric buddies in the jail dining room till he got here."

My scalp tightens. "Are they here now?"

"Yes, sir. I put 'em right where the sheriff said."

This actually brings me some relief, though I'm not sure it's justified. "Did they bring a lawyer?"

"No, sir. None so far."

"No sign of Claude Devereux?"

Spanky Ford laughs. "Man, I ain't seen old Claude in here for two, three years at least. He stays drunk out at the lake or drives up to the casinos for high-stakes poker."

"Where's Agent Kaiser?"

The smile vanishes again, and Ford's eyes go hard. "In the sheriff's private office. He's acting like he owns the damn place."

I nod in sympathy. "Feds are the same all over. I'll go make sure he's not rifling through Walker's files."

"Good idea."

A lot of eyes follow me as I cross the office to the mahogany door, but I don't return anyone's gaze.

When I open the door, John Kaiser looks up as if I'm exactly the person he expected to see. "Morning, Mayor," he says. "Your fiancée had quite a few interesting stories in her paper this morning."

Kaiser doesn't look like he got much sleep after our intensive session with Dwight Stone last night. "I'll tell her you enjoyed them."

"I wouldn't say that. What I'd say is that she seems to have a lot of information that I don't. I think she's been holding back on me."

Seeing Kaiser behind Sheriff Dennis's desk is like seeing a trim, combat-blooded colonel take over the desk of a heavyset captain at a stateside army post. When I first saw Walker in that chair, he looked like he'd be happy not to have to get out of it often. Kaiser looks like he could organize and implement a Rhine crossing at a moment's notice.

"Sheriff Dennis is AWOL," he says. "Any idea where he might be?"

"None. By the way, thanks for e-mailing me that assessment of the Knox family."

Kaiser ignores this. "I also find it odd that with six Double Eagles waiting patiently in the jail dining room to be questioned, we haven't seen hide nor hair of an attorney. Doesn't that strike you as odd?"

"A little."

"It could only mean one of two things. One, Snake and his crew have nothing to hide—which we know is absurd. Or they don't really expect to be questioned today. And so far as I know, the only person who could guarantee that outcome is Sheriff Walker Dennis, who appears to be missing."

"If you think Dennis is going to lift a finger to help Forrest Knox, you're crazy. He blames Knox for killing a family member. Not to mention two deputies yesterday morning."

"Then where is he?"

I glance at my watch. "I guess time will tell."

"You know exactly where he is, don't you?"

"No, I don't." I sit in one of the chairs opposite Walker's desk. "I thought you were going to skip this little party, John."

"The more I thought about it, the more certain I became that I couldn't afford to."

"Why's that?"

"Because if the Double Eagles are going to be questioned, I should be the person doing it. You have no legal authority here, and between Walker Dennis and myself, I'm the more experienced interrogator by far."

"Didn't I tell you that Dennis deputized me? Special Deputy Penn Cage. I even get a tin star."

Kaiser rolls his eyes. "Well, as soon as Marshal Dennis gets finished at the Long Branch, or wherever he is, we need to sort out a batting order for these interrogations—if they absolutely must happen."

"John, you won't talk Walker out of questioning these guys."

Kaiser reflects on this for a few seconds, then veers in a new direction. "Dwight landed in Colorado about midnight last night."

"When does he go under the knife? Or has he already?"

"He should have, but his blood pressure was too high. If they can get it down, they're going to cut on him this afternoon."

I shake my head, seeing no point in belaboring Stone's plight.

"Yesterday's trip probably pushed that pressure up," Kaiser says. "But he has no regrets. He told me to tell you it meant a lot for you to listen to him last night."

"I wish I could have told him more."

Kaiser shrugs. "We'll learn the truth eventually, if you guys don't blow it today. But I doubt Dwight will live to hear it."

The bang of a door down the hall makes us both turn toward the office door. Four seconds later it flies open, and Spanky Ford comes in with wide eyes. For a moment I'm afraid he's about to tell us that Sheriff Dennis has been killed.

"You guys gotta clear the office! Sheriff's back."

"And?" Kaiser asks. "You look like the president just got shot."

Before Ford can answer, I hear the swell of excited male voices. As Kaiser and I look at each other, heavy boots pound up the hall.

Walker Dennis pushes in behind Deputy Ford, his red face grinning, his big hands holding a Ziploc bag taped into a tight brick. "You like my office, Kaiser?" he asks with almost electric good humor.

"I needed some privacy," Kaiser says warily, his eyes on the bag.

Dennis laughs like a man who no longer has to care what other men think. At least four deputies crowd the hall beyond the door.

"What's that in your hand?" Kaiser asks.

"You noticed that, huh? This, my federal friend, is four hundred and eighty grams of crystal methamphetamine, enough to put a man in Angola Prison until his curly hairs turn gray, if they ain't already."

"Where did you find it?"

Dennis's grin is so wide it looks painful. "This particular bag came from underneath Snake Knox's house. I found more just like it under the houses of Sonny Thornfield, Billy Knox, and two other Double Eagles."

My heart thumps at this last revelation. I told Walker not to try to plant anything at Billy Knox's house, since it's probably monitored by armed security, or at least cameras. That thought of digital cameras recording Sheriff Dennis's felonious mission sends my heart into overdrive. But for now, I have to roll with the punches.

"This is a joke, right?" Kaiser says, looking back and forth between us.

I shrug in feigned ignorance.

The sheriff's grin has disappeared. He looks back into the corridor and motions for his men to get back to work. Then, with deadly calm, he says, "What do you mean, a joke?"

Kaiser doesn't shrink from his stare. "Yesterday you guys had virtually nothing on the Double Eagles. Today you find matching evidence bombs on the three perps you'd most love to nail? I'd say that's more than convenient."

Dennis takes an ominous step forward, and I step between him and the desk. Kaiser is right, of course: Dennis is guilty of planting evidence; but no human being is more self-righteous than one who's been caught committing a crime.

"Sometimes a pitch just breaks the right way," Walker says, trying to regain his equanimity.

"At *exactly* the right time?" Kaiser asks, a mocking tone in his voice.

Dennis draws himself up a couple of inches. "This ain't none of your business, Mr. Kaiser. We local yokels have got this one under control. Why don't you get back to draining ponds, or whatever your main business is?"

Kaiser looks to me for help, but I'm not inclined to give him any. This meth bust gives us irresistible leverage against the Knoxes, who would otherwise be uncrackable as a unit.

After taking several seconds to collect himself, Kaiser says, "Sheriff, I'm sorry if I was out of line. But these cases involve some of the most important unsolved crimes in this country. And if any . . . *overzealousness* on the part of law enforcement endangers the convictions we might otherwise get, that would be a tragedy for a lot of people."

The stubbornness in Dennis's face looks almost bovine. Kaiser isn't going to change this man's mind.

"What exactly are you suggesting I do?" Dennis asks at length.

"Don't arrest the Eagles for those drugs. Not yet, anyway. Let me talk to them. They came in voluntarily. They're feeling cocky. So far, they don't even have an attorney present. We have a lot of information that they don't know we possess, and we might learn a lot that could help our cause. But if you arrest them for that meth, they're going to lawyer up. And it'll be a very long time before we learn anything that could help anybody." Kaiser looks at me again. "I include Dr. Cage in that."

It was a good try, but he can't sell me. Not with the Knoxes holding almost all the cards. Dennis is watching me for some kind of signal. When Kaiser looks back at him, I give my head an almost imperceptible shake.

"I'm sorry, Mr. Kaiser," Dennis says. "But I didn't lose good men just to shoot at the hump. I'm arresting those bastards right here and now."

Kaiser raises his hands to protest, but Dennis is already yelling down the hall for some men. When they come running, he tells them to draw their weapons.

Kaiser and I follow this hyped-up posse down the

narrow paneled hall to a small dining room where the Double Eagles are waiting. By the time I stand on tiptoe and get a look into the room, I see pure shock on the faces of the six old men gathered inside. This is clearly the last thing they expected to happen.

"Sonny Thornfield?" Dennis says loudly. "Snake Knox? You are under arrest for possession of and trafficking in crystal methamphetamine. You other boys are under arrest on suspicion of conspiracy to traffic in methamphetamine. And I'll tell you this right now: the first son of a bitch to come clean with me gets to walk, but the rest are gonna die on Angola Farm."

Snake Knox looks defiant, but several other pairs of eyes widen in fear.

"Get off your asses and hold out your hands!" Dennis shouts. "*Now*, by God. I ain't got all day!"

"I want a telephone," Snake says calmly.

"I want a blow job from Angie Dickinson," Walker replies. "Don't mean I'm gettin' it."

"You've got to give him a phone call," Kaiser says from behind us.

Dennis barks out an abrupt laugh. "Thank *God* you boys got the FBI lookin' after you, Snake. Next best thing to the ACLU. I'll bet you never figured the Bureau would be pickin' up your slack, did you?"

"Fuck you, Dennis," Snake growls. "You're a dead man. You and yours, boy."

Sheriff Dennis crosses the room in two bounds and seizes Snake Knox by the throat with one hand. Snake tries a judo chop on the sheriff's massive forearm, but his blow barely leaves a pink mark on the muscle.

"You can threaten me all day long, scum," Dennis says softly, backing Snake against the wall. "But if you threaten my family again, you'll be eatin' through a straw the rest of your life, *if* you live."

Snake's eyes bore into the sheriff's with no fear in them at all. For a moment they almost seem to have the vertical irises of his reptilian namesake. In a raspy whisper, he says, "Both your boys, dipshit. And your old lady, too. Though that'd be a mercy fuck, from what I've seen."

Walker Dennis closes his hand like a man crushing a beer can.

Snake's eyes bulge, and his face goes red, then purple.

"*Sheriff!*" yells Kaiser. "Release that man!"

Two deputies bolt forward and try to pull their boss's crushing hand from Snake's throat, but they can't do it. The old crop duster's eyes have gone glassy. One deputy holds his nightstick over his boss's head as a last resort, but Dennis finally comes to his senses and releases Knox.

"Throw that fucker in the drunk tank," Dennis says, stumping toward us with blood in his eye. "Put Thornfield in there with him. Process the rest and put 'em in the main cellblock. We'll separate 'em later."

"What about that phone call?" Kaiser asks.

"Fuck him," Dennis mutters, walking past the FBI agent without even a glance. "And fuck you, too. Stay out of my way."

AFTER TWENTY MINUTES OF flying over the Lusahatcha Swamp, Caitlin realized that hunting for the Bone Tree in a boat would have taken weeks without a guide like Toby Rambin. From five hundred feet in the air, the swamp appeared vastly larger than it had on Google Earth, which Caitlin had used to scan the terrain this morning. The cypress forest seemed endless, and the thick undergrowth was caught in the transition from fall to winter, an uncertain process in the South. Though it was late December, a lot of green still dotted the landscape below, and a greenish-brown scum floated at the edge of the black water between the big trees. Caitlin now understood why Henry and the FBI had not found the Bone Tree during their relatively brief searches. With half a million trees between the east and west borders of the swamp, the odds of finding a single one by pure luck were practically zero.

"The X on your map," Danny McDavitt said over the headset, "appears to lie in the borderland between the federal wildlife preserve and the private hunting club in this area. Some of it's disputed borderland."

"What do you mean, disputed?" Jordan asked.

"I've always heard that fence down there is in the wrong place," Danny replied. "Some say the hunting club fenced in more land than they own. But they claim they actually own more than they've fenced. I never heard of any litigation over it, though. Too many senators hunt at that place."

Caitlin figured this was her chance. "Have either of you hunted at the Valhalla camp?"

"I went once," Carl said. "Sheriff Ellis took me. He's tight with the people who own it."

"The Knoxes?" Caitlin asked as casually as she could.

"That's right," said Danny. "Some of them are old Klansmen, but one is a big dog in the state police. I think that Brody Royal was a member, the one who died the other night."

Caitlin wondered if Danny knew that she'd been in the room when Henry Sexton immolated the old multimillionaire. Of course he did. That would have been the talk of the county this morning, and certainly the sheriff's department.

"I didn't care for the place," Carl said.

"Big surprise," Danny cracked. "You're definitely the wrong color."

"Yeah. The sheriff only took me over there to show those assholes he's got the best rifle shot in the state on his payroll."

Caitlin looked over at Jordan, who was gazing out the window as though this were a commuter shuttle from New York to Boston.

"What the hell is with those huge fences?" Jordan asked. "We saw them on the way in. The whole place felt like a goddamn concentration camp."

"That's what it is," Carl said glumly. "But for animals."

Danny tilted the chopper so that they could see more landscape below. Caitlin scanned the swamp for cypresses noticeably larger than the others.

"What's it cost to belong to one of those hunting clubs?" she asked.

"Ten grand a year for some, others ten times that much. Depends on what you're after."

"Unless you're a senator or a titan of industry," said Danny. "Then you can order what you want off a menu, just like going to a restaurant. They take you out to an electric feeder where the game of your choice eats every day, and you execute the animal while he's having dinner."

"Real sporting, huh?" Carl said. "It's like hunting in a zoo."

"Pathetic," Jordan said. "You see how those deer run when we roar over them? That's exactly how people run from choppers in some countries I've been to. Only slower."

"Yeah," Carl said, his voice suddenly somber. "I've seen that myself."

"Is that the way Valhalla is run?" Caitlin asked. "Like a hunting zoo?"

"For the customers, yeah. But the owners do some crazy stuff, like the spear hunting."

"There are politicians who have wet dreams about being asked down to those camps for a weekend," said Danny. "They've got chefs and waiters and whores on call for those boys. It's redneck heaven down here."

"And Sheriff Ellis is tight with the owners?" Caitlin asked.

Carl nodded. "The sheriff's okay. He's a redneck, but he's basically a decent man."

"Are we getting close to the X?" Caitlin asked.

"Not long now," Danny said. "This map wasn't exactly drafted by the U.S. Geological Survey."

"I'm sorry about that."

The pilot laughed, then looked over his shoulder at Caitlin. His eyes were hidden behind dark sunglasses. "You ladies going to let us in on what's supposed to be waiting under that X?"

Caitlin felt a chill of suspicion.

"It's not Jean Lafitte's pirate treasure, is it?"

"How did you know?" Jordan said with a laugh. "If it's there, we'll cut you in for five percent."

Carl laughed. "I think this chopper rates a four-way split, don't you?"

Caitlin forced herself to laugh, but she wondered how the pilot would react if they actually discovered the Bone Tree this morning. As a young black man, Carl obviously sympathized with her cause, but Sheriff Ellis wasn't going to be happy to have his county become the new epicenter of civil rights cases that would draw the attention of the whole world.

Out of nowhere, an image of Tom Cage rose in her

mind. Without intending it, Caitlin prayed as she never had before. She prayed for Tom's deliverance, of course, but more than that, she prayed that Penn would never discover that she'd known where Tom was and kept it from him.

She started as Jordan's hand fell on her knee.

"I'm okay," she said, looking up at her new friend. "Just a little airsick."

Jordan smiled, but she wasn't buying it.

CHAPTER 54

WALT STOOD WITH his back to the wall of the rear-most upstairs bedroom of the Bouchard lake house and listened to the muted hum of voices from the deck. Only a glass door covered by a curtain separated him from Knox and Ozan now. He had accomplished a minor miracle in getting this far. After the Redbone arrived, Walt had put on some rough clothes he'd found in the neighbor's house, then crossed the open ground wearing a gardener's cap and gloves and carrying a short shovel. Once he'd gained the house undetected, he'd quickly searched the garage. After determining that Tom wasn't inside Ozan's pickup truck, Walt had taken out his pistol and begun searching the house, room by room.

With every room he cleared, the embers of hope in his heart burned lower. After ten minutes, he found himself standing here, in the final room, which was as empty of human beings as the others. This huge house contained only Walt Garrity, while Forrest and Ozan talked in low tones on the deck. Walt clenched his pistol against his chest and tried to make out what the men were saying.

He couldn't do it.

Unless he put his ear to the glass window, there was no point in even trying. His only hope now was to confront the bastards directly. At two to one, the odds were against him, but he'd faced worse as a Texas Ranger. Much worse, in fact, and he'd survived.

Truth be told, the safest plan would be to shoot Ozan outright and then force Knox to give up Tom's location. But if he did that, he'd have little choice but to finish off Knox as well. Both men certainly deserved to die, but Walt found the idea of blowing Ozan away without any warning more difficult than he would have expected. Perhaps he could get the drop on them so cleanly that they wouldn't go for their weapons. . . .

"No," he whispered. "Right now, I'm Tom's only chance."

Walt edged over to the window, where a thin crack of light offered a view of the deck. He could just make out Ozan standing in profile, while Forrest remained out of sight. Throwing open the door before firing was out of the question, a sucker's play. Better to slide the curtain aside and fire through the glass—multiple times, if necessary.

Walt tried to calm himself the way he did before shooting at a distant deer. But no matter what he did, his heartbeat grew louder, and his ears began to pound.

One shot, he thought, focusing on Ozan's brick-colored face. *For all I know, Tom is dead already, and that bastard killed him. . . .*

FORREST HAD FELT SOME relief after Ozan joined him. Having a man who was willing to follow any order without question gave you a certain confidence. But the plain fact was, they were in a tough spot. Something had clearly gone wrong with his plan to bust Sheriff Dennis. He didn't know what it was, but he wanted Snake and his crew out of the sheriff's office. Somehow, a dumb ex–baseball player had turned the tables on him. Forrest wasn't really worried about Walker Dennis; he was worried about the sheriff giving Penn Cage and John Kaiser access to the Double Eagles. Forrest had reviewed the records of both men, and both had proved themselves expert at wringing the truth out of hardened criminals. If he couldn't find a way to get Snake and his crew out of that jail, Cage and Kaiser would get a real shot at turning somebody. The fallout from Glenn Morehouse's deathbed confession had yet to be controlled, and if one more Eagle decided to unload the sins of his youth, Forrest could say good-bye to all his ambitions for the future.

He cussed his own stupidity when it hit him that he'd been wasting time waiting for Claude Devereux to come through. The simplest solution was just to call Snake and tell him to walk the Eagles right out of the building. After all, they hadn't been arrested. They were free to leave anytime they chose. They could flip Sheriff Dennis the bird as they walked out! Instead, they were sitting there—on Forrest's orders!—patiently awaiting an interrogation they were confident would never happen, because they expected Dennis to be busted by his own men at any moment.

Forrest picked up his burn phone and speed-dialed Snake's cell phone. The phone rang several times, then kicked him to voice mail. Ozan asked what he was doing, and Forrest explained. Then, while Forrest tried Sonny Thornfield's phone, Ozan began dialing the other Eagles at the station.

None answered.

Something began to thrum in Forrest's chest, like a wire stretched taut between his heart and his voice box.

"What do you think happened?" Ozan asked.

"Nothing good."

"Where the fuck is Claude Devereux?" muttered the Redbone. "He should've been down there by now. He should've called you back, at least."

Forrest licked his lips and thought about Devereux. Given Brody Royal's death, and the manner of it, the crafty old Cajun might just have bolted. . . .

"Maybe Claude *is* down there," Ozan suggested.

"I don't think so. I want you to alert every trooper in the southern half of the state. Claude's daughter lives in Lafayette. Tell them to look out for Claude's car. If they see it, pull him over and tell him to get his ass back to his office and wait for instruction."

"Do you think he—"

Forrest's StarTac was ringing.

"That's probably him now," Ozan said, grinning.

Forrest shook his head and answered the phone. The caller was his primary mole at the sheriff's office.

"Talk," Forrest said.

"Sheriff Dennis just arrested everybody, Colonel."

Forrest balled his left hand into a fist. "Define 'everybody.'"

"Snake, Sonny, and the other four old guys."

"On what charge?"

"Meth trafficking. Dennis and two deputies found a

shitload of crystal under Sonny's and Snake's houses. He's strutting around here like goddamn rooster."

Forrest's pulse began to pound. "What about Billy's houses?"

"I haven't heard anything about Billy. But Mayor Cage and that FBI guy are here, too. This is some serious shit, Colonel. I gotta go, but I knew you'd want to know."

"Hold on! As soon as you can get word to Snake, make sure he knows I had nothing to do with this. I don't want him thinking it was some kind of setup."

"Ten-four."

"And tell him I'll get them out. *Today*. You hear me? Tell them I've got a lawyer on the way."

"Yes, sir. Will do."

The connection went dead.

"What the hell happened?" Ozan asked.

Forrest told him.

The Redbone shook his head, his eyes bright with outrage. "Why would Sonny and Snake have meth at home? You think they been skimming or something? Putting back a nest egg?"

"Hell, no! Don't you see? Sheriff Dennis found the meth we planted under his house and planted it on *our* guys. Goddamn it!"

"How the hell could he have found that? A K-9 unit?"

Forrest nodded. "Had to be. But he'd never think to look for it. Not Walker Dennis. Kaiser, maybe. But an FBI agent would never risk planting dope like that. They leave that kind of shit to the DEA."

"Then who?"

"Penn Cage. The old prosecutor. I'll bet he saw every trick in the book out in Houston. He's probably sent cops to the pen for planting dope to get a conviction, but now that his old man's life is on the line . . . Yeah, it was Cage."

Ozan's mouth twisted into a jagged line. "Maybe it's time we did something about that fuck."

Forrest nodded thoughtfully. "Maybe. I was hoping to do a deal with that boy."

"I don't see that happening now."

"This definitely puts a kink into things. But first things first. We've got to get Snake out of jail ASAP. I guarantee you he's going to think I set him up. Because I'm the one who made him march in there for this. He didn't want to do it. And it looks like he was right. *Shit.*"

"Snake can't screw you over without screwing himself, can he?"

Forrest rubbed his chin and stared out over the lake. "I don't know. Snake's a lot smarter than people think. That crazy act is just that—an act."

"What's our play, then?"

"First, find Devereux. Claude's the only lawyer who knows the whole backstory, and he's got as much to lose as we do. Second, have somebody search my house in Baton Rouge. For all we know, they planted a pound of meth on me, too."

"Christ. Good thinking, boss."

"And last . . . find somebody local who knows somebody at the hotel where the FBI is staying. I want wireless bugs planted in their rooms by noon, and somebody stationed one floor above them monitoring the bugs. I'm getting the feeling there's something personal about Kaiser's interest in me. And it's starting to piss me off."

"You got it, Colonel. Is that it?"

Before Forrest could answer, he heard a car door slam on the other side of the house. A couple of loose guys from the Black Team were scheduled to arrive, so he relaxed. Then something shifted inside the house. The sound hadn't been loud, but Forrest had been here long enough to know it wasn't part of the normal background noise of the place. He looked over at Ozan, who nodded once.

"Go," Forrest whispered.

WALT HAD BEEN AIMING through the glass door when he heard something from the other side of the house. It sounded like a car door.

The voices on the deck went silent.

Walt listened, frozen in space. He heard the sound again. It *was* a car door. Then footsteps on the deck moved toward the glass.

As lightly as he could, Walt retreated through the bedroom door, then rushed around a landing and down a back staircase he'd found while passing through the kitchen. He could hear voices in the garage. At least two. Instead of standing still, he slipped into a dark pantry and waited as the voices neared, then passed and moved upward.

Instinct told him to get out while he could, but he forced himself to remain in the pantry. Either Knox or Ozan was hunting him. Walt kept his pistol aimed at the door. After what felt like five minutes, he opened the pantry door, walked straight into the garage, and picked up the shovel he'd left there. Then he shoved his pistol down his pants, left the shadows of the garage, and started shuffling up the driveway with the gait of a man in his eighties.

For forty yards he felt as though a laser scope was burning a hole in his back, but he forced his brain to short-circuit the urge to run. When he was fifty yards from the Bouchard house, he turned right and started across the open ground to the neighbor's home. Given that Tom was not with Knox or Ozan, and he had no way to question them, Walt could hardly stand the delay. As soon as he reached the house, he would take out his cell phone and do what Tom had forbidden from the beginning.

It was time to call Penn.

SONNY AND SNAKE WERE sitting on the lower bunk in their two-man jail cell when Deputy Spanky Ford made a pass through the cellblock. After surveying all the Double Eagles, he stopped before the cell and beckoned the two of them over. Snake looked up and walked over to the bars.

"How's it hangin', Spanky?"

"Not too good," the deputy replied. "Seems like the whole world's turned upside down."

"You're goddamned right it has," Snake muttered.

Ford looked over his shoulder, then whispered, "I've got a message for you."

Snake glanced back at Sonny, then said, "None too soon. Let's hear it."

"Forrest says to hang tough. He's gonna get you out today. He's got a lawyer on the way. Just hang tight, he said."

"Hang tight?" Snake spat on the floor near Spanky's boots. "I've got a message for the young colonel, Spanky. You be sure and remember every word. Tell Forrest I said, 'Go fuck yourself.'"

Spanky Ford's eyes went wide.

"Tell him we'd better be out of here in an hour. *One fucking hour*, you hear me?"

"Yeah." Ford was sweating now, clearly fearful of any further interaction with Forrest Knox—especially this kind.

"And one more thing. You tell him I've got Tom Cage."

Spanky gulped.

"Yeah, you heard right. Tell Forrest I've got the doc, and what I decide to do with him will be based on what Forrest does in the next sixty minutes."

Ford looked ready to bolt. "Is that all of it?"

Snake chuckled. "You don't think that's enough?"

Ashen-faced, Ford hurried out of the cellblock.

Sonny waited for Snake to back away from the bars. Then he said, "Do you think that was the smart way to play it?"

Snake looked down at Sonny, his eyes cold. "Are you kidding? Who do you think put us in here, Son? The same guy who's promising to get us out today. Grabbing Tom Cage last night was about the smartest thing I've done in a long time. All we gotta do now is sit tight and watch Forrest jump to it."

Snake chuckled, then walked back to the bars.

"Listen up, boys," he said. "We're gonna be out of here in two shakes of a lamb's tail. We all know that dope was planted on us. All you gotta do is sit tight and keep your mouths shut. Most of you are pretty good at that, and the ones that ain't . . . well, you know the price of flappin' your gums."

"Damn straight," said an older Eagle named Will Devine, a contemporary of Frank Knox's, and the seventh Double Eagle initiated into the group. "We know what to do, Snake."

"Good man, Will. Everybody just take this chance to catch a nap. Meanwhile, I'll be thinkin' on how we're gonna pay back the fools who put us in here. Okay?"

A low murmur of agreement passed through the concrete cells.

Sonny stretched himself flat on the hard mattress of the bottom bunk. He shivered as the stink of mildew entered his lungs. He had a feeling they might not be leaving these accommodations quite as quickly as Snake expected.

CHAPTER 55

WALKER DENNIS HAS reclaimed his desk, and now Kaiser sits before the furious sheriff like a supplicant, just as Henry Sexton and I did three days ago. Walker has deigned to give the FBI agent ten minutes to make his case, unless the Double Eagles can be processed and booked in less time than that. Kaiser's face was taut with anger when he first came back into this office, but he's managed to calm down and present his objections without quite accusing Sheriff Dennis of planting evidence on the Double Eagles. Walker has listened with surprising patience, though he's checked and sent several text messages during the monologue.

"Agent Kaiser," Walker says during the first sufficient pause, "I realize you've questioned a lot of serial killers and such, and that's real important work. But what we've got here is a drug trafficking case. Open and shut. And I've got some personal experience in handling that kind of case."

Dennis points at me. "Mayor Cage here also has considerable experience handling felony cases. In the big city, too. From drug cases right up to capital murder. And he's been duly deputized by me as a special deputy of Concordia Parish, so there won't be any bullshit about jurisdiction from the ACLU."

"Sheriff, let me stop you there," Kaiser interjects. "Penn has not come here to solve civil rights cases, or even drug trafficking cases. He's here to save his father."

I feel my face reddening.

"And while I can empathize with that goal, I can't allow it to torpedo criminal cases of historic significance."

Dennis starts to reply, but Kaiser beats him to the punch. "Sheriff, I know you lost a relative a couple of years back—a deputy you believe Forrest Knox had a hand in killing. You also lost two deputies to that booby trap at the warehouse. I've lost agents, myself. I lost fellow soldiers in Vietnam. A lot of them. But you can't give in to the hunger for quick payback. It never works out like you think it will." Kaiser glances at me, then back at Dennis. "What I want from these sons of bitches is the truth, no matter who gets jailed or exonerated. The *truth*, men. That's why if anybody goes in to question them today, it should be me."

"But you're not even convinced they *should* be questioned," I point out.

Kaiser shrugs. "Obviously, we can't unbreak that egg. They're in custody now."

"Damn straight," Sheriff Dennis says.

"But I need you to understand something, Sheriff. I've been working to nail these bastards longer than you think. I know things about them that even Henry Sexton didn't know. With all due respect, you don't know who you're dealing with."

"I know the Knox family, all right."

"Do you?" Kaiser reaches into a thick leather bag beside his chair and drops a stack of worn files on the sheriff's desk. "Why don't we see how well you know them?"

Dennis sighs heavily, glances at his watch, then motions for Kaiser to get on with it.

As I pray I won't have to listen to a rehash of the file I read last night, Kaiser pats the top file with the flat of his right hand, then launches into a more concise version of exactly that. Sheriff Dennis appears surprisingly interested in this information, particularly the tales of mutilation carried out by Knoxes serving in the armed forces.

"There were official records of this?" he asks, taking a pinch of Skoal and tucking it into the right side of his lower lip.

"Absolutely," Kaiser says. "And they weren't unique to the Knoxes. The practices were so widespread that the brass couldn't stop them. In 1944, one 'picture of the week' in *Life* magazine showed a U.S. sailor's girlfriend writing him a thank-you note for a Japanese skull he'd sent her from the Pacific. Vietnam vets took a lot of heat over severed-ear stories, but that kind of savagery has always been a part of war—especially in societies that value hunting as proof of masculinity."

"Like the Deep South?" I ask.

"The South has no monopoly on brutality," Kaiser says without missing a beat. "A Pennsylvania senator gave President Roosevelt a letter opener made from the arm bone and tanned skin of a Japanese soldier. Roosevelt only returned the gift after a scandal broke about it. Hundreds of gold teeth and ears were taken by American soldiers on Guadalcanal, sometimes from living owners."

"So you're saying that normal men committed these kinds of acts?"

"Yes—if the word 'normal' means anything when it comes to war. But the Knoxes don't belong in the middle of the curve." Kaiser lets me see the passion behind his eyes. "I believe the Knoxes are sociopaths—all of them, to one degree or another. And I believe that America's wars—and later the civil rights struggle—offered them an arena in which to exercise their particular appetites."

"Henry Sexton had a similar theory," I tell him.

"The damned thing of it is," says Sheriff Dennis, "it sounds like Forrest Knox was a hell of a soldier. Killing all those VC out on his own like that, and leaving half-dollars in their mouths . . . he scared the hell out of the Cong."

Kaiser smiles strangely. "Sociopaths often make effective soldiers, at least in small-unit actions. Killing is the objective, after all. But over time, their various paraphilias have a corrosive effect on morale."

Dennis gives a somber nod. "I swear to God, when I read Caitlin's article this morning, about the Double Eagles slicing off those black boys' service tattoos, I damn near puked. Anybody who did that to a vet ought to be hung."

"I'm working on it," Kaiser promises. "Just like Henry was."

"I thought the Double Eagle gold piece was the Eagles' sign," Dennis says, glancing at his watch. "Why did Forrest use half-dollars on the VC?"

Kaiser smiles like a patient college professor. "Only the older guys had gold pieces. The mints stopped pressing the Double Eagle in 1933. All the younger members car-

ried '64 JFK half-dollars. Confidentially, that may have
had to do with the Kennedy assassination."

"You said something about that in the hospital yesterday morning," Dennis recalls. "What's the deal on that?"

I sigh wearily, dreading a Kaiser soliloquy on his pet
conspiracy theory, but he says, "We don't have time to
go into the details, Sheriff. And I don't have the authority to give them to you. Let me just say that one or more
of the men in your jail at this moment may know who
killed John F. Kennedy. They may even be related to the
assassin. Most important, they may possess evidence that
could prove his guilt."

Dennis can see that Kaiser is serious, and he's appro-
priately impressed. "Well, since they're facing mandatory
thirty-year sentences, why don't you take this opportunity to squeeze the truth out of them?"

Kaiser takes his time with this question. The idea must
surely be tempting to him. But his response is exactly
what I expect.

"Because," he says, "anything I get them to say based
on a threat that might later be proved, ah . . . less than
genuine, shall we say, would be inadmissible in court. I
can't risk a case that big under those circumstances."

Dennis has the grace not to take this as a personal
insult. "Those charges are going to stick, Mr. Kaiser. And
they should stick. Because those bastards have been selling that poison in this parish for years. And people have
died from it."

"I know they have, Sheriff." Kaiser fans through a file
without looking at it. "But the men you're trying to nail
aren't simply meth dealers. Nor are they merely violent
racists. They're serial rapists and murderers related by
blood and tribal ties. I don't think there's any comparable
case in the literature, at least not on this scale. The link-
ing crime signature is the trophy taking. It crosses all the
generations. Two separate sources have mentioned that
Elam Knox had a Bible bound in human skin, possibly
given to him by his youngest legitimate son, Snake."

"Holy Christ," Dennis says, as if finally appreciating
the scope of the battle he has taken on. "I should have
gone ahead and crushed that asshole's windpipe back
there."

"Then we'd be booking you for murder," Kaiser observes. "Sheriff, I'm begging you to look at this thing objectively. If you won't postpone these interrogations, at least let me handle them. I'm an expert on the Knox family, and I have far more experience than either of you at questioning sociopaths."

"On that point," Dennis says, "unless I'm mistaken, you also nearly killed a convict you were interrogating as part of an FBI research project. A handcuffed convict."

Kaiser's face colors. "That's true. He was trying to get under my skin, and he did. He described a little boy he'd violated and killed eight years earlier with a power drill. I snapped and went for him, just like you did earlier with Snake. It was a mistake, and I'm lucky he didn't die. You should—"

Someone has knocked at the office door.

"*What is it?*" bellows the sheriff.

A tall deputy pokes his head in. "Everybody's printed and processed and locked up tight."

"I'll be there in a second, Silas."

"Who you want first, Sheriff?"

"Snake fucking Knox."

Kaiser clears his throat. "Sheriff, could I have another sixty seconds before you make that decision?"

Dennis tells the deputy to wait for confirmation on who to bring to the interrogation room.

After the door closes, Kaiser looks back and forth between us. "You two probably figure that Snake Knox is the leader of the Eagles that we have here and therefore possesses the most information. You're right on both counts. But Snake is also the toughest of all six suspects. You just threatened to kill him, and he spit your threat right back in your face. He's not worried about that crystal meth, Sheriff. You can't break a guy like that. Not legally, anyway. And maybe not even with torture."

Dennis's face darkens. "Well, who would you question first, hotshot?"

"Sonny Thornfield. He's got a daughter and two grandkids that I know about, and maybe more. One grandson is in the army. Sonny was probably present at most of the Eagles' worst crimes, but nothing in his background indicates the kind of sociopathic behavior that the Knoxes and some others have displayed. Sonny's also got severe heart disease, and he knows he'd never survive prison. Hell, he nearly died three days ago after Dr. Cage and Garrity questioned him in that van. If any Eagle ever had incentive to cut a deal, it's Sonny Thornfield. I think that's why Dr. Cage picked him."

Sheriff Dennis turns up his palms as if it makes no difference to him. "So I'll start with Sonny. Thanks for the tip."

Kaiser shakes his head wearily. "No . . . if you do that, you'll tip Snake that we know Sonny is the most vulnerable. The thing to do is start with Snake, but don't truly go after him. I'll show him the gun we pulled out of Luther's Pontiac, maybe a bone or two. I'll keep hammering at him with that, and he'll keep stonewalling. Then we swap him for Sonny. But once Sonny's in there, we show him what we *really* have. Not the meth, but everything I know about the Double Eagles and the Knoxes."

"Compared to the meth, that's nothing," Dennis says. "If you had enough to nail him, you'd have arrested him already."

"Sonny won't forget about the meth," I think aloud, as I realize what Kaiser is doing. He's not going to make himself party to using planted evidence, but he doesn't mind exploiting the fear that evidence has produced.

"Trust me, Sheriff," Kaiser says. "If I make it plain that Sonny's going to spend the last years of his life in Angola if he doesn't turn state's evidence—and at the same time offer him and his family federal witness protection— Thornfield will crack."

Kaiser is right. In terms of planning his interrogation, Walker Dennis probably never got much past walking in, slamming the meth down on a table, and giving Snake an ultimatum. And that would be effective enough to accomplish my initial goal—distracting Forrest from hunting my father. But if Kaiser is willing to use the fear created by the planted meth, and pile what he knows on top of that, then Sonny might actually agree to flip on his comrades. If he does that, we might learn not only where Dad is, but also who killed Viola—not to mention getting enough testimony to send Forrest and Snake to prison. Closing deals like that often takes days, of course, not hours; but if I don't at least admit the logic of Kaiser's argument, he'll suspect I was part of the planted meth gambit from the start.

"He's making sense, Walker," I say, still wondering if Sheriff Dennis condemned himself to prison by planting meth at Billy Knox's residence.

Perceiving my wavering support as a betrayal, Walker launches into an impassioned defense of his jurisdiction and his need to prove to the people of his parish that the era of police corruption has come to an end. While Kaiser suffers patiently through this, my cell phone vibrates. Slipping it partway out of my pocket, I see a text message from a number I don't recognize. I almost ignore it, but then a little voice tells me I can't afford to ignore anything today. Sliding the phone farther out of my pocket, I see this message:

This is Walt. Ur father's been taken. I'm on my way to Natchez. ETA 8 mins. If we don't find Tom quick, he's dead. He could be already. (Yeah, it's me, boy. We first met on the Alvarez case.)

The final parenthetical sends a chill across my neck and scalp. Someone trying to lure me outside might claim to be "Walt" or "Walt Garrity," but no one involved with this case could possibly know that Walt and I first met during a murder case in Houston, when he worked as an investigator for DA Joe Cantor.

If we don't find Tom quick, he's dead. He could be already. . . .

Walker is still pontificating to Kaiser, who quietly responds in logical counterpoint that has no effect whatever on the sheriff. While this clumsy dance continues, my mind slips quietly but inexorably free from its moorings. Too much has happened too quickly over the past few days, and I've had too little rest to process this new information with anything like objectivity.

"Penn?" says Sheriff Dennis. "Did you hear me?"

"I'm sorry. What?"

Kaiser is watching me with an inquisitive gaze, and I can't summon a mask to put him off. All I can think about is marching back to the cellblock and sticking a gun in Sonny Thornfield's mouth and forcing him to tell me where my father is. Given the circumstances and the time frame, it seems the only logical thing to do.

"Penn?" asks Kaiser. "What's the matter?"

"I'm fine," I lie, blood pounding in my ears. Walt's desperate text message is unspooling continually across my field of vision, like the news crawl on CNN. "I just hit a wall. All this talk . . . not enough sleep."

Sheriff Dennis is watching me with equal concern from behind his desk. Before Kaiser can say anything else, Walker leans forward and says, "Agent Kaiser, you've gathered a lot of valuable psychological information. And you seem to have had it for quite some time. I suppose you were going to act on it sometime in the future, but in the meantime, Henry Sexton is dead. Sleepy Johnston is dead. And two of my deputies are, too."

Kaiser tries to interrupt Dennis's flow, but I don't hear a word he says. If we're going to find my father, neither Kaiser's tactics nor Walker's will be fast enough. I need answers *now*. After closing my eyes a moment to settle my nerves, I take out my cell phone and text Walt:

Understood. Wait for me or Sheriff Dennis in the Conc. Parish sheriff's west parking lot.

Then, after a covert glance at Kaiser, who's speaking earnestly to Sheriff Dennis, I text Walker the following:

You have to let Kaiser question Snake. I just got a life or death message about my father. Hostage situation. I need instant answers or he's dead. As soon as Kaiser gets going with Snake, isolate Sonny where no one can hear him scream. Retired Texas Ranger Walt Garrity will be waiting in west pking lot in 5 mins. Bring him inside to assist. Text me when it's set up. Walt is old school, tough as a boot heel. Help me, buddy. I'd do it for you. P

Walker may not want to comply with my demand, but he can't refuse the only man who knows that he planted drugs on the prisoners now locked inside his jail. While Kaiser continues his impassioned plea, I hold up my cell phone where only Dennis can see, then quickly lower it. Sheriff Dennis isn't the most subtle man alive, but he manages to cover his confusion quickly enough to prevent Kaiser from noticing our exchange. When his cell phone pings a few seconds later, Walker takes it out casually and glances at it as if dealing with some routine request from one of his men. Then his big eyebrows knit like those of a wise old hound pondering some unfamiliar animal.

"John," I say, to distract Kaiser, "you're crazy if you don't use the meth against the Double Eagles. You'll never have more leverage than you do right now."

Before Kaiser can reply, Walker sighs heavily, as though in surrender, then says, "I tell you what, Agent Kaiser. You've convinced me to give you a shot. One shot. Let's walk over to the interrogation room, and I'll have Snake Knox brought in. I'll give you your chance to play him the way you want. We'll see how you do. After that, we'll reevaluate the situation."

Kaiser blinks in surprise, but he loses no time getting to his feet and following Walker into the hall. As he leaves the office, I pick up the vibe of a man who feels he's been manipulated but isn't quite sure how. I shut the door and call Walt's cell phone back.

"Talk to me, Penn," he says. "What's your status?"

"I'm still inside the CPSO. We were about to interrogate Snake Knox and his crew."

"I'm real close to you. There isn't time to catch you up on everything. From the signs I saw, I think Tom is probably being held by some of Forrest Knox's SWAT guys, but I don't know where. Snake Knox might, though."

"We can't get to Snake. But Sonny Thornfield might know, and we can get to him. Where's Forrest now?"

"Less than five miles from you, at a house on Lake Concordia. But that Redbone's with him, Ozan. I sneaked into the house and searched it. Tom's definitely not there."

"Do you think Dad could be at that hunting camp in Lusahatcha County?"

"Not likely. I just got out of there myself."

"It's a big place, though, right?"

"A few thousand acres, at least."

"Then we need to get a look at it."

"You'll never get a warrant fast enough. These guys have connections all over Mississippi and Louisiana. We've got to twist the truth out of somebody who knows."

"I'm on it. I want to check out Valhalla. With some luck, maybe I can arrange an overflight of the property. One that won't require a search warrant. Meanwhile, you get your ass into the CPSO parking lot and wait. I'll either come out to get you or send Sheriff Dennis out. And you be ready to twist somebody hard."

"I'm past ready, son. Just get me in the room."

FORREST KNOX THREW HIS StarTac phone against the wall of the lake house so hard that Alphonse Ozan jumped, and one of the two Black Team officers inside came running to the glass door.

"That double-crossing old son of a *bitch*," Forrest shouted, turning to Ozan. "He told me to go fuck myself!"

Ozan didn't know what to say.

"Snake's taken Tom Cage!"

"*What?*"

"I had trouble reaching the Black Team guys in Garrity's van this morning, but I put it down to the crappy reception down near Monterey. I guess you'd better send those two inside back down to the oil field and see what the damage is."

Ozan's face had gone dark. "You don't think they shot any of our guys. . . ."

Forrest thought for a moment. "I don't think Snake is that crazy, but you never know."

"If he snatched Cage from the Black Team, there's no way they're gonna let that pass. They'll kill his ass."

Forrest snorted. "They had their chance last night, apparently, and they didn't manage it. It never pays to underestimate Snake Knox."

Ozan started to open the glass door, but Forrest said, "You know what? I'm worried Dr. Cage is already dead. Snake's wanted him dead since Monday afternoon."

"Yeah," Ozan agreed. "I got that feeling myself."

"We've got to find out. If he is alive, we can still use him. We have to think about where Snake could stash him and feel like he was safe on ice."

"You don't think the FBI could have the doc, do you?"

Forrest felt a chill run up his back. "Hell, no. If they did, why would Snake tell us he had him?"

"He might be working with 'em."

Forrest considered this for exactly three seconds. "No chance. He'd castrate himself first. But that doesn't mean he wouldn't fuck me if he thought I betrayed him. And he said I'd better have him and his crew out of jail in an hour."

"Ain't no way," said Ozan. "Not with that much dope hanging around their necks. Not unless we take over the whole damned department."

Forrest nodded. "I was considering that last night, but now that Dennis has pulled this meth switch, and with the FBI involved—and Snake being my uncle—there'd be too damned much scrutiny."

Ozan grunted in agreement.

"Still no word on Mackiever resigning?" Forrest asked.

The Redbone shook his head. "Nobody's texted or e-mailed me."

"All right, then. If we're going to bust Snake out of there soon, we're going to have to think outside the box. We need reliable people, but they have to be several layers removed from us."

Ozan nodded but offered no names.

Forrest looked out over the lake and considered the problem for a while. The low December sun had finally hit the water, and he could see fish jumping among the cypress knees. As he watched them, an ironic idea came to him. Ironic, and inspired.

"I think I know just who to call," he said.

"Who?" asked the Redbone.

"You'll find out. But we need to keep up the appearance of playing by the rules. You don't have any word on Claude Devereux yet?"

"Nothing."

"That lying Cajun. I'm going to roast him over a slow fire when this is all over."

"Amen to that," said the Redbone. "He's always gotten on my nerves."

"Then find him, Alphonse."

Ozan nodded and punched a new number into his phone.

CLAUDE DEVEREUX WAS HALFWAY to Lafayette, Louisiana, driving a careful seven miles over the speed limit. It had taken him longer than he'd hoped to pack, but that came from not preparing sooner. He should have known that after Brody Royal's death, the old order would start to break apart, with all the attendant chaos and risk that accompanied such changes.

He was taking a risk going to Lafayette, but he couldn't bear to leave the country without seeing his grandchildren one last time. Given the crimes in which his employers had embroiled him, he might have to stay away for some time, years even, and at his age, he could easily die before he got a chance to return. In case of that eventuality, there were certain papers Claude wanted to give to his daughter. He could have mailed them, of course, but it wouldn't be the same. He wanted to see Adeline's lovely face when he told her there were millions that she had no idea existed, and that every dollar would pass to her someday.

The problem was, traveling from Vidalia to Lafayette meant driving through Baton Rouge (unless you wanted the trip to take twice as long as necessary), and Baton Rouge was Forrest's home base. Still, Claude figured he had a couple of hours before Forrest realized something was really wrong. By then, he would have hugged his family, given them their gifts, and headed west to Houston, where he would board a plane bound for the Cayman Islands.

Devereux's Catholic faith had lapsed more than six decades ago, but as he reached the outskirts of Baton Rouge, Claude began a litany of Hail Marys that would not cease until he had passed over the Atchafalaya Swamp to the west.

CHAPTER 56

THE CPSO INTERROGATION room looks pretty much like the ones in Houston, only without the sophisticated video system. It does have a camera though, trained on the table from a tripod in one corner. Deputy Spanky Ford led me to the soundproof observation room on the other side of the traditional one-way mirror, where I stand now. Through it I see John Kaiser sitting on one side of the interrogation table, studying a file. His large leather briefcase stands beside him on the floor. In a few moments, Snake Knox will be led into that room and chained opposite him. Kaiser has the confident look of a soldier who's just won an important skirmish. If only he knew that somewhere in this building, Sheriff Dennis is separating Sonny Thornfield from his fellow prisoners and moving him to more private quarters, where he can be questioned without constitutional restraint. Under any other circumstances, I would be ashamed, but with my father in the hands of Forrest Knox, I can't afford to observe the rules.

As soon as Spanky Ford left me, I dialed Carl Sims, a deputy I know in Athens Point, Mississippi, forty miles south of Natchez. A former marine sniper, Carl was born and raised in Lusahatcha County. He's done security work for me in the past, during off-duty hours, but he has two more important qualifications. One, he's a good friend of the Lusahatcha County sheriff's chopper pilot. If anyone can organize an aerial search of the Valhalla hunting camp, Carl can. Second, Carl has a bit of a crush on Caitlin, as well as carrying some guilt about a mistake he once made in protecting her. Carl's phone rang eight times, but he didn't answer. It didn't seem that luck was on my side, but Lusahatcha County is rural and infamous for spotty cellular coverage.

While I wait for Walker Dennis to let me know that Sonny Thornfield is ready for me, a CPSO deputy leads Snake Knox into the interrogation room. Kaiser doesn't look up as the old man takes his seat, or even when the deputy chains Snake's hands to a steel ring set in the metal tabletop.

I don't know how Snake got this nickname, but at that table, separated from his aged subordinates, he does exude the cold-blooded menace of a venomous serpent. He might be asleep, for all the signs of life he shows. But like a cottonmouth moccasin coiled beside a pond, he's ready to strike. With his slit eyes, pale skin, and stringy muscles, Snake seems a strange crossbreed of mammal and reptile. If emotion could be measured externally, he would likely register zero. The totality of his indifference to Kaiser reminds me of some killers I encountered in Houston—the ones who immediately went to sleep after being arrested for the most heinous of crimes. And yet . . . staring through the one-way glass, I also perceive the face of a young soldier and pilot beneath Knox's sagging, weathered skin.

"I know you," Snake says in a flat voice. "You're John Kaiser, out of New Orleans. You're married to that photographer."

This knowledge worries me a little, which is exactly the response Snake intends to arouse in Kaiser. But Kaiser doesn't look up from his file.

"You know that fatass planted that meth on us," Snake goes on. "So you'd better say your piece while you have a chance. I won't be here long."

"I don't care about the meth," Kaiser says, setting down his file at last. He picks up the case and sets it flat on his lap.

"No?" Snake sounds surprised.

"No." Kaiser opens the briefcase, takes out the rusted Nambu pistol that his agents removed from Luther Davis's sunken Pontiac, and sets it carefully on the table between them.

Snake regards it like a pile of dog shit.

"Been a while since you've seen Frank's gun, eh?" Kaiser asks.

Snake looks up, amusement in his eyes, but he says nothing.

Kaiser reaches into the briefcase and takes out the rusted handcuffs his divers found locked to the Pontiac's steering wheel. These he sets beside the Nambu.

Snake studies the cuffs without touching them. Then he says, "Fond memories, my man."

Given Kaiser's sober demeanor, it's hard for me to remember that he's merely acting out a ruse for Snake Knox. He knows he has no chance of making this man talk by any legal means. Every move is designed to buy him equal access time to Sonny Thornfield. But nothing about Kaiser's posture or facial expression communicates this. In this moment, Snake must feel he is the prime target of an experienced interrogator.

The FBI agent's silent presence is so compelling that I've forgotten to try Carl Sims again. As I dial, Snake says: "Tell me something, Mr. FBI man."

Kaiser inclines his head slightly to the side. "What's that?"

"How do you know Adam and Eve weren't black?"

When Kaiser refuses to rise to the bait, Snake says, "You ever try to take a rib from a nigger?" A slow grin spreads across the old Double Eagle's face, the first real expression I've seen from him.

"What's with this comic book racist act?" Kaiser asks. "I know you're just putting on a show. Don't you ever look around and realize you didn't accomplish a damned thing with all your violence?"

Snake smiles expansively. "Oh, you're right about that. We lost the war, all right. Yes, sir. The world we got now is the proof of that. How do you like it, Agent Kaiser? The liberals got what they wanted, and everything we feared came true."

After six rings, Carl's phone kicks me to voice mail again.

"You auditioning for Fox News?" Kaiser asks, still expressionless.

Snake laughs. "They could use me, that's for sure. See, I figure the niggers have had civil rights—for real, not just by law—for about three decades now. And they're probably worse off as a group than they were during slave times. It's plain as day, man, but nobody wants to talk about it. Every city with a high concentration of blacks

has the worst statistics in the country on crime, education, unwed mothers, infant mortality. And don't give me
that poverty bullshit, because no other ethnic group has
disintegrated like that."

Kaiser rolls his eyes.

"You think I'm wrong?" Snake asks. "Last weekend,
black gangs in Chicago and Detroit killed more niggers
than the whole Ku Klux Klan killed between 1960 and
1970. *Last weekend.* Most of 'em can't read any better than
a white fourth grader. They won't work half as hard as a
Mexican—not even at drug dealing—and the black family
pretty much ceased to exist when the black church women
who kept them together started dying off."

"I see. And you think they were better off as slaves?"

"Well, sure. Hell, son, the black male just ain't equipped
to handle freedom. It discombobulates him. Look at
Africa. Once the European powers pulled out, the whole
place went to hell. The black revolutionaries became everything they claimed they hated. The only country on
the whole continent worth a spit is South Africa, and that's
because it was the whitest the longest. You sure don't hear
American jigs yelling, 'Back to Africa,' anymore, do you?
No, sir. Before long, starvation and AIDS will empty that
whole damned landmass, and somebody with real genetic
potential can start over."

"You're a walking artifact, Snake."

"Hey, you asked. And don't kid yourself: half the people
north of the Mason-Dixon line have asked themselves
what their ancestors were thinking when they fought a
civil war to free the slaves. See, back then, the niggers
were all down *here.* But once they started moving north,
those Yankees started singing a different tune."

"Speaking of a different tune," Kaiser says, "why
don't you tell me why your brother Frank didn't take that
second Mannlicher-Carcano with him to Dealey Plaza
back in '63?"

This question hits Snake like a blindside punch. He
works his mouth around for a few seconds, absorbing the
possible implications of the question. Then, instead of answering, he turns to the one-way mirror and looks right
into my eyes. "How you doing, Mayor? Yeah, I saw you
earlier, when Sheriff Fatass was choking me. Your daddy's

in a world of shit, ain't he? Spent his whole life helping coons, and now he's going to jail for killing one. Don't seem fair, does it? In jail for doing the world a goddamn favor."

As I feel my blood pressure rise, I can't help but admire Kaiser for remaining so cool before Snake Knox.

"My files tell me you're a Holy Roller, Snake," Kaiser says, trying to bring Knox's attention back to him. "Like your old man."

Snake slowly looks back at the FBI agent, his eyes flat and cold again. "Well, I don't know. I've prayed mighty hard on occasion. One night, about ten thousand Chinese communists in quilted pajamas came pouring over the wire in my sector, and my squad had exactly five hundred bullets between us. That night I prayed like a man trying to polish coal into diamond with his asshole."

Snake glances in my direction again. "You can ask your daddy about that, Mayor—if you ever see him again. Dr. Cage knows all about that kind of religion."

Snake is speaking of my father in the present tense. But is he doing it unconsciously or not? Whatever the case, Kaiser doesn't take the bait.

"You want to tell me about the night you crucified old Elam?" Kaiser asks in a neutral tone. "How does it feel to kill your own father?"

Snake's face slowly ratchets around to Kaiser again, like a sniper returning his aim to his primary target. "Who you been talking to, boy? It don't pay to listen to liars."

"I don't. That's why I'm not asking you about killing Martin Luther King. I know that's whiskey talk. But I know you killed Elam, Snake. You and Frank both. Oh, you killed a lot more than that, I know. But you must have felt something when you killed your own father, even if he did molest you. Unlike when Frank killed Kennedy. I'm betting that killing a president—that president—was one of the high points of Frank's life."

To my surprise, Snake is smiling again, as though at some private joke. "You obviously found those rifles in Brody's basement, huh? You ought to sell 'em on eBay. I always wanted to."

"I could use the money," Kaiser admits, "but selling evidence is illegal. I know one of those rifles is real, Snake.

Just like the Carcano Brody kept upstairs. I know Frank
was supposed to use that to lay part of the blame on Eladio
Cruz, the Cuban student from New Orleans, but he decided not to take the risk."

For the first time doubt flickers in Snake's eyes, and
Kaiser cannot mask his satisfaction. "How does it feel,
Snake?" he asks. "That fear? Been a while since you felt
that?"

"I'm a crop duster, son. You can't make it in my business if you're the nervous type. So you just wear yourself
out. You've got till my lawyer gets here, and not a second
longer." Knox's expression slowly morphs from a good-ol'-
boy smile to a cobralike spreading of the lips, and there's
only death in his eyes. "But if *you* ain't scared, you've mis-
understood the situation. Them pretty girls you and the
mayor sleep with at night? You ought to stick closer to 'em.
Because I know some boys who'd love to spend a few hours
in that company. And they'd never be the same afterwards."

Kaiser stares back at Snake without expression. Jordan
Glass is supposed to be headed to Moisant Airport in New
Orleans, but I know Kaiser is wishing he could call her
and verify that right now.

"Planting that meth on us was breaking the rules,"
Snake goes on. "It surprised me, I'll admit. But it also
got my attention. So I'm gonna be giving you both some
thought after I get out of here. Yes, sir. A lot of thought."

Kaiser appears to be reading a file without the slightest
concern for Snake's words, but I can tell the old Klansman
has gotten to him.

The door behind me suddenly opens, and Sheriff
Dennis pokes his head in, puffing from exertion. "Thorn-
field's cooling his heels in a utility closet, and your man
Garrity's babysitting him. You ready?"

"Do the other Eagles know we have Thornfield?"

"They know he's not in the cellblock. No way to avoid
that."

"Okay, I'm coming. But let me go in with Snake for a
sec, so Kaiser thinks we're out here watching his every
move. That'll buy us the time we need."

"Well, get to it. Thornfield looks scared shitless to me.
I think he's ready to crack."

Walking up to the one-way mirror, I lay my fingers

against the cool surface and listen to the conversation. Kaiser has gone back to tapping at Snake, searching for weak spots. The name Carlos Marcello crackles out of the speaker above me, but Snake simply stares across the metal table like a man reconciled to waiting all day at the DMV to get a new license plate. Kaiser is maddeningly patient, like all good interrogators, but it's plain that he was right about the futility of trying to break Snake Knox.

It's time to make my play.

Before walking into the interrogation room, I try Carl Sims once more. I'm about to hang up when I hear a click, a burst of digital static, and then a familiar voice speaking out of a rhythmic pounding that sounds like nothing so much as a helicopter.

DANNY MCDAVITT HAD SLOWED the JetRanger down to a figurative crawl. He had been having trouble matching up what he'd seen on the hand-drawn map to the monotonous topography below him. Beneath the chopper lay a vast stretch of black water and cypress trees that reached westward to the glittering line of the Mississippi River. Carl had moved up to the copilot's seat to try to help, but both of them seemed to have lost the game fence Danny had been following. The trees were especially thick here, and Caitlin saw no sign of the fence.

The chatter between the two men suddenly stopped, and Carl removed his helmet to take a phone call. Caitlin watched him listening for a few seconds. Then he turned back to her with wide eyes.

Caitlin glanced over at Jordan, who had missed nothing.

Carl moved back into the cabin and motioned for Caitlin to remove her headset. Once she had, he covered the mouthpiece of the phone and leaned very close to her.

"This is Penn on my phone."

She flushed. How the hell had Penn found her?

"He doesn't know you're here," Carl whispered. "He called because he wants me to organize an overflight of Valhalla. Without a search warrant, if possible. He thinks Dr. Cage might be being held prisoner there. I'm going to talk it over with Danny, but I figured I'd ask if you wanted to talk to him."

Caitlin took a deep, fearful breath, then expelled it. This morning she had told Penn that she would be working in Natchez all day. Admitting that lie might make him furious, but given that this was about Tom *and* Valhalla, she couldn't refuse. She only hoped that their discussion wouldn't require her having to tell Penn she'd met Tom secretly last night.

She held out her hand to Carl.

Carl passed her the phone, then clambered forward again to talk to Danny.

"Penn, this is Caitlin."

At first there was only silence. Then Penn asked her to hold on, thinking she'd somehow called him and broken in on his connection with Carl. It took a while to convince him that she was in fact *with* Carl, and already in a helicopter not far from the land Penn wanted searched. She could hear the anger in his voice, but she also knew that was nothing compared to the rage he would feel if he learned she had kept Tom's location from him.

"Did you drive down there by yourself?" he asked.

"No. Jordan came with me. It was on her way to the New Orleans airport."

"Jesus. You realize Kaiser has no idea she's with you?"

"Yes, but is that really the issue right now?"

"You're right. Has McDavitt decided whether he'll do the flight for me?"

She gestured forward at Carl, and he came back into the cabin and took the phone from her.

"Penn, Danny says he'll do it. But this is a big favor, bro. I don't think *I'd* do it except that I don't think you'll ever get a warrant to search that place. Not unless it's a federal one, and you might not even get that."

Carl nodded at whatever Penn answered.

"We can't take the girls with us," he went on. "Danny says no way. If we find something and have to set down, they can't be any part of it. Even if we don't set down, we might have to fly straight back to the departmental helipad. . . . Right. I'll call you when we're on our way. You want Caitlin back? . . . You sure? . . . Okay. Out."

Carl stuffed the phone back into his pocket and shrugged in apology.

"It's all right," Caitlin said. "Finding Tom's more important than anything else right now."

"The problem," Danny said in the headset, "is what to do if we find him. He's still wanted for killing a state trooper."

"We'll burn that bridge when we come to it," Carl said. "Let's get these ladies back to their vehicle."

"Just a second," Jordan said.

"Yeah?" Carl asked.

"We don't have to go all the way back to the car. Set us down by that fisherman—Mose. He can help us find the X on the map while you guys search Valhalla."

Carl didn't look wild about this idea. He did not want to have to explain to Penn that he'd let her go searching for the Bone Tree with only Jordan and an old man to protect her. "It'd take too long to find Mose."

"No, it won't," Danny said from the cockpit. "He keeps a two-way radio with him for emergencies. I can call him right now. If Mose answers, I can set down on a little tussock, and you can hop right into his boat."

"Great," Carl muttered.

FIVE MINUTES LATER, DANNY McDavitt flared the chopper and settled his skids onto a little hummock of earth at the center of a big black pool. Mose Tyler stood his boat off at a safe distance while the JetRanger's rotors buffeted the mirrored surface into a stinging hail of icy droplets.

As they prepared to exit the chopper, Carl said, "I don't think Penn will appreciate me dropping you two into this swamp with only Mose Tyler for protection."

"Penn's not in charge of this hunt," Caitlin told him. "I am. And we're both carrying guns."

"Show me."

Caitlin reached into her bag and pulled out the 9 mm Springfield Penn had bought her a month earlier.

"You know how to use that?"

"Yep. Dr. Cage taught me."

Carl looked at Jordan. "I guess you're an expert with that nine mil I saw earlier?"

Jordan smiled. "I hit what I aim at."

"Well, then. I guess you two can handle anything but a platoon-sized assault. But I'm still going to give you one of our departmental walkie-talkies. About all you can do with your cell phone down here is play games on it, or run down the battery while it pings for a tower every minute."

"I've gotten a couple of bars down here before," Danny interjected. "Depends on where you are, weather conditions, who your carrier is, a lot of things. Leave them on just in case."

"In case of what?" Jordan asked. "In case we find ourselves in a *Deliverance*-type situation?"

Carl laughed appreciatively. "I've got a feeling you could handle that just fine."

Jordan jumped out of the chopper, and Caitlin followed. The shock of the ground jolted her bones, but she managed to keep her feet. As Danny lifted off and beat away toward the west, Caitlin waved for Mose Tyler to bring his boat in.

CHAPTER 57

STANDING OUTSIDE THE room where John Kaiser probes in vain at Snake Knox, I try to maintain my composure in the face of a painful reality: yesterday, when Caitlin made love to me at my house on Washington Street, she did not do it out of desire, but because I had raised the possibility of sending Stone and Kaiser in search of the Bone Tree. Instead of answering me, she removed her pants and made sure that my newest brainstorm evaporated quickly and completely. She knew then that she planned to spend today searching the Lusahatcha Swamp, and she would only be doing that if she had a lead on the Bone Tree that she didn't tell me about. I suppose I can't resent this, since I've held back most of the Kennedy information, but the idea that she could—and did—manipulate me so easily is more than a little troubling. It begs the question, how many times has she done that before?

Taking a deep breath, I open the door to the interrogation room, walk through, and become part of the movie being recorded on the video camera's cassette.

"Hello, Snake," I say amicably.

Knox looks over at me with the flattened lips of a smile, but his eyes are ice cold. "Well, well, Mayor Cage is in the house. You look more like your daddy every year. Minus the beard, of course."

Kaiser glares at me, waiting for an explanation of my interruption.

Now that I'm physically in the room with Snake, it's difficult to remember that our real target is Sonny Thornfield. Because this smug bastard clearly knows everything we want to know. He knows where my father is, at this moment. He knows who killed Viola Turner. He knows who murdered all those civil rights victims, because he was there himself when most of them died. He may even know who really killed John Kennedy.

But he's never going to tell us.

Ignoring Snake's chatter, I motion for Kaiser to follow me outside so I can tell him about Jordan and Caitlin's airborne adventure. When he hesitates, Snake says, "Did you hear Mister Kaiser say he thinks my crew killed President Kennedy? I think he's angling for a book deal, Mayor. Can you help him out any?"

"I can probably get *you* one, Snake. But you'd better write it quick. You can't keep the profits from a book written in prison."

Kaiser follows me into the hall and shuts the door behind us.

"This better be serious," he says. "Don't tell me Claude Devereux has shown up to spring the Eagles?"

"No. But you're not going to like this. Jordan isn't on her way to New Orleans right now."

Kaiser tenses himself for bad news. "Where is she?"

"She and Caitlin sneaked down to Lusahatcha County to hunt for the goddamned Bone Tree. They're flying around in a chopper with two guys I know."

"You're fucking kidding me."

"You know I'm not. Don't worry, these guys are deputies. Carl Sims is a former marine sniper, and Danny McDavitt was a decorated chopper pilot in Vietnam."

Kaiser shakes his head in exasperation. "I had a feeling she was up to something, but she played it damned cool."

"Same here. Well . . . now that you know, why don't you get back in there and finish up with that asshole so you can move on to Sonny Thornfield?"

"I will. But remember what I said: I can't rush it with Snake. Every minute I spend with him buys me another minute with Sonny. I'm going to spend at least fifty more minutes with him."

I try to look downcast, and it works.

"I'm sorry, Penn. I know you want your father home. But you know a plea bargain is a slow process."

I nod. "Yeah, I get it."

The FBI agent pats me on the shoulder. "Thanks for telling me about Jordan. Snake got to me a little with that threat."

"I saw."

Kaiser clucks his tongue. "That means Snake saw, too."

After he returns to the interrogation room, I count to ten, then hurry to find Sheriff Dennis's utility room.

The big man is waiting for me two corners down the hallway. Drafting behind his broad back, I move down a second hallway, then take a sharp turn into a concrete-floored area that stinks of disinfectant and old vomit. Dennis turns right, into a cul-de-sac, then opens a door to a dim, ten-by-ten room crowded with cleaning supplies, paper towels, toilet paper, and mops. Unshielded pipes and conduit run along the walls and hang from the ceiling. It is to one of these ceiling pipes that Sonny Thornfield has been chained by his wrists. His dark Creole skin cannot hide the nearly bloodless state of his face. This man is a quivering mass of fear, which makes me wonder what Walt said to him during Sheriff Dennis's absence. Thornfield actually looks relieved to see me as Walt looms at his side. *Does Sonny think I've come to rescue him?* Walker closes the door behind us, then takes up a position behind me.

"Thank God," Sonny almost whimpers. "Help me, Mayor. This guy's crazy! He already tried to torture me a couple of days ago."

With his cowboy hat pulled low and his expression grim, Walt Garrity certainly looks the part of the professional torturer.

"Listen to me, Sonny," I say. "I'm going to ask you some questions, and you're going to answer every one. Nobody's ever going to know where I got my information. I promise you that much protection. *But*—if you don't answer, Captain Garrity there is going to do whatever is necessary to make you talk. Is that clear?"

"Just tell me what you want! My heart can't take no more strain, Mayor. I don't know nothing anyway."

"I hope that's a lie, Sonny. For your sake."

"What do you want?"

"I want to know where my father is."

Sonny's eyes go wide, and he looks from me to Dennis, then back. "I don't know! The last time I saw him was Tuesday night. Him and this fella here kidnapped me from my fishing camp. They tortured me in a van, and then they killed that trooper!" Spittle flies from Thornfield's mouth in his panicked state. "I don't care about that trooper, 'cause Deke Dunn was an asshole anyhow. But this'un here wanted to kill me afterwards! Thank God Dr. Cage made him take me to the hospital. Doc's a good man, and I know you are, too. *Please* don't let him hurt me. I've got grandkids, and my heart can't take it. I already had one coronary this week. I can't stand no more, I swear."

One glance at Walt tells me Sonny is telling the truth about Tuesday. But my gut says he's lying about my father. Unfortunately, he's not lying about his heart condition.

"I don't want to hurt you, Sonny. But I will. And you're right: you could have another heart attack at any moment. If you don't want to die for Forrest Knox, you'd better tell me where Dad is. I don't care about any of the rest of it. Tell me the truth, no matter how bad it is. Is my father dead?"

The old man shakes his head, on the verge of tears. "No . . . he ain't. At least I don't think he is."

My heart leaps and begins to pound. "Tell me where he is!"

"Forrest took him last night. Doc was hiding out at that colored lawyer's place in Jefferson County. But Snake didn't want to come in here without some kind of insurance. He was worried about some kind of setup, something like that planted meth, I guess."

"So what did he do?"

"We took the doc back from Forrest last night."

"Where is he now?"

"You swear to God you won't tell Snake or Forrest I told you?" Sonny's eyes go to Dennis. "They'll kill me, Sheriff. Ya'll will just go get the doc and say you found him, right? If I tell you where he's at, will you do that?"

"There's no 'if' to you telling, Sonny," Walker says from behind me. "*Talk.*"

"Okay, I'm trusting you. Dr. Cage is at my little fishing cabin on Old River."

I can scarcely believe this. Old River is less than ten miles from where we stand. "Are you lying, Sonny? Are you trying to stall me?"

"No! I swear by Jesus!"

"That's where we picked this guy up Tuesday," Walt

says. "There's no legal record of the place. We found it using a GPS tracker."

"Who's guarding my father?" I ask Sonny.

"Nobody! We're all here. I swear, Mayor, he's just tied up good."

"Is he hurt?"

"He ain't in the best shape, but he's breathing." Thornfield's voice betrays how little confidence he has in his captive's well-being.

"My truck's outside," Walt says excitedly. "Let's go get him."

"Wait," says Sheriff Dennis. "What do we do with Sonny meanwhile?"

"Nothing yet." I'm surprised by the emotionless tone of my own voice. "I've got one more question. Who killed Viola Turner, Sonny? No bullshit. Your life depends on it."

The old man's chin and lips quiver as he shakes his head. "I don't know. I swear to God, Mayor. Snake might know, but I don't."

I've watched too many suspects lie to be fooled by Thornfield's false sincerity. "You're lying. Make him tell me, Walt."

Sonny's eyes bulge as Walt grabs a long, wet towel, throws it over the pipe, and quickly ties a knot. With the dangling end he ties a second knot around the hanging cloth, making a functional noose.

"Oh, no, now," Thornfield cries, starting to weep. "My heart'll blow out if you lift me up there! I don't know nothing about that nurse, I swear."

I lean forward until my eyes are only inches from his. "Who killed Viola, Sonny? I know you saw her die."

Thornfield is too terrified to retreat from his lie. He shakes his head like a thousand suspects I've seen driven into a corner, clinging desperately to what they believe is their only currency.

"Lift him up there, guys," I say coldly.

Walt grabs Sonny by the shoulders and positions him beneath the noose. Sheriff Dennis steps around me in the tight space and grabs the old man by the waist.

"Jesus, no," Sonny pleads. "*Don't do it!*"

Sonny screams, but I lose the sound when the door

behind me flies open and bangs against the cinder-block wall. When I turn, I see John Kaiser staring wide-eyed at us with a combination of amazement and disgust.

"Have you lost your fucking minds?" he asks.

Nobody answers.

"Let go of him, Garrity," Kaiser orders.

Walt doesn't move.

With calm deliberation, Kaiser draws a pistol from an ankle holster and aims it at Walt's head. "Step away, Captain. Anybody reaches for a weapon, I'll fire. Does anybody doubt that?"

"Do what he says, Walt," I say softly. "Walker, you too."

"Hey, I'm done," Dennis says, dropping his hands from Sonny's waist.

After a tense few seconds, I hear the slap of wet cloth on Sonny's head as Walt drops the noose.

"Everybody out in the hall," Kaiser says, backing out of the doorway. "*Now.*"

We step into the hallway, but Kaiser doesn't stay with us. Instead, he moves into the utility room and closes the door. I hear muffled voices inside.

"We done stepped in the shit now," Walker says. "If only he'd waited another minute before busting in there. Goddamn it."

"If we wait here, Kaiser might arrest us," I think aloud. "We know where Dad is. We'd better get going."

"It's his word against ours," Dennis snaps. "He can't arrest us. This is my department."

"Don't kid yourself. He'll do it. Normally, he'd call in the state police, but Kaiser's not about to do that. Forrest and Ozan might show up in response. But it doesn't matter. Walt, you've definitely got to get out of here. You're wanted for murdering a cop. I'll call you as soon as I'm outside."

Walt nods, then trots up the hall and disappears around the corner.

"I guess we're standing our ground?" I ask Walker.

As the doorknob of the utility room rattles, I whirl, and the sheriff jams something into my back pocket.

Kaiser steps out of the room and glares at Dennis. "Sheriff, I'm taking custody of all your prisoners until such time as the governor can make a determination about your fitness to continue in office. You will either confine yourself to your office or go home for the day. I suggest the latter."

"You've got no authority over me," Walker says. "It's your word against mine, and unless you call the state police, you can't do a thing. And you don't want to call them."

An odd smile touches Kaiser's lips. "Sheriff, a wanted cop killer just fled the premises and you made no attempt to arrest him. That's dereliction of duty. You may have noticed that Forrest Knox is not here to challenge federal authority today. I suggest you take a page from his book."

Without waiting for Walker to respond, Kaiser turns to me and says, "You're done here, Penn. Go home to your daughter."

"John, they've—"

"I don't care what they've done! You can't torture people. You know that. This is a perfect illustration of how unhinged your father's situation has made you. Don't make me jail you, Penn. Go home."

"I didn't see any cop killer in here," Sheriff Dennis says.

"Louisiana," Kaiser mutters. "I guess it never changes after all. Get out of my sight, both of you."

WALT, SHERIFF DENNIS, AND I huddle between a CPSO inmate van and a mobile crime-lab trailer. Sheriff Dennis is burning with rage and frustration, but Walt looks ready to roll.

"I've got Dr. Elliott's truck and plenty of guns," he says. "Let's go get Tom."

"Did you get the phone I put in your pocket?" Dennis asks me.

Reaching into my back pocket, I pull out a StarTac cash phone. "Whose is this?"

"I took it off Deputy Hunt this morning. I think he was using it to talk to Knox's people. I'm thinking it might be a line to Forrest himself."

"Did you try any of the numbers in it?"

"There's only one. Nobody answered."

"Where's Deputy Hunt now?"

"I had my nephew lock him up at the gun range. I wasn't sure how I wanted to handle him."

"Go get him. Take him somewhere that no one could possibly find him. If Forrest knows he's been taken, he's already got men trying to kill him. We may need Hunt before we're finished."

"Don't you want me to come to Thornfield's cabin with you?"

"Walt and I can handle it."

Walker hesitates, then nods. "If that's how you want to play it, okay. Call me if you need me. And be careful."

As the sheriff trots away, Walt starts toward Drew's truck.

"I'm going to take my car," I call to him. "You're still a fugitive, and depending on what Kaiser has done about our little hanging party, you may need to rabbit one more time."

"Okay."

Adrenaline flushes through me as I sprint for my Audi.

"THIS THING'S GOING OFF the rails," Forrest said, pulling his coat around him as the wind over the deck picked up. "I can feel it."

"What you want to do, boss?" Ozan asked.

Forrest shook his head and wished he had a cigarette. He couldn't move any faster than he was already. He'd hoped to reassure Snake by phone—and also to ask for a proof of life on Dr. Cage—but when the mole offered Snake a cell phone, Snake's only answer had been to point at his watch. Forrest understood that message well enough. But now that so much time had passed, he was starting to worry that his worst fear was true.

"I think Dr. Cage is dead, Alphonse. There's no other reason for Snake to put off talking to me like this. Not that I can see, anyway. And if Dr. Cage is dead . . . there's no deal to be made with Penn Cage. Not one that'll hold, anyway."

Ozan pulled his hands from his pockets and rubbed them together in the wind. "I reckon not."

"I've got to know, one way or the other. But Snake's the only person who can tell me. Claude's bugged out, and I'm not bringing in a new lawyer this late in the game. We're going to have to get Snake out of that jail regardless of the risk."

"Just Snake?"

"No. All of them. Otherwise, somebody's going to start thinking about cutting a deal. But getting all of them out is going to take some precision timing combined with reckless daring." Forrest sucked his teeth, reflecting on his choice of manpower.

"You know that Black Team can handle it," Ozan said.

"I'm not so sure anymore. They'd *better* handle their end."

"Who was that you called earlier?"

"Glenn Morehouse's sister. Wilma Deen. She's as cold as they come. Not many women would stand by quiet while you killed their brother, much less help you do it."

"She done that?"

Forrest nodded. "This past Monday. She's old school, boy. Like that Madame Defarge in *A Tale of Two Cities*."

Ozan looked blank.

"I also called Billy about a bastard child of Snake's. Alois Engel's his name. The kid's only twenty-five but he's a mean little fucker. He's already affiliated with a couple of white supremacist groups. Cold as ice. Reminds me of a Hitler Youth poster. He's done work for Billy in the meth trade, too. Anyway, the point in using him and Wilma is that, if anything goes bad with the end of the op—which is the biggest risk—Kaiser will think Snake brought 'em in. Not me."

Ozan gave a malevolent grin. "Now you're talkin', babe."

"Let's start assembling the team. We're going to need the whole goody bag, too."

"It's time, boss. Waiting never helped anything."

CHAPTER 58

AS WALT AND I race toward Old River, a dead-end channel still connected to the Mississippi River by a narrow chute, the atrocities Kaiser wrote me about spin through my mind like curling strips of black-and-white film. To accept that men capable of such acts have control of my father is tantamount to resigning myself to his death. For while Snake Knox and his crew are behind bars at this moment, they had half the night to work their will on my father, and Forrest—the feared ghost of the Vietnamese Highlands—had him before Snake did.

As I focus on holding the wheel steady on the gravel road, Walt points along the row of bizarre stilt houses that line Old River. This part of the parish always floods when the river rises, hence the tall metal stilts beneath every structure. The little cabins look like ugly cranes on long, thin legs, waiting for an unwary fish to swim down the brown channel behind them. Most of the cabins have a crude elevator system, fashioned from a welded iron cage and an electric truck-winch to lift it.

I'm suspicious of Sonny's claim that Dad is unguarded, but Walt insists that speed is everything now. As soon as I pull into the driveway he tells me to, Walt leaps out with his pistol and boards the cage that will carry him to Sonny's raised deck. Walt tests the machine by gripping the rail and heaving himself from right to left, then lays his hand on the lever that will start the winch.

"You take the staircase," he says. "If somebody comes out, start shooting, because I'm a sitting duck in this thing."

I look at the four flights of steps that lead the thirty feet up to the cabin. "My fire will be blocked as I near the top."

"Then get up there before I do, and if they start shooting, kick in the back door and kill them from behind."

"Okay."

Walt flips the start lever on the winch, and with a grinding hum he begins rising toward the tree house–like structure. I sprint for the base of the staircase, then start pumping my legs as I did running the bleachers as a high school football player. In seconds my chest is pounding and my throat burning, but the door isn't far away. I'll beat Walt to the cabin by ten seconds.

Once I reach the deck behind the cabin, I tiptoe to the back door, my ears tuned to the slightest sound. I hear nothing. A clang from the winch around front tells me Walt has reached the front platform. The fact that no one has opened up on him must be a sign that Sonny was telling the truth about no guards.

The back door is locked. As I raise my foot to kick it in, Walt yells, "Front door's open!"

Worried that someone might be lying in ambush for him, I kick open the flimsy back door and burst into the den of the little structure. The cabin stinks of mildew and looks to have been furnished with cast-off pieces or actual junk. A plywood square has fallen from a footlocker that served as the base of a makeshift coffee table, and the Naugahyde sofa against the wall has been patched all over with silver duct tape.

"I'll check the back," Walt says, gesturing at a narrow doorway with his pistol.

I nod, but my belief that Dad might still be here is evaporating fast. Two medicine bottles lie on a square of shag carpet that looks like its purpose is to serve as a toilet for an incontinent dog. Picking one of them up, I read the label: *PATIENT: Thomas Cage. PHYSICIAN: Drew Elliott, M.D. Nitroglycerine, 0.4 mg.*

"He's not back there," Walt says, emerging from the doorway. "Maybe he got away?"

I shake my head. "He'd never have left his drugs. There's nitro and pain pills on the floor. He couldn't do without either. Not for long, anyway."

Walt kicks the plywood sheet against the wall, plops down on the patched sofa, and kicks his feet up on the footlocker. "You think they knew we were coming?"

"How? Sonny couldn't have told them. More likely, Forrest figured out where they were and took them back."

"Damn it. What about Sheriff Dennis? Could he have warned them by phone?"

"No fucking way. Dennis hates the Knoxes."

"Yeah. I was reaching."

"It had to be Forrest, Walt. Unless . . ."

"What?"

"Unless Snake came back here and moved him somewhere else. I think Sonny was telling the truth. He believed Dad was here. But you heard him. He said Snake was worried about a setup. He wanted insurance. Maybe Snake worried that Sonny was too weak to stand much interrogation, so he made sure that nobody but him knew where Dad really was."

"Well, we can't question Snake. Kaiser won't let us near him."

I think back to Snake's smug countenance. "Nope. And questioning Forrest is pointless, unless we're willing to do what we just did to Sonny. And even if we were, that's easier said than done with him."

Walt nods thoughtfully. "I know where Forrest is. The Bouchard lake house, Lake Concordia. Forrest and Ozan were on the outside deck, and I searched the whole place."

"Could you have missed Dad?"

"No. Tom could've been in the boathouse, I suppose, but I just don't think Forrest would keep a hostage that close to him. Much more likely Tom would be out at Valhalla."

"But you were there, too."

Walt shrugs. "They could have moved him back to either place since I left. If we can't talk to Snake, then Forrest is our best chance. But we'll have to fight our way in there, unless either Sheriff Dennis can get us a warrant—"

"That won't happen."

"—or you set up some kind of negotiation with Forrest."

"The way I did with Brody Royal? That didn't end too well."

"I didn't say it was a good plan. But it might be the only one."

"No matter what happens, Forrest could order Dad killed, then say he died while resisting arrest. Not only that, he could arrest you as a fugitive, and me for interfering on your behalf."

"Can you get a warrant for Valhalla?" Walt asks.

"Lusahatcha County is in our court district, and I know the circuit judge in Natchez. I can probably get a warrant, but I don't know that Sheriff Ellis would serve it. From what I've heard, he's pretty cozy with the local hunting camp owners, including the Knoxes. Plus, Valhalla is known to be connected with the Knoxes. I don't think they'd stash him in a place we could find using common knowledge, paperwork, or computers."

"Shit," says Walt, spitting on the floor.

"You just left your DNA here," I observe.

"Fuck some DNA. We're way past that now."

We sit in silence for several seconds, and in the strange vacuum, a profound fear begins to flow through me. "Walt," I say in a flat voice. "What does your gut tell you? Do you think they've killed him?"

"I've worried from the start they meant to kill him so he'd go down as Viola's killer, and that investigation would stop. And with the trooper hanging around our necks . . . we just made it too easy for them."

Walt's tone of despair leaves me feeling hollowed out. Short of getting Snake Knox in that CPSO broom closet with Walt and a wet towel, I don't see that we have an option.

"Hey," Walt says, shoving the old footlocker with his foot.

"What?"

"You see this? This is a marine footlocker, World War Two vintage. It's made of wood. I saw a few of 'em in Korea."

"So?"

"So it's got a brand-new padlock on it. A Chubb. Take a look."

Looking down, I see a pitted, flimsy-looking latch with a heavy, shining padlock on it. Above the circular latch is a metal nameplate with the letters CPL. SONNY THORNFIELD stamped on it. The same letters are stenciled on top of the oblong box, but they've faded to near invisibility.

Walt taps his thighs, his eyes on the padlock. "Why

does an old gomer like Sonny lock up his piece-of-shit footlocker like it's holding the crown jewels?"

"Maybe it's all he's got in the world."

Walt slides up to the edge of the sofa and leans forward. "Let's find out."

Reversing his pistol in his hand, he hammers at the latch and lock, but they refuse to yield.

I get up and go through the drawers beside the plastic sink against the wall, hunting for a screwdriver. I don't find one, but in the back of the drawer I find an old rat-tail file, as rusty as some tool left behind by the slaves who built the pyramids. Taking it in my hand, I go to the footlocker, wedge it into the latch, and with one savage twist snap the latch free from the lid of the case.

"Good man," says Walt. "Let's see what that old fool thinks is worth protecting. Probably ten years' worth of *Hustler*."

My stomach feels strangely hollow as I lift the lid, just the way it did when as a boy I secretly unpacked my Christmas presents after finding them hidden in a closet. In the dim light of the cabin, I see mementos of Sonny Thornfield's younger life stacked carefully in layers. A woman must have packed this locker. Digging patiently through it, I find war ribbons and medals; a pistol and bayonet; an ancient tube of Barbasol shaving lotion; a marine forage cap; a Ku Klux Klan hood and several Klan pins—one a fiery cross wrought in gold—lying on what appears to be a folded white robe; a stack of baseball cards from the early 1940s, bound by a dry-rotted rubber band; a cup of multicolored marbles; a *Playboy* magazine from 1953; a snapshot of a Ku Klux Klan rally in Natchez, probably the big one held in the summer of 1965; two hand grenades that have been emptied of explosive; Thornfield's birth certificate, along with several other yellowed legal papers, including his honorable discharge from the Marine Corps. But at the bottom of the footlocker, pressed between two ancient hymnals, lies a memento of a different sort—the sort that Kaiser dealt with in his previous life.

What I first think is just a chamois cloth is actually a soft swatch of leather with the letters *USN* needled into it with dark blue ink. Above these letters are an anchor and a rope. About five inches long, and brown as stained walnut, the skin has rolled a little at the edges. Fighting the urge to gag, I lift the thing from the bottom of the footlocker. The obscene trophy is soft and buttery, like the finest grain leather. It *is* leather, I remind myself. Tanned to perfection by someone with a deep knowledge of such things.

"Son of a *bitch*," Walt intones.

I try to speak, but my throat has sealed shut. The ragged edges of the thing in my hand make it plain that it was cut from Jimmy Revels's arm. I only hope he was dead when it happened.

"This is my ticket back into the sheriff's office," I finally whisper. "To talk to Snake Knox."

"Is that where we're going?"

After hastily repacking the footlocker, I fasten it shut, then look up at the old Ranger. "No. Not yet. Kaiser won't let us do what we'd need to do to Snake."

Walt nods gravely. "Where then?"

"It's time to talk to Forrest Knox."

His eyes narrow. "You gonna call him on that cell phone Dennis gave you? Try to cut a deal with him?"

"There's no deal to be had. We're going to find out where Dad is, no matter what that takes."

An unspoken question rises in Walt's eyes. I lay the tattoo in his callused hand, then get to my feet and check my pistol. The old Ranger looks down at the tanned skin for several seconds without speaking, feeling it between his fingers. Then he brings it closer to his face so that his aging eyes can focus on the inked letters.

"Jesus wept," he says finally. "I had a brother who served in the navy. No matter what happens at Knox's place, I'm gonna kill the motherfucker who done this."

CHAPTER 59

THE BOUCHARD LAKE house sits on the side of Lake Concordia farthest from the Mississippi River. A modernist, metal-skinned anomaly, it stands out among the older ranch houses and contemporary McMansions. At my request, Walker Dennis waited for us four miles up the road in the parking lot of a small grocery store that serves the lake residents. There I parked my Audi and climbed into Drew's truck, while Walker followed us in his marked Tahoe.

During the drive here, Walt told me two things I could scarcely believe: first, that he'd planted the derringer that killed Trooper Deke Dunn inside Forrest Knox's Baton Rouge home; and second, that while exploring Forrest's computer, he'd discovered a video of a state police SWAT unit murdering what appeared to be black drug dealers during Hurricane Katrina. Walt rather unwisely turned this video over to Colonel Griffith Mackiever, but so far as he knows, the derringer still remains in Knox's house. The implications of this information are too explosive for me to predict, yet I will be facing Forrest himself in less than five minutes.

When we reach the driveway of the Bouchard house, Walker Dennis pulls in after me and blocks the drive with his Tahoe, then climbs out with an AR-15 mounting an ACOG sight on its top rail.

"What's the fire signal?" he asks.

"If I raise my right forefinger, blow him away."

"Forrest first?"

"Whoever's the most immediate threat."

Dennis nods, then walks behind the Tahoe and rests his rifle on the hood, making a bench rest of his vehicle.

Walt drives slowly up the driveway: thirty meters, forty . . . I lay my hand on his arm and wait for him to turn to me. When he does, I say, "Tell me one thing, Walt. Did Dad kill Viola? I don't care either way at this point. I just need to know."

The old Ranger's eyes don't waver. "I honestly don't know. I just came to help the man, because he's my friend."

I actually believe this. Walt and my father are from a different era, almost a different nation. The code by which they live probably precluded Walt from even asking the question.

"What if they just open up on us from the house?" he asks.

"They won't. If they're watching, they'll have seen Walker's bubble lights already."

Walt doesn't look reassured. "You sure you don't want to try to call Knox on that cell phone?"

"Nope. I've got other plans for that phone."

The brakes squeak as Walt rolls to a stop twenty meters from the house. I can just see the corner of the rear deck jutting out from the second floor. As I stare, a head appears, silhouetted against the sky. After several seconds, it withdraws.

"We just lost the element of surprise," Walt deadpans, glancing into the backseat, where the veritable arsenal of firearms he brought from Texas lies in a padded duffel bag.

"I don't think we ever had it. I'll get out and wait for them. You stay in here until I clarify the situation. We don't want them shooting you before they understand the price."

Climbing out of the truck, I stand with my .357 hanging in plain view against my leg. In less than a minute, the side door of the house opens and two men emerge, one of average height, but well built and with the grace of an athlete; the other shorter and built like a small refrigerator. As they approach, the second man's brick-colored skin becomes obvious. Alphonse Ozan.

"Hello, Mayor," says the taller man, whose dark face has now resolved into recognizable features. Forrest Knox looks like the actor Kenneth Tobey, but with a dark suntan, pocked skin, and black hair. He's square jawed and almost handsome, but a badly disfigured ear and his disturbingly direct eyes make me uneasy. "What can I do for you?"

"Tell me where my father is."

Forrest gives me a bemused smile. "How would I know that?"

"You kidnapped him last night, and then your uncle snatched him from you. Now something tells me you've taken him back. In any case, I don't have time for a long explanation. Just tell me where he is now."

Forrest drums the fingers of his right hand against the knuckles of his left. "Who's that in the truck, Mayor? Looks like he might be a wanted cop killer."

"He is. And he's going to get out. But before he does, I want you to note the sniper at the end of your driveway. He's got you zeroed right now."

Forrest chuckles softly. "Can that clown hit me from there?"

"The deer heads on his office wall tell me he probably can." I turn to Drew's truck and motion for Walt to get out. As he does, I give Alphonse Ozan a warning glance. "I don't want either of you touching a cell phone. If you do, Sheriff Dennis will fire and I'll swear you went for your guns."

Forrest laughs softly. "You've got some balls for a lawyer, don't you?"

"You called this play. I'm only doing what I have to do for my family."

Knox gives me a measuring look. "What do you really know about me, Mayor?"

"I know you used to leave JFK half-dollars in the mouths of men you killed in Vietnam."

"That Kaiser does his homework, doesn't he?"

"It wasn't all book work. He was at FSB Ripcord when you were there."

"No shit?" The intelligent eyes narrow with curiosity. "Well, now. If we're going to speak any further, I need you wanded."

Without further prompting, Ozan takes a black wand from his pocket and runs it the length of my body. I can imagine Walker Dennis tensing for a shot, thinking Ozan is making a move on me. The wand beeps when it passes the cell phone in my back pocket, but I show Ozan that it's switched off.

When the Redbone wands Walt, the instrument begins beeping loudly near his ankles.

"My throwdown," Walt informs him. "Try to take that, and I'll beat you to death with it."

Ozan chuckles like Walt's a funny old codger.

As he straightens up, Forrest says, "Who planted the meth on my relatives?"

"This conversation's drifting off point, Colonel. I'm only concerned about my father."

"Your daddy murdered a state trooper, Mayor. That makes this a problematic conversation."

"Bullshit," says Walt. "I killed that asshole Dunn, and he was no cop. He was a disgrace to his badge. I stopped him from committing murder."

Forrest gives Walt a hard look, then motions for me to follow him away from the other men. "Let's move downwind and keep this civil," he says. "Otherwise there may be casualties."

When we're out of earshot, Forrest turns to me. "You tried to cut a deal with Brody Royal, didn't you? That was your mistake right there. Brody was a megalomaniac. I'm a pragmatist."

"Is that right?"

"You can find out right now. Let's hear your offer."

"I'm not here to make an offer."

"That's too bad. Because I did speak to your father last night, and his main hope was that we can all come to a mutually satisfactory arrangement. His idea is to blame the casualties up to this point on dead people—Brody, Regan, and Morehouse, say—and you and your fiancée back the fuck away from this stupid Double Eagle story, and everything you think goes with it."

Trying not to read anything into his verb tenses, I say, "Where did you speak to my father?"

"That doesn't matter. But we had a good visit last night. Talked about the old days—and my old man, of course. Daddy thought a hell of a lot of Dr. Cage."

"I don't imagine the feeling was mutual."

Forrest barks a laugh. "Are you kidding? Your dad and mine got along great. They'd both been through the same meat grinder in Korea. They had different politics, sure, but they respected each other. Hell, Daddy even knew Dr. Cage used to patch up the black agitators when they got hurt, but he didn't care."

I try to imagine my father respecting Frank Knox, but I can't see it.

"Doc got into some trouble over in Korea," Forrest says in a confiding tone. "He ever tell you about that? Bad trouble. He nearly went to prison, I believe. Daddy said he got fucked over by the army for doing the right thing, whatever that means. But I guess old Tom didn't want you worrying he might not be the hero you thought he was." Forrest smiles with what appears to be genuine nostalgia. "You know, Dr. Cage had to stitch me up five or six times when I was a kid."

"Do you remember Viola assisting him?" I ask quietly.

The nostalgia goes out of Knox's face, but his eyes still gleam as though from an inner heat. "I sure do. She wasn't the kind of woman you forget."

Could he possibly be Lincoln's father? I wonder, noting the dark color of his skin, which looks like the result of Creole blood and not a suntan in December. He's actually darker than Sonny Thornfield, but I won't accomplish anything here by going down that road.

"I made a mistake with Brody," I tell him. "I thought he was the man behind all this. But I was wrong. It's been you all along." I step closer to Forrest, and as I do, I get the feeling not many people invade this man's personal space. "I'm not here to cut a deal. I don't know whether you've got Dad right now or not. But if you don't, you've got the best chance of finding out where he is. So I'm giving you until six this evening to put him safely in my care. After that, if he's not back in the bosom of his family—"

"Are you seriously about to threaten me, Mayor?"

"Not physically. But let me finish. If you don't get my father back safe in the bosom of his family, I'm going to do what I do best."

"Which is?"

"There's an old saying, Colonel. The mills of the gods grind slow, but they grind to powder. You know that one?"

Forrest cocks his head, which gives me a better look at the scarred nub of his ear. "I suppose you're God in this hypothetical?"

"No, I'm the grinding wheel. I sent sixteen killers to death row in Houston. Thirteen have been executed. I'm no longer very proud of that, but it's a fact. So . . . you return my father, and I won't much care what happens to you. But if you don't, I'm going to resign the mayor's office and turn all my attention to you. All my legal ability and experience, my law enforcement and political connections, all the resources of my future father-in-law's media conglomerate—all that I will relentlessly focus on you. I'll peel you open, layer by layer. I'll dig up every enemy you ever made, every woman you betrayed, every cop you ever paid off, every lie you told, every corpse you buried, every dollar you moved offshore, every tax return you ever filed. Then I'll grind you to powder, bone by bone. I won't stop until there's nothing left."

Forrest Knox is looking at me as though seeing me for the first time. He doesn't speak for a while, but when he finally does, he sounds anything but rattled. "That might be tougher than you think, Counselor. You see, my enemies are dead. Their bodies no longer exist, my women know better, my brothers in uniform *are* brothers, my money is safe, and I've paid my taxes. I'm basically bulletproof."

"Nobody's bulletproof." The time has come for my bit of theater. "To illustrate my point, I've got a message for you."

"Yeah? From who?"

Moving very slowly, so as not to trigger a shot by Sheriff Dennis, I take Deputy Hunt's cell phone from my back pocket.

While Forrest watches, I power up the phone and wait for it to acquire a signal. Knox is squinting at the device as though it looks familiar. When two bars show on the screen, I pull up the number last called and hit REDIAL. After a pregnant pause, during which Knox leans forward to better see the phone, a cell phone in his pocket begins to ring. At the second ring, his eyes widen like those of an ice fisherman who realizes he's walked too far out on the lake.

"Technically," I say, "I guess this message is from Deputy Hunt. But in a larger sense, you *could* say it's a message from God. He's telling you to cut your losses while you can."

Forrest looks like he's thinking about snatching the phone from me.

I nearly wag my finger at him, but then I remember that

would trigger a shot from Sheriff Dennis. "Six o'clock," I repeat. "After that, I'm giving Deputy Hunt to the FBI, turning Caitlin and her father loose on you, and going to work myself. If that happens, you can forget taking over the state police. They'll be processing you into Angola within six months, I guarantee it. And I can't imagine a much worse hell for a dirty cop who uses snipers to take out his black competition. That would be a fitting end, but it's one you have the power to avoid."

Forrest hasn't blinked for maybe a minute. He probably looked like this when he staked out trails at night in Vietnam. After a few more silent seconds, a tight smile broadens his mouth, and he reaches out as though to shake my hand in acceptance of my terms.

Don't do it, says a voice in my head. *He's playing you. Raise your finger and have Dennis blow his brains out. Any other choice is giving this man a chance to tear your life apart.* If Walt weren't already wanted for killing a state trooper, I might raise my finger and take my chances in court. But that's not really an option now.

Suppressing my revulsion, I take Forrest's hand and shake it. "We're going to leave now," I say evenly. "If either of you touch your weapons, Walker will fire. He won't hesitate, trust me. He lost a cousin to one of your men, and he'd love some payback."

Again Knox's dark eyes glint with interest. "This has been an enlightening visit, Mayor. I look forward to our next meeting."

"One more thing, Forrest. I'm not your problem. The federal government is. Special Agent Kaiser is running Sheriff Dennis's department now, and he wants your ass bad. I think he's wanted you for a long time. You need to get my father back, so you can focus on staying out of federal prison."

I walk away from Knox without waiting for a response, nor do I speak when I pass Walt. All that matters now is Walker Dennis and his rifle. Without them, Walt and I would already be dead.

WALT GARRITY WATCHED FORREST Knox follow Penn with his eyes, then turn and walk back toward the lake house. Walt was about to follow Penn to the truck when the Redbone reached out and grasped his arm.

"What the hell are you doing here, Granddad? You sure as hell can't be no bodyguard."

Walt pulled his arm free and started to leave, but Ozan said, "So you shot Deke Dunn, huh? I find that pretty hard to believe."

After watching Forrest walk back into the lake house, a cell phone pressed to his ear, Walt finally gave his full attention to the combative trooper.

"That's because your head's full of stump water. Why don't you crawl back to whatever slough you crawled up out of?"

The Redbone's eyes blazed. He balled his right fist and stepped toward Walt, but Walt didn't move.

"You must be crazy," Ozan said. "Is that it? Alzheimer's got you?"

Walt spoke in a voice so low that the trooper had to lean forward to hear him. "I've known many a Redbone in my day, you know? Especially down around Galveston in the fifties. Some were hardworking boys you could trust to tote the key to the smokehouse. Others could wear a top hat and walk under a snake's belly. But I sized you up the second I saw you. There ain't much worse than a dirty cop. I don't mean a patrolman who takes his share of the pad to pay for his kid's braces. I'm talking about pricks who use their badge to extort and kill people. Pricks like you and your boss. I wouldn't be surprised if I bent my Colt over your daddy's head back in the day. And you could ask him about it, if you knew who he was. But I'm bettin' you don't."

As Ozan's cheek twitched, Walt said, "Tom Cage is worth two of me and ten of you. And if he don't come out of this thing alive and in one piece, I'm gonna cut the blood out of you. And I'll do the same to your boss."

"You mouthy fuck," Ozan said, reaching back and drawing a switchblade from his back pocket. The blade sprang out with a chilling snick.

Walt looked at the knife with disdain. "Crab apple switch? I figured you for an Arkansas toothpick."

"What the hell you talkin' about, old-timer?"

"You'll find out soon enough." Walt pointed at the lake

house. "Run home to Papa, son. We'll have our day, you and me."

Ozan waved the knife under Walt's chin. "Laugh it up now, Texas, but get ready. I'm gonna gag you and gut you and sit you in front of a mirror while I do it."

Walt spat within an inch of the trooper's boot. "I'll look forward to that party."

I STAND BY THE Tahoe with Walker Dennis, who is still sighting down his AR-15 at Ozan as Walt makes his way to Drew's pickup truck.

"I'd like you to cover us until we're clear here," I tell him. "Then escort me back to Vidalia."

"What about Garrity?"

"He needs to stay on these guys. As soon as I'm back in Vidalia, I want you to go to wherever you have Deputy Hunt and move him again. Find out everything he knows about the Knoxes, but don't kill him. Right now he's the only leverage we have against Forrest."

"Understood."

Drew Elliott's truck starts up and begins rolling toward us. "And Walker? Switch vehicles before you do it. We're not the only ones who know about GPS trackers."

Walker nods, his rifle still trained on the lake house.

When the truck reaches me, I pat Walker on the shoulder, then climb into the passenger seat beside Walt.

"Does Knox even know where Tom is?" he asks.

"I don't think so. I think Snake has stashed Dad somewhere."

"Oh, man. Lord, just give me ten minutes in a cell with Snake Knox and no cameras."

"You're not going to get it. That's why we're splitting up."

"What?"

"I'm going back to the sheriff's office. I can use Sonny's tattoo to buy my way back into the interrogations. You find a good spot to lie up and monitor Forrest by GPS. If he and Ozan make a move, stay with them. If they go to where Dad is, and you feel you have a chance, kill them and get him out of there. Or call Dennis and me, and we'll help you hit them."

Walt thought this through. "And if that call Knox just made was to order Tom killed?"

"There's only so much we can control, Walt. Let's get to it. Take me back to my Audi."

He shifts into Drive and pulls onto the narrow lake road.

"What was that between you and Ozan there at the end?" I ask.

"Just a little flirting. Nothing to worry about."

CHAPTER 60

THE VIEW FROM Danny McDavitt's helicopter had been overwhelming in its way, but the view from Mose Tyler's johnboat was oppressive. Traveling through the cypress swamp at water level felt like trying to navigate the delta of a great jungle river. Part of the time the boat was driven by a small, outboard Evinrude, but at other times the old man had to switch to an electric trolling motor. Tyler appeared to be over eighty, and he moved with an arthritic slowness that Caitlin recognized from her father-in-law's careful motions.

Their guide said little, even in response to questions, and Caitlin soon began to doubt that he could even see well enough to read the map they had shown him. But he'd been happy to take two hundred dollars from her, and right now she had little choice but to trust the old man.

Just as she began to wonder whether they should head back to their car, a stand of massive cypress trees came into view. They dwarfed the ones she had seen up until now. Their trunks were as thick as economy cars, and the great knees that jutted out of the water around them looked like boulders made of wood. Several trees had wide cracks in them, as the story in Henry's files claimed the Bone Tree did. But Mose Tyler seemed disinclined to stop and investigate these gigantic specimens. When Caitlin turned to Jordan for support, the photographer merely shrugged and went on shooting pictures with her plastic-wrapped Nikon.

Amazingly, the trees grew even larger as they sailed deeper into the swamp. Many stood on grassy tussocks that rose like hobbit hills out of the water, and these trees seemed somehow more alive than the oaks and pines Caitlin was accustomed to seeing. The wildlife became more abundant, too. Caitlin saw a water moccasin swimming like a slowly curling whip, its wedge-shaped head lifted above the water. A young alligator rested on a log in a single shaft of sunlight. And farther on, a pair of deer swam with surprising speed between two grassy hummocks.

"I didn't know deer could swim," she said with awe.

"Deer be good swimmers," Mose mumbled. "Better get your raincoat on, if you got one."

As though summoned by the old man's words, Caitlin heard a high-pitched hiss over the water. A silver gray curtain was rolling toward them through the trees. The mirrored surface of the swamp suddenly erupted into chaos, and the hiss grew into the crazed snapping of water thrown on a hot griddle. The cold rain quickly worked its way under the collar of her jacket, soaking her bandanna and running down her back. Caitlin made sure that Carl's walkie-talkie was staying dry in her zippered bag.

Mose tolerated the downpour with the equanimity of a cow, and Jordan reacted much the same. Caitlin shrugged away the rain and focused on the forest around them. The massive trees with their great gnarled knees reminded her of the Tree of Life in the Animal Kingdom at Walt Disney World in Florida. They weren't *that* big, of course. That tree was fourteen stories tall, and riddled with hidden passageways. But the giant cypresses here looked fifty feet around, and their fibrous trunks seemed like natural models of the great columns at Karnak.

"I read that some of these trees could be seven hundred years old," she told Mose and Jordan.

"These trees ain't nothing," said the fisherman. "When I was a boy, you couldn't hardly come through here. Then a rich man sent saw-gangs in here one summer. They cut all the oldest trees. They'd cut them down, then wait for the winter rains, chain them together, and float 'em out to be sawed up for lumber. All them trees gone now. Nothing left but these littl'uns."

Caitlin could scarcely imagine trees that dwarfed the ones before her. "Are we anywhere near that X on the map?"

The old man killed the Evinrude, then leaned to his left and pointed past Jordan in the bow of the boat.

Caitlin followed the line of his weathered hand. An

eight-foot-tall fence like the ones they had seen on the way in blocked their path.

"What's that?" she asked.

"Hunting club fence," Mose said.

"Is the X on the other side of that fence?"

"Best I can tell, it is."

"Have you ever been on the other side?"

"No, ma'am. Dat private property."

Caitlin didn't believe him. She looked hard into the old man's bloodshot eyes. "I don't care if you run illegal trotlines, Mr. Tyler, or hunt game out of season. I just want to know what's on the other side of that fence."

Tyler's eyes narrowed and he looked away from Caitlin.

"I didn't mean to suggest you were doing anything wrong," she said.

"We despise the people who put up these fences," Jordan said. "We'd tear every one of them down if we could."

"You can't," Mose said solemnly. "You tear down them fences, you'll find yourself sunk in a hole out here. Food for the panthers."

"There aren't any panthers out here," Jordan said. "Panthers are extinct in the United States."

Mose laughed for the first time, an eerie cackle that set Caitlin's nerves on edge.

"Will you take us to the other side of that fence?" Caitlin asked. "Please?"

"Not for no two hundred dollars, I won't. And not today."

"Why not?"

"Lots of reasons. But I'll earn my money. I'll tell you something most people don't know. That fence ain't on the rightful boundary."

"What?"

Mose nodded with conviction. "Just 'cause you puts a fence in a certain place don't make the land yours."

"How do you know that's not the boundary?" Jordan asked.

"'Cause I was here before that fence was. Lots of times, with my daddy. And that fence be in the wrong place."

Caitlin felt a chill go through her that had nothing to

do with the rain. If Mose Tyler was correct—as Danny McDavitt had suggested—then the Bone Tree might stand on federal land. And committing murder on federal land—even dumping a body on it—meant that the killers could be tried in federal court, even if they had been tried and set free decades ago in a state court. It was one of the very few ways around the double-jeopardy statute.

"Nobody checks this fence?" Jordan asked.

"Guv'mint ain't got the men to do it," Mose said.

Caitlin was about to ask him another question when the old trapper raised his hand. She had no trouble interpreting that gesture as a call for silence. Caitlin listened, but all she heard was the steady hissing of the rain. A slight wind was blowing, enough to have made the boat drift farther away from the fence, but she saw nothing threatening in that.

"I think it's time we get out of here," Mose said. He yanked on the Evinrude's starting cord, but the motor didn't catch.

"Wait," Jordan said in a commanding voice.

Mose ignored her, and this time the engine caught. As he started to throttle up the motor, Jordan stood in the bow and held up her hand. The old fisherman had little choice but to kill the motor.

"What's the matter?" he asked, anxiety in his voice.

"I smell something," Jordan said.

"No, you don't."

"Yes, I do. Something dead."

"They's always somethin' dead down in here. Half this swamp be dyin' and rotting, while the other half growin' so fast you can almost see it. You ought to come down in here at night sometime. There's logs glowing, under the water like the bodies of dead men lookin' up at you."

"What I smell is human," Jordan said without any doubt in her voice.

"How you know that?"

"I've been in a lot of war zones, that's how. I know what a dead body smells like." Jordan turned slowly in the unsteady boat, peering off into the trees as the cold rain fell upon her. "That way," she said, pointing toward an opening in the trunks, not far from the fence.

"Oh, hell no," Mose said.

"We'll pay you extra," Jordan said. "Take us down there."

Tyler shook his head like a scared little boy.

"Five hundred more," Caitlin said.

"How much you got?" the old man asked.

"A thousand. It's all yours." Keeping her envelope in her jacket, she dug out ten more bills and handed them over. "There you go. Now, take us."

With a resentful look, Mose switched on the electric trolling motor to propel the boat in the direction Jordan was pointing.

Ten seconds later they saw buzzards circling above the cypress trees in the distance.

WHEN I LAID JIMMY Revels's navy tattoo on the desk Kaiser had commandeered from Walker Dennis, the sight stunned him speechless. Before he could question me, I gave him an edited version of how I'd found it and where I'd spent the time since he'd kicked me out of the sheriff's office. I told him that Forrest Knox had used a SWAT team to kidnap my father last night, and that Snake and the old Eagles had then snatched Dad from Forrest's men, to keep as insurance in case Forrest was setting them up to be arrested this morning.

I didn't tell Kaiser I'd seen Forrest Knox in person, nor did I tell him anything Walt Garrity had told me about his activities relating to Forrest. If Kaiser was unwilling to use planted meth to pressure the Eagles, he wasn't going to use a planted derringer to go after Forrest. I was tempted to tell Kaiser about the video of the Katrina sniping, but since it didn't show Forrest himself (and since Walt no longer had possession of the video) I knew Kaiser wouldn't go for that. After a couple of Kaiser's men photographed the tattoo, he wrapped it carefully in a dry towel, then asked them to give us some privacy.

Once they had, he said, "Why did you bring this back here, Penn?"

"Because Snake Knox is probably the only person alive who knows where my father is, and if he's alive or not."

"This tattoo isn't going to make Snake talk. You saw him in there. You talked to him. He's not going to tell us where your father is."

"No. But he might tell Sonny Thornfield."

Kaiser drew back, his face darkening. "Oh, no. If I sent Sonny into that cellblock to try to trick that information out of Snake, Snake would tip to what's going on in two seconds flat. I can't take that risk."

"John—"

"I'm sorry, Penn. This isn't the way I wanted it, but I now have a chance to turn a Double Eagle. With that tattoo, I can break Sonny Thornfield. And I have to try it. Now. I'm sorry, but that's the way it is."

"You wouldn't even have the chance without that tattoo."

"Probably not. And I'm grateful for it."

"John . . . I could walk out of here and tell the world that Walker Dennis planted that meth on the Eagles. And I could say I never saw that tattoo in my life until you pulled it out of your briefcase."

Kaiser looks like he doesn't believe I'd do it, but then doubt enters his eyes. "You'd blow the chance to turn a Double Eagle and solve a dozen murders on the off chance of saving your father?"

"If that's my only option."

"Two can play that game. I could jail you for obstruction. Under the Patriot Act."

"You'd have to take me to a black site to keep me from telling what I know."

Kaiser groans angrily. "Goddamn it."

I look at my watch. "Okay, let's say you succeed in flipping Sonny. If he agrees to a deal with you, will you send him back and ask him to see if he can find out where Snake sent Dad?"

The FBI agent runs his fingers along the rolled towel that contains the tattoo. "Maybe. If you can come up with an approach for Sonny that will convince Snake he's not a traitor."

"Okay, I'll think about it. Let's go."

"Where?"

"I'm going to watch you try to flip Sonny. That tattoo's my ticket, and you know it."

"From the observation room," Kaiser says. "That's as close as you get."

"Fine. Let's go."

BEYOND THE ONE-WAY WINDOW of the observation room, Sonny Thornfield stares anxiously at the rolled white towel in Kaiser's hands. It probably reminds him of the towel Walt slung over the pipe in the utility closet. If he knew what that towel contained, it would scare him more than being hung from a pipe.

"Sonny?" Kaiser says gently. "Mayor Cage and the sheriff just searched a fishing cabin over on Old River. They didn't find Dr. Cage there. But they did find two bottles of his medicine, and signs of a struggle."

Sonny blinks and swallows involuntarily. "If the doc ain't there, I don't know where he's at. Snake must have moved him. Or else Forrest found him again."

"Once you get back to the cellblock, I'd like you to find out which."

Sonny looks at Kaiser like a little boy whose father has asked him to stand up to a bully in the schoolyard. "You got no idea what you're askin', mister."

"Yes, I do, Sonny. But before you go back to your comrades, we need to address a different issue. Mayor Cage also discovered a footlocker in your cabin." The old man's chin begins to quiver, and the blood slowly drains from his face. He looks like a patient waiting to hear a terminal diagnosis from his oncologist. Kaiser posted a deputy trained as a paramedic outside in case Sonny has another heart attack, and it's looking like that was a good idea.

"Apparently, your footlocker contained all sorts of memorabilia. Your marine forage cap and battle ribbons, a Ku Klux Klan hood, an old pistol, and a *Playboy* magazine from 1953."

Beads of sweat have popped out on the old man's wrinkled forehead. "That locker ain't mine," he says.

"No? It has your name on it, and your marine discharge inside it."

Sonny's pale lips move, but no sound emerges.

Kaiser lays the rolled-up towel on the table between

them. "I'm going to unroll this cloth, Sonny," he says gently.

"Don't," the old man whispers.

"I have to."

"How come?"

"You know why."

Thornfield wipes his eyes. "I can't help you. Even if I wanted to, I couldn't."

Kaiser sighs softly. "Yes, you can, Sonny. You can send Billy and Snake to death row. Forrest too, unless I miss my guess. And you can spend all the years you have left with your family. Safe from harm."

Sonny bends his head and covers his eyes with a shaking hand.

As a prosecutor, I saw many men confronted by the evidence of their most secret sins. Some showed no emotion; others, those like Snake Knox, actually laughed at photographs of dead or mutilated victims. But a few, like Sonny Thornfield, enter something like a fugue state. The knowledge that their most depraved act on earth will be revealed to all is more than they can endure.

He's going to break, I realize. *When he sees that tattoo, he's going to fall apart. The only problem is, he's the wrong target. Sonny doesn't know where my father is. Only Snake knows that.*

Kaiser slowly unrolls the cloth.

"Please don't," Sonny whispers again, begging now.

Why did Sonny keep that tattoo? I wonder. An FBI agent asked the same thing when I showed it to Kaiser in Dennis's office. *Because that's what men do,* Kaiser answered. *Didn't you ever keep something that belonged to a girl you had sex with? A lost earring? An article of clothing?* Blood rose into the agent's cheeks when Kaiser said that, but the old profiler was already rolling the swatch of skin into the towel.

Now the tattoo lies exposed under the harsh UV light—a thing that has probably haunted Sonny Thornfield since the day he cut it from a living man. *Did Sonny really slice off that skin?* I wonder. *Or was it Snake?* I remember reading about the Hells Angels, and how it was actually a small core of sadistic members who carried out punishments like rape and savage beatings. *I'd be willing to bet the Double Eagles worked in a similar way. I can see*

Snake Knox laughing as he cut a man's balls off, but it's hard to imagine this shivering old man mutilating an innocent victim. Killing one, yes, out of some twisted sense of mission. But not torturing for pleasure—

"Sonny?" Kaiser asks, his voice still gentle. "Can you hear me?"

The old man's shivering has grown more pronounced, and as I look beneath the hand shielding his eyes, I see tears dripping down his wrinkled face.

"Nod if you can hear me," Kaiser says in a louder voice.

The old man's head bobs once, like he's ducking a blow in slow motion.

"That tattoo came from the arm of Jimmy Revels. We know it, and you know it. DNA testing will prove it. This little souvenir is your ticket to the lethal injection chamber. But you're in a special position today. You're in a position to trade this ticket in for a very different one. You can trade it in for freedom."

"No, I can't," Sonny whispers. "You don't know what you're dealing with, mister."

"I know it very well. I know Forrest Knox is standing in the shadows behind you. I know he's got a knife at your back. And behind him you see Snake, Frank, and even old Elam Knox. You've known some depraved men, Sonny. And you've done terrible things yourself. But now you have a chance those men never had, or will. A chance at redemption. At peace. I can give that to you. I can protect you, Sonny."

Thornfield actually laughs at this, a dry sound like rustling leaves.

"Have you ever heard of the Witsec program?" Kaiser asks.

Sonny doesn't respond.

He's shuddering violently, and I wonder how much stress he can stand before he throws a clot and dies right in front of us.

"No jargon," I whisper from the observation room, urging Kaiser to speak as plainly as he can.

"The Federal Witness Protection Program," Kaiser clarifies. "I'm sure you've seen shows about it on TV. Nod if you know what I'm talking about."

It's as though the man inhabiting the body across

the table from Kaiser has dropped down some hole of pain and grief from which he might never emerge. I've seen this before, and Kaiser has, too. In normal circumstances, you send the guy back to his cell and give him time to adjust to the new reality, but thankfully Kaiser seems to understand that, on this day, we don't have that time.

With slow deliberation, the FBI agent leans across the table and speaks just above a whisper. "Do you want to die in prison, Sonny? Do you want to ride the needle?"

"It don't matter," Sonny croaks. "I'm dead either way. All I care about now is my family."

"What if we could protect your family too?" Kaiser asks.

Thornfield slowly looks up, his desolate eyes now alive with a glimmer of hope. "All of them?"

It's all-or-nothing time, and Kaiser knows it. "You've got one daughter and two grandkids. Right?"

Sonny nods quickly, surprised by Kaiser's knowledge. "My grandson's got a baby on the way. A boy."

"Where do they live, Sonny?"

"My daughter lives in Oklahoma. Her girl lives there, too. But my grandson's in the service, been going back and forth to Iraq."

"Is he stateside now?"

"He's just about to ship out for another rotation. He's in California."

"That's everybody?"

"Everybody I care about. Or that cares about me."

"Do you think they would be willing to enter witness protection? Would they change their identities in order to protect you from retaliation? Or to protect themselves?"

Thornfield sighs wearily. "I don't know. My daughter and me have had some hard words between us. She don't like me much. You'd have to talk to her."

"She has a phone, right?"

Sonny shakes his head. "We're not doing this by phone. No way, no how. You gotta bring 'em here. Use a phone, and Forrest would know about it before you could say 'boo.'"

Kaiser looks exasperated. "We're the FBI, Sonny. We have some very secure communications gear."

Sonny snorts. "Says you. No, you want a deal with me, you bring my kids here."

"It would be tomorrow at the soonest before we could do that. Do you really want to go back into the cellblock with your Double Eagle buddies?"

The old Klansman laughs again. "Man, I been living with them guys my whole life. I reckon I can make one more night. But if you get my grandson and grand-daughter here, and lemme talk to 'em, I believe they'll do it. My grandson don't want to do that last rotation. Not with that baby on the way. He's afraid he'll catch a packet this time."

Kaiser gets to his feet and stares down at the old man, his eyes like lasers. "If I do this, Sonny, it will cost the tax-payers a lot of money. Millions of dollars over the years. Before I can commit to that, you have to convince me I'm not wasting that money."

Sonny looks up at the FBI agent, his face as sincere as any child's. "You protect my family, mister, and I'll do whatever I gotta do to keep them safe. I swear."

Kaiser's gaze hasn't wavered. "I'm afraid I need you to be more specific than that. I need you to convince me, Sonny. I need you to tell me what you know."

The old man shakes his head. "I can't do that till you live up to your end of the deal. You keep your promise, I'll keep mine. Ain't that how it works?"

This stumps Kaiser for a bit. He stares at Thornfield for several seconds, then looks up at the window and mo-tions for me to come in. I dart to the door before Kaiser can second-guess himself. As I enter the interrogation room, Sonny's eyes go wide in panic, but Kaiser quickly reassures him.

"Mayor Cage is only here to observe, Sonny."

"I don't know where Dr. Cage is at!" he cries. "I told you!"

"We know that," Kaiser says, signaling me to keep my distance. He sits again, then says, "I tell you what. I'm going to mention some crimes, and I want you to nod if you know who's responsible for them. Okay?"

The old man's cheek twitches. He looks like a retiree suspicious of a loan officer's pitch. "I guess."

"First and foremost, the Double Eagle murders. I'm

talking about Pooky Wilson, Albert Norris, Joe Louis Lewis, Jimmy Revels, Luther Davis—"

"You already know who killed Albert and Pooky," Sonny breaks in. "That was in the paper yesterday morning. Brody Royal was behind that."

Kaiser nods. "But the Double Eagles did the dirty work. What about Jimmy and Luther? And Joe Louis Lewis, the busboy?"

After several seconds of hesitation, Sonny nods once.

Kaiser turns to me, his eyes glinting with excitement, but I feel like throwing up. We're nowhere close to saving my father, assuming Dad's still breathing.

"Okay," says Kaiser. "Let's move forward in time a bit. How much do you know about Forrest Knox?"

The old man starts shaking his head before Kaiser can get the whole name out.

"Come on, Sonny. I already know a lot about him. I know he started taking part in Eagle operations when he was a teenager, and I know he was party to some of the worst crimes. But I'm just as interested in his present-day drug business, and also his activities during Hurricane Katrina. Can you link him to that?"

Thornfield looks surprised by the extent of Kaiser's knowledge. "Would I have to testify in court?"

"Probably so, yes."

Sonny closes his eyes like a man asked to confront Satan incarnate. "I ain't saying shit about Forrest, man. Not until me and my family are safe and living under new names."

Kaiser grimaces, then tries another tack. "I know Forrest means to take over the state police. What about his ties to the power brokers in Baton Rouge and New Orleans? Can you identify any of the people he's been dealing with in that regard?"

Thornfield rakes his wrinkled hand over his chin, but then he shakes his head. "Nothing about Forrest. Not until the deal is done. Don't waste your breath."

"All right, then. Let's talk about Dallas."

Sonny blinks as if he doesn't understand the word. "Dallas?"

"Yeah. President Kennedy. Dealey Plaza."

Sonny shakes his head as if he's clueless.

Kaiser smiles as if in appreciation of good entertainment. "Come on, Sonny. I know all about Frank drawing the three *K*'s in the sand on the sandbar. The day he founded the Double Eagles? I know about Carlos Marcello. I know about the Rose Garden photo and the red circles. JFK, RFK, MLK? Right?"

Sonny's eyes have gone wide. "Where'd you hear that? Did Glenn Morehouse tell you that?"

"He told Henry Sexton."

"Jesus. Glenn really lost it at the end, didn't he?"

"He couldn't live with himself anymore. Can you blame him?"

Thornfield shrugs sullenly.

"Tell me about Dallas, Sonny. About Frank."

The old man looks cagey now. "How much does it mean to you?"

Kaiser cuts his eyes at me. "What do you mean?"

"I mean . . . if I could tell you who killed Kennedy, would that be enough to get my family federal protection without going to court against Forrest?"

"Fuck, no," I snap. "Tell him, John!"

Kaiser holds up his hand to silence me.

"Ask him who killed Viola," I bark, moving toward the table. "He knows that much, and there's not one reason he can't tell you right now."

"Stay over there, Penn," Kaiser orders. "Or get out."

I force myself to stop and back up a couple of steps. I don't want Kaiser to have me removed before Sonny says something I can use.

"What about that, Sonny?" Kaiser asks. "Do you know who killed Nurse Turner?"

Sonny cuts his eyes at me, then looks back at Kaiser and gives a slight nod.

"I want a name," Kaiser says.

Thornfield shakes his head.

At last Kaiser sighs in frustration. "Compared to what you say you know, that's nothing, Sonny. If you don't give me that name, you're not getting any deal at all. As of now, naming Viola's killer is the price of me calling your family."

Sonny stares at the table for a while. Then he looks up at Kaiser, the tight smile of a mischievous little boy on his face. "No, it ain't," he says softly. "Because I've got the first-class ticket now."

"What are you talking about?"

"The big D, boss. I *can* tell you about Dallas. And about Frank. I can tell you *all* about it. And then you can be a big hero up in Washington. They'll probably make you the head of the goddamn FBI, after I tell you what I know. *That's* my ticket out of this place." Sonny gives Kaiser a smirk. "Tell me I'm wrong."

"You're wrong, Sonny."

The smirk doesn't falter a bit. "No, I ain't. I may not be no rocket scientist, but I know that much."

THEY HAD FOUND WHAT had drawn the attention of the buzzards. Jordan had been right. Beneath the circling carrion birds, the body of a Caucasian man lay wedged among the limbs of a fallen tree. The reek of death was suffocating. Mose Tyler had stopped his boat thirty feet from the mostly submerged corpse, but even from here Caitlin could see that the dead man was missing his head.

"I ain't goin' no further," Mose said flatly. "Not for all the damn money in the world."

"Yes, you are," Caitlin said, her heart hammering in her chest.

"No, I ain't."

"Jordan," Caitlin said, peering over the water, "Dr. Cage couldn't have been killed more than . . . I don't know, fifteen or sixteen hours ago. Could his body already stink like that?"

"I wouldn't think so. Not with the temperature this low."

A new terror struck Caitlin. "But other people have gone missing over the last few days. Those three boys from Concordia Parish, remember?"

"I didn't pay much attention to that."

"They worked for Brody Royal's oil company." Though Caitlin couldn't let her mind rest on the thought for more than a split second, some part of her was already certain that the dead man in the water was Tom Cage. "They might have dumped Tom where other victims were dumped earlier this week."

"Don't borrow trouble. Let's just get over there and find out."

"You gonna have to swim," Mose said.

"For God's sake," Jordan snapped, "he's just a man who drowned."

"No, he ain't. A blade cut dat head off. See dat dere?" He pointed at the severed neck, but Caitlin had already noticed the wound. "They used to hunt men back in here in the old times, you know."

"How long ago were the old times?" Caitlin asked.

"Back in the twenties, I know. Maybe the forties and fifties, too. My daddy told me about the year of the Great Flood, how they brought colored men in to hunt that year. And in slave times, too, he told me. A man ain't the fastest or the strongest game, but he's the smartest. And some men got a taste for dat meat. Call it 'long pig.'"

"I don't care," Caitlin said. "You take us up to that body so I can try to identify it."

"No, ma'am. I ain't got to do dat. I'm takin' you back to your car."

Almost crazed with fear and exasperation, Caitlin remembered the radio Carl had given them. "Jordan, call Carl and tell him to get his ass back here."

Jordan wasted no time, and she seemed quite at home with the radio. But when Carl's voice came from the speaker, Caitlin's feeling of dread only deepened.

"We're on our way back to the airport," Carl said. "I was just about to call you and tell you to get out of there."

"Why?" Jordan asked, peering into the trees as though an army might emerge from the shadows.

"We weren't over Valhalla for more than sixty seconds when the sheriff called us. Somebody at the camp called in and complained. He ordered us to get the hell out of their airspace. Said we were ruining a hunt and spooking their breeding animals. Can you believe that?"

Jordan was shaking her head. "All that's academic now," she said. "We just found a body in the swamp. I presume the sheriff won't write that off to natural causes."

"What do you mean, a body?" Carl asked.

"A dead man in the water. And he doesn't have a head. If you guys could start this way, we damsels in distress would sure appreciate it."

The radio crackled and hissed for half a minute. Then Carl said, "We're coming to you. I'll call you in a few minutes to guide us in."

"Thanks. And while you're at it, would you tell our guide to take us in where we can get an idea of who the deceased might be? Caitlin is worried it might be Dr. Cage."

The radio crackled some more. Then Carl said, "Mose, you do whatever those ladies tell you to do, or I'm bustin' you for all the stuff I know you do when you think we're looking the other way."

In the stern of the johnboat, the old fisherman hung his head.

"Ten-four," Jordan said. "I think he got the message. Out."

KAISER SHOULD NEVER HAVE asked Sonny Thornfield about JFK. Not until after the plea deal was done. The old Eagle is sitting as smug as a mob soldier who knows his godfather will have him out of jail in time for happy hour at his favorite bar.

"John, come on," I say in the most reasonable voice I can muster. "Don't let him play you like this. How critical is the Kennedy stuff, given the overall situation? Even if he tells you Frank Knox killed JFK? Frank is as dead as Kennedy, and he has been for nearly as long."

As tense as a pointer nearing a quail, Kaiser holds up his hand to silence me. "It's not enough to say Frank killed him. He has to *prove* Frank killed him. Can you do that, Sonny?"

Again the little-boy smile animates Sonny's mouth, and his eyes flicker with secret knowledge. "I can give you chapter and verse, boss. Frank himself told me the story one night, when he'd drunk damn near a gallon of moonshine."

Kaiser looks like Ahab after having sighted the milky head and spout of the white whale. Nothing could turn him aside from his obsession now. I feel like slapping him upside the head.

"He's read you like a book," I say angrily. "He's telling you what you want to hear, and there's no way to cross-check anything he says. Make him give you details on crimes we know about. The Double Eagle killings. Then we'll know whether he's full of shit or not."

Thornfield gives me a ratlike glare. "I ain't sayin' shit about that until my family is here and they agree to protection."

As Kaiser works his mouth around in frustration, my cell phone vibrates. This time, when I take it out of my pocket, I see Carl Sims's name in the LCD window.

"Carl?" I ask. "What's up?"

A burst of static makes me jerk the phone away from my ear, but then Carl's voice pops from the speaker with a tinny timbre. *"Penn . . . girls found a body . . . swamp. . . . No ID yet. . . . Caitlin trying to reach it. . . . Altitude, Danny. . . . Penn?"*

"Carl!" I cry. "I can't hear you! The girls found a body?"

"Ten-four. . . . Lusahatcha Swamp. . . . Haven't reached it yet. . . . Going down to try to help. . . . Call you soon as we know. . . . Out."

My pulse pounds in my ears as the phone goes dead. *A body in the swamp?* From the sound of Carl's voice, he wasn't talking about old bones, but a fresh corpse. An image of my father floating facedown in the swamp rises behind my eyes, and my legs go weak. What if I had to call my mother and tell her that Dad had been found dead? *Impossible—*

"What's happened?" Kaiser asks. "Is it your father?"

"It sounds like it. Caitlin and Jordan found a body in the swamp. They haven't ID'd it yet, but Carl wouldn't have called me unless he was afraid it's Dad. Goddamn it!"

I take two steps toward Thornfield, then force myself to stop, my face burning with rage. "Did Snake kill my father and dump him in Lusahatcha Swamp?"

Sonny gapes at me in genuine terror. "I don't know! I truly don't. I hope he didn't, but he could've. Or that Redbone, Ozan. He's a bad sumbitch."

Kaiser pulls me away from Sonny, then interposes himself between us, his back to me.

"This is getting out of hand, Sonny," he says in a cold voice. "Let me tell you something. My superiors badly want to talk to Dr. Cage. If he turns out to be dead, it's going to be tough for me to make any kind of deal for you. My bosses won't approve it. I can't believe Snake wouldn't tell you what he was going to do with him."

"That's the whole ever-lovin' point!" Sonny cries. "He didn't trust the rest of us not to break under pressure. Not after what Glenn done. And I reckon he was right not to, wasn't he?"

"If I sent you back to the cellblock, could you get it out of Snake?"

"Shit. I do that, I might as well tell him I'm in here trying to cut a deal with you."

"If Snake Knox doesn't trust you anymore," Kaiser muses, "I can't believe *Frank* Knox ever did. If you want your family brought here on a government plane, you've *got* to give me something to justify your deal."

Thornfield grimaces so hard he bares his teeth, which makes him look like a possum cornered between two garbage cans.

"Look, I *know*," he insists. "I know all there is to know—twice as much as Glenn ever did. But how can I prove it without giving away the store?"

While Kaiser wrestles with this dilemma, my mind fills with an image of Caitlin rolling over a bloated white body in the black water of the Lusahatcha Swamp. I've seen many floaters in my career, rotted and half eaten by turtles, snake, and fish. I can't bear thinking about my mother having to view my father's body in such a state. I'm not sure I could bear it myself.

"Turn off the camera, John," I say sharply.

"What?"

"Just do it. And find us a bedsheet to cover the observation mirror."

"What exactly do you have in mind?" he asks, getting up and walking to the camcorder.

"A way for Sonny to let us know what he knows without implicating himself or giving away the store."

Sonny looks worried now. "I ain't saying nothing you guys can record. I know you got all kinds of fancy hidden microphones and shit."

"It's nothing like that," I assure him.

"Then what is it?"

"Have you ever worked a jigsaw puzzle, Sonny?"

He gives me the cornered possum look again, but finally he nods.

"This is just like that." I sit down in Kaiser's chair and start writing in his notebook. "Get the bedsheet for the mirror, John. You'll need some duct tape to hold it up."

"All right, hell. But I'm not leaving you in here alone with him. I'll send one of my men."

As he goes to the door, I begin writing words across the top of a page.

VICTIM
KILLER(S)
WEAPON/METHOD
DUMP SITE

"And bring some scissors, too."

Kaiser pauses at the door. "You can't bring scissors into an interrogation room."

I look up angrily. "You want to break these cases? Bring me some goddamn scissors!"

FORREST HAD FINALLY TIRED of fighting the wind out on the deck. He'd moved into the great room of the Bouchard lake house, and Ozan had built a fire in the stone fireplace. A hidden gas jet made it easy work, and Forrest had moved forward to warm his hands when his cracked StarTac rang.

"I'm waiting," he said.

"Bad news," said Spanky Ford. "I think one of your guys may be talking."

A shiver ran the length of Forrest's body. "Who?"

"Thornfield."

Sonny? he thought skeptically. But after a few seconds, it made sense. Sonny was probably the smartest of the Eagles. He would sense that things were spinning out of control. And Sonny had family that didn't actually hate him outright.

"They've got him locked in the main interrogation room," Ford said. "Snake and Will Devine are locked in questioning rooms, too, but there's nobody in with them.

I think Kaiser stuck them in there so they wouldn't know what was going on."

"Have you told Snake about this?"

"I just managed to before an FBI agent took up station in front of his door."

"What did he say?"

"He said tell you that Dr. Cage is alive but he's where he can't hurt anybody. Don't waste effort looking for him, Snake said."

Relief washed through Forrest. If Tom Cage was alive, then he still had some flexibility in dealing with Penn Cage and his fiancée. Of course, if Sonny Thornfield turned state's evidence, everybody was going down. Then a new possibility came to him.

"Deputy . . . do you think Snake was telling the truth about Dr. Cage?"

Ford didn't answer immediately. Then he said, "I didn't know he might have a reason to lie, Colonel. I really couldn't say, sir."

"Okay. But you believe Sonny's really flipping?"

"All I know is, Cage and Kaiser are the only ones in there with him, and they've taped a sheet over the observation window."

"Okay." Forrest thought furiously. "Here's what I want you to do. The first chance you get to pass a message to Snake, tell him I said to get ready to shut down any talk, and for good. Tell him I'll get him his chance. Snake will know when to move. You got that?"

"Yes, sir."

"You'll have a job, too, but I'll get back to you with it."

"I'm ready."

"Last thing . . . you tell Snake he'd better bring Dr. Cage to me on a silver platter after I get him out of there."

"Will do, Colonel. Is there—"

"Boss!" Ozan called, walking into the room with an armload of firewood. "I got news! Good and bad. What you want first?"

"Gimme the bad. Is Dr. Cage dead?"

"I don't know, but the Black Team found the guys they left to guard the doc tied up in the Roadtrek at the back of that oil field. They said Snake and his crew took the doc, all right. They're ready to rip his lungs out."

Forrest nodded slowly. He'd never really doubted that Snake had taken Dr. Cage. The question was, what had he done with him?

"What's the good news?"

"One of our highway units stopped Claude Devereux on the causeway outside Lafayette."

Forrest pumped a fist in the air. "I've got to go," he told Ford. "You tell Snake what I said."

"I will if I can."

"And call me in fifteen minutes if they're still talking to Thornfield."

"Will do. Out."

Forrest clicked off and pocketed his phone, then turned to Ozan. "You tell whoever stopped Claude to escort him all the way back to his office in Vidalia. And if Claude raises a fuss, arrest him."

Ozan nodded. "So Dr. Cage is alive?"

Forrest blew out a lungful of air. "I don't know. Snake sent word that he is, but that doesn't mean a thing now. He's just trying to get out from under those meth charges. For all I know, the doc has been dead since last night."

CHAPTER 61

TO SPARE MYSELF the torture of waiting to hear whether or not the body in the swamp belongs to my father, I've designed a puzzle that will allow Sonny Thornfield to tell us what he knows without it being recorded in any way. I did this by drawing a grid on a piece of notebook paper, then listing the known murder victims vertically on the left side of the page. Across the top I created columns for the killers, the murder weapons or torture methods, the dump sites. Then I gridded a second page and filled it with names, murder weapons, torture methods, and dump sites (multiple copies of each place name). Finally, using Kaiser's scissors, I cut that page into small rectangles with one word on each. As I did this, an FBI agent helped Kaiser tape a bedsheet over the one-way observation mirror. And though he did it quietly, I also heard Kaiser post an FBI guard at the cellblock door with orders not to let me inside under any circumstances. After what he witnessed in the utility closet, he isn't going to let me near Snake Knox again.

With the interrogation room's two doors shut and the camcorder unplugged, I spread the columned page on the table in front of Sonny Thornfield and pile the rectangular "puzzle pieces" beside it. Then Kaiser and I take up stations on either side of the old man so that we can watch his progress, like parents watching a toddler work a puzzle.

Thornfield is hesitant to begin, but Kaiser finally convinces him we have no way to record what he might do. That's the beauty of this method. The revelation only exists for a moment, and once the puzzle is completed, Sonny can simply toss the rectangles in the air, obliterating all evidence of what he's "told" us.

After staring at the collection of names and words for

a while, Sonny finally sets to work. His wrinkled hands move tentatively across the page, trembling as though he's in the early stages of Parkinson's disease. Time seems to slow as the quivering hands slide the rectangles across the page, and every second that ticks by feels like weight being piled on my heart. At any moment Carl Sims could call back and say they've found my father dead.

I feel trapped in some bizarre, real-world demonstration of the physics paradox known as Schrödinger's cat. At this moment, while an old murderer uses a child's puzzle to reveal the knowledge that resides in his aging brain, a body floats facedown in the Lusahatcha Swamp. At this moment, that body both is and is not my father. It exists as a superposition of probabilities, and I must somehow hold myself together while accepting both outcomes as possible. But soon Caitlin—or Carl Sims, or Jordan Glass— will turn that body over, and all possible states will collapse into the single observed reality: the corpse will either be my dead father or it will not. And even if one believes that this choice has already been made, or is known, until it is made known *to me*, both realities must be endured.

"Look," Kaiser whispers, pointing over Sonny's shoulder.

Thornfield hasn't filled in the second column—the killers' identities—but the third and fourth columns: the weapons and methods of torture or killing, and the dump sites.

Albert Norris		flamethrower	
Pooky Wilson		flamethrower	Bone Tree
Joe Louis Lewis		flayed	Bone Tree
Jimmy Revels		shot	Bone Tree
Luther Davis		shot, drowned	Jericho Hole
Viola Turner		overdose	Home
Glenn Morehouse		overdose	Home

"You haven't filled in the killers' column," Kaiser points out. "I get you leaving the dump site blank for Norris, because he died in the hospital. But if you want lifetime protection for your family, you've got to give me every name of the killers."

Sonny looks up like a reluctant child. Then, slowly, he tears off a new sheet of paper, writes about twenty names on it—many of them repetitions—and asks Kaiser to cut them into rectangles. Once Kaiser has complied, Sonny slides most of the new squares onto the paper. After he's finished, Kaiser stands so still that I'm sure he's stopped breathing. The first two columns of the puzzle now read:

Albert Norris	Frank Royal Snake Glenn
Pooky Wilson	Frank Snake Royal
Joe Louis Lewis	Frank Snake Glenn
Jimmy Revels	Snake Glenn Forrest Royal
Luther Davis	Snake
Viola Turner	
Glenn Morehouse	Royal Snake Forrest

As I stare at the gridded page, I note that our prisoner has not only omitted his own name from every murder, he's listed no killers beside Viola Turner's name. Before I can comment on this, he lifts the makeshift puzzle and shakes it in the air, creating a snowstorm of paper. While the rectangles flutter to the floor, he puts his head down on his desk like a schoolboy.

I give Kaiser an angry, questioning look.

"All right, Sonny," he says, "we've got two problems. First, if you're not willing to implicate yourself, this is worthless. You'll be given immunity, but you have to tell the *whole* truth. And second, we need to know who killed Viola."

"*I* need to know my grandkids are safe," Sonny replies without looking up. "I ain't saying nothing else, or doing no more damn puzzles."

Crouching beside the table, I look into Thornfield's one exposed eye. "Did you love your father, Sonny?"

The eye widens, then blinks slowly. "My father?"

"You see . . . if that corpse in the swamp turns out to be my father, my mother won't be able to stand it. My little girl, either."

"They can stand it," he says. "People can stand almost anything, when they have to."

Kaiser taps my shoulder, but I don't move. "I'm not letting myself believe that corpse is my dad, Sonny. Any minute, I'm going to get a call saying it was some other poor bastard who crossed the Knox family. And when that happens, you're going to go back into the cellblock and find out where Snake took my father."

"Get up, Penn," Kaiser says sharply.

As I stand, I say, "If you don't, I'm going to flush this deal you two are making straight down the toilet."

"No, he won't," Kaiser says, pulling at my arm. "He can't, Sonny."

"You don't think so? All I have to do is let Forrest Knox know who's been blabbing in here. I talked to him face-to-face less than an hour ago, and I've got a phone that'll put me right back in touch with him."

Thornfield's eyes have locked onto mine, and the terror in them gives a measure of the fear Forrest inspires in his ranks.

"Get your ass out of here, Penn!" Kaiser explodes, his face bright red. "Now!"

"Not until I find out whether my father's dead or alive."

WHEN MOSE FINALLY BROUGHT his boat within reach of the corpse, Caitlin felt no relief. She had hoped for some distinguishing mark that would tell her the dead man wasn't Tom, but she saw nothing like that. The skin of the back was pale, as Tom's was, and since most of the corpse was jammed under some limbs, she couldn't turn it over. She looked for the red marks of psoriasis she had sometimes seen on Tom's back, but the water had probably soaked the skin to the point that they wouldn't show, especially under the surface.

Mose cut the motor.

"Do you have a pole or something?" Caitlin asked.

"Pole no good for that. You need a hook. Grappling hook."

"I think we're going to have to wait for Carl," Jordan said. "Maybe even for divers. Or at least waders."

The longer Caitlin stared at the submerged corpse, the more terrified she became. She had to know whether that was Tom or not. Carl was probably going to call Penn on the way over here, and the first question he would ask would be who the dead man was.

"We have to identify him," Caitlin said.

"How?" Jordan asked. "He doesn't have a head."

"I have to know whether or not it's Tom."

"Dat body missin' a leg, too," Mose said, craning his neck. "Look. A gator took it off."

Caitlin squinted into the muddy water, but she couldn't tell.

"How did the body get caught up in the branches like that?" Jordan asked.

"Gators do that," Mose said. "They stuff their kill up under a bank or in some tree roots underwater, just like us puttin' meat in the Frigidaire."

A shiver ran the length of Caitlin's body. She had been close to a feeding alligator before, and she wanted no part of it again.

"We gotta get out of here," Mose said. "Dis business for the high sheriff."

"How deep is the water here?" Caitlin asked, slowly untying the bandanna from her neck.

"Can't be sure," the fisherman replied. "Could be four feet, could be ten."

"Guess."

The old man surveyed the trees that bordered the patch of clear water, then studied the fallen tree that held the corpse in its branches. "Probably six, eight feet deep here."

A sun-faded life jacket lay in the bottom of the boat near Jordan's feet. Caitlin picked it up, slipped it on, and tightened the straps as best she could.

"What the hell you doin'?" Mose asked, starting to stand. "This boat ain't gonna turn over."

Before he could reach her, Caitlin bent her knees, then let herself fall backward over the gunwale, the way she'd been taught to enter the water when scuba diving in the Caribbean. She prayed that the splash would scare away any scavengers.

The black water enveloped her like an icy blanket. She'd expected it to be cold, but not this cold. After a stunned second or two, she bobbed to the surface, the life jacket bringing her upright. Jordan and Mose were screaming from the boat, telling her to get back in, but having gone this far, she wasn't about to stop now. She didn't think she could climb back into the boat without tipping it over anyway.

She couldn't feel bottom beneath her, so she kicked toward the corpse. The reek worsened as she got closer, and her shoes grew heavy in the twenty seconds it took her to come within reach of the body. Catching hold of a waterlogged branch, Caitlin catalogued the physical traits that might identify Tom. The cold made it hard to concentrate, and the stink worsened the problem, but her fear was stronger than her revulsion.

Deformed fingers, she thought. *Spooned fingernails. Coronary bypass scar . . . Tom had his chest cracked in 1987. Would the scar still be visible after all these years? Gray chest hair . . .*

The way the corpse was situated, Caitlin realized that

the quickest way to see anything was to simply swim under it rather than try to shift it. As she struggled to shed the life jacket, Jordan began shouting at her again, but Caitlin ignored her. She simply had to know.

The buckles of the life jacket were stuck. Caitlin pressed and jerked as hard as she could, but none of the damned clasps would come undone. Some part of her knew she must be doing something wrong, yet she couldn't solve this simple problem. The life jacket was strangling her! At last Jordan's shouts broke through her wild frustration.

"Catch this!" Jordan yelled. "There's a knife in it!"

Caitlin's head cleared as though she'd been slapped. Looking up, she saw a dull flash of metal and somehow snatched it out of the air. Jordan's multi-tool. Flicking open the largest blade, Caitlin sawed through the three straps. Then she looked up and threw the knife back at Jordan. By the time the tool clanged against the bottom of the boat, she had kicked free of the life jacket. With that freedom came the memory that Tom had been shot in the shoulder on Tuesday night.

Which shoulder was the bandage on? The left.

Caitlin screeched in terror as something bumped against her leg, then scooted away. It hadn't felt like a fish, unless it was a damned big one. A gar, maybe. Or a catfish.

"*Caitlin!*" Jordan shouted. "*Get back in this boat and wait for the chopper!*"

Caitlin shoved all her fear down into a deep hole, took a huge breath, then dived deep under the tree and kicked hard. When she felt mud, she rolled over and opened her eyes.

She could see amazingly well, but what she saw almost made her vomit. The corpse had no left shoulder. It had been eaten away. Likewise both hands. Fighting panic that scrambled in her chest like a crazed animal, she grabbed a limb that was jammed into the mud and tried desperately to remember her thoughts only moments ago.

Gray chest hair . . .

She couldn't see any hair on the chest. As she stared, something long and dark passed between her and the body, then disappeared. Primal terror surged through every fiber of her being. She let go of the branch and drove her feet against the bottom, desperate to reach the surface. As she broke through to air and sunlight, the last thing she had seen finally registered in her cerebral cortex.

Black pubic hair.

At the crotch of what remained of the dead man's legs, a thick thatch of black hair had been plainly visible. Caitlin had never seen Tom naked, but Penn's father was seventy-three years old, and he had silver-white hair and a beard of the same color. No way was his pubic hair black.

Jordan had braced one hand against the gunwale of the johnboat and was holding out a small boat paddle.

"*Grab it!*" she cried. "Grab it, goddamn it!"

"It's not Tom!" Caitlin shouted. "It's not Tom!"

"Thank God. Now get your crazy ass back in here."

She grabbed the paddle but found herself too weak to pull. Mose Tyler took the paddle from Jordan and hauled Caitlin to the edge of the boat with surprising strength. Then an eerie hissing sent adrenaline surging through her again. She jerked her head in every direction, looking for snakes or any other threat, but it was only the sound of fresh rain on the water. As her heartbeat steadied, Mose and Jordan reached down and dragged her up into the listing boat. When Caitlin came over the gunwale and collapsed onto the green metal bottom, she heard the heavy beat of approaching rotor blades.

"It's not Tom," she said again, relief flooding through her like a drug.

Jordan knelt above her and looked into her eyes like a doctor examining a patient. Apparently satisfied that she was not seriously hurt, Jordan said, "Not bad, little sister. Not bad at all."

"Crazy is what dat was," Mose said. "Craziest damn thing I ever saw."

Caitlin felt a sudden panic, as in a nightmare when she'd lost something but didn't know what it was. Then she knew.

The map.

She dug into her pocket and pulled out what remained: a soggy mess like wet toilet paper, faintly stained with blue ink.

"I lost the map," she said. "Toby's map."

"Don't worry about it," Jordan said, squeezing her hand. "It's nothing."

TEN SECONDS AGO, KAISER took out his phone and summoned two agents to drag me out of the interrogation room. As pounding feet sound in the hall, I see Sonny Thornfield pick up the pen I used to create the puzzle pieces and begin writing on the large page.

"Look!" I cry. "John, look!"

The door crashes open, and two agents rush into the room. Kaiser holds up his hand long enough to look where I'm pointing, then walks to the metal table. After looking down at the page, he motions me forward.

With his trembling hand, Sonny Thornfield has written seven uppercase letters in the blank square next to Viola Turner's name. My breath goes shallow as I read the childishly written letters:

TOMCAGE

Sonny lays down the pen and then looks up at me, his eyes filled not with triumph or revenge, but with some unreadable emotion.

"You happy now?" he asks hoarsely. "Is that what you wanted?"

I cannot voice the thought that has arced through my mind like a rocket against a black sky: *Two nights ago, Brody Royal told me my father killed Viola. Now Sonny Thornfield has told me the same thing.*

"Let's go, Penn," Kaiser says, signaling the two agents to help me out of the room.

"He's lying, John," I insist, as much to myself as to Kaiser. "How could he possibly know that?" I lunge at Sonny, but strong hands yank me back, and a thick forearm locks around my neck. "*How could you know that unless you were there?*" I shout.

Kaiser lays the flat of his hand on my chest. "Penn, I'm on your side, but you need to step out of this room."

I start to protest when my cell phone rings. "Let me answer, John!"

Kaiser nods, and after a moment the agents release me. I pull my phone from my pocket and answer it. "Caitlin?" I ask, my arm and voice shaking.

"Penn! Can you hear me? Stay on . . . we're airborne and climbing!"

My heart leaps at the sound of her voice. "I hear you!" I yell into the static. "Whose body was it? Was it Dad? Tell me now!"

"No! It wasn't Tom! Repeat, *not* your father. It was a much younger man. The sheriff's office down here thinks it's one of those missing boys from Vidalia, Casey Whelan."

"It wasn't him," I echo, though my brain has spun into some zone where it feels disconnected from my voice. "It was one of those missing kids . . . Whelan."

Thornfield's head whips up at the mention of the name.

"Thank God," says Kaiser, squeezing my shoulder. "What about Jordan? Is she okay?"

Dizzy with relief, I half fall toward the metal table. Kaiser steadies me by taking hold of my shoulders, and I rest one hand against the table's edge to regain my balance.

"Tell John Jordan's fine," Caitlin says, the connection much clearer now. "We'll probably be stuck down here talking to Sheriff Ellis for a while, but we're both good. There's no other word on Tom?"

"No."

"Please call me the moment you hear anything."

Already the euphoria of relief has begun to evaporate. "All right."

"I love you!" Caitlin shouts.

"Okay . . . okay. I love you, too."

And then she's gone.

I look down at my hand, and a shock of revulsion goes through me. I'd thought Kaiser was squeezing my wrist, but the hand wrapped around my arm belongs to Sonny Thornfield.

"I'm glad for you," the old man says.

Yanking my arm free, I shake my head and speak with open disgust. "You knew who was in that swamp. You killed Whelan, didn't you? Or you saw it done. I saw it in your face just now."

Thornfield's watery eyes go wide. Then he shuts them tight and covers his face with his hands. Kaiser jerks me away from the old man and shoves me toward the door.

"Get out, Penn. You've had some luck just now, but don't push it."

I plant my feet at the door and stop us. "Luck is for fools, John. Are you going to give Thornfield his deal?"

He looks anxiously back at the old man.

"You've got to get him back to the cellblock soon. You already kept him longer than you did Snake."

"Hold Penn here," Kaiser says to his agents. Then he walks back and squats beside Thornfield, just as I did earlier. "Why didn't you put your name by those victims, Sonny? The only way you could know who killed them was to be there yourself. Come on, man. Take the final step."

The old man's body is trembling like a scarecrow in a rainstorm.

"Give me something I can believe," Kaiser pleads. "Then your family can have a new lease on life. New names, a new town, far out of Forrest's reach."

Thornfield's bloodshot eyes slowly focus on Kaiser. "Something you can believe? How about Jimmy Revels's last words?"

Kaiser glances back at me. "How do you know them?"

Thornfield shakes his head like a sinner facing his maker. "They've haunted me for the last forty years . . . that's how. That boy whispers in my ears when I sleep."

Kaiser swallows in anticipation. True detectives live for these moments. "What were they, Sonny?"

"'*I forgive you,*'" Thornfield says with utter desolation. "Can you believe that?"

When Kaiser bows his head, I know Sonny's confession has rung the bell of truth within him.

"Jimmy tried to forgive me with them words," Sonny says, weeping openly now. "But he damned me forever."

TWO MINUTES AFTER THORNFIELD'S confession, Kaiser and I stand alone in the observation room while two agents flank him at the interrogation table.

"You've broken him," I say. "But you've spent too long with him. If you're going to fly his family in, you'll have to send him back to the cellblock in the meantime. Send him in with one mission, John. Find out where my father is."

Kaiser shakes his head. "Not yet, Penn."

"You're going to blow it, man. Don't get greedy. I know what you want, but you can't spend another hour in there with Sonny asking about the Kennedy assassination. Snake will realize that he's flipping. You've got to question the other Eagles to keep Sonny safe."

Kaiser shakes his head, his expression adamant. "I can have other agents question the other Eagles. I've already separated them from one another. None of them knows what's going on in here. Snake sure as hell doesn't know. I've got one of my agents questioning him right now to throw him off."

"But Snake *will* know. You know he will."

It seems incomprehensible, but Kaiser is deaf to my appeals.

"You'll get the Kennedy stuff with all the rest of it. There's no deadline on that stuff. Why is it more important than half a dozen civil rights murders? Why is it more important than my father?"

Kaiser clenches his jaw, and for a moment I believe I've shamed him back to sanity. But then he grabs my shoulders, his eyes blazing with passion.

"Why do you think, Penn? Dwight Stone is going under the knife in ninety minutes. Once they put him under, he may never wake up again. If I can give him the peace of the answer he's sought for twenty years, I'm going to give it to him."

"At the cost of all the other cases? Of Sonny's *life*?"

"Sonny's not going to die."

"My father might. He's stuck somewhere without his medicine, if he's alive at all. He doesn't have nitro or insulin . . ."

"Fifteen minutes, Penn. That's all I need. In fifteen minutes Sonny can confirm or deny every critical detail of the assassination. I just want to know whether Marcello was behind it, and whether Frank Knox fired the kill shot."

"That's a sixty-second conversation."

"Christ, can't you see? After this session, the director will authorize total protection for Sonny's family, and I'll bet any amount of money he'll do the same for your father."

"Like that matters now?"

Kaiser clutches my arm. "Don't you want to know whether your father was complicit or not in writing that medical excuse for Frank Knox? Sonny might know that."

I pull my arm free. "I already know. Whatever's at the root of my dad's behavior, it isn't evil. I know that, even if you don't."

"Then at least let's do this for Dwight. After that, we'll see if Sonny can wheedle your dad's location out of Snake."

At this point, I surrender. Nothing is going to stop him anyway.

CHAPTER 62

WILMA DEEN TURNED the stolen pickup right on Auburn Avenue, cruised for a quarter mile, then turned left on Duncan Avenue. This took her once more past the house that Penn Cage had pulled out of this morning, and where Forrest Knox had told her Tom Cage might be hiding. For the second time she saw a tall, broad-shouldered man in blue jeans walking in the front yard of the two-story house. Wilma was sure he was a guard, and she'd wanted to know if there was another in back. After she crossed over a rise in the street, she pulled over to a tall stand of hedges and stopped.

A blond, wiry twenty-five-year-old roustabout named Alois Engel stepped out of the hedge and climbed into the backseat of the truck. All Wilma knew about Alois was that Snake Knox had fathered him by some honky-tonk slut, and he worked for the Double Eagles in some capacity. She thought she remembered Sonny Thornfield once telling her the kid was into white supremacy, but he didn't look like much to her. The most distinctive thing about Engel was the anger that bled steadily from his eyes. He looked hungry for retribution, but Wilma had no idea for what. Nor did she care. She was here for one reason: to make sure her brother had not died for nothing.

"Any guards in back?" Wilma asked, accelerating down State Street, which was lined with expensive cars.

"One," said Alois. "An old nigger. I think he's a city cop, or used to be. The guy out front looks like an old hippie or something, doesn't he?"

"He looks pretty tough to me. I think I've seen him doing dirt work across the river."

"Fuck him. We just need a diversion to make sure we can get the bombs to the door."

"We don't have a go order yet, do we?"

"We will. I heard it in the colonel's voice."

Alois jerked a dirty towel off the box sitting beside him on the backseat. In the box were three sealed wine bottles filled to the neck with a mixture of gasoline, kerosene, tar, and potassium chlorate. Taped to the side of each bottle were two windproof matches.

"Who did you say designed these things?" Wilma asked. "The Russians?"

"The Finns," Alois said irritably. The kid fancied himself a connoisseur of World War II weaponology. "They used them in the Winter War."

"Against the Russians?"

"Against the *Germans*."

"Okay, okay, BF deal. Somehow they don't look like real Molotov cocktails without the rag hanging out."

Alois grunted. "Do you want to look cool while you set yourself on fire, or really hurt the people who wasted your brother?"

Wilma said nothing. This kid had no idea what was really going on. To him Glenn Morehouse had been just a fat old guy who'd lived in her house, not an unstoppable force that could be pointed at a target like a tank.

"How well do you know Forrest?" Wilma asked.

"Well enough to know that when he asks you to do him a favor, you do it. He's about the baddest son of a bitch I ever met, and I've met some."

Wilma laughed. "I just bet you have, blondie."

The truck jounced over a speed bump, and the bottles clanked ominously in the box.

"Stuff that fucking towel in there!" Wilma snapped. "Wedge it between the bottles. I don't plan on burning up in this truck."

Alois obeyed with surprising delicacy. Then he reached down to the floor and brought up a heavy Sig Sauer pistol.

"You know, if that guy doesn't go in for a break pretty soon, I'm just going to walk up and blow his shit away."

"Forrest didn't say anything about shooting guards," Wilma said.

"Well, he doesn't want us waiting on the street all day."

"Just hold your water. He'll have to take a leak soon. You got the masks?"

Alois lifted a Walmart bag from the floor. "You get the Harry Potter. I'm taking Spider-Man."

She shook her head in derision. *Kids.*

ONLY ONCE IN HER life had Peggy Cage had her faith in her husband tested as it was being tested now, and she wasn't sure she was up to the challenge. Still, she put the best possible face on things, as she'd been taught to do from birth. Despite her protestations to Penn, having Kirk Boisseau close by had improved her sense of security. Like a lot of Natchez men of his generation, Kirk had been taught English by Peggy at St. Stephen's Prep back in the early 1970s. He'd grown up to be quite an imposing adult, and today she was glad of it. Tom's elderly patient James Ervin was guarding the back of the house—unless it was his brother Elvin; Peggy could scarcely tell the difference between the retired cops. With both James and Kirk on guard, it seemed that physical security was not a problem, and yet Peggy felt deeply unsettled.

One reason was Annie. As the mayor's daughter, Annie Cage had become even more adept than her grandmother at putting on a public face, but the girl couldn't fool Peggy. Though she'd managed an animated discussion with Kirk, Annie was clearly worried about her father and Caitlin—and terrified for her grandfather. Annie had also suggested to Peggy that Penn and Caitlin were having "relationship trouble." Though she had only her intuition and Caitlin's continued absence to support this assertion, Peggy suspected she was right.

Early that morning, Annie had sat down in the den and made a great show of reading Caitlin's most recent articles aloud from the newspaper Kirk had brought with him. Peggy tried to look interested, but the only stories that held her interest anymore were those dealing with the murder for which Tom had been indicted, and there had been precious little information printed on that case after the initial story.

"Gram!" Annie cried, getting to her feet with her cell phone held aloft. "Caitlin just texted me!"

Peggy clenched her abdomen in preparation for whatever might follow. "What does she say, honey?"

Annie read from the screen: "*Hey punk, sorry I haven't been around much. You can see from the paper I'm working around the clock. Today I'm doing Lara Croft meets Nancy Drew. I may be on CNN tonight, so watch the news. With any luck, I'll be there to watch it with you. Love, Cait.*"

"Who's Lara Croft?" Peggy asked, relieved and thankful that Caitlin had thought to reassure Annie.

"Just a character from a video game," Annie said, her face glowing. "I wish Dad and Papa would text us like Caitlin does."

"Me, too. I'll be right back, sweetie," Peggy said, getting to her feet. "I'm going to check on Mr. Kirk."

"He's just plain Kirk," Annie corrected her. "He told me not to call him mister. He was four years ahead of Dad in school, but they played football together."

Peggy smiled and went into the den, where Kirk Boisseau was leaning against the wall and watching an old western in black and white.

"Are you all right, Kirk? Can I fix you a sandwich or something?"

"No, ma'am," he said with a smile. "I'm good."

Unable to think of any small talk—which was rare for her—Peggy looked at the television. On-screen she saw a black-clad cowboy brandishing a bullwhip, and the sight cut her to the quick. The actor was Lash LaRue, a Saturday matinee cowboy from the 1940s and '50s. Peggy recognized him because she and Tom had once seen an impromptu performance by LaRue at New Orleans' Dew Drop Inn, a Negro nightclub that Tom sometimes visited to hear certain black musicians. Tom and Peggy were allowed admittance because Tom had treated several employees while working as an extern. As a boy, Tom had worked as a theater usher during the 1940s, and he'd been ecstatic to find a star from his childhood onstage. He watched spellbound as the black-suited LaRue played his guitar with the Negro musicians, then cut paper from the mouth of a waitress with a bullwhip someone had produced from the back of the bar.

"Are you all right, Mrs. Cage?" Kirk asked.

"What?" Peggy asked, wiping a tear from her eyes. "Oh, yes. This has just been hard. I'm not used to doing without Tom."

Boisseau smiled. "I'm sure it's all going to work out."

"Are you?" she said quietly. "Because I'm not."

"Penn will get it worked out."

Peggy somehow summoned a smile. "Do you feel like we're pretty safe here?"

Kirk smiled back, and Peggy thought his eyes looked too gentle to belong to a real soldier. But when he spoke, his voice held the hard edge of steel.

"I won't let anything happen to you or that girl. You can count on that. I gave Penn my word. You just try to relax."

"Thank you. We'll try."

"I saw that pistol in your purse," Kirk said. "You know how to use it?"

Peggy nodded. "Tom taught me. A long time ago. But I hope it won't come to that."

"What are you guys doing?" Annie asked from the door. "What won't come to what?"

"Me eating healthy food!" Kirk said easily. "Your grandmother was trying to sell me on a salad. I want a big old skillet-fried grilled cheese sandwich."

Annie looked suspicious for a second, but then she started laughing.

"I'm going to make another pass around the house," said Kirk.

"And I'm going to make you that sandwich," Peggy said. "Come help me, Annie."

Annie looked longingly after Kirk as he went out the front door.

ALOIS ENGEL BRAKED AT the stop sign at the corner of Auburn and Duncan Avenues and depressed the electric cigarette lighter. The hippie who'd been guarding the front of the house was still nowhere to be seen. There were no cars behind Alois, and none on the intersecting streets. Duncan Avenue felt like it had been transplanted from the Garden District in New Orleans. Facing a golf course dotted with black and white men in their seventies, this sleepy lane was due for some excitement.

The cigarette light popped out, ready to go.

Alois removed the little metal plunger with its red-hot

eye, then picked up the Molotov cocktail and carefully ignited the windproof match taped to the bottle's side. Then he wedged the bottle between the passenger seat and the console of his pickup. The match burned with a snakelike hiss.

Alois scanned 360 degrees around the intersection. *Still no traffic.* Picking up his cell phone, he texted a question mark to Wilma Deen, whom he'd dropped off on Ratcliff Place, near a home whose yard abutted the yard of the mayor's safe house. Ten seconds later, his phone pinged.

Wilma's text read: *Still in position. Ready 2 rock.*

Alois picked up the Spider-Man mask from the passenger seat and pulled it over his head. Then he let his foot off the brake and rolled forward.

The mayor's house was fifty yards away.

Alois had rolled only ten yards when the blond hippie walked out the front door and surveyed the street.

"Goddamn it," Alois muttered. "I'm gonna blow your shit away."

But he didn't. He snapped off the head of the sizzling match and grabbed for his cell phone.

CHAPTER 63

I'M ABOUT TO observe the most surreal interrogation of my legal career, and I'm not even sure it's legal. John Kaiser hasn't set up this session to gather evidence for a court case. He wants to uncover a long-buried truth, one he believes to be bigger than any single case, and more important than the fate of my father. For this reason, Kaiser has allowed things I've only rarely seen in a sheriff's office, and never during an FBI interrogation.

First, the video camcorder is unplugged. This occasionally happens, and for a variety of reasons (but not usually to help the suspect). Second, the bedsheet is still hanging over the observation window (a sensible precaution). But strangest of all, Kaiser has submitted to a physical search by his prisoner, so the Double Eagle can be sure the FBI agent isn't wearing any recording device. I had to endure the same treatment in order to be present, and since I hold out some hope that Sonny might recant what he wrote about my father on the puzzle I created, I consented.

Sonny Thornfield has relaxed considerably since I was last in this room. The reason is simple. Kaiser's agents have already tracked down his grandson, the one preparing to depart for his second tour in Iraq. Kaiser actually brought in an encrypted FBI phone and allowed Sonny to speak to the kid on it. By then I knew the backstory: the boy saw his best friend maimed during his first tour, and he has no interest in sharing the same fate. Kaiser promised Sonny that if his grandson agreed to go into federal witness protection, he would not have to return to Iraq. I have no idea whether this is true, but Kaiser's confidently delivered answer—combined with the fact that he's already arranged to fly three of Sonny's family members here on FBI aircraft—told me that the FBI agent is pulling out all the stops for this case.

So . . . here we sit, watching a former Ku Klux Klansman and Double Eagle prepare to reveal a secret he's carried for forty years, on pain of death, in order to save himself and his family. Among my regrets—and they are many—is that Henry Sexton did not live to sit beside me in this moment. Whatever Sonny Thornfield knows, it might mean more to Henry than even to Dwight Stone.

"I want to make one thing clear," Sonny begins, licking his lips and glancing over at the bedsheet to make sure it's still taped over the one-way mirror. "I'm not going to talk about any other case but the big one. Dallas. And when I say the name Frank, I'm referring to Frank Sinatra. Nobody else, got it? Frank Sinatra."

"Got it," says Kaiser. "Let's hear what Old Blue Eyes did in Dallas in 1963. I always heard that he and JFK were friends."

Sonny shrugs and turns up his palms. "What do you want to know? I can't just start talking. Ask me something."

"All right. To your knowledge, who was behind the assassination? I mean the man at the very top."

Thornfield rubs his stubbled chin as though pondering what answering that question would have cost him forty years ago.

"Come on," Kaiser urges. "Nobody can hear you."

"It was Carlos Marcello's show," Sonny says finally. "All the way."

When Kaiser turns to me, I see something like rapture in his eyes.

"Who fired the kill shot? The one that blew Kennedy's brains out?"

"You already know. Frank Sinatra."

Kaiser doesn't react at first. But I can see from his frozen stillness how badly he wishes this were a legitimate interrogation. "How do you know that?" he asks.

"He told me."

"Who did?"

"Frank."

"When?"

Sonny shakes his head.

"What year, then?"

"Nineteen sixty-seven, I believe. About a year after he . . . had a family tragedy."

Kaiser looks back at me. We're both thinking the same thing. *A year after Frank Knox lost his son in Vietnam.*

"Was he sober when he told you this?" Kaiser asks.

"I don't think Frank was ever sober after 1966."

"Fair enough. How did Marcello approach Frank about that job? Or did someone else do that?"

"I think Marcello did it. We'd done a few jobs for him over the years, mostly in Florida. But Carlos knew Frank from the anti-Castro training camp in Morgan City. That's how Frank knew, ah . . . the other guy, too."

"What other guy?"

"The other guy who was in on it."

"Oswald?" Kaiser asks, but I know this is a feint to test Thornfield.

"No. Frank didn't know that nut job."

"Who, then?"

Sonny practically whispers the name. "David Ferrie."

Kaiser closes his eyes and exhales slowly. I have to admit, I feel a profound sense of satisfaction at hearing Dwight Stone's theory confirmed, and since Stone can't be here himself, I let myself enjoy it.

"What was Ferrie's part in the operation?" Kaiser asks.

Sonny shrugs as though the answer is self-evident. "He's the one who knew Oswald."

"How?"

"They were both from New Orleans. Ferrie had known him since Oswald was a kid."

"Known him how?"

"Frank told me they were queer. I don't know if that's true. But that's what he said."

Kaiser cuts his eyes at me again. So far, he and Dwight are batting a thousand.

"Did Frank know why Carlos wanted Kennedy dead?"

"He told me JFK and his brother were going to run the Little Man out of the country. Carlos had tried everything he knew to stop it, but nothing worked. This was the last chance."

"Okay." Kaiser glances at his watch. "Let's talk about the actual hit. Dealey Plaza."

Sonny scratches his nose and looks at the bedsheet once more. "You guys ain't got some kind of X-ray camera or anything in there, have you?"

"No cameras," Kaiser says, treating it as a serious question.

"Are you sure Snake don't know what's going on in here?"

"Positive. We're questioning Snake in another interrogation room right now."

Sonny clearly gets a fair dose of relief from this knowledge. "What else you want to know, then?"

"Tell us about the rifles, Sonny. The ones from Brody's house. Penn says one was displayed in Brody's basement as the assassination rifle, but that was a Remington Model 700. So why did we find an exact copy of Lee Harvey Oswald's rifle upstairs in Brody's study?"

Sonny smiles strangely. "You can thank Frank for that. See, Carlos and Ferrie wanted him to use a rifle like Oswald's for the hit, and then leave it at the scene. They wanted to sell a big Commie conspiracy and blame Castro."

"To deflect suspicion from Carlos?"

"Sure, and to get Carlos's casino action back. They figured if they could get the public mad enough at Castro, LBJ would invade."

Kaiser happily clucks his tongue. "So, why didn't Frank use the Carcano to kill Kennedy?"

"Because it was a piece of junk! The aftermarket Jap scope that came on it wasn't good enough for a BB gun. Frank told 'em he'd use his own rifle for the hit but leave the Italian one at the scene. But Ferrie didn't like that idea. He'd given Frank bullets from the same box as Oswald's, and he said Frank had to use those. The bullets had to match, he said."

I can only see Kaiser in profile, but an anticipatory smile has appeared on his face. "So what did Frank do?"

"He told Ferrie no problem. Frank was a genius with guns, see? Any kind of weapon, really. But guns were his specialty. He told Ferrie he could use his Remington and the bullets would *still* match—if the cops found any fragments at all."

Kaiser's face is practically glowing. "How could Frank manage that?"

Sonny chuckles with obvious admiration for his old sergeant. "First, he took those 6.58 Carcano bullets and removed them from the cartridges. Then he scraped the lead out of the copper jackets, so he'd have a lead-antimony mix that would match Oswald's bullets to a T, or at least as well as could be done."

"And then?"

"Then he used that lead to cast some .243 bullets to fit the cartridges for his Remington. He drilled out the cores so they'd blow apart on impact, and then he tested them to be sure."

"How did he do that?"

"On some pigs."

"Pigs. Did the bullets work as he wanted?"

"Hell, yeah. I told you he was a genius. The damn things exploded when they hit the skulls, and they hardly left a trace."

Kaiser quietly considers all he has heard. "If Frank went to all that trouble, then why didn't he leave the Carcano behind him after he made the shot, like he'd promised?"

Sonny settles back in his chair and folds his arms. "A couple of reasons. He said totin' it around was too risky. He already had to carry the Remington—broke down, of course. Carrying two guns doubled the risk. But that wasn't all. He was worried there might be forensic tests he didn't know nothin' about. Space-age stuff, you know? He'd handled that rifle himself, and he didn't want it winding up in the Sandia National Lab or someplace like that."

"Smart thinking."

"Frank didn't miss much, boy." Sonny looks anxiously around the interrogation room. "Is that enough? Can I go back to the brig now?"

Kaiser shakes his head. "Not yet. You haven't told us where he shot from. Was it the grassy knoll?"

Kaiser is testing Sonny again. There's no way the kill shot could have been fired from the grassy knoll. In my view, this testing is a waste of time. Thornfield is obviously telling the truth as he knows it. The real question is, *Was Frank Knox telling Sonny the truth when he told him all this?*

"Sonny?" Kaiser prompts. "The grassy knoll?"

"Hell, no. That's Hollywood bullshit. Frank shot from the building next to the Book Depository. Catty-corner to it. The Dal-Tex Building."

"How do you remember the name?"

"I've seen some TV shows about it. Documentaries. Hell, I watch the History Channel. It's pretty funny, the stuff they come up with, when you know what really happened. Everybody overthinks it, you know? Frank always took the shortest path between two points. I can't tell you how many times he said to me, 'Simplest is best, Son.' From back when we were kids, all the way to the Pacific . . . he lived by the same rules."

"How did he get into the Dal-Tex Building?"

Sonny chuckles again. "He went in as an elevator repairman, with a toolbox."

Kaiser thinks this over. "And how did he get out? The Dal-Tex Building was one of the first to be shut down after the shots were fired."

"As a *cop*," Sonny says, amazement in his voice. "Isn't that great? What could be simpler? He carried a Dallas police uniform in with him in the toolbox, wrapped around his rifle parts. Kept the gun from rattling. He put on the cop's uniform as soon as he got to the office he shot from. After he fired, he just walked out carrying the rifle. Everybody assumed he was part of the security detail, hunting for the shooter. Even the Secret Service. Always hide in plain sight, right?"

"Did he carry the toolbox out?"

"Nope. He left it in the elevator machine room. Empty." Sonny looks at me, then back to Kaiser. "Can't I go? This is taking too long. And the mayor wants to know about his daddy, don't he?"

"Yes, he does," I say in a taut voice, my eyes on Kaiser.

"Just a little longer," says Kaiser, not looking at me. "Tell me about Oswald, Sonny. Was Frank meant to fire the kill shot all along, or was he a backup for Oswald?"

"Backup. See, Ferrie thought Oswald could make the shot. Shows you how much he knew about rifles. Frank said the way that scope was attached, Oswald was lucky he hit anything. With only two mounting screws, you couldn't even zero the damned thing."

Yet another perfect correlation with Stone's theory. "Did they mean for Oswald to be captured?"

"Found dead, more like." A new light shines from Sonny's eyes. "That was where the operation went wrong.

Frank was supposed to kill the idiot right after the hit. Oswald was told to meet him in that stockyard parking lot behind the Book Depository, but on the day, he didn't show up."

"Why not?"

"Frank figured that when Oswald saw the president's head explode in his scope, he knew he hadn't made that shot. And that scared the shit out of him. That's why he panicked and ran home to get the pistol he hadn't even brought with him to Dealey Plaza. The one he used to shoot that cop later. Tippit."

"If Oswald didn't know anything about Frank, who did he think he was going to meet in the stockyard parking lot?"

"Ferrie, of course. That fool thought Ferrie was going to fly him to Havana! What a joke, right? But Frank told me Ferrie had actually run guns to Cuba, back before Castro allied with the Russians. And Oswald knew that. So maybe he wasn't so dumb to believe it."

"All right," I say in the most conclusive tone I can. "You've got what you wanted. Time to get on with the next act of this show."

Kaiser looks at his watch. "I think we're okay, Penn."

I try to mask my growing anger. "Sonny's not. Wanting doesn't make it so, John. Time's passing. Send him back to the cellblock with Snake and give Dwight his victory call. That's the gift you wanted to give him, and he deserves it. Then start interrogating all the other Eagles. Spend just as much time with each of them as you did with Sonny. And maybe—just maybe—you'll get away with this."

At this moment Kaiser regrets bringing me into this room. But at some level, he brought me in here to keep him from losing sight of his priorities.

"Then it's time for the big question," Kaiser says. "Sonny, you've given me a lot of details today, and I appreciate it. But do you have any way of proving anything you've told me? Anything besides what you say Frank told you?"

Sonny looks perplexed. "Like what? Like something physical?"

"Exactly."

"You know . . . I think there was something he kept. Frank never told me about it, but Snake said something once."

"What are you talking about? Something besides the rifles?"

"Yeah. A letter, maybe. Some kind of insurance."

"A letter written by Frank?"

"No, no. Somebody else. Ferrie, maybe. Or even Oswald. It sure wouldn't be Carlos. Carlos was like Frank. He never wrote nothing down. He was famous for that."

"How would Frank get a letter from Lee Harvey Oswald?"

"I don't know. But he followed the kid around for a while. A day or two, maybe. With Frank, you never know. I wouldn't be surprised if he screwed Oswald's Russkie wife while he was in town. That's how Frank rolled."

Kaiser isn't laughing. "You're joking, right? Because that's just absurd."

"Hey, I was just thinking out loud." Sonny shrugs. "You had to know Frank. He was something else."

Kaiser finally turns to me, one eyebrow raised. "Don't you have a question for Sonny?"

I close my eyes and ask myself if I want to give Sonny another opportunity to implicate my father. But in the end, I guess I have no choice. Standing and moving into Thornfield's sight line, I say, "Did my father have any connection at all to this plot?"

Sonny looks confused by my question. "Dr. Cage?"

"Yes."

He looks blank. "Not that I know of. What could he have had to do with it?"

"Some people say he had a relationship with Carlos Marcello when he lived in New Orleans as a young man. And he was the company doctor for Triton Battery, right? He knew Frank."

"Sure, yeah. He took care of all of us." Sonny suddenly holds up a forefinger. "Wait. . . . I believe Doc did sign Frank's sick card for the time he was gone."

My stomach flutters at his memory of this detail. "Did Frank mention that specifically?"

"Yeah, he did."

Kaiser gives me a regretful glance.

"Wasn't no big thing, though," Sonny says. "Frank spun Doc a story about having an affair with some floozy, said she was going to blow up his marriage unless he stayed with her awhile and calmed her down. So Doc just put what he wanted on the medical excuse."

The relief that flows through me is like a powerful narcotic. Forty years ago, any male, even a doctor, would have accepted a story like Frank's without question, and many would have provided the requested cover. When I turn to Kaiser, he's looking at me with an expression I can't read. Does he accept this as exculpatory evidence? "That's all for me," I tell him. "Let's get him back to the block."

"Just one more question," says Kaiser. "How did Frank get to Dallas and back?"

"Shit, come on," I mutter, imagining Dad in a diabetic coma somewhere.

"Ferrie flew him out there," Sonny says. "Snake flew him back."

Kaiser nods slowly. "And how did Frank get around *while* he was in Dallas?"

A faint smile widens Sonny's mouth. "He used a car that some of Carlos's people left for him."

"What people?"

"The Dallas mob out there, you know. I forget the name. Something that ends with a vowel."

"Civello, maybe?"

Sonny shrugs. "That sounds right. An Eytie name like that."

"And Frank was out there the whole week?"

"I don't know for sure. But at least from Wednesday on he was. He reconned Dealey Plaza the first day he got there. Then he staked out Oswald. He wanted to know who the other shooter was, see? He wanted to be sure he killed the right guy."

"Frank was a detail guy," Kaiser says with only light sarcasm.

Sonny gives Kaiser a hopeful look. "Are we fuckin' done now?"

I rise from my chair and retrieve my cell phones from the box where Sonny asked that I put them. The first one I switch on is the StarTac that Walker Dennis took off

Deputy Hunt when he caught him this morning. I can't deny that I'm hoping for a message from Forrest, but the screen only reads out the time.

"Hey," Sonny says to Kaiser. "You were being straight about my grandson, right? About getting him out of that second tour? 'Cause he's really scared about going back to Iraq."

Kaiser gets to his feet. "That's one thing I can do, Sonny. I'm the government today, and we are definitely making a deal."

"It really messed him up when his buddy got hurt like that. I saw that kind of shit all the time in my war, of course. Back then, you just had to choke it down and go on. But these kids today didn't come up the way we did, through the Depression. They're not as hard. I don't judge 'em. I'm glad, you know? But they can't stand the same stuff we could."

Kaiser gives him an understanding nod. "I hear you, Sonny. And after you sign that plea agreement, I will take care of him like he's my own. You have my word."

"I just hope my daughter doesn't screw this thing up."

"Me, too," Kaiser says worriedly. "I think we're done, Sonny. Let's get you back to your cell."

The old man grins. "I'm ready, believe it or not."

"I'm going to have a word with Mayor Cage outside. My guys will be in to take you back. If you get anything from Snake about where Dr. Cage is, act like you're having another heart attack. I'll get you out of there quick."

"Got it."

Kaiser follows me into the hall, where the electro-mechanical sounds of the open office out front filter back to us. Phones, printers, HVAC, the dispatchers' radio—

"Do you realize what we just heard in there?" Kaiser asks, his eyes glowing with excitement.

"Yeah, I heard it."

"What do you think?"

"I think he was telling the truth. The question is, was Frank Knox telling *him* the truth?"

"But the details—"

"I know. It's like you and Dwight scripted everything

he said. I'd say you guys had it figured pretty close. I'm glad Dwight's going to hear that before he goes under. Hopefully it'll help him through."

Kaiser nods like someone who can't quite believe he's been so fully vindicated. "And good news about your dad. How do you feel about that?"

"Compared to his present crisis, I don't much care what he did forty years ago."

"I understand. Well, with luck, Sonny can get Snake to tell him where Dr. Cage is."

"Maybe. But how long will it take him?"

Kaiser shrugs. "With Snake, Sonny gives us a better chance than using a car battery and jumper cables. Where will you go in the meantime?"

"No idea," I answer truthfully. "I can hardly think right now."

"Go see your little girl, Penn. I swear I'll call you the second I have any news. You did good work today, buddy. It was the tattoo that broke him."

Kaiser grips my shoulder, then steps back into the interrogation room and closes the door. As I make my way through the open area of the office, I recognize few of the remaining deputies, but Spanky Ford gives me a thumbs-up as I pass and walk through the main doors, out into the winter sun.

CHAPTER 64

"IF I HADN'T had tickets on that flight to Cuba," said Jordan Glass, "I think that redneck sheriff would have kept us in his office all afternoon."

"Cuba wasn't what did it," Caitlin countered. "If you weren't married to an FBI agent, good old Billy Ray Ellis would have jailed us as commie sympathizers."

Jordan laughed and led them out to her car, which Carl Sims had kindly sent a deputy to retrieve.

Caitlin looked back at the sheriff's office, thinking of the hour of her life she had wasted inside it. Billy Ray Ellis had a lot in common with Billy Byrd, and during his rather hostile interrogation, she'd gotten the feeling that he had spoken to his Adams County colleague. The only kindness he had shown was to give Caitlin a prison jumpsuit to wear while a matron dried her wet clothes.

"Look at that building," Jordan said. "It looks like four glorified mobile homes nailed together, but he's got a concrete helipad with klieg lights, a windsock, and the biggest Mississippi flag I've ever seen."

Caitlin looked up at the Stars and Bars in the corner of the state flag, which hung just below an equal-size version of the Stars and Stripes.

"The only good thing I got out of there was the peppermints," she said. "I'm still starving."

Jordan laughed and pulled a handful of cellophane-wrapped peppermints out of her pocket. "Me too. I emptied that secretary's jar."

"We need to get some lunch."

Jordan shook her head and moved on toward the car. "I don't have time. If I don't leave in the next twenty minutes, I'll miss my flight."

Caitlin felt an anticipatory sense of loss at the realization that she would soon be without Jordan. She had already called Terry Foreman, a girl from the *Examiner*'s marketing department, to pick her up at a local service station, but Terry was no substitute for Jordan Glass.

When they reached the car, Caitlin stood rather awkwardly by the door and stared at her friend across the roof. "I can't tell you how much today meant to me."

Jordan waved her hand dismissively. "I'm glad I came. But the day's not over yet. I've got a surprise for you."

Caitlin was confused. "Surprise?"

Jordan gave her a mischievous, almost elfin look. "You're about to owe me sooo big. Before you jumped in the drink, I shot two pictures of Toby Rambin's map."

"*What?*"

Jordan's eyes twinkled with pleasure. "While you were studying it earlier, I shot a couple of pics and made sure we had a copy. I didn't tell you in the boat because I didn't want Mose to hear."

Caitlin still couldn't work it out. "But Sheriff Ellis had us searched when we got to his office."

"Mm-hm."

"He confiscated your memory cards."

"He confiscated *a* memory card."

Excited laughter burst from Caitlin's throat. "Where was the real one?"

"They were both real. But while we waited to see the sheriff, I figured he might try something like that. It's what all third-world policemen do. So I put the card with the most pictures on it where they wouldn't find it and left the other one in the camera for him to steal."

"You are *crazy*."

"You don't know the half of it. When I went to the bathroom, I stepped into an empty office, plugged the card into a computer, and printed you a copy of the map."

Caitlin gasped in disbelief. "Oh, my God."

Jordan pulled a folded sheet out of her back pocket and passed it to Caitlin. "I'm pretty sure you can see everything."

Caitlin unfolded the page and saw a high-resolution copy of Toby Rambin's map, her own thumbs showing above it on either side.

"You're a superhero," she said. "Seriously."

"Well, don't show it to every deputy in the parking lot." Jordan unslung her camera bag and tossed it into her car. "Come on. Let's get you to your new wingman."

"Wait a second. Where did you hide that memory card?"

"Trade secret." Jordan winked. "Let's go."

SONNY THORNFIELD TURNED HIS head slightly to the left as a big deputy named Isbell led him into the cellblock and toward his cell. When Snake caught Sonny's eye through the bars, Sonny winked, then put his eyes front again.

"Open number seven!" Isbell barked.

Someone outside the block pressed a button, and the door to Sonny's cell opened. He went in and sat on his cot without looking back at the deputy.

"Close seven."

A deep buzzer sounded repeatedly, then the heavy motorized door slid down its track and clanged shut.

"Hey, Sonny, when the fuck we gettin' outta here?" asked Skillet McCune, a flat-faced welder who had once been a Double Eagle squad leader. "They can't keep us here like this without a phone call."

"FBI says we can," Deputy Isbell cut in. "Patriot Act. They can leave you in this hole till Judgment Day if they want. They can pull out your fucking fingernails, too. They can *waterboard* your ass, and the Supreme Court can't say shit about it."

As the deputy passed Snake's cell, Snake said, "What's that chubby wife of yours get up to while you're standing guard over drunks and crackheads, boy?"

The deputy's baton was off his belt in less than a second. He cracked the wood against the bars of Snake's cell, only missing his fingers because Snake jerked them clear in time. Snake got a good laugh from that. Isbell whacked the bars twice more, but Snake only laughed louder. The red-faced deputy cursed and stomped out of the cellblock.

Sonny lay on his cot with his hands behind his head. He felt like a man balanced on a tightrope, with hell on one side and purgatory on the other. As a Baptist, he didn't believe in purgatory, but he felt like that intermediate state of punishment was about the best he could hope for, given his past sins, with the hope of getting into heaven someday if he could atone in the time he had left.

He was starting to identify with Glenn Morehouse, who had complained so bitterly during the last weeks of his life about all the sins he'd been dragging behind him like lead weights chained to his dying body. For Sonny, the prospect of starting over with his estranged family in some new town was like an unexpected gift. He couldn't afford to let himself believe too much in it, in case his daughter screwed it up for everyone—which, if the past was any guide, was a real possibility.

He tensed up as he heard Snake sidle up to the bars of the adjacent cell. He could feel suspicion radiating like heat from that direction. Then Snake's voice floated to him, coarse but insinuating.

"I hear you were gone an awful long time, Sonny. You makin' new friends out there?"

"Fuck, no. I got no control over how long they keep me. They're acting like I'm the weak link or something, probably because of my heart attack. But fuck them."

Snake nodded, seeming to buy Sonny's brazen act. "How'd they pitch you?"

"They asked me a lot about Dr. Cage, actually. They want to know where he is."

Snake laughed softly. "You didn't tell 'em, did you?"

For a couple of seconds Sonny considered saying that the FBI had already raided his cabin and found it empty, but his sanity stopped him. "Right. When the cabin's in my name? That'd be a genius move."

Snake didn't comment on this.

"They also kept telling me I was gonna die in Angola. That fed Kaiser asked me if I thought I'd last a week in a jail full of niggers, once they found out who I was."

Snake chuckled. "He's got a point there. It's a good thing none of us will spend a day on that farm."

"You really think we should be talking like this? They could be taping everything we say in here."

"No, they can't," said Snake. "That's against the law."

"You heard Isbell," Skillet said from the cell to Sonny's right. "We're talking feds here. They don't give a shit about the law on this thing. Not with that Patriot Act. Hell, they planted that meth, didn't they? And you can see the cameras right up there in the corner."

"Those cameras are there to keep morons from killing themselves," Snake said. "Keeps the state from gettin' sued. But they don't record sound. What, you think Kaiser has a platoon of lip-readers out there, watching us?"

"I wouldn't be surprised," said a reticent man named Gene Christian, a retired electrician's helper. "Sonny's right. Let's keep our mouths shut. Remember what Frank used to say. A man's worst enemy in this world is his mouth."

"That's what Frank used to say, all right," Snake said. "Didn't he, Sonny?"

"Sure," Sonny mumbled, closing his eyes and wishing he'd thrown out that goddamn navy tattoo thirty years ago. Kaiser had promised to make no mention of the eight-inch swatch of human skin when talking to his family about the Witness Protection Program. If Sonny's daughter heard about that, she might tell Kaiser to put her son back on the plane to California, even if he had to pull another tour in Iraq.

Sonny thought back to the awful day they'd taken the tattoos from Revels and Davis. Snake had been the instigator, of course, as always. Only that day it was worse, since he'd been consumed with grief for his older brother. Frank had just died, and Snake had assumed the role of leader. The rest of the men had egged Sonny on like he was a virgin at a whorehouse, waiting to lose his cherry. What could you do in the face of that?

Even though it had been almost forty years since that day, Sonny could hardly own up to what he'd done to that boy. He could still remember Revels's anguished screams as Morehouse held his skinny arm against the workbench so that Sonny could cut the blue-black anchor from his bloody skin.

"*Sonny?*" came a faint whisper.

Snake again.

"You're awful quiet in there, brother."

"Get me out of this cell and I'll talk a blue streak for you. But till then, leave me the fuck alone."

But Snake couldn't do that. "I'm worried about Will," he said. "They've had him out as long as they had you.

And Will ain't got your sand. He's a couple of years older than you, isn't he?"

"That's right. What are you saying?"

"I'm worried he might do what Glenn did, that's what. He's the oldest Eagle left, and the idea of jail—or even the possibility of it—might just be enough to break him."

"Bullshit," Sonny said, thinking how easy it had ultimately been for him to tell Kaiser what he'd wanted to know. "Will was the seventh man sworn into the group. Frank gave him his Double Eagle. He won't say anything."

"Maybe," Snake conceded. "But what if he did?"

"Then we'll worry about it *then*."

"That could be too late. We learned our lesson with Glenn, didn't we? You wait too long, and they start talkin' before you can stop 'em. Right?"

Sonny nodded.

"We might have to try some preventive medicine. In here. You up for that?"

Sonny's stomach rolled. "Any son of a bitch tries to cut a deal by naming names, he needs to die. We all took the oath."

"That's right, brother. You stay ready."

JORDAN PULLED INTO A diagonal parking space beside the Crossroads Service Station, which stood at the intersection of Highway 24 and the main drag of Athens Point, Mississippi. The town proper lay a mile closer to the river, but this intersection saw most of the commercial action. Three corners were occupied by service stations, the fourth by a large grocery store. The Crossroads Station was the largest of the three; it held a full-service bait shop, an ice cream counter, and a café with booths and tables. The fueling bays did a brisk business with everything from semi trucks to pickups hauling bass boats and ATVs on trailers.

Caitlin had told Terry Foreman to meet them here, and the girl was waiting outside with two red-faced FBI agents standing like bookends at her shoulders, drawing stares from the mostly black clientele of the station.

"Ms. Glass, you scared the crap out of us," said one of them.

"You also got us in deep shit," said the other, who obviously knew Jordan better.

Jordan smiled her mischievous smile again. "Look at the bright side. You got the pleasure of hanging out with Terry here."

Terry blushed. With her blond hair, blue eyes, and trim figure, she still looked like a high-school cheerleader.

"We'd better get moving if you're going to make your plane," said the second agent. "We're cutting it really close."

"Give me thirty seconds."

"We're in the black Suburban."

"I never would have guessed."

Jordan took Caitlin's arm and led her around the corner of the station. Once there, she took Caitlin's hand and gave her a wholly unguarded smile.

"I had a blast today. I'm sorry we didn't hit pay dirt, but that's the way it usually goes. The big coups take a lot of prep work."

"Thanks for all you did to help me," Caitlin said. "And thank you for inspiring me when I was a kid. And—"

"Stop it," Jordan said. "We're colleagues now, right? Get that through your head. I hope I'm back to shoot the photo spread of the Bone Tree when you find it."

Caitlin nodded, a strange elation flowing through her.

"Oh, shit," Jordan said, mock-slapping the side of her head as though she were an idiot. She reached into her camera bag and pulled out the multi-tool she'd lent Caitlin to cut her life jacket loose in the swamp.

"This is for you. I've carried it through at least two dozen countries, and it's never let me down. Time to pass it on to somebody who needs it more than I do."

Caitlin reached out to take the scarred metal tool. When Jordan dropped it into her hand, she realized that no gift had ever meant more to her. "Can I ask you something cheesy?"

"Sure."

"Will you be one of my bridesmaids?"

Jordan laughed so loudly that one of the FBI agents walked out to the gas pump island to peer around the corner at them.

"Christ, I'm more like matron-of-honor age now."

"You're same age as Penn. Anyway . . . just think about it. And come back soon—and safe."

"Safe?" Jordan rolled her eyes. "Cuba's like Miami circa 1955. You're the one who needs to be careful."

"I will."

"Bullshit. You're just like I used to be. You'd walk into a minefield for a story. And you have the map now. Promise me you won't try to find the Bone Tree without Carl or some equivalent with you." She jabbed Caitlin's chest with her forefinger, only half playfully. "Promise."

"I won't. I promise."

The photographer smiled and then hugged her. "*Have babies and be happy,*" she whispered fiercely in Caitlin's ear. "There's plenty of time for work."

Jordan's urgency sent a shock through her, but before she could analyze the feeling, Jordan hiked her camera bag higher on her shoulder and walked toward her car the way Caitlin had dreamed of walking since she was a girl. Like she'd been everywhere in the world at least twice and was on her way to one of the few places she hadn't seen yet. But the truth was, Jordan had already been to Cuba. She'd flirted with Castro, for God's sake. And what she wanted more than anything now was what Caitlin already had.

So why can't I be content? Caitlin wondered.

Jordan didn't look back as she drove out of the parking lot and turned onto 24, headed back toward Highway 61 South, the black Suburban on her tail.

Terry Foreman walked up to Caitlin and shook her head. "Those guys were pretty cool. Are we heading back now?"

Caitlin looked down at the multi-tool in her hand, wondering what kind of crazy jams it had gotten Jordan out of over the years.

"Caitlin?"

Caitlin looked up at Terry. Actually, she saw no reason to go home just yet. Natchez was filled with reporters, all working the same story, and all hunting for a lead like the one she had folded in her back pocket. Penn and John were still interrogating the jailed Double Eagles, trying to force a confession out of one of them, like stonecutters looking for a crack in the face of a rock. And worst of all, Tom was still missing.

But I still have the map, she thought.

Mose Tyler might have fled the area, but somewhere in Athens Point or Woodville had to be someone who knew the location of the Bone Tree. There were probably quite a few. Most would be white—ex-Klansmen or Double Eagles who'd been there for god-knows-what rituals that made widows out of wives. Those men would never show Caitlin where that tree was. But there must also be black men who knew the tree's location, as Toby Rambin had claimed he had.

She just needed to find one of them.

"What's that?" Terry asked, pointing at the multi-tool.

"Just something Jordan gave me to remember her."

"Huh. Wow."

Caitlin shoved the tool into the pocket of her jeans.

"Hey," Terry said, sounding worried. "Don't look now, but there's a black guy staring at us. He's creeping me out."

"Where?"

"Behind you, at the gas pumps, gassing up a truck."

"Let's go in the café, then."

"Shouldn't we just head back to Natchez?"

"Not yet," Caitlin said. "He might follow us down the road."

Terry's eyes widened. "God, you're right."

Caitlin wasn't worried about any black guy following them to Natchez. She just wanted to buy some time to think. It would be abnormal if men gassing up their vehicles *didn't* stare at two reasonably attractive young women standing outside a combination bait shop/café. She simply wasn't ready to leave Athens Point yet. In fact, if she had an extra vehicle, she would send Terry back without her, then search for a reliable guide to take her back into the swamp.

"Order me a cheeseburger," Caitlin said, nodding at the quick-service counter. "And get yourself something. I need to run to the bathroom."

"Okay."

Caitlin walked toward the restroom but didn't go in. The dining area was a collection of booths with bright orange plastic seats and wood-topped tables. The smell of hot grease and onions permeated the air. Most people probably bought food from the counter, but there was a waitress who would come to your booth and take your order if you wanted to sit for a while. Three booths were occupied, all by groups of men. Two groups were black, one white. The black men were older and drank coffee as they pored over racing forms. The white men looked like truckers. She wondered what would happen if she approached one of the black men and struck up a conversation.

Jordan wouldn't think twice about doing that, she thought, trying to work up her nerve.

CHAPTER 65

PEGGY HAD LAID out a platter of roast beef, cheese, lettuce, and tomatoes in the kitchen. She and Annie were making sandwiches for themselves and for Officer Ervin. The iron skillet crackled and popped with melted butter as Ervin's grilled cheese crisped up. (He'd seen Kirk Boisseau's earlier and decided he wanted to try one himself.) Annie had the den television tuned to the Baton Rouge station and turned up loud, so that she could hear any relevant news that might break in on regular programming. Earlier she'd heard on the Jackson, Mississippi, station that an interview with Caitlin would be broadcast on WJTV during tonight's six o'clock report.

Peggy scooped the heavy grilled cheese out of the skillet with a spatula, then cut it in half and poured some potato chips onto the plate from a bag.

"You take that to Mr. Ervin," she said.

As Annie disappeared through the back door, Kirk Boisseau entered the kitchen from the den and asked if there was any coffee.

"I can make you some," Peggy offered. "Or I can offer you iced tea. I just made a pitcher."

Kirk looked suspiciously at the pitcher by the kitchen window, then walked over to it and tapped its glass rim. "It's not that syrupy sweet stuff like we drank when I was a kid, is it?"

Peggy laughed. "The kind you can pour over pancakes? No, these days even my tea has Sweet'N Low in it."

Kirk laughed and said he'd try a glass after he made one more round of the house.

Peggy fixed two roast beef sandwiches and set them on the counter for herself and Annie, then poured the tea and walked to the front door to find Boisseau. Her former student was just walking up the steps, and he accepted the glass with a grateful smile. Over his shoulder Peggy watched a blue pickup truck roll up Duncan Avenue, then slow as though its driver was watching the foursome playing on the eighteenth fairway. Seeing her sight line change, Kirk turned toward the street. As she looked past him, the face in the driver's window caught her attention. Oddly, it didn't look human, but almost like a cartoon. Then she recognized the character: *Spider-Man* . . .

As she registered a flicker of flame in the truck, Kirk shoved her back through the door. Falling backward, she saw an arm hook over the truck's roof and throw something toward the house, the way one of her newspaper deliverymen used to heave the *Examiner* at her old house. A gun appeared in Kirk's hand, but before he could fire, a whirling object smashed against the steps and the air burst into flame.

Peggy smelled kerosene, and then the truck tires screamed.

Kirk Boisseau fired a fusillade of shots at the departing truck, then grabbed his leg and started to yell for Officer Ervin. With the unreality of a nightmare, Peggy saw fire run up Kirk's pant leg and gather around his waist. The floor vibrated like a drum beneath her, and then James Ervin ran past her, dragged Kirk down the steps, and rolled him onto the ground. Then he wrapped his jacket around Kirk's leg and smothered the fire. Peggy scrambled to her feet, her mind on one thing: *Annie—*

"*Gram, what happened?*" the girl yelled from behind Peggy. "Something's burning!"

Her frightened voice filled Peggy with relief, but instead of wasting time with conversation, Peggy pulled Annie into the kitchen, opened her purse, and took out the .38 that Tom had bought her long ago. Then she led Annie into the den and made her crouch behind a big club chair.

Heavy footsteps hammered on the hardwood, and then Officer Ervin came pounding back into the den, his beagle-like face animated with anxiety.

"You all right, Miz Cage?"

"We're fine, James. Was that a Molotov cocktail?"

Ervin nodded. "I b'lieve it was. Call 911 and tell them we need the fire department. I'm going back outside."

Peggy's phone was stored in her purse and powered

down, as Penn had insisted. She started to get to her feet, but Annie already had her cell phone in hand and was entering the numbers while it searched for a signal.

As Officer Ervin went back out the front door, two explosions sounded behind the house. Then Peggy heard a roar and crackle that could only be fire. She leaped to her feet and pulled Annie up with her.

"We've got to get out!"

Annie was speaking into her cell phone, but she let Peggy lead her toward the front door. Halfway there, Peggy stopped. What if the fire was meant to drive her and Annie into the open, where they could be shot or taken? She thought frantically. The best solution she could come up with was to hunker down just inside the front door, protected from gunfire but near an escape route.

"We need a fire truck!" Annie cried into her phone. "Two hundred Duncan Avenue! A bomb just blew up at our house. . . . Yes, a bomb!"

Through the open door Peggy heard a man roar in anger and pain. She knew it was Kirk Boisseau. Pulling Annie down to the floor, she took the phone from her granddaughter and tried to remember the last number Penn had given her.

I'M PARKED IN THE drive-through lane of the Vidalia Burger King when my BlackBerry rings. It's Kaiser.

"What's up?" I ask him. "Did Sonny get Snake to tell him about Dad?"

"No. Where are you, Penn?"

"Getting food."

"Okay, stay calm. Your mother and daughter are fine, but there was some kind of attack on the house where you have them staying. A Molotov cocktail, it sounds like."

"*What?*" A blast of adrenaline brings me straight up in my seat. "How the hell did they find it?"

"I don't know that yet. Your mother called the sheriff's office looking for you. Whatever number she has for you didn't get answered, so she got me instead."

I take out my burn phone, which I set on silent before meeting Forrest and neglected to switch back on after hearing Sonny's JFK story.

"They just hit our satellite dish, too," Kaiser says, "at the hotel. This was a coordinated attack, Penn. Nobody was hurt at the hotel, but our secure communications with Washington have been knocked out. The Natchez PD and fire department are over at Duncan Avenue now, and they're covering your mother and daughter. I'm going to head over myself, because my guys can handle the hotel scene."

"I'm on my way, John. I'll talk to you there."

I honk my horn, but the cars in front of me don't move. Rather than wait for a response, I wrench the wheel right and drive over the concrete curb, then squeal out of the parking lot.

Once I'm on Highway 84, I speed-dial Walt's burn phone.

"Talk to me," he says.

"The Knoxes just hit the house where I was hiding Mom and Annie. They're okay, but the war has definitely started. Where's Forrest?"

"I'm following him south on Highway 61. He could be headed back to Baton Rouge, or he could turn east for Athens Point and head back to Valhalla. I'm hoping that's his plan."

"Is Ozan still with him?"

"Yep. They could easily have ordered the attack over the phone, though."

"Don't lose them, Walt. We can't afford to now."

"I won't. You take care of Peggy and your baby. I got these bastards covered."

"Thanks." As my front wheels hit the eastbound Mississippi bridge, I push the gas pedal close to the floor.

SPANKY FORD WAS SITTING at his desk when the dispatcher informed him that the courthouse had received a bomb threat. Even though he'd known it was coming, his stomach flipped and his mind went blank for a few seconds. *What's the protocol?* Sheriff Dennis wasn't in the building (and hadn't been since he'd stormed out and Agent Kaiser had announced that the FBI was taking over the department). Since the sheriff's department occupied much of the western end of the courthouse building, a bomb threat meant a twofold crisis, and Spanky set down the phone in a kind of daze.

"What's the matter?" asked the FBI agent sitting at the desk with him, a man named Wilson.

"We just got a bomb threat. Apparently it has something to do with JoJo Menteur."

"Who the hell's that?" Wilson asked.

"One of the meth prisoners. He's downstairs in the holding pen."

"He's not one of the specials, is he?"

"No. He's nobody. A Cajun who moved up here about five years ago."

"What's the protocol? Do you guys have an EOD squad?"

"Not really," said Spanky. "We're supposed to evacuate, both the department and the courthouse."

"For every phoner? Or only credible threats?"

"How the hell do you know what's credible? JoJo's got some crazy-ass cousins. We've got to evacuate!"

Wilson thought for a moment. "Well, we can't move the special prisoners out of the cellblock."

"Why not? Sheriff Dennis left me in charge, and I'm not going to have deputies *or* prisoners blown to pieces on my watch. We already lost two men raiding these meth dealers."

Wilson's face had colored. "Agent Kaiser will shit a brick if we let those prisoners out of there. Did the threat come with a time frame?"

"Right now! How's that?" Spanky showed some temper. "What do you think your boss'll do if those assholes get blown up or die of smoke inhalation?"

"Good point. I'd better call him."

"You do that. I'm calling an evac."

Spanky hit the panic button at the front desk, and a loud alarm began blaring through the building. As deputies scattered to perform pre-assigned tasks, Agent Wilson stood and peered at the exterior windows as though some answer lay outside the building. "Who the hell would bomb a courthouse over some low-level Cajun meth dealer?" he asked. "A meth charge might get you a stretch in the pen, but bombing a courthouse is a ticket to death row."

Spanky was about to reply when the floor rocked beneath his feet, a vibration that went into his bones. The sound only arrived afterward, a muted blast that triggered a combination of awe and fear in him.

"That was the near the courtrooms!" Spanky cried.

Two more explosions sounded from outside the building, reminding Spanky of transformers exploding during a thunderstorm. Then the sprinkler system unleashed a torrent of water upon them. The lights went dim, wavered, blacked out. Seven seconds later, they switched back on as the emergency generator came online. Spanky saw Special Agent Wilson standing with surprising coolness, holding his phone to his ear.

"Nobody would do this for some meth cooker," he said, wiping water from his eyes. "They're trying to get us to evacuate the cellblock. They want to break the old guys out."

As the two men stared at each other, a second detonation rattled the building. This time the room went dark and silent, as all the computer drives and fans spun to a stop.

"They took out the backup generator," said Spanky. "What do you think now?"

At that moment an FBI agent raced into the office from the hall that led to the courthouse. "Dan!" he cried, waving at Wilson. "Somebody just blew up two of our cars!"

"Son of a bitch," Wilson said, raising his hand to point at Spanky. "This may be an escape attempt. Don't let a soul in or out of the cellblock until I get back."

"Don't worry," said Spanky, stunned by how perfectly Forrest's predictions were being borne out. "You guys be careful out there."

WHEN THE FIRST SHUDDER rolled through the cellblock floor, all six Double Eagles came up off their cots. As the lights dimmed and came back on, a babble of questions bounced off the cinder-block walls. The fear in the voices was plain. After seven or eight seconds, Snake shouted everyone down, and the block fell silent.

"What the fuck, Snake?" whispered Gene Christian from his cell.

"That was a bomb," said Skillet McCune.

"C4, sounded like," said Snake. "Did you think Forrest was gonna leave us in here to rot?"

"Hot damn!" cried Skillet.

"Keep your yap shut. I want to listen."

Sonny Thornfield had known it was a bomb within two seconds of the blast. During the war he'd been inside buildings that had taken direct hits from mortar rounds. That bone-rattling shudder of masonry and earth was unique to blast waves, at least in this part of the country.

Sonny sat frozen on his cot, wondering what Snake might know that Sonny didn't. Would Forrest really try to stage a mass escape with FBI agents crawling all over the courthouse?

A second detonation rocked the building, and this time the lights went out. Now the only illumination reaching the cells came from gray light spilling through the high slit windows.

"Jesus," someone breathed. "Were you expecting that one, Snake?"

"Right on time, boys. This is it. Okay?"

As Sonny wondered what Snake meant, all eight cell doors slid open simultaneously.

"Holy shit," Skillet marveled.

"*Go time*," said Snake.

In the darkness Sonny heard the hiss of sock feet sliding across the floor. The sound seemed to come from all directions at once.

He was no longer alone in his cell.

The fear hit Sonny's chest like the boot of that Texas Ranger who'd kicked him in the sternum three days ago. He prayed that the pain was only angina and not another heart attack.

"*Stand him up*," ordered Snake. "Quick, now."

Powerful hands seized Sonny's arms below the shoulders, then hoisted him to his feet. In the dim haze he saw Snake's slit-eyed face inches from his own, and then a pair of hands looped something thick and dark around his neck. A towel, maybe? He tried to pry his arms loose, but the hands that held them were far too strong, and the towel quickly choked off his air. He thought briefly of

Glenn Morehouse's giant hands twisting Jimmy Revels's coffee-colored arm down to the workbench . . . but Glenn was dead now. Sonny blinked in confusion. Everything he saw and felt was distorted by the prism of agony in his chest.

"*Traitor*," spat a venomous voice near his head.

The words that followed penetrated no deeper than Sonny's eardrums. The terror he'd felt when the cell doors opened had yielded to an eerie sense of separateness—as though he were some Gemini spaceman whose tether had been cut, so that he drifted steadily away from his ship with its life-sustaining oxygen. Was this how Jimmy Revels had felt when he spoke the three words that had haunted Sonny every day of his life?

I forgive you. . . .

Sonny couldn't forgive Snake Knox for stealing the last few years of his life—the only ones that might have really mattered. Sonny couldn't even forgive himself. He'd bitten so hard on the deal Kaiser had offered him, the dream of a life unburdened by association with men who'd goaded him to do things he would never have done on his own. How could he have been such a fool? When you'd gone as far down the road to damnation as he had, there was no getting back.

Snake's face loomed before him, the familiar flattened smile of the hooded cobra swaying before its prey. "You know the rules, Sonny," he hissed, his eyes filled with wounded pride. "Damn, but I never figured it'd be you who turned."

Sonny's eyelids began to close. He wanted to speak, to tell the rest of the boys to get away from Snake as fast and as far as they could, but whatever they'd wrapped around his neck had sealed his throat shut.

"Next stop, Hell, brother," Snake whispered. "Say hello to Glenn for me."

Sonny thought of his grandson, flying toward Louisiana at five hundred miles per hour, hoping to see his grandfather and to get a reprieve from war. He thought of his daughter, who would see his murder as a fitting end for a selfish old man. Then he thought of the eager-eyed FBI agent back in the interrogation room, who longed to tell the world who'd really killed President Kennedy. What could it matter after all this time? America had swerved so far off course since then that nothing would ever bring the country back to what it had been. As the last light winked out in Sonny's mind, his final thought was a prayer that God had heard Jimmy Revels forgive him in the shadow of the Bone Tree.

CHAPTER 66

CAITLIN HAD INTENDED to approach one of the black patrons of the Crossroads Café without Terry, but in the end, her nerve had failed her. It was the audience of white men that had stopped her. Instead, she'd sat down in the booth farthest from the white men and taken Jordan's map photo from her pocket. Toby Rambin's hand-drawn graphic left a lot to be desired, but it was better than anything the FBI had. More even than the Lusahatcha County Sheriff's Department had—unless they'd known where the Bone Tree was all along.

A waitress walked up to Caitlin's booth and asked if she needed help. Caitlin explained that her friend was ordering from the counter, but she asked for a cup of coffee and borrowed a pen from the waitress—a clear hexagonal Bic like the ones she'd used in grade school. Just holding it gave her a surprisingly nostalgic feeling. She pulled a napkin from the dispenser on her table and began drawing a map of where they'd found Casey Whelan's body.

While Terry waited for their order at the counter, Caitlin stole glances at the men who were doing the same to her. In between looks, she would go back to her napkin, her mind on whether or not she might be able to lure Carl Sims away from work to help her locate the X on Rambin's map.

She nearly jumped out of her skin when a boy of about nineteen walked up to her booth and stared down at her. At least six foot two, he wore the traditional uniform of the gangbanger, with a bright designer sweatshirt and oversized shorts that hung so low that his butt crack had to be on constant display.

"You pretty, baby," the boy said, shifting his package with his hand. "You got a boyfriend?"

Caitlin glanced over at the men in the booths, but no one seemed inclined to come to her aid.

"I'm married, baby," she said, holding up her engagement ring.

"'Course you is, hot as you are."

A table of truckers were now watching the interchange, but no one interrupted.

"That's a big rock," the boy said. "Your husband rich?"

Caitlin looked up with all the hardness she could muster. "Listen, *baby*. I work for the DEA, and I'm in town to consult with Sheriff Ellis on the crack trade. Do you really want to sit down and get to know me better?"

The boy gaped at her for a few seconds, then shuffled back toward the glass-fronted beer cases, his ass crack in plain view. The men in the booths went back to their papers. A couple chuckled softly.

The waitress brought Caitlin her coffee. Someone left the café, and two more men walked in. Caitlin sipped the harsh mixture, then jotted some numbers on the napkin, trying to remember exactly how long she'd been off the Pill when she'd conceived. She didn't care that people were going to realize she'd been pregnant before she was married. She just wanted to know that her body had cleared the artificial hormones before her egg was fertilized.

About the time she'd figured out the relevant math, another young black man decided to hit on her. This one didn't merely approach the booth, but slid onto the bench seat opposite her as though he belonged there.

Caitlin was so shocked that she didn't protest immediately. This boy was older than the first one, maybe twenty-five. Not a boy, really, but a young man. He was also dressed in work clothes—reasonably clean jeans and a flannel shirt worn over a red long-john top. His hair was cut close to his scalp, he was clean-shaven, and his eyes were large and bright. The only thing that tweaked her radar was the sharp tang of cigarette smoke that wafted off him when he leaned toward her and whispered so that the men in the booths could not hear him.

"You the lady lookin' for the Chain Tree?" he asked.

"Excuse me?" she said, a wave of heat coloring her cheeks. "The what?"

The young man turned around far enough to check on the men in the booths. "The Chain Tree. Big cypress with old rusty chains on it, where the Klan killed all them boys back in the old days?"

A couple of the men were watching now, and Terry was staring fearfully from the counter. Caitlin leaned forward and said, "How do you know that?"

The young man smiled faintly, and his eyes twinkled. "My daddy goes to Reverend Sims's church. Beulah Baptist. He was asking about the Tree, whether anybody knew where it was. He talked about the Cat Lady a little, the one whose son got beat to death out there, and his wife got raped."

The Cat Lady? Caitlin thought, trying to work through the boy's words. It struck her then that he was the one who had been watching from the gas pumps when she and Terry first arrived. "How did you recognize me?"

The boy laughed. "You don't exactly look like you fit in around here, you know? But I've seen your picture in the Natchez paper before. I saw you a minute ago, when I was getting gas. I figured you had to be her. Carl Sims said you looked like a movie actress."

"Do you know Carl?"

"I know his cousins, the Greens."

Caitlin didn't bother digging any deeper. "So why did you come over here? Just to chat me up?"

The boy's smile broadened. "No, ma'am. I came to check if you still want to go see where that tree be at."

A dozen different thoughts tumbled through Caitlin's mind. At the counter, Terry looked like she was about to call 911. Caitlin gave her the okay sign, then slid the photo of the map across the table.

"Do you recognize that?"

"Who drew this?"

"A friend."

The boy chuckled softly. "I know who drew this map. Ol' Toby Rambin."

The kid was sharper than he looked. "Do you see that X on it?"

The boy nodded.

"Is it in the right place?"

He pursed his dark lips, then laid his long fingers on the edges of the map and regarded it from different angles. After several seconds, he took Caitlin's pen and drew an X about an inch from the one that Rambin had drawn.

"Right there looks better to me."

"What's there?"

The boy looked up at her, his eyes like dark pools. "A place no black man ever went by choice."

"Is everything okay?" Terry was standing at Caitlin's side with a tray in her hand. Her eyes were locked onto Caitlin's as though she was afraid to make eye contact with the stranger in the booth.

"Everything's fine," Caitlin said. "Sit here by me."

After some hesitation, Terry slid into the booth.

"Terry, this is . . . ?" Caitlin gave the boy an inquisitive look.

"Harold," he said. "Harold Wallis."

Caitlin looked steadily into his eyes. "Show me your driver's license."

After a couple of seconds, he took out his wallet and opened it for her. The name under his driver's license photo read *Harold Wallis*.

"You don't have a middle name?"

"Nope. Mama couldn't think of one. I got eight brothers, and she said she ran out by the time she got to me."

Caitlin pointed at the map and lowered her voice still further. "How do you know where that X goes, when nobody else seems to?"

"Easy. My granddaddy trapped and fished that swamp all his life, same as old Toby. He used to take me back there to help with the trotlines. I seen that tree a dozen times, even though Daddy cut a wide circle around it."

"How long ago was this? You're not that old."

Harold shrugged. "Fifteen years, maybe."

"Did you ever see it up close?"

"Yes, ma'am. One time. And that's all I ever wanted to see it."

"Is it hollow, like the legends say?"

Harold nodded. "I shined a light through the crack in that big trunk."

Caitlin's pulse quickened. "What did you see?"

"A pile of bones."

She looked past Harold at the men in the booths. No one seemed to be eavesdropping. "Human?" she asked.

"Some was. I saw a skull. But I saw deer bones, too. Set of antlers. Looked like a mess up in there, and I didn't look long. Granddaddy was about to skin me."

"Where's Toby Rambin now?"

"Gone. Took off somewhere, I heard. He long gone."

"Why?"

"Chicken, maybe. Or smart. I don't know."

"What's he scared of?"

Harold shook his head slightly. "Not in here."

Caitlin leaned toward him. "Do you know why I want to find that tree?"

He nodded. "You lookin' for them dead boys."

"What boys?"

"Them musicians from Ferriday, went missing back in the sixties. Used to play the blues clubs round here."

The men in the nearest booth got up and went to the cash register, keys jangling on their belts.

"What else do you know?" Caitlin asked.

Harold shrugged. "More boys than that got killed back in that swamp. Newspaper say you lookin' for them, too. That's what Stoney told me."

"Stoney who?"

"Stoney Jackson. He go to Reverend Sims's church." Harold suddenly looked nervous, or maybe just impatient.

"Do you think those bones are still where you saw them?" she asked.

"Why wouldn't they be? 'Less somebody moved 'em. And why would they do that?"

"Because they know the FBI is looking for them," Caitlin said.

Silent laughter animated Harold's dark face. "The men who own that hunting camp down there ain't scared of no FBI. They got senators and governors coming down here to hunt and get wit' women. Besides, the FBI didn't find nothin' back in the day, so why should they find anything now? Sheriff Ellis ain't gonna help 'em none. And without help, they couldn't find their way out, if they ever did get in. That swamp ain't hardly been *logged*, lady. You saw it.

It's like a dinosaur movie. You got to know exactly where you goin' to get anywhere."

"How do *you* get in and out?"

"Boat. That's the only way."

"Do you have a boat?"

"Got a pirogue. For settin' out trotlines and such."

Caitlin tried to imagine what a pirogue might look like.

"So . . . you wanna see them bones or not?"

"Why are you willing to take me to them?"

A cagey look came into Harold's face. "I hear you gave Mose a grand to take you through the game fence on that map."

"I see. You want money?"

"Who don't?"

"What do you want it for? Drugs?"

"Hell, no. I want to get out of this town, just like everybody else. Everybody black, anyway."

Caitlin spoke so softly she doubted the boy would be able to hear. "Mose told me the Bone Tree is behind that fence. He said there was no way through without cutting it."

Harold smiled. "Mose don't know half of what he think he does. I know where there's a hole. Deer know it, too."

"Are you a poacher, Harold?"

The smile disappeared. "I do what my granddaddy taught me. I live off the land. Ain't nothin' wrong with that. You want to see that tree or not?"

Caitlin didn't hesitate. "Yes."

"A grand ain't gonna cover it. I need double that."

"Two thousand dollars?"

"Hazard pay. Soon as I bring you back, I'm blowing town. Won't be able to stay after that. Once you get the police in there, the men who use that tree gonna start looking for whoever showed it to you. I got to be long gone by then."

"Are you sure you're not just trying to screw me out of this money you think I have?"

The look of hurt pride on the boy's face actually made her feel guilty. "If all I wanted was your money, I could just run you off the road and take it—which some brothers around here would be happy to do. Crackers, too. I'm only askin' what's fair. You'll see what I mean when you see where we got to go."

Caitlin nodded. "All right. Two thousand. But that's it."

Harold thought about it, hard. "Okay," he said finally. "It's a deal."

Caitlin turned to Terry, whose eyes were as big as fried eggs. She laid her hand on Terry's arm. "You told me once that you envied the reporters, who get to do important work. Well, this is it."

Terry swallowed hard but said nothing.

"Can we go today?" Caitlin asked.

Harold looked at the big window to their left. An MP&L truck rumbled up to the nearest gas pump, water steaming off its hood.

"It's rainin' again. But that's the best time for us. Won't be nobody else back up in there."

"The sheriff's men are down there, working a crime scene."

Harold smiled. "If they are, they won't stay. Not in this rain. Even the men at the huntin' camp will stay inside. But once this rain stops for good, you don't want to be caught back there. We could all wind up like that boy you found."

"Give us a minute to talk," Caitlin said. "Go to the men's room or something."

Harold looked at Terry for a couple of seconds, then got up and went to the quick-serve food counter.

"Oh, my *God*," Terry said. "I know you're my boss, but are you *crazy*? That's the guy who was staring at us before we came in here!"

"I know. I need you to calm down, Terry."

"I'm not going down into that swamp with that guy."

"That's right, you're not."

Terry's eyes narrowed, then went wide. "You're not either!"

"Yes, I am. I need you to stay here and field my calls. There's almost no reception down in that swamp, not unless you're in a helicopter. I'm going to text Jamie to route all my calls to you. If Penn calls you while I'm gone, tell him I'm interviewing somebody and I can't talk to him until I'm done."

Terry grabbed her wrist. "Caitlin, you can't do this.

You don't know this guy, and even if he's okay, you know that swamp is full of crazy rednecks."

"That swamp has about as many living people in it as the Natchez cemetery. I'll be fine."

"Oh, this is *not* happening."

"Terry, how do you think people like Jordan Glass got famous? You think she went back to her hotel whenever the bullets started flying?"

"I don't know, and I don't want to."

"Well, I do. She got where she is by going farther into the shit than anybody else was willing to go. Compared to that, what am I doing? Taking a boat ride with a poacher. You've seen the guy's face and read his driver's license." Caitlin lowered her voice to a whisper. "He's *black*, for God's sake. He's not about to take his boat where the Knoxes can find us. Okay?"

Terry shook her head like a frightened little girl. "I still don't like it. You should call the FBI and tell them about this guy. He can take *them* to that Bone Tree."

"I'm not about to give them this guy. And you're not either. You hear me? I need two hours to myself. That's all."

Terry's eyes darted back and forth like she was looking for an escape route.

"Promise me, Terry."

"Do you have pepper spray or something?"

"I've got more than that." Caitlin opened her purse and showed Terry the butt of her 9 mm pistol.

"Oh, my God."

"Do we have a deal?"

Terry closed her eyes and struggled with her fear. "Okay," she said finally. "But if you're not back here in two hours, I'm calling Mayor Cage and the cops and anybody else I can think of."

Caitlin squeezed her arm. "Good girl."

She waved at Harold, who walked back to the booth with some chicken fingers wrapped in wax paper.

"We all set?" he asked, sliding into his seat.

"Yep, I'll be your only passenger. Terry's staying here to man the phone for me. And if we're not back in two hours, she's calling the cavalry."

Harold looked discomfited by this news, but then he

shrugged and said, "You're paying the fare, you make the rules."

"Can we make it there and back in two hours?"

"Probably so. Long as we don't run into company."

"Is that your boat in the back of your pickup?"

"Yeah. And we'd better get moving, before this rain lets up."

"I'm ready."

"One more thing," he said, his face hardening.

Caitlin raised her eyebrows.

"You got a gun?"

She nodded.

"What kind?"

"Nine mil. In my purse."

"Okay. I feel better already."

"Do *you* have a gun?"

Harold looked embarrassed. "All I got's a .22 rifle, for shootin' snakes and such. I had to pawn my pistol. But we'll be all right with your nine."

"Okay, then. I'll come out to your truck a minute after you leave."

"Yes, ma'am."

Harold Wallis walked back to the counter, bought a pack of cigarettes, then sauntered out into the rain as if he had nothing to do for the rest of the day. A man in the far booth watched him for a few seconds, then went back to his coffee.

Caitlin folded the map and slipped it into the side pocket of her purse. Then she looked at Terry and gave her a confident smile. "Don't worry, okay? Just drive around for a while, walk through a couple of stores. I'll be back before you know it."

Terry Foreman looked like she was about to cry. "You'd better be."

"Two hours from now, you and I are going to be headed into the history books."

"I don't care about that."

"Well, I do. And I sign the checks."

"Great." Terry got up so that Caitlin could get out of the booth.

Caitlin shouldered her purse and walked to the door without looking back.

She could hardly contain herself as she trudged through the rain toward the beat-up truck with the knife-like brown pirogue jutting from its open bed. Harold Wallis was already inside, and blue-gray exhaust puffed steadily from the tailpipe. With a silent prayer of thanks, Caitlin climbed into the truck.

CHAPTER 67

DRIVEN BY PANIC, I crossed the Mississippi River and reached the police barricade at the intersection of Auburn and Duncan Avenues in record time, topping a hundred miles an hour on short stretches, weaving in and out of traffic like a PCP-crazed fugitive on *COPS*. Thanks to a radio call by Chief Logan of the Natchez police, no police cars tried to stop me. I don't think half the drivers I passed even saw me until I'd blown past them.

My well-known face was enough to get me past the Natchez cops at the Duncan Avenue barricade, but it takes Kaiser to get me past the FBI agents and up to the Abrams house. A bright red fire engine is parked in the driveway, its crew spraying water on the face of the house, which still seems to be standing. As we move closer, I spy Annie and my mother sitting on the Abramses' front porch, watching the firemen work. Kirk Boisseau leans against one of the porch columns, his pants scorched, his face lined with pain. James Ervin is sitting against the column at his feet, his face covered with soot.

"Daddy!" Annie cries, leaping off the porch and running to me.

I lift her into my arms and squeeze tight. Beyond her, I see tears running down my mother's face.

"Kirk feels really bad," Annie says in my ear. "But he was awesome."

She pulls back and begins chattering with eyes so bright and alive that I can only stare. "The house isn't messed up too bad. The fire department was so close, and the sprinkler system worked just like it's supposed to. The back looks bad, all black, but the fire chief already said the damage is mostly superficial."

"Sam Abrams is going to have a heart attack," I murmur, looking past her at Mom again.

"Tell Dad how Kirk saved you, Gram!" Annie cries. "Come here, Kirk."

Hugging my mother, I wave at my old friend. After patting Ervin on the shoulder, Kirk limps toward us.

"He got burned bad on his leg," Annie goes on. "But he pushed Gram back through the door when Spider-Man threw the bomb."

"Spider-Man?" I ask in confusion.

"The guy who threw the bomb was wearing a Spider-Man mask. Kirk said it was a Molotov cocktail."

I lower her to the street and reach out to take Kirk's hand.

"I'm so sorry," he says. "I should've reacted quicker."

"Don't be stupid, man. You did great. I'm just glad you're alive. You obviously went far beyond the call of duty."

"He did," Mom says. "He was wonderful."

"I'll second that," John Kaiser says from behind me.

As I turn back to Kaiser, my cell phone rings. I take it from my pocket and check the LCD, then stop. The screen reads JORDAN GLASS.

"Dad, listen," Annie says, pulling on my arm.

"Hang on, babe." Jordan must have tried to reach Kaiser and failed, then decided to try me. But if my memory serves, she ought to be winging her way to Cuba now, or at least headed to the airport. I press SEND and say, "Hello? Jordan?"

"Penn, yeah, it's me."

"What's going on? Are you trying to reach John?"

Kaiser moves around in front of me, his eyebrows raised.

"No, I wanted you. I'm worried about Caitlin."

Thirty yards to my right, a window shatters and falls to the ground. I whirl and see a fireman aiming his hose into the new opening in the house.

Kaiser is still looking hard at me, but I signal for him to be patient.

"After we finished with the Lusahatcha sheriff's people, we split up at an Athens Point gas station. A girl from the *Examiner* had driven down, and she was supposed to drive Caitlin back to Natchez. Her name was Terry. But as I drove toward Baton Rouge, something told me I ought to be sure they'd done that. So I started calling Caitlin."

"She didn't answer?"

"No. She could have been busy, of course, but I had a funny feeling. I kept calling, and her phone started kicking me straight to voice mail. I tried five more times before I called you. Have you heard from her?"

"No. I've assumed she was on her way back."

"What's the cell reception like between Athens Point and Natchez?"

"Good, most of the way. Couple of dead spots."

"Maybe that's it. Or maybe she switched off that phone for some reason. But when I started thinking about her being out of range, I thought of that swamp. We had no reception at all at ground level—only in the chopper. And . . . well, I know how badly she wants to find the Bone Tree. I made her swear that she wouldn't go back until Carl or Danny could help her, but I don't know. . . ."

"I do. Do you remember the last name of the girl she's supposed to be with?"

"Terry, that's all I know. She works in marketing at the paper."

"Okay, that's enough to work with. Do you need to talk to John? He's about five feet away from me."

"No, listen. I called you because I don't really have the right to tell John what I know about Caitlin. She has a lead that nobody else did. Henry had found a poacher who claimed to know where the Bone Tree was. The guy didn't show today, but he sent a map that supposedly showed the tree's location. Long story short, Caitlin still has that map, or at least a photo I shot of it. Also, she's not only after old bones from those cold cases. Frank Knox apparently hung on to some kind of document that he used as insurance against Carlos Marcello. It was supposedly written in Russian, and it was supposed to have been kept inside that tree at some point. You know Caitlin. She's not about to let somebody else get down in there and find that stuff before she does."

"No, shit. But how could she get back into the swamp?"

"That I don't know. But if there's a way—"

"She'll find it. Thanks, Jordan. I'll call you if I reach her. You do the same."

I hang up without waiting for a good-bye, then dial Caitlin's office.

Kaiser lays his hand on my forearm. "What the hell was that about? Where's Jordan now?"

"Headed to the New Orleans airport." I give him the quickest summary I can, omitting any mention of Frank Knox, but my narrative is terminated by a chipper female voice saying, "*Natchez Examiner.*"

"This is Penn Cage. I need to speak to Jamie Lewis, immediately."

While the call is transferred, I tell Kaiser that Caitlin might be trying to get back into the swamp.

"This is Jamie Lewis."

"Jamie! I need to know which female employee Caitlin took out of marketing today, and I need her cell number right now."

"Ah . . ."

"This may be life or death, Jamie. Don't fuck around."

"It was Terry Foreman. She hasn't come back yet. It may take me a minute to get her cell number."

"Hurry."

Kirk, Annie, my mother, and Kaiser close around me as I wait for the number, then dial it. The worry in my mother's eyes looks deeper than I would have expected, but Annie's face is almost bloodless.

"This is Terry," says a young female voice.

"This is Mayor Penn Cage. I need to speak to Caitlin. Immediately."

"Oh. Uh . . . she's doing an interview right now. She told me not to disturb her until it's over."

"Drop the lie, Terry. Jordan Glass called me, worried sick. Are you with Caitlin?"

She hesitates only a moment. "No, sir."

"Do you know where she is?"

"Not really. To be honest, I'm scared myself. Caitlin told me not to worry, but I'm not used to this kind of stuff."

"What kind of stuff? Did she go back into the swamp?"

"Yes, sir."

"How could she do that?"

"A black guy was going to show her where it was."

This answer throws me. "A black guy? Was it Carl Sims?"

"I don't know who that is."

"Was he a deputy?"

"Oh, no. No way. He was just a guy at a gas station. The Crossroads Café. He was some kind of fisherman or something."

Oh God . . . "Why didn't you go with them?"

"There was only room for two in the boat. Seriously. It was the littlest boat I ever saw. He called it a pee-row, I think. It was a Cajun boat."

"A pirogue?"

"That's right."

"Where are you now, Terry?"

"I'm still at the Crossroads Café. That's where she told me to wait for her."

"Have you tried to call her?"

"Yes, sir. I can't reach her."

I close my eyes and try to stay calm. "I want you to stay right where you are, in case she comes back. If she contacts you by phone, call me right away. I'm coming straight down there, and I'm going to get the police involved. They'll probably come by the station to talk to you."

"Oh, God. I knew she shouldn't have gone with that guy. I'm so sorry—"

"It's not your fault. You couldn't have stopped her. Tell the police everything you remember. Even the smallest thing could be important. Do you understand?"

"Yes, sir. I was just trying to help Caitlin."

"I know. You sit tight. We're going to find her, Terry."

As soon as I click off, my mother asks me to explain the situation, but I'm too freaked out even to summarize it.

"I'll go with you," Kaiser says. "I'll bring in Bureau assets."

"I won't turn down FBI agents, but if you're going to protect Sonny, you need to keep questioning the other Double Eagles."

"I know. I intend to. But I'm going to try to expedite some air assets down there. I'll also call ahead and inform the Highway Patrol you're going to be coming through, but don't kill yourself."

"Oh, Lord," my mother intones. "There must be some other way."

"Daddy, is Caitlin really in trouble?"

I clench my daughter in a tight hug. "She's just exploring in the woods, babe. She's fine, but I want to make sure she doesn't get lost. I'm going to find her. You take care of Gram while I'm gone." Reaching to my right, I squeeze Kirk Boisseau's hand.

The marine shakes his head and says, "You don't think I'm staying here, do you?"

"Hell, yes. You've done enough for one day."

"You need to get to an ER," Kaiser tells him. "And don't worry about the Cage ladies. They're going to have a steel curtain around them."

Before Kirk can argue, Kaiser's cell phone rings, and he answers with such authority in his voice that everyone falls silent. I give him a quick salute and start to move past him, but he grabs my arm and holds me in place. When I try to pull away, he tightens his grip, forcing me to look into his face, which has gone pale.

"Forget that," he says sharply. "Forget the bombs, forget the crowd, forget everything. Get into that cell-block and get Sonny Thornfield out of there."

Bombs?

"I don't give a damn about an escape! Get Thornfield secured!"

"What happened?" I ask, after he slaps the phone against his thigh.

"Some kind of explosive attack on the courthouse. And since the courthouse is attached to the sheriff's department, they had to evacuate it. I've got to get over there."

"What in God's name is going on?" my mother asks.

Kaiser drops my arm. "Call me from the road, Penn. Let me know what you need."

"I will."

After giving Annie and Mom a final hug, I sprint toward the police barricade, speed-dialing Carl Sims on the way.

WALT HAD FINALLY MASTERED the art of driving with his left hand while monitoring the GPS tracker that he held in his right. He'd followed Forrest and Ozan along Highway 61 as it wound through the pine and hardwood forests between Natchez and Woodville, then watched them turn east toward Athens Point. When the cruiser passed the turn to Valhalla without slowing, Walt feared the worst. His secret hope had been that Tom had been moved from Sonny's Old River fishing cabin to the hunting camp. But if Knox and Ozan weren't stopping . . . then he was probably elsewhere.

The next time Walt looked down at the tracking screen, he did a double take. The cruiser had turned east off Highway 61 on a road about two miles past the turn to Valhalla. Maybe it led to some other destination on the camp property? He felt a fillip of excitement in his chest, but also concern. They might be nearing some hiding place unknown to anyone. In a matter of minutes, he might have to decide whether to try to rescue Tom himself or call for backup and hope for the best.

Walt made up his mind then and there that if the pair led him to Tom, he would go in with his pistol-grip Benelli shotgun and finish them once and for all. The time for talking was done. It was kill or be killed.

The question was, would he even get that chance?

THE GERMAN AUDI S4 can do 180 miles per hour, but my American version is computer-limited to 135. Despite a lightly falling rain, I've hit the maximum several times during the past ten minutes, especially on the long stretch where Highway 61 climbs from Adams County into Wilkinson. I've spent much of the drive on the phone.

Carl Sims quickly located Terry Foreman at the Crossroads Café. Reviewing the security footage there, Carl found video recordings of Caitlin speaking to a young black man inside the café, then getting into his truck in the parking lot. A Cajun pirogue was clearly visible in the back of his truck. A teenager eating in the café identified the black driver as Harold Wallis, a local fisherman, poacher, and sometime drug dealer. Carl told me that Caitlin didn't look as though she was under duress at any point on the tape.

Carl also told me that Danny McDavitt was ready to

do anything he could to help me locate Caitlin, but that Sheriff Ellis hadn't yet okayed the use of his chopper. If the sheriff stalled much longer, McDavitt would take me over the swamp in his own fixed-wing plane.

I've tried to call Caitlin several times from the road, but she hasn't answered once. As I roar past the private prison north of Woodville, Mississippi, my cell phone rings again. My heart leaps, but it's only Kaiser again.

"What have you got?" I ask.

"Sonny Thornfield's dead."

"No. How?"

"They got him in his cell. Someone opened the cells during the mandatory evacuation. There goes our star witness."

"Jesus, John." I don't remind him of my warnings that the extra time he took with Thornfield would put his life in jeopardy.

"Oh, and the meth Dennis planted was stolen from the evidence room during the alarm."

Yet again, the Knox family is two steps ahead of us. "Was it obviously murder?"

"No. It looks like a heart attack, but I know better. At least one of Dennis's deputies had to be involved, but that's no surprise. We've got real trouble in this parish."

That's probably how Snake or Forrest learned of our special interrogation.

"I'm sorry," I tell Kaiser. "I still need your help, though."

"Tell me."

"I need the Lusahatcha County helicopter in the air and searching for the truck Caitlin left that gas station in. Carl says the sheriff down there hasn't okayed it, and he may have ties to the Knox family. I'm not saying he's dirty, but he's definitely hunted out at Valhalla. He might be as obstructive as he can about us searching that land."

"I'll take care of it."

"The sheriff's name is Billy Ray Ellis. He's eating lunch with some hunting buddies now."

"Yeah? Well, I'm about to ruin his day. Good ol' Billy Ray is about to feel the full weight and power of the federal government."

I thank Kaiser and click off, then push the accelerator to the floor. The S4 eats up the miles like a starving beast, its Quattro drive holding me in the curves when most other cars would spin off the steep shoulders and into the trees below.

I reluctantly brake as I reach the outskirts of Woodville, Mississippi. The turn for Highway 24 East isn't far ahead, but my cell phone rings yet again before I reach it.

It's Carl again.

"Talk to me, buddy," I tell him.

"Danny and I got the chopper! Agent Kaiser lit a serious fire under the sheriff's ass. Billy Ray's spittin' mad, but we're cleared to go into Valhalla if we need to. A judge is signing the warrant now. Right now we have to decide where to search. Do we run the roads and turnarounds? Or do we start searching the swamp first? We'd rather you make that call."

"The swamp, no question. She's got a map to follow, and she wouldn't hesitate."

"I thought she lost her map when she dove on Whelan's corpse."

"She did, but Jordan Glass shot a picture of it before it was lost. But if this Harold Wallis is a poacher, he may know where the Bone Tree is anyway. That's what she's after. How much do you remember of Rambin's map?"

"Enough to get us in the general area of where that X was." There's a static-filled pause. "But there's a million or so cypress trees down there, Penn. The only way to find that tree without the map is to grid-search the whole area, tree by tree."

"Screw the tree. We can search for Caitlin's cell phone, if you have the equipment."

"We're already up and trying, but we haven't found a trace of it."

I look at the Audi's nav screen and make a quick calculation.

"Carl, in two minutes, I'll be on Highway 24 and moving toward you guys at close to a hundred miles an hour. Can you set down on the road in front of me? Will Danny do that?"

"He'll do it. You still driving that black convertible?"

"Yep. I'll have my headlights on."

"We'll see you in a minute."

"Thanks, buddy."

Dropping my cell on the passenger seat, I slam the accelerator to the floor. The Audi's rear end nearly slings out from under me as I start around a sweeping curve, but at the last instant the tires catch the wet pavement and the increasing G-force presses me back in the seat.

"Come on, Caitlin," I whisper. "Call me. . . ."

CHAPTER 68

CAITLIN SAT IN the bow of Harold Wallis's narrow pirogue, the rain shell of her jacket pulled tight around her as they trolled slowly under overhanging cypress branches. The steady hiss of rain on the black water was as familiar now as the stink of decaying vegetation. Beneath the hiss ran the hum of the trolling motor Harold had bolted to the side of the pirogue's stern. Pirogues were usually powered by a human with a pole, but the boy had cleverly worked out a way to save himself a lot of labor.

Harold navigated the swamp much more deftly than Mose Tyler had earlier in the day. Perhaps it was his youth—and the better vision that came with it—but he threaded his slender boat through the tangled jungle almost noiselessly, leaving no trace of their passing. Only the hum of the trolling motor marked their passage.

Caitlin had brought along the little point-and-shoot camera she carried in her glove box in case of traffic accidents, and she'd already shot a mother alligator lying on a half-sunken log, four babies clinging to her back. The pirogue passing ten feet away hadn't fazed the gator at all. This was her territory, not theirs. If Harold actually led Caitlin to the Bone Tree, she was going to wish she'd borrowed Jordan's Nikon, but in that event, a hundred professional photographers would descend on this swamp. Today her tiny Casio would have to do.

In the pocket of her fleece jacket, Caitlin clutched her cell phone. She'd checked it every two or three minutes since they put in to the water, but the LCD had yet to register a single bar. This worried her a little, she wouldn't deny that. Because Harold Wallis, while a companionable guide, had begun acting like a nervous point man on combat patrol five minutes after they put into the water. She'd considered calling Penn before they left Athens

Point behind, but he would have forbidden her to go into the swamp without Carl Sims as an escort. Nor could she call upon Carl or Danny. They were already in serious trouble for helping her, and she didn't want to jeopardize their jobs any further. Besides, she was armed, and Harold had his .22. She hoped that would be enough to drive off anyone who might have come out to the Bone Tree to remove whatever incriminating evidence lay inside it.

But the deeper they penetrated into the ghostly stands of cypress trees, the clearer her memory of Henry Sexton's Bone Tree journal became. Not the legends of ghosts and demons riding through the fog-shrouded swamp, but the real men on horseback who'd surely prompted those legends, men who had killed for a dozen different causes, but always with ruthlessness, rage, or hatred. Today she was more likely to encounter angry rednecks riding souped-up ATVs rather than horses. The thought made her clench the pistol in her jacket pocket.

She was glad that most of the Double Eagles were in jail today. Of course, Forrest Knox remained free, as did his cousin Billy—not to mention the intimidating Redbone who served as Forrest's right-hand man. Caitlin shivered at the memory of his flat, cruel stare the night she'd encountered him outside the Concordia hospital.

"You know where you are?" Harold asked softly.

Caitlin took the map out of her left pocket and studied it, then peered through the rain, trying to orient herself.

"No. Where are we?"

"Close to where you found that boy's body earlier. We just comin' at it from a different way, in case there's still cops out here."

Are we? she wondered. The pirogue soon glided out into a circular pool like the one in which she'd wrestled Casey Whelan's torso into a helicopter's rescue basket. But was it the same? *Yes.* . . .

An exhilarating shudder of recognition went through her. "We're close to that game fence, aren't we?"

"Yeah," Harold said. "You don't see any deputies, do you?"

"No."

"Hear anything?"

She listened for a moment. "No. Nothing."

"Like I said . . . Sheriff Ellis don't want anybody to find that tree."

"Are you saying he already knows where it is?"

Harold shrugged. "I know he hunts over on Valhalla every fall."

"How do you know that?"

"I done worked over there as a guide. I seen the sheriff cozying up to country singers and football players."

"How far away is the hole in the game fence?"

"A little farther on. This rain will make it easier to get to by boat. When the water's low, you got to walk the last fifty yards."

Harold eased back on the throttle, then cut the motor altogether as they drifted into a narrow channel between two grassy tussocks.

"Look," he whispered, and something in his voice made the hair on the back of her neck stand up.

"Where?"

"You can't see that hog?"

Caitlin froze as her eyes locked with the eyes of a wild hog even larger than the ones she and Jordan had seen by the road earlier.

"Is it dangerous?" she whispered.

"I wouldn't get out of the boat if I was you. She might have babies close by."

As Caitlin stared at the massive animal in the eerie silence, she heard a low whine from somewhere to her left. It sounded like a truck passing on a distant road. "What's that?"

"Boat," Harold whispered. "Somebody's still down here."

"What do we do?"

"Keep going."

He restarted the trolling motor and left the two tussocks behind. As they hummed through the trees, she realized that the trunks of the cypresses were getting closer together.

A cracking boom like thunder echoed through the trees from somewhere to their right. Whirling, she saw Harold cock his head as though gauging distance and direction.

"Was that a rifle?" she asked.

"Yeah. Somebody's shooting over at Valhalla. Probably took a deer."

"How far away?"

He rubbed his chin with an audible scratching sound. "A mile. Maybe two."

"Is it hunting season now?"

"Ute season."

"Ute? What's that?"

"That's when little boys can hunt, but their daddies can't."

"Ah . . ." She felt embarrassed for misunderstanding him the first time.

Harold increased speed through the narrow channel. The tall wire fence appeared to the right of the boat. Caitlin experienced the disturbing feeling Jordan had spoken of, that they were at the edge of a prison camp. This afternoon Caitlin wasn't sure whether she was on the inside of the fence or the outside. Suddenly Harold cut the motor, and the pirogue drifted to a stop.

"What is it?" she whispered.

"Listen. Outboard again. That other boat's closer now."

"I don't hear it. Where?"

He pointed at the fence. "It's on that side."

"What do you think?"

"I think you didn't pay me enough for this gig."

A tingle of fear and frustration went through her. "I'll add five hundred to the pot. Let's just get to that damned tree."

Harold stared through the fence, seemingly weighing odds.

"Get your pistol out," he said. "Keep it in your hand."

Caitlin's fear kicked up several notches. She let go of her phone and took the 9 mm from her pocket. As she did, she saw her Coach purse lying in two inches of water at the bottom of the pirogue.

"Cock it," Harold said. "But be careful you don't shoot me by mistake."

Caitlin cycled the slide with a violent motion. The metallic snick of machined parts echoed off the trees and back over the water. Then she tensed both forearms, holding the gun the way Tom had taught her.

"What am I watching for?" she asked in a quavering voice.

"White men," Harold said. "Maybe in a boat, maybe on foot. Maybe even on horseback. You never know what them crackers get up to."

Caitlin shivered at this prospect. "What do I do if I see somebody?"

"Keep your gun lower. Yeah, like that. Out of sight. Let me do the talking. You a smart lady. You see it goin' bad, you start pulling that trigger and don't stop."

"Okay."

"Can you hit what you aim at?"

Caitlin remembered Tom teaching her how to shoot. "I can hit bottles on a fencepost."

"Then you can hit a man. Just be on the lookout."

Harold started the motor and continued up the channel. They followed the game fence for a couple of minutes, then Harold guided the bow onto a shallow slope of mud until they scraped to a stop.

Caitlin's heart thumped in anticipation.

With the cold gun butt clenched in her hand, she scanned the surrounding trees while Harold tugged on a pair of knee-high rubber boots and climbed out. Wading into the dark water, he went to the game fence, took a pair of pliers from his jacket, and pulled open a four-foot-by-four-foot gap.

"What about the other hole?" she asked.

"Somebody might be watching that. Could be a game camera there, no telling. We gonna go through here to be safe. The Chain Tree ain't far."

He tugged the pirogue back into deeper water, then climbed in, started the motor, and steered them through the opening as sweet as you please.

"What would the white men do if they knew you put a hole in their fence?"

Harold laughed softly. "Hang me on one of them hooks they got in their skinning shack. They'd skin me like a buck, then mount my head on the wall."

Caitlin shuddered at the dark undertone in his laughter. Numbing fear competed with the electric anticipation she felt as they neared the object of her quest.

"How far are we from the tree now?"

"Couple minutes, no more."

Sweat had broken out beneath her jacket. Every cypress tree they passed seemed larger than the one before, and the air grew dark and close beneath the overhanging limbs.

"You want to hear a scary story?" Harold asked.

"Hell, no."

Harold chuckled softly. "You know what a mandrake is?"

Caitlin thought she remembered some John Donne from college that referred to a mandrake. *Go and catch a falling star. Get with child a mandrake root, tell me where all past years are, or who cleft the devil's foot.*

"It's some kind of plant, isn't it?"

"That's right. My granny used to fool with some witchin'—charms and stuff like that. Voodoo from New Orleans. She said a mandrake will scream when you pull it out of the ground, and the scream will kill anybody who hears it."

Caitlin rolled her eyes at this quaint superstition, and a little wave of relief rolled through her.

"Granny said you have to harvest the mandrake a special way." Harold peered into the dimness ahead. "You tie a dog's tail to it, then run away. When the dog runs after you, he pulls up the plant. Then you can go back safe and get it."

"What made you think of that story?"

"Granny made Granddaddy bring her out here one time. She said the real mandrake only grew where the seed of a hanged man spilled on the ground." He paused a beat. "You know what I'm talking about?"

Caitlin thought about it for a few seconds, then grunted in the affirmative.

"Granny knew some boys had been hung out here, see? More than one with his clothes off. And some people say they cut them boys' manhood off. The ones hung from the Chain Tree anyway. So Granny figured there would be mandrakes growin' under it."

Caitlin gripped the pistol tighter. "That's enough. You're creeping me out."

"Hey, I'm scared, too. I wouldn't even be here without you payin' me that money."

Instinctively, she pulled open her jacket and checked her phone. Still no reception.

"There it is," Harold said, a note of awe in his voice. "Just like I told you. Man alive, look at that."

Caitlin jerked up her head. Before her stood the near-mythical object of so many fruitless searches. Just as the legend said, the Bone Tree towered more than a hundred feet over the water, its lower branches joining the crowns of other trees to form a tangled canopy. The fibrous bark of the massive cypress looked like the leathery skin of some great creature, not dead but only sleeping. At its bottom, the trunk divided into leglike partitions that plunged into the muddy tussock that supported the tree. What lay inside that vast trunk? she wondered. Were Elam Knox's bones really wired to the inside wall of its organic cave?

As the pirogue glided toward the tussock, Harold was forced to slow the motor and thread his way between giant knees that protruded from the water like the backs of prehistoric animals basking in the water.

"Where's the opening?" she whispered.

"Other side," Harold answered softly. "There's the chains."

Caitlin followed his pointing finger. From a twisted limb fifteen feet above the ground hung two thick, rusting chains of iron. Wild euphoria surged through her at this confirmation of her hopes. At last she was close to the consummation of her dream—and Henry Sexton's, too.

As she said a silent prayer for Henry, the chain-saw whine of an outboard motor smothered her joy and made her duck down in the boat. The motor was much closer than before, maybe fifty yards away. She could see nothing through the ranks of cypress trunks, but when she turned and looked to the stern of the pirogue, she saw pure terror in Harold's eyes.

"*What should we do?*" she hissed.

"We need to get out of here." He reached for the trolling motor.

"No!" she whispered. "Not before I see what's inside that tree. We've come too far."

"Then get out and do it! Quick! 'Cause two minutes from now, I'll be gone from this motherfucker."

JOHN KAISER SAT ALONE on a bunk in the cellblock of the Concordia Parish jail, staring down at the corpse of Sonny Thornfield. He felt like a fool. He'd fallen for the oldest trick in the book—a diversionary attack. Both the shotgunning of the FBI satellite truck and the firebombing of Penn's family's safe house had been timed to draw him and his men away from the courthouse, making the murder of Sonny Thornfield possible. This meant that someone with connections in both the criminal and law enforcement spheres was pulling the strings.

Forrest Knox.

He should have known that a former Lurp like Forrest would employ military tactics. Kaiser's second mistake had been placing confidence in Sheriff Dennis's men and the facilities under their command. Dennis himself had been absent during the attack—and he still hadn't shown up—but of course Kaiser had effectively banned him from the premises after the torture fiasco in the utility closet.

Kaiser had examined Thornfield's body inch by inch, and his best guess was that a Double Eagle had strangled or suffocated Sonny with something soft—a shirt or towel—while the others gently held him down. Thornfield's arms showed faint bruising, but he'd been far too weak to fight hard—or for long. Murder was going to be hard to prove. The grim truth was, his heart might have given out even before his oxygen.

No one could understand how the killers had gotten into Thornfield's cell, but Kaiser was pretty sure of what had happened. In the event of a power failure, the emergency generators kicked on, which powered the electronic gate system controlled by the duty guard. But after the second bomb had taken out the generator, the cell doors would have had to be operated manually. There hadn't been enough time for someone to crank open those doors, allow the Eagles to get to Thornfield, then close the doors again while Agent Wilson had been absent from the sheriff's office. But Kaiser had examined the door mechanism, and there was a dual DC-controller for the unit, which meant that you could hook a car battery to it and operate the doors in an emergency. He suspected that someone with advance knowledge of the bombs and their targets had done just that. Spanky Ford had claimed this was practically impossible—and Kaiser planned to hook Ford up to a lie detector as soon as possible—but the damage was already done.

He was about to go down to the garage-level holding pen where Snake and the remaining Double Eagles had been moved when he heard boots approaching the cellblock door. A few seconds later, the broad silhouette of Walker Dennis filled the space, and then the sheriff stumped down between the cells and stopped outside Sonny's. He didn't even nod to Kaiser, but only stared down at the body with what looked like cold fury.

"Where the hell have you been?" Kaiser asked between gritted teeth.

"None of your goddamn business," Dennis muttered.

Kaiser shook his head in amazement. "You're going to have to do better than that, Sheriff. Four bombs go off at your courthouse, your department falls apart, a star witness is murdered in your jail, and you don't show up until a half hour after the fact?"

"I don't answer to you, Kaiser."

"No. But that begs the question: just who *do* you answer to?"

Dennis looked up at last, his eyes burning with rage. "Fuck you."

Kaiser fought to control his temper. When he spoke, it was in a low voice that almost any man would recognize as dangerous. "Sheriff, either you come clean and tell me everything that's going on, or I'm going to federalize your department. In all frankness, I may have to do that regardless of your actions."

Dennis studied Kaiser for several seconds. Then he turned and walked out of the cellblock.

CHAPTER 69

CAITLIN SCRAMBLED OUT of the pirogue with her pistol in her right hand and clambered onto the grassy earth beneath the Bone Tree. Her left hand held a cheap flashlight Harold had passed to her.

"Which way?" she asked. "Where's the opening?"

"Go to your right. Around to the other side. And quiet down. Jesus. We ain't the only ones out here."

"Sorry," she panted. Fear and excitement were making her hyperventilate.

She kept her eyes on the wet ground as she moved around the great legs of the trunk, watching for cottonmouth moccasins, which were plentiful out here. She felt like she was moving in slow motion, but she knew this was only adrenaline distorting her sense of time.

The trunk of the Bone Tree was so vast that the johnboat disappeared as she worked her way around it. Again she thought of the Tree of Life in the Animal Kingdom at Walt Disney World. But this tree had been made by God, or nature. And it was no tree of life, but of death.

As she worked her way to her right, a black opening like a cave mouth showed between two of the cypress's elephantine legs. Her breath stopped in her throat. The inverted V was more a crack than a door, but certainly wide enough for men and animals to pass through.

"Harold!" she cried, forgetting all caution. "Come around here. Hurry!"

"*Shut up!*" hissed her guide. "Them bones ain't going nowhere, if they even in there."

He appeared about five feet behind Caitlin, his old .22 rifle clutched in his hands.

"I know, I know, I'm sorry. This is just freaking me out. This is a major deal, Harold. You have no idea what's going to happen behind this. Do you think it's safe to go inside?"

"Prob'ly safer in there than out here."

She started to venture in, but Harold held up his hand.

"What is it?" she whispered.

"I heard that motor again."

"Shit. It's just hunters, right?"

"You think that's good news?"

"I don't care anymore. Just stand guard while I check out what's inside. Five minutes is all I need."

Harold turned and scanned the darkness under the canopy of trees. With his dark skin and the primitive atmosphere around the Chain Tree, Caitlin couldn't help but picture a runaway slave from 150 years ago, afraid of being lynched.

"If you want to stay five minutes," he said, "give me your gun."

Caitlin hugged the pistol to her belly. "My gun? Why? You've got a rifle."

He snorted. "This lil' .22 ain't worth spit against the deer guns them hunters carry. They'll blow a pound a meat out of me. I need some firepower."

Caitlin thought about it. "What if there are animals inside the tree?"

Harold took the stock of his rifle and banged it against the trunk of the Bone Tree. The wood made a dull thump against the fibrous bark. He watched the black opening for several seconds, then said, "Anything but a snake would have scooted right out of there. And you wouldn't hit a snake with that pistol anyway. You got boots on. Just give 'em a wide berth."

"I'm not giving you my gun," Caitlin said. "I'm sorry. I'll hurry, I promise. Now, promise you won't leave me."

"You gonna pay me the extra five hundred?"

"Absolutely. I'll pay you an extra thousand if those bones are in there. Hell, you'll be going on talk shows for the next six months."

This notion didn't seem to impress her guide. He flicked his hand like she should get on with it, then turned and gazed out over the water with his rifle clenched in his hands.

Closing her left hand tight around the flashlight, Caitlin inched toward the lightless opening with the pistol held in front of her. She felt like an archaeologist carrying a flaming torch into an undiscovered tomb. The fissure in the tree was tall, and narrower than she'd first thought. A man Penn's size would have difficulty squeezing through, but she was thin and could pass with relative ease. Pausing on the threshold of the strange doorway, she shone the flashlight's weak yellow beam into the darkness at the heart of the tree.

She saw bones, far more than she'd expected. Some were white as chalk, while others looked brown and coated with moss. There seemed to be no order to their arrangement. She would have to move closer to understand exactly what she was looking at.

Shining the beam just inside the crack, she saw no snakes on the dry-looking floor of the cave. She sucked in a deep, preparatory breath, then turned sideways and stepped through the fissure.

A small animal scrambled out of her path, and she jerked backward, shining the light around in a panic. A possum stared at her from ten feet across the floor, its red eyes glazed with terror. She aimed her pistol at the gray-furred animal and started to squeeze the trigger, then stopped. A gunshot might send Harold into panicked flight across the swamp. Instead, she moved several feet to the side of the fissure, crouched, picked up a long bone, and hurled it at the possum. The animal started, froze, then scuttled around the inner wall of the cave and vanished through the crack of light that led to freedom.

Caitlin heard Harold laughing softly.

Now that she was alone in the hollow heart of the cypress, a profound transformation overcame her. She sensed the great age of the tree, an ancient, hoary temple of fiber more resilient than any bone. She understood why wounded animals might seek out this silent chamber to die. It was literally a mausoleum, and it felt like one, only without the artificiality of the stone sweatboxes in human cemeteries. In one curve of the round room, it appeared that animals or humans had mounded up earth and moss against the wall.

Remembering the need for haste, she dropped to her knees, set her pistol beside her, and began to examine the bones. Caitlin knew little about anthropology, but she seemed to be looking at a mixture of deer and human bones. Then her flashlight played across the hollow eyes of a human skull lying sideways beneath a pile of arching rib bones, and her breath stopped. Five feet away, she saw another. Something coiled beside the second skull caused her to scrabble backward, then jerk up her pistol and squint into the darkness. It wasn't a snake, she realized, but a thick rope. Picking up the flashlight again, she saw that the rope was rotted half through. With sickening certainty she realized that someone had probably been bound with that while being tortured.

She gasped as she started breathing again. Forcing herself to relax her diaphragm, she shone the light upward to give herself a break from the horror. What she found was horror magnified, and confirmation of the story Jason Abbott had told the FBI back in 1972. Wired to rusted nails driven into the walls of the tree were enough human bones to make a skeleton. The collection had lost much of its original composition, but the bones had clearly been posed to represent an inverted crucifixion. It brought to mind the cross of St. Peter, but Caitlin knew that Elam Knox's death was no martyrdom.

She dropped the beam and let it play over the bones on the floor again.

"I can't leave these here," she said softly. "God."

Hot tears slid down her cheeks. She had come here looking to make her reputation, but she'd found something so profoundly sad that it humbled her beyond all thought for herself. As soon as she came within range of a cell tower, she would call John Kaiser. This obscene place was the business of the FBI, not a swarm of ravenous reporters craving the latest titillating story. She pocketed her flashlight and pulled out her Casio camera to start photographing the bones.

"Harold?" she called over her shoulder while shooting pictures methodically. "Could you come in here, please?"

Getting no answer, she looked back at the vertical crack of daylight behind her. "*Harold!*"

No reply.

She felt a moment of panic at the thought that he'd

abandoned her, but then his dark silhouette blotted out the lower two-thirds of light shining through the crack.

"You find what you was lookin' for?" he asked.

"Yes. I'm going to pass you a skull and a few bones. It's terrible crime-scene procedure, but I'm worried that whoever's in that boat might come back and get rid of the evidence before the FBI can get here. Preserving some of this is far more important than any damage we might do. Okay?"

The boy didn't answer.

Fear struck her like an arrow as she confronted the dark and silent silhouette in the crack. *Is that even Harold?* she thought crazily. *Of course it is. He just doesn't want to take the bones.*

But something odd about the figure's posture stoked Caitlin's fear into panic. Was someone standing *behind* him? Did Harold have a gun jammed in his back? Moving as naturally as she could, she dropped her camera, closed both hands around the butt of her pistol, then shifted her feet so that she was facing the crack.

You're being paranoid, she told herself. *Just take out your fucking light and shine it on him.*

When she did, she saw Harold watching her with a strange intensity.

"What's the matter?" she whispered, trying to look past him. But her eyes had adjusted to the dimness, and the light beyond the door was blinding.

"I'm about to do you the biggest favor of your life," Harold said.

A spit of flame erupted from the center of the silhouette, and a blazing dart punched through her chest.

Stunned, Caitlin wavered, then fell to her knees, trying to draw breath.

"Don't fight it," Harold said. "I don't want to have to shoot you again."

From pure instinct, she raised her pistol and fired five rounds at the shadow in the opening. The blasts of her pistol deafened and blinded her, but they must have driven her guide away from the tree, because a few moments later, her traumatized retinas again perceived the blue-gray light of the crack. Every instinct told her to lie

down and try to catch her breath, but what remained of
her reason argued that doing so would mean death.

Flattening her left hand on the cool floor, she struggled
unsteadily to her feet, even as someone turned a giant
screw at the center of her chest, driving it into her heart.
She nearly collapsed twice, but somehow she managed to
stay erect.

Her plan was to stagger through the crack with her
pistol in front of her, then take the boy's boat by force. She
told her right foot to take the first step, but more primitive fibers than her cerebral cortex now had control of her
brain. After two labored breaths, she backpedaled until she
collided with the wall of the Bone Tree, then sat down hard.

For half a minute, she could do no more than force
breath into her lungs. The stink of burnt gunpowder
in the closed space sickened her. She laid the flashlight
beside her. Then, shifting the pistol to her left hand, she
raised her right and slipped her fingers inside her jacket.

"Oh, God," she gurgled, feeling warm fluid soaking
her top. Then she felt the small, ridged hole a couple of
inches below her left nipple. *My heart is under that*, she
thought. *I'm dead.*

"Hey, lady," said a soft voice. Harold's voice. "Can you
still talk?"

Caitlin squinted at the crack of light, searching for a
target, but she saw nothing. She still wasn't sure what had
happened. Had Harold shot her? Or had someone standing behind him shot them both? Or had they shot her and
knifed him?

"What happened?" she croaked.

"I know you've got more bullets. That Springfield
holds ten."

Caitlin didn't want to believe that the boy had shot her.
If he had, then she had no hope of getting out of here
alive.

"What happened?" she asked. "Is somebody else out
there?"

"No. And you owe me for that. Captain Ozan told me
to call him when I got you out here, but I didn't. And I
ain't gonna. I got a walkie-talkie right here, and I ain't
even turned it on. You're a nice lady. You don't need to go
through that."

A wracking sob burst from Caitlin's throat. "You shot me?"

"I had to. But it's way better than what could have happened, believe me. Pretty thing like you . . . they'd rape you for sure. All day long, front and back. Even shot like you are now. They don't care. That Ozan, and Colonel Forrest, man . . . they're *sick*."

Gasping for breath, Caitlin tried to understand why a black man would be working for the likes of the Knox family.

"Look up to the left of those wired-up bones," Harold said. "Shine my flashlight. You see what's up there?"

Caitlin didn't try to lift the light. But in a shaft thrown from the door, she saw a woman's leather coat hanging on a nail, brown and tattered where the waist hem should have been.

"That ain't what you think it is," Harold said. "That's a skin. That lady wasn't much older than you, either. Mexican lady. She got in the wrong car one night. Po-lice car. Now there she is."

Caitlin struggled to hold down the few bites of cheeseburger she'd eaten at the Crossroads Café. She thought of Terry Foreman waiting there, her bright cheerleader's face lined with worry.

"Will you help me?" she asked, trying not to sound pathetic. "I'll pay anything you ask. A hundred thousand dollars. Two hundred."

"You shoulda said something sooner. It's too late now."

Caitlin thought of her father, sitting in his office in the glass tower high above Charlotte. "My father will pay you a million dollars if you take me to a hospital, Harold. A *million dollars*. No questions asked. I mean it. He doesn't care about any of this crap. Not the bones . . . nothing. Only me."

Caitlin realized she was crying.

"Shit," Harold muttered from outside the fissure. "After what I done just now, your daddy would stake me to the ground and back his car over me."

"He wouldn't!"

"This ain't what I wanted," said the boy. "My brother's stuck in Angola. Twenty-year sentence. Now that I done this, Colonel Forrest will get him out. Next month, when his parole hearing comes up."

Caitlin finally understood what had happened. Harold Wallis was probably a low-level drug dealer. He'd recognized her the moment he saw her standing outside the service station with Terry, and he'd called someone in the Knox organization. Probably Captain Ozan. Ozan had made him a proposition, or given him an order, and he'd strolled into the café to make his pitch. And she'd been so gullible! She'd brushed Terry's doubts aside like the fears of a nervous child. After all, wasn't she on a crusade for justice? Justice for murdered black activists? Surely a young black man would be on the side of the angels.

Caitlin cursed as the pain in her chest intensified. She'd made an assumption based on race—exactly what she'd always told others not to do—and it had proved her undoing. The irony was that she'd made a *positive* assumption, and thus hadn't seen it as an assumption at all.

"*You won't get away with this!*" she screamed. Every word caused her agony, but she kept shouting. "Terry saw you at the café! She saw your *driver's license*. They have security cameras back there! The FBI will find you, no matter where you go!"

"Lady, you got no idea how things work down here. Colonel Forrest can make them tapes disappear. He can make that Terry disappear if he wants to. She's liable to be in a car with Captain Ozan right now, thinking he's trying to save you."

Caitlin moaned. She felt as though a strong man were pressing down on her breastbone.

"Colonel Forrest, he's connected all over this state. Even up in Washington. That's how it's always been down here. My granddaddy told me that. Forrest's daddy was just like him. He kept all the niggers round here in line for the Man."

She wanted to speak, but her lungs felt like they'd shrunk to a quarter of their normal size. *Maybe it's panic*, she thought.

"You still awake?" Harold called.

When she didn't reply, he said, "Come on, now. Don't play games with me."

A terrifying thought came to her. "Harold, please," she gasped. "I'm pregnant."

The boy said nothing to this. Had she struck a chord of compassion?

"I just found out. I was . . . supposed to be getting married next week, and . . . I'm already pregnant. If you let me die here, you're killing my baby, too."

After a long silence, a spooked whisper said, "You're lying."

"I'm not," Caitlin sobbed. "I wouldn't lie about that."

"Women lie about being with child all the time."

"Oh, God," she croaked. "Why don't you just . . . fucking get it over with?"

"'Cause I know you've got more bullets. It'll be over soon enough."

She wondered why Harold had only shot her once. He must be worried about attracting attention, in case there were still deputies in the swamp. Honest deputies like Carl Sims. Harold had been genuinely frightened by the sounds of the boat motors during the trip in.

With desperate effort, Caitlin raised her pistol, then shut her eyes and fired two shots at the crack of light. Then she opened her eyes and watched for the slightest movement at the edge of the fissure.

A shadow deepened at the right edge of the crack.

She fired.

Harold cried out in pain, then screamed in fury.

Caitlin gritted her teeth and scooted about three feet to her left. Seconds later, the barrel of the .22 rifle appeared in the crack and orange flame shot from it. The impacting rounds knocked stinging wood chips into her face, but at least no lead struck her.

"*Fuck you!*" she yelled, and fired another round. "You missed!"

One shot left.

She waited for the barrel to appear again, but it didn't. Twenty seconds later, she heard the trolling motor start up. Panic shot through her like a jolt of electric current. She tried to roll sideways and crawl across the dirt floor, but it was useless. Before she'd made it two feet, she heard the hum of the motor fading. Ten seconds later, all was silent.

But not for long. For some reason her ears began ringing, making a harsh sound like her junior-high-school bell, only this bell wouldn't stop. She drew all the breath she could into her lungs, then slowly, agonizingly, forced herself back into a sitting position. She only managed it because the earth humped against the wall helped her get herself out of a prone position.

Taking the flashlight in her hand, she shone it around once more in hopes of finding something that might somehow help her. This time she played the beam around the seam where the trunk legs met the earth, where dirt and other organic matter had been mounded up in the darkest part of the cave. As the beam came closer to her, she realized that the mound she had clung to as she pulled herself up was not all made of earth.

It was human.

There was a body lying facedown against the wall of the tree. Whoever that person was, they had to be dead. He or she had not stirred during the gunfight, and that could mean only one thing.

Knowing she was probably only minutes from death herself, Caitlin let her body fall sideways, then used her elbows to crawl close enough to the head to shine her light on it. The hair was gray and white. She steeled herself against her fear, then held the flashlight closer with her left hand, took hold of the hair with her right, and pulled the head as far back as she could. The moment the beam fell on the face, she recognized what would have been—but now would never be—her father-in-law.

Tom Cage.

HIGHWAY 24 IS A serpentine track of asphalt cut through deep, encroaching woods and bordered by eleven-foot game fences. With the leaden sky above and no other cars in sight, it feels like I'm driving through some Central European country during the darkest days of the Cold War. But somewhere between the tiny hamlet of Lessley and Lake Mary, the Lusahatcha County Sheriff's Department JetRanger swoops out of the sky ahead and drops toward the wet asphalt like a gunship on a strafing run.

I brake as hard as I dare, and finally skid to a stop mere

yards from where Danny McDavitt has flared the helicopter to land. Grabbing my pistol from my glove box, I
shove it into my belt, then snatch up my cell phone, leap
from the car, and run to the chopper as it settles onto the
road.

Carl pulls me through the side hatch and starts strapping a four-point harness over my chest.

"Any signs of Caitlin's cell signal?" I ask.

The deputy points to the headset muffling his ears,
then slaps an identical one over my head.

"*What'd you say?*" he asks, working at my harness
buckles.

"Have you seen any sign of Caitlin's cell signal?"

"Not yet."

"Kaiser called. The last tower her phone pinged was
four miles west of here. I don't think she's far away."

"Yeah, well. I don't want to bring you down, but you
haven't seen that swamp yet." Carl slaps my chest, then
gives McDavitt a thumbs-up.

"You secure, Mayor?" asks the pilot.

"Go!" I shout. "*Get her up!*"

The JetRanger rises slowly at first, but then its nose
tips forward and we beat our way into the dark sky like a
mother hawk in search of a lost fledgling.

CHAPTER 70

CAITLIN SAT WITH her back against the inner wall of the Bone Tree, staring at Tom's motionless face. She'd recoiled in horror upon first recognizing the corpse as Penn's father. But then, realizing that he might be the last person she would ever see, she'd placed her hand on his cheek and murmured a prayer. As she did, she realized Tom could not have been dead long, because his cheek was not yet cold.

Then he breathed on her wrist.

At first she jumped back in terror, but then she understood what that breath meant. Leaning over the body, she spoke Tom's name, shook him, then pinched his cheek, hard—but nothing brought him around. His breaths were faint and frighteningly far between. He might be so close to death that he could not be revived—even by doctors. That would explain why he hadn't stirred during the gunfire.

Caitlin knew she needed to attend to her own injury, but the terrible truth was that without Tom's knowledge and skill, she wouldn't live more than a few minutes. The pain in her chest had begun to drive out all thought when an obvious realization struck her.

Tom is diabetic.

If he'd been dumped here without food, he might have gone into diabetic shock. Low blood sugar could send a diabetic into a coma . . . even kill them. And if Tom had gone hours without sugar—

Shifting her body painfully, Caitlin dug her hand into her pants pocket, searching for the peppermints she and Jordan had stolen from the Lusahatcha sheriff's office.

She had one left.

Her hands shook terribly as she unwrapped the cellophane, but she finally got it out. Since Tom was unconscious, she forced his mouth open and pushed the peppermint between his tongue and the roof of his mouth. He might choke on the candy, but she could address that if it happened.

If she was right, then that sugar was his only hope.

The next minutes passed with the slowness of a nightmare. Tom did not move or make a sound. Caitlin, by contrast, grew steadily more agitated. She stared down at the hole in her chest, which she'd exposed by removing her jacket and shirt. It was so small, the skin hardly puckered around it, though a little distended rim of flesh had begun to swell under a slow but steady flow of blood. As best she could tell, the bullet had grazed the lower left edge of her sternum and passed between two ribs, entering her chest just below her bra. She hadn't known whether the slug had passed through her body entirely until she'd gotten her shirt off and seen that its back was free of blood.

The bullet was still in her chest.

Caitlin knew enough anatomy to understand that her heart, lungs, and several major blood vessels might lie in the path of that chunk of lead. Yet she was still alive and conscious. For the first couple of minutes after Harold fled, breathing had become a little easier. But now it seemed harder to fill her lungs with each passing breath. The pressure in her chest felt like the flat of someone's hand pressing down on her sternum, harder and harder.

She checked her cell phone for the hundredth time: still no reception.

I've got to get outside this tree, she thought, with a last hopeless look at Tom. *I've got to find a signal. . . .*

With a supreme act of will, she packed her phone into her jacket, then managed to flex her thighs hard enough to slide her back up the inner wall of the tree and get to her feet. Using the wall as a brace, she slid her way around to the crack in the trunk and turned sideways. She'd planned to marshal her strength for a few moments, but as soon as she was at a right angle to the crack, she fell through, crashing to the ground with an impact that blacked out her vision for a few seconds.

"*Unnghh*," she groaned, feeling tears on her face. "This is bad." Even as she said this, a thought went through her mind. *What would Jordan do?*

"Jordan wouldn't be here," she said. "TSTL, that's me. Too Stupid To Live."

She rolled onto her stomach, reached into the pocket of her fallen jacket, and pulled her phone up to her face. The LCD still read NO SERVICE. Fighting back panic, she looked around the tree.

The rain had stopped.

All she saw were more cypress trees jutting from the black water, the largest of them standing on tufts of earth. Between the trees, an endless mere stretched into the distance. She couldn't walk through that water, and she hadn't the strength to swim it. Even if she had, she'd seen enough alligators during the ride in to know that slogging through a swamp trailing blood wasn't a good idea.

You have to climb, said a voice in her head. *Get high enough, and your phone will find a tower. . . .*

"I can't *climb,*" she wailed with self-disgust. "I can't even walk."

It wasn't a matter of will. The pain in her chest was so intense that she'd be lucky to stand again.

There are people nearby, she thought. *Within gunshot range. Fire the bullet you have left and hope to attract attention.* This idea wasn't completely stupid, except for the fact that she'd left her pistol back inside the tree. *If I can't get out of here on my own, then I have to stay alive until somebody comes for me. Terry will call someone eventually.*

Caitlin thought back to a night two months ago, when she'd been trapped in a building with another woman and death seemed certain. She'd summoned extraordinary strength that night, and done things most people wouldn't have been able to do. The police and paramedics had told her that. She was a survivor; she'd proved it in spades. But somehow the bullet in her chest made a mockery of all her confidence. A tiny lump of lead fired from a plinking gun, a child's rifle. But a plain old .22 could kill you if it hit a vital organ or artery.

The bullet, she thought in a haze of confusion. *That's my problem.*

Bracing herself for further pain, she fought her way onto her knees and elbows, then crawled to the wall of the cypress trunk and sat against it, just beside the fissure.

What would Tom do if he were conscious? Call a fucking

medevac chopper, that's what. But the phones don't work. So what else? He'd do what he could on the spot. The bullet obviously hit something important. The pressure's increasing, so I must be bleeding. Unless my lung has collapsed. . . .

"Pneumothorax," she whispered, recalling Tom telling her how he'd once saved a car accident victim on the side of a highway by punching a hypodermic needle between his ribs and reinflating the lung.

Sucking chest wound—

She stopped laboring to breathe and forced herself to listen. Then she slowly drew in a lungful of air. She heard no wheeze from the hole in her chest. *Not my lung,* she thought. *Which is good, because I don't have a needle anyway.*

What else could it be?

The bullet had punched through her chest on the left side of what Tom had always called the "midline." Caitlin was pretty sure the aorta lay under that hole, as well as her heart. *If he'd hit my aorta,* she thought, *I'd be dead now. What else could the bullet have hit? I* must *be bleeding internally—*

A wave of terror hit her as she imagined drowning in her own blood. She saw Penn looking down at her dead body, a froth of clotted blood on her face and chest. Seconds or minutes later she realized that her brain was wavering between consciousness and sleep. *That's not sleep,* she realized. *That's death. Think, goddamn it. THINK!*

A strange sound came from the interior of the tree. It sounded like a cat with something caught in its throat. An electric shock of possibility flashed through her. Could Tom be choking? If he was choking . . . he was *alive.*

Caitlin started to crawl back through the opening but found she couldn't move. Tears of desperation flowed down her face.

"Hello?" called a rough voice from the darkness inside the tree.

"*Tom!*" she cried, sobbing with relief. "It's Caitlin! Can you hear me?"

A moan of pain came from the opening. Then Tom said, "Where are you?"

"Outside! I can't move! I'm in trouble. Can you get outside the tree?"

"I don't know. My hands are tied behind me. Handcuffed, I think. Is anybody else out there?"

"No. And I'm shot. In the chest."

Tom was silent. Then he said, "Hold on, darling. I'm coming."

Half a minute later, Tom Cage knee-walked through the opening in the trunk of the cypress, his hands bound behind him. With his dirty gray face and bloody clothes, he looked like a man who'd just crawled out of his own grave. But to Caitlin he looked like an angel. Her angel didn't waste time with small talk, either. His eyes were on her chest as he lurched toward her.

"How long ago did that happen?"

"Eight or ten minutes?" she wheezed. "I'm not sure. It was a .22 rifle."

Tom tucked his chin into his chest as he studied the wound, but then he looked up at Caitlin's neck.

"What is it?" she asked anxiously.

"Are you having trouble breathing?"

She nodded.

"And pressure in the neck?"

She nodded again, her fear blooming into panic.

Tom leaned forward and studied the right side of her neck. The second he did, she saw his eye darken.

"What is it?"

"Your jugular veins are distended. Touch your neck."

She put her hand against the skin beneath her jaw, and the bottom dropped out of her stomach. Tom was right—one blood vessel felt like a hose filled near to bursting.

"What's the matter with me?"

Tom laid his right ear against her chest and pressed it hard against her. "I can barely hear your heart. It's pericardial tamponade."

"What's that?"

"The bullet probably nicked your heart."

Caitlin shut her eyes tight, trying not to scream.

"Take it easy," Tom said in his reassuring voice. "Not all heart wounds are fatal. When the heart is hit by something that doesn't destroy its ability to pump outright, it bleeds into the pericardium—the protective sac around it. As blood flows into the sac, it creates external pressure on the heart, like a crushing fist. What you feel now is that pressure making it harder for your heart to beat."

Caitlin's stomach fluttered again. "How long until it stops altogether?"

"That depends on the rate of bleeding. Never, if I have anything to do with it. Do you have any tools with you? Anything?"

"Not much. What do you need?"

"In an ideal world? A six-inch needle to aspirate the excess blood."

"Sorry, fresh out. Will anything else work?"

Tom bit his lip and looked around the muddy tussock beneath the tree. "We need a tube of some kind, the longer the better."

"Like a reed?"

"In principle, but it has to be rigid. A reed wouldn't be near strong enough."

As he searched the edge of the water with his eyes, she dug into her pocket and fished out the multi-tool Jordan had given her when they parted. With spastic fingers she unfolded knife blades, screwdrivers, a bottle opener, scissors . . . everything but what she needed. Nothing even *resembled* a needle.

"What's that you've got?" Tom asked.

"A multi-tool. Nothing hollow on it, though."

"We can use that knife blade. We still need a tube, though. Without it . . ."

"I'm dead."

Tom grimaced but didn't argue the point. Instead, he kept searching the area around the tree, although what he hoped to find, Caitlin had no idea.

What else do I have? she thought desperately. *A useless cell phone . . .*

She remembered the handheld walkie-talkie Mose had carried, with its old-time metal antenna. If she'd taken that, she could snap off the antenna, shove the tube into the bullet hole, and ask Tom to suck the blood out of her pericardium like a gangbanger siphoning gas from a Mercedes. Of course, if she had a walkie-talkie, they could radio Danny McDavitt to airlift them out of this fucking swamp—the deus ex machina of her dreams.

She blinked in silent shock. *Harold said he had a walkie-talkie.*

Caitlin struggled to her knees, then scanned the

ground like a strung-out addict hunting a dropped bag of crack. She saw nothing other than a cigarette butt near a footprint in the mud. No walkie-talkie.

"How's your breathing?" Tom asked, turning back to her.

"Somebody's sitting on my chest."

"I want you to sit down. Your blood pressure's going to drop as the pericardium fills. Do you feel light-headed?"

She went still, her panic morphing into something close to shock. As carefully as she could, she leaned back against the tree and sat down. She fell harder than she'd intended, scraping her back and landing on something that jabbed her right buttock. Leaning to her left so that she could reach whatever it was, her fingers touched hard plastic, then froze. Wedged tight along the vertical seam of her right pocket was the clear Bic ballpoint she'd borrowed from the waitress in the café.

"Tom!" she cried, taking it out and extending her hand to him. "I hope to God you can pull some kind of Mac-Gyver shit with this thing."

"Hallelujah!" he said, moving back to her. "It's thick, but it's about the best we could hope for."

"You mean it's thicker than the bullet hole?"

"We'll find out. With a .22, the track through your body will have swelled shut, but not permanently. Which means . . ."

"What? Tell me!"

"To drain the pericardium, you've got to get the tip of that pen barrel to it. To get *that* tube to your pericardium, you'll have to reopen the wound."

"So?"

"The pain will be severe. And with my hands cuffed behind me, I can't do the procedure."

"Then tell *me* what to do!"

Tom stared at her for a few seconds, then at the wound. He shook his head slowly. When she began to sob, he sighed and said, "Take the ink tube out of the pen barrel and throw it on the ground. Then open that knife and get ready to use it."

Caitlin stuck the pen's point between her teeth, bit down, and yanked out the ink-filled insert. Then she slid a fingernail under the edge of the blue end cap and popped it out. What remained was a strong hexagonal tube about six inches long. Awfully thick for a needle, but better than nothing.

"What about sterilization?" she asked.

Tom actually laughed. "Infection is the least of our worries. You just worry about getting that Bic to your heart."

"I'll do it. Tell me what to do."

Tom knelt before her, then allowed himself to fall onto his butt. As he coached her, his eyes moved constantly between her eyes and the bullet hole. Caitlin felt like she was about to climb Everest or jump out of an airplane, and Tom was the only instructor she would ever have.

"In a clinical setting we'd have an ultrasound machine to guide the needle. You're going to have to go by feel. But first you have to widen the hole. You're going to insert the point of the blade, then work it along the track of the bullet by touch—widening the track as you go. It won't be easy—first because it will hurt like hell, second because the point might hang up in tissue all along the way. You've got to ignore the pain, but not altogether, because if you blot it out totally, you might go too far and hurt yourself worse, or pass out."

"I understand. How do I keep from going too far?"

Tom considered this question. "That's my job. I'm going to watch you closely. Once you have the blade halfway in, you're going to guide the pen barrel along the blade, then push both toward the pericardium. Don't be surprised if you get a squirt of blood. There's quite a bit of pressure in that sac right now."

"Won't there be blood the whole time?" she asked.

"Not that much. When you reach the pericardium, you'll know."

She had a feeling he was underplaying the horror she might soon experience.

Tom tried to smile. "All right, let's do it. If you pass out, this isn't going to get done."

Dropping the Bic between her legs, Caitlin picked up the multi-tool and looked at the knife blade. Three inches of tempered steel with a glittering edge . . .

"Don't think about it," Tom said. "Just do it."

As she contemplated shoving that blade into her chest,

something froze her hands. She was thinking of a scene from *The Texas Chainsaw Massacre* in which a character slices open his own palm with a pocketknife.

"Cait . . . ? Come on, girl. You can do it."

"I know. Fuck it." She grabbed a twig from the mud, stuck it between her teeth, and bit down as hard as she could. Then she shoved the point of the knife into the bullet hole and pushed it slowly but steadily toward her heart. The twig flew out of her mouth when she screamed. She saw keen empathy in Tom's eyes, but also resolve.

"Keep going," he urged. "If you stop, you won't start again."

She pressed the blade deeper, and fire seared her chest. When she wiggled the blade in the wound, the pain was nearly unbearable.

"Back it out a little," Tom advised. "The point's probably buried in tissue."

She did as he advised, and blessed relief was her reward.

"Okay, back in. You've probably got another inch to go."

She shut her eyes and drove the knife deeper into the wound track. It was like threading a catheter into your bladder, only a catheter that had been heated to a thousand degrees Fahrenheit.

"Stop," Tom said. "It's time to put the pen barrel in there."

Christ, she thought, shivering from adrenaline. She picked up the clear barrel of the Bic and held it along the knife handle, its narrow end near the bullet hole.

"Be deliberate," Tom said.

The pen barrel actually hurt worse than the blade, because of its thickness. She groaned and screamed each time the tube penetrated deeper into her chest, and as it disappeared, she realized that her breathing was even more difficult.

"That's as far as I can go without cutting more," she gasped. "What's the fucking problem?"

"Stay still. I want to try something." Tom bent at the waist and put his gray lips around the pen barrel. After taking a deep breath through his nose, he began sucking as hard as he could.

How can he do that? she wondered. And then she realized something that brought tears to her eyes. Tom loved her. Her, and the child that she carried within her. This procedure was a brutal act of self-preservation, not for themselves alone, but for each other and for their family.

"Keep going," she urged, as Tom's face reddened.

Despite his effort, nothing darkened the clear tube. At length, he pulled back his head, gasping for breath. "I'm light-headed. You've got to go deeper . . . and faster. I think my sugar's bottoming out again."

"Did you finish that peppermint I put in your mouth?"

"I didn't know I had one. All I knew was I was choking on something."

"You should find whatever's left so you can eat it. That's all I had with me."

"I'd better look. Getting to the pericardium is only half the job."

A blast of panic went through her. "What are you talking about?"

"Take it easy. Now, what's keeping your heart from bleeding out—probably the left ventricle in this case—is the pressure of the blood in the pericardium. Since we have no way to plug the hole in your heart, if we drain too much blood from the sac around it, there's no more pressure to hold in the blood. You understand?"

"You're telling me that if we somehow succeed at this, I'm going to bleed to death."

"No, you're not. The trick is to drain out enough blood to let your heart pump well, and get your blood pressure back up, but not so much that you bleed to death. We can do that by plugging the end of the pen barrel with a finger. Okay?"

"Okay."

"But to do that, at least one of us has to be conscious."

Caitlin gritted her teeth against the fire in her chest. A runnel of blood slid down her bare belly. She looked up at Tom, her jaw set tight. "Go find that goddamn peppermint."

While Tom knee-walked into the Bone Tree, Caitlin gingerly held the knife and pen barrel as steady as possible in her chest. She feared that any second a jet of blood would burst from the tube, and she would die. To block out that image, she focused on the pain, which reminded her of going to the dentist when she was a child. Her father had always taken her to an elderly practitioner who seemed not to have heard of Novocain. He took forever to fill teeth, and she always felt like he was drilling directly into a living nerve. Ice and fire living together in the heart of a tooth: that was what she felt now beneath her breastbone.

"I couldn't find it," Tom croaked, falling beside her again. "Most of it probably melted before I came to. How do you feel?"

Caitlin nodded, unwilling to waste breath answering.

Tom gave the buried steel an appraising look. "Time to try again."

She took a deep breath, then drove the steel and plastic still farther toward her heart. When she'd probed as deeply as she dared, Tom leaned down again to begin sucking, but before he could, dark blood spurted into his eyes.

"Oh, my God!" Caitlin cried, as the blood kept coming. "Oh, shit. I'm sorry!"

Tom pulled away and shook the blood out of his eyes. "Cover the end with your finger! We've got to control the flow!"

The jet had slowed to a dribble by the time she capped the pen with her fingertip. As she leaned back against the cypress trunk, she realized that Tom was right: unless one of them remained conscious, she would bleed to death through a Bic pen. *Why couldn't that waitress have kept the freaking blue cap on it?* she thought, picturing a chewed-up pen cap from her junior-high days.

At that moment she remembered the tiny flat end plug she had dropped on the ground. She could see it in the mud between her thighs. If she felt light-headed, she could plug the tube with that.

"How do you feel?" Tom asked again, studying her neck. "Your venous distension looks a lot better."

She hadn't thought about the result of her efforts, beyond the blood. But the very fact that she hadn't must mean that her condition had improved.

"It's better . . . everything's better. But what do we do now? If we're going to get out of here, one of us has got to climb high enough up a tree to get cellular reception, so someone can pull us out."

She thought of Carl Sims and Danny McDavitt and their beautiful JetRanger. How easily they could drop down and lift both her and Tom out of danger—

"Tom?" she cried, suddenly afraid.

He'd started coughing violently, and as she gaped in horror, he rolled onto his back, fighting for air.

"*Tom!* Roll over on your stomach!"

He didn't seem to hear her. Caitlin tried to push herself off the ground and go to him, but she didn't have the strength to change positions, especially while holding the pen in place. If she wasn't careful, she'd fall over and not be able to get up again.

Tom had finally stopped coughing, but he was no longer moving either. His face was gray except for where her blood still marked it, and his eyes were closed. A chill like the one Caitlin had felt inside the tree when she first recognized him went through her again. Only this time, she feared she was right.

"Tom?" she said, almost pleadingly. "Tom, *say something.*"

He didn't move.

"Tom, please!" she screamed. "Don't leave me! *TOM, WAKE UP!*"

CARL ASSURES ME THAT Danny is pushing the envelope as far as he dares, but the JetRanger slides over the tops of the cypress trees at a maddeningly slow pace. Ever since I learned that Caitlin left the service station with a young black man, I've tried to convince myself that she knew what she was doing and that she's all right. But every neural fiber that drives my instinct tells me she's not. In the heat of chasing a story, Caitlin sometimes loses the judgment that serves her so well the rest of the time.

"Can't we go any faster?" I ask. "Just a couple of knots?"

"We can," Danny says in my headset, "but we shouldn't. Her phone will only be pinging for a tower every one to three minutes. If we pass over her too fast, we could miss it."

"You realize we were doing this very thing only two months ago?" I say in a shaky voice. "Searching for Caitlin."

"That was different," Carl says in my headset. "Then

we were flying at night, and we were using FLIR to look for her body heat. We were trying to pick her out of thousands of false positives created by animals, and we didn't have any decent idea of where she was."

"And now?"

"Now we're scanning for a ping with a two- to four-mile range, line of sight. If we fly close enough, that phone will come up on this scope like a lighthouse in the night. We can fly straight to her."

"*If* her phone's on," Danny says in a grim voice. "And if she still has it."

"Fuck that noise," Carl snaps in a rare display of temper. "The girl knows what she's about. She's a survivor. She'll have it on."

"If she's such a survivor," I mutter, "how does she keep winding up in these situations?"

"You know how," Carl says. "She can't stand to sit by and do nothing when she sees something messed up. Keep your eyes on the deck, Penn."

What I can see from the window is far less valuable information than the electrons on the Raytheon screen Carl is studying on the scope behind my seat, yet I can't take my eyes from the cypress trees passing steadily beneath the chopper.

"Watch for boat wakes," Carl says. "Anything."

"No wakes so far," Danny says. "I've been watching."

"Caitlin's smart," Carl insists, almost like a mantra. "If she hears this chopper, she'll find a way to signal. She's got a gun on her, too. I saw it."

Thank God, I say silently. "How are you choosing your course, Major?"

"I'm riding the border between the federal preserve and the private hunting land. That's our best shot, right?"

"Right," says Carl.

Time passes with inexorable slowness. I feel more like I'm riding in a cable car than a helicopter.

"Carl?" I say into my headset mike. "Nothing?"

"Not a beep, bro. Just keep the faith. . . ."

A frantic pressure is building in my chest, so strong that I wonder if I've inherited my father's propensity for heart attacks. "What are we missing?" I ask in desperation. "Are we making some stupid mistake? Maybe the problem is that she doesn't know she's in danger. Maybe she's actually hiding from us. Or from someone else she thinks is out there."

"That's a good point," McDavitt says.

"Bullshit," Carl insists. "If she's in trouble, she knows it. This is like fishing. We've just got to stick with it."

"I hate fishing," I mutter.

"*Hold it!*" Carl yells. "I got a ping! Decent strength . . . I think she's trying to make a call."

"Which way?" Danny asks.

"Sixty degrees. Strong, too. Eyes open, Penn! She's down there. Watch for that pirogue!"

Danny banks to the right for what feels like a quarter mile, then goes into a hover. Carl studies his screen like a sonar operator tracking a torpedo that could kill him. Agonizing seconds pass.

"Carl?" I prompt.

"Hold it . . . I've lost the signal. Backtrack, Danny!"

"Oh, God," I whisper.

"Hang tight, Penn. We're close."

CHAPTER 71

CAITLIN HUNCHED AGAINST the trunk of the cypress tree, gasping for breath, every atom of consciousness focused on the bloody tube protruding from her
chest. Shock had set in—she knew from the uncontrol-
lable shivering. Her visual field had darkened at the edges;
the world was fading to a small circle, to the tube in her
hand. Most alarming, her jugular vein had swollen again,
so badly that it was hard to bend her neck. Every few seconds she looked skyward and twisted her neck; the motion
seemed to help keep her conscious.

As her symptoms worsened, Caitlin had tried to drain
more blood from her chest, but to her horror she'd discovered that the tube had clogged shut. The blood must have
clotted inside the pen barrel. She figured she might be
able to expel the blood from the tube if she pulled it out of
her chest and blew as hard as she could, but she knew she'd
never get the damned thing back into her pericardium.

Her panic over Tom passing out again had become
anger, then rage at his weakness. But after screaming for
half a minute, she'd realized two things: first, that Tom
was never going to wake up again; and second, this situation was as much her fault as his, for lying to Penn last
night when she could easily have told him that Tom was
hiding at Quentin Avery's house. If she'd only done that,
everything that followed would have been different. . . .

Faced with the reality that she would die unless she
could relieve the growing pressure on her heart, she
tried to contort her neck sufficiently to suck on the
barrel herself. This was akin to trying to suck her own
nipple—which she'd once done at the request of a college
boyfriend—only much more difficult. Because the pen
was three inches lower than her nipple, and also because
as the end of the pen barrel neared her lips, she felt its tip

slip out of her pericardium. Dizzy with pain and terror, she drove the pen to its maximum depth again.

A dark rivulet of blood ran down her belly.

At first she thought the fresh pressure of built-up cardiac blood had driven the clot out of the tube. A surreal image of herself on television rose in her mind: she was making the talk-show rounds, like that kid who'd cut off his own arm to get free from a cliff. *And I'm just as stupid as he was for running off to a blank space on the map, where no one knew where to look.*

"I'm a media whore!" she cried, giggling hysterically as the echo of her voice rebounded through the swamp.

But her exultation evaporated almost instantly. The rivulet of blood had come from her wound, not the pen barrel. The plastic tube was still clotted shut.

"No," she whispered, fighting the urge to drive the barrel deeper into her suffocating heart. "*No, no, no.*" Her back and chest felt as though someone had been pounding them with a mallet. "Please, God," she moaned, remembering the blessed relief after the first jets of blood had drained enough smothering fluid for her heart to find its rhythm again.

Staring down at the clogged tube, she began to sob quietly. *I'm going to die because I don't have a six-inch needle and a syringe.* "For want of a nail," she whispered. "One motherfucking nail."

She probably had only minutes to live. Tom lying motionless on the ground made her future all too plain. A wail of desolation forced its way up through her constricted throat, but the strangled squawk that emerged probably traveled less than fifty feet. Her vision flickered, faded to black. Panicked again, she shook her head and shifted position; the world returned.

Magic, she thought. But soon the light would vanish forever.

A soft hiss sounded in her ears. Then little splashes threw water droplets off the surface of the swamp like glass beads over a black floor. Only a few dozen at first . . . then hundreds, thousands . . . *millions*. As Caitlin stared, each impacting raindrop registered in her brain as a separate event. Time had slowed, or dilated somehow, every second stretching to many times its usual duration. The chilling drops fell indifferently on Tom's gray face, and he did not move.

Somewhere above the canopy of branches, she knew, beyond the leaden clouds, glorious sunlight streamed over the horizon onto this part of the world. A few miles to the west, the Mississippi River rolled over the land as it had for millions of years. And somewhere to the north, Penn had probably heard from Terry Foreman by now. He might be racing toward Athens Point even now. But long before he found Caitlin, she would have vanished from the world.

Her baby, too.

The thought of a new life growing inside her did not drive Caitlin to fight harder. The last thin filament that held her to the world—an umbilical as fine as a strand of spiderweb—had stretched to the point of breaking. The old part of her, the super-competent control freak, was finally laying down her weapons and giving in to the ebb and flow of eternity. She recalled how safe she'd felt inside the ancient tree behind her, the sacred chamber, a centuries-old repository of bones. Why not use her last reserve of strength to get out of the rain? Even dying animals had the sense to find a warm, dry place to lie down for the last time.

She tried to scoot to her left, but she couldn't manage it. She could no longer even shift her own body weight. She would die here, and before long, animals would crawl up out of the water and devour what remained of her.

Circle of fucking life, she thought. *So it goes.*

The rain fell cold upon her face, but she didn't care. Now that she'd accepted the inevitable, her thoughts drifted to Penn, and to Annie. She wished she could say something to them, explain that she'd had no intention of abandoning them when she came on this crazy quest.

She picked up her Treo and checked the screen again, praying for a miracle. One bar could be considered divine intervention at this point. But there were none.

She pressed 911 anyway.

Nothing happened.

Staring at the silver device, Caitlin realized that she had one last way to speak to Penn and Annie, or at least to leave them a message. After gathering her thoughts as best she could, she activated the Voice Memo program and began talking softly. She had to pause every few words to take replenishing breaths, but this effort brought her a feeling of peace that nothing else had. She tried not to cry, but tears came anyway. She felt like a mountaineer trapped on a storm-shrouded peak, leaving a final message for her family. As she ran out of words, she realized with a jolt that she was losing consciousness.

Is this how it ends? she thought dully.

She still had enough neurons firing to know that if she could clear the clot from the pen and drive it back into her pericardium, she might be able to save herself. As she lowered her gaze, the world began to shrink again, tunneling down to the small plastic tube. Then a new train of thoughts flashed through her mind, not images from her past, but from the future: She lay on a hospital bed, a pink baby swaddled in her arms. Tom stood beside the bed, grinning through his white beard. He had somehow delivered the baby, even though his arthritic hands made that all but impossible. Peggy stood on the other side of the bed, Annie smiling beside her. The scene was pure Norman Rockwell. Yet as corny as it was, Caitlin wanted it more than anything else the world had to offer.

But where was Penn? He wasn't in the picture. He wasn't even in the room. But Caitlin could hear him. He was shouting at her, seemingly from far away. What was he saying? He wanted her to do something. But what?

Pull it out! he cried. *You have to do it now. Pull it out and clear that clot. . . .*

"Do it now," she echoed, her voice slurred.

Caitlin raised her right hand to the two inches of plastic protruding from her chest. Her fingers, slick with blood, could barely grip the pen barrel. She tried to squeeze harder, but her fingers lost their purchase. The hexagonal tube stayed in her chest. With her last pulse of energy, she seized the tube, yanked it from her body, stuck it in her mouth, and blew with all the force left in her.

"GOT IT!" CARL SHOUTS, as Danny holds the hover with perfect steadiness.

"If it *is* her," Danny says worriedly. "It could be one of the search teams."

"We must be right on top of her!"

"No boat wake," I say, desperately scanning the black water as Danny shifts the bird thirty yards to starboard. The surface of the swamp is empty of human signs for as far as I can see.

"Ten o'clock!" cries Carl. "What do you see, Penn?"

"Holy shit," I breathe, catching sight of the crown of a massive cypress tree in the distance. "Look at that, Carl."

"Son of a bitch," he says. "That's gotta be it. Danny?"

The chopper is already rolling right, picking up speed as we bore in toward the ancient giant.

"Got it again!" Carl says. "This is it."

As Danny slows to a hover fifty yards from the tree, I catch sight of something too white and clean to be part of the natural environment.

"Under the tree!" I shout. "Something white."

"I see it," says Danny.

The JetRanger dips forward, then descends toward what now looks almost like a white flag of surrender. As we draw closer, I recognize the red stripe across the back of Caitlin's jacket.

"It's her!" I scream, straining against the four-point harness that holds me in my seat. "That's her jacket."

I'm suddenly terrified that Caitlin's been dumped in the swamp like Casey Whelan. "Back off a little bit. Get down close to the surface, so we can see under the branches."

"It's gonna be close," Danny says in a taut voice. "Those branches are a problem."

"Screw the branches," Carl growls. "Take this bitch in, Danny."

The JetRanger edges up to the colossal tree, chopping branches into kindling like the world's biggest Weed-wacker. A choking lump rises in my throat. Caitlin is sitting with her back against the cypress. She's still too far away for me to see if her eyes are open or closed, but if she were all right, she would be jumping and waving at the helicopter.

"Get us down, Danny! Hurry!"

With an expert hand, Danny noses the chopper still closer to the enormous cypress, descending all the while.

Suddenly Carl is at my shoulder, staring through the side window with me.

"I'll go down first," he says. "With the hoist."

"Bullshit you will." I grab the handle on my chest and pop the harness free.

Carl opens the side door, then begins prepping the rescue basket. When I look forward, Danny is holding a pair of field glasses to his eyes.

"What do you see?" I ask, dread filling my chest.

"She's got blood on her chest. A good bit. Her eyes are closed. We've got to get her out of there ASAP. Let Carl go down first."

"I'm going down."

"Penn, wait." Danny looks back, his eyes searching mine from beneath his helmet. "Your father's down there, too. He's lying face-up, his eyes are closed, and he's not moving."

I scramble back to where Carl is prepping the aluminum mesh basket for descent and drop to the floor. From here, I can see the pilot was right. Dad is lying on his back about ten feet from Caitlin, near the water's edge.

How the hell did this happen? How did he get here? In less than a second I know the answer: *Snake Knox brought him here.*

Carl checks the hoist's cables, then gives Danny a thumbs-up. We're only six feet above the water now. I'm going to jump. As though reading my mind, Carl grabs for my arm, but I twist away and leap through the door before he can stop me.

My feet dig into soft mud as icy water closes around my chest. The chopper's rotors fling a stinging storm of spray and debris into the air, nearly forcing my eyes shut. Just above me, Carl slides the rescue basket through the open door.

At six foot one, I can bull my way over to the cypress without swimming. Pushing through the sulfurous water, I see a dark vertical slash in its trunk, like a great scar left by the sword of a giant. *She really found it*, I think. *That's the fucking Bone Tree.* This realization transforms the cold iron of dread into molten terror—not of the tree and its legends, but of the men who use it as their killing ground.

Clawing my way out of the water, I scrabble up onto

the tussock beside my father. "Dad!" I shout, shaking him. "Wake up!"

He doesn't move. Checking the pulse at his throat, I feel nothing, but my fingers are already stiff from the cold water. Leaving him for the moment, I crawl to Caitlin, whose stomach and lap are red with sticky blood. My right hand goes straight for the artery beneath her jaw. Her lips are blue and her neck strangely swollen, but she's faintly warm, as though life still thrums somewhere beneath her skin.

There's no pulse in her throat.

"Caitlin!" I shout, taking her cheeks in my hands and squeezing tight. "*Caitlin, can you hear me?*"

She doesn't move. With rising panic I turn and wave to Carl for help. He's fighting through the water now, nose and eyes just above the surface, dragging the rescue basket behind him. Turning back to Caitlin, I slide my hand over her belly, searching for her wound. My palm hits something hard: a Bic pen, stuck to the blood on her stomach. Six inches above it is a small hole beneath her left breast. *A bullet made that. . . .*

A loud splashing sounds behind me, and the ground thumps as Carl drops to his knees at my side. "Any pulse?"

"Nothing. She's bled out, Carl. She's dead!"

His dark fingers go to her throat, where mine were moments ago. "My *ass*," he says. "I feel something!" He presses his ear to her chest. "This girl ain't dead till a doctor tells me she is. Let's get her in the chopper. We can make Baton Rouge General in fifteen minutes!"

"The basket?" I ask numbly.

"Fuck the basket! Danny's practically on the surface. I'll carry her. You get your old man. He's bigger."

As Carl turns to the hovering chopper and waves Danny still lower, I run to my father and grab him beneath the arms. Struggling with his heavy bulk, I see Carl drag Caitlin away from the Bone Tree, lift her slim body over his shoulders, and charge into the blast of spray coming off the water. Replaying the scene in Brody's basement two nights ago, I drop to my knees and heave my father's body over my shoulder, then march down into the black water while Danny's screaming rotors smash bone-thick branches off the towering tree above me.

CHAPTER 72

WALT HAD KEPT nearly a mile between himself and Forrest's cruiser as he followed his quarry southward. The GPS tracker allowed him that luxury. He prayed that Knox and Ozan were driving to wherever Tom was being held. If they weren't, then Forrest might already have given the kill order, and Tom could be dead or dying at this moment.

For the thousandth time Walt cursed Mackiever for not bugging Knox's car, but there was nothing to be done now. All he could do was follow Knox and the Redbone to wherever they were bound. The cruiser was following a roundabout back road that looked as though it might lead around the Lusahatcha Swamp, toward the Mississippi River. Walt couldn't actually see any water, but he could smell it. When you lived in a dry state like Texas, you got to where you could smell rain from a hundred miles off.

When he slowed Drew's pickup to soften the sickening drop of a pothole, the guns in the bag on the floor behind him made a reassuring clank. Thinking himself at the end of this empty, winding road, Walt visualized various scenarios. No matter what odds he confronted, he could not hesitate to fire, as he'd done back at the Bouchard lake house. In fact, he decided, he would shoot the bastards in the back if he got the chance. Kidnapping was a felony, after all.

I ain't proud today, he thought. *Or particular.*

FORREST KNOX LEANED AGAINST the side of his cruiser and watched the pirogue glide toward him out of the cypress trees. Ozan looked back from the water's edge and gave him a thumbs-up sign. If the boy in the boat had done as instructed, then Caitlin Masters was no longer a problem.

Forrest had parked his cruiser right beside the boy's junk pickup truck. He left his engine running, so he couldn't hear the hum of the trolling motor as the pirogue neared the shore. Harold Wallis raised his left hand and waved. Ozan waved back. As Wallis cut his motor and drifted toward them, Forrest could see the kid was surprised to find them waiting for him.

"Hey there, Colonel!" Wallis called. "I didn't expect to see ya'll out here."

The pirogue's bow bumped the shore.

"I guess you didn't," Ozan said, "since you didn't call us back."

Harold opened his mouth but no answer emerged.

Forrest took a couple of steps toward the water's edge. It surprised him that a drug courier like this boy couldn't sense the danger in what he had done.

"That was a big job you did for us, Harold," he said. "We want you to know we appreciate it."

The boy relaxed a little, but he didn't move to get out of the boat.

"What about the girl?" Ozan asked. "She dead?"

Harold ducked his head with an exaggerated nod. "Yes, sir. She gone. Long gone."

"How many times did you shoot her?"

Wallis's eyes flicked back and forth. "Oh, three, fo' times. Right in the chest. She died inside the tree."

"You checked to be sure?"

"Yes, sir. She bled to death right there."

Ozan had taken a step closer to the water. "What'sa matter with your arm? Is that blood on it?"

Wallis shook his head quickly. A stupid lie.

"Did she shoot you?" Ozan asked.

"It ain't nothin', Captain. She winged me after the first couple of shots. But I finished her off good."

The kid was definitely lying, Forrest decided. He'd shot her, all right, but he hadn't stuck around to watch her bleed out.

"It's too bad she had to die," Forrest said. "She was a hell of a pretty girl, wasn't she?"

The boy looked at the bottom of his boat. "Yes, sir."

"Did you think about fucking her? As a little bonus?"

Wallis shook his head. "No, sir. I just done my business, so my brother could get out of Angola." He looked up at last, clearly frightened. "You gonna take care of that next month, Colonel? Like the captain said?"

"Absolutely," Forrest said. "Least I can do, after what you did today."

The boy's face was still troubled. "That lady told me she was pregnant, Colonel. She was lyin', right?"

Why would Masters tell the kid that? Forrest wondered. She must have figured that killing a pregnant woman might move a simple young man to mercy. A smart play, considering the softness of this kid. She'd probably been lying, of course, but they'd never know, because no one would ever find her body and perform an autopsy.

"Sure she was lying," Forrest said. "She was trying to play you, Harold. Play on your sympathy. She sensed you're a good boy."

Wallis didn't look convinced. "It's wrong to kill a doe that's carryin', Colonel. Every hunter knows that."

"Let me help you out of there, kid," Ozan said, reaching out his left hand.

"I'm good," Harold said. "You men got important things to do, I know. I can pull the boat out and load it. I do it dern near every day."

"No, it's no problem," Ozan said, his hand still extended.

Harold hesitated, then stepped to the bow of the pirogue and took Ozan's hand. Forrest saw the Redbone's other hand slip into his back pocket and take out his knife. In a single motion Ozan released the spring-loaded blade and drove it up beneath Harold Wallis's sternum.

Nobody ever looked as surprised as people stabbed without warning. It wasn't like the shock of a bullet, which often scrambled the brain in a millisecond. A blade gave people time to comprehend what had happened to them. The force of Ozan's blow had surely knocked the wind from Wallis's lungs, and the knife had probably punctured his heart, but his eyes were wide open and still full of life. The kid looked like some blackface cartoon from the 1920s, drawn to illustrate the question: *What the heck?* Or maybe, *Why me?*

Ozan lifted Wallis off the ground by main strength. The boy hung there, folded around the knife, his eyes bulging.

Forrest heard a low rumble that rose in volume, then faded. Probably an eighteen-wheeler back on the highway. He stepped up to the dying boy and looked directly into his stunned eyes.

"Your brother's gonna rot in Angola, son. But I do appreciate the favor."

Forrest nodded, and Ozan twisted his hand.

The light in the boy's eyes went out. His body hit the ground with solid finality.

"What you want I should do with him?" Ozan asked as Forrest walked back to his cruiser.

"Load him into his truck. Have one of the boys drive him down to Baton Rouge and leave him behind a crack house. Too many eyes around here right now. The security cameras from the café will ID him as the person last seen with her, and after we get rid of her body, they'll eventually write it off as a homicide."

"True dat, boss. See you back at the camp."

Forrest's hand was on the door when a helicopter stormed over them at treetop level, its throttle wide open. For a moment Forrest stood paralyzed, back in Vietnam, trying to recall map coordinates for an artillery strike.

"Son of a bitch!" Ozan yelled. "Who the fuck was that?"

"Lusahatcha County Sheriff's Department!" Forrest cried, shading his eyes and peering after the bird. "I saw the gold star on the door. That's Billy Ray Ellis's chopper."

"Looked to me like it was coming from Valhalla."

"From the Bone Tree is my guess," Forrest said. "God-*damn* it."

"What would Sheriff Ellis be doing there?"

"That wasn't Billy Ray, Alphonse. *Shit.* We've got trouble."

"You mean you think they found the girl?"

"That's exactly what I think."

"What you wanna do?"

Forrest's mind was gearing down into combat mode. If Penn Cage had somehow discovered the Bone Tree, then a tectonic shift had occurred in the situation. A curtain

was about to be stripped from the past, which meant casualties were inevitable.

"Boss?" Ozan asked softly.

"We've got an hour before the cavalry gets here. Maybe
half that. We've got to move fast."

"Where to?"

"First Valhalla, to clear out the safes and get some
diesel fuel."

Ozan gave him a puzzled look. "And then?"

Forrest smiled the way he once had before going out on
night patrols when he expected contact.

"The Bone Tree, Alphonse. Where else?"

WALT HAD JUST WORKED his way into a spot from
which he might see something when a Bell JetRanger
came blasting over the treetops above him. Whatever
Knox and Ozan had stopped to do, the appearance of the
chopper had startled them. Even before the sound of the
rotors faded, he heard an engine start up. Then a pickup
truck he had never seen trundled over the hill with Ozan
at the wheel and a pirogue in back.

Walt ducked down and waited for it to pass, then started
running back toward his own truck. Knox was bound to
be right behind the Redbone, and Walt had a feeling that
things were going to happen fast from this point forward.

Just as he reached his truck, Forrest's cruiser came
racing past on the road. Walt cranked his engine and
started to follow, but then he realized that he shouldn't
do that before driving back and checking the spot where
they'd stopped. It might be that Tom had been held prisoner by whoever owned that truck and pirogue, and Knox
and Ozan had killed both guard and captive.

Cursing like a sailor, Walt manhandled the truck out of
the trees, then pointed it back into the woods and floored
the gas pedal.

CHAPTER 73

I HAVE A friend whose son was accidentally shot in the chest by his brother during a hunting trip outside Natchez. For thirty-five miles my friend cradled his dying son in the backseat, trying to stanch the bleeding while the sobbing fourteen-year-old brother drove toward St. Catherine's Hospital at nearly a hundred miles per hour. Twelve miles from Natchez, the boy's heart stopped.

I used to wonder what those last twelve miles were like. Now I know.

Under a sky so dark we could see the lights of the capitol from thirty miles out, Danny McDavitt piloted the JetRanger southward toward Baton Rouge at over 130 knots. In the chopper's belly, Carl Sims gave Caitlin continuous and violent chest compressions while I got on the radio and fought to get landing clearance at Baton Rouge General Hospital. They had an active delivery in progress, and since we weren't an authorized LifeFlight, they were trying to divert us elsewhere.

During the first minute of flight, Carl had determined that my father had a faint pulse and a heartbeat. After I used a fence-cutting tool to remove the handcuffs from his hands, I'd plundered Danny McDavitt's flight bag, found a Snickers bar, and stuffed a chunk into Dad's mouth. We couldn't be sure that blood sugar was his problem, but there was little else we could do without real medical help.

Caitlin was another matter.

Ten miles out of Baton Rouge, Carl could no longer detect a heartbeat in her chest. While Danny pushed the chopper's engine beyond its operational limit, I telephoned Drew Elliott and begged him to do anything he could from Natchez. Thirty seconds later we were over Baton Rouge and boring in on Baton Rouge General. Danny started to land in their automotive parking lot, but space was tight and the risk to bystanders real. While Carl and I stared wild-eyed at each other over Caitlin's bloody chest, Drew called back and told me to divert to Our Lady of the Lake. A med school buddy of his was a trauma surgeon there, and he was ready to get Caitlin into an OR the moment she arrived. Danny instantly aborted the parking lot landing and got us over Our Lady in less than a minute.

As we dropped toward the rooftop helipad, John Kaiser called and told me we'd been cleared to land at Baton Rouge General. I thanked him and shut off my ringer as Danny flared and settled the JetRanger dead center on the white-painted ring. Crouching against our rotor blast, a trauma team rushed to the chopper and moved Caitlin onto a gurney within ten seconds of the skids touching concrete. Carl and I followed them into the elevator, watching in stricken horror as they started large-bore IVs and searched in vain for a heartbeat. A technician diagnosed pericardial tamponade even before the doors opened on the next floor.

Drew's buddy was scrubbed and waiting in the OR when they shoved Caitlin through the big double doors and ordered the security guard to keep me outside. Four minutes later, using a long pair of tweezers and a portable fluoroscope, the surgeon pulled a deformed .22 slug out of Caitlin's heart with as little trouble as a boy pulling a doodlebug from a hole with a stick.

Then he declared her dead.

She'd apparently been dead when they bundled her off the chopper. The surgeon had only opened her chest because the nature of her injury sometimes offered hope of an "exceptional save." There was also the unspoken reality that the doctor had been doing Drew a favor.

When I close my eyes, I still see Drew's friend coming through the double doors, pulling off his mask, and reciting his stock speech with solicitous eyes: *Mr. Cage, your wife was shot, as you probably know. The bullet struck her heart. We tried every means at our disposal to resuscitate her, but in spite of our best efforts, she died a few minutes ago. I'm sorry.*

"She's not my wife," I said, which was legally true but made no sense or difference to the well-meaning surgeon.

He apologized again, and I mumbled that he should forget it while it struck me that no matter what the law says, I am twice widowed, which must be a fairly rare mark of distinction among forty-five-year-old American men these days.

Carl Sims put his hands on my shoulders and in a cracked voice said he was sorry. Then he told me that Danny McDavitt would have been there, but the hospital had asked him to move the chopper to a secondary landing site near the car lot. Then, to my surprise, the trauma surgeon spoke some more, telling us things that brought tears to our eyes. He told us that Caitlin was brave, even heroic, and that she and my father had used an ingenious method to try to relieve her cardiac distress. The remarkable thing, the surgeon said, was that Caitlin must have done all the cutting and probing herself. For since my father's hands had been cuffed, he could not have done it. Had Dad not gone into a diabetic coma, he might have kept Caitlin alive long enough for the trauma team to save her.

I was in no mood to hear praise for my father, and I did not react well. The surgeon shook my hand and bade me farewell, and then a nurse came out with a hospital bag containing Caitlin's personal effects.

All that happened twenty minutes ago.

Now I stand alone with Caitlin in the OR—"viewing the remains," as I heard a nurse say, in what she thought was a whisper. Someone had draped a sheet over Caitlin's body, covering her to the neck, but I removed it as soon as the nurse left me alone with her.

Standing in the awful silence, I relearn lessons that I learned when my wife died, then forgot out of self-preservation. Lesson one: the stillest thing in the world is the corpse of someone you loved. A hunk of cold granite seems more alive than a dead human being. You don't expect a stone to move. A person robbed of all motion and cold to the touch is the most alien object in the world. Natural instinct drives us away from the decaying body, and quickly. Yet love compels us forward, to kiss the empty vessel of the soul departed.

Lesson two: there are many fates worse than death. The most common is surviving the death of a loved one.

For the dead, all questions have been answered or made ir-
relevant. For the survivor, some questions have been rendered unanswerable. When my wife died, I had months to
prepare, yet even then the final reality stunned me. But
Caitlin has been snatched away like the son of my deer-
hunting friend: alive and vital one moment, permanently
AWOL the next. The cruelty in this feels personal. Many
in my circumstance would lay it at the door of God. Yet I
know where the true blame lies.

But that is for later. . . .

For now I must say good-bye. Unlike my wife, Caitlin is beautiful in death. Sarah was beautiful in life, but
cancer stripped away her loveliness piecemeal until all
that remained was a living husk. On this table, Caitlin reminds me of stories from London during the Blitz, when
lovers seated on park benches had the life snatched out of
them by the blast of a V-2 rocket they never even heard.
The bullet wound in her chest is obscene, as is the thora-
cotomy window the surgeon cut in her side, but the rest
of her body bears no mark. Her skin was always china
white, and with her veil of black hair, she looks more like
an actress playing a murder victim in a film than an actual
corpse. For a surreal moment, I half expect someone to
yell "Cut" and to hear the footsteps of the crew rushing in
to congratulate her and give her sips of Perrier.

But no one does.

Looking closer, I see that Caitlin died without a trace
of makeup on. Jordan Glass's influence, no doubt. Beneath her frozen perfection, though, I sense that the process of decay has already begun. Her cheeks sag in a way
they never did in life, and her breasts lie flatter than I
ever saw them. This woman will never bear a child, never
nurse one, or watch one take its first steps. She will never
sit proudly at a graduation, or grow old and touch the
wrinkles on her face with exquisite sadness over slowly
encroaching mortality. For Caitlin Masters, mortality arrived all at once, in a tiny package of lead and copper that
rearranged her vibrant heart just enough to smother it in
its own blood.

Questions swim like ravenous fish below the surface
of my consciousness, yet something of almost terrifying power holds them at a certain depth. Since Caitlin

cannot answer questions for me, the fish must wait to be fed. Some part of me understands that this will be the last time I spend with Caitlin in her natural state. As a prosecuting attorney, I know too well the clinical rituals that follow death. After this brief lacuna in the rush of events, she will be violated by the pathologist's saw; her organs will be weighed upon the scales; her blood will be pumped out by the embalmers and replaced by chemicals; all the other ghoulish sequelae we inflict upon the dead will follow in train. Yet all this leaves me strangely cold. My temporarily cauterized nerve endings transmit no signals of agony; my brain experiences revulsion as a concept, not an emotion. I know that pain will come—in minutes perhaps, or hours, or even days—and when it does, I may not be able to endure it.

But for now . . .

I reach out and take the cold hand of the woman I would have married next week, had my father not taken leave of his senses, and gently squeeze it as I did in life. She does not squeeze back, but I still remember with absolute clarity what the reciprocal squeeze felt like: the proof of love returned.

The OR's double doors open behind me, but I do not turn. A nurse gently suggests that I rejoin my friend outside.

I ask her to leave.

Perhaps I was not as polite as I should have been, for I hear voices just outside the door. Some male, others female. Someone is talking about shock, suggesting I might need to be seen by a doctor.

Shock.

Am I in shock?

"Penn?" says a hesitant voice from behind me. "It's Carl. Can I talk to you?"

"Talk," I say without turning.

Carl walks slowly up beside me.

"I'm sorry we couldn't save her, man. I did everything I could."

"I know you did."

"I think I broke her ribs, doing CPR. I'm so sorry about that."

"That means you did it right."

"You don't—" Carl's voice catches, and he has to pause to regain his composure. "You don't think I made her worse, do you? That pericardial thing?"

In truth, he probably did, but nobody could have wanted Caitlin to live more than Carl Sims in those moments. "She wasn't going to make it, man. You did all you could."

Carl sobs once, then wipes his nose on his sleeve. "You heard what that doctor said? Your daddy tried hard to save her. And Caitlin did all she could to save herself. She did shit even a combat soldier might not do."

My throat constricts painfully, cutting off a single wracking sob.

"Your daddy's awake now, they said. Down in the ER. He went into sugar shock. A few more minutes and he would have been dead."

I grunt but say nothing.

"I didn't tell them who he was, but that trauma doctor knows. And I mean . . . he's still a fugitive. You better think about how you want to handle that. State police could show up any time."

"It doesn't matter now."

"Well . . . I just thought I should tell you. They're getting kind of antsy out there. The hospital folks."

"It doesn't matter, Carl."

The deputy makes a sad sound deep in his throat. "Look now, Sheriff Ellis ordered me and Danny back to Athens Point. We told him you didn't have a ride back, but he said you weren't our problem, that we had a job to do out in the swamp. But then I got a call from Agent Kaiser. Kaiser said we weren't to leave this hospital without you on board, and he would take care of the sheriff. And I guess he did, 'cause the sheriff ain't called back once."

I nod but don't take my eyes from Caitlin's placid face.

"Penn," Carl says, stepping closer to the table, then turning to look up at me. "I never got a chance to ask you. Why'd she go back out there, man? She didn't say nothing to me about it, I swear. Did she tell you she was going back?"

"No."

"Lord, I just can't believe it. I feel for you, brother. I know that don't mean nothing right now. You just tell me and Danny what you want us to do, and we'll do it. I don't care what it is."

"I want to take her back to Natchez."

Carl says nothing for a few seconds. Then he says, "I don't figure the local law would look too lenient on that. But if that's what you want . . . then say the word. We'll put her on a gurney and roll her down to the chopper and fly her back home."

As insane as this would be, it's what I want. Though Natchez was never really Caitlin's home, taking her back would spare her the impersonal butchering that awaits her here—at least for a little while. Her father and mother might be able to see her as she is now, tranquil and relatively whole.

"I'm afraid you can't do that," says a deep voice from behind us.

I turn. Behind us stands a man in his sixties, wearing the uniform of the Louisiana State Police. The sight of that uniform sends me into a rage. Blood pounds in my ears, and I surge toward the stranger, but Carl hooks his muscular arms beneath mine and locks his hands behind my neck.

"Easy, Penn! Easy now! Listen to what the man's saying."

"He's one of Knox's people!"

The newcomer holds up both hands and shakes his head. Then he steps closer, apparently confident that Carl can restrain me. The old trooper's eyes look more sad than angry or gloating, and his voice communicates empathy when he speaks.

"Mayor Cage, my name is Griffith Mackiever. I understand why you're angry, so I'm going to tell you something that's not to leave this room. A long time ago, I used to be a Texas Ranger. And I've been in contact with Captain Walt Garrity for the past two days. I'm also in contact with Sheriff Walker Dennis. We're all trying to work together to handle the shitstorm that Forrest Knox and his people have unleashed in this state. Forrest does work for my agency, yes, but I've been investigating him for some time, and I am most assuredly *not* one of his people. In fact, he's trying to destroy me as we speak."

Mackiever pauses, as if to ensure that what he's saying

is sinking in. Apparently satisfied, he continues. "This is a tragic thing that's happened, and it's not the only murder of the day."

His words are registering about the same emotional response as if he'd told me a dump truck ran over an armadillo on the highway.

"I'm still trying to ascertain what happened out in the swamp," Mackiever goes on, "and I'd like to speak to you for a few minutes before the media descends on this hospital. If you're up to it, that is. Now, obviously Ms. Masters is going to have to remain here for the time being. There'll have to be a postmortem, as you know."

"She died in Mississippi," I say flatly. "They can do the autopsy there."

Mackiever gives Carl a worried look, as though he's uncertain of my sanity. "She was declared dead in Louisiana, Mr. Cage. That puts the autopsy here."

I say nothing.

"I think you can let the mayor go, Officer," Mackiever tells Carl.

"You okay?" Carl murmurs in my ear.

"Yeah."

Carl lets me go, and my hands tingle and ache as the blood flows back into them.

"The FBI is about to pour massive resources into Lusahatcha County," Mackiever informs us. "Agent Kaiser has already dispatched Bureau choppers from New Orleans to secure that Bone Tree and whatever was inside it. Apparently your fiancée uncovered a trove of bones and other evidence that could solve up to a dozen murders."

"Then you don't need me."

"Mayor Cage—"

"Please don't call me that." With careful movements, I pick the sheet up off the floor and lay it over Caitlin's body, leaving only her face exposed.

"Mr. Cage, I think you'd better come with me," Mackiever says gently. "Pay your last respects, and then meet me outside in the hall."

The colonel nods once, then leaves the way he came.

"I know it doesn't make you feel any better," Carl says, "but Caitlin did find what she was looking for, and I know she'd be proud she did."

"Proud?" I echo. "Yes, she would have been proud. And for what?"

"For the families, man. All those boys that got killed, and the families that suffered. They can finally have some peace."

I look back and find his earnest eyes. "Is that why she did it, Carl?"

The young ex-marine shrugs awkwardly. "I think so, yeah. She wanted to do good."

A strange laugh comes from my throat. If only Carl had known her as I did.

"Well," he says. "You knew her a lot better than me. All I know is, she was the prettiest woman I've seen in a long time. She still is, even now. Ain't she? Even lying there now."

I turn back to the table. "Yes. She is that."

Taking two short steps forward, I lean over and kiss her forehead. She's not as cold as stone, not yet, but the skin beneath my lips sends a shudder of revulsion down my back. The woman I loved is no longer present. Death has taken her, and it mocks me now from within her. The tears I leave upon her face might as well have fallen on the floor. When at last I turn and walk from the room, part of me is as dead as she is.

CHAPTER 74

TOM HAD BEEN awake for less than five minutes when he saw the first cop walk past his door. It looked like a city uniform, not the brown of the state police. A nurse had asked him his name, and he'd acted as though he was unable to hear her, but he knew the troopers wouldn't be long in arriving. A man with a gunshot wound would always trigger a message to the police. At least he wasn't handcuffed to the bed yet.

From staff chatter he'd gleaned that he'd suffered diabetic shock and gone into a coma. It couldn't have lasted long, he figured, because he felt reasonably alert, and his wounds looked just as they had when he last checked them, albeit cleaner. His memory was sketchy, but he clearly remembered trying to save Caitlin beside the huge cypress tree in the swamp. He had no idea how she'd gotten there, nor had he even thought to ask her. He had no idea whether she'd survived her wound or not. The only thing he was sure of was that if Caitlin had not appeared at the Bone Tree, he would be dead by now.

The next time a nurse came through, he asked how Caitlin Masters was doing. The woman told him she'd been taken into the OR and a trauma surgeon was working on her. Tom would have given all the money in his name to rest on that bed and wait to hear the outcome of Caitlin's surgery, but if he did, he would almost certainly be arrested by cops who reported to Forrest Knox.

He rolled onto his side, then slowly sat up on the treatment table and waited to regain his equilibrium. Once he had, he pulled the IV out of his wrist, held his thumb against the hole, and walked over to a chair, where a white coat had been left by the ER physician. After struggling into the dirty clothes they'd removed from his body, he slipped on the lab coat, then opened drawers until he found a surgical mask, which he placed over his nose and mouth.

He knew he should check his appearance in a mirror, but he didn't have time. A nurse or tech could come in at any moment. He walked to the door and paused long enough to steel himself against the pain signals pouring into his brain from every extremity. Then he marched through the ER as he had ten thousand times in Natchez, walking with the purposeful tread that nurses would instantly read as the gait of a physician in a hurry to get somewhere he was needed.

Though Tom had never been in this emergency department, he'd worked in enough of them to sense the flow of people, and within seconds he was in the ambulance bay and walking through the parking lot. A spray of rain hit him as he moved out under the gray clouds, but he didn't break stride. The lone security guard was staring at what appeared to be an illegally parked car as Tom approached. When the guard looked up, Tom gave him a quick salute and kept walking.

"Yo, doc," said the guard, "have a good one."

PEGGY CAGE STOOD AT the kitchen stove of Penn's Washington Street town house, watching Annie and waiting for the six o'clock TV news. Kirk Boisseau had finally agreed to go to the hospital for treatment, and after that she and Annie had been moved here, where they would be surrounded at all times by at least a dozen cops and FBI agents. The Natchez police chief had told Peggy that a prisoner had either died or been murdered in the Concordia Parish jail, but he knew few details. As for Penn, Peggy knew only that he had raced out of town to try to find Caitlin in the swamp near Athens Point.

Peggy had tried to persuade Annie to rest, but all her efforts were in vain. Annie meant to sit up until her father returned. Peggy had thought she knew Annie pretty well, but right now she couldn't tell whether the eleven-year-old was on the edge of cracking, or whether she was stronger than her own grandmother. Peggy was feeling pretty fragile after the events of the afternoon. Had Kirk Boisseau not reacted as quickly and selflessly as he had, she might have been badly burned. And there had been no word, neither open nor via a secret channel, about Tom or Walt.

When Peggy was stressed, she cooked, even if there was no real need. She'd decided to prepare chicken jambalaya for Annie, even though the child had claimed all she needed was a peanut butter sandwich. The policemen outside would certainly appreciate it. As Peggy stirred the chicken and rice mixture, she wondered whether the time had come to trust her son above her husband. During their life together, Tom had rarely made a bad decision about the big things. But this time, Peggy had come to believe, he was wrong. Even if he was right, he was wrong, in the sense that his choices might cost him and Walt their lives—not to mention what might happen to the rest of the family.

"Come sit down, Gram," Annie said, beckoning her to the kitchen table.

"I'm cooking, sweetie."

"What will Mr. Abrams think about his house? It smelled pretty terrible when we left, and some of the windows got knocked out by the fire."

"Mr. Abrams's son and your father are good friends. Your father will pay to fix it like it was before."

"The news is on!" Annie cried, pointing at the living room. "I hear it. Come on! Should we watch Baton Rouge or Alexandria?"

"I'm not sure we should watch either. You can't be sure they have accurate information."

As the announcer gave a précis of the night's report— which included a possible murder in the Concordia Parish jail—the house phone began ringing, triggering a rush of fear in Peggy. She forced herself to calm down, then picked up the kitchen extension.

"Penn Cage's residence."

"Mrs. Cage?"

The voice sounded familiar, but Peggy wasn't sure she recognized it. "Yes. Who is this?"

"Special Agent John Kaiser. I met you this afternoon, with Penn."

"Yes, I remember." Peggy's throat tightened in dread. "Do you have any news?"

"I do. And I'm afraid it's not good."

Peggy stopped breathing, and her gaze flew to the kitchen door, to be sure Annie wasn't eavesdropping from the den.

"Is my husband all right?" she whispered. "And my son?"

"Yes, ma'am, Penn's alive and well. Dr. Cage, too, as far as I know. But . . . I'm afraid that Caitlin Masters has been killed."

The world seemed to distort around Peggy, and a claustrophobic silence blanked out the sound of the television from the den. "Are you certain?" she whispered.

"I'm afraid so, Mrs. Cage. She was airlifted to a hospital in Baton Rouge, but she expired before she arrived. Penn was in the helicopter with her."

Peggy shut her eyes against tears. *Dear God, could things get any worse?* But she had lived long enough to know the answer to that question: things could always get worse. Much worse.

"Where's Penn now?" she whispered.

"He'll be headed home soon. But, Mrs. Cage, there's more."

Peggy's hand went to her mouth, and she felt her heart pounding. She knew before the FBI agent said anything that it had to do with Tom.

"Tell me," she said.

"Dr. Cage was apparently with Ms. Masters either when or after she was shot. He tried to save her, but he wasn't able to. He went into diabetic shock."

"Oh, God." Peggy closed her eyes. "You said he was all right!"

"Yes, ma'am. He was on the chopper when they flew into Our Lady of the Lake Hospital in Baton Rouge. They stabilized him, but after he regained consciousness, he walked out of the ER. Nobody knows where he is now."

"Oh, no. Are you sure? How do you know he wasn't kidnapped?"

"Security camera footage shows him walking out under his own power. I believe he knew he was going to be arrested by the Louisiana State Police, so he fled the scene."

Peggy didn't know what to say.

"Mrs. Cage, I called you for two reasons. First, I'm

concerned about Penn's state of mind. According to two officers who were on the scene, he was extremely upset. I was thinking you might even want to call one of Dr. Cage's partners to check him out. I know that may sound extreme, but Penn's going to be feeling a lot of anger—at your husband, unless I miss my guess—and grieving men in shock can be pretty unpredictable."

"I understand," Peggy said, thinking of all the widows and widowers Tom had been forced to sedate over the years in the first hours after a death.

"Obviously the question of telling Penn's daughter the news is going to come up. I don't know how you feel about that. But given what I've heard tonight, you might want to handle that job yourself. Penn may not be in a condition to do it."

"Of course," Peggy said automatically, though dread had begun to fill her heart. Annie had lost her biological mother at the age of four, and she hadn't handled it well. Now—on the verge of gaining a new one—she too had been snatched away?

"I didn't want Penn driving a car," Kaiser was saying. "That's why he's returning by helicopter. He left his Audi on a highway in Wilkinson County, so I sent agents to retrieve it and bring it back to the house. Don't be alarmed if you see his car pull up outside. I've alerted my men there."

"Thank you, Agent Kaiser," she mumbled, even as her ears picked up the news announcer in the next room saying: "*We're getting news of a breaking story in Lusahatcha County, Mississippi, one that involves yet another death and possibly a break in the unsolved civil rights murders being investigated in the Natchez–Concordia Parish area. . . .*"

"Oh, I've got to go," she said.

"Wait, please," said Kaiser. "There's a good chance your husband will try to contact you. It's time to bring this circus to an end, Mrs. Cage. I'm doing everything I can to arrange protective custody for Dr. Cage. If he should contact you, please try to persuade him to call me. Any FBI office can patch him through to me. Tell him to identify himself as Dr. McCrae. Which I believe is your maiden name."

"It is, and I'll try. I've really got to go now."

Peggy hung up and rushed into the den, meaning to

grab the remote and shut it off. Annie was holding it, of course. The child whipped her head around, then froze as she saw Peggy's face.

"What's the matter, Gram? What happened?"

Peggy's throat had sealed shut.

Annie's eyes widened. "Gram . . . ?"

"Your father's on his way home, sweetie."

"Then why don't you look happy?"

Peggy glanced at the television. The newscast had cut to a commercial, but it would return any second with the story that John Kaiser had already relayed to her.

"Annie, let's turn off the TV."

"How come?"

Peggy stepped forward and held out her hand. "Let me have that, sweetheart."

Annie looked down at the remote control. Then she began to cry.

CHAPTER 75

AS THE LUSAHATCHA County Sheriff's Department helicopter storms northwest through gray towers of cloud, I huddle in its belly, my back pressed against the chopper's metal skin. From across the cabin, Carl Sims stares at me like he's been assigned to a suicide watch. Carl cares about me, I know, and at some level he loved Caitlin, but right now he might as well be a stranger. The only thing that really joins us is that once he was paid to protect Caitlin and failed in his duty. So Carl knows that pain, at least to some extent. But in the last analysis, Caitlin's death is a tragic but transient event for him, whereas I have suffered a physical and spiritual amputation. Caitlin is gone forever, and from bitter experience I know I will feel her loss every day (as I did that of my first wife), for at least several years. The effect on Annie I cannot even begin to contemplate; I must spare myself that pain for now.

Between my legs rests a small cardboard box containing what the duty nurse at Our Lady called Caitlin's "personal effects." I only glanced inside the box, half hoping for some clue to what happened to her. But all I saw was her cell phone (which Carl had instinctively saved during our attempted rescue), her engagement ring (the very modest one she'd asked for), one plain gold earring (the other had somehow been lost), a navy blue hair scrunchie, and a scarred Gerber multi-tool with clotted blood still on it. The nurse seemed torn about the multi-tool, wondering aloud whether the police might want it as evidence; but the trauma surgeon believed that Caitlin herself had bloodied the tool in a failed effort to save her life.

Again and again I hear that surgeon marveling at how Dad had contrived to drain the blood from Caitlin's pericardium with a ballpoint pen, but even more that Caitlin had carried out the painful procedure herself. Once I left the hospital, I couldn't shut out the image of Caitlin steeling herself against the fire of that naked blade, then cutting her own flesh in a desperate attempt to save herself. God knows she didn't lack nerve. Caitlin once put four stitches in my lacerated foot under my father's watchful eyes, after I'd ripped it open walking through a creek on the Natchez Trace. I did similar things as a boy, when Dad tried to instill in me a love for medicine. But despite his effort, that love never developed, and instead I followed my talents for reading people, for seeing through the fog of lies, and for persuading people of certain realities. How odd that I would ultimately turn to writing fiction: telling lies to persuade people of things that never happened. Of course, the secret that all good novelists know is that the "lies" they tell are truer than any factual history could ever be.

I wish I had a good lie now. If I did, I would tell it to myself and then, before I saw through it, call Caitlin's father and tell it to him. Because . . . how do you tell a man that his daughter has been murdered? What do you say when he asks you whether his little girl suffered before she died? And how do you answer when he asks you what you intend to do about what happened to her? In that father's ideal world, you would say, *I promise you this, sir, the son of a bitch who killed her won't see another sunrise.*

For that is one thing about the South: it's still a place where, if a man catches someone molesting his child and beats that man to death, he can reasonably expect a jury of his peers to conclude that the pervert fell down twenty-six times on his way to the morgue. *Not guilty, Judge, and by the way could we shake the defendant's hand?* The same principle would hold true for a killer of women, at least in some circumstances.

But in reality, most times the man in my position does nothing. I saw this soul-deadening dilemma too many times as a prosecutor. The desire for revenge is primal, bred deep in our species. But the fear of losing everything is greater still. Most times, a man who contemplates revenge realizes that he must throw away not only his freedom but his family in order to get it, and in the end, he turns his anger inward. There it mixes with guilt and poisons him until, with luck, the passing years eventually dilute the toxins to a tolerable level. Sometimes, though—particularly with the parents of missing or murdered children—that dilution never happens.

Sometimes the poison kills them.

I may not turn to murder for revenge, but neither will I be one of those poisoned men. Whatever responsibility Caitlin bears for her fate, I have failed in my duty to protect her. What can I do now? Killing her killer for revenge would go against everything I've stood for all my life. It would go against everything my father taught me. But as this thought flashes through my brain, I realize that in the past week, my father has broken every precept he ever tried to instill in me. So why do I still jump to the false tune of his teaching?

Danny McDavitt's voice crackles in my headset: "I just heard on the radio that somebody set that Bone Tree on fire."

This brings me out of my fog. "Set it on fire?"

"That's what I heard. Trying to destroy evidence, looks like."

Snake Knox, says a voice in my head. *Or Forrest . . . or that Ozan.*

"Danny?" I say into my headset mike.

"What is it?" Carl asks, his lips not seeming to move beneath his helmet.

"Can you fly over Valhalla on your way back to Natchez?"

"I think the FBI's pretty active in there right now," McDavitt says. "And Sheriff Ellis is mad as hell at them for diverting this bird. I'd hate to have to explain what we're doing in that airspace when we're supposed to be delivering you elsewhere."

I guess I expected this answer, or one like it.

"We already passed it anyway," Danny says. "I didn't know the tree was on fire, but the swamp to the south of Valhalla was lit up like a firebase under attack."

"Thanks," I mutter, visualizing Kaiser and his men standing around the burning Bone Tree like angry Crusaders around a burning altar.

"Is there anything else I can do for you, Mayor?" Danny asks.

"No. Just take me home."

"I'll sure do that."

After closing my eyes for nearly a minute, I take out my BlackBerry, scroll through my contacts, and find the home number of John Masters. Somewhere in North Carolina, the self-styled southern media baron sits in blissful ignorance of his daughter's fate. For a few more seconds, he can believe he has been blessed by providence. But after he answers my call, his life will implode as surely as mine has. Where another man might pray, I simply stare across the deck at Carl Sims and give John Masters a little more time to feel alive.

A little mercy.

TOM CAGE STOOD SHIVERING on a street corner in the pouring rain, watching a line of vehicles douse him with gutter spray as they passed. Two blocks from the hospital, he'd stopped a man wearing a business suit and told him he'd just been mugged, then asked if he could use the man's cell phone to call his son. The businessman had hesitated only a moment; the physician's coat, white hair, and professional manner—along with Tom's ragged condition—convinced him that Tom must be telling the truth.

"Punks ought to be hung," the man said, shaking his head. "This city's gone to hell since those Katrina refugees flooded in. Am I right?"

"When you're right, you're right," Tom replied, turning away and praying Walt would answer.

To his surprise, Walt had, his normally strict phone discipline overruled by his desperation for news of Tom. More surprising still, Walt had been parked outside state police headquarters only a few miles away, surveilling Forrest Knox and Alphonse Ozan. Thirty seconds after arranging to meet, Tom had tossed the white coat in a Dumpster and set off across Baton Rouge on foot.

Now he cupped his hands over his eyes and peered into oncoming traffic, searching for Drew Elliott's old pickup. After two freezing minutes, Walt pulled to the curb in front of him, ignoring the honks and curses of the irate drivers behind him. Seeing Tom's state, Walt jumped out and helped him through the driver's door. Tom slid carefully across the bench seat and sagged against the passenger door. He felt Walt fasten the seat belt around his waist, then a lurch as Walt put the truck in gear and rejoined the flow of traffic.

"We should never have split up," Tom said, his feverish face pressed against the cold glass.

"You got that right," Walt said. "Whose idea was that anyway?"

Tom couldn't raise a laugh. "Should we turn on the radio? Find out how hard they're still looking for us?"

"You don't want to do that."

Tom looked up then, and he saw pain in Walt's face. The kind of pain that often filled his own when he passed on terrible news. "What is it? Has something happened to Penn?"

Walt shook his head. "No."

"Who?" Tom felt a shiver of dread. "Not Peggy or Annie?"

"No, no. It's the girl. Caitlin."

Tom's heart turned to lead. "Tell me."

"She died on the table. Mackiever just called me."

Tom stared at Walt, slowly shaking his head, refusing to believe it. Then he put his face in his hands and began to shudder. He had failed at so many things over the past few days—over his lifetime, really—but failing to save Caitlin was beyond bearing. For Tom knew in that moment that he had lost not only Caitlin and the child she was carrying, but also Penn. He had crossed into a country beyond forgiveness.

He had lost his son forever.

CHAPTER 76

PEGGY CAGE HAD watched her son endure tragedies before, but she had never seen him come unhinged. During the past few minutes, Penn had started to do just that. She already regretted not calling Drew Elliott so that he could sedate Penn; but in truth, Drew would have refused to do such a thing unless Penn requested it, and Penn would never request it. Yet sedation was exactly what he needed.

If watching Caitlin die in his arms had not driven Penn beyond the point of endurance, having to tell his daughter about it had. Peggy had done all she could to help, and more than half the battle had been fought before Penn ever arrived. Peggy had never suffered as she had while watching Annie's face as she absorbed the news that the woman she'd viewed as a second mother would never walk into this house again. Peggy had worried that Annie might not believe the news, but she had—instantly. She had, in fact, been waiting for it. Apparently, Annie's fears for Penn, for Peggy, and for Caitlin had been so great that she had scarcely slept the past few nights. She had covered it well, but once Peggy confirmed one of her worst fears, Annie had begun a sort of high-speed infantile regression.

Peggy had never forgotten the effects of Annie's mother's death. The then three-year-old had developed severe separation anxiety, which was the main reason Penn had moved her to Natchez. Prior to that move, Annie had refused to leave her father's side, and even insisted on sleeping in his bed, one little hand always in contact with his wrist or arm, an early-warning system of impending loss. After that move, Peggy had taken Penn's place to some extent—as had Tom—until over time the child had grown secure enough in their love and constant attention that she learned to be independent again.

But Caitlin had played an important role as well. She had entered their lives as soon as Penn and Annie arrived in Natchez, and despite being only twenty-eight and career-oriented, Caitlin had proved amazingly intuitive at earning Annie's trust. The depth of their bond had been displayed tonight, when Annie shattered before Peggy's eyes.

After the first tears of shock, Annie had voiced an almost obsessive concern with Caitlin's body. Where was she now? Was she alone? Why wasn't Daddy bringing her home with him? The rational answers did nothing to allay her concerns, and once Annie realized that Caitlin's body was almost sure to be autopsied, she had grown even more distraught. After a very difficult hour, Peggy had given her a couple of teaspoons of Benadryl, with the excuse that it would make her burning eyes feel better. The adrenaline-depleted child had almost instantly collapsed in her lap and gone to sleep.

Annie still lay there now, while Penn steadily vented the emotions boiling in his mind and heart. At first he had spoken softly, but as he revealed more of his feelings, he got louder, and Peggy grew worried that he would awaken Annie. On the advice of their FBI guards, they had moved down to Penn's basement office. Thankfully, that isolation also prevented the guards from hearing what Penn was saying now, which was a blessing. Peggy didn't want anyone to know how angry he was at his father, or how irrational he sounded when he spoke about the Knox gang—particularly Forrest Knox. She worried that Penn actually might take it on himself to go after the state police officer with a gun. Part of her was glad to see Penn's anger diverted from Tom, but she knew his focus on others was probably some sort of transference. His deepest anger was reserved for Tom, and there Peggy was at a loss. She didn't know how to argue without appearing to be giving her husband the blind support of an ignorant or deluded wife. She was looking down at Annie when the best solution came to her.

"Penn, would you take Annie from me? My legs have gone to sleep. She's way too big for my lap now."

He stopped pacing and glared at her, but then his face softened, and they made the transfer with the smoothness imparted by long practice.

"I'm going to make you a drink," she said.

"I don't need a drink."

"Yes, you do. If you don't slow that brain down, you're going to talk yourself into something crazy. You *have* to calm down, son."

He sighed heavily and looked over at his desk. "All right, one drink."

"Gin and tonic?"

He nodded.

Peggy swished up the stairs before he could think twice, then went to the kitchen cabinet where Penn kept the liquor. A young FBI agent sat at the kitchen table, but he merely nodded to her and smiled encouragingly.

"Is there anything I can do for you, ma'am?"

"No, thank you." Peggy quickly poured a triple serving of gin.

"Don't hesitate to ask."

"I won't," Peggy said, covertly reaching into her purse for the bottle of the temazepam she took to help her sleep. She swallowed one of the yellow capsules, then quickly pulled apart three others and stirred the white powder into Penn's drink with her forefinger. It didn't dissolve very well, but she thought the bitter gin would cover the taste.

"I wish my husband would call," she said, just to keep the agent focused on what she was saying rather than what she was doing.

"I think Agent Kaiser wishes the same thing."

"Oh," Peggy said brightly, "I'm sorry, I forgot to offer you a drink."

The agent smiled. "I'm on duty, Mrs. Cage."

"*Peggy*, I told you. Please."

"I'm fine, ma'am."

She smiled, then picked up the glass and carried it back to the basement, the ice tinkling as she negotiated the stairs. She thought she might have to press Penn to drink, but when she got to his office, she found Annie asleep on the couch and Penn standing by his desk with his hand out. He took a big gulp from the glass, then gave her a hug so tight she could feel him shuddering against her. As she hugged him back, she spied a suede zip bag lying on his desktop. It hadn't been there when she left to get the drinks. Tom owned several bags like that one. Every one contained a pistol.

"Mom . . . last night Dad was hiding at Quentin's house in Jefferson County. I didn't know that, but Caitlin did. She found him somehow. She went to see him, she talked to him, but she never told me about it. I think Walt knew, but he held it back to protect her. I only found out because I called Melba to check on her. She let it slip by mistake. If Caitlin had told me last night where Dad was . . . none of this would have happened. Don't you see? It's like she killed herself. Because she wanted an *exclusive story*. Can you believe that?"

Peggy was stunned, but she didn't want to play into Penn's anger. "I imagine Tom made her promise not to tell us about it."

"Of course he did, but still. You've got to draw the line somewhere with loyalty. That's what I was telling you yesterday."

Peggy just hugged her son and willed the drug to take effect.

"Can you believe Dad just walked out of that hospital? Caitlin was dead upstairs, and he just . . . walked out. Like he didn't even care."

"He couldn't have known she'd died, honey." Peggy prayed this was true.

Penn drew back, his bloodshot eyes like those of an angry and disillusioned teenager. "If he didn't, then it's *worse*. He knew she was barely holding on."

"Don't talk that way!" Peggy snapped.

"Why not? I'm sorry, Mom, but I have to say it: how many chances has Dad had to do the right thing?"

Peggy went and sat beside Annie, stroked her silken hair. All she'd withheld from Penn roiled in her stomach like something she needed to vomit up, yet still she did not speak.

"I wonder if he'll even come to Caitlin's funeral?" Penn asked bitterly.

A wrenching abdominal ache nearly doubled Peggy over. She almost couldn't bear to hear these words come from her son's mouth. When would those three pills take effect? Penn's face had grown steadily redder, but he showed no sign of collapsing. As she stroked Annie's hair, Penn spoke with almost fearful softness.

"Mom . . . do I know everything you know?"

Peggy closed her eyes and thought of Tom running through the night. Every fiber of her heart urged her to stand, take Penn in her arms, and do all she could to make him understand the true stakes of their situation. But she had sworn to Tom not to reveal her knowledge without his permission, not even to save his life. She hadn't wanted to make that promise, but she had. Earlier she'd considered breaking her oath, but now, with Penn like this . . . she knew Tom had been right.

"I can't help you," she said simply. "I wish I could, but your father is the only one who knows what really happened back in those dark days."

"I'm not talking about the old days," Penn said, his eyes leveled at her.

Peggy's heart fluttered with fear. After taking a slow breath, she folded her hands together and spoke with absolute conviction. "Son, the violence that exploded this week was like the bombs the work crews used to find in Germany when they worked on the streets after the war. It's been waiting in this ground ever since the sixties, rusting away. Sooner or later, somebody was going to sink a shovel into the wrong place. That was Henry Sexton. And once he shoveled out enough dirt . . . nothing was going to stop the explosion."

Penn shook his head, his eyes unmerciful. "That's not what happened, Mom. Henry had been digging around that bomb for years and it never went off. It was Viola Turner who triggered it. And why? Why did she come home? To die? Maybe. More likely, it was to make Dad—"

"*Stop!*" Peggy hissed, and a door slammed shut in her mind. "I won't listen to that kind of talk. Even if you're right, I don't care to discuss it."

"Mom, we have to—"

She shook her head and looked resolutely down at Annie's face. "We'll cross that bridge when we come to it. If we do."

"If we're not going to discuss that, why are we even talking?"

Peggy took another deep breath, then slowly exhaled. "I know there's a pistol in your bag. What are you planning to do with it?"

He looked over at the suede pouch. "I'm not going to hurt myself, if that's what you're worried about."

"It's not. I'm worried you'll try to hurt someone else with it. Because of what happened to Caitlin."

Penn shrugged angrily. "I don't know who killed her."

Peggy gave him a long look.

"Mom, I've been carrying that gun since Monday. None of us has any business leaving this house unarmed."

"None of us has any business leaving this house period. Not tonight. And especially you. Your daughter needs you."

Penn walked up and stood over Annie, looking down with a mixture of love and grief in his eyes. "Where's Dad, Mom?"

"Dear God, son. If I knew, I would tell you. Don't you know that?"

Penn looked over at her then, his eyes more lost than she could ever remember. "I don't," he said. "That's what all this has done to us. What Dad has done to us. And now Caitlin's dead." He started to continue, then checked himself. His mouth opened and closed as though he were testing the function of his jaw.

Thank God, Peggy thought, seeing confusion in his eyes. *The drug is finally working.*

"Tom still might not know what's happened to Caitlin," she thought aloud. "He could be lying unconscious beside a road somewhere. He could have been kidnapped from that hospital."

Penn made a contemptuous sound and flipped his hand in the air. "The security cameras filmed him walking out. He put on a doctor's coat and . . . *sneaked out.*"

Penn sounded like Tom after four or five whiskeys. Peggy started to worry that he might hurt himself if he simply passed out.

"Why don't you sit down? You're exhausted."

"Dad knows what happened, all right. Earlier today Walt and I were working together. He was glad to take my calls. But now . . . he won't answer. That tells me he's hooked up with Dad again."

"I hope that's true! I just pray they're not dead in a ditch somewhere."

A snort of laughter came from Penn's nose. "No chance of that," he slurred. "If those two get killed in this mess, they'll be the last to die. No . . . he and Walt are sitting pretty somewhere . . . playing whatever game they've been playing from the start. Unless Walt doesn't know the game either. He might be just like the rest of them, acting out of blind loyalty to a man who doesn't exist . . . who never really did. Like Drew, Melba, even Caitlin. And . . ."

"And what?"

Penn shook his head. "I forgot what I was saying. I was thinking about the bone creek."

"You mean the Bone Tree?"

"That's what I said."

Penn looked at the floor and shook his head like some despairing drunk. "I had to call her father," he said, wavering on his feet. "Did I tell you that? I called the estimable Mr. John Masters to tell him his daughter had been murdered."

"I know that was hard."

Penn's glassy eyes found hers again. "Do you know what he said to me? What the great John Masters said to me . . . after I told him I'd let his favorite daughter get killed?"

Peggy shook her head.

Penn opened his mouth but no sound emerged. She was about to slide Annie's head from her lap when he turned in place and fell across the club chair beside his desk.

He was out.

As carefully as she could, Peggy reached into her pocket, took out her cell phone, and dialed Drew Elliott's home number.

After three rings, a reassuring voice said, "Dr. Elliott."

"Drew, this is Peggy Cage."

"Oh, Peggy. I'm so sorry about Caitlin. Is everything all right over there? Can I do anything to help?"

"Actually . . . you can. Penn isn't handling Caitlin's passing very well. I slipped him three of my sleeping pills and got him down, but it's going to take more than that to keep him asleep until morning. I'm worried he's going to wake up in the middle of the night and go hunting for someone."

"Okay. I'll be right over."

"Thank you, Drew. We're in the basement."

"Have you had any word from Tom?"

"No. Have you?"

"I'm afraid not. But sit tight. I'm on my way."

"Bring something strong, Drew. Penn's just like his father. It's not easy to get him angry, but once he is, there's no stopping him."

CHAPTER 77

WALT GARRITY SAT half-conscious in the backseat of a massive silver Bentley, Tom's head cradled in his lap. The only light came from the dashboard, but the muscular shoulders of the young man called Xerxes looked a yard wide in the passenger seat ahead. To Xerxes's left, his more conventionally sized father, Darius, gently steered the vehicle through the night without benefit of headlights.

It had taken Tom's last conscious effort to guide Walt to the front gate of Corinth, which was one of the most magnificent plantations Walt had ever seen. Eighty-eight acres of virgin land right in the middle of Natchez, fenced from prying eyes and owned by a woman who had loved Tom for more than forty years. No better sanctuary existed in the world for the two fugitives, and they'd been lucky to reach it at all. Only moments after the great iron gate came in sight, Tom had finally collapsed from exhaustion.

As Darius and Xerxes carried Tom from Drew's pickup truck to the gleaming Bentley, Walt had felt lost in a dream. Once inside the car, he'd nearly fallen asleep himself. Now, after what he judged to be a slow ride of about a minute, the heavy Bentley came to a gentle stop like a boat settling against a dock.

Walt leaned over to make sure that Tom was still breathing, then looked between the shoulders of the two men in front and saw a pair of white columns as thick as oak trees beyond the car's winged hood ornament.

"Home safe," Darius announced from behind the wheel. "Tell Doc hang on jes' half a minute."

Walt felt a cold rush of air as both back doors opened and Tom was slid off his lap. Tom groaned but did not wake. Walt clambered out of the luxurious backseat and trudged up the steps of a *Gone with the Wind*–era palace. As Darius and Xerxes approached a great walnut door with Tom in their arms, the door receded before them as if by magic.

Walt followed the men into some sort of entry hall, where they laid Tom out on a worn red sofa. Thirty seconds later, a door at one end of the hall slowly opened, revealing an old woman seated in a motorized wheelchair. Behind her stood a black woman who had clearly once been beautiful, but now looked as stern as any general's batman. The wheelchair whirred forward, and in the dim light Walt gradually made out its occupant's features. The woman was at least ten years older than he, but age had not stolen the refinement from her face. Her paper-thin skin was the color of bone china, and Walt could see that it had once been soft as cream. The eyes beneath her high brow held many things, but most of all intelligence. They settled upon Walt and seemed to take in the whole of his being at a glance. Then her gaze moved to Tom.

"Can he survive without a hospital?" she asked.

"For a while," Walt replied. "If his heart doesn't give out. He needs medicine, though. Insulin, antibiotics, nitro—God knows what else. And it sure wouldn't hurt to get his partner here to look at him. I was a medic in Korea, but that was a long time ago."

The woman looked back at him, her eyes filled with something he couldn't quite make out. "Was it? To me that was yesterday."

Before Walt could analyze this, she said, "Take Dr. Cage upstairs, Darius. My old chamber, if you please."

The two men moved as one to obey.

"He'll get all he needs here, Captain Garrity," the woman said. "I'll see to that. You need rest now. Can you make it up the stairs? Or do you need to use my elevator?"

Walt was now certain he'd fallen into a dream, or maybe a hallucination. He blinked several times, waiting to awaken in a gully off Highway 61.

"Who are you?" he asked dully, but *What are you?* was the question that ran through his mind.

"I'm Pythia Nolan. You may call me Pithy."

"Pithy," Walt repeated. "Yes, ma'am."

The spectral woman reached into a bag attached to

the arm of her chair and brought out some sort of mask, which the stern maid fitted over her face with an elastic strap. Then she pointed up the hallway like a military officer ordering a charge.

Walt followed blindly, glad to be only an infantryman once again.

WALT AWAKENED SOME TIME later in the half darkness of a guest room on an upper floor of Pithy Nolan's great mansion. Darius and Xerxes had installed Tom in a hospital bed just up the hall from Pithy's bedroom. When Walt found him, his first thought was that he was watching his old friend die.

It had been fifty years since he'd done any real medicine, and back then most of his patients had been soldiers in their twenties with various holes in their bodies. Treating a wounded seventy-three-year-old man with a multitude of co-morbid conditions was far beyond his abilities. Drew Elliott had done a good job with Tom's shoulder wound on Tuesday, but Tom belonged in an ICU now, not on the second floor of a decaying antebellum mansion.

Still, you worked with what you had. Afraid to risk calling Dr. Elliott yet again, Walt dispatched Xerxes on a dangerous mission to Tom's clinic to retrieve a list of medicines and equipment. After the young man succeeded, Walt caught Tom up on his cardiac and diabetic drugs, then hung an IV "banana bag" by duct-taping it to the four-poster bed. But what really worried him were the rales he'd heard when he put a stethoscope to Tom's chest. Wet rales could be signs of pulmonary edema secondary to congestive heart failure, which Tom had experienced long before the crisis of the past few days. Walt had little choice but to pray that the diuretic he'd administered would drain some of the fluid off Tom's heart.

Pithy Nolan had twice driven her electric wheelchair into the room, but Tom had been asleep both times. The matron's breathing sounded even more labored than Tom's, but her oxygen mask seemed to give her some relief. If Walt was honest with himself, the old lady gave

him the creeps. She seemed almost incorporeal, masked
and wrapped in her voluminous blanket, yet her love for
Tom could not be questioned.

Xerxes remained outside the door like a sentry, ready
to run whatever errand Walt might command. Walt had
already sent his father, Darius, to Walmart to buy four
more TracFones. No matter what course of action he and
Tom took now, they were going to need secure lines of
communication to get out of this mess alive.

It was one of these phones he used to call Griffith
Mackiever when he checked his old burn phone and saw
that the embattled superintendent of state police had tried
to reach him only minutes earlier.

"What's the situation?" Walt asked when Mackiever
answered.

"We'll get to that," Mackiever said. "Did you check
the GPS coordinates on Forrest's car around the time the
Masters girl was killed?"

"Why?"

"I figure he was within eight miles of that Bone Tree
when she was shot."

"That's about right, I'd guess."

"I'd like to prove Forrest killed her, but we also have
a videotape of Ms. Masters leaving the Crossroads Café
with a black kid."

"I'll go you one better. I saw Ozan drive away from
the swamp in that kid's truck. And I found blood on the
ground at the edge of the water."

"*What?* Christ, Walt. I could do something with that."

"A statement from a fugitive cop killer? Wake up, son.
You'd be a lot better off using that Katrina video I gave
you."

"I'm working on it. I haven't had any luck reaching
my former friends in state government. I think my only
choice now is the feds."

"I agree. What's happening at the Bone Tree now?
Who's got control of the scene?"

"It was shaping up to be a jurisdictional dispute, but
then the FBI went in there like the goddamned Marines
and cordoned off about twenty acres. A U.S. attorney
issued some kind of special directive under the Patriot

Act, and they ran the goddamn Lusahatcha County sheriff right out of there. The senior agent is Agent John Kaiser out of the New Orleans field office."

"That's who you want to see, Mack. He and Penn Cage know each other. Do you know where Penn is now?"

"They flew him back to Natchez in the Lusahatcha County air unit. He and his family are under twenty-four-hour FBI protection at his residence."

Walt sighed in relief. "Okay, good." Walt hesitated as Tom stirred in the bed, but he didn't awaken. "Are you going to go see Kaiser now?"

"That's my plan. I wish to God I didn't have to bust open this Katrina sniping mess in order to do it. But I guess that's the only way to take Forrest down."

"There's always my derringer."

"Don't even mention that." Mackiever was silent for a few seconds. "I tell you, Walt, when I think about what happened this afternoon—those Eagles killing Sonny Thornfield right in that jail, while it was under FBI control—I wonder if even the feds can stop Forrest. It's like he's three steps ahead of us all, no matter what we do."

"No," Walt said. "He's scrambling just like the rest of us. Worse, he's got dissension in his ranks."

"How do you know that?"

"Trust me. Him and his uncle, Snake, don't exactly see eye to eye. Sooner or later, one of them's going to have to go."

"Not soon enough for me. I'm gonna talk straight to you, Walt. I've got a bad feeling about those Knoxes. They remind me of a couple of crews back in Texas, in the old days. I don't think even the FBI scares them much. And I think that rather than let themselves be taken, they'll try to take down everybody. I think a lot of people could die."

"What are you saying, Mack?" Walt asked, but he already knew.

He and the LSP chief had been Texas Rangers in an era when they'd gone after certain outlaws with the tacit understanding that they were not to return with a prisoner. And to Walt's ear, Mackiever's voice had echoed into the present from that time.

"It's not 1955 anymore, Griff. Not even 1965."

"You could have fooled me, these past coupla days."

Walt listened to the phone hissing in his ear. Mackiever wasn't speaking hypothetically. He saw a malignant cancer eating his department from within, and he wanted a fellow Ranger to rip it out by the roots.

"I've got a wife now," Walt said.

"I know. I've got no right to ask anything of you. But the situation is fluid, and I just want you to know that . . . if anything were to happen to Knox, I can promise you'd have an angel on your shoulder in the aftermath. I'd move heaven and earth to protect you. You and Dr. Cage both."

"I hear you. And my advice is, take everything you've got to Special Agent Kaiser."

Mackiever was silent for several seconds. Then he said, "I'll do that, Cap'n. Just don't forget what I said."

The connection went dead.

Walt stared at Tom for a long time after he set the phone down. Then he reached over to the bedside table and opened a box of Tom's precious cigars. Xerxes had retrieved them earlier when he'd gotten the drugs from Tom's clinic. Walt knew that lighting one would be bad for his friend's lungs, but he needed to settle his nerves. He also knew Tom would thank him for the vicarious pleasure he would experience upon waking. Biting off the end of a Partagas, Walt picked up the lighter Xerxes had brought in and lit the cigar, savoring the flavor of one of the few luxuries Tom Cage allowed himself each day.

Tom stirred, but thanks to a hefty dose of oxycodone, he did not awaken.

Walt smoked thoughtfully, watching the man he'd fought with like a brother through the killing snows of Korea. In the deep shadows, he turned his mind away from the war and thumbed back through the years he'd spent chasing desperate men across Texas, first on a horse, then in motor vehicles of various types. He recalled times that he'd followed the rules, and other times when he'd thrown the book away and simply done what was necessary. He wasn't proud of those occasions but he wasn't ashamed, either. While Tom slept fitfully, Walt wondered whether John Kaiser and the FBI could take on Forrest Knox—who personified the endemic corruption of an entire state—and win. Even if they did, how many more people would become casualties in that war? Caitlin Masters's death had already come close to destroying Tom. As the cigar slowly burned down, Walt pondered Colonel Mackiever's final words, and what it might cost him personally to relieve the world of the burden of Lieutenant Colonel Nathan Bedford Forrest Knox.

CHAPTER 78

CLAUDE DEVEREUX HAD waited nearly two hours before the FBI agreed to admit him to the visiting room in the Concordia Parish jail. In the end it took not constitutional arguments, but threats to go public with the Bureau's use of the Patriot Act to supersede the Bill of Rights to gain him access to his clients. An agent confiscated Claude's cell phone at the door of the visiting room, then patted him down for weapons, but as Forrest had anticipated, they left the cigarette pack in his briefcase alone.

Claude had worried that an FBI agent would stay in the visiting room with them, but after searching it thoroughly, the agent posted himself outside the door. As Claude waited for Snake, he cursed himself for trying to see his daughter and grandkids before fleeing the country. Forrest had put out a statewide APB, and they'd caught him easily. Had he run north to Memphis—through Mississippi—they never would have found him.

The door opened behind him, and two deputies ushered Snake into the room. The Double Eagle looked down at Claude, gave him a game wink, then sat in the chair across the scarred old table. Claude got out his legal pad as if to take notes, then looked up at the deputies and waited for them to leave.

The two men glared at him as though they'd like to kill him—which was no surprise, considering they'd lost two fellow deputies in the past thirty-six hours—but at length they turned and left the room.

"So what are you doing here?" Snake asked. "I'm supposed to be out of here."

"We're working on it. Somebody wants to talk to you."

Snake chuckled softly. "You got smokes in that pack?"

"Four." Claude lowered his voice. "But I've got something else for you in there."

Claude ripped off the taped-down top of the pack and brought out an analog flip phone and a thin wire with an earpiece wrapped around it.

"It's encrypted," he whispered. "Hit star-one, and Forrest will pick up."

Snake smiled.

FORREST JUMPED WHEN THE burn phone finally rang. He and Ozan had been waiting two hours in Forrest's home office in Baton Rouge, and he'd just about given up hope that Devereux would be allowed into the CPSO jail. But the caller ID told him that, unless the FBI had discovered the cell phone hidden in Claude's briefcase, the man on the other end of the call was his Uncle Snake.

Forrest clicked SEND and said, "Identify yourself."

"This is Jerry Lee Lewis. The Killer."

Despite the circumstances, Forrest laughed. It was just like Snake to cut up at the very moment the world was crashing around him. Snake had known Jerry Lee his whole life, and he'd often used that connection to get bar sluts to sleep with him.

"I'm going to talk fast," Forrest said, clicking on the speakerphone, "in case they figure out what you're doing. Keep your answers short, and don't use names."

"Well, get with it, *Tahyo*."

Ozan scowled in confusion, but Forrest smiled. "*Tahyo*"—a Cajun expression that meant "big, hungry dog"—was a childhood nickname that only Snake and very few others would remember.

"Did your lawyer bring you up to speed on recent developments?"

"I hear the girl's dead, shot at the Bone Tree."

"That's right. And she met somebody else there. Somebody she didn't expect."

"And he lived?"

"He walked out of the hospital under his own power."

"He's a tough one, I'll give him that. Do you know where he is now?"

"No."

"Find out. He knows way too much about too many people in our past. If that doesn't pucker your asshole . . ."

"I'm working on it. There was a fire at the Bone Tree. You understand? Somebody went to a great deal of trouble to destroy whatever evidence was there."

Snake chuckled. "That was mighty nice of somebody."

"That same person also cleared out the safe. Everything that was there is somewhere else."

"Sounds good."

"It's not going to be enough. That's why I'm calling you. I wish I could tell you you're going to be okay, but the FBI isn't going to let this go. Neither is Penn Cage. You were part of everything the Eagles ever did, and no matter how much evidence was destroyed, they're eventually going to tie you to one of those killings. And one's all it takes. If that doesn't happen, somebody's going to flip on you. Whichever it is, your days are numbered."

Snake grunted but didn't comment.

"At least *here* they're numbered." Forrest watched Ozan's expressionless face for clues to how his pitch was playing. "It's time to use your golden parachute, Uncle."

Snake still did not reply.

Forrest thought he heard his uncle blowing out cigarette smoke. Right now the old man was thinking about the arrangements Forrest and Billy had been perfecting for the past five years: new identities, clean passports, three separate properties in Andorra—one of the few nonextradition countries left in the world where a white man could live well. But something told Forrest that his uncle wasn't itching to retire in the Pyrenees.

"You still there?" Forrest asked.

"I'm here. And I hear what you're saying. But all in all, I think I'd rather take my chances where I'm at. I got no desire to spend my last years with a bunch of foreigners. I don't ski or hike or hang-glide, and I don't care to live with a bunch of Pernod-sippin' faggots who do."

Ozan groaned softly.

"Do you realize what you're saying?" Forrest asked. "How long do you think you can—"

"What you don't seem to understand," Snake cut in, "is that I don't give a shit what they accuse me of. They've been calling me a killer for forty years. So what? A few more accusations ain't gonna matter. Proving guilt in forty-year-old murders is a tough job, and it gets tougher with every passing day. I don't think they got the evidence to do it."

"Maybe not, but half a dozen people have died in the past week."

"I don't know nothing about those killings. Do you?"

Forrest shook his head at Ozan, who cursed in exasperation.

"You sound nervous, nephew," Snake said. "Take it easy. Have a drink. I'm not nervous. See, I'm not in the position you're in. With me, they can either prove a crime or they can't. But you? Even the appearance of wrongdoing could end your career. So maybe it's time for *you* to pull that golden ripcord."

"Goddamn it, Snake."

Snake laughed softly. "Have you shoved your boss out of his job yet?"

"Not yet."

"That doesn't sound promising. What's your next play?"

"I'm not going to get into that on the phone. We'll talk when you get out."

"When will that be?"

"Soon. Tomorrow, probably."

"*Probably?* Shit, boy. Sounds to me like you don't know whether you're going or coming."

Forrest slammed his hand down on the table. "What the fuck were you thinking taking the doc like you did?"

"Covering my bets, *Tahyo*, the way Frank taught me. Now, seriously, when do you see me walking out of this dump?"

Forrest forced himself to try to calm down. "That depends. The meth disappeared during the bomb scare, so they have no drug evidence to hold you on. In theory, you could be released tomorrow morning. But I don't know what forensic evidence they may get from Sonny's corpse."

"Don't worry about it, nephew. I've figured my own way out of this place. All five of us will walk out before noon tomorrow. You watch. I'll give Claude instructions on how to pick us up."

Forrest didn't like the sound of this. "What are you planning?"

"That's my business. Now listen. You need to calm down. Things are actually falling our way. The girl's gone. So's our latest traitor, and none of my crew's gonna open his trap to the government again. The next thing that needs to happen is for Doc to be shot as a fugitive. And that Texas Ranger needs to die with him. As for the FBI, you just get your ass into Mackiever's job and the federal hassle will die down quick."

Forrest was far from sure about this. Worse, Snake was right about one thing: he could endure anything the FBI threw at him and laugh, while Forrest could not. If the moneymen in New Orleans decided he was a magnet for scandal, they'd cut him off like a gangrenous limb.

"I know you're thinking about pulling in your horns," Snake said, "but Frank would have done the exact opposite right now. When the enemy comes for you, you don't turn tail or lie low, you hit back so hard that nobody will ever think about fucking with you again. Right?"

"I told you I'm not going to talk about tactics."

"You don't have to. I know how your mind works. If I'd agreed to retire into the sunset, you'd have made sure all the loose crimes around here got blamed on me. Since I'm refusing that option, you're gonna start exploring other options. But you know me well enough to know I'll see bad news coming. So be real careful if you're tempted to think in that direction. You could wind up on the row yourself."

Ozan actually rose from his seat at that remark.

"Don't worry, Uncle," Forrest said. "You want to stay in Louisiana and take the risk, be my guest."

"Always a pleasure, *Tahyo*. I'll see you tomorrow, when I get out."

Snake clicked off.

Forrest tossed the phone on the table and joined Ozan standing to pace.

The conversation hadn't gone anything like he'd hoped. He hadn't actually had much faith that it would. Where Snake was concerned, nothing could be predicted. It had been that way for as long as he could remember. That was why Carlos Marcello had canceled the RFK plan after his father died in '68; the pragmatic old mobster had known Snake was too crazy to trust with an operation like that.

"That didn't sound too promising," Ozan said.

"He's not going to leave the country, that's for sure."

"Then they're going to get him. And sooner rather than later. He's popped too many people, boss. They're going to find some forensic evidence, or somebody will flip, and then he'll be sitting in an interrogation room playing *Let's Make a Deal*."

Forrest sat on the edge of his desk. "There's only one thing to do now."

"What's that?"

"Let Snake do what he wants."

"What do you mean?"

"He's not going to sit still and wait for the Bureau to come at him, no matter what he said on the phone. And with Caitlin Masters dead, her paper might come at us twice as hard as they did before. Snake won't sit still for that. He figures we'll take Tom Cage and Walt Garrity out of the equation—as fugitives—so he'll move against the mayor, and maybe even Kaiser."

"Bullshit. You think he'd hit an FBI agent?"

"Alphonse, Snake would kill the pope and twelve nuns if he thought it would keep him out of jail. He does not give a fuck."

"And you're saying we should let him do that? The heat would be unbearable."

A tight smile came to Forrest's lips. "You've forgotten the plan I brought up the night Snake missed killing Sexton and Brody got killed instead."

"Which was?"

"We let Snake hit the people he wants to hit. Then we paint him as an out-of-control psycho. Once the pursuit starts up, he'll come to me for an escape route. I'll send him to what he thinks is a safe house, then when he's cornered, I'll go there myself to 'arrange a surrender.' Once I'm inside . . . I'll blow him away. After that, I'm not only washed clean—I'm a hero. I was willing to kill my own uncle in the name of justice."

Ozan nodded steadily. "That's a cold play, boss, and a ballsy one. Which pretty much makes it perfect. But Snake has to be out of jail to make that work. Do you really think he can get himself out?"

"If he says he can, I believe it."

"You think he's planning on *busting* out?"

"I hope so. The bloodier it is, the better."

Ozan looked like he was thinking hard.

"What is it?" Forrest asked.

"I had another idea. Didn't you say our hotel bugs told you the FBI's planning to fly their evidence up to D.C. on that Bureau plane out at the airport?"

"They're still discussing it."

"If you tipped Snake about that flight . . . he'd probably go after the plane."

Forrest shook his head. "We don't want that. For one thing, the feds might capture Snake alive. For another, Snake might actually succeed in destroying the evidence."

It took a while, but a smile slowly spread on the Redbone's face. At last he understood the reason Forrest had thrown more than fifty bones into the water near the Bone Tree before they'd set it afire.

"Once Snake's dead," he said, "you're gonna bury him in blood and bones."

"That's right." Forrest snapped his fingers. "I want him to look so demonic that I look like a saint by comparison."

Ozan rubbed his eyes, then shook his head. "One thing. I've read up on the mayor a little bit. He's been in some scrapes before, and he did what he had to do to get out of them. He's killed some people. And after what happened to his girl today, he's never going to stop trying to nail us. Never."

"That's what Snake is for," Forrest said. "It was probably always coming to this. Sometimes you just have to wait and see which way things break."

JOHN KAISER STOOD IN the study of the Valhalla hunting lodge and stared into the eyes of the seven-hundred-pound hog that stood opposite the desk. He'd spent most of the night working beneath the Bone Tree, in shadows thrown by klieg lights like the ones Londoners had used during the Blitz. Kaiser had visited countless crime scenes during his career, especially during his time with the Investigative Support Unit, but few could compare in scale or horror to the Bone Tree. From the Civil War–era chains hanging from the limb outside to the inverted skeleton wired to the wall within—now badly charred by the diesel fire—the whole scene forced you to contemplate the essential savagery of the human species.

The tree had still been burning when Kaiser arrived. From the helicopter it looked like a colossal column of flame burning on a vast landscape. After bringing in some pumps on airboats, a fire department team from Baton Rouge had managed to douse the flames. Even so, Kaiser and his team had been forced to wait to get inside the tree. He lost no time getting divers into the water around the gigantic cypress, and they'd already brought up more than a hundred human bones. Once the interior of the tree cooled sufficiently, an evidence team began using archaeological picks and brushes to sift through the layers of bone and human remains buried beneath the new ash.

All that time, he had been haunted by an image of Tom Cage trying desperately to save Caitlin Masters, sucking blood from her wounded heart with his hands cuffed behind him. Kaiser found it hard to view a man who would do that in a negative light.

A half hour ago, he'd tired of slogging around in hip waders, so he'd air-boated to their base of operations on the shore, then ridden an ATV to the main Valhalla lodge, which stood on a high ridge over the Mississippi River.

The search team here had already uncovered two floor safes in the study, but they had been cleaned out. A file cabinet contained some corporate papers from Billy Knox's media company, the one that produced an outdoors show for cable TV. They found no computers in the lodge (despite it having a Wi-Fi connection), and no other papers that could implicate Forrest Knox in any crime. As far as weapons, there were some samurai swords mounted on the walls, and there was a gun room that held about thirty hunting rifles, but Kaiser didn't see anything that looked suspicious. Still, he would have them checked against any unsolved murders in the state.

The real question now was whether the Bone Tree stood on federal land or property owned by the hunting camp. If you judged by the game fence, then it was on Valhalla land, which meant the corpses inside the tree were automatically tied to the men on the Valhalla deed. But there was apparently some question about the real property line, and Kaiser had a feeling that the great cypress might actually be on federal land.

"Sir?" said one of his agents from the study door. "Somebody to see you."

"Who is it?"

Before the agent could answer, a trim man wearing the uniform of the Louisiana State Police walked into the study. For a second Kaiser thought Forrest Knox had decided to show up and make a turf battle of it, but then he saw gray hair, deep wrinkles, and heavy black bags like bruises beneath the man's eyes.

"I'm Colonel Griffith Mackiever," said the newcomer. "Superintendent of the Louisiana State Police."

"You're out of your jurisdiction, aren't you?"

"Technically, yes."

Kaiser got up and shook Mackiever's hand. "How can I help you, Colonel?"

"I'm hoping we can help each other. I'm here to talk to you about Forrest Knox."

CHAPTER 79

TOM WASN'T SLEEPING but floating in a fog of oxycodone and Ativan. His limbs felt no contact with the bedclothes, and only the pulsing memory of his shoulder wound kept him from sinking into oblivion. A few minutes ago his mind had cleared enough for him to see Walt sleeping beside him on a cot, as he had half a century ago in Korea. But Tom's mind had now turned inward, slipping beneath the surface, into a layer of awareness where time had no meaning.

In this place all things happened at once. Caitlin was as dead as the young GIs who had perished in the ambulance after running the Gauntlet south of Chosin Reservoir, and Tom was as responsible for one death as for the others. In truth, he was more responsible for what had happened to Caitlin, because if he had made different choices, he might have prevented that. The boys in the ambulance would have died anyway. Caitlin lingered in his mind because he had lied to her. The night she'd come to him at Quentin's house, she'd asked him many questions. One was about the Kennedy assassination, and Tom had claimed he knew nothing.

That was a lie.

It hadn't bothered him to tell it at the time, because he'd told himself he was doing it for Caitlin's good, as he had so many other times on behalf of others. That was how it went with lies of omission: you could always rationalize staying silent when to speak would cause pain or injury. But now that Caitlin was dead, Tom would never be able to tell her the truth.

Perhaps that isn't such a terrible thing, said a voice he knew too well.

It was the voice of self-preservation. He had made friends with that voice over the decades. The last time he had resisted it was 1990, the year he'd last seen Carlos Marcello. Tom had nearly fainted when the Mafia boss summoned him. He'd had no direct contact with Marcello for at least twenty years and had not even treated any of his soldiers for a decade.

The summons had been delivered by Ray Presley, of course, the former Natchez police detective who'd once worked as a New Orleans cop on the Marcello payroll. Ray had stopped by the office late one Friday, as he sometimes did, and told Tom that "the Little Man" wanted to see him at his Metairie home. So much time had passed since the bad old days that Tom had actually tried to beg off, but Presley had only laughed and said he would pick Tom up on Sunday morning.

During the drive down to New Orleans, Ray explained that the don had not been doing well since his release from a Rochester, Minnesota, prison hospital the previous year. While in the maximum-security prison in Texarkana, Marcello had suffered a series of strokes, and "someone" had arranged for his BRILAB conviction to be overturned, allowing him to return home. Originally, many had assumed that the "strokes" were simply a scam to spring the don from prison, but Ray had heard that Marcello's health was truly declining. Now Carlos himself had apparently asked to see the "jail doc" from the parish prison, and someone close to him had remembered the doctor from Natchez.

Tom tried to hide his anxiety during the drive, but Ray Presley had the predator's instinct for weakness, and he sensed Tom's discomfiture. Over the years Tom had come to an uncomfortable truce with his conscience over his relationship with Marcello. In a perfect world, he would have had nothing to do with the Mafia kingpin. But when that kingpin provided the umbrella of protection that kept Viola Turner alive, Tom had little choice but to bow to his wishes.

The hardest thing to grasp was how tiny turns of fate resulted in inextricably complex relationships. Tom had entered his externship at the Orleans Parish Prison with the dewy eyes of a schoolboy. Still only a medical student, he'd done his best every day, treating cops and criminals alike with equal courtesy. Tom had always been that way:

he'd treat a black sharecropper just as he would have treated the Prince of Wales. But in the Orleans Parish Prison, his attitude marked him as different. His dedication was noticed by guards and cons alike, the difference being that cons—or the men behind them—came from a culture that believed strongly in rewarding good turns. It was this informal system, which in Louisiana had been a way of life for centuries, that resulted in Tom being sold a twenty-five-hundred-dollar Ford for three hundred dollars cash.

A bookie named Cookie Pistolet had been serving a thirty-day stretch in the Orleans Parish Prison for beating his wife. Tom had been treating Cookie's gout. Pistolet was apparently a man of some stature in the Marcello organization, because he received daily deliveries of food and liquor, not to mention a regular envelope filled with various papers and receipts, which he worked on far into the night—with police assistance when necessary. Tom had never seen anything like this, but it was the way of the world in New Orleans, so he turned a blind eye.

Twenty days into Cookie's sentence, the godfather himself had showed up to visit his subordinate. Marcello had apparently been suffering from a wracking cough that had prevented him from sleeping for nearly a month. His doctors had diagnosed bronchitis and prescribed antibiotics, but they hadn't helped. When Cookie discovered this, he praised Tom to the skies and sent a guard in search of the "jail doctor." Tom soon found himself being led before the real ruler of the State of Louisiana, where he was asked to "take a look at" the don's chest.

After examining the short but powerfully built Marcello, Tom had questioned the don about his symptoms. Half a dozen questions convinced Tom that the godfather was suffering an acid-reflux cough, a condition likely exacerbated by Marcello's late-night consumption of acidic Italian-Creole cuisine. The don had brushed off Tom's diagnosis as "old-women's talk" and departed the prison. But one week later, a smiling stranger had shown up and handed Tom a set of keys to the prettiest 1957 Ford Fairlane he'd ever seen. Apparently Marcello had grown so frustrated at losing sleep to his cough that he'd tried Tom's advice and avoided eating sauces and spices after 8 P.M. After five days of this discipline, the cough had subsided.

Naturally, Marcello had wanted to thank the man who'd relieved his discomfort. Through the prison grapevine, Carlos discovered that Tom and Peggy had no working vehicle: their twelve-year-old truck had been sitting dead in front of their apartment for the past three months. The don's answer to this problem was the Fairlane, which could be Tom's for a little more than one-tenth of the sticker price. Tom had tried to resist the gift, but one older cop whom he trusted had advised him that refusing gifts from the godfather of New Orleans was the surest road to ill health that a man could take. So Tom had withdrawn most of his nest egg from savings, paid the three hundred dollars, and accepted a bill of sale from a grinning young Italian who was surely a Mafia foot soldier. Then he'd concocted a story for Peggy that his wife, thankfully, had never analyzed too closely. After all, her daily grind involved trudging through torrents of French Quarter rain to ride the ferry over to the West Bank to teach English to immigrant grade-school kids. The car literally transformed her life for the better.

From this humble beginning had grown an unwanted relationship that ultimately provided Tom with the god-like power of saving Viola Turner's life nine years later, when the worst Ku Klux Klan offshoot in the South wanted her dead. Carlos had been all too happy to accommodate the doctor who had cured his cough, especially when the favor was as trivial as safeguarding the life of a colored woman in Chicago. Of course, Carlos had not accommodated Tom gratis. Since he was doing a favor, he required a favor in return, and that favor turned out to be covert medical treatment for his men during any emergencies that might occur "in Tom's neighborhood." Tom had been in no position to refuse these terms. And both he and Carlos had lived up to their word for the next twenty-five years, though thankfully the burden had lessened for them both as time passed.

But the connection had never been forgotten. That's what had placed him in the passenger seat of Ray Presley's truck in 1990 as it turned into a secluded section of Old Metairie, Louisiana, and then into the driveway of the white marble home of Carlos Marcello.

Despite what Ray had told him, Tom expected to find

an older version of the saturnine boss he had met back in 1959. But the don he viewed on that day was a man beset by Alzheimer's disease and fast regressing toward infancy. Tom had no idea why he'd been summoned, unless someone in the family had decided to humor a casual whim of the old boss.

Marcello's disease, combined with the sequelae of several strokes, had left him unable to care for himself. A team of nurses tended him around the clock, and with more than thirty years of medical practice behind him, Tom knew that the deathwatch had begun. He'd been as kind as he could be to the family, then made his exit as rapidly as possible. He never found out whether Marcello himself had requested his presence, and the question would vex him greatly. Because thirty seconds after he left the godfather's sickroom, he realized that the shield that had protected Viola since 1968 would soon crumble into dust.

As soon as he got back into Presley's truck, he asked Ray what would happen when Carlos died. "Is it like a royal succession? Will his oldest son take over, or one of his brothers?"

"Neither," Ray said. "They've already lost most of what they had. Frank Carraci and Nick Karno have controlled the French Quarter for a while now. But Carlos always knew his brothers could never hold his empire together without him. So he made sure that when the time came, the family would be legit enough to make it without the old part of the business. And they are. They own more land than the goddamn Catholic Church, and they've got all kinds of other businesses. So Carlos is going to do something not many mob bosses get to do."

"What's that?"

"Die free in his bed. And his brothers are gonna do the same. His kids, too. See? He was always smarter than the other bosses."

Tom found no comfort in this. He'd hoped that the business would be passed down to a son or brother who would honor the don's old commitments, including the protection of Viola Turner, but this was apparently not to be.

"All the new players have been trying to carve pieces off

the carcass. The Asians, the Jamaicans, the Russians . . . there's always a free-for-all for a couple of years, till things settle out. Lots of blood, lots of payback."

Tom wanted to ask whether there might be any way to extend the protection of Viola, but he didn't want to start Ray thinking about her. Because that would give the crooked cop leverage he might try to exploit in the future.

A few miles passed in silence. All Tom wanted now was to get home as soon as possible, and home still lay nearly three hours up the Mississippi River.

"It's fuckin' hard to believe," Ray said suddenly, "you know?"

"What's that?"

"That lump of cauliflower we saw back there was about the most powerful boss who ever lived. To think he changed history like he did . . . changed the whole world. And now he ain't no better than some gomer in a nursing home. Needs to be diapered like a damn baby."

"What are you talking about?" Tom asked.

"What do you mean?" Ray asked.

"You said he 'changed the whole world.' "

"What did you think I meant?" Ray asked, cutting his eyes at Tom. "I'm talking about Kennedy."

"Kennedy?" Tom asked. "What Kennedy?"

"John Kennedy. Who else?"

"What about him?"

Presley drew back his head as if Tom were trying to play him. "Come on," he said. "I know you know."

"Know what?"

"What the Little Man did back in '63."

"I don't know. Spit it out, Ray. What are you saying?"

"Shit. Don't give me that. I know you know."

"I don't know anything. Why don't you spell it out for me?"

Presley snorted and drove another mile. Then he said, "Carlos killed Kennedy, Doc. You know that. Why're you making me say it?"

"Are you serious?"

"Am I fuckin' serious? Sure he did."

"Carlos himself?" Tom asked incredulously.

"Himself? That's like asking if Patton kicked the Germans' asses himself. 'Course not. Carlos didn't kill anybody himself, not after about 1955, anyway. Unless he finished somebody off for the fun of it out at Churchill Farms."

"Then who did it?"

"Shit," Ray said, laughing uncomfortably. "I know you're fucking with me now."

"The hell I am!" Tom said angrily.

"Okay, then, okay. Play your games. I've said too much anyway. The Little Man ain't dead yet, and he's got damned big ears. Always has."

"Ray. Are you telling me you know who assassinated President Kennedy?"

Presley turned to him then, peering deep into Tom's eyes. "You know, too," he said. "Unless you're a lot dumber than I think you are."

Tom shook his head. "How could I know?"

But Presley just looked straight down the highway. "If you want to know the answer to that, think about who you knew who had the balls, the brains, and the talent to kill a protected president. That's gotta be a pretty short list."

Tom stared back at Ray for a long time, but he asked no more questions, nor did he think too hard along the lines Ray had suggested. Some deep part of him had already realized he might not want to know the answer.

Two nights later, despite his best efforts to distract himself, Tom had come awake in the middle of the night with an image of Frank Knox in his head. Of all the men he knew—or had known—Frank was the one with "the balls, the brains, and the talent" required to kill a president. A few minutes later, Tom's heart nearly seized in his chest when he remembered Knox asking a favor of him the first year that he'd joined Dr. Lucas's Natchez practice. There'd been a story about a woman, a mistress threatening to ruin his marriage. Frank had told Tom he desperately needed to be excused from work for several days to calm the woman down. Tom might have balked at such a request from just any patient, but on more than one occasion Frank had mentioned training Cuban troops at a Marcello-owned camp in South Louisiana. Frank's connection to the Little Man had been enough to tip the scale. Tom wasn't sure about the exact dates, but an awful feeling in the pit of his stomach told him that the time frame would match John Kennedy's rendezvous with death in Dallas.

While Peggy snored, he'd put on his clothes, retrieved a flashlight, and climbed up to his attic to go through his old Triton Battery records. A steady current of fear ran through him as he breathed suffocating dust and flipped through yellowed files, but the thing he feared most he did not find. Frank Knox's health file was not among his records.

Tom didn't sleep much after that night. He worried constantly about Viola in Chicago, and also about the favor he'd done for Frank back in '63. He lost weight, hair, and his peace of mind. Peggy begged him to have one of his partners check his health, but Tom knew the source of his problem. What he didn't know was what to do about it. Eventually, he crafted a request based on fabricated medical grounds, which he sent to the Triton Battery Corporation. Tom claimed to need information on Frank Knox's medical history, in order to better treat one of his descendants. Though the Triton company had recently been sold, a clerk responded to Tom a month later, telling him that he'd been unable to locate Knox's medical record. Tom initially felt relief, but then a second missive from the helpful clerk arrived, informing him that the bulk of Knox's personnel file had been transferred to the FBI in 1965 and had never been returned to the company. The clerk forwarded a few photocopied sheets covering Frank's employment from 1965 until his death in '68, but this chronicle of suicidal alcoholism held no interest for Tom. The relevant year's record was in the hands of the FBI, and this sent his paranoia into overdrive.

The first Saturday after receiving this letter, he drove down to the clinic's rented storeroom, rolled up his sleeves, and began tearing through every box of extant medical records. It took him six hours, but he finally found the answer he had both sought and feared. It waited in a bellied old box containing the medical records of deceased patients from 1968. There, in the file of Frank Knox, was a notation in Tom's scrawled hand recording a visit by Frank on November 18, 1963, during which Tom had ordered Knox to stay home from work for five days. The medical reason: chronic hepatitis. Tom sat alone in the storeroom, his heart pounding, his blurred eyes skimming the final page of Knox's file, where he'd recorded Frank's "accidental" death by industrial mishap. As terrible as that lie had always seemed, it paled in comparison to the implication of freeing Frank Knox from work during the week of the Kennedy assassination.

Tom returned home that evening a changed man. He had satisfied his curiosity, but the price had been a piece of his soul. He told no one about his discovery. After all, Carlos Marcello was still alive, and the FBI already had its own copy of Frank Knox's absentee record. Though Tom lived in constant dread of being contacted by the Bureau about Frank, he never was. And while he half expected to receive tragic news about Viola any day, he never did. Eventually, the demands of his practice and the passage of time drove his anxiety into the background, and three years passed before he was forced to confront his fears once more.

On March 3, 1993, Carlos Marcello finally died.

Naturally, the first Tom heard of it was when his nurse ushered Ray Presley into his office at the end of a workday. The rawboned former detective held a brown paper bag in his hands. In that bag was a bottle of expensive bourbon, which Ray took out, set on Tom's desk, and said, "The king is dead. Long live the king."

"What are you talking about?" Tom asked.

"The Little Man passed."

A cold shudder went through Tom: it was fear that Viola's days were now numbered—possibly in single digits.

Ray opened the bourbon and poured shots, and Tom drank three in a row. After Ray waxed poetic for a few minutes about the old days in New Orleans, he fell silent and looked into Tom's eyes. Then he asked whether Tom was still confused about who'd killed JFK.

Tom shook his head and said, "Frank, right?"

"Good old Frank," Ray confirmed, nodding.

"So what happens now?" Tom asked.

"What do you mean?"

"Well . . . Frank's been dead for a quarter century. Now Marcello's dead. Kennedy's been dead thirty years. Are you going to carry the secret to the grave? Or are you going to do something else with it?"

Presley's eyes narrowed to slits. "Like what?"

"You know what. You're a history buff, like me. We're talking about the biggest murder case in American history. You can set the record straight, let the world know what really happened. Hell, that story's probably worth millions of dollars."

Ray thought about this for a while. Then he said, "I'd never live to spend it."

"But you told me his family had lost most of its power, that his brothers were going straight. Where's the danger?"

Presley chuckled softly. "Not from his brothers. I'm thinking about the Corsican."

"Who the hell is that?"

"Another guy who was involved in that hit."

"Another shooter?"

"No, no. He was the cleanup man. If anything went wrong, he would have cleaned it up."

"Meaning?"

Ray laughed at Tom's ignorance. "Meaning kill everybody involved. Oswald, Frank, Ferrie . . . everybody."

"Who was he?"

"Shit, I don't know. He was Corsican, a CIA contract man. He worked as an instructor at one of the Mongoose camps, like Frank did. Hell, you met him yourself."

Tom blinked in disbelief. "What? When?"

"On the fishing boat, remember? That time down on the coast. With Brody Royal and Devereux?"

A wave of heat rolled across Tom's face. "That Frenchman who got so drunk and ranted about Dallas?"

"That's right, *cher*. That's him. They speak French in Corsica, don't they? And I heard some real horror stories about that guy. Frank killed people, but that fucker *liked* it."

"Christ." The bourbon soured in Tom's mouth and gut. "Is that guy still around?"

"Who knows? But you never leave a guy like that out of your calculations."

"Hm. But . . . with Carlos dead, why would he take the risk of killing somebody who talked now?"

Presley laughed again. "Because he was involved in the hit. Because he's a pro. Because he's a sick fuck. Need I continue?" Presley threw back a shot and shrugged. "No,

I'll carry what I know to my grave, because I want that grave to be a long way off. I'd advise you to do the same, Doc."

Later that night, Tom decided he would heed Ray's advice. Keeping such knowledge secret went against every principle he believed in, but the logic seemed inescapable: If he contacted the authorities about what he "knew," what would really happen? First, he had no objective proof of anything. There was the medical excuse, of course, but all that proved was that Frank Knox had lied about why he'd skipped work during the week in question. That didn't place him in Dealey Plaza, or even in Texas. Second, Ray Presley would never corroborate anything Tom said, and he might well kill Tom for dragging him into the mess. Third, the Corsican assassin remained an enigma who might or might not be out there somewhere, ready to silence anyone who talked. If Ray was scared of the guy, that was sufficient for Tom. Finally, who would see Tom's tale as anything more than just another crackpot conspiracy theory?

Ethically, his dilemma wasn't as thorny as some. Unlike the Albert Norris case, the perpetrators in the JFK assassination were as dead as the victim. No one had been wrongfully imprisoned. Nothing would bring the victim back. At the empirical level, Tom would be risking his family's lives in order to set the historical record straight—and with only the slimmest circumstantial evidence to back up his accusations. Tom was far more concerned that with Carlos Marcello physically gone, Snake Knox and his old Double Eagle comrades would take the opportunity to silence the one person who could send them to death row for murdering her brother and Luther Davis.

But that did not happen.

Tom's original deal with Marcello had stipulated that so long as Viola did not return to Natchez, she would be left alone, and it seemed that the Double Eagles were content to abide by that arrangement. Maybe they figured that since Viola had held her silence for that long, she never intended to speak. And until a few weeks ago, history had proved them right. But at some point during her journey toward death, Viola *had* decided to return home.

In so doing, she had attracted the attention of Henry Sexton. And through Henry, she'd drawn the notice of the other local men who knew that Viola possessed information that could alter not only the perception of the past, but the reality of their futures. The Double Eagles.

Through the chemical fog that held him in his suspended state, Tom heard a distant voice calling his name. *Tom? Tom . . . ?*

"Tom," said a voice in the dark. "Can you hear me?"

Someone shook him. Then Walt's face appeared above his, eyes bleary in the weathered brown skin. "You were moaning something. Then you stopped breathing."

"Did I?"

"Were you having a nightmare?"

"I don't . . . Must be the drugs."

Walt nodded, then took Tom's pulse. "Not good," he said. "But you can dance to it. Can I get you anything?"

Tom shook his head in exasperation. "I need the goddamn urinal again."

"You and me both. Let me get enough light on to find it."

While Walt searched the floor beside the bed, Tom lay back and remembered Viola in the year he'd first gone to work at the clinic. But then, flowing through and over those memories, came images of Peggy during those summers in New Orleans when they'd been as poor as Viola and her husband would be later, when a meal in Mosca's Italian Restaurant and a tableside visit from Carlos Marcello had made Tom feel like he was more than a penniless student, and when the smooth rumble of the Ford Fairlane carrying his wife and him back to their apartment with good wine and food in their stomachs was as solid and comforting as anything he'd ever known. For it was only later—much later—that Tom realized the three-hundred-dollar Fairlane was the costliest possession he would ever own.

CHAPTER 80

JORDAN GLASS WALKED slowly along the Malecón in Havana, watching young couples stroll down the promenade while old men fished the surf along the seawall. The night air was warm, and Jordan could hardly believe she'd been in the chilly swamp of Lusahatcha County only hours ago. Her Nikon hung around her neck, but she hadn't taken a single photo since the afternoon, when she'd shot Raúl Castro in his office in El Capitolio. The president had been too ill to be photographed, and Jordan had done a poor job of hiding her disappointment at being passed to his younger brother. Before the session was done, however, she'd had a brief encounter that from her husband's point of view had made the trip worthwhile.

Jordan couldn't agree, since she felt certain that had she not left Caitlin alone in Athens Point, the young newspaper publisher would still be alive. Even if Caitlin had insisted on the two of them pushing on to find the Bone Tree using Rambin's map, with two guns they might have driven off the young man who killed her. In fact, Jordan thought, if she'd stayed in Athens Point, Harold Wallis might never have summoned the courage to approach them. But maybe she was flattering herself. She'd survived many combat zones, but even a seasoned veteran could be killed by making assumptions about people. And in the end, that was what had killed Caitlin.

She'd been so hungry for that story—so ready to go to the end of the trail Henry Sexton had blazed, and then farther, making the story her own—that her normal defense mechanisms had been blunted. Where normally she might have felt suspicion of a stranger approaching her with information, the fact that the young man was African-American had lulled her into thinking he was naturally on her side. Caitlin probably assumed he'd heard of her quest through Carl Sims's minister father, who'd put out the word for information on the Bone Tree the previous night. Caitlin would have known she stuck out like a TV actress in the dingy café at the Athens Point crossroads, so it was only natural that someone might recognize and approach her—

A burst of salsa music from the street startled Jordan, and she turned in time to see a gleaming relic of Detroit metal roar past, complete with tail fins and fisheye headlights. The laughing girl in the passenger seat was stunningly beautiful, as most young women down here seemed to be, and watching the antique car race past a dozen others like it gave Jordan the feeling of being lost on a film set. This feeling was magnified by the depressing fact that most of the occupants of the classic cars were tourists who'd paid locals to drive them around Old Havana. More disturbing still, she'd noticed that except for a couple of large ships visible in the harbor, the sea was empty of boats. The government knew that its citizens would not hesitate to strike out for Miami in even the flimsiest craft that offered the promise of a new life.

God, Jordan wished she'd stayed in Mississippi.

Her mind returned to the afternoon's photo shoot, which had begun as a study in anticlimax. Raúl Castro was a poor substitute for Fidel, or at least the Fidel that Jordan remembered from her visit twenty years earlier. But as she was concluding her work, the president himself had stepped into the room unannounced and told her he remembered her from their previous meeting. Back then, the Cuban leader had been vital and filled with restless energy, and he'd flirted shamelessly with Jordan. The man facing her now was only a shadow of his younger self, a bent figure with a grizzled beard, swept aside by the tides of history.

Speaking softly in Spanish, Jordan told him that her husband had asked her to inquire whether he might answer a couple of questions. Having been briefed before the meeting, Fidel knew that Jordan was married to an FBI agent. In response to her request, he gave her a noncommittal tilt of the head and asked what the subject of her questions might be.

"John F. Kennedy," she said. "New evidence has been discovered in America."

Castro gave her a polite smile, but she thought she saw a flicker of interest in his eyes. "You speak much better Spanish than you once did, I believe," he said.

"I got a lot of practice in El Salvador and Honduras in the 1980s."

"Excellent. Tell me about this new evidence."

Jordan had lowered her voice. "I'm not free to do that. But my husband would like to know if an American pilot named David Ferrie once ran guns to your government, before you aligned yourself with the Soviet Union."

Castro considered the question for some time. Then he said, "This is true. Señor Ferrie was an unstable man, but in those early days we could not be selective in our choice of allies."

"Thank you. The Bureau also has a reliable report that when you heard of the death of President Kennedy, your first reaction was to say it was a terrible thing for Cuba."

Castro nodded firmly. "This is also true. Kennedy's administration worked against us, and even tried to kill me, but privately we were working toward a sort of détente between our countries. Also, the man who stood waiting in the wings in America—and the men behind *him*—were far worse than the Kennedy brothers, from my perspective. It was Cuba's good fortune that those men became ensnared in Vietnam. Otherwise, I fear we would have been next on the menu, and the world itself might now be only a memory."

Again, Jordan thanked him for his candor while struggling to remember the questions John had given her. Pulling out a notecard didn't seem like an ideal move in a situation where informality was the lubricant for conversation.

"At that time, you also seemed to imply that the CIA or a right-wing cabal was behind the assassination."

Castro tilted his palm from side to side. "At that time, you must remember, this was a reasonable suspicion, given the events at Playa Girón—excuse me, the Bay of Pigs. And of course the Caribbean Crisis—our blockaded missiles—and the subsequent activities involving Operation Mongoose. It was very easy to see Lee Oswald as the dupe of more devious men. He tried to emigrate here, but we wanted him no more than the Soviets." Castro waved his hand dismissively. "But that is ancient history. I no longer believe in a CIA conspiracy regarding Kennedy. Such men could not have kept that secret for so long." The president regarded her curiously, then said, "Does your husband have a new theory about the events in Dallas? What has been discovered?"

Jordan tried to keep her answer as short as possible. "I'm afraid I don't know that myself. But my husband and some of his colleagues now believe that the president was killed by a Mafia figure that Robert Kennedy was trying to deport from America. Do you have an opinion on that?"

The old dictator's eyes seemed to deepen as he studied her. "I've had a good deal of experience with gangsters, *mi cariño*. They are venal men. They care only for themselves; they have no morals or mercy. If you seek a man who would murder the president of his country—one who is not a political extremist—then a gangster fighting to survive would be very easy for me to accept. Which *mafioso* do they have in mind?"

"The boss of New Orleans. Carlos Marcello."

Castro's eyes filled with some of the intensity she remembered from an earlier decade. "Ah, *sí*. Some of my people had dealings with this man. He was a crony of Santo Trafficante, who I held in jail here for some time. Marcello had an interest in the Lansky casinos, and . . ."

"Yes?" Jordan asked, willing him to continue.

"Marcello's people also had dealings with Señor Jack Ruby, who paid a visit here in connection with the release of Trafficante during the early days of the Revolution."

"Do you know whether Marcello and David Ferrie knew each other?"

"This I do not know, I'm afraid. But"—the president smiled—"I will inquire among certain men of my acquaintance."

"Thank you. Can you tell me anything more that might be helpful?"

"Perhaps. But first you must tell me something. I watched you while you were photographing my brother. You seem very sad, *mi cariño*. Not like the girl I remember from before. Has your trip been made unpleasant in some way?"

Jordan felt heat come into her face. "I lost a friend today. A young woman, only thirty-five."

The old man's eyes released the tension they had held. "I see. I am sorry. I experience the same thing often now . . . more with each passing year."

Jordan forced herself to stay on point, not so much for John as for Caitlin, who would have tried to milk this opportunity for all it was worth. "Can you tell me any more about Carlos Marcello or the other men?"

Castro's eyes flickered again. Jordan noticed his brother watching carefully from across the office, but the president kept his eyes on her. "Perhaps," he said finally. "But I shall not. Not today, anyway. I wish to reflect on what you have told me."

At that point the dictator had nodded with enough formality to let Jordan know that her impromptu interrogation was over.

"Please let your escort know if there is anything we can do to make your stay in Havana more enjoyable. And next time bring your husband with you. I would like to speak to him on this matter. Like so many, I, too, would like to know with certainty who was behind the death of Kennedy."

And that was the end of it.

After she left the capitol, Jordan had gone to the restaurant in her hotel, but found she had no appetite. She did feel thirsty, which had led to her drinking four Russian vodkas in quick succession. Then she'd begun her walk along the Malecón, watching the dark blue surf hammer the seawall, the waves hurling cold spray over her more than a few times. She'd wanted to fly home immediately, but to New Orleans, not Natchez. With Caitlin dead, the town was forever tainted for her. Yet John was still there, leading a forensic team as they excavated the heart of the tree that had drawn Caitlin to it like a moth to flame.

Jordan could still hear Caitlin laughing in the car as she'd talked about Elizabeth Taylor and Montgomery Clift filming *Raintree County* in Natchez, and how the Bone Tree was like a dark manifestation of that myth. More than ever, Jordan thought of Caitlin as a younger incarnation of herself. Only unlike Jordan, who had cheated death all over the world, Caitlin had walked into its embrace in her own backyard.

Realizing that she'd just walked past the door of her hotel, Jordan backed up and turned in, meaning to buy a double vodka to carry up to her room. But before she reached the bar, the desk clerk called her over in an excited voice. The fiftyish man she remembered as arrogant was a living stereotype, with slicked-back hair and a mustache that looked drawn on with a grease pencil.

"What is it?" Jordan asked, afraid that something had happened to John.

The man's eyes sparkled with innuendo. "You have a present, Ms. Glass. A very special gift."

The newly unctuous clerk turned and lifted a breathtaking bird-of-paradise blossom that Jordan had assumed was part of the hotel's décor. This he presented to her with a suggestive smile. Jordan couldn't imagine John sending this to her. For one thing he was busy, for another he knew nothing about flowers. If anything, he would have sent roses.

"I think there's been a mistake," she said.

The desk clerk gave her a leer. "No mistake, Ms. Glass. *El presidente*, madam. See? There is a note."

Jordan opened the sealed envelope and read the brief lines written in what appeared to be painstaking English script on common white notepaper.

> *I am sorry for your loss, mi cariño. Thirty-five is far too young for anyone to die. As for the other matter, please tell your husband that I agree with him about Señor Marcello. A man who knows much of these things tells me that the pilot Ferrie had close dealings with Marcello's people. I would be interested to receive a report on this matter, though I do not expect to see one. And anyway, the truth is depressing and simple. The president's brother pushed too hard against the shadow, and the shadow pushed back. This is the way of life. I doubt we will meet again. Like your young friend, we all share the fate of this flower.*
>
> *Farewell.*
> *Fidel*

Jordan looked down at the flamboyant signature with a disturbing sense of dislocation. She felt a visceral echo of the excitement Caitlin would have felt to hold that piece of paper.

"Well, *Señora*?" asked the desk clerk. "Will they be sending a car for you?"

Jordan looked up with a glare that backed the clerk up a step. "I'd like a double vodka sent to my room. Two, in fact."

Then she turned and walked toward the elevators.

"And the flower, Ms. Glass?"

Jordan pressed the elevator button, then looked back at the desk clerk. "You can send that up, too."

She'd decided to return to Mississippi after all. She would take the bird-of-paradise and leave it beside Caitlin's grave. The brave girl deserved some symbol of the exotic journalist's life she'd always wanted, even if in truth that life did not exist.

CHAPTER 81

COLONEL GRIFFITH MACKIEVER watched Special Agent Kaiser's face as he studied the computer screen on the desk in the study of the Valhalla hunting lodge.

"How long have you had this video?" Kaiser asked, shaking his head as he replayed it.

"I got it yesterday," Mackiever replied.

"Where?"

"I'd rather not say just yet."

Kaiser looked up momentarily, then reviewed the video again. "Those are definitely your SWAT officers?"

Mackiever nodded. "I'm sure of it. That's definitely one of our spotting scopes, and I know I've heard those voices before."

"And they just killed those kids in cold blood."

"I think that's the only possible interpretation of that footage. I'm trying to identify the two speakers based on their voices, but I have to be careful. I'm not sure who I can trust in my tech division."

Kaiser pushed the computer away and leaned back in the chair. "If that goes public, it'll do irreparable damage to the state police."

"I realize that. I've been struggling with this decision, and in all honesty, I'd prefer not to use it."

"But . . . ?"

"It may be the only way to bring down Forrest Knox. And if it is . . . then I'll use it."

Kaiser nodded thoughtfully. "How can you tie Forrest Knox to this video if you don't know who the men in it are?"

"The video was found on a computer in Knox's residence."

Kaiser looked up sharply. "You searched his home?"

"I didn't say that."

Kaiser mulled this over. He obviously had enough experience to know he should not ask questions he did not want the answers to. "Why bring it to me?" he asked finally.

"I have a feeling you want to stop Knox as badly as I do."

Kaiser's reaction was difficult to read. "Let me ask you a question, Colonel. I've read Forrest's LSP record. You promoted him twice after you took over the state police. You elevated him to his present position. Can you explain that?"

Mackiever had asked himself this a thousand times. And the answer was depressingly simple. "He was the smartest son of a bitch under my command. He tested off the charts on paper, and he was the best man in the field, bar none. By any objective standard, he ought to be sitting in my chair."

"I see. But . . . ?"

"It took me a few years to recognize his problem, because he's so good at hiding it."

"Which is?"

"He's a pure sociopath. But he's not like the robot types we've both arrested before. He's got a genuine warmth that people relate to. He's more like a highly intelligent wolf than a shark. A thinking predator, if you get my meaning."

Kaiser smiled strangely. "That's basically the definition of a human being."

This brought Mackiever up short. "Well . . . multiply that times ten, and maybe you'll know what I'm trying to get across. Am I wrong about you wanting to nail Forrest?"

Kaiser closed the computer, slipped the flash drive into his pocket, and stood. "No, sir. You're not. I've got a lot of evidence to process, but this could be the straw that breaks that bastard's back. We've got to find the men in this video."

"What do you want me to do?" Mackiever asked.

WELL AFTER MIDNIGHT, A steady knocking awakened Jordan from alcohol-induced sleep. When she got to the door in one of John's T-shirts, she found a Cuban army officer standing in the hall. The captain was in no mood to be patient, but she forced him to take the time to convince her that the Cuban president was summoning her to his estate for a legitimate purpose, and not for some fantasy of a late-night booty call. After she dressed, Jordan carried her camera bag into the hall, but the officer shook his head and said she would have to rely on her memory. No recording devices of any kind would be allowed—not even a notebook and pen.

The car that carried her west past the Bay of Pigs was a black vintage Cadillac limousine with bulletproof glass. The captain did not once look into his rearview mirror to check Jordan out. She didn't know whether this was out of fear of his commander in chief, or because he'd driven so many women to see Castro in this way that he no longer had any interest in the process.

Their destination proved to be a mansion on the beach with its own private marina, a palace guarded by at least a dozen soldiers and fully staffed by maids and a butler. This was an eye-opening experience, considering that the tenant was theoretically the leader of a Communist revolution.

The butler escorted her to a well-appointed study whose walls displayed dozens of framed photographs dating to the 1950s and '60s. Rubbing the sleep from her eyes, Jordan walked slowly down the wall and tried to identify various African and Central American leaders. She recognized Patrice Lumumba, Thomas Sankara, Evo Morales, and of course the pale Soviet premiers grinning as they smoked cigars with Fidel. She was a little surprised to see Castro with his arm around Che Guevara, since she'd heard the Cuban president had been jealous of his more glamorous comrade-in-arms.

"Thank you for coming," a voice behind her said in Spanish.

She whirled to find the president standing inside the door, watching her.

"I'm told you were sleeping," he said. "I'm afraid I'm at the age where sleep has deserted me, at least as anything but a torment."

Jordan elected the direct approach. "Why have you brought me here?"

Castro came farther into the room, then sat in a heavily padded chair and put his slippered feet on an ottoman. All she could think about was how frizzy his white beard looked beneath the pasty face. Gone was the virile, black-haired firebrand who had so impressed her twenty years ago.

"The things you asked me today started me thinking," he said. "I found myself unable to stop. I finally decided that the time has come to pass on some information to the U.S. government. I will not do it officially, but . . ." The president looked up at her with a flash of his old intensity. "It's my understanding that your husband may be working with some older men who remember the Kennedy years as clearly as I do. They call themselves the Working Group. Do you know anything about that?"

While Jordan considered how to respond, the president motioned for her to take the seat opposite him.

"Maybe," she said. "I know he's working with a retired agent named Dwight Stone." She perched on the edge of the chair. "Stone's very ill, and my husband wants to find out who was responsible for what happened in Dallas before time runs out for Stone."

Castro gave her a tight smile. "Just so."

"You obviously know more than you told me today, or in your note."

"Oh, yes, the flower. How childish of me, yes?"

"It was beautiful."

The president inclined his head. "So . . . let us speak of assassination. I myself have survived over six hundred attempts on my life since taking office."

"Six hundred?"

"That I know of. Nearly a dozen of those were planned and carried out by the CIA at the direction of the Kennedy administration. Some of those were facilitated by what you call the Mafia. This is well documented, of course. Not news, as you say."

"Yes, I've read about that."

"Then let me tell you something about which you have not read."

Jordan waited.

"In 1967, a man with a rifle tried to assassinate me in the Plaza de la Revolución. Had my security services not been warned by one of the man's confederates, he probably would have succeeded. He was set up to shoot me from seven hundred yards away, and he had the skill to make such a shot."

"What nationality was the shooter?"

"French Corsican."

"I see. Was he killed?"

"Not immediately. He was wounded during his capture. Then he was questioned by the security services. He subsequently died during this process, but not before telling most of what he knew."

Jordan had the feeling that the Corsican's confession was what she had been brought here to hear.

"And?"

"The story he told was quite interesting. He had been hired to kill me by two American Mafia leaders. Santo Trafficante and Carlos Marcello."

Jordan felt an unexpected thrill. "Have you confirmed that he was telling the truth?"

This time Castro's smile had a reptilian quality to it. "He was telling the truth, you can believe me. But I wasn't very interested in his story. The Mafia has wanted its casinos back ever since 1959. They will never get them. Sometime after I die, Cuba will revert to capitalism and the Walt Disney company will have Mickey Mouse running the damned casinos."

For a moment Jordan wondered if the Cuban leader were drunk. In any case, he now seemed to be lost in his own memories. She decided the best thing to do was let him ramble.

"The story that interested me also involved Señor Marcello. By 1967, I had of course heard the craziest theories imaginable about who killed Kennedy. Like Robert Ludlum stories, you know?"

"Yes."

"Justice Warren's commission probed many of these theories. But one name that never appeared in the Warren Commission Report was Carlos Marcello. It was as though this man had been rendered invisible during the investigations. But the Corsican told me a very simple story. He said Robert Kennedy had been in the process of deporting Marcello permanently from the United States, and the only way Marcello could stop this was to neutralize the attorney general. To do this, he decided to kill the president. It was no Machiavellian stratagem by the CIA, the military, or corporate America. It was simply a matter of survival."

"Did this Corsican claim to have been the shooter?"

"No. That was partly what convinced me he was telling the truth. He was not claiming to be the assassin and asking to be spared because of it. He was simply emptying his brain to spare himself further pain."

Jordan shuddered at the thought of the agony concealed behind the clinical coldness of that phrase.

"He said the shooter was a man who had trained exiles in preparation for Playa Girón at camps in Louisiana. He was one of the white-robed racists, a KKK man. He was also a former U.S. marine, like Oswald. Unlike Oswald, however, he was supposedly a man of great competence."

"Did the Corsican give this man a name?"

The president vouchsafed Jordan another tight smile. "*Sí*, he did."

"What was it?"

Castro closed his eyes for a moment, then shook his head. "I think it best not to go that far at this time."

Jordan struggled to contain her frustration. "If you learned this in 1967, why has it never been made public?"

"For several reasons, *mi cariño*. First, my security services did not want anyone knowing that a foreign assassin had come so close to killing me. Second, quite frankly, it served the purposes of the Revolution to have the American public mistrust its leaders. Far better for the man in the street to fear that the CIA or some corporate big shots had murdered their King Arthur, and not some Sicilian gangster trying to save his business."

Jordan sat quietly, trying to process what she'd been told, and why. "And the Corsican died?"

"*Sí*. Badly."

"What do you want me to do with this information?"

The president studied his fingernails for a while. Then he said, "I want you to pass it to your husband. Tell him not to try to contact me for confirmation. I will not confirm it. I tell you now, tonight, because you presented me with a completely unofficial way to let the right people know what we know."

Jordan didn't know whether to thank him, ask more questions, or prepare to leave.

"You are a beautiful woman, Ms. Glass. You have aged very well since that day we met in 1987."

"Was that the year?" Jordan asked. "I wasn't sure."

"Yes. I, sadly, have not aged nearly so well. Were I ten years younger I would ask you to stay the night."

Jordan shifted on the chair. She'd been afraid this was coming. "You know I'm a married woman."

Castro gave her a jaded smile. "Different women view marriage in different ways. I notice you have not taken your husband's surname."

"No. But I'm afraid I'm the one-man variety, neverthe-less."

The light of flirtation died in his eyes. "Pity. Well . . . you've heard what I wanted to tell you. My driver will take you back to your hotel."

Jordan got to her feet before he could have any second thoughts and moved toward the door. As she passed the president, he touched her arm, and looked up at her.

"Any more questions before we say good-bye?"

She knew she should go on, but she stopped anyway. She fought the urge to ask what he was doing living in opulence while his people struggled, but she figured she knew the answer already. Power corrupts, regardless of nationality or philosophy. Instead, she asked, "What will you do if someone makes this information public?"

The old man shrugged. "It's an American problem. I leave it in their hands. I only have one regret."

"What's that?"

"I wish I had let Mrs. Kennedy know this information before she died. Perhaps it might have brought her some peace."

She gave the dictator a last generous smile, then walked into the hall and hurried toward the mansion's door. She thought of Caitlin as she passed between the luxurious an-tiques and crystal lamps, but once she was outside, in the tropical air, she remembered that Dwight Stone was fight-ing for his life in a Denver hospital. As the army officer shut her into the backseat of the limo, she wondered whether the Corsican's story would bolster Stone's will to live. If not, at least it might give him some peace before he died.

IN THE WELL OF the night, Walt looked up from Tom's unquiet bed and saw Pithy Nolan's electric wheel-chair silhouetted in the door to the hall. This time the old woman did not remain at a distance, but whirred softly into the room and came around the bed so that she would be close to Walt. Her eyes glimmered in the spill of light from the hallway.

"I smelled your cigar in my room earlier, Captain."

"I'm sorry about that. I needed to settle my nerves."

"Don't apologize. It's good to smell men in this house again. It reminded me of Tom. He never smokes in my presence anymore, but I can always smell that cigar on his clothes."

Walt smiled to himself. Many times during his life he had looked up or turned at the smell of certain cigars and expected to find Tom Cage standing there.

Pithy Nolan let her gaze fall on Tom for half a minute. "I've heard some upsetting news," she whispered. "About the girl Penn was set to marry."

"I know about that."

"Have you told Tom?"

"He knows. It's weighing mighty heavy on him, too."

The old woman regarded Tom again. Walt had the feeling she saw very deeply, despite her lack of medical knowledge.

"How much danger is he in?" she asked. "I don't feel that he's dying, but . . ."

"He could die, all right. He should be in a hospital. But this is the way he wants it."

Pithy nodded. "He's a stubborn man."

"Do you know why he's doing this?" Walt asked.

The wise eyes returned to Walt's face. "Do you not?"

"Up to a point, I guess. But no further."

Pithy Nolan reached down and sucked a deep inha-lation from the oxygen mask on her lap. Then she said, "He's not doing it for himself. Tom Cage almost never did anything for himself. This man takes care of people.

That's his purpose on earth. And he'll die fulfilling it, if the gods require it."

Walt thought about this. "Makes it a mite tough on the people who care about him."

Pithy nodded, the ghost of a smile upon her lips. "Those who love heroes must walk a stony road." Then the smile vanished, and her eyes pierced Walt to the quick. "Sometimes we must share their end, as well."

At some level, Walt figured, he had always known this. "I understand."

"I read Classics at university," Pithy said, a hint of wistfulness in her reedy voice. "Do you remember the Spartans?"

"I think so, ma'am."

"I didn't care much for them. The Spartans didn't deserve the glorification they got. But they did have a rather succinct saying that's never left me. Nothing is more apt when things come to the sticking point."

"What was that?"

The piercing eyes found his eyes. "'Come back with your shield—or on it.' Did you ever hear that saying?"

"Yes, ma'am. And I've been in that situation myself. With Tom, as a matter of fact."

"You must have acquitted yourself well."

Walt wasn't so sure.

"My husband never returned from the war," Pithy said quietly. "He's resting somewhere at the bottom of the Pacific Ocean. But his shield is with him. He's sleeping in it. A Curtiss Warhawk."

In his mind, Walt saw a brave American boy in an aging P-40 being cut to ribbons by a swarm of quicker-turning Zeros. He jumped when Pithy reached out and laid her papery hand on his. It felt featherlight, and neither warm nor cold. But through her thin skin Walt felt something like an electric current running into him.

"I'm going to send Flora in with food and tea," she said. "Then you need rest, Captain. Marshal your strength. There's no telling what might be required of you before this business is concluded."

The regal old woman gave him a sad smile, then turned her chair with the touch of a finger and whirred out of the room like a queen borne upon a royal litter.

SATURDAY

CHAPTER 82

WALT AWAKENED TO pale light leaking through the heavy drapes of the guest room. His back ached from sleeping on the cot, and his head throbbed from lack of caffeine. Rising onto one elbow, he saw that Tom was not in his bed, and his heart began to race. He scrambled up off the flimsy cot and hurried around the bed, afraid he would find his friend lying dead on the floor.

The floor was empty.

Walt rushed out to the hallway, into darkness. A column of light rose from the well of the staircase, filled with dust motes, and through its lambent swirl he saw a crack of brighter light beneath a door at the end of the corridor. Relieved, he rubbed his eyes and trudged down the hall to the bathroom.

When he opened the door, he saw Tom standing before the sink in shorts, hacking at his face with a safety razor like a man who'd decided that his beard offended God. The IV bag hung from the brass stem of a wall sconce, still trickling saline into Tom's arm. Last night's exhaustion had vanished from his eyes. Now they looked . . . not quite *wild*, but filled with almost messianic intensity.

"What the hell are you doing?" Walt asked.

"Shaving." Tom hadn't even looked in Walt's direction. "You finally got some sleep?"

"*Why* are you shaving?"

Tom shrugged and kept hacking at his face. "It's been a while." He rinsed white hair from the blade and went back to the task.

Yeah, like fifty years, Walt thought. He hadn't seen his friend without facial hair since Korea. Tom's white mus-

tache and beard had become so much a part of his identity that their absence was almost tangible. The new face
being revealed in the mirror disoriented him. The strong
jawline Walt remembered from the army had emerged,
taking ten years off his friend.

"You look like a man with a plan," Walt said.

"Maybe. Where's Caitlin's body?"

Walt didn't like the sound of that. "I imagine they've
got her down in Baton Rouge, awaiting autopsy. She was
DOA from a gunshot, so it's a coroner's case."

Tom closed his eyes and breathed like a man forced to
expend a significant fraction of his energy just to move
his diaphragm.

"Are you okay?" Walt asked.

"I'm functioning. Which is more than I can say for
that poor girl."

Walt waited for whatever was going to come next.
Grief did strange things to people, and Tom was unlikely
to be an exception.

He turned to Walt, squinching his mouth up so that
he could shave the whiskers between his lips and chin.
"What was Caitlin doing down in that swamp? I didn't
even ask her."

Walt shrugged. "Searching for bodies, probably. And
if she hadn't gone down there and found you, yours would
have been the next one."

"So she took my place. You think that's a fair trade? A
thirty-five-year-old with her whole life ahead of her for a
man at death's door?"

Walt shook his head. "Life don't work that way, pard,
and you know it. What happens, happens. There's no
sense to it."

Tom rinsed the razor again, examined his face, then
went back to scraping off the remains of his beard.

"Come on," Walt said. "What are you thinking?"

"First . . . I need to call Penn. I need to apologize."

"I don't think that's a good idea. Not unless you're
ready to turn yourself in. Penn's being guarded by the
FBI, and he's probably pretty upset with you today. If you
call him, they're going to trace you, and—"

"I am ready, Walt."

Walt blinked in confusion. "Ready for what?"

"On top of everything else I've done this week, I got Caitlin killed and I've turned you into a fugitive. It's too late for me to help Caitlin, but not to help you. I figure we're down to two choices. We can either kill Forrest Knox, or I can turn myself in to the FBI."

Walt didn't answer right away. He'd given the first option considerable thought during the night, and he'd decided it was suicidal. Of course, Tom already knew that, and he was probably resigned to it. Or maybe *resigned* wasn't the right word. He was at peace with it. Drawn to it, even. The way a lot of guilty men were drawn toward death.

"As for door number one," Walt said, "I'm not anxious to make Carmelita a widow. And I can't see us getting out of that play alive."

Tom turned to him and held out his right arm. "Then will you pull this damned IV out? I did it once yesterday, and it wasn't much fun."

"I will, if you tell me about that second option."

Tom dropped his arm to his side. "On Thursday, Caitlin told me that Agent Kaiser would offer me protective custody if I could give the Bureau information about the Kennedy assassination."

Walt had to think about this for a minute. "The Kennedy assassination?"

"That's right."

"What the hell do you know about that?"

"More than you'd think, I'm sorry to say. I knew Carlos Marcello back in New Orleans, when I was a medical extern at the parish prison. Our paths crossed a few times after that, and I got pulled into something I didn't really understand."

Walt felt as though the floor had shifted beneath him. "Well, ain't you full of surprises."

"The point is, I may be able to buy protection from Kaiser with what I know. Hopefully for you and me both. And I think it's high time I did."

"How exactly are you going to do this without getting killed?"

"You're going to coordinate the negotiation, with those burn phones of yours. And I'm going to arrange a surrender in a very public place."

"It sounds like you already have somewhere in mind."

"I do."

Walt sighed, dreading the answer. "I'm afraid to ask."

"It's somewhere I would have gone anyway. Henry Sexton's funeral."

"Oh, hell. That's crazy. You'd be recognized and arrested before you could cross the church parking lot."

Tom patted his clean-shaven face. "I don't think so."

"*That's* your idea of a disguise?"

Tom nodded with surprising confidence.

Walt had to admit he might not have recognized his friend in a crowd if he hadn't known about the missing beard ahead of time. And even then . . .

Tom tossed his wet towel into the bathtub, where it landed with a slap. "I'm the last person the Knoxes would expect to show up at that funeral. And if *they* show, we'll let Kaiser worry about them."

"Where's Sexton's funeral gonna be? Louisiana, I'd guess."

"The Early Funeral Home in Ferriday," Tom confirmed. "Jim Early owns that business. I've known him thirty-five years. He's buried many a patient of mine. Visitation probably doesn't start until nine A.M. at the earliest. It's only six thirty now. Jim'll let us in before anybody gets there, and then he can smuggle us over to the church without anybody the wiser."

Walt slapped his thigh. "You're some damn piece of work, I swear. You've got cops from two states and the FBI on your tail, and you want to visit a funeral home to see a dead man who'll never even know you were there? If you want to turn yourself in, call Kaiser and arrange to do it in the middle of nowhere. Hell, do it *here*! This old mausoleum is perfect."

Tom's gaze remained on Walt, his eyes cold and leaden with intransigence. "Henry Sexton died in part because of things I did. Also things I didn't do. I'm going to pay my respects to him, even if it is too late."

Walt shook his head. "You're suicidal, bud."

"What if that was you lying dead over in Ferriday?"

"I'd yell up from the fiery furnace for you to light out while you could and pour a whiskey for me later, once you were safe and dry."

"No, you wouldn't. So get this damned IV out of me." Tom held out his arm and made a fist.

"Mrs. Nolan ain't gonna like this plan," Walt grumbled.

"Wait and see."

Remembering last night's strange conversation, Walt decided Tom might be right. "I think she's had some sort of vision about the end of this business. And I think maybe we die in it."

Before Tom could answer, Walt yanked the IV catheter out of his wrist and pressed Tom's free thumb against the bloody hole.

"We all die," Tom said, scanning the floor for something. "I've been watching it from the bedside for fifty years. It's *how* you go that matters—not when. You know that. That's why you came to Mississippi when I called. Now, help me find my goddamn pants."

CHAPTER 83

SPECIAL AGENT BOYD Bertolet watched Snake Knox and four other men in their seventies walk out of the main entrance of the Concordia Sheriff's Department and pause at the top of the stairs.

"Looks like a geriatric walking club," said his partner, Sheila Stowers.

Boyd saw at least three vehicles waiting to pick up the newly released Double Eagles. "Watch who gets in what car. Do you recognize Snake?"

"Oh, yeah," Sheila said. "He's the wiry old fucker. The crankiest-looking bastard in the bunch."

"I don't even get why the boss is letting them out. You know they killed Thornfield yesterday. Even if that meth disappeared, we could have held them—especially with Kaiser invoking the Patriot Act."

"Kaiser knows what he's doing," Sheila said. "If he's letting these guys walk, he's got a damn good reason. But you and I won't ever be told what it is. We'll just have to pay attention down the line."

Three Double Eagles walked down the steps, then climbed into the waiting cars and pickup trucks. Snake accompanied the last man, but Boyd didn't see him get into any vehicle. Instead, Snake seemed to be walking along the front wall of the courthouse, away from the vehicles.

"Where's he going?" Boyd asked.

"I don't know," Sheila said, a note of concern in her voice.

"Do you see anybody waiting to pick him up over that way?"

"Nope. Just parked cars."

Bertolet grunted and watched Snake Knox walk toward the edge of the parking lot, which abutted the parking lot of a single-story shopping center on the east side of the courthouse.

"I'll bet somebody's waiting for him in a car over in that lot," Sheila guessed. "Whoever it is didn't want the courthouse cameras to record their face. Let's see if we can get a look."

She picked up her radio and called a second surveillance car, asked them to pull into the shopping center lot and be sure they saw Knox get into whatever vehicle was waiting for him.

"He moves pretty good for a seventy-year-old man," Boyd commented.

"He still flies crop dusters, which means he's a long way from dead. Let's pull out to the main road. We'll pick them up when they leave the lot."

"Let's give it a minute," Boyd said, keeping his eyes on Snake's diminishing figure.

"Uh-oh," Sheila said.

"What?"

"Look." She pointed toward the shopping center. Snake Knox had just climbed onto an orange-and-white motorcycle and kick-started it. Bertolet could see smoke blooming from the exhaust pipe.

"Tell me that's not a dirt bike," he said.

"It's a dirt bike. Looks like a 250."

"Fuck."

Boyd jammed the Ford into gear and hit the accelerator, but even as he did he saw Snake pull onto the grass lawn beside the shopping center, then spin a shower of gravel into the air as he took off toward the tree line far behind the stores. His front wheel lifted off the ground from the force of his acceleration.

"Look at that shit!" Boyd cried.

"I told you," Sheila said. "A goddamn crop duster. What do you expect?" She keyed her radio and said, "What are you waiting for? Get this car up onto the grass and try to stay with him."

"There's no way," Boyd said. "He'll be in those trees in thirty seconds, and without air support, he might as well be in Mexico. He's gone."

"I know."

"We need a goddamn drone."

"I wonder if we have an aircraft close," Stowers said. "Kaiser might divert the chopper to keep eyes on Snake Knox."

"Give it a try," Boyd said, aiming the Ford at the space between the courthouse and the shopping center. "I sure wish this was a rental."

SNAKE WAS THREE MILES from the courthouse when he stopped the Honda. He'd lost the FBI after the first half mile, as he'd known he would, so he'd taken care to ride the last two miles under heavy tree cover. He'd found the pistol and the cell phone he'd requested in a leather bag attached to the handlebars, and during the ride over, he'd called his illegitimate son and told him to be parked by a certain borrow pit fifteen minutes later. Unlike the pit where Deke Dunn had died, this one lay north of Highway 84, but otherwise the topography was the same.

Snake put the motorcycle back in gear, rode to the edge of the water, then stashed the bike behind some thick cottonwoods and waited. If Forrest meant to kill him, it was likely to happen here, now.

After two minutes, a navy blue pickup truck nosed up the little dirt road, stopped thirty feet from the water, and fell silent. Through the windshield Snake saw two familiar faces. One belonged to Alois Engel—his son—the other to Wilma Deen. He wondered how far he could trust them. Most bastard sons carried a heavy burden of anger, and Alois was no different. And while Wilma was no fan of Forrest's, she didn't like Snake much better, considering how he'd treated her over the years. He'd screwed her when she was young and attractive and ignored her all the decades since.

Snake listened hard for other engine sounds, but he heard none.

After another minute, he walked into the open with his pistol in his hand and beckoned them out of the truck. They moved naturally as they got out—no shared glances or any other signs of nerves—so Snake calmed down a little.

"Everything cool?" Alois asked.

"Worked like a charm," Snake said, walking toward the truck. "The Fibbies don't know what hit 'em."

"What do we do now?"

Snake studied the boy before he answered. Alois looked nothing like him. Snake saw his mother in the blond hair and too-close-together eyes. "Dump the bike in the water," he said, "and get the hell out of here. It's over behind those trees."

Alois nodded and went to take care of it. When he was out of earshot, Wilma said, "I don't like your boy much. Thinks he knows everything."

"Shows the apple don't fall far from the tree."

She laughed bitterly. "You got that right." Wilma looked over her shoulder and watched Alois run the Honda into the black water. "Look, before he gets back," she said, "I heard something you might want to know."

"What's that?"

"I got a friend who works part-time at the motel where them FBI agents are staying."

"And?"

"She tells me her manager asked her to plant some bugs in their rooms yesterday."

Snake went on alert. He'd heard nothing about this from Forrest. "Keep going. Who's this manager?"

"Name's Wade Kimball."

Snake smiled. Kimball's father had been a Klansman back in the day, and the son fancied himself a right-wing blogger. "Little Wade," Snake said. "Forrest must have put him up to that. Where else would he get the bugs? Does your friend know who's monitoring the transmissions?"

"Kimball himself, she thinks. He's been locked up in his office ever since the bugs went in."

Snake couldn't believe his luck.

Alois walked back up to them and said, "What now?"

"Now?" Snake grinned. "Now we're gonna kill some people."

The boy's mouth twitched a couple of times, then broke into a slit of a smile. After years of waiting, the hard-core action he'd been craving was at hand. Snake had figured Alois would be more than ready.

"Who?" Alois asked.

"Penn Cage and his old man. Maybe even that FBI agent, Kaiser."

Wilma drew back her head, her eyes unbelieving. "That sounds pretty damn stupid to me."

"You want to go sit home and watch your soap operas, go ahead."

"I'm ready," Alois said. "Where are they?"

"The mayor's home right now and covered by about twenty cops. But later on, he won't be. And neither will his father."

"Where'll they be?"

"I'd lay odds on Henry Sexton's funeral."

"How do you know that?" Wilma asked.

"Because that's what guys like them do. They follow the rules, observe the social niceties. And that makes it easy for us to pick them up."

"Are we going to hit them *at* the funeral?" Alois asked, his eyes wide.

"Depends on who else is there. We might do it there, or right after. Or we might wait and stage something interesting. But either way, we move today."

CHAPTER 84

WALT FELT MORE than a little anxious crossing the river back into Louisiana after killing the state trooper only four days ago. Thankfully, Darius had agreed to drive them (and in Flora's Lincoln, not Pithy's Bentley, which would have been like driving through India in Queen Elizabeth's golden carriage). Walt had tried to enlist Pithy in his effort to dissuade Tom from visiting Henry's remains, but as he'd feared, the old woman had predicted that no evil would come from Tom paying proper respect to the dead. This hadn't reassured Walt, but neither Tom nor Pithy had paid him any mind. He felt like the insignificant shield bearer that Pithy seemed to think he was.

The miles flowed by under Darius's sure hands and feet, Tom as silent as a pilgrim nearing a holy shrine, and soon they reached the west side of Ferriday, where Early's Funeral Home stood. The business occupied a columned two-story Greek Revival house, while the owner lived in a simple ranch-style home next door, a bass boat parked on a trailer to the side and martin boxes on poles in the yard.

Walt felt some trepidation as Darius went to the door to summon Mr. Early to the Lincoln, but once the owner of the funeral home stopped gawking at Tom's missing beard, he couldn't move quickly enough to please his guest. Two minutes after they'd pulled up, Jim Early was letting them into the funeral home through the back door.

Tom thanked Darius and asked if he'd mind going to a convenience store and picking up a couple of Diet Cokes, and their driver agreed without a word. Walt didn't like the idea of losing their transportation, but once again Tom ignored his concern.

Mr. Early led them to the room where the pre-service visitation was to be held for Sexton. A gleaming metal casket lay at the head of the room, already surrounded by flowers. By necessity, Early informed them solemnly, the funeral would be a closed-casket affair. The reporter had been burned beyond all recognition. Brody Royal had suffered the same fate. After shaking both their hands, Early excused himself to begin preparations for the day's operations.

Walt told Tom to get on with his business, since they were basically sitting ducks. Tom had already arranged his surrender to the FBI, but Agent Kaiser didn't expect him to turn up until midway through the church service, after the crowd had been seated. Walt had brought a pistol along, but he knew better than to think he'd get the drop on another state trooper like he had with the one by the borrow pits. This time, if the staties came, it'd be the SWAT boys with body armor, tactical sights, and pump Remingtons.

Tom walked up to the casket and laid his hand on the lid, right about where Henry's chest would be. He was speaking softly when a woman who had to be eighty entered the back of the room. She started when Walt nodded at her, as if shocked to find someone here. But then, after staring at Tom's back for a while, something in her gaze softened, and she shuffled forward.

Walt followed softly behind her, more out of curiosity than anything. As she neared the coffin, Tom turned and looked at her. Walt saw then that his friend's eyes were wet. Tom held out his right hand to the woman.

"Hello, Virginia."

The newcomer gave Tom her quivering hand, and Walt saw that it was a working woman's hand, callused and scaly from many washings.

"Dr. Cage?" she said hesitantly. "Is that you?" She laughed self-consciously. "I didn't recognize you at first."

"It's quite all right, Virginia. I shaved my beard."

Mrs. Sexton looked blankly around the room, then shook her head like someone lost. "Lord, Doc . . . you're one of the few people I could stand seeing right now. What are you doing here?"

Tom's face reddened. "I came to pay my respects to your son. You may have heard that the police are looking for me, and I hope you're not offended."

Mrs. Sexton dismissed his concern. "No, no. I'm glad to see you. You were so good to us back in the old days. It meant so much to me, and to Henry."

"I was just doing my job, Virginia."

"Oh, no. You do your work the way my Henry always did his. It's not a job to you. It's a *calling*. That's mighty rare these days, I'm sad to say."

Tom nodded. "Henry was working with my daughter-in-law, you know. Caitlin Masters. Or my future daughter-in-law, I should say. I lost her yesterday. She was killed by the same bunch that got your boy."

Mrs. Sexton laid her hand on Tom's forearm and squeezed, and her eyes said, *Have strength.*

"Caitlin loved to chase big stories," Tom said. "And she was good at it. But your son was different. He reminded me of my boy, actually. Henry was a crusader, like Penn. He didn't work for the glory, but for truth. For real justice. *That's* what's rare in this day and age. You taught him well, Virginia. Henry believed right and wrong are as plain as day and night, and it's a man's duty to stand up and be counted, no matter what the cost."

Tears welled in Mrs. Sexton's eyes, then slid down her cheeks. She did not wipe them. "You're right, Doc. But Lord, what that costs."

"The last full measure," Tom said softly.

"Beg 'pardon?"

"I was quoting President Lincoln. Henry gave the last full measure of devotion to his cause."

"Oh . . . yes. I remember now," Mrs. Sexton said in a voice of detached wonder. "Did I have to memorize that in school?"

"You probably did."

Virginia Sexton looked over at Walt, who smiled awkwardly, being a stranger. Then she said, "Dr. Cage, I wonder if I could ask you something?"

"Anything."

"It would mean the world to me if you would say a few words over Henry. It would have meant a lot to him, too."

Tom looked stunned by her request. "Actually—"

"Don't say no, now. I struggled and fretted over who to ask for a eulogy, and I'd about decided on his publisher. But somehow I just haven't felt settled with it. And the

way you put that just now . . . that's what I want people
to understand about my boy. And coming from you, well,
it would really mean something. Everybody knows what
kind of man you are, no matter what any law says. Folks
know you. And they care about what you say."

"Actually, I came here expressly to ask you if I might
say a few words during the service."

The old woman's eyes brightened. "Really?"

"Yes. Henry's passing affected me a lot more than
you might suspect. It made me realize some things about
myself."

Mrs. Sexton looked flabbergasted by this turn of
events. "Well, I never . . . of course. You say whatever you
feel called to."

Tom took Mrs. Sexton's hands in his and squeezed
them. "I'm going to leave you alone with him now, Virginia. But I'll see you at the service. And if you would,
please don't mention to anyone that I'll be speaking. I'll
have Mr. Early inform the pastor."

"I understand. But . . . could you stay here a little
longer, Doc? You see, I don't have anybody left now that
Henry's gone."

Tom looked back and gave Walt an apologetic glance,
then put his right arm around Mrs. Sexton and stood
before the coffin in silence. Walt wondered what his
friend was thinking. Tom never went to funerals, seeing
them as a reminder that in the end, a physician always lost
his battles with death. For his part, Walt was thinking
about the hours still to pass between now and the moment
when the FBI would take Tom into protective custody.
So long as they were in Louisiana, someone could alert
Forrest or Snake Knox to that fact. And if they did, then
Mr. Early would be doing a land-office business in caskets
before the day was through.

CHAPTER 85

"FBI'S PULLING OUT," said Alphonse Ozan. "I just got word. They're staying down at the Bone Tree, but they're pulling out of the lodge."

"Wasn't anything there for them to find," Forrest said.

The two men faced each other across Forrest's kitchen counter. His wife had left for her yoga class fifteen minutes ago, and Forrest had brewed a second pot of coffee.

"So what now?" Ozan asked.

"We go right back in there like we have nothing to hide. I'll call Billy and get him headed toward Valhalla in his plane. I want Kaiser and Mackiever to see I'm going to brazen this through."

"And Snake?"

"Snake did what he said he was going to do. At this point, the best thing is to let him be himself. Given what I read in the paper this morning, I'm betting somebody's not going to live through this day."

"Who?"

"I'm not sure. But I'll make one prediction. The mayor's under round-the-clock protection, but I think there's a good chance he'll show up at Henry Sexton's funeral. Dr. Cage will want to go too, out of guilt, but he won't be able to risk it. There's bound to be some FBI agents there—paying their respects, if nothing else."

"You think Mayor Cage will want go to that funeral right after his fiancée was killed?"

"Especially after that. I figured he might be a pall-bearer, but he's not."

Ozan looked unconvinced. "Would Snake really try to hit Cage at a funeral with FBI agents present?"

"Why not? This isn't like the hospital, where he had to shoot through glass. The service is at Early's Funeral Home. Mourners have to walk in from their cars, then walk out again. Probably wait in line, too, at this service. Snake could stand off with his sniper rifle, pop anybody he wants from five or six hundred yards out, and still get away clean."

Ozan thought about this. "I guess it's a good thing he's not coming after us, huh, boss?"

Forrest felt a ripple of foreboding along the skin of his arms. "You're damn right. Snake's gotta believe we're on his side right up to the second I put a hollow-point in his head."

THE TWENTY-EIGHT-STORY state capitol building dominated the Baton Rouge cityscape like a spike against the sky, and it was the key offices in that building to which Colonel Griffith Mackiever had been trying to gain access for two days. Stymied at every turn, he'd finally been forced to settle for a glass-and-steel box within sight of the capitol: a branch of one of the wealthiest private banks in Louisiana. Victor Marchand, its chairman, was not only an architect of the secret plan to transform post-Katrina New Orleans into a much whiter city that could bring back the corporate tenants it had lost in recent decades, but also one of Forrest Knox's most powerful supporters in his bid to be the next superintendent of state police. Marchand's influence in the political corridors of Baton Rouge was second only to his power within the less visible conclaves of New Orleans. Short of the capitol, there was no better place to test the power of the weapon Walt Garrity had given Mackiever than Marchand's office.

The colonel watched the banker sit behind his desk and fold his arms in what Mackiever could only interpret as a combative position. A handsome and urbane fifty-five, Marchand was dressed to the nines—probably for some fund-raising luncheon—but Mackiever couldn't imagine an honest citizen giving this man any money. An executive assistant stood behind his boss like a cross between a bodyguard and an attack dog.

"I assume," said the banker, "you understand that I don't relish being asked to come into my office on a Saturday to see a child molester."

"*Alleged* child molester," Mackiever said, nervously gripping the notebook computer in his lap.

"It's only at the strong insistence of the FBI that I've agreed to see you."

But here you sit, Mackiever thought. After being publicly pilloried by the media, he could not deny the degree to which he would enjoy the next two minutes.

"I'm sorry to have to say this," said Marchand, not sounding sorry at all, "but I see absolutely no reason to postpone your resignation, which frankly we expected long before now. No matter what you have to show me, neither I nor my associates in government can possibly intervene in a matter that will soon be under adjudication. We're going to have to let law enforcement and the courts settle this."

Mackiever opened his computer and made sure it was powered up with the appropriate file cued in the viewing program.

"I hope that contains your resignation letter," the banker said.

Mackiever stepped forward and set the computer on the desk, the screen facing Marchand. "If you'll just hit Play, I think you'll understand a lot better where things actually stand."

"What am I about to see?" the banker asked irritably. "Not anything illegal, I hope?"

"Very much so, I'm afraid."

"I'm not going to look at child pornography."

"Just hit Play. You'll understand."

After a heavy sigh, Marchand started the video. Mackiever knew from watching Kaiser's face what he should expect, or he thought he did. But the banker's eyes went so wide during the executions that he looked as though he were watching the kiddie porn that Mackiever had been accused of trafficking in.

"Are those men doing the firing police officers?" he asked.

"At least two are. And they are under the direct command of Forrest Knox."

Marchand swallowed, then glanced at his assistant. "When did this happen?"

"One day after the storm made landfall, before General Honoré took over the city."

"Jesus, Mary, and Joseph. And who was that I saw shot?"

"Drug dealers. Specifically, African-American drug dealers."

"Why were they shot like that?"

"Because they were cutting into the profits of Forrest Knox's ongoing drug operations. And by that I do *not* mean his *anti*-drug law enforcement operations. I mean his family's drug *sales* operations."

The banker blinked in disbelief. "Are you saying—"

"That Forrest Knox uses his troops as a private enforcement arm of his family's drug smuggling and sales organization? Yes."

Marchand closed his eyes. He had just glimpsed the beginning of a PR disaster that could bring down not only politicians, but also any known private sponsor of the man who had ordered these murders.

"Do you have proof of what you just said?" Marchand asked.

Mackiever let the banker twist in the wind for a few seconds, so he could better appreciate the abyss yawning beneath him. "As we speak, the FBI is interviewing the man giving the kill order in that video."

Marchand's face went completely white. "You went to the Bureau before you came to us?"

"No one in the state government would even return my calls. About the manufactured charges Knox leveled against me? They went straight to the media and called for my head."

"But this could destroy . . . destroy the effectiveness of the state police for years."

"It could destroy a lot more than that," Mackiever said softly.

Marchand looked back at his assistant, who obviously had nothing to offer.

"Son of a *bitch*," he muttered. "What are we going to do about this?"

LESS THAN FIVE MILES from Victor Marchand's bank, Special Agent John Kaiser sat in the backseat of a black FBI Suburban. Beside him sat the state police sergeant whom Griffith Mackiever's son-in-law had finally identified as the man giving the kill order in the Katrina sniping video. Kaiser's agents had snatched the sergeant right off the street as he walked out of a coffee shop down the block from the parking lot where they now sat, watched over by four heavily armed FBI agents.

"You can't fuckin' do this," the sergeant growled. "I don't give a shit who you are. There's laws in this country."

"And you've broken the most serious of them," Kaiser said calmly. "Keep your eyes on the screen."

Once the filmed replay of the murder began, the SWAT sergeant knew exactly what he was about to see. He didn't wait for the shots to begin defending himself. His first instinct was to use the classic Nazi defense—*I was just following orders*—only in this case he was clearly the man giving the orders.

Kaiser finally silenced him with a wave of his hand.

"You're not under arrest," Kaiser said. "Although I'll be happy to oblige you right now if you'd prefer it. Second, we are operating well outside the parameters of what you think of as normal procedure. The special provisions of the Patriot Act give me truly frightening power over your ass, so please keep your mouth shut while I finish. You have only two choices: one, you turn state's evidence and tell us everything you know about Forrest Knox and his illegal activities before, during, and after Hurricane Katrina—"

The SWAT sergeant's eyes bugged.

"Or two, you become the epicenter of the biggest police scandal in modern American history, after which you spend the rest of your life in a maximum-security prison, praying that no relatives of the black drug dealers you murdered during the storm put out a gang hit on you behind bars."

The SWAT officer turned to stare out the window at the people walking up and down the street. The world of which they were a part had just shifted forever beyond his reach.

"Forrest Knox will never be head of the state police," Kaiser said with finality. "Somebody in this video is going to flip. Maybe it's just me, but I'd rather risk Forrest's retribution than what will happen to the guys in this video once it hits the Internet, and you're all identified."

It took the sergeant less than a minute to make up his mind. He insisted on speaking to a lawyer before signing any plea agreement, but in principle he agreed to give up everything. After all, he had no blood stake in the Knox organization.

"One thing," Kaiser said, as an agent in the front seat put the Suburban into gear. "Do you know if Forrest is planning any sort of hit today?"

The sergeant shook his head. "Not that I know of. But he ain't the one I'd worry about. I'd worry about Snake. 'Cause that motherfucker is crazy."

Duly noted, Kaiser thought.

"Two of my agents will drive you to our New Orleans field office," he said. "Your attorney can see you there. This is obviously a politically sensitive matter, so we'll play it by ear as the day progresses."

Kaiser leaned over the sergeant and opened the door, and two FBI agents unceremoniously pulled the man from the vehicle, then closed the door.

Kaiser tapped the shoulder of his driver. "Let's get back to Concordia Parish, and fast. We've got a funeral to go to."

CHAPTER 86

WHEN I ENTER the broad door of the AME Church for Henry Sexton's funeral, less than eighteen hours have passed since I cradled Caitlin in the shadow of the Bone Tree. Were it not for Annie, I probably would not have come here. But after awakening groggily from what I would soon learn was drugged sleep, I found her sitting beside my bed, dressed for church.

"Where are you going?" I asked her.

"We're going to Mr. Sexton's funeral," she said.

I blinked and tried to think of ways to dissuade her, but before I could voice the first objection, Annie said, "That's where Caitlin would be today, and she'd want us to go in her place."

There was no arguing this point, and after my mother sided with her, I resigned myself to the fact that sulking in my tent was not a viable option. After a shower and three cups of coffee, I found myself in Mom's Camry, driving across the river I'd come to curse in the past few days. Annie had appropriated Caitlin's cell phone from the box of her personal effects, and though my daughter could not break the passcode, she held the phone tightly as a kind of talisman. She also asked whether she might wear Caitlin's engagement ring around her neck on a chain, but this request I gently refused. I could see that my mother agreed with me, and that made me feel a little better as we left the house. We can't let Annie slip back into the kind of paralysis she experienced when my wife died.

I assumed that Henry would be buried from a white church in Ferriday, Louisiana, but as we crossed the bridge, Mom informed me that he would be buried from a black church in Clayton, a few miles away. Knowing this, I expected to come upon a white saltbox standing at the edge of an empty soybean field, with maybe fifty cars in the parking lot. Instead I saw a white saltbox that appeared to be floating on a sea of automobiles, with more lining the highway for at least a quarter mile.

Inside that box I found a crowd that probably violated the fire code by a factor of five. Like most black churches in this part of the South, this one was built from cheap pine and stands on wedge-shaped concrete blocks. If set alight, it would burn to the ground in less than twenty minutes; yet it has stood for nearly seventy years.

The demographics of this parish are simple: 70 percent black, 30 percent white, give or take a few percent, with no mixed churches or cemeteries, and the white kids in segregated private schools unless they can't afford the tuition. Today, however, quite a few white faces salt the pews of the AME Church. They look slightly confused at finding themselves here. Yet here they have come, to honor Henry Sexton. I recognize Jerry Mitchell from the *Clarion-Ledger*, and one older reporter from the *Atlanta Journal-Constitution*. Beyond the smattering of journalistic luminaries, I see John Kaiser and at least half a dozen FBI agents standing near a door behind the altar. This comes as a surprise, since Kaiser must surely have more pressing business than Henry's funeral.

Spying me as we move up the crowded aisle, Kaiser points to a few empty seats in the front rows that have been reserved. As we take our places, he walks over, leans down to me, and whispers, "How's your daughter coping?"

At least he didn't ask me how I'm doing. Rising again, I say, "Better than I am, so far. What are you guys doing here? Has there been a bomb threat or something?"

Kaiser shakes his head. "They found Harold Wallis early this morning, dead."

"Where?"

"Behind a Baton Rouge crack house."

I close my eyes, absorbing this news at the gut level. "Doesn't matter," I say softly. "He was just the bullet. I want the man who aimed the gun."

Kaiser's eyes tell me he remembers telling me the same thing about the Kennedy assassination. "You probably don't know, but the Double Eagles were released this morning."

This penetrates the haze of my grief. "*What?* After killing Sonny Thornfield?"

Kaiser gives me a cagey look. "There's a method to my madness. I have them all under surveillance. But Snake Knox has temporarily lost his tail. Keep your eyes peeled for him, if you're out and about."

"Great. Where's Forrest Knox now?"

"Holed up with his sidekick at the Valhalla hunting camp."

"You haven't gone after him?"

"We're close. I'm working with the Louisiana State Police now."

"Forrest *is* the state police."

Kaiser shakes his head with confidence. "Not quite. We're going to get him, Penn. I can't tell you how, but it's only a matter of time now. And not much, at that."

"So what are you doing here?"

The FBI agent smiles and nods at Annie and my mother. "I'll explain later. Just be cool, no matter what happens."

Before I can ask what he means, he drifts back toward the door beyond the rail.

The hum of voices in the church is like the low rumble before a big high school graduation. People are still squeezing through the double doors at the back, and after the younger men give up their seats to women, the rear of the room swells with bodies, and the balcony creaks from the collective weight of children. I start to offer my seat to a woman standing against the wall, but Annie holds me firmly in my spot.

As we wait for the service to begin, I look to my left and right. The deeply creased faces around me have seen more toil and pain than I ever will. Life here has always been hard. In 1927 the river inundated the Louisiana Delta for miles inland, trivializing the flooding caused by Hurricane Katrina. Raccoons and poisonous snakes filled the trees, while rat-covered logs and rotting cattle floated between the hacked-through roofs serving as islands of grim survival. On the levees near the river, Red Cross camps struggled to treat refugees suffering from pellagra and other maladies. Out here, the only food or medicine arrived on small boats sent by the federal government. Yet still these people refused to leave their land. More than a few of today's mourners look like they lived through the '27 flood, and most of them probably remember the 1960s like they were yesterday.

The humming voices drop to nothing as two men wearing suits wheel in a coffin of dull gray metal. After they depart, a tall black man who must be at least ninety walks out to the lectern carrying an ancient Bible. He is the Reverend John Baldwin, a legend in this parish. Probably six feet four during his prime, Baldwin now has the subsident stoop of osteoporosis, but the wise eyes behind his large gold spectacles communicate dignity and compassion.

A hatted matron seated at an upright piano up front begins the service with a hymn I don't recognize, but none of the black people in the pews need a hymnal. They sing with full-throated passion, tempered by the sadness appropriate to the occasion. After the last chord fades and dies, Reverend Baldwin looks over at another preacher who appears to be a younger version of himself. When that man nods, Reverend Baldwin begins to speak.

"Greetings, brothers and sisters," he says in a deep baritone ravaged by time and cigarette smoke, "friends and neighbors. My son Richard recently took over as pastor of this church, but today I will preside over the funeral of my good friend, Henry Sexton. I ask you new folks to be patient with me. I'm ninety-two years old, and it takes me a while to say what I mean to, but I can only hope that you find what I say worth the waiting."

Reverend Baldwin turns his head slowly and takes in the sea of faces upturned to his. Then he smiles with a generosity of spirit that makes many of the whites in the pews smile in return.

"This is more white folks than I've preached to since 1964, when the children from the white colleges up north came down to help in the struggle. That makes me happy, despite the sad occasion. People say the most segregated day of the week in America is Sunday, and they're close to right. But today, in this church, that's not true."

Reverend Baldwin looks down at his Bible, but he's

not reading anything. He's thinking, or perhaps praying. Then he turns around to where the long coffin lies on a bier draped with a cloth to hide the trolley wheels beneath it.

"First I want to answer the question some of my parishioners are asking themselves. Why is that white man lying here, in our church, instead of in the white church down the road? Ain't that the way it's supposed to be? Well . . . yes and no. That's the way it *is* most times, I'm sad to say. But it's not the way it *ought* to be. When a man gets to where Henry Sexton is now, he ought to be where he belongs, and Henry belongs *right here*. His mother knew that, and that's why she asked me to preside over his funeral service. And when she asked, I knew this was something I had to do—indeed, I'm *proud* to do. Why, you ask? Because every member of this church owes Henry Sexton something. What, you ask? What do I owe that white man?

"First, your prayers, brothers and sisters. And your thanks."

Reverend Baldwin takes out a white handkerchief and dabs sweat from his brow. "Last night I thought about comparing Henry to a hero from the Bible. But that was an age of heroes, if the stories aren't exaggerated. Being a hero in our time seems particularly hard. Our children don't even know the names of the martyrs who freed them from the chains of bondage. They know Martin Luther King, and Malcolm X, and Medgar Evers *maybe*. But ask them who Wharlest Jackson was, or Jimmy Revels, and watch the blank look come over their faces. If it's not on the TV, they don't know it. Well, Henry Sexton—the man who brings us together today—is a hero from *our* time.

"The scripture says, 'He who lives by the sword shall die by the sword.' Well, Henry Sexton did not live by the sword. Yet he died by it. Henry never resorted to violence—not until his last day on earth, anyway. And even then, he only did so to save the lives of others. I have preached nonviolence all my life, but that's not an easy road, I can tell you. I served in the navy during the war against Japan. But I wasn't allowed to carry a gun, not even in a combat zone. I was a cook, like Jimmy Revels. And there were times, such as when we were being attacked by kamikaze airplanes, that my greasy, shaking hands itched to have a gun in them. But they never did.

"After the Lord brought me home, though, I finally picked up a gun, to defend my family and protect my flock. Henry wrote an article about us, the Deacons for Defense. He must have asked me five hundred questions for that story." Reverend Baldwin smiles in fond remembrance. "He pestered me night and day. Henry asked what I'd think about when I laid in a ditch all night with a shotgun to keep marauders from burning down our churches and homes. I told him that when I wasn't praying, I was asking myself the same question my good friend Wharlest Jackson used to ask: 'How can we change the white man's heart? How can we make him see that we're all the same inside?'

"Over the years, I've asked myself what made Henry different from other people. One answer is that he spent his younger years in the company of Albert Norris and his family, some of whom we have with us today."

"*Amen*," says a soft voice.

Stretching my neck, I try to see who the pastor might be talking about, but this is foolish. I wouldn't recognize any of Albert Norris's family even if I saw them.

"For another," Reverend Baldwin goes on, "Henry was a musician, and music always brings a man closer to his fellow man, and to the Lord. I've known very few men with music in their hearts who hated their brothers and sisters."

"Hallelujah!" someone calls.

"Yes, Lord!" chimes in another.

"But as much as Henry loved music, that was not his calling." Reverend Baldwin looks slowly around the room, as though he has all day to speak to this crowd. "Do you know what Henry's calling was?"

"Tell us, Reverend."

"Henry's calling was *truth*."

"*Praise Jesus.*"

"Henry's calling was *justice*."

"*Yes*, Jesus!"

Annie looks around to find the authors of these cries, but she doesn't seem disturbed by them in the least.

"When other men reached for swords," Reverend Baldwin says in a stronger voice, "Brother Henry reached for a pen. And with his other hand he reached for a shovel. And with that shovel, he dug for the truth. You know, the truth isn't hard to find, if you're willing to get your hands dirty. Truth waits just under the surface for any man brave enough to scrape a little dirt away. But most people are too afraid or too lazy to get dirty. They're afraid to ask the right questions. The *hard* questions. Brother Henry asked the hard questions. And after he got his answers, he took his pen and wrote them down."

"*Yes, Lord.*"

"Henry wrote the whole truth, too. Not half the truth. Not a sanitized truth. He wrote the *signified* truth, and he wrote it down for everybody to read. From his tiny little newspaper, right down the road, Henry shook the foundations of this great nation. He shook the capitol in Jackson, Mississippi, and he shook the FBI building in Washington, D.C. Look around at all the strangers sitting here with us today, and you'll see what one man can do with a pen and the truth."

"*Yes, Jesus.*"

"Brother Henry," Reverend Baldwin says softly. "Our brother Henry proved an old saying that we all hear from the time we're children, but one we never quite believe." The old man holds up his long right arm, and in his hand is a fountain pen. In full voice he cries: "The pen is mightier than the sword!"

A swell of emotion fills the church, and cries of praise ricochet through the echo chamber created by the seasoned wood that holds us. When the calls finally subside, Reverend Baldwin still holds the pen high, like a wand that might spew lightning at any moment. "'The word of God is sharper than a two-edged sword,'" he quotes, "'penetrating even between soul and spirit, joints and marrow, and able to discern reflections and thoughts of the heart.'"

"Amen!" shouts a woman close to us, and Annie's mouth falls open in wonder.

Reverend Baldwin pauses, and the brief silence is filled by the sound of shifting bodies and gurgling babies. Then he speaks in the voice of a grandparent recalling his grown child as a toddler.

"Henry must have asked me ten thousand questions during his life. He was like a child that way—always another question. Who? Where? What time was it, Rev? How many were there, Rev? But most of all, he asked the question the youngest children ask—the hardest question of all to answer. *Why?* 'Why did they do that, Reverend Baldwin?' Or 'Why *didn't* they do such-and-such?' You wouldn't know that from reading Henry's stories, because newspaper stories aren't generally about the *why* of things. But I believe Henry was saving up all the *why* answers to put in a book someday—a real book, like Mayor Penn Cage writes—but not fiction. A *true* book. Henry's book of 'Why?' And now . . . now that book will never be written."

Reverend Baldwin turns and walks solemnly to Henry's casket, then lays his hand on the polished metal. "A lot of history died with this man. Satan will bury a world of truth with Henry Sexton. And the same is true of that poor young lady who published the Natchez newspaper. On Wednesday night Brother Henry gave his life to save Caitlin Masters, and when she died on Friday, she did it following in his footsteps."

Annie grips my hand hard enough to stop my circulation.

"One more bullet flew," Reverend Baldwin says, "and more truth fell into darkness. But hear me, friends and neighbors. *Bullets can't kill truth.* They can kill flesh, but *truth does not die*—no more than the soul does. The truth is all around us still, waiting for someone to find the courage of the fallen champion we mourn today. And though it might seem like the dark times of forty years ago have returned, I tell you now: the truth that Brother Henry and Miss Masters died for must not be buried with them."

"No, Jesus!"

"Because the truth *shall* set us free."

"AMEN! Yes, Lord!"

After the thunder of *amen*s subsides, Reverend Baldwin's voice drops to a confiding murmur. "I said that Brother Henry reminded me of a child with his questions.

But Henry Sexton was *not* a child. And if you've asked yourself what this white man is doing in this church of ours, I say this to you"—Reverend Baldwin looks out and seems to find every pair of eyes in the room—"Henry Sexton was *not a white man*."

This time no one cries out. Everyone in the church leans forward with bated breath, even the children, waiting to see what Reverend Baldwin will say.

"Henry wasn't a white man," he repeats. "No. Henry Sexton was a *man*. Just a man. Do you hear me, brothers and sisters?"

The exhalation doesn't come for several seconds, and when it does it's like a gasp of comprehension.

"A *man*," echoes a woman near the back, as though speaking the word for the first time.

Reverend Baldwin looks down at the coffin and speaks softly. "A man is a hard thing to be, friends. And my final word on Henry is taken not from scripture, but from one of the musicians Henry loved so much: Mr. Muddy Waters."

"Lord, Lord," moans an old man near us.

"What did Muddy say?" asks a female voice.

"'*Ain't that a man?*'" quotes Reverend Baldwin, pronouncing *man* as *main* as he points at the coffin. Now his voices rises, and he stabs his finger at the coffin. "I said, *Ain't that a man?*"

"*Yes, Lord! Praise Jesus!*" comes a counterpoint of impassioned voices.

Out of this chorus rises a soft flurry of piano notes, and then the younger Reverend Baldwin walks to the lectern.

"Brothers and sisters, we're going to be blessed today by a unique musical performance. A song by two performers who've traveled two thousand miles to be with us today. The first grew up in Ferriday, but she hasn't been back for more than twenty years. Brothers and sisters, friends . . . Miss Swan Norris."

A thrill of shock and anticipation races through the crowd, as though the pastor has announced the presence of a recording star. *Swan Norris*, I echo silently, the name hurling me back to Thursday night when Caitlin and I made love at Edelweiss after my face-off with Sheriff

Byrd. As we lay in the shadows of the master suite upstairs, Caitlin told me a story she'd read in one of Henry's
journals, a tale of childhood innocence and passion that
had moved her profoundly. How happy it would have
made Henry to know that the love of his young life would
return to Ferriday to sing at his funeral.

A woman who looks closer to fifty than the sixty she
must be rises from the front pew and walks to the lectern
while the Baldwin men vacate it. As Caitlin told me, the
daughter of Albert Norris is indeed beautiful. Her face
is lined at the corners of her eyes but otherwise smooth
as polished wood, and her high cheekbones and forehead
give her an aristocratic mien. Wearing a simple black
dress, Swan gazes out over the congregation like a dark
angel who long ago left the mortal world but has returned
to bring comfort to those who remain.

"Accompanying Swan on the piano," says the younger
Reverend Baldwin, "will be James Revels Argento."

A handsome, light-skinned man of twenty rises and
walks to the piano with the unself-conscious manner of a
natural painter walking to a canvas.

"James is the grandson of Swan Norris and Jimmy
Revels, who was tragically lost to us in 1968."

This time the response is electric. A symphonic cas-
cade of piano notes cuts through the awestruck buzz that
follows, silencing all conversation. Gradually the notes
diminish in volume until they settle into a slow, rhythmic undercurrent. Then, out onto that current, like a
sleek canoe of rough-hewn timber, sails the voice of Swan
Norris.

I was born by the river, in a little tent . . .
Oh, and just like the river I've been runnin' ever since . . .

Sam Cooke's immortal anthem is one of those songs
that few singers are really up to, but the restrained power
of Swan's voice brings chills to the back of my neck. One
senses that, like a dammed river, it could break loose at
any moment and wash away all before it. Swan doesn't
ruin the song with exhibitionist melismas, the way so
many modern singers do, yet her sinuous phrasing easily
matches Cooke's original. When she pauses after the

second verse, her grandson's piano fills the space like an eddy of water. Then she goes on, catching the main current again.

In the third verse her timbre changes, morphing into a more angelic tone, one reminiscent of a boys' choir. Then I realize that Swan is no longer singing; she's watching her grandson carry on what she started. As James Revels sings of being denied help from his brother, his voice seems to float above the crowd, into the high spaces of the church. But just as it seems in danger of drifting away, Swan's rich, earthy alto fills the building from the floorboards to the apex of the ceiling.

> *It's been a long, a long time coming,*
> *But I know a change is gonna come.*
> *Oh, yes it will.*

When the last resonant echoes of the piano fade into silence, awe fills the church. For the natives of this area, a prodigal has returned—two, in this case—one a daughter, and the other the descendant of a man they believed martyred long ago, and without children. All I can think of is how profoundly moved Caitlin would have been to know that Jimmy Revels left a child in the world, and by Swan Norris. Then a piercing question comes to me: *Did Henry ever know?*

As Swan returns to her seat, the elder Reverend Baldwin rises once more, presumably to dismiss the mourners. But when he reaches the podium, he looks out and says, "Brothers and sisters, our final guest today was asked to speak by Henry's mother. Almost all of you know him, and I ask that you remain seated and give him the courtesy of silence."

In the front pew, John Kaiser gets to his feet. Several FBI agents do the same. When the door behind the altar opens, I half expect a black celebrity to walk to the podium, but to my surprise the man who appears is white—with white hair, a clean-shaven face, and piercing eyes.

"My God," whispers my mother, clutching my arm so hard it hurts.

"Brothers and sisters," says Reverend Baldwin, "Dr. Thomas Cage."

I start to get to my feet, but a strong pair of hands presses me back down. When I turn, I find Walt Garrity's face only inches from my own, his eyes filled with empathy.

"Just sit tight," he says softly. "Hear him out. Then decide what you want to do."

CHAPTER 87

AS MY FATHER walks to the lectern, obviously bent with pain, Walt keeps one hand on my shoulder. The whispers in the church rise like a wind before a storm, but Dad looks unfazed. My mother is blinking in openmouthed shock, but Annie is smiling broadly, Caitlin's cell phone still held tight in her hand.

"What the hell is he doing, Walt?" I whisper.

"You'll see. Just wait."

I quickly scan the pews behind me. "A hundred people are using their cell phones. Forrest Knox will have men here in ten minutes, and we'll have a war on our hands."

"No, he won't. Check your phone."

I slip my mobile from my inside coat pocket. The LCD reads NO SERVICE.

"Jammed," Walt says with satisfaction. "Courtesy of the FBI. Your father's turning himself in, Penn. But he's doing it in his own way."

"To who? Kaiser?"

"That's right."

"Jesus. Does the FBI know you're here?"

"Officially? No. In reality, yes."

A flood of confused emotions is surging through me. Dad stands silently at the lectern, a gray pinstripe suit with high, wide lapels hanging off his frame. He looks as though he barely has the strength to hold himself upright.

"I don't believe this."

"Penn—"

"What the hell is he *wearing*?"

"A suit that belonged to Pithy Nolan's husband," Walt hisses. "It was made in 1940."

Pithy Nolan, I think, stunned by my stupidity. *Of course! Where else would they be hiding?*

"He's lost his mind, Walt. This is insane."

"Just listen, for God's sake."

Dad looks down at the lectern, but he has no notes. He seems to be considering what he wants to say. When at last he begins speaking, his usually strong voice sounds weak, but his words are clearly audible.

"I know some of you are surprised to see me here," he says. "I haven't come to disturb this service. I've come to pay my respects to Henry, and to the cause for which he worked so hard."

Dad looks out over the crowd, and recognition is the dominant expression on his face. His eyes pause as they take in Annie and my mother, but they slip right over me and move on. *He can't bear to look at me*, I realize. When he speaks again, his voice seems to have gained strength.

"This morning, I told Henry's mother that he had given the last full measure of devotion to his cause, which was justice. I was quoting Abraham Lincoln describing the fallen at Gettysburg. But Henry's bravery wasn't the kind I saw demonstrated by my fellow soldiers in Korea, charging into bullets and dying in a foreign land. Henry proved his courage alone, in the face of apathy, resentment, and open hostility. Having experienced battle myself, I wonder whether Henry's bravery isn't a higher form of courage. There's nothing harder than fighting alone, with no one to keep you company in your foxhole. There ought to be a special medal for that. But like most soldiers I knew during my service, Henry wasn't looking for medals."

"Amen," says a soft voice behind me.

In the pew reserved for family, I see an old woman who must be Henry's mother nod and wipe her eyes.

"It says in the Good Book," Dad goes on, "'No greater love hath any man than he who lays down his life for his friends.'"

"That's right," says a bass voice from the rear of the church.

Dad bows his head as though paying homage to this principle. "Henry laid down his life to save my future daughter-in-law, Caitlin Masters, who I've thought of as a daughter for years now. As Reverend Baldwin told you, Caitlin was murdered yesterday, despite Henry's sacrifice. She died following a trail that Henry blazed, and her greatest hope was to complete his work. If she hadn't managed to discover that Bone Tree, I wouldn't be standing before you now, but lying on a cold slab somewhere. Instead, that brave young girl is the one awaiting burial."

Dad pauses to catch his breath, and I can tell this speech is costing him dearly in physical terms. Then I see his chin quivering with emotion, and a knife of pain goes through me.

"To paraphrase what President Lincoln said in 1863: We here cannot consecrate or hallow the ground in which those honored dead will lie, for their actions stand far above our power to add or detract. The world will not remember what we say here today. But it *will* remember the battles that Henry and Caitlin fought. What remains for us is to rededicate ourselves to the task for which they gave the last full measure of devotion. We *must* resolve that they shall not have died in vain."

All the whispered conversations have ended. Everyone in the church sits with rapt attention. Something is coming, and the congregation senses it like a flood swelling one bend up the river.

Dad looks around the church, taking in each face in its turn. "How can we do that, you ask?"

"Tell us, Doc."

My father raises his right hand, his finger pointed skyward, and the spirit of the crowd rises with it. As angry as I am at him, he somehow radiates the conviction of a prophet when he continues.

"Hear me now," he rumbles. "For the hour of justice has come."

Excitement sweeps through the church like a strong wind.

"That I, a white man, stand here and speak to you, the descendants of slaves, about justice is almost absurd. Yet speak I will. Because someone *must*. The wound that slavery dealt this country has never healed. Speaking as a physician, the efforts to heal it have been pathetic. Four months ago, a hurricane swept through New Orleans and revealed just how broken this country is, how deep the divide between black and white. The scenes we saw play out after that storm would not—could not—have happened in a white city in the North."

"You're damn right," murmurs a voice from the crowd, and Reverend Baldwin glares at his congregation.

"Some people argue that your community is destroying itself," Dad goes on. "Your children are killing each other, accomplishing a genocide that the Ku Klux Klan never could. The terrible truth is, all that death is a legacy of the great crime that came before, that shattered families and stained these rich fields red for generations. But nothing is simple. I wish I could tell you that the enemy is all of one tribe, but I'd be a liar if I did. It seems that the young man who killed my daughter was black, a drug user manipulated by white men to do their dirty work for them."

A few sharp inhalations cause me to start.

"We in the South know just how complex and porous the boundary between black and white truly is. Our communities touch each other in a thousand ways, but not always in the light. We try to bridge the great gulf between us at our peril. In my life, I came to know and love people on your side, but I don't know whether I helped or hurt them."

Dad pauses to wipe sweat from his brow. I suppose this is as far as he will go toward acknowledging his relationship with Viola. After gathering himself again, he continues, speaking as intimately as he would to his own family.

"Some of you here today, I delivered into the world. Others watched me hold the hands of your parents or brothers or sisters, or even your children, as they passed out of it. I relieved pain where I could. But in the last analysis, I've been nothing but a conductor on the train of life. I took people's tickets as they boarded, attended to a few needs while they rode, then punched their tickets as they got off. In my own life, I did things I should not have done, and I left undone things that will haunt me to my grave. For the most part, other people paid the price for my sins. Henry Sexton was one of them, and I can't change that.

"But the lesson of Henry's life is that you don't cure the great ills of the world by grand gestures. You start small. Like all great men, Henry began in his own backyard. He saw injustice and tried to remedy it. He knew that murder—especially the murder of those who had no voice, no champion—could not be allowed to stand. So he took up the work that his government had failed to do. He lit the lamp for the rest of us. Henry pointed the way."

"Amen," says Reverend Baldwin.

"If we're to follow Henry's path, then we must be as brave as he was. We must risk his fate, and Caitlin's, too. There are always a thousand reasons to do nothing. We tell ourselves the past is better left undisturbed, that stirring up old trouble will hurt everybody, white and black. That only when the oldest among us have died will change be possible. Even the Bible warns of the terrible price of looking behind us. 'Don't look back,' said the angel to Lot's family, 'lest you be swept away.' But Lot's wife did, and she became a pillar of salt."

"*Sho' did*," says a woman's voice.

"Unlike Lot's family, we live in the modern world. And in this world there is only one path to healing. As a physician, I learned long ago that denial, no matter how fervent, will not cure the afflicted. Nor will prayer, I'm sad to say. If prayer could cure cancer, that scourge would long ago have been wiped from the earth. No . . . if we hope to leave a better world for our children, we must cut deep into living flesh and rip out the tumors we've left alone too long.

"That's hard and bloody work. Practicing medicine over the years, I came to know secrets that might have altered the future of our little postage stamp of America. But I feared what might happen to my family if I exposed the terrible deeds of which I had knowledge. I did small things to ease my conscience along the way. I even wrote to Henry—anonymously—and tried to point him in the right direction on some cases, but that was far too little. Henry lying dead in that casket is the proof, and also my reprimand. Today I am shamed by his example."

This time no one calls out in support or affirmation.

"But I will be ashamed no longer," Dad says with an edge of anger in his voice. "I will live in fear *no longer*. They've shot me once already, and if necessary they can shoot me again, because I've already lost a daughter. But no matter what they do, the crimes of the men who killed Henry and Caitlin *will not stand*."

"Praise Jesus!" calls an older woman.

"Two nights ago I was kidnapped by Colonel Forrest Knox of the state police—not legally arrested, but kidnapped and taken to a secret place to be held hostage. A few hours later, I was kidnapped from Forrest by his uncle, Snake Knox, who meant to murder me."

The name Knox has silenced the church. Not one breath do I hear, and to the side of the altar, John Kaiser's face has gone white. But Dad has no intention of stopping. He was always a commanding speaker, but now, despite his obvious physical frailty, his voice is gaining power like a heavy rocket leaving the gravitational pull of the Earth.

"You all know these men. You know their history, and that of their family and fellow travelers. None of that's a secret anymore—if it ever was—thanks to Henry Sexton and his newspaper. Like Brody Royal, these men not only mock the law, but wear its mantle and twist it to their own selfish purposes. You in those pews know more about that kind of injustice than I ever will."

I hear bodies shifting, angry whispers, and murmurs of resentment, but Dad pushes on with irresistible force.

"Today, in the shadow of Henry's coffin, I call you all—not to arms, for this is a house of worship—but to *witness*, to speak the truths you know, and to demand the justice for which Henry gave his life. Set aside your fear. Refuse to be silent one minute longer. For justice delayed *is* justice denied. Force those who come in the night to terrorize and kill to flee in terror themselves. Deny them the sanctuary of silence. Deny them all refuge but the bars of a prison cell. Deny them all rest but the grave. And by so doing, let Henry, and all the grieving families for whom he sought justice, rest in peace at last."

Dad sags forward on the lectern, and half the people in the church lurch forward as though to prop him up. But after a moment, he pushes himself erect again and gazes out over the congregation with empathy and sadness.

"Thank you for hearing me out. And now . . . I go to answer for those things I've done and left undone. I go to speak the truth as I know it, and pray there's still time for redemption. But please . . . remember my charge to you: do *not* let them die in vain. God bless you all."

With that, my father turns and shuffles to Henry's coffin, then lays his hand on it, head bowed.

My mother sobs once beside me, overcome with emotion, and then her quivering hand closes around mine. "That's your father," she says, her voice filled with vindication.

"I know that," I mutter, more confused than I've ever been in my life.

After his silent communion with Henry, Dad straightens up and walks back through the door whence he came, this time escorted by two FBI agents.

The buzz of voices that rises in his wake sets the walls of the church to vibrating. The energy in this building is palpable, electric, a living force that craves a balancing of the scales. If the surviving members of the Double Eagle group were brought through the doors behind me now, I doubt they would escape this crowd alive.

"Does Kaiser have men out back?" I ask Walt as the pallbearers slowly walk to the bier.

"He's got everything covered."

"Are they taking Dad into custody now?"

"Probably. Quentin Avery's back there, too. Kaiser's coordinating this with Colonel Mackiever, the Concordia Parish DA, and the big boys in Washington. It's going to run like clockwork."

"You're forgetting the Knoxes, aren't you?"

Walt squeezes my shoulder again. "I'll talk to you outside, Penn."

He starts to rise, but I turn and grab his arm. "What did Dad trade for this, Walt?"

"I don't know."

"The JFK stuff?" I whisper. "Or is he going to come clean about Viola?"

"I don't know, man. And I don't care. This was the only way to end this nightmare with him alive."

"And you?"

"I'll be okay. He's seen to that."

I shake my head, then release Walt's arm.

As the old Ranger hurries through the back door, Mom clenches my knee. "Penn, what's happening? Did Walt say Tom is turning himself in?"

"Yes."

She nods and shudders with conflicted relief. "Do you think the FBI would let me see him? Just for a minute?"

I can hardly answer, so profoundly shaken has this turn of events left me.

"Penn?" Mom says again.

Henry's funeral is over. The coffin has departed, Reverend Baldwin has released the crowd with a barely audible prayer, and the doors at the back of the church have been thrown open, letting in a broad shaft of gray-white light.

"Walt said Quentin's out back," I tell her. "Go through the door behind the lectern and find him. He'll help you."

Mom grabs my hand and places it over Annie's, then rushes through the door beside the altar.

As the excited mourners stream outside, and a couple of the journalists scrawl in notebooks produced from their suit jackets, Annie tugs at my sleeve. When I look down, I see her holding Caitlin's cell phone to her ear. Her eyes are wide with an emotion I cannot read.

"Daddy, you need to listen to this."

"What, Boo?"

"I finally broke Caitlin's passcode! She left a message on her phone."

Only then do I remember that Caitlin originally bought the Treo because it had a Voice Memo function that allowed up to an hour of voice recording, an invaluable tool for a journalist. "That's a new phone, Boo, but she's probably got an hour of memos on there already. I'll listen to them after we get home."

As Annie speaks again, a commotion erupts outside, so loud that I can hear it through the back wall. Several voices shout out for someone to stop something, and then *"Leave him alone!"*

"Daddy?" Annie asks worriedly.

"Dr. Cage!" someone screams.

Caitlin's cell phone forgotten, I grab Annie's hand and race through the door by the altar, into the blinding sunlight.

"Over there!" Annie cries, pointing at the crowded parking lot.

A burly man in a black T-shirt is gripping my father's arm with one hand and aiming a pistol at him with the other. Four FBI agents and Walt Garrity have surrounded the gunman, but they seem helpless as the big man yells, "This man's a fugitive! I'm making a lawful arrest!"

Only when I get close enough to read BAIL RECOVERY AGENT on the T-shirt do I understand what's happening. Half of Kaiser's men have their weapons out, but they're not aiming them at the bounty hunter yet.

"Penn, do something!" cries my mother, who's being restrained by an FBI agent.

"Everybody back off!" the big man yells. "This man's wanted for the capital murder of a Louisiana State Police officer! I'm taking him into custody."

As I let go of Annie and run toward the group, Walt's hand disappears under his jacket. A voice that sounds like Kaiser's yells for Walt to stop, but Kaiser might as well have shouted for a meteor not to fall. Out comes a black semiautomatic, and Walt orders the bounty hunter to release my father. Recognizing the steel of an armed lawman's voice, the bounty hunter turns toward Walt and finds the barrel in his face.

"Texas Rangers," Walt says. "Just take your mitts off him, junior. Nice and easy."

"Take it easy, Captain Garrity," Kaiser says in a level voice, motioning for his agents to holster their weapons. "Put that gun away."

The bounty hunter stares back at Walt, and then his eyes narrow in suspicion. "Texas Ranger, my ass. This son of a bitch is wanted, too! What the hell's going on around here?"

"You're disturbing a funeral," Walt says with eerie calm. "And that's bad manners in any jurisdiction."

"Manners?" the big man scoffs. "I just made a lawful arrest. There's a hundred witnesses here. You'll get the death penalty if you shoot me in front of all these people."

Walt shakes his head so slightly that only the men who have witnessed lethal violence realize how close they are to it.

"I'm Special Agent John Kaiser, FBI," Kaiser says to the bounty hunter. "I've already taken Dr. Cage into protective custody. If you don't holster that weapon and leave now, you'll be spending tonight in a federal lockup."

This threat should be sufficient to defuse the situation, yet somehow it doesn't. I can't understand why the bounty hunter would disobey Kaiser unless . . . *unless he's waiting for some kind of backup.*

"John, you need to get Dad out of here," I say in a taut voice. "Right now. Walt, too, if you can. Something's wrong about this."

"Put down that gun, Garrity," Kaiser orders.

"Him first," Walt says, and for the first time I sense that Walt may be the sanest one of us.

I step closer to Kaiser. "This guy could be working with Forrest, John. He could be waiting for state SWAT to show, or for a kill shot to come out of the trees across the road."

This prospect galvanizes Kaiser beyond anything I expected. He whips out his service weapon and plants its barrel on the temple of the bounty hunter. "You're under arrest for violation of the USA PATRIOT Act. Drop your weapon now or I will fire. You have three seconds. One, two—"

"*Wait! Shit!*" The bounty hunter's gun hits the ground and his hands fly skyward, his eyes bugging in shock and fear.

Two FBI agents hustle him through the crowd, while another jerks Walt's pistol from his hand. One agent starts to arrest Walt, but Kaiser waves him off. Then I hear tires spinning as an FBI vehicle leaves the lot, hurling gravel behind it.

The standoff has stunned everyone within sight of it. The faces in the crowd run the gamut from green looks of seasickness to fascinated stares. As I pull Annie into my arms, a black Suburban with tinted windows rumbles up beside Dad, who is hugging my mother like he'll never see her again. Kaiser gently separates them, then shepherds my father toward an open door halfway down the passenger side. Dad turns, possibly looking for me, but I look down and put an arm around Annie's shoulders so that I don't have to endure whatever he wants to communicate to me.

After he's been closed into the SUV, it waits only for Kaiser to board. The FBI agent climbs in, then rolls down the window and addresses us through it. "We've federalized the Concordia Parish Sheriff's Office. I emptied out the jail. Let us get Dr. Cage processed into custody, and then you can see him."

My mother clenches Kaiser's hand and thanks him,

and then the Suburban speeds away. As Mom falls into my arms, I hear a strange whir to my right. Turning, I see Quentin Avery rolling up in his motorized wheelchair. Despite missing both legs, he manages to look more debonair than any male present, thanks to his still-handsome face and his five-thousand-dollar suit.

At least a hundred people stand behind him, watching expectantly. Beyond them I see Swan Norris on the church steps, looking serene and resigned as people mob her with what politeness they can manage. Her grandson, too, is shaking hands with well-wishers. Quentin rotates his chair to face the mourners and, in the voice of a man with an enviable ability to stop and smell the roses, says, "That Swan sure sang Sam Cooke pretty, didn't she?"

"She sho' did," someone agrees.

Annie tugs anxiously at my trousers. "Daddy, where were they taking Papa?"

I lean down and give her a reassuring squeeze. "Don't worry, Boo. Mr. Quentin's going to take care of Papa."

"How? That man with the gun looked really mean. The guys in the black truck looked scary, too."

Quentin leans toward her with a confident smile and then winks. "Don't you worry, pretty girl. Bullies are my specialty."

"But they were a lot bigger than you are. And . . ."

The old lion's smile broadens. "And they're not in a wheelchair?" Quentin reaches out and taps Annie's forehead. "Looks can be deceiving, darling. That's an important lesson. Ask your daddy about it on the way home." He gives me a mock salute. "I'm off, my brother. Keep your chin up, and remember what's important."

"Which is?"

"Those women on either side of you."

As Quentin's wheelchair hums off toward a white Mercedes van, Doris Avery climbs out and opens the side door, then deploys the ramp. She sees me watching, but she does not wave. This is exactly the kind of situation she wanted to avoid when she urged Quentin not to take Dad's case, which already seems a lifetime ago.

Looking around for Mom, I see that Walt has taken her aside to explain what happened with the bounty hunter. For a brief moment I feel released from the weight of supporting her, and into that vacuum rushes all my grief and anger at my father. The logistics of getting to Henry's funeral—and the intensity of the event itself—had distracted me from it for a while, but now the nearly unendurable reality returns with shattering force: *Caitlin is still dead, and two days from now we have another funeral to attend.*

"Daddy?" says Annie. "You need to listen to that message now."

"I told you, babe, I'll listen to it when we get home. I promise."

"*Now*," she insists, her face angry. "It's important!"

There's a desperate note in my daughter's voice that I can't ignore. "All right. Okay. You start it for me."

Annie goes to work on the keypad with fingers as deft as her mother's once were—and Caitlin's, too.

"The passcode was ya'll's wedding day," she says. "Or what it was supposed to be. All numbers. Lean down by me to listen."

I do.

Annie presses a button, and then—as though calling from some plane beyond the grave—the second love of my life begins to speak in a strained whisper:

"*Penn . . . this may be the last time you hear my voice. I've been shot. In the heart, according to your father.*" The rasp of labored breathing comes from the phone's tiny speaker. "*Tom was . . . trying to help me, but his hands were cuffed, and . . . now he's passed out. I'm afraid he may be dead. I'm going to try to save myself, but . . . in case something goes wrong . . . I want to tell you some things—*"

"Daddy?" Annie asks, her eyes wide. "Daddy, are you okay?"

CHAPTER 88

THE ROAD FROM the AME Church to the Valhalla Exotic Hunting Reserve has passed like a hallucination. I couldn't say whether I've been driving thirty seconds, thirty minutes, or thirty hours. All the way I've played back Caitlin's last words, spoken into her cell phone before she performed that last, desperate self-mutilation in an effort to save her life. Her message is a sequence of broken sentences punctuated by gasps, gurgles, wheezes, and wracking coughs. Each sound of distress makes it plain that she has little time to live. Yet I'm as powerless to stop listening to it as I am to stop breathing.

"I did something stupid, Penn. . . . I went looking for the Bone Tree by myself. I found it and . . . got myself shot . . . my own damn fault. A black kid offered to show it to me and . . . because he was black . . . I just assumed we were on the same side. Anyway . . . he shot me with a .22. Otherwise I'd be dead. . . . I scared him away with my pistol, but . . . doesn't matter now . . . wasn't him anyway. . . . Forrest Knox . . . did this to me. The kid . . . who shot me told me . . . Forrest promised to get his brother paroled . . . from Angola . . . if he killed me.

"After the boy ran . . . I realized Tom was in the tree . . . don't know how he got there. He was unconscious . . . sugar shock, I think. . . . Thought he was dead at first . . . revived him with . . . a goddamn peppermint. I'm sorry I sound this way. . . . Veins in my neck are filling up. . . . Can't get my breath. Tom said I have . . . pericardial something . . . my heart's being smothered by blood . . . in the sac around it. Sorry . . . the point was to tell you some things. . . . I feel like that guy on Mount Everest . . . who got to talk to his wife on the radio before the end. . . . I heard a chopper a couple of minutes ago. I hope it's you . . . or at least Danny and Carl. Anyway . . . here goes nothing."

There were more savage wheezes, and then she said, "First, I love you. I . . . don't know why the hell we waited so long . . . to get married. . . . Stupid, I guess. Second . . . you have to forgive your father. There's stuff . . . stuff you need to know. Viola and Tom killed Frank Knox. . . . Frank was hurt, but . . . Viola finished him off. She shot his heart full of air . . . and Tom stood by while he died. . . . Covered it up. That's why Tom kept silent all those years. . . . He thought Viola would go to prison . . . he'd be jailed and taken from his family, or . . . killed by the Double Eagles. . . . Oh, God, I feel like my neck's going to burst. . . . I don't want to pass out."

There was only gasping and wheezing for a few seconds, and when Caitlin spoke again, her voice was much weaker, and far less coherent. ". . . to think about. . . . Forrest raped Viola . . . when he was a teenager. He raped another woman, too . . . here at the Bone Tree. . . . I think Forrest may be Lincoln's father. . . . Look at his skin color. Anyway . . . can't believe I actually found the Bone Tree. . . . I'm leaning against the thing . . . but didn't find what I was really looking for. . . . Tell John that Frank Knox kept something . . . something from the assassination. . . . It tied him to Marcello. . . . Frank killed JFK, Penn. . . . I believe that now. . . . Tell John to look for a letter written in Russian. . . . Snake told Morehouse about it. . . ."

At this point her voice constricted into a strangled squawk, and I feared I would hear no more. Then she coughed and somehow went on:

"I've got my multi-tool . . . tell Jordan it saved me . . . fucking pen in my chest. . . . Need some kind of suction . . . but Tom can't help me. . . . I'm afraid he's dead, Penn. . . . Oh, God. . . . If I don't make it, tell Annie . . . I loved her . . . like she was my own. . . . I want to tell her myself, though, because . . . I don't want to die in this fucking swamp. Okay . . . this is me, babe, signing off. . . . Heard rotors again . . . hope to God you're in that chopper. . . . Don't ever blame yourself for this. . . . I asked for it and . . . I got it. I love you. . . . Bye for now."

The first ten times I listened to this recording, her voice was like a blade shaving shreds of muscle from my heart. Then I started to curse Caitlin for talking so long, talking to me when she could have been trying to save herself. But finally I realized the terrible truth: she'd known all along that without my father's help her efforts would be futile.

Whatever she said into that cell phone would be the last words I would ever hear from her. Typical that she spent so much of that precious time catching me up on facts, as though the message were her final news story.

When I get within a mile of where I expect the Valhalla road to be, I start watching the turns that lead into the woods between the highway and the Mississippi River. I try two that lead nowhere, logging roads that wind through the dense trees and then peter out. But then I come to an asphalt lane blocked by a wrought-iron gate set between two enormous stone pillars. A gleaming sign on one reads:

VALHALLA EXOTIC HUNTING RESERVE
Absolutely No Trespassing

Seeing no other option, I press a small black button on the keypad and wait while the wind blows through the dry leaves still clinging to the trees. A fire is burning somewhere nearby, but the scent of woodsmoke brings me no pleasure. To the right of the gate I notice a small sign nailed to a tree trunk. It reads: FORT KNOX. The letters look as though a child made them with a woodburning iron.

"Who's there?" asks an accented voice that reminds me of Captain Ozan.

"Penn Cage."

The silence from the intercom lasts a long time. Then the same voice, laced with amusement, says, "Come on in, Mayor. But if you've got a weapon, be advised I'm going to take it off you."

"I didn't come here to kill anybody," I say in a robotic voice. "I came to talk."

Five seconds later, the great gates slowly part. For a moment I'm reminded of Corinth, Pithy Nolan's mansion, but then I realize that the two places could not be more different. Corinth is essentially a sanctuary, while Valhalla has always been a killing ground. Approaching the lodge, I see a large rough-hewn timber building served by central air and heat. The telephone wires, satellite dishes, and antennas make the place look more like an army outpost than a hunting camp.

Alphonse Ozan awaits me on the porch, a pistol in one hand and his black wand in the other. The sight forces me to accept a grim reality: before I can speak to Forrest Knox, I must give up my ability to defend myself. I could leave my gun in the car, but some primitive impulse makes me jam it into my waistband at the small of my back.

As I get out of my mother's car, Ozan watches me as he might a rabid dog. He doesn't take his weapon off me for a moment. After I climb the steps, he instructs me to lean against the porch rail, and I comply like the most docile of prisoners. The Redbone kicks my calves apart, then pats me down from shoulders to ankles. Yanking the .357 from my belt, he pulls me away from the rail and, with a flourish like an overzealous doorman, motions for me to enter the lodge.

The great room of Valhalla is a surreal museum filled with dozens of stuffed animal heads. Some appear to be endangered species. A fully grown mountain gorilla squats in one corner, its glassy gaze trained on the massive flat-screen TV across the room.

Ozan prods me toward a cypress door at the far end of the room.

As I make my way toward it, four gleaming samurai swords catch my eye. To the right of them hangs a photograph of an American sergeant beheading a Japanese officer in a World War II uniform. It makes me think of John Kaiser and his psychological history of the Knox family, but Kaiser is a million miles away from here.

In a study beyond the door, Forrest Knox sits waiting behind an antique desk, his freshly pressed state trooper's uniform worn like protective armor. He regards me with curiosity but does not speak as I survey the room. His trooper's hat hangs from an iron coatrack in the corner to his right. A finely tooled leather holster containing a semiautomatic pistol hangs beside it. Opposite the desk stands a massive feral hog, stuffed and mounted on an ash pedestal against the wall. A long spear protrudes from the animal's back, but it's clear to me that whoever killed that tusked giant must have struck it through the heart in order to get away alive.

"Seven hundred pounds," Forrest says. "A worthy opponent, wouldn't you say?"

"An armed man against a pig?"

Forrest smiles. "Get out there in those woods on horse-back and you'll change your mind." He glances at Ozan. "He's clean?"

"As the sheets in a convent."

"Give us a few minutes, Alphonse."

Obviously disappointed, the Redbone slips through the door and pulls it shut behind him. Knox smiles enigmatically, then motions for me to take the chair that faces his desk. As I sit, he leans back in his leather chair and cradles his hands behind his head.

"Alphonse told me you want to talk," he says. "You here to give me another ultimatum? That last one didn't work out too well."

Yet again I note that Forrest is darker even than Sonny Thornfield was, and could well be Lincoln Turner's father.

"Maybe I can save us some time," he says, impatient with my silence. "You made some serious threats yesterday. I don't know what your plans are, and you don't seem in a very talkative mood. But I know one thing without you saying a word. Today you know something you didn't know yesterday, which is that loss is not theoretical."

I say nothing, and he takes my silence as encouragement to go on.

"Mayor, sooner or later, your fiancée was bound to die like she did. She nearly died two months ago during that gambling mess, didn't she? See, her way was to grab the snake by the tail and try to pull it from its hole. Henry Sexton had the same problem. He lacked an appreciation of nature's laws. It may be a cliché, but when you enter a lion's territory, you become prey."

Forrest waits for me to object, but I don't.

"Let's look at how things stand as of today." He ticks off points on his fingertips. "Your mother and daughter are still alive, which is a blessing. Your father is also alive, which isn't ideal from my perspective, but something I can tolerate under certain conditions. Besides, Doc hasn't got that much time left, from what I understand. As for me . . . any minute now I'll be superintendent of the state police. The FBI may have an army wading through the swamp a few miles from here, but nothing they find there

will ever be tied to me. They already searched this lodge."
He gestures around us, then leans back again, satisfied.
"They found nothing. So, no worries here. The Double
Eagles aren't going to say a word to anybody, especially
since that planted meth disappeared from the evidence
room at the Concordia Parish Sheriff's Office."

Forrest stops talking and regards me with the seemingly detached interest of a poker player. But the animal
cleverness in his eyes tells me that, despite his calm affect,
he's trying to decide whether I'm an annoyance that can
be mollified or a threat that must be eliminated.

"The long and the short of all this," he concludes, "is
that I'm content with the way things stand. You paid a
heavy price, granted, but I'm hoping you're smart enough
to count the blessings you still have, rather than dwell on
what you lost."

When my silence becomes intolerable to him, he gives
me an odd look and says, "I think it's time for *you* to talk,
Mayor."

"You ordered Caitlin's death," I say softly. "I can prove
that."

Knox blinks twice but otherwise shows no surprise.

"You also raped Viola Turner when you were sixteen.
Like father, like son, right? Grandfather, too."

Now some color has come into his cheeks. With any
other man, I'd have expected to see blood drain from
them, but Forrest Knox is not a man to run from threats.
"Go on," he says, "if you have more to say."

"You raped another woman, too, at the Bone Tree. I
don't have her name yet, but I will. You probably raped
a dozen or more over the years, right? Killed them, too."

Forrest cocks his head as though unsure of my sanity.
Then he gives me a broad, conspiratorial smile that re-
veals gleaming yellow teeth. "Let me tell you a little
secret, Mayor. If you've never taken a woman by force,
you've never *had* a woman. Do you understand?"

"I can't say that I do."

Knox gives me a skeptical look. "Are you sure? See, it's
the same as with killing. Until you've killed a man, you
haven't become a man. I know you know that, because
you've killed men. You know it transforms you. Most men

don't, these days. That's why I'm paying you the courtesy of this audience. But there are many levels to the mystery of life, Mayor. And at bottom, what you learn is that there *is* no mystery. There are sheep and there are wolves. That's it. You follow?"

"Maybe you'd better enlighten me."

"Since you're not wearing a wire, I will." Knox takes a tin of Copenhagen from his desk drawer and stuffs a plug behind his bottom lip. "The only gods who ever existed were men who had the courage to *live as gods*. You follow? Men who seized the power of life and death, embraced it, ruled through it."

"You're the Ubermensch, huh?"

"You think I'm ignorant," he says, betraying some bitterness. "Unread, like my father. But you're wrong. You, your father, Henry Sexton . . . do you know what kind of men you are? You're the ones who plant crops in the river valleys, who invent gods, who pray for rain. You build houses and write laws, then beg forgiveness for every natural impulse."

Knox leans forward, puts his elbows on his desk, and speaks with naked disdain. "I'm *nothing* like you. I'm like my father was. We're the men who swept down off the steppes on horseback like a storm. We burned your cities, devoured your crops, salted your fields, pillaged your treasure, raped your women, and left them pregnant and wailing. Men like your father took black slaves to do the hard work, then mated with them and corrupted both races. But to us, you're *all* slaves: to be used, worked, fucked . . . and finally killed, if necessary."

"You did some mating yourself, I believe," I say in a neutral voice. "In fact, I'm pretty sure you're Lincoln Turner's father."

Forrest barks a laugh. "So? What could I possibly care about that?"

"You're as guilty of corrupting your race as anybody else. That's my point."

Knox leans sideways and spits in a trash can. "The difference is, I don't give a shit whether some nigger whelp lives or dies. A man takes his pleasure where he will and moves on, same as the buck."

"You're full of shit, Knox."

Startled from his rant, he regards me as he might some a mentally defective child. "How's that?"

"You think you fucked Viola Turner, but she fucked you ten times over."

Suspicion comes into his face. "What are you talking about?"

"Viola Turner killed your father, dipshit. She killed the great Frank Knox."

At last my words have struck home. The whites of Forrest's eyes have grown larger. "Are you drunk?" he asks softly.

"I wish I was. It's hard to think about this shit sober. But I'm going to, because you need to hear it. See, two days after you and your father's crew raped Viola, Frank was brought into my father's office, hurt. Viola saw her chance at payback and took it. She injected him with enough air to stop his heart. That doesn't sound much like a sheep, huh? I'll tell you something else, too. My father saw it happen, and he didn't do a damned thing to stop it. He watched your father die like a dog, Forrest. Not a lion. A *dog*. Or a sheep, maybe."

Knox's Adam's apple bobs in his throat.

"Frank Knox died in terror on a cold tile floor," I press on. "He died helpless and begging for mercy from a black woman who cursed him while he bled out."

Forrest has gone so still that I wonder if he's even breathing. The blood has finally drained from his face. He raises a callused hand and rubs his jaw, the sound like the scrape of sandpaper.

"Doesn't sound like the death of a Hun to me," I say simply. "Sounds like one more broke-dick factory worker too dumb to see death coming for him."

Knox's eyes have narrowed to slits, yet I sense that he no longer sees me. Rather, he sees his father dying under the hand of a woman they both raped nearly forty years ago. Suddenly his eyes clear, and I feel the single-minded stare of a true predator upon me.

"You just signed your daddy's death warrant," he whispers. "Your mother's, too. And your kid. And last of all . . . you. You're going to watch them all die, Cage. And then, when you least expect it . . . I'll step out of the shadows and gut you."

In the wake of Caitlin's death, his threats mean nothing to me. Perhaps this is a sign that my mind has come unmoored from reality.

"I'd like to do it now," he says. "But too many people know you're here." His eyes suddenly flash with comprehension. "Or do they?" He raises a hand and points at me. "You came here to kill me, didn't you? You want to cut my fucking throat. Only you can't do it without going to jail." A weird glint comes into his eyes. "Shit, Cage, you might just have some potential after all. Same as your old man. I guess Daddy was right. The blood never lies."

I take a deep breath, then slide back my chair and get to my feet.

"You going somewhere?" Forrest asks.

"Yes. But you haven't seen the last of me."

"Oh, I know that. Well . . . there's one thing I forgot to mention. I'd spare you, but the medical examiner's going to tell you anyway, so I might as well enjoy it."

Something in me rises to his goad, like iron filings to a magnet. "What are you talking about?"

Just before he answers, I feel a sickening dread that he's going to tell me he raped Caitlin—which I could not bear. Because of her past experiences, Caitlin had a special hatred for rape, and it was an ever-present fear.

"Your fiancée was pregnant," Forrest says. "Ain't that a shame? You thought you just lost one person, but you lost two."

For a moment I lose track of his voice, so loudly is my blood rushing in my ears. "How do you know that?"

"She told the nigger who killed her, when she was pleading for her life. She figured he might spare her, I guess. And the truth is, he might've. He was awfully upset about shooting her when he came out of that swamp. He was talking crazy. Scared to death."

"But you killed him," I say in a flat voice.

Knox laughs again. "Alphonse did. Stuck a knife in his gizzard, to make sure he stayed quiet. You know what Daddy always said: a man's worst enemy is his mouth."

My next breath is a gasp, and I realize I haven't breathed for so long that I'm dizzy from oxygen deprivation.

"He was right," I whisper, more to myself than to Knox. Without looking away from his eyes, I gauge the distance to the holster hanging in the corner. *Twelve feet.* Knox's knees are still under the desk. . . .

Two backward steps cause me to bump into the giant razorback standing on its pedestal. Turning as though surprised, I lay my hands on the shaft of the spear.

"That's no toy," Forrest says. "That's a man's weapon. You think you could kill a monster like that?"

"What do you call this thing?" I ask dully.

"A spear, or a dart. But you throw it with an atlatl, which comes from a Nahuatl word, which is Aztec."

My eyes go once more to the pistol in the corner. It's too far away.

"That's gotta hurt about your girl," Knox says with mock sympathy. "She could've been carrying a son. Guess you'll never know now, unless you ask the M.E. to check."

He's pushing me to go for the gun. With the speed and power of a man with everything to lose, I yank upward on the shaft of the spear. For a sickening moment the whole animal rises, and I sense Forrest aiming a gun at my back—but then the shaft slips free and I'm whirling with the gleaming black point before me.

Forrest is moving too, shoving back his chair and reaching for something below my line of sight. I lunge toward him, but the distance is too great. Then, just as his bright pistol clears the desktop, the wheeled chair skates backward and he grabs for the edge of the desk with his free hand. In that instant of uncertainty, I drive the spear into the hollow at the base of his throat. His blinding muzzle blast scorches my face, but I cling to the shaft and drive forward until the point strikes bone.

Knox's hands fly to his throat, and his gun caroms off the wall behind him. His eyes follow its path, but instead of chasing that pistol, he hurls his body toward the corner, reaching for the gun on the coatrack. The spear point goes with him, but the shaft remains in my hands. As his right hand closes on the holster, I twist the shaft with all my strength and jab it forward. There's a sharp crack, then Knox drops like a puppet whose operator has snipped its strings.

His weight tugs the spear from my hands, but the

threat is no more. My final thrust must have severed his spinal cord. Forrest Knox lies on his side, the spear lodged in his neck, blinking mechanically and gasping like a catfish dying on a riverbank. His gray lips are fast turning blue, and the only emotion I see in his eyes is horror.

The sound of the door behind me registers too late.

By the time I turn, Alphonse Ozan is aiming his pistol at my chest. He takes two steps into the room, far enough to see what's happened to his boss. When he looks back at me, his eyes blaze with rage.

"You just killed a cop," he says. "You die for that. And nobody will even question why."

I'm weaponless, but it hardly matters. He's got me cold. All I can think about is Annie wondering why she had to lose her father as well as her mother. But I can't simply stand helpless and wait for his bullet.

As my legs tense to spring, a soft creak comes from behind Ozan, and he whirls. Before he can fully turn, a silver blade flashes down, slicing through his shoulder and deep into his chest. The blasts from his pistol deafen me, but the rounds blow harmlessly through the floor.

When Ozan falls, I see Walt Garrity standing framed in the doorway behind him. He looks as dazed as a sleepwalker awakened in the midst of traffic. The curved blade of the *katana* jutting from Ozan's back pulses for a few seconds, then goes still.

"Walt! Are you okay?"

"Is Knox dead?"

Forrest's eyes are closed, his face gray.

"He's dead."

"Come on, then." Walt beckons me forward. "We've got to get out of here."

"What's the point? There's no running from this."

He starts to reply, but then he touches the back of his head. When his hand comes away, I see blood. Lots of it.

"Ozan hit me with his pistol," he explains. "I'm foggy, Penn. We've got to move." Walt rolls Ozan over, wipes down the hilt of the sword with his shirttail, then pulls me to the door. "Did they take anything that belongs to you?"

"I didn't bring anything but my gun."

"Find it. I'm going to do what I can in here."

As I hunt through the main room, Walt calls from the study: "I saw game cameras on my way in. Mounted on trees. I avoided them, and I took the memory cards on the ones I saw. We'll just have to hope I got them all."

At last I find my .357 in the drawer of a maple cabinet. "We can't get away clean on this," I shout. "You need a hospital."

The old Ranger marches out of the study and grabs my shirt front, his eyes wild. "Listen to me, goddamn it. Think about your kid, okay? Even if Tom gets out of jail, he doesn't have long to live. Which means you're the only one left to take care of the women. You get it? So get your ass moving!"

"Okay," I tell him, following toward the front door. "But you're hurt, man. You need a doctor."

"All that matters now is getting clear of this place. We don't know who else might be out there."

He stops me at the door, then opens it a crack and peers through. "We've got to run for it. We'll take the car you brought and drive to mine. I'm down the drive a ways. I don't know if anybody's out there, but we've got no choice. You ready?"

"I'm right behind you."

"If I'm hit, don't stop. Get the hell away, and call Kaiser or Mackiever. Nobody else."

I nod, recalling the night I told Henry Sexton something similar.

Walt shoves open the door and goes flying down the stairs with amazing speed for an old man. I leap off the porch and quickly pass him, racing for my mother's Camry.

"Go!" he yells. "*Go, go, go! Start the car!*"

When the Camry's engine roars to life under my hands and feet, a manic exhilaration blasts through me. Then Walt slams into the door, yanks it open, and gets in beside me. Three seconds later, we're fishtailing down the road toward the highway.

"I'll tell you where to stop," he says breathlessly, one hand cupped behind his bloody head. "I'm in Pithy's maid's car."

"Screw that. You're coming home with me."

"I can't. I've got to take care of something."

"What?"

Walt digs in his pants pocket, then opens his hand beside the steering wheel. In his palm lies a small silver key.

"What's that?"

"I found it in Forrest's pocket."

"What does that fit?"

"I don't know. But I think it may be a padlock. I mean to find out."

"How?"

"Stop here! I'm parked right through those trees."

I slam the brake pedal and skid to a stop near where he pointed. "You're crazy if you go off by yourself now. You could die, Walt."

When he shakes his head, the look in his eyes tells me it's pointless to say another word.

"Get back to your mother, Penn. Your mother and Annie. You were never here."

CHAPTER 89

THE BLOOD WAS still wet when Billy Knox walked into his office at Valhalla and saw his cousin lying dead in the corner with Alphonse Ozan sprawled across his legs. Billy had asked his pilot to wait down at the airstrip in case he wanted to make a swift exit, and he thanked God he had. But after the first rush of panic eased, he decided to learn what he could before running back to Texas.

Taking a small Walther from his ankle holster, Billy moved quickly through the office. The floor safes behind the desk were open—open and empty. His second instinct was to call Snake, but then it struck him that his father had been out of jail long enough to have done this himself.

Billy propped his butt on the edge of the desk he'd sat at for so many hours and stared at the sword jutting from Ozan's back.

What's the smart move? he wondered. *What would Forrest do?*

Then he realized that the man he'd always looked to for guidance was dead. For the first time in his life, he was truly on his own.

Before he could make any decision, he had to know whether his father was behind this or not. This desire triggered the first brilliant idea Billy had had in a long time. Keeping his pistol in his hand, he slipped out through the glass doors and trotted around to the front of the lodge, moving swiftly from tree to tree. There were eight or ten game cameras between the lodge and the main road, and at least fifty more on the larger property. But it was the ones near the drive that interested Billy.

The first three he checked had had their SD cards removed, which made him suspect Snake even more. But in the fourth camera he found a card in the slot. In the remaining six he found four more cards. There were no computers left in the lodge (Forrest had removed them prior to the FBI search), but Billy had a laptop in his bag in the plane.

Racing back to the ATV he'd ridden up from the airstrip, he cranked the engine and took off down the rocky trail that led to the bottomland where they'd graded out a runway. If luck was with him, he would soon know who had killed the most dangerous man he'd ever known.

Billy hoped to God it wasn't his father.

CHAPTER 90

I HAVEN'T BEEN inside a jail cell since my time working as an ADA in Houston, and then it was to visit prisoners. Today I'm the inmate, and the unforgettable ambiance hurls me right back to my former career in Houston. I'm sitting on a plastic-coated mattress on the lower bunk of an eight-by-ten cell. The chemical tang of disinfectant can't mask the reek of mildew, urine, old vomit, and worse things. The toilet is a stainless steel hole with no seat, and I wouldn't sit directly on it for a thousand dollars. The scarred walls have been scrubbed and painted countless times, but there's no shortage of artwork. Above a child-like drawing of a massive phallus entering exaggerated labia lined with teeth, a recent occupant scrawled the encouraging missive *Im goin home, but YOUR fucked!*

From the mouths of babes.

The Adams County Sheriff's Department was waiting for me when I finally drove up to my house on Washington Street. The deputies didn't even let me go to the door before hauling me the six blocks to the jail. Mom and Annie ran out onto the porch as they handcuffed me and forced me into the back of a cruiser, and I could hear Annie's screams through the glass.

All I remember of the drive home from Valhalla is forty miles of oak and pecan and pine trees covering the rolling land. A few times I flashed back to Forrest Knox lying in the corner of his study like a bag of bones, but I felt no emotion. I now believe I was slowly decompressing from a state of mind that attorneys used to call "irresistible impulse." At one time this principle was an important component of the insanity defense. Essentially, it was a way for sane people to plead diminished capacity, by arguing that even though they knew the difference between right and wrong, they could not have restrained themselves from killing. It was sometimes called the "policeman at the elbow" defense. In other words, if I would have killed my victim even with a policeman standing at my elbow, then surely I could not be responsible for my actions. After John Hinckley was declared not guilty by reason of insanity, most states threw out this component of the defense, and it's a shame. Because I'm a living argument for the validity of that statute.

It was the memory of Walt Garrity that reawakened my emotions: faithful Walt, who despite being badly wounded had insisted on going God knows where to check out the key he'd found in Forrest's pocket. As he drove away from me, the silver Lincoln he'd borrowed from Pithy Nolan's maid had weaved all over the road, but then he got the car centered in a lane and disappeared over the hill.

After I reached Natchez, I drove aimlessly around the city, much the way I once had as a teenager. I drove down Broadway and paused in front of Edelweiss, the house that Caitlin will never live in. I suppose I was waiting for some insight, or even a blind impulse to push me in a particular direction. But none came. Walt was right: my only real choice, other than to turn myself in for murder, was to go home.

And there I found Billy Byrd's welcoming committee. The speed with which they identified me as Forrest's killer was impressive, and during the booking process Byrd lost no time bragging about what had gone down. Forrest Knox's cousin Billy had flown into the Valhalla airstrip from Texas and discovered the bodies shortly after Walt and I left the camp. After calling the Lusahatcha County sheriff (yet another Billy, albeit Billy *Ray*), Billy Knox got the idea of checking the deer cameras strapped to pine trees on the Valhalla property. Several had missing SD cards, but in one Billy found not only a card, but also a photograph of me. The photo was dated and time-stamped, which definitively placed me at the scene of the crime near the time the two men were killed. Sheriff Ellis immediately issued an APB for first-degree murder, and based on this, Sheriff Byrd had started combing Adams County for me. Since I drove straight home, more or less, I was an easy catch.

I'm surprised that Shadrach Johnson hasn't come up to

my cell to gloat, but perhaps Shad senses that right now, any punch he lands on me will strike an anesthetized man. Better to wait until the awful reality of my situation has sunk fully into my soul.

My prospects are grim indeed. When I tore out of Clayton, Louisiana, bent on confronting Forrest Knox, I laid my daughter's future down on the green felt of God's roulette table and spun the wheel. So long as that wheel remained spinning, I felt the wild rush of seizing fate in my hands and twisting it to my purpose. When I impaled Forrest on his own spear (and Walt spirited me away from the scene of the crime), the gleaming ball appeared to drop into my chosen color: black. But at the last possible moment—thanks to forces beyond my control—that ball skipped over into a red slot. Now, less than one hour later, I'm locked behind bars, the remainder of my life held in escrow.

Sheriff Byrd gave me my own cell, something I know enough to appreciate even in my deadened mental state. At best, cell mates are an irritating annoyance; at worst, they're sociopaths who will beat you, rape you, kill you, or provoke you to murder in self-defense. My block has six cells, five of which hold two or more men, a mixture of blacks and whites. Most are here on drug charges, but two have been charged with armed robbery, and one—the lone Mexican—with murdering his wife. My father isn't housed on this block, and for that I'm grateful. I have no desire to see him now. According to a man two cells down from me, Dad was here for a while, but they transferred him out half an hour before I was brought to my cell. To my knowledge, Walt has not been arrested or even found, so perhaps the deer camera didn't capture his presence at Valhalla.

A harsh buzz announces that the block door is about to open, and with a low clang, it does. A big black deputy enters and walks slowly down the line of cells as though checking for mischief. The closed-circuit TV system monitoring the cellblock doesn't show every inch of every cell.

"What you lookin' at, mook?" he challenges someone down the block. "Lemme see them hands. Both of 'em! Thass right."

He moves steadily up the block, getting closer to me.

"Miss Francine say we gon' have chicken and greens tonight, boys. What you think about that? Maybe even a biscuit for every man this time."

The whoops and hollers that greet this news tell me fried chicken and biscuits is a rare treat in these environs. As excited conversation breaks out, the deputy pauses in front of my cell and focuses heavy-lidded eyes on me.

"Come here," he says. "Move."

I get up from my cot and shuffle warily toward the bars, expecting some kind of taunt. But when I near him, the guard whispers, "I got a message for you. Quentin say don't say nothing to nobody, no matter what they tell you. He'll be up here soon as he can."

My pulse kicks up several beats. "Who told you that?"

"Mr. Q.," he whispers.

I start to ask the deputy for more detail, but before my first word emerges, he bellows, "I can't do nothin' 'bout that, dumbass! I don't care if you the governor's *brother*!"

For emphasis, he whangs the bars of my cell with his billy club and marches back toward the door, mumbling, "Man wants to see his kid. Everybody *up* in this motherfucker got kids."

"No shit!" shouts someone down the block. "Who that motherfucker think he is? The president?"

"He be Dr. Cage's son," says a wiseass voice. "Little Lord Fuckleroy."

Scattered laughter reverberates through the cells. Then another voice says, "He's the mayor, man. I guess his power don't quite extend to the *jail*, though."

"I guess it don't!" hollers someone else, as the block door clangs shut.

I walk back to my cot and sit, hoping to lessen my silhouette in the consciousness of my jail mates.

So . . . Quentin Avery has enough juice to send me covert messages via Billy Byrd's own deputies. I shouldn't be surprised. Quentin has contacts all over the South. If I asked about this, he would only laugh and say something about the "soul-brother network" or something similar. And I have no doubt that the black deputy feels far more allegiance to Quentin than to a redneck like Billy Byrd, despite working for Byrd. If he'd passed me a more substantive message, I might doubt its authenticity. But "don't say nothin' to nobody" is the first law of the jailhouse, and I'm surprised Quentin felt he needed to send that advice to a former assistant district attorney. Then it hits me: if Quentin felt he needed to tell me that, then he seriously doubts my present mental state.

Maybe he should, says a voice in my head. *You couldn't have fucked up much worse than you did.*

But once Forrest told me what he did about Caitlin, I had no choice in what followed. I don't think I even made a conscious decision to kill him. At some level I realized that Caitlin had known she was pregnant but had decided to spare me that pain by omitting that information from her last message to me. And in some unquantifiable fraction of time after that realization flashed through my brain, every nerve and muscle fiber in my body fired.

The buzz and clang of the cellblock door don't signify anything at first, or else I think it's my imagination. But then the clack of expensive shoe heels sounds between the cells, and Shadrach Johnson appears before my cubicle.

"How are you doing, Mayor?" he asks, straightening the lapels of his expensive suit.

I remain on my cot and say nothing. Whatever Shad has to tell me will be calculated to hurt me in some way, so I might as well sit and take it and give him the least possible amount of pleasure during the process.

"I just gave a press conference on the courthouse steps," he announces. "Two Jackson TV stations were there, a half-dozen print reporters, and producers from the BET network and Court TV."

"Congratulations. Next stop, CNN."

"With any luck. Anyway, I informed those outlets that the prosecution of your father for the murder of Viola Turner will proceed as scheduled in three months. March first on the court docket—just in time for Spring Pilgrimage."

Despite my familiarity with Shad's boundless ambition, this surprises me. "I thought my father had been placed in protective custody by the FBI."

Shad gives me a knowing look. "I don't know what kind of strings you pulled with the Bureau, but we both know that they can't grant him immunity on a state murder charge. They may find some way to shake him and Garrity loose from that dead state trooper, but not even the president can make Viola Turner go away."

"So you're a happy man. I really appreciate you coming by with the bad news."

The DA shrugs. "I wanted you to hear it from me first. This is going to be a high-profile case, Penn. Historic."

"Maybe you can kick-start your mayoral campaign for the special election they'll be having after they throw me out."

Shad snorts with what sounds like derision. "I'll be shooting a lot higher than that, after this case is over. But that brings up the real reason I came. The Lusahatcha DA will probably want to try you in his county. Since they're in our judicial district, you'd normally get one of our circuit judges. But since you know them all so well, the attorney general will probably bring in an outside judge. My office could prosecute your case, but I haven't yet decided whether to take it on. Given our history, the AG may decide to appoint a special prosecutor."

"That must really rankle, Shad. You'd probably rather convict me than my father."

He looks philosophical. "A week ago, I'd have said yes. But given the issues in your father's case? No. You killed a dirty cop who's going to be looking like a world-class dirt bag by tomorrow. I'm happy to leave you to the special prosecutor. By the way, my condolences on Caitlin's passing."

I can't tell if he's feeding on my pain or hoping I'll give him some sort of absolution. "Seriously?" I whisper. "You do realize that if you hadn't grabbed onto Lincoln Turner's accusation and turned it into a three-ring circus, she'd still be alive?"

"That's absurd," he snaps, but he knows it's true. "Caitlin was killed by her own ambition. You know that as well as I do."

"Get out of here, Shad. While you still can."

His dark face cycles through several changes of expression I can't quite read. Then he says, "I have something else to tell you, but you'll have to come closer if you want to hear it."

He's worried about the closed-circuit cameras. "Not interested," I tell him.

"It's about Forrest Knox and your father."

Forrest and my father . . . What could Shad know about Knox and my father? Whatever it is, I'd rather find out now than sit here wondering about it for the next few hours. After a long sigh, I get to my feet and move up to the bars. Shad's eyes become clearer as I get closer, and in them I see a strange, hyperexcited light.

"I'm telling you this," he says in a near whisper, "because you're one of the few southern white males I've met who's capable of appreciating irony. Two days ago, Forrest Knox came to me and told me he was either going to kill your father or let him go free. If Dr. Cage went free, he said, I was to drop all charges and leave the crime unsolved. If I didn't, Knox would destroy me. I don't know if that bastard had the power to do it, but he talked like he did."

Shad's eyes flicker in the shadows between us. He's watching me for signs of emotion. "Do you see?" he whispers. "If you'd let Forrest live today, I'd have had no choice but to drop the charges against your father. And *you would never have been charged with killing him*. That almost beggars belief, doesn't it?"

I can tell from Shad's voice that he's telling the truth. And what he said fits with what I know. Forrest probably went to see Shad before he offered me the deal for my father's safety. He wanted to be sure the district attorney could and would kill the case against Dad. Which means that Forrest meant to stand by that deal, if he believed I could compromise my principles and do the same. This terrible irony sinks into me like the spear I drove into Forrest's throat, and this time I can't hide the pain.

Shad's eyes devour my anguish the way death row convicts in solitary drink in their allotted hour of sunlight. "Strange, isn't it?" he asks. "I've dedicated so many hours to paying you back in kind, and in the end I didn't have to do anything. You've destroyed yourself. It's positively *Greek*, isn't it?"

As he stands mulling over my fate, the irrational rage that possessed me a few hours ago lights up my nerves like copper wires, and my muscles fill with blood. Shad perceives the change, but he doesn't recognize it for what it is.

"I never thought I'd see you like this," he goes on, a distinct note of pleasure in his voice, like that of an oenophile drinking a rare wine. "Not in my wildest fantasies. Your father, yes. But you? . . . Never. Just goes to show you. I suppose your mother will have to raise your daughter. Unless your sister takes her back to England. I only hope Mrs. Cage lives long enough to—"

Without even thinking I grab Shad behind the neck and snatch his head against the bars with a muted clang. The security footage of this assault might tack attempted murder to my charge sheet, but at this point, what does it matter?

As Shad screams and tries to jerk himself free, the other residents of the cellblock shriek like crazed zoo monkeys. Before Shad can get away, I bring up my right fist and drive it against his skull with all the follow-through I can muster.

The impact hurls him against the opposite cell, where another prisoner kicks him in the back, knocking him to the floor. When he rolls over, I see pure terror in his eyes. Something crunched when I struck him—either my hand or his skull—and rather than try to get up, he covers his face with his hands and lies there shuddering.

Ten seconds later, two white deputies rush into the block and help Shad to his feet while a bigger black one charges my cell with a Taser. I back against the wall with both open hands held high. The deputy roars something at me, but his warnings are drowned by those of Shad Johnson, who's now yelling that I'm going to get the death penalty for killing Forrest Knox, just like my dad will for killing Viola.

My fellow inmates' cacophony has reached such a frenzied ecstasy that I expect a half-dozen armor-suited deputies to flood in and blast us with pepper spray, but no one else appears. The two deputies with Shad help him limp to the steel door, while the black one remains in front of my cell. Just before exiting the block, Shad turns back to me, his face dark with rage and shame.

"I told them about Lincoln," he says. "The reporters at the press conference. I told them you two are brothers, and that your father killed that boy's mother. You should have seen them eat it up. Like dogs gobbling raw hamburger. Your life is over, Penn. Life as you know it, anyway. Your mother won't even be able to walk down the street. They'll hiss her out of church. And your daughter? Wait till she gets back to St. Stephen's. Can you imagine what they'll be calling her?"

Shad strides out of the cellblock door under his own power, the deputies flanking him. Only then do I realize that the black deputy with the Taser is the one who brought me the message from Quentin Avery. Amid the prisoners' rabid screams, he looks at me sadly and shakes his head.

"You shouldn't have done that, Mayor. No matter what he said to you. I figured you'd know better."

I lower my hands, then shrug. "What does it matter now?"

The deputy's sad eyes linger on me with a sort of clinical empathy. "Everything matters in here, Mayor. You'll see."

CHAPTER 91

TWO MONOTONOUS HOURS have passed since I assaulted Shad Johnson. When the big deputy appears before my cell again to announce that I have a visitor waiting, I assume Billy Byrd is about to inform me that new charges have been added to my sheet. I do the convict shuffle as I follow the deputy out of the cellblock, so that my leg manacles don't abrade my ankles. But when he takes me into the visiting room with the solitary chair and the wire screen, I find not Billy Byrd but Special Agent John Kaiser waiting for me.

"All those years in the Houston DA's office," he says, "and you never learned that punching a district attorney is a bad idea?"

"I actually wanted to punch the DA about once a month over there."

When Kaiser forces a smile, I realize he's doing it because of Caitlin. He looks as though he hasn't slept since I last saw him, and his shoulders seem bowed beneath some great weight.

"Why the long face?" I ask him. "You must have found a treasure trove of evidence at the Bone Tree."

"Yes and no. Plenty of bones, but they'll take a long time to process. All in all, though, this is shaping up to be one of the crappiest weeks of my life."

"What do you mean?"

"For one thing, I was about to nail Forrest Knox's hide to the barn door when you decided to relieve him of the burden of living."

"I hope you don't expect me to apologize."

Kaiser sniffs and bites his bottom lip. "That's not all. Dwight Stone died this morning."

This bald statement hits me like a gut punch.

"His daughter was with him, at least."

"Shit. You told him everything Sonny Thornfield told us, right?"

"Yeah." Kaiser rubs his right thumb against his fingertips with a dry, urgent rustle. "It meant a lot to him. His daughter told me that."

"That's something, at least. So . . . is that what you came to tell me?"

"Partly. But I've also got some more news for you. Quite a bit, actually."

"Good or bad?"

"I think you'll like it. Do you know who Griffith Mackiever is?"

"Sure. Forrest Knox's boss. The one accused of child pornography."

"Right. Well, Colonel Mackiever is going to quite a bit of trouble to get you released from jail."

"Released? Why would he do that?"

"A couple of reasons. First, Walt Garrity has been doing some undercover work for him for at least two days."

"While he was being hunted for killing a state cop?"

Kaiser gives an ironic chuckle. "Yeah. It seems Walt and Mackiever go back to their days as Texas Rangers. Forrest was the one smearing Mackiever, trying to take his job. Mackiever promised Garrity that he'd do all he could for him and your father if Garrity would help him bust Forrest."

"Bust him?"

"I think 'remove' might be more accurate. In any case, you ended up performing that function, and you happen to be very dear to Captain Garrity. Also, according to Walt, Mackiever is one of those rare men who understand gratitude. He's the personification of 'old school.'"

"Great. But how the hell can he get me out of killing Forrest?"

Kaiser leans forward and speaks in a nearly inaudible whisper. "Don't ever let those words pass your lips again. You drove south on Highway 61 and walked through the Valhalla property, but you never entered that lodge. You were distraught, but you came to your senses and drove back home. You never saw Forrest Knox."

"John . . . how the hell can he make that fly?"

Kaiser speaks a little louder but keeps his voice low.

"That's where I come in. You see, Garrity's not exactly alone in trying to help you."

After Shad's gloating certainty about my fate, the recognition of compassion in Kaiser moves something within me. "I think you'd better explain."

"Do you remember Garrity telling you he'd found something in Knox's pocket after he died?"

"Sure. A key. I saw it."

"No, you didn't."

Okay . . . "Go on."

"Well, Garrity figured he ought to do what he could with that key before events took on their own momentum. All he knew was that it went to a Chateau brand lock, which is a very common disk-type padlock. That wouldn't have meant a damned thing to most people, even most cops. But being the old bloodhound he is, Garrity did something pretty remarkable. He drove to Baton Rouge and looked up rental storage units in the Yellow Pages, and he found two that were within a mile of Forrest Knox's residence. They contained hundreds of individual units, of course, but that didn't stop Garrity. He drove to both places, and saw that one had security cameras, while the other didn't."

"Forrest used the one without cameras," I think aloud. "In case whatever he kept there was ever discovered."

"Exactly. And did Garrity stop there? No. That wounded SOB walked up and down the lines of units, checking every Chateau lock he could find, until he found the one that Knox's key fit."

"That sounds just like him, actually. What did he find inside?"

"The jackpot, Penn. I shit you not."

"Not a body."

"Better than a body."

"Goddamn it, John, tell me."

"Most of the stuff was locked in metal containers, and some were even booby-trapped. Walt figured he'd better leave that intact for a later search—an official search. But just inside the storage unit's door—like it had just been dropped there—he found two boxes of crap that probably came from the floor safes at Valhalla."

"What was in them?"

"Not much. But two items were of particular interest to me. One was a U.S. Navy tattoo on a swatch of human skin."

A chill races up my back. "Jimmy Revels's tattoo!"

Kaiser nods, his eyes shining. "The one stolen from Sheriff Dennis's evidence locker yesterday, and now back in our hands. The other item"—he digs into his back pocket—"was this."

The FBI agent brings up some folded sheets of paper and holds them in the air, just out of my reach.

"What's that?"

"A letter."

"From who? To whom?"

Kaiser looks like he can't decide whether to tell me or not. Then he says, "Lee Harvey Oswald."

"What?"

The FBI agent nods. "It's a letter from Oswald to his wife, Marina, and it's dated November twenty-first, 1963."

"John . . . that's impossible."

"Not if Frank Knox killed John Kennedy. The letter was still in its envelope, by the way."

Yesterday I wouldn't have cared one whit about more assassination information, but for some reason, Kaiser's revelation has stirred something within me. I try to imagine a sequence of events that could have produced the scenario he's describing, but my mind is too detached to do it. "That can't be right. No letter like that was ever found. Marina Oswald sure never mentioned it."

"I don't think she ever got it. The envelope was addressed and had a stamp on it—five cents—but it wasn't postmarked."

"So . . . what are you thinking happened?"

Kaiser lays the letter on the table and folds his arms in front of him. "I think Frank Knox was following Oswald the day before the assassination. As Sonny told us, he wanted to get some idea of who the primary shooter was. He was supposed to kill him the next day, remember? I think that sometime late that day or night, Frank saw Lee drop this letter in a public mailbox. At that point he had to decide whether to keep following Oswald or try to get hold of the letter, and I think Frank chose the second option. He had to, didn't he? In one day, he and Oswald were going to be part of a team that was going to kill the president. Oswald didn't know about him, of course, but that was the reality. Frank was only the backup shooter, so his actions depended on Oswald's. He had to know whether Lee had any other plans or surprises in store."

The idea that Frank Knox somehow obtained an artifact no one ever knew about has triggered a strange apprehension in me. "What does the letter say?"

Kaiser looks as though he'd like to tease me, to pay me back for my skepticism in the hotel, but in the end— probably because of Caitlin—he lays it flat where I can see it. The moment I do, my hand and face go cold. The paper is covered with Cyrillic letters.

"Is that Russian?" I ask.

Kaiser's grin is filled with triumph. "Yes, it is. And it's a known fact that whenever Lee wrote his wife, he wrote in Russian. Marina was a native Russian, after all."

All I can think of is Caitlin's final message. "What the hell would Frank Knox have made of that?" I ask, my mind still on Caitlin's unfulfilled quest.

"God only knows. He probably worried that Oswald was telling Marina to tell the Soviets what he was about to do, or maybe even Castro. Who knows? But Frank didn't waste time in getting it translated."

Kaiser lays the second sheet of paper over the first. This one is covered with blocks of Courier text, which were obviously hand-typed on an old machine.

"Walt found this translation in the same Ziploc bag that held the original. These are both photocopies, of course. Would you like to read it?"

In my present state, I don't think I could even reach out for the paper. "How about you read it to me?"

Kaiser nods and begins reading in a low voice.

> *Marina, I am writing because I cannot tell you what I am about to do. I wanted to tell you earlier tonight, because I thought it might convince you to give me one more chance. But for once I can afford to be patient. If all goes as planned, by the time you read these words, I will be on my way to Havana. I can't write how I have arranged this, finally, but by the time you read this, you will know. Tomorrow,*

*everyone who doubted my commitment will finally
see how wrong they were. I mean to bring you and
the girls to Cuba as soon as this can be arranged, so
prepare yourself. No snow this time! Only sand and
sun.*

*I have only one reservation. I don't completely
trust the man who is making this possible for us.
I knew him long ago, when I was a boy. I never
told you about him. He and I no longer share the
same politics or motivations, but we do want the
same end, at least in this matter. But in spite of my
reservations, this opportunity is so historic that I
could not in good conscience refuse it. Fate has chosen
me to alter the history of the world. Tomorrow you
will see how I was placed in a position to change the
future, and no man of conscience could refuse such a
call.*

*After you finish this letter, burn it and flush
the ashes down the toilet, so that Hosty and the other
agents will have no evidence against you to prevent
you from leaving the country. (I'm mailing this
because I did not want you to find it too soon, and
we can't be sure that the FBI doesn't enter the house
at times, even with the cleaning woman there.) If
anything bad should happen, know that I gave my
life to change things for the better, for us and for the
world. When the girls are old enough, tell them what
I did.*

  Lee

By the time Kaiser falls silent and looks up from the
page, the table before us is wet with my tears.

"My God, man," he says. "What's the matter?"

"It's not the letter. It's Caitlin. She found out about the
letter on her own, through something of Henry's, I guess.
She actually knew it was in Russian. That's really what she
went back to the Bone Tree for. She left a final message
on her phone, and one thing she said was to pass that on
to you. I'm sorry I forgot. But . . . you found it anyway,
so . . ."

Kaiser is blinking in disbelief. "Henry knew about
this?"

"Christ, man . . . She died for something that wasn't even out there. Do you think it was ever out there?"

Kaiser shrugs and says, "Who knows, with those old guys? It might have been, and for a long time. We'll probably never know, until a Double Eagle tells us about it. I'm sorry, Penn. But at least we've got it now."

"Do you believe that letter is real?" I ask.

"I already checked the Russian handwriting against known samples of Oswald's other letters. It's real, Penn. No doubt."

I sit in silence, trying to process the implications. "The way that's written certainly implies a conspiracy."

Kaiser nods. "He's talking about Ferrie, Penn."

"He doesn't mention a name."

"No. But I got independent confirmation of a tie between Ferrie and Oswald late last night."

"From who?"

"Fidel Castro."

"*What?*"

Kaiser's eyes light up again. "Jordan asked him about it. And that wasn't all. Castro told her about a French Corsican who made an attempt on his life. I think it was the man in the fishing boat with your father and Brody Royal. Under torture, he told Castro that an American instructor at one of the Cuban training camps killed JFK for Marcello. He said the man was a former Klansman."

Even in my numbed state, this revelation sends shock through me. "Did Castro mention Frank's name?"

"No. But goddamn it . . . what more could we ask for?"

I shrug. "Frank's name, obviously. Not to mention Dwight and Caitlin living to learn about this."

"Dwight did find out. I told him late last night."

My face probably doesn't express it to Kaiser, but this does bring me at least some comfort. "Well . . . I'm glad of that. But all this is kind of off-track for me, actually. My problem is a murder charge."

"No, it's not. Don't you get it? This letter is your ticket out of here."

"I don't follow."

Kaiser gives me a sympathetic smile. "When Garrity found this stuff, he knew how big it was. He called Mackiever right away, and by then, Mackiever and I were working together. He told us what he found, and he made some very clear demands. He wanted Forrest blamed for the murder of Trooper Deke Dunn, which would clear him and Tom of that killing. By some method I won't let myself think about, the derringer that killed Dunn turned out to be hidden in Forrest Knox's Baton Rouge home."

I nod slowly.

"I see that doesn't surprise you. Well, maybe this will. Garrity also wanted you cleared of any possible charges that might come from the death of Forrest Knox or Alphonse Ozan. At first it seemed that I couldn't use this letter—or even the evidence from Forrest's storage room—without revealing that you and Garrity had been at Valhalla and done what you did there, which allowed Garrity to find the storage locker."

"I'm listening."

"After some discussion, we decided that Colonel Mackiever would say *he'd* discovered the key at Forrest Knox's house during a legitimate search. He was actually searching Knox's house while you were driving to Valhalla. He found the derringer, but there's quite a bit of other evidence against Forrest, too. We have a video of Knox's SWAT guys carrying out a multiple murder during Hurricane Katrina. Using that, I forced one of the snipers in the video to turn state's evidence. And last night, when I was questioning Double Eagles about Sonny's death, I actually turned one of them."

"Are you serious?"

Kaiser nods. "Will Devine. The guy was scared to death, especially after what happened with Sonny. Devine's the oldest Eagle left alive. He's haunted by things he did. A bit like Glenn Morehouse, I imagine. That's why I let those guys out this morning, to protect him. He couldn't have kept up a front while I worked out his plea deal. That's what I was hinting about at the funeral. Anyway, taken in toto, all that gave us quite a bit of power to shape the narrative that would emerge in the wake of Forrest's and Ozan's deaths."

"Your code of ethics seems to have relaxed a bit since yesterday."

The FBI agent sighs deeply. "I'd rather not discuss that just now. What matters for you is the new narrative. The official story. Now it's *Mackiever*—not Walt—who discovered the key, hunted down Forrest's storage unit, found the evidence, and contacted me about the Oswald letter."

"Okay. But I still don't see how that gets me out of here. Sheriff Ellis from Athens Point has game camera photos of me at Valhalla right around the time of death."

Kaiser gives me a strange smile. "Does he? Well . . . the significance of those photos is all in the interpretation, isn't it?"

"Come on, man. Out with it."

"This is where another friend of yours proved to be a great help. Carl Sims? The former marine sniper?"

"How did Carl help?"

"Once Sheriff Ellis issued the APB on you for killing Knox, Carl decided he had information I might need to know. And he was right. Carl told me that if I poked my hand into certain holes, I'd find evidence tying Sheriff Ellis and his department to the Knox family and Valhalla. Turns out Ellis went on all-expenses-paid hunts in Alaska and Canada every year, on the Knoxes' dime. But that was only the tip of the iceberg. A lot of drugs move through that county, and a lot of murders have gone unsolved. Turns out, I didn't have to work very hard to convince Sheriff Ellis that a double murder in his county involving endemic police corruption wasn't something he wanted me looking into too closely. He was perfectly willing to take my word that your presence at Valhalla was wholly unrelated to the crime."

This statement leaves me almost breathless. "How the hell is that possible? Who killed Forrest, then?"

A self-satisfied grin animates Kaiser's face. "As a novelist, you'll appreciate this. Captain Alphonse Ozan is now the hero of this revised opera. Ozan was the brave internal affairs officer assigned by Colonel Mackiever to infiltrate Forrest Knox's cabal of corrupt cops. Earlier today, Forrest discovered that Ozan had been working against him for months, and the two men killed each other in a vicious hand-to-hand struggle."

I can hardly get my mind around this revision of reality. "Mackiever's going to stand by that?"

"He's drafting his statement as we speak. Spear-versus-sword makes pretty compelling news. The media's going to eat it up."

My brain has gone into overdrive. "Okay, but . . . even if Dad and Walt are cleared of the Dunn killing, and I go free as well, that still leaves Dad charged with the murder of Viola."

Kaiser nods with somber deliberation. "Mackiever's got no control over that, Penn. Neither do I. Your father was always going to have to face that on his own. That's why attacking Shad Johnson wasn't the best idea you had today."

"Oh, but I enjoyed it." I sigh heavily, then lay my hands on the scarred table. "How soon can I get out of here?"

"It shouldn't be long. I'm about to go downstairs and give Billy Byrd a heads-up on what to expect. He won't like it, but I'll make him take it. Also, Mackiever tells me that he may have some leverage against Shad Johnson."

This takes me by surprise. "What kind of leverage?"

"I don't know. But he told me to tell you, 'Every dog has its day.'"

A slow smile spreads across my face. "I think I know."

"All right. Well, just sit tight and don't assault anybody else, no matter how badly they provoke you."

"Don't worry."

He reaches up to the wire screen and flattens his hand. "I know this is a fucked-up time, but I'm glad for you, Penn. And as for Forrest . . . I wanted to be the one to take him down, but if I'm honest, what happened was probably the best thing in the end. That guy had too much power. He could have had every one of us hit while he was awaiting trial."

With an almost overwhelming rush of emotion, I raise my hand and press my palm against his. "Thanks, John."

"I'm so sorry about Caitlin," he says, his jaw set tight. "But you know what? She went down swinging. What more can any of us do?"

I nod but say nothing. I don't trust myself to speak.

CHAPTER 92

THE NEXT TIME a deputy tells me I have a visitor waiting, I assume it's Quentin Avery and follow him without question. But this time my surprise guest truly stuns me speechless. The black man sitting in the adjacent room is not Quentin, but Lincoln Turner. Lincoln offers us an expansive smile.

"I've got nothing to say to this man," I tell the deputy, a comically skinny white man of about thirty. "Take me back to my cell."

"Can't do it. Sheriff says you gotta stay here ten minutes."

Thanks, Billy. "The sheriff can't make me see a civilian I don't want to see."

"He's your goddamn brother," says the deputy, backing through the door with a smirk on his face. "You don't have to say nothin' to him if you don't want to. But you gotta sit there."

"What about these?" I ask, holding up my handcuffs.

The deputy grins, then closes the door.

Lincoln's smile has vanished. Now he simply watches me through the wire screen, his face inscrutable. Just as I did in the black juke out by Anna's Bottom, and beside Drew Elliott's lake house, I find myself searching his face for similarities to my own. But now I don't really expect to find them. All my instinct tells me Caitlin was right: if this man's father wasn't Sonny Thornfield, it was Forrest Knox.

"I don't know why you're here," I tell him. "But you pushed that case against my father for the wrong reason. He's not your father, no matter what your mother told you. You're going to find that out eventually."

Lincoln shakes his head as though he's dealing with an idiot. "I guess you haven't heard."

"What?"

"Dr. Cage had a DNA test done on some baby teeth of mine that Mama kept. He got the results back today. It was positive. He's my father for sure."

I don't want to believe him, but I see no a trace of deception in his face.

Lincoln's eyes play over my face like those of a man trying to read a hidden code. "I had a feeling he might not have told you. You never really believed it, did you? That you and me were brothers."

"Half brothers, you mean. No. I guess I didn't."

He shrugs again. "Blood don't lie, man."

"Well . . . now you've told me."

Lincoln just sits there staring as though he has all day to study me. "Maybe you know how I feel now," he says at length. "That Knox guy killed your woman, and you killed him right back. Well . . . Dr. Cage killed my mother, and I feel that same hole. I want him to pay, too."

"I don't believe you," I say in a flat voice. "I know you're hurting, but you're hiding something. I've dealt with too many witnesses in my day, Lincoln. Dad may be your father . . . I can believe that. But there's more to it somehow. I know there is. And if you push this thing, the rest of the story's going to come out, I promise you. I hope you're ready for that, because it always does."

A resentful hardness comes into his eyes. "Well, you won't have to worry about it. You'll be on trial yourself, for murder."

"I don't think so."

"What do you mean?"

As if on cue, the door to the visitation room bangs open behind Lincoln. I first see the big deputy who first brought me into this room, but with surprising grace he steps sideways so that the man behind him can see into the room. That man is Quentin Avery, seated in a motorized wheelchair with two stump supports jutting out from the seat. Quentin's wearing a beautiful three-piece suit, the pant legs sewn shut beneath what remains of his legs. For a moment there is only silence. Then Quentin raises his right hand and points a long forefinger at Lincoln.

"Get this bum out of my sight, Larry."

Black rage darkens Lincoln's face. "You don't talk to me like that, you Tom motherfucker."

The big deputy leans into the room and glowers at Lincoln. "Don't be callin' Mr. Avery names, now. I'm the one gon' escort you out, remember."

"You kiss my ass, too, *Larry*," Lincoln spits. "I'll kick your fat ass down those stairs and sue you out of a job."

The deputy shakes his head without rancor, but I remember him charging into the cellblock like a blitzing linebacker, and I wonder about Lincoln reaching the exterior of the jail without injury.

"Don't pay that chump any mind, Larry," Quentin says affably. "Just make sure he gets outside in one piece."

"All right, Mr. Q."

"Yassa, boss!" Lincoln mocks. "Anything the house nigger say do, I gwine to hop right to it!"

Quentin's deep-set eyes focus on Lincoln. "Like I said, Larry . . . ignore him."

"I'm a lawyer, too, old man," Lincoln says. "Just like you."

A rumbling chuckle comes from Quentin's chest. "There aren't many lawyers like me left, boy. And Lord knows you're not one of them."

"I'm glad of it. You're long past your prime, dog. I checked you out. You sold out a long time ago, and you're in this fight for the wrong reason. You've made a lot of enemies over the years, too. And when you go down in flames on this case, a lot of people are going to be glad to see it, you old crip."

For the briefest instant I see doubt in Quentin's eyes, and it frightens me. I expected a deft riposte from him, but what I hear instead is the ringing impact of Lincoln's head being slammed against the wire screen by Larry. Lincoln is a muscular man, but his struggles against the deputy are like the thrashing of a toddler against a full-grown man. Lincoln tries to yell, but Larry mashes his mouth against the steel and jams a knee as thick as a tree stump against his spine.

Quentin lets this go on for perhaps eight seconds, then calmly tells Larry to let Lincoln go. When my half brother finally slides off the screen, he gasps like a winded fighter on his last legs.

"That's battery, goddamn it," he croaks.

"I guess he is a lawyer," Quentin says, his equanimity restored.

"Disbarred," I inform him.

"Good to know. Take him out, Larry. And don't worry. If he sues, I'll defend you in court."

Ignoring Lincoln's parting threats as Larry drags him out, Quentin carefully navigates his black wheelchair through the door.

"One thing you never are," I say to the old lawyer, "is boring."

Quentin smiles, but his once proud and handsome face is lined with pain and care. "I've got good news for you."

"Your face doesn't show it."

"Well, things aren't so good for your father."

I let this slide past me. "Kaiser told me that Griffith Mackiever was working on getting me out."

Quentin nods. "They ought to have you processed in a few minutes. I was surprised that Brother Shadrach would go along with this little maneuver. Do you have any thoughts on why our esteemed district attorney would accede to this?"

"I can think of one. Shad told me that Forrest threatened to destroy him unless he agreed to do certain things. That means Forrest had some sort of leverage over Shad. He and Mackiever were both state cops. I'm betting they have a file on Shad dating back to the dogfighting stuff in Louisiana. Maybe they have a photo like I had, or even a videotape. Sheriff Byrd neutralized mine by saying he'd testify that Shad had been working undercover for him, but Billy Byrd's not going to line up against the Louisiana State Police and commit perjury. Not to save Shad's ass."

"You have the FBI to thank as well," Quentin adds. "Agent Kaiser has spoken up for you where it counts."

I raise my eyebrows at that. "Kaiser's a good man."

"Good for you. But none of that helps your father."

"Bullshit. Mackiever is clearing him and Walt of the cop-killing charge, and John has spared him the hell of Billy Byrd's jail by taking him into protective custody. I think that's about the best Dad could hope for, considering."

"You sound like you want to see him go to trial over Viola Turner."

I look down, trying not to let my anger engage. "I think that may be the only way we'll ever find out the truth of what happened in Viola's house that night, Quentin. In a court of law, under oath."

Avery closes his eyes and sighs like a weary old wizard. Then he opens them and shows me his irritation. "Don't be naïve, Penn. That's like saying we're going to measure the position of an electron by having twelve scientists watch it for a week and then take a vote. No jury ever found out the truth of *any* damned thing. Not the kind of truth you mean."

"That's a pretty remarkable statement for a trial lawyer. If you really believe that, you've stayed in the profession too long."

"If you think I'm wrong, you were right to get out when you did. Now"—Quentin claps his hands and wrinkles his nose—"let's get the hell out of this dump. That stink reminds me of my wayward youth."

AFTER BILLY BYRD'S FUNCTIONARIES process me out of the lockup—a ritual at which the sheriff chooses not to appear—Quentin stops me in the corridor that leads to the ground floor lobby of the sheriff's department.

"What is it?" I ask, itching to get out of the building before someone realizes they've made a mistake and set a cop killer free. Through a glass window to my left I hear a dispatch radio and the clicking of an actual typewriter being pecked with painful slowness.

Quentin looks up from his wheelchair with some trepidation. "Don't be angry, but your mother and daughter are waiting out there for you."

A ball of ice forms in my chest. "Where? Outside the building?"

"In the lobby."

"With the pimps and hookers?"

"Ain't you high and mighty for a jailbird? Look, Peggy hasn't left that lobby since they brought you in. It's like she's standing vigil in a surgical waiting room, waiting to hear the worst. Even Walt Garrity's out there, and he ought to be in a hospital bed."

"Annie hasn't been down there all that time, has she?"

"No. She's been at home, with Kirk Boisseau and half a dozen Natchez cops. But she's here now. An FBI agent drove her over."

To my embarrassment, hot tears are rolling down my face. They're tears of shame, a special variety I saw on the faces of many men in my former life. "Just tell me one thing," I say, wiping my face on my shirt sleeve. "And don't bullshit me. Did Dad run a DNA test on some baby teeth of Lincoln's?"

Quentin mutters something under his breath. "Goddamn that boy."

"What was the result, Quentin?"

The lawyer looks up like a man who'd rather be anywhere but here. "Viola was telling the truth. Tom fathered Lincoln Turner."

I nod slowly, taking it all the way in. "All right, then. So now we know. Let's go see Mom and Annie."

"Wait." Quentin grips my wrist with surprising strength. "You don't want to hear this, but I've got to say it. Right this minute, your father's sitting in a cell exactly like the one you just left. And he's in a lot worse shape than you, physically speaking. He wants to see you, Penn. He wants to talk to you."

The ice in my chest has begun climbing up my throat. "After a week of running from me? Quentin, I told you—"

"I'm not asking you for Tom's sake! I'm asking for Peggy's. If your mother asks you to go across the river with her, you need to go."

"Quentin, I'm not—"

"I ain't flappin' my gums to hear myself talk, boy!"

His shout stuns me into silence. A shocked face appears in the window to my left. I signal that we're okay.

"You know what's going on here?" Quentin asks. "You're like the angry parent who thinks the best thing for a wayward child is to spend a night in jail. But this is your *father*, Penn. He probably won't even live until his trial date. He might not live to see next Sunday, if he doesn't get something to hope for soon. And Sunday is tomorrow, in case you forgot."

I look down at the floor, Caitlin's last message playing in my head. *You have to forgive your father,* she said.

"What can Dad want from me but absolution, Quentin? And I'm not empowered to give him that. That's up to Mom."

Quentin drops his hand from my wrist. "Penn, you've got a lot of growing up to do yet. Your mother forgave that man the day she married him. You've got to swallow your pride and face the world as it is. You just lost the woman you loved, and you feel like you've lost your father, too. You've also got a brother you never knew about. A soul brother, as it happens. That's not the end of the world, but you want to blame all that on somebody. Well, that's natural. But there's plenty of blame to go around. You've got to be a man now."

"I'm forty-five years old, Quentin."

The old man shakes his head sadly. "Age got nothing to do with it. I know eighty-year-old men still obsessed with the slights of their youth. They wouldn't know forgiveness if they stepped in it. You've got to open your heart to let the pain out. Ask any nurse, she'll tell you. Doesn't matter what you're talking about. *Better out than in.*"

I haven't the energy to resist Quentin's gift for persuasion. "You know, sometimes I really do believe you spent time in jail with Martin Luther King."

"Hell, that's established fact. Now— Hang on." He takes his cell phone from his coat pocket and checks it. "Doris just sent me a text message. The reporters out on the steps just left. Must have gone to get something to eat. Let's get out while the gettin's good."

His whirring chair leads me to the wide swinging door monitored by a video camera. When the door buzzes open, Quentin rolls through the door like an aged black knight on a charger, ready to do battle with anyone who would obstruct us. Beyond him I see a motley crowd lining the seats against the walls, wearing clothes that look like they were snatched out of a Goodwill bin and worn directly to the jail. Half the people in the crowd are talking on cell phones, while several toddlers bound through the lobby as if playing in their own backyards.

In the midst of this chaotic scene my mother stands like a duchess at the center of a Renaissance painting. With her perfectly coiffed silver hair and sky-blue pantsuit, she clutches a purse under one arm and holds my daughter's hands in hers. Walt Garrity stands beside them like a tired cowboy who mistakenly wandered into the painting and can't find his way out.

Annie sees me first, and her eyes light up like diamonds in the beam of a spotlight. With no regard for the propriety so important to my mother, she shouts "Daddy!" then jerks her arm free, sprints toward me, and leaps into my arms. This barely elicits glances from the veteran visitors, but my mother raises her chin to get a better look at me. After convincing herself that I am indeed her son, she sags against Walt as though her storied strength has finally given out. Walt hooks a comforting arm around her, then raises his other hand and gives me a thumbs-up and a wide grin.

CHAPTER 93

DURING OUR WALK from the jail lobby to the court-yard outside the sheriff's department, Quentin must have communicated to my mother that I now know the results of the DNA test. Otherwise, she would have already asked me to ride over to Vidalia with her and visit my father. She hasn't, and after a few awkward moments, I realize she doesn't intend to. She will cross the river with Walt as an escort and only asks that I take care of Annie while she's "busy."

Quentin straightens in his wheelchair to accept a bent-over hug from my mother, then follows Doris to their Mercedes van. Backing his wheelchair onto the mechanical lift, he watches me while it raises him into the van's belly. His reproving eyes tell me he expected more compassion from me than this. My last image of him is of a proud man looking determinedly forward as his younger wife and de facto nurse drives him away from a block where he'll be spending a great many hours during the next six months.

We four who remain exchange hugs, but as we separate, John Kaiser walks briskly through the main lobby doors, scans the sidewalk, then turns directly toward me. I can see from his face that something has changed, and not for the better. At this point, having tasted freedom, my greatest fear is that Billy Byrd has decided to keep me in jail until a judge orders him to release me. Giving Annie's shoulder a squeeze, I meet Kaiser at the foot of the steps leading down to the sidewalk. Up close, I see his face is deathly pale.

"What's happened, John? Don't tell me I'm going back inside."

"I wish that was it," he says.

Now I'm truly afraid. "Don't tell me my father died."

"No. We just had a plane go down."

"A plane? What plane?"

"A Bureau jet. A small Citation. It took off from Concordia Airport fifteen minutes ago, headed for Baton Rouge and then D.C. Looks like it crashed in East Feliciana Parish, not far from Zachary."

"Who was on board?"

"Two pilots. But they weren't the target."

"*Target*? What do you mean?"

Kaiser's face looks as grim as I've ever seen it. "Somebody brought that plane down on purpose. It was loaded with most of the evidence we've gathered over this past week."

"You're kidding."

Kaiser shakes his head. "The bones, Jimmy Revels's tattoo, even the Marina Oswald letter."

"Jesus, John. What brought it down?"

"We don't know yet. All I know is that it took off from the same airport that Dr. Leland Robb's plane took off from thirty-six years ago—the same airport where Snake Knox's crop-dusting service is based."

Unbelievable. And yet . . . "Where's Snake now?"

Kaiser pulls his lips back over his teeth like a man suffering bone-deep pain. "We lost him two minutes after he was released from jail this morning. And two minutes ago, I called Will Devine, the Eagle I turned last night. He gave me an emergency number. I got no answer. I think they played me, Penn."

There's nothing I can say to this.

"Your family's going to need protection," Kaiser goes on. "Around the clock, most likely. These guys aren't going to lie down and wait for us to round them up."

"My mother's going over to Vidalia to see Dad. Can I have a couple of minutes with my daughter before we head home?"

"Sure. Yeah."

I walk back to Annie, then tell Walt that he and Mom should start for the Concordia Parish jail. Walt raises his eyebrows for an update, but I shake my head. After Mom kisses Annie and they depart, my daughter leads me westward down the street, toward the bluff and the river. Our Washington Street house lies four blocks in the other direction, but Annie whispers in my ear that she wants to visit "our new house" before we go home. Taking her hand in mine, I lead her slowly down the slope to Broadway, where Edelweiss stands above the vast emptiness that stretches west from the bluff over the river.

As soon as we reach Broadway, everything changes. The wind is stronger here, racing up over the face of the bluff after its long journey across Texas and Louisiana. As we turn the corner in front of Edelweiss, I look back and see John Kaiser following at a discreet distance. He means to make sure we're safe, even if he has to provide the protection himself.

Annie and I climb the steps side by side, then walk to the rail of the wide gallery that overlooks the river. A long string of barges is rumbling downstream toward the twin bridges, the red-and-white pushboat behind them looking almost festive against the dark water. I expect Annie to chatter as she so often does, but the loss of Caitlin has affected her as profoundly as it has me. We still have each other, of course, but the road we've anticipated walking for so long has disappeared, and the way forward feels far from certain.

"Is Papa going to be all right?" Annie asks without looking up. "Gram's really scared. She won't say so, but I can tell."

"I know. I'm not sure yet what's going to happen with Papa. We're just going to have to do all we can to make sure Gram gets along as best she can."

After some thought, Annie says, "Okay."

She waits until the barges vanish around the bend. Then, very softly, she says, "Somebody at the jail said you killed the man who killed Caitlin. He whispered it, but I heard him anyway. Did you really do that, Daddy?"

I consider lying, but what would that achieve? One day she's bound to learn the truth. I suppose today is as good a day as any.

"Yes, Boo," I tell her, squeezing her shoulder. "It's a secret. We can't tell anyone else. But I did."

Annie blinks twice, then looks up at me with wide eyes I can't quite read. After studying my face for a while, she takes my hand again and looks out over the river. "I'm glad," she says. "I've been really scared, too."

This hurts me more than anything I've heard in the past week. "You don't have to be scared anymore, Boo."

A mile downriver, another long string of barges appears, pushing slowly upstream. We watch it labor through the current for a while, then Annie points to a spot in the middle of the river, where two tiny kayaks glide and bob like reeds over the surface. Though they're far away, I can just make out the sea bags secured to the sides of the boats. Those voyagers probably began their journey up in Minnesota, or even Canada. If so, they've traveled far, but they still have many tortuous miles to go before they reach New Orleans and the Gulf. For nearly a minute, the colossal train of barges threatens to overrun the little craft. Annie's hand tightens on mine as their courses converge, but at the last second the kayaks squirt from under the bow of the iron giant, and she relaxes.

"They made it," she says with relief.

"They did," I agree. *This far, anyway.*

CHAPTER 94

FIFTY MILES SOUTH of Natchez, Snake Knox piloted a Cessna 182 along the floor of the cloud ceiling above Zachary, Louisiana. His son Billy sat beside him, trying to hide his fear. This was a dangerous area to depart from regulation procedures. Baton Rouge's main airport lay only ten miles to the south, and even though Snake had filed no flight plan, commercial airliners might pick him up with their anti-collision radars, not to mention the possibility of an actual collision. Snake had already been challenged once by an air-traffic controller from the airport, but he'd ignored the call. If he hung around much longer, he might find an F-16 on his wingtip.

"Keep your eyes peeled to the northeast," he said. "There's a little town over that way. Ethel, it's called. I'm thinking that's where it went down."

"How do you know it went down at all?" Billy asked, shielding his eyes from the sun glaring through the scratched Plexiglas.

"Because I knocked it down."

Billy blew out a rush of air and lowered his face into his hands. "I haven't heard anything on the radio about it."

"You will, any second."

"Wait," Billy said, the moment he looked up. "I see something! Can you drop a little lower out of these clouds?"

"Sure, if you want to go to prison for the rest of your life. What do you see?"

"Fire. Fire in the trees."

Excitement ran through his son's voice like an electric current. Snake banked so that he could make a pass with the fire on his side of the plane. Just as he was coming into position, the Baton Rouge air-traffic controller said, "This is Metro Center. All aircraft, be advised, we have reports of a downed aircraft in the vicinity of Ethel, Louisiana. Aircraft is U.S. government Cessna Citation. Please report any visual evidence of debris in the vicinity of Metropolitan Airport."

Snake felt the primal pleasure he'd always experienced after making a kill shot as a sniper, or even hunting game—only magnified by a thousand.

"How can you be sure all the FBI's evidence will be destroyed?" Billy asked.

"I couldn't be, if all I did was bring the plane down. That's why I used two devices."

"Two bombs?"

"Bingo. The first one brings down the plane, the second sets the fuel on fire. If I'd blown the thing to pieces in the air, the fuel would have been wasted, and most of the evidence would eventually be recovered. But by bringing down the plane relatively intact and then setting the fuel on fire, *abracadabra*—nothing left. No bones, no guns, no nothing."

"Are you sure, Pop?"

"You're damned right I'm sure," Snake said irritably. "Jet fuel's what melted the steel in the Twin Towers."

Snake could see the crash site now, thirty feet of white-hot flames climbing out of a charred section of scrub pine. At least two vehicles were moving on the ground nearby. *Time to bug out.*

He climbed fifty feet higher into the clouds and started his last turn.

"Where are we going now?" Billy asked. "I feel like we ought to head for fucking Mexico."

Snake laughed. "To hell with that. We're going back to your place on Toledo Bend, just like I told you. We're gonna sit this thing out in style."

Billy's eyes filled with disbelief. "Is that even possible now?"

"Sure it is. The Bureau will hang everything that's happened around Forrest's neck, just the way he was gonna hang it around mine. And I'm gonna give 'em a little help, too."

Billy rubbed his head with his hands as though trying to hold himself together. "I still can't believe Forrest is dead."

Snake shrugged. "He pushed somebody too hard, just like I told you he would someday. And he paid the price."

Snake checked the GPS and smiled with satisfaction. There was nothing like flying VFR on a pretty day in the good old USA.

"So what about Penn Cage?" Billy asked. "And his father? You just going to let them go?"

Snake could hardly believe it, but his son sounded almost hopeful.

"Christ," he muttered. "You gotta know me better than that, boy."

Snake craned his neck around and took one last look at the burning wreckage on the ground. Then he opened the throttle to maximum and headed for Texas.

ACKNOWLEDGMENTS

First and foremost to Stanley Nelson, the heroic reporter who cracked the Silver Dollar Group cases. Watch for his upcoming nonfiction book on those cases, *Devil's a-Walkin'*.

To David Highfill, Liate Stehlik, Tavia Kowalchuk, Danielle Bartlett, and Eric Svenson (and all the reps who worked so hard), my heartfelt thanks. And to Laura Cherkas, a special thank-you.

To Charlie Redmayne, Julia Wisdom, Louise Swannell, Stuart Bache, and all the rest of the crew at HarperCollins UK. Great times and great work!

To Ed Stackler, my copilot.

To Dan Conaway and Simon Lipskar of Writers House, and Kassie Evashevski of UTA, for enthusiastic support and sage advice.

To Betty Iles, Madeline Iles, Mark Iles, Joe Iles, Larry Iles, Geoff Iles, and Betsy Iles, for constant support.

To my team of Southern Philosophers: Courtney Aldridge, James Schuchs, Jim Easterling, Rod Givens, and Billy Ray Farmer.

For brilliant life insights and an infinite number of dissonant chords: Scott Turow, Stephen King, Dave Barry, Michelle Kaufman, Sam Barry, Erasmo Paolo, James McBride, Roy Blount Jr., Mitch Albom, Amy Tan, Lou DeMattei, Ridley Pearson, Ted Habte-Gabr, and Lisa Napoli (and Josh and Gary!).

Medical research: Dr. Michael Bourland, Dr. D. P. Lyle, Dr. Kellen Jex, Dr. Roderick Givens, Dr. John White, and Dr. Brad LeMay.

For other valuable research assistance: Judge George Ward, John Ward, Joseph Finder, Sheriff Chuck Mayfield, Mimi Miller, Keith Benoist, Darryll Grennell, Joe Mitchell, Tom Borum, Gary Abrams, Rusty Fortenberry, and Alan Kaufman.

For unstinting physical support: Rick Psonak, Richard Boleware, and Blake Carr at UMMC Prosthetics. Also thanks to Sarah Greer for friendly diagnosis while partying on the bluff.

Finally, to new friends (and wonderful writers) Tom Franklin and Beth Ann Fennelly, who made London a blast. To Regina and Doug Charbonneau, for the rehearsal dinner! Thanks always to Lyn Roberts and the gang at Square Books, and to John Evans and the gang at Lemuria.

All mistakes are mine.

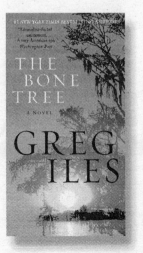